Texas Forever

Jack White

TEN YEARS IN TEXAS

By Jack White

Copyright © 2007 Jack White
All rights reserved.

ISBN: 1-4196-8025-0
ISBN-13: 9781419680250

Visit www.booksurge.com to order additional copies.

FORWARD

As with most historical novels I took a few liberties with some of the real people. For instance I extended the life of the Baron De Bastrop, because he is such an interesting person and history knows very little about him. I also needed him to live another few years so he could help integrate my hero, Bud Miller, firmly into the story. Of course, conversations involving real people who lived the ten years Texas was an independent republic are what I think they may have said, unless there is recorded history of their actual conversations.

I wanted to contrast the difference between my fictional family, the Satterwhites, and the Mavericks, who are real Texas heroes. I wanted to show the hardships people like the Saterwhites endured to come to Texas, while those with money and slaves like the Mavericks arrived in comfort.

My main character, young Bud Miller is named after my best friend in high school. Like young Bud in the book, the Millers came from Kentucky. My hero possesses some of the wonderful traits as that of the real Bud Miller.

The story begins with my sixteen-year-old hero on his way to Texas to kill those who murdered his father in the Goliad Massacre. He is filled with hate and revenge. In time he reaches his arc and becomes one of the foundation stones that makes Texas such a great state. He survived in no small part to my allowing the Baron De Bastrop to live longer and mentor young Bud. If you purists can live with that embellishment I think you will find the story of Texas and our fight for freedom on the money. I have a hunch you will enjoy my story telling.

I want to dedicate this book to my mate Mikki for being my rock and number one fan. I also wish to thank my editor, Libby Kirk for her endless hours correcting my typos and misspelled words. I want to thank Sharon Smith who first encouraged me to write. I am so blessed to have such marvelous support. Make no mistake, this broken down football player and cowboy is appreciative that I was born in Texas. I'm a sixth generation Texan and remain one today by choice.

Jack White
Official Texas State Artist
Admiral in the Texas Navy

TABLE OF CONTENTS

Chapter One | Calamity	Page 1
Chapter Two | David	Page 17
Chapter Three | The Island	Page 29
Chapter Four | Cold Country	Page 35
Chapter Five | The Raven	Page 43
Chapter Six | A Visitor	Page 55
Chapter Seven | Turmoil	Page 75
Chapter Eight | Fame and Glory	Page 81
Chapter Nine | Cesarean Birth	Page 89
Chapter Ten | Survival	Page 95
Chapter Eleven | Trip Interrupted	Page 99
Chapter Twelve | Manhood	Page 109
Chapter Thirteen | Party Time	Page 123
Chapter Fourteen | Aftermath	Page 125
Chapter Fifteen | Change	Page 131
Chapter Sixteen | Divided	Page 139
Chapter Seventeen | Together	Page 145
Chapter Eighteen | Murder	Page 153
Chapter Nineteen | Unraveling	Page 167
Chapter Twenty | Harassment	Page 175
Chapter Twenty One | Peace	Page 183
Chapter Twenty Two | Fear	Page 195
Chapter Twenty Three | Maturity	Page 201
Chapter Twenty Four | Conflict	Page 213
Chapter Twenty Five | Mustangin'	Page 219
Chapter Twenty Six | The Revolver	Page 229
Chapter Twenty Seven | The Reunion	Page 237
Chapter Twenty Eight | Taylor White	Page 255
Chapter Twenty Nine | Unrest	Page 261
Chapter Thirty | Reality	Page 267
Chapter Thirty One | War	Page 275
Chapter Thirty Two | Disaster	Page 287
Chapter Thirty Three | Change	Page 301
Chapter Thirty Four | Sorrow	Page 323
Chapter Thirty Five | Houston	Page 337
Chapter Thirty Six | Maverick	Page 351
Chapter Thirty Seven | Devil Yack	Page 357
Chapter Thirty Eight | Goliad	Page 371
Chapter Thirty Nine | Dillard	Page 381
Chapter Forty | Statehood	Page 399

Chapter One
Calamity

The bilious black waters heaved angrily below the bow of the overloaded steamboat *Destiny*. As she traversed the raging ocean waves, her well-worn wooden deck creaked and moaned like a new leather saddle with each lunge into the unrestrained indigo sea. The *Destiny* was not constructed to sail the open ocean and its weakening body verified the mistake made by the naive Captain Gene Yelton in attempting such a perilous voyage. His cunning, bellicose passenger had pressured the Captain into transporting his merchandise across the crescent cove of the Gulf of Mexico in a vessel designed to paddle up and down the smooth waters of the Mississippi River. Out of desperation, paranoia, and the fear of being arrested, the old passenger used all his persuasive skills to coerce Captain Yelton to transport his goods to Galveston Island. When the Captain had wavered, the old trader resorted to cajoling and flattery, and a generous bribe.

Both the Captain and his passenger acknowledged the riverboat was built for calm river waters; yet, Captain Yelton disregarded his better judgment and gave in to his lust for money. Contrary to his knowledge of the sea and the limitations of his vessel, the Captain piloted his fragile steamer headlong into the Gulf of Mexico and the fury of a powerful hurricane.

The first day out of port, the waters were silky smooth and the riverboat paddled along with ease in the warm shallow water, as if on a tranquil lake. On the second day a violent tropical storm suddenly struck, threatening to tear the old ship into splinters. Unlike a ketch, frigate, sloop, clipper or brigantine, the riverboat *Destiny* had no keel extending below the surface for ballast and stabilization. The vessel was completely dependent on the extra weight of the merchandise in its belly to prevent capsizing. Bobbing like a giant coffin waiting to join Davy Jones at the bottom of the sea, the ship, the Captain and crew were helpless against the forces of nature.

The six months between June and November are never an ideal time to cross the Gulf of Mexico, and the fall of 1836 was shaping up to be the worst hurricane season in recorded history. The unusually late hurricane appeared without warning, churning the salty waters into a solid sea of white foam along the Louisiana/Texas coast. The powerful storm squalls reached out like octopus tentacles for miles in every direction. The ninety mile-per-hour winds caused wave surges over thirty feet to roll across the shallow surface of the Gulf, lifting the flat bottom boat as if it were no more than a leaf in the wind. The vessel was not built to withstand the turbulent seas, but the shortage of available sailing ships had forced the old merchant, Baron de Bastrop, to hire the *Destiny*. Had he remained in New Orleans, the Americans would have arrested him, sent him to jail back in Baltimore and would have surely extradited him to his home country after time served in a Union jail. But Bastrop had successfully eluded authorities and was able to procure the much-needed merchandise for his new general store. Suppliers in New Orleans had allowed him to load his goods, fully expecting to be paid before the ship's departure, but Bastrop and his supplies pulled out of port long before daybreak. Now he was so near freedom he could taste Texas cornbread; yet one more giant wave and he could lose everything, including his life.

A waning full moon illuminated the darkness, turning the white sea foam into a picture of blowing snow. The blue moon's glow bathed the sky with a brilliant cerulean hue between each flash of lightning. Moonbeams transformed the belching smokestacks' steam into mysterious streams of gray, swirling with the whim of the winds. Each powerful blast rendered the paddle wheel ineffective as the aging freighter struggled to keep afloat, groaning like a wounded animal with each wave surge.

In the early morning hours of October 1, 1836, the lone man stood tethered to the teakwood railing, his size diminished by the massive storm's wrath. The thick rope secured around his protruding waist provided a precarious lifeline as waves slammed the vessel. The lumbering man shouted into the howling wind, "French, you dastardly French. It's all your fault I stand here facing death."

He lamented into the pitch darkness that if the French had never controlled Louisiana, he would not be a fugitive. In his warped and frightened mind, his troubles started in the 17th Century when a Frenchman sledded his canoe from Canada down to the mouth of the Mississippi River into the Gulf of Mexico. The French explorer claimed valleys and tributaries from the Rocky Mountains east to the Appalachians as French land, naming the area Louisiana in honor of his King Louis XIV. In his panicked thinking, he didn't feel the territory had been France's to sell. The old passenger felt the French should have allowed the ownership of Louisiana to remain under Spanish rule; with Spain in control, he would still be a resident of New Orleans and enjoying the finer things of life. When Spain lost the territory to the French, his only option was to flee to Spanish Texas. Then, when the Union took over, his dangers increased yet again.

His rage soon turned toward the despotic Napoleon Bonaparte who sold Louisiana to the United States for virtually nothing. In 1803, with Napoleon's army dying of yellow fever in Haiti, the French dictator surprised Thomas Jefferson by offering Louisiana for a relatively small amount of desperately needed cash. Napoleon's thirst for money and the United States' vision of Manifest Destiny made the Louisiana Purchase move quickly. The transaction gave the Union 800,000 square miles of land and Napoleon, $15 million dollars.

When facing death, the mind conjures up scores of dreadful scenarios. Standing waterlogged on the deck of a doomed ship, the big man thought about the arrest warrants issued against him in the Netherlands and Baltimore. With a modicum of luck and fast thinking, he had managed to avoid capture in both places, but it appeared as if his good fortune might be running out. He was facing death on a rickety ship paddling from New Orleans to the new Republic of Texas; a Republic he helped build.

With the rain stinging his face, he turned his thoughts away from the French and directed his wrath toward the Spanish. Under his breath, he muttered profanities against the cowardly Spanish for not fighting harder to hold Louisiana. Looking skyward into the swirling rain, he wondered how long he had to live. The ship appeared to be coming apart beneath his feet. As lightning flashed, he saw no one was on deck, no one was at the helm; not even the Captain. The best he could tell the wheel was lashed with ropes to keep the vessel on course. His lone figure clinging to the railing was the only visible sign of life on the *Destiny*. He thought to himself death shouldn't be solitary.

The old riverboat freighter tossed high, slamming back into the foaming surf with each gust of wind. Rain poured from the sky as if being released from giant buckets, drenching the lone figure as the squalls circled above. He wanted to smoke his fresh store-bought Cuban cigar to calm himself, but that was not an option. A mug of rum would calm him, but none was available. This giant of a man could only stand and hope the weakening vessel held together until the main force of the hurricane passed. Anger interlocked with fear welled up inside of him. No matter how he shifted his mind, he was unable to shake his anguish at the thought of dying at sea. He conjured up the memory of his crossing from Europe to America; and how a young sailor had been buried at sea. How sharks had ripped the canvas coffin to shreds and consumed the cadaver in moments. The memory of the sharks ripping the flesh from the sailor's bones was more than his mind could handle and caused him to vomit over the railing into the churning black water.

He chastened himself for not having purchased a Christian Cross from a street vendor a few days earlier. Not being a religious man, he wasn't sure how to pray; nevertheless, he felt the urgency to make an attempt. Grabbing some semblance of composure, he remembered learning the *Lord's Prayer* in grammar school. He was unsure if he could recite all the words, but decided a partial prayer would be better than no prayer at all. In a thundering baritone brogue, the six-foot-two, 270-pound man turned his gaze to the heavens and bellowed, "My Father who art in heaven, hallowed be thy name..."

The ship shuddered under his feet. The bow leapt high and then crashed deep into the surf, pitching side to side in a desperate dance against the sea's fury. In one deafening instant, a bolt of lightning slammed into one of the smokestacks, shooting sparks high into the blackened sky. A blast of wind ripped the damaged tower from its base and sent the column crashing across the deck and out into the darkness. The flying debris barely missed the old man. Before he could pray another line, he heard a voice speaking from the blackness somewhere behind him. "God ain't goin' to listen to you prayin' like that mister."

The big man froze, thinking perhaps an angel was answering his prayer and telling him God was no longer accepting requests. Being turned down would serve him right for his sinful life.

Once more a voice broke through the howling winds and crashing waves. "Mister, that ain't no way to talk to God. You gotta jus' tells God whut you wants and not go saying whut you done learned someplace."

Reluctantly releasing one hand from his white-knuckle grip on the railing, the man spun around and saw a young lad standing on deck behind him, feet spread wide apart for balance. He looked down at the boy, trying to figure where he came from. In a boisterous voice, the frightened man blurted out, "Boy, what on God's green earth are you doing above deck in weather like this?"

"Kaint sleep with all them sailors cryin' and prayin' down there so I 'cided to come up and see whut all the fuss wuz 'bout," he answered as his voice cracked into a youthful falsetto.

Momentarily putting aside his fear, the older man became harsh in his delivery as he sternly inquired, "How old are you lad and where in the deuce did you come from?"

The youngster did his best to deepen his voice and answered with contrived confidence, "Seventeen goin' ons twenty. I reckon I'm a hog and half tall." Wanting not to reveal his true age for fear of being turned over to some mysterious authority, the young man rose up on his toes to appear taller. He didn't tell the old man that in three days he would be sixteen. Not telling the truth troubled the boy because he was taught never to lie, but he feared revealing his age would cut short his important journey. He had been told no one would let a boy his age immigrate and even if he was older, he might still have trouble being allowed to come ashore. The Republic needed productive men, not children begging off the locals.

He had been warned several times in New Orleans not to proceed, but his mission was too important. He must do everything in his power to get his feet on Texas soil. It had been his mother's dying wish; a request he must fulfill, or die trying.

"Boy, where are your kinfolk and what puts you on my ship on a night like this? You better have a good answer," the old man demanded. "This isn't a passenger ship, but one I leased to transport my merchandise. I have the say so on who sails and who is made to walk the plank."

The boy moved over to the railing, grasping the smooth teak with both hands just as a mammoth wave engulfed them both. He waited until the riverboat crashed back down into the water to answer. Suddenly the winds and rain ceased. The brash boy once more spoke in his deepest voice. "I ain't got no kinfolk. I done slipped on the ship in a bushel a corn. Please don't tell the Captain 'cause he'll fling me overboard. I hear tell of how they feed peoples' bones to the sharks for stealing a ride. I don't think God can find us if a shark eats our bodies, do you Mister?"

The thought of sharks jumped back into the mind of the older man. He shook his head vigorously back and forth, then put on a brave face in front of the young boy. He didn't want to even think about sharks tearing him limb from limb should the ship come apart. Instead, he demanded, "You mean to tell me you are in the middle of the Gulf of Mexico heading for the Republic of Texas as a stowaway? You have no parents and no means of supporting yourself? I can tell you one thing. You are lucky you ran into me, the Baron de Bastrop. I'm a man of compassion. I can also tell you the Captain will have you bagged and tossed overboard. That's the way they treat stowaways. If you have a good excuse, I might be able to spare your life."

The boy answered, "Alls I knows is I got to git to Texas and kills me sum Meskins. It was them dirty Meskins that dun killed my pa. After my pa wuz killed, my ma grieved herself Plum to death. I promised ma 'for she passed on I'd go and kill them that dun murdered pa." The wafer thin lad never wavered as he explained his reason for being on the ship. The crime of stealing a ride was justified in his young mind because of the vendetta he needed to exact upon those who had killed his father. There was no doubt in his mind that his voyage was sanctioned by God. He was to follow God's will and kill the people who murdered his father. After all, his uncle read him passages from the bible where it said "an eye for an eye." His Uncle Charlie explained the passage meant "a life for a life."

Bastrop was no Baron. His real name was Phillip Hendrik Nering Boegel, or as the Mexicans would call him, Felipe Enrique Neri. He gave himself the propitious title after fleeing his native Netherlands when the government discovered he had embezzled tax funds. Like so many before him, once he arrived in Texas, he could be anyone he desired. Many newcomers to Texas were escaping a shady past, debt, or the law, and simply assumed a new identity and started over.

For years he had looked over his shoulder, wondering if a bounty hunter was on his trail. He knew the French would be pleased to capture him and turn him over to the Netherlands. Considering the consequences, he obtained a Spanish passport, slipped into Spanish Texas and became a Mexican citizen, which offered him immunity from deportation. He could not risk being returned home because a very lengthy prison term awaited him there. Even worse, he had swindled a widow of her life savings in Baltimore, Maryland. A jail cell waited as patiently as a giant blue heron in both countries for the man now calling himself a Baron. He had risked greatly sneaking back into New Orleans, buying merchandise and hiring a boat. He counted on the fact he could be in and out with haste and depart before anyone recognized him. After all, he had not lived in New Orleans in thirty-plus years. His plan had worked to perfection, but now he may die by the hand of God, buried with his swindled goods at the bottom of the sea.

Baron de Bastrop knew the importance of appearances. He was dressed in a rich velvet coat, softly woven wool trousers, and a splendid stovepipe hat. His gray hambone sideburns met his bushy mustache at a perfect juncture, each hair set in place by wax to ensure he always looked splendid. His father had instilled in him the idea that clothes make the man. The elder Boegel told his son: "If all men were nude, no one would know who to follow."

His fancy clothing meant nothing to the young boy from Kentucky, and certainly offered him no protection from the impending calamity. Once more, the old con man pulled himself together and addressed his young companion. Always a salesman, first he asked a question to bring the boy into his confidence. "Where do you hail from lad?" He paused and waited for the boy to answer. He learned at an early age that the first person to speak after an editorial question, loses. The big man waited and waited; yet the young boy spoke not a word. Bastrop was tempted to ask again; nevertheless, he stood quietly. He became impatient, but knowing the rule of controlling a conversation, the Baron waited for the boy to speak first.

Finally, the bold lad answered, "I cum frum Allan county Kentuck' not far from the big river by Scottsdale. My pa done up and leaved us and headed to Texas. Ma said he went to git sum land of our own. Pa been told men get a bunch of land by jus' saying he wants some down here in Texas.

Alls I knowd is my pa wuz a fighting them Meskins at some place I can't exactly recall. It was a church or sumthin' like that when they done run out of dry power. Pa and 'em stuck up the white flag. Them dirty Meskins done killed them all anyhow. Shot 'em like dogs. My Uncle Charlie said they killed 'bout a million good men after they done raised their hands and told them Meskins they were dun a fightin'. Them stinkin' Meskins done up and killed my pa shore as shootin'.

Then sum men cumed and telled ma my pa wuz killed; she up and passed in two weeks. My ma wuz a good woman. My ma's brother, Uncle Charlie took me in after she passed. Charlie only got one leg he can use or he would have come along to kill us sum Meskins."

The young man stopped talking as homesickness weighed down on his countenance. He looked up into the face of the Baron and changing the subject, continued, "Uncle Charlie makes sum good corn lickker. He don't use no sugar er stuff like that. Charlie fixes his Kentuck' corn lickker and then puts the hooch in hickory barrels. His lickker is not like the white lightning most make that gives a man Jake-leg. Uncle Charlie's lickker looks like pure gold when you pour a slug in a clean fruit jar. I have to tell you Uncle Charlie's lickker kicks like a mule. He wanted to give me his rifle, but felt he might need it when them Revenuers cums to collect taxes on his lickker."

The boy abruptly stopped talking and his mind seemed to wander. He never looked up at the older man, calmly keeping his empty gaze facing into the darkness as tears filled his eyes. He missed Kentucky. He missed his Uncle Charlie. He missed his mother. Feeling the lad's loneliness, Bastrop mellowed his tone. "The Goliad Massacre. You are talking about the Goliad Massacre. Truly a sad day in the history of our great Republic. So your pa was with Colonel James Fannin at Goliad when they surrendered in good faith to General Urrea. Then that reprobate Santa Anna ordered 330 innocent men murdered in cold blood. The men were told they were free to go, marched into an open field, made to kneel down and then shot down like dogs. After he killed the able-bodied men, he hauled the sick and dying into the front of the mission and shot them one by one. General Jose Urrea was not to blame for the slaughter for it was Santa Anna that gave the final order. My blood runs cold when I think of the loss of so many brave men in that battle."

The Baron pondered for a few moments and continued, "I lost several friends at Goliad to those butchers from Mexico City. I would have cut General Antonio Lopez de Santa Anna's tongue out and nailed the forked sliver to a tree if I'd been in San Jacinto. I'd have loved to see that little brown weasel squirm. When our boys grabbed the little coward, he tried to act like he was just a regular foot solider. My bum knee prevented me from marching, and besides, I was tied up with urgent business over in Galveston. But, mind you, had I been there, I would have strung Santa Anna from the oak tree under which General Houston negotiated the peace treaty with him."

The young boy was receiving more information than he could possibly absorb. He wanted things kept simple. Where were the Mexicans and how could he kill them? Names meant nothing to him; his one and only goal was to settle his personal vendetta with the men who killed his father and return home to Kentucky.

The Baron, for a moment, forgot the danger they were facing and began to berate a man he had been jealous of since the early 1820s when he first arrived in Texas. "That worthless Houston. He treated that little reptile Santa Anna like he was royalty or someone of importance. He is now getting ready to send him back to Mexico City. Santa Anna is a murdering dictator and should have been burned at the stake."

The boy listened without saying a word. There was nothing to say. The Baron was talking Texas history; a subject unfamiliar to the lad. The storm banged their drenched bodies into the railing as the Baron continued to berate Houston. "He is too weak to lead a great nation like ours. Even that sorry scoundrel Burnet is a better man. I have no respect for Sam Houston. What we need is another Jim Bowie who wasn't afraid of hurting a few feelings and sure was never a redskin lover. Or General Lamar; a great man and one who believes that the only good Indian is a dead Indian."

The Baron suddenly realized the boy was not interested in his words. He paused before turning to what he knew best, selling. In a deep, concerned voice he implored, "Son, please tell me your name?"

The rain vanished as quickly as it had appeared. The moon bathed the boy's face in a soft manganese glow; his deep black eyes looked like chunks of coal in the soft light. He didn't answer for a few minutes, unsure if he could trust the Baron. His Uncle Charlie told him his father had enemies in Texas. Someone might try to steal the land granted his father, but the old Baron looked harmless and as best the boy could detect, he was not carrying a weapon. After a long delay, the lad blurted out, "My name is Miller, Benjamin Miller, but everybody back home jus' calls me Bud."

With some firmness in his voice, he answered, "Well Mister Benjamin Bud Miller, do you really know what you are getting yourself into? The Republic of Texas is not an easy place right now; we have been independent for only a few months. One year ago tonight Colonel John Henry Moore and his men forded the Guadalupe River and moved against the Mexican Lieutenant Francisco Castaneda and his one hundred dragoons. The Lieutenant had gone to Gonzales to retrieve a cannon Mexico loaned the city, but the Texans refused to give up the four-pound cannon. One of the local women made a flag out of a petticoat that read 'Come and Take IT.' That brief scrimmage was our Lexington."

The Baron never worried about facts when he was telling a story. He continued his diatribe, ignoring his own past. "Things around here are pretty unsettled right now. We are inundated with a lot of bad people running from the law. They change their names, making it impossible to know who you are dealing with. Young Miller, Texas is no place for a lad like you. I know you can't be older than fourteen at best. You don't even have any peach fuzz on your cheeks."

Bud Miller was small for his age from lack of proper nutrition and months living on almost nothing. He didn't dispute the Baron, but forcefully restated his purpose. "Mister Bastrop, I gotta git to Texas so I kan kill me sum Meskins. I dun promised my ma I'd cum as soon as I git ol' nuff. Heck fire, I'm ol' nuff. My sis dun already married and got a house full of kids 'fore she wuz my age. She's got three kids with one a cumin' and she ain't even nineteen." Bud realized his slip of the tongue and prayed the Baron hadn't picked up on his carelessness. He knew even sixteen wouldn't be old enough to satisfy the crusty old man. Perhaps the Baron was correct; Texas wouldn't want a young boy. Of course, Bud had no way of knowing how many young boys his age had already died fighting for Texas' independence. The old man failed to mention boys as young as thirteen were killed in the Goliad Massacre.

Bastrop smiled to himself, but didn't let little Bud know the boy's words had betrayed him. Just as he started to speak, another squall swirled over them, dousing them with sheets of cold, stinging rain. The force made the big man duck his head, causing him to look down into the surf. He could swear he saw a shark as one of the big waves came level with the railing. Shouting at the top of his voice he asked, "Did you see that?"

"I ain't shore whut you're' talkin' 'bout Mister Baron."

Frustrated and fearful, Bastrop screamed, "The shark. I saw a shark. It was forty feet long. I hate sharks 'cause I saw them eat a dead sailor on my way to America. I can still see the water turning red as those sharks shook their ugly heads back and forth in their frenzy. It's a horrible sight to see a body devoured by those man-eaters."

"I ain't ever seed a real shark Mister. I hear tell they will gobble up a grown man in one big gulp. That's whut Uncle Charlie said when he wuz telling me how to git to Texas."

Bud's cavalier attitude didn't help alleviate Bastrop's tension. The lack of fear on Bud's part was not sitting well with the old man. Once the squall passed, he asked, "So you want to get to the Republic of Texas to kill the men who slaughtered your father? Do you have any idea what you are facing in Texas?" Not waiting for Bud to answer, the Baron continued, "Well, let me share a few things that might change your mind about trying to slip into my Republic. After I finish, I suspect you will just stay on this ship and head back to your Uncle Charlie and the great state of Kentucky. Do you have any idea how many different tribes of savage Indians we have in Texas?"

Undeterred, Bud replied, "We got redskins back home. They don't go 'round killin' folk. One old buck heps Uncle Charlie make his corn lickker."

Bastrop laughed out loud and for a moment forgot the salt water spraying over the sides of the ship and the danger of sharks lurking in the ocean. The lad was so young and naive. How could he not know about the Indian Wars and what he was getting into? What kind of an uncle would send a child into the mouth of a monster called Texas without at least giving him some idea of the dangers that lay ahead?

The Baron and the lad stood together pressing against the squall. Within minutes, off the portside, sunrays peeked over the horizon as the glow rose upward to illuminate the day. Like a miracle, the sky transformed from ominous gray into a cool blue. Rays of yellow and brilliant orange sunshine washed away the darkness and filled the sky with hope.

Becoming fatherly, the Baron scolded, "Son, we have more savages than should be allowed. Down near Campano Bay, along the Gulf of Mexico, we have a port similar to what you will find on Galvez Island. Down there, we got a cluster of the most brutal Indians ever known to mankind. They were living on Galvez Island until the Buccaneer Lafitte and his band of outlaws ran them off twenty-five years ago. It's a fact that bunch of Karankawa Indians are man-eating cannibals. Most of the men are six feet or taller and when they go on the warpath, they paint half of their faces red and the other white. They cover their bodies with alligator and skunk grease to keep the mosquitoes from biting them. They can pull a bow as long as they are tall, and shoot a Buffalo's eye at three hundred yards. These warriors can shoot a dozen arrows a minute; a lot faster than we can load and fire our rifles. They don't have to worry about dry powder or if their flint will spark. Just two months ago they raided a farm down near Victoria and killed a mother and her three young boys and took the little ten year old, blonde haired girl to their camp. These animals live in the swamps and are impossible to track. They have no soul and I don't even think God considers them human."

Bud looked up as he responded, "Seems to me them Meskins ain't the only ones who need killin'. Sounds likes we need to go git that little gurl and kill us sum of them Injuns."

"Wanting to and doing the actual killing is easier said than done. Our Citizen Rangers have been tying to lay an ambush for them since Steve Austin formed our first company back in 1823. Our rangers are a salty bunch, but have been unable to eliminate the Karankawas. I doubt if a lad like you and an old codger like myself would have much luck. Besides, they are not the only Indians. Son, Texas is swarming with Redskins. We got the Waco, Biloxie, Creek, Muscogoee, Delaware, Caddo, Seminole, Mescalero-Apache, Lipan-Apache, Cronk, Tonkawa, Coahuilecan, Kickapoo, Chickasaw, Choctaw, and Shawnee. The Coahuiletecans kill their own daughters to keep their tribe's population small. There is very little game in the territory they occupy, forcing them to forage on grasses, seeds, cacti, insects, and fish when they can find water. And of course, there are the brutal Comanche. They make the Karankawas look like Sunday school teachers. You have no idea how treacherous some of those savages are."

Catching his breath, the old man continued, "You know what the name Choctaw means? I'll tell you, 'man-eater'. That's right; the Choctaw eat white boys like you for breakfast. The Apache; now there is a vicious bunch. The very name *Apache* means 'enemy'. Son, Indians kill babies and eat them like you would a rabbit. They make slaves of boys your age and take the young girls for their wives. Old men like me, they just leave in the wilderness to wander till a mountain lion eats us or we starve to death. Those redskins make Texas an unsafe place for a lad like you."

The Baron knew his words were not making much of an impact on the determined, naive boy, so he decided to complete the boy's education about the hazards of living in Texas. The Baron continued, "Even Houston's dear Cherokee have been known to kill and kidnap."

Bud interrupted, "Did you say Cherokee? That redskin who heps Uncle Charlie make his lickker, he's a Cherokee. He is pretty nice, fur an Injun. Always treated me good. I kaint see no reason to be afraid of no Cherokee."

Bastrop shrugged his shoulders and responded, "The only good Indian is a dead one. Don't ever get to thinking you can trust one of those savages. They may look human, but they are not. It's a proven fact that they are part man and part animal. I have that from a good reliable source. I know a doctor who cut one open and found he had a stomach like a wolf. It's just a matter of time till that Cherokee turns on your uncle and has him for lunch."

His words fell on deaf ears. Bud knew the Cherokee working for his Uncle, and nothing the Baron could say was going to sway his mind. Not to be deterred, the Baron bellowed on. "Boy, you have no business getting off in Texas. You need to stay on this boat and return home. I'll give you grub money so you won't starve before you are back with your uncle. Texas is sure no place for an orphan like you."

Naturally Bastrop failed to tell Bud the Kickapoo and Lipan were not only friendly with the Texans, but helped to track and also engaged in battles with the hostile Indian tribes. As always, Bastrop painted word pictures to prove his point rather than portray things as they really were.

Bud shot back, "But Uncle Charlie said the word Texas means friendly. That's what he dun told me. If it's so darn friendly, then how cum there be so many savages running round tryin' to kill folks?"

"Boy, your Uncle Charlie is thinking about how some say we got our name. Texas is the American way of saying Tejas. Tejas is Caddo for friend or friendly. I don't want to imply that the people of Texas are not friendly. We are without question the friendliest folks you will ever come in contact with. It's the savages and Mexicans that challenge our friendly nature. But there is a difference with Mexicans from Texas and those living in Mexico. You won't find a better bunch of folks than the Tejano Mexicans who live in Texas, they helped us fight for our freedom."

Baron de Bastrop found himself frustrated that he was not able to focus the boy's attention on the dangers awaiting him in the new Republic. The boy was so consumed with blinding vengeance, he refused to see the deadly barriers standing between him and his goal. With uncharacteristic compassion, the Baron inquired, "Son, who was your father?"

A wind surge slung Bud against the railing and almost pushed him overboard. Grabbing the railing, he steadied himself. After regaining his balance, he answered, "My pa was Stump Miller."

Bastrop's face flushed red. He knew Stump Miller all too well. His last encounter with the boy's father had cost him a pair of matching dun mules. Stump cheated him out of his mules in a rigged card game. Only after Stump was gone with the Baron's mules did he discover the scam perpetuated by the lad's father. He also knew Stump Miller was among those murdered in Goliad. Not wanting to hurt the young boy more, he opted to spin a lie. Not looking down into the bright-eyed boy's face, the Baron responded, "I did indeed know your father. He was a brave man who died as a hero fighting for the people of Texas. You can go to your grave knowing he died fighting for freedom and independence."

Bud seemed to take the fact his father was a hero for granted, but had other questions. "Mister Baron, kan I ask you sumpin'?"

"Sure, ask me anything you desire, as long as it's not my age." Bastrop was sensitive about being sixty-nine, keeping his otherwise white hair dyed midnight black.

The boy's eyes told a story of sadness that was all too familiar during these trying times in Texas as he asked, "How come you knowd 'bout where my pa wuz killed?"

The Baron looked out toward the horizon to organize his thinking. The truth of the matter was he was remembering how he met the lad's father and who had introduced them. Bastrop was trying to decide just how deeply he should get into the details. Finally, after what seemed like five minutes, he answered, "I think I met your pa in thirty four or maybe thirty three. He fought with Jim Bowie when they took San Antonio back from General Cos. It is my understanding he had a place down near Victoria. When the war heated up, Stump went off to fight with George Collingworth from Mississippi. A handful of them captured the fort at Goliad. A while after that, he joined Fannin. I've often wondered, what was your father's given name?"

"Folks back home called my pa Stump 'cause he wuzn't real tall. His name wuz Joshua Washington Miller, but ma jus' called him Josh. She never took to calling him Stump. She said that made him sound like a half a man or somthin' like that. I wuz nine, going on ten the last time I seed him. Ma said he was liked by all. She really missed him when he up and went to Texas. She wuz gonna bring us to Texas when he got some land. B'fore we could go, we got word 'bout them Meskins killing 'im." Tears flowed from the young boy's eyes as he spoke in loving terms about his parents. Even the crusty old Baron de Bastrop got a lump in his throat. As the ship swayed, the sun shot a flash of gold across Bud's face and the old man could see just how young the boy really was. As brave as the young man appeared to be, he was still just a frightened boy facing the unknown.

The wise old man knew the truth about Bud's father was not what the boy needed to hear. Stump was a small man with a hot temper, quick to kill and loathe to forgive. Even before Texas gained independence and became a sovereign Republic, the attitude was 'short on suspicion and long on hospitality'. Stump Miller never would have been a good Texan. He was selfish and a known card cheat who spent his winnings on prostitutes.

The Baron hoped he could cheer up his new young friend by embellishing some stories about Stump Miller. Finally Bastrop did what he knew best and lied to Bud. "Yep, I knew your father. A mighty fine man. No, let me back up a little and say he was a great man and would have been a leader in our new nation, without question, had he been spared.

Our Vice President Mirabeau Lamar is the man who introduced me to your pa. Lamar is a good man of high moral character. Lamar is an educated man, not anything like that unschooled, drunkard Houston. Even though they are our president and vice president, they hate each other and for good reason. Houston is an egomaniac if I've ever known one. He had a town named after him so the Republic's money would have his name on the bills. I find that disgusting. I wonder if it has something to do with people from Tennessee. Davy Crockett was almost as bad. I never met him, but several of my friends had dealings with him and said he was a braggart."

A bolt of lightning played tag on the remaining smoke stack, bouncing back and forth as if a warning to the Baron for expanding the truth. The Baron continued, "That blasted Houston's head has gotten too big for his body and at six foot six, he's got a good-sized noggin. The town of Houston won't ever amount to much. It is located in the wrong place. I cannot see that area ever thriving. They should have set the capital up in my town. When the good people at Mina decided to rename their town Bastrop in my honor, I was humbled. The name change was not something I lobbied for. The town had originally been named for a French General who defected to the Mexicans. The citizens of Mina renamed it after me because of my contribution to help tame the wild land so we could become a civilized nation. You are talking with the man who one day will be called the Father of Texas."

For some reason, talking helped calm him so he rambled on and on about things that young Miller had no interest in or knowledge of. This didn't stop the Baron. He kept on chattering, "If it had not been for me, there would be no Texas. When old Moses Austin came to San Antonio de Bexar begging to be allowed to bring in Anglo families, he was kicked out on his ear. Lucky for him, he bumped into me. I marched him back to Governor Martinez and pointed out how Moses possessed a Spanish passport, was a good Catholic and besides, we needed able-bodied men to fight the Indians. I don't know if Austin was a Catholic, but I know he had a Spanish passport and men who could shoot, and that was what the Governor needed to combat the savages. Because I gave my word to supervise the immigration, Austin was granted permission to bring in three hundred families."

Bud was confused, but didn't know how to stop the older gentleman. He started to ask another question, but decided to keep listening. Bastrop continued, "Old Moses died before he could get back to Texas. I took over for his sickly son, Stephen. God rest his soul, young Austin was in pretty bad shape. Frankly, I doubt if poor Stephen will last the winter. Last time I saw him, he was very weak. He always has been a frail man and I think the stress of being in a Mexican jail for eighteen months was more than his body could endure.

Anyway, I had the vision to build a great nation out of this wilderness. You can tell by speaking with me, I'm a humble man even though I have accomplished great things for this country. One day you will see a headstone on my grave, '*Here lays Baron de Bastrop, the Father of the Republic of Texas.*' Remember, it was me giving out the land titles and forming new towns. I was the one who got Mexico to let Anglos come to Texas in the first place. Son, you are in the presence of greatness, if I might humbly say so."

Bud was distracted. He could hear the flat-bottomed ship creaking loudly with the pressure of the waves. He knew if they didn't find smooth water and a lessening of wind, he would not live to reach Texas. Finally he blurted out, "That's mighty good thangs you are saying Mister."

That was the encouragement that Bastrop needed. His voice became louder as he proclaimed, "Lamar is a good man and the one I cannot wait to see as our leader. If I understand the way things are set up, he has a good chance to become our next president. Lamar liked your father."

The Baron stopped talking as he recalled an incident a few years earlier in San Antonio at the *Bear Claw Tavern*. Stump Miller had been caught cheating and challenged to a duel by one of the men at the table. It was rumored that Miller turned around half a step early. Nothing ever came of the early shot because the witnesses refused to testify in court against Stump, in fear for their own safety. Bastrop rambled on, making up a few more tall tales about the bravery of Stump Miller so little Bud would feel good about his pa.

Bastrop would lie even when the truth would have been better. He had lied when he tried to pretend that the settlers of Mina just decided to honor him by changing the name of their community to Bastrop. He failed to disclose the fact that Stephen Austin made the suggestion because of favors the Baron had granted to help his father in the early years, as well as the assistance Bastrop provided in his powerful position as land commissioner. The locals in Mina despised the arrogant foreigner and frankly resented their town bearing his name. But since Austin was given near dictatorial powers by Mexico City, they were forced to comply.

There was one thing the Baron said that caused an immediate reaction with the young man in wet buckskins. Bastrop blurted out a shocking statement. "If you ask me, it was Houston who got your pa killed. Travis asked the men from Goliad be brought over to help defend the Alamo. With the Goliad 400 and the 180 with Travis, they could have defeated the Mexicans. Houston could have sent another 500 men if he had the inclination. The Alamo had two-dozen cannons and plenty of supplies. They had large numbers of beef to slaughter and bushels of corn inside the compound. Water was plentiful because they had two wells. With a thousand men to handle the twenty four cannons, the Mexicans would have been fools to attack our boys, especially since they were armed with fine 'Betsy' rifles."

The truth was Houston had arrived in Gonzales to find only a few men. By the time he reached Gonzales, the Alamo had already fallen. The Baron's bald-faced lie was typical of his mode of operation. He slandered those he didn't like with impunity.

"No doubt in my mind it was Houston who killed your father. Instead of being a hero, he should be hanged as a traitor and I don't mind saying that's what I wanted to happen. All I can say is he got lucky when he captured General Santa Anna."

The Baron could never bring himself to admit General Houston had two horses shot out from under him at the Battle of San Jacinto, mounted a third and continued to lead the charge with a shattered ankle. Even in excruciating pain, Houston negotiated a treaty for the Independence of the Republic of Texas. The real reason the Baron was so bitter toward Houston was because Houston had long known of the fraudulent land script the Baron handed out. Upon becoming President of the Republic, he immediately relieved Bastrop of his position as Land Commissioner. The old fraud was not a forgiving man; he despised Houston with every ounce of his obese body. Now he realized he would have to soften his tone or his vitriolic statements might just provoke this feisty young boy into getting himself hanged for treason.

Bud nonchalantly said, "I guess I'll jus' have to kill that there Houston feller 'long with them there *Injuns* and Meskins. Don't matter nothin' to me. I don't mind killing. I had to kills me a black buck on the way down here from Paduke, Kentuck'. We wuz on two river rafts tied together when the storms done started to make the water go real fast. We couldn't stop 'em and couldn't git 'em over to the bank cause the water wuz goin' too fast. When we hit one of them huckleberries sticking up in the middle of the river, the stump dun split us apart like a railing chopped with a sharp ax. Black Tom grabbed my belongins and jumped to the other raft. He got my five dollars Uncle Charlie gave me and the pitcher of my ma and pa when they wuz young. I went one way down the river and he went t'other. He didn't think I'd be able to find him. That darkie didn't know he wuz a messin' with a Miller. I don't cotton to nobody stealing from me. We went over the waterfalls 'bout the same time. His raft got stuck on some rocks and I managed to git mine over to where he wuz hung up. I slipped my frog sticker out of my pocket and when I got over on his raft, I stuck him in the gizzard. He croaked like a bullfrog and then fell into the brown water, turning it red. Guess the turtles had him for supper. I got my belongins back and my raft carried me to Nu Awlins. Like I said, I don't mind killin' when folks do me wrong. Sounds like that Houston feller done me wrong. Shore glad Mister you told me about him. I might just have to kill 'im too."

The Baron had not planned to incite a murder plot. No doubt he needed to discourage this angry boy from getting off the ship in the event they made it through the storm. He knew for sure he had to change the subject about his personal dislike for President Houston. Too many citizens saw the ex-Tennessee Governor as a modern day hero. Houston's popularity was at an all time high. The lad's excitement about killing the president was the Baron's fault… if he would have just kept his big mouth shut. Baron de Bastrop knew he would need to stifle the simmering rage he had ignited, or the boy would surely not live long enough to become a man.

The dissipating storm was still firing gusts across the ship's bow and from time to time, knocking the hull sideways. With each burst of wind, their bodies slammed against the railing, knocking them breathless. Young Bud stayed calm, even managing a laugh while pinned against the railing.

The sun rose higher and cast a welcomed warmth upon their cold, wet clothes. In the brighter light, the old man could now clearly see the young boy was wearing handmade buckskins. The wet deerskin sagged and pooled over his shoes, if you could call what he was wearing on his feet, shoes. He had taken strips of deerskin and wrapped them like a physician's bandage around his feet. The bottoms were paper-thin and worn slick. He knew Bud would not be able to do any serious walking until he had real shoes.

Once more, the Baron de Bastrop decided to see if he could discourage the young man and talk him into heading back home while he was still in one piece. "Hey boy, you cannot walk in Texas with those shoes. We have grass that grows burrs as sharp as wallpaper tacks. We got the goat-heads, sand burrs, cockleburs, and thistles. All of these can do some serious damage to your feet unless you have real shoes. Son, even the trees have thorns and you have never seen so many sharp plants. The algerita bush protects its berries with leaves that will rip your skin. All the cacti are covered with 'horse cripplers' five inches long. Our yucca has swords for leaves. You have to cover your legs when you ride or the brush will rip your skin to the bone. And I suspect you don't have any money to buy any shoes."

Young Bud replied, "Mr. Baron, I know I got to git a job and make me sum money so I kan stay in Texas."

"What can you do boy? You don't have a gun. Son, you don't even have a horse or mule. How do you plan to go Mexican hunting without a horse and a gun?"

"I guess I'll jus have to barra me a horse and rifle."

The Baron's patience was wearing thin. He was getting angry with the single-minded boy. "Son, we hang horse thieves in Texas. Stealing a horse is worse than committing murder down here."

"I don't plan to steal nobody's horse Mister. I wuz jus' gonna barra one when no one wuz looking. If'n one day I brung the horse back, then it wouldn't be stealin' would it? Now if I planned to keep the horse, then that would be stealin'. Ma told me God hates a man who steals, but I ain't seen nowhere its wrong to barra. I won't barra one no longer than two or three years."

Bastrop just shook his head in disbelief. The rain stopped and the winds calmed, allowing him to see land to the northwest. He assumed the ship was nearing the Texas shoreline. Tapping his gold-tip cane four or five times as he exhaled a sigh of relief, he was now sure they would make port, even well ahead of schedule. The best part was he would be out of the reach of the United States arm of the law.

The Baron was unclear how to handle the young boy. He knew immigration authorities would refuse entry to a vagrant with no apparent skills or means of supporting himself. From the glint in the lad's eyes the Baron thought, with some education and gentlemanly training, the boy could become a productive Texas citizen. In a few years, Miller would be old enough to start a family and take up residence in the township of Bastrop.

The Baron hoped once Lamar became President of the Republic, he would move the state capital to Bastrop. The town was centrally located and far enough away from San Antonio not to be in the path of a Mexican invasion. The strategic location was also enough off the frontier to minimize Indian raids. The Baron also had an ace up his sleeve. He knew a dark secret on Vice President Lamar. Unless Lamar went along with his plans to relocate the epicenter of the Republic of Texas Government to the town of Bastrop, he may be forced to expose the dalliance of the religious vice president. The Baron de Bastrop had not survived for sixty-nine years without knowing where the bones were buried and had no hesitation in exposing their location for his own benefit.

Bud said nothing as the Baron untied the wet rope from around his waist. The boy was deep in thought, sorting through all the information the old man had thrown at him during the night. Texas sure was not the Garden of Eden his Uncle Charlie painted for him. He was starting to wonder if his uncle had not embellished the beauty and downplayed the danger just to get rid of him. Uncle Charlie had his own children and Bud's younger siblings to feed. Bud realized he was an extra burden for his Uncle Charlie, but it was not as if Charlie had just given him the five dollars and buck knife. The knife had belonged to his pa and Charlie sold off the Miller property after Bud's ma had died. He got several times more for the land than the measly five dollars he had given to Bud. Realizing an uncle he loved used an excuse to get rid of him caused an empty feeling to well up in the boy's stomach.

The Baron was beginning to feel some sympathy for the orphan boy. Replacing his gold-tip cane under his belt after tapping the fine walking stick on the deck a few more times, he asked, "Are you hungry boy?"

"Does a skunk stink? Shore, I'm hungry enuff to eat a piece a leather. I ain't had no vittles since a day or so 'fore I slipped on board."

"Well Bud, this is your lucky morning. You are going to be my guest at the breakfast table. I need to put some meat on your bones. You might blow away when a Texas norther comes storming through."

"Mr. Baron Sir, I kaint go to eat with you. That Cap'n ull make me walk the plank."

Bastrop smiled for the first time since the ship left the dock in New Orleans. He patted the boy on his well-worn beaver hat saying, "Son, Captain Yelton is a friend of mine and besides, I own the cargo he has on this vessel. He is hauling dry goods, gunpowder and weapons for the new trading post I'm opening in Bastrop, Texas." The Baron liked to hear his voice say, Bastrop, Texas. So he repeated the words in the thin morning air several times. "Bastrop Texas, Bastrop Texas, Bastrop Texas, Bastrop Texas, yep that's my town." Those two words when spoken together had a nice ring in his ears. A town named after him was more than he ever dreamed possible when he slipped away from his native country at the age of twenty two, just steps ahead of the law.

He had survived the storm. He had his merchandise and had made it to Texas. Now in Texas, he would be a respected businessman with political ties to the vice president of the grand, new nation. The Baron felt he was once again at the top of his game. Captain Yelton was not going to give him any grief over a rag-tag lad with a vendetta to settle. The Baron knew Yelton's pedigree included some freebooting in the Caribbean under an assumed name when pirates sailed those azure-green waters. Bastrop had used this knowledge of the Captain's days as a sea wolf to persuade Yelton to risk the precarious voyage.

Bud followed the Baron down one level, through a small mess hall, and into a tiny room where the Captain ate. The Captain's table was a small rectangular plank with a thin, one-inch lip around the perimeter to keep utensils from sliding to the floor during rough seas. In his gruff voice, the Baron grumbled, "Grab a bench lad and I'll get the cook to bring us our breakfast. For the amount of money I'm spending, I expect special service."

Young Bud had never seen a Chinaman before. He couldn't keep his eyes off of the short man with the jaundice-colored skin. The constant bowing and unusual accent captivated the boy from the backwoods of Kentucky. As starved as Bud was, he could hardly eat because of his fascination with the Oriental cook.

Bud's porcelain cup of steaming black coffee slid across the table and landed against the Baron's side, and would have tipped over if the cook hadn't grabbed it. "Hey, must hold cup. Burn if spill." The cook's voice expressed his displeasure with being stared at.

A few minutes passed and out came the Chinese cook again. This time he was carrying a tray with two tin plates piled full of food. The Baron had slipped him a quarter and in return, the cook loaded their plates to the brim. Each had three large biscuits with a heaping of flour gravy, four eggs scrambled with jalapenos and onions, fried potatoes, and two of the largest pieces of ham the boy had ever seen. Bud was mopping his plate clean before the Baron even started cutting up his ham. Once more the Baron smiled. He was starting to like this brave young lad from Kentucky. He remembered back how frightened he was when he had headed for America, and here this boy was, a baby really, feeling no fear.

Bastrop took his time eating; he wanted to work out a plan to help the boy and at the same time, have one more person in his debt. The old swindler believed there could never be too many people owing him favors.

"Do you want more coffee? Once we get into the heart of Texas, you will find coffee is mighty hard to find. It's too expensive to import overland. I'm lucky if I get one cup a week once we go inland."

Pulling a Cuban cigar from his jacket's inner pocket, the Baron motioned to the cook for another cup of coffee as he pushed his plate over to the boy. He still had one slice of ham and a thick biscuit left and didn't want the food to go to waste. Bud said nothing as he held his cup up for more coffee, his head down as he carved away at the meat.

The tide was up, which allowed the ship to enter the bay through a channel. The Galveston Port had been discovered long before the Buccaneer Jean Lafitte made the oblong island his home. But the old bandit had been wise enough to put a pier on the backside of the island where the waters remained calm in the bay between Galveston and the mainland. Even with a storm at sea, docking was easy once they got out of the Gulf and into the bay.

The Baron stood on the portside near the gangway as the boy followed alongside, carrying a ball of clothes dangling from the end of a stick. The old man had consummated a plan in his mind to help the boy. Once more patting Bud on the crown of his wrinkled hat, he softened his tone. "Lad, you seem like a fine boy. How would you like to go to work for me? You will need to learn some things before you go off killing Mexicans. First, I must teach you which are the good ones and how to spot the bad ones. The Tejanos helped us fight that evil dictator from Mexico City. Several good Mexicans like Navarro, Ruiz, and Lorenzo de Zavala risked their lives when they signed the Declaration of Independence. They were signing a death warrant when they penned their names on that piece of paper."

The Baron stopped talking for a few minutes so he could watch the workmen secure the ship to the dock. During the Baron's silence, Bud said nothing for fear one wrong word could cause Bastrop to change his mind. The boy from Kentucky's fears were relieved when Bastrop inquired, "I bet you can't even read nor write?"

Bud shot back, cutting the old man off in the middle of his thought. "Kan too. I knowd my ABCs and kan sign my own name."

"That's a good start boy, but you will need to know more than that if you are to become a leader in this new Republic. You will need to be able to read books and learn to master a quill. I can see a person with your spirit becoming an important man in our great nation a decade from now. Travis was only twenty-six when he commanded the men at the Alamo. One of our best Texas Rangers is no more than twenty. Jack 'Coffee' Hays is not much bigger than your pa and he has already become a leader of men. Won't be long before he is a Captain. I want you to understand there is a place for young men who are willing to learn and improve themselves. If you will go to work for me, I'll see to it you get an animal to ride, a place to sleep, and three squares a day. From time to time, I'll slip you a dollar or two. When you are ready, I'll give you a gun and one of my men will teach you to shoot. What do you say to my proposition?"

Bud was unsure if he was hearing the offer correctly, so he asked, "You means to tell me you goin' ta hire me without seeing whut I kan do? How do ya knowd I kan do the work? I gots to tell you Mister, my Uncle Charlie showed me how to shoot. I kan knock the tail off a coon at two hundred yards." Bud then took a deep breath and shouted, "Yeaaah Whooo, this Texas shore is Paradise on Earth jus' like Uncle Charlie done said it wuz. Its got the friendliest folks in the world."

Bastrop took a puff of his fresh cigar and proceeded to blow smoke rings into the brisk autumn air. Between puffs, he responded, "Any lad that can make his way from Kentucky to Texas by himself has a place in my operation. There is plenty to do and we will just have to see where your strengths lie."

"I'm ready to git to work," young Bud enthusiastically replied.

"Well Mister Benjamin Bud Miller, you are in for the surprise of your young life when we dock shortly. Galveston is crawling with ladies. They will have your gold before dark if you are not careful. That's how the town got its name. The town is named after a naked woman. *Gal-vest-on* was run together so it sounds like Galveston. That means she only wears a vest and nothing more. There are a few that say the island was named after a Viceroy of Mexico, Bernardo de Galvez, but I prefer to think of Galveston as a town filled with women running around in vests. Of course, the French called it Saint Louis, but that never stuck. The French can never get anything right. I do like the Indian name best. They called this God-forsaken sliver of land, Snake Island. It's still covered with scrub brush, salt cedar and snakes. If you are afraid of snakes, you had best not get off this ship."

The Baron's talk of naked women passed over the boy from Kentucky's head. He was not interested in town names or women for that matter. All he could focus on was the need to get his feet on Texas soil.

Bastrop exhibited two sides. On one hand, he was an out-and-out fraud. On the other, a benevolent man where those who were down and out were concerned. The Baron then solicited the young man's answer to his earlier question. "Well young Miller, do we have a deal?"

Bud tossed his head back like a young colt and quickly answered, "Duz a goat eat trees? Ya dang tooten' we have a deal. I'll be your 'blackie' if'n you do all you said you's gonna do."

"Bud, if you were a colored man I'd be happy to pay the going rate of a dollar a pound. I could buy you for seventy dollars, soaking wet. But I, the Baron de Bastrop, am a man of honor and always keep my word. I'm not buying you, but hiring you.

First thing we have to do is head for the local dry goods store where my credit is good and get you some shoes and decent clothes. You simply cannot sit at a gentleman's table in such a disheveled state. Besides, with winter coming on, your feet will freeze. I can't have my apprentice walking around with stubs for feet." The Baron blew one more set of smoke rings just as the shipmates finished securing the ship to Hedley's Wharf.

Off in the distance was the Messrs. Williams and McKinney warehouse, where his merchandise would be consigned until he made arrangements for shipment. The Baron knew he would need to raise the capital to pay the warehouse fees and to hire wagons to transport his supplies inland. The gun powder, coffee, sugar, salt, flour, cloth, tea and a sundry of other items would translate into a nice fortune for the old con once he was able to pay for storage and delivery to his new trading post. He knew some new mark with money would land on Galveston Island eager to invest. The first to make the mistake of bringing money onto the island would find themselves under the Baron's spell.

The stevedores were mingling on the dock, unloading the vessel. Bastrop took one last drag from his cigar before he flipped the butt into the deep blue-green bay and motioned for the lad to pick up his luggage. The Baron was ready for a bath and a bottle of whiskey. He could feel things were finally falling into place. The coming year his company was going to break over the top. The lad would work out just fine in his bigger picture. Bud was without question, brave, adventurous, and eager to learn. The Baron was confident he had found a rare gem in young Bud Miller who was truthful and honest to a fault. These were traits which the Baron never troubled himself with in his own dealings, but did recognize as valuable assets in those beholden to him.

The Baron de Bastrop's large stomach pressed against his wide leather belt as he exhaled a sigh of relief to be home. As the two waited for the gangplank to be lowered, the Baron started tapping his gold-tip cane on the deck. He glanced down at Bud, offering the lad from Kentucky some Texas lore. "When Texas was created, one lone star danced the night away in the heavens in her honor. That's the truth, so help me God. That's why we are called the *Lone Star Republic*. Master Bud Miller, prepare to set foot on Texas soil."

Stepping through the crowd undetected by the Baron were two men dressed in black, each wearing a brace of .46 caliber A. Whiting pistols. The two men with a score to settle would welcome him before he set foot on Texas soil. Bud's chances of reaching land had diminished greatly as the pair of intruders stood in silence, waiting for the old man and boy to disembark.

Chapter Two
David

McLemoresville, Tennessee August 9, 1835.

Congressman David Crockett waited for the ballots to be counted. He had just completed a brutal Congressional race in which President Jackson's camp and the press had lambasted the native hero. David was aware that their vitriolic attacks, portraying him as a buffoon and swindler, had dealt a critical blow to his popularity. His opponent, Adam Huntsman had accused Crockett of incurring excessive expenses and proclaimed he had accomplished nothing for his constituents while in office. Huntsman was a war hero, having lost one leg fighting Indians and he made sure not to camouflage his peg leg, stomping it on the floor when making a point. The one-legged man never failed to mention the pain he suffered fighting Indians for his beloved Tennessee. Huntsman hoped this strategy had provided the popularity he would need to take the election from the Tennessee legend. Crockett's own fiery attacks on President Jackson had contributed to his declining support as well. As he had pounded his hatred of Jackson deep into the red Tennessee clay, one by one Crockett's loyal supporters had drifted away. His lead had steadily declined, and the race was now neck-and-neck down the homestretch.

When the votes were tallied, the results failed to swing in Crockett's favor. 4,400 for the man many said was half-horse and half-alligator and 4,652 voted for his opponent, Adam "Blackhawk" Huntsman. Losing the hotly contested race to Blackhawk was a bitter and painful defeat for Crockett. The loss of his seat in Congress killed any hopes of being his party's nominee for president the following year. He had been touted as his party's presidential candidate should he be re-elected to Congress; now they would throw their support behind Van Buren. The Tennessee legend stood shaking his head in disbelief as the final tally was read. He was forty-nine years old and just missed the opportunity to be a candidate for the president by of the United States by only 252 votes.

David debated calling for a recount; however, his friends assured him that doing so would not be in his best interest. Unknown to Crockett, unscrupulous supporters had voted for him more than once in various parts of the state. A recount would, without question, reveal voter fraud on both sides. Crockett didn't need a voting scandal should he decide to run again.

Later in the day, a dejected David Crockett made his farewell speech and painfully conceded defeat to a man he felt was inferior. During the campaign, Crockett had told anyone who would listen that if they voted for Blackhawk, he would "go to Texas and they could all go to Hell." Now that the voters refused to send him back to Washington, he would have to make good on part of his threat. He might not be able to send them all to hell, but he would go to Texas where his skills would be appreciated. The first time the voters had failed to send him back to Washington, Crockett left the next day for a three-month hunting trip to the interior of Tennessee. This time he would leave the state, in protest, for good.

The seasoned politician raised and lowered his voice as he spoke, expounding on the virtues of leaving Tennessee to the devil and moving where God had meant for men to live in abundance and freedom. "Texas is the true paradise and the sooner we get there, the better. I feel certain when Christ returns for His own, He will visit Texas first." David encouraged his supporters to follow him, adding, "Land is almost free and the soil so rich all you have to do is sprinkle your seeds on the ground, and I promise on my good name, you will see corn grow taller than an elephant in no time." To the sharecroppers in the audience, his words appealed to their desperate hope for a better life.

In the rear of the crowd stood a twenty-seven year old farmer, twenty-two years Crockett's junior; Johnny Satterwhite was one of those disenfranchised sharecroppers. Wide-eyed, Johnny hung on every word the dejected leader was espousing. Mesmerized by the promise of a better life in Texas, he fell under Crockett's spell. When Crockett finished speaking, Johnny Satterwhite waited patiently for the crowd to disperse before timidly approaching the legend. Johnny's voice cracked as he spoke to the man he dreamed of emulating. "Mr. Congressman, Sir," he said, as his words came in jerks instead of a steady flow. "Mr. Congressman, Sir, you will always be my man in Washington. That Blackhawk is nothing like you. He can't carry your bags. You are a true and honest man of the people. We named our youngest boy after you. We christened him David Crockett Satterwhite. Hope that's okay with you Sir."

For a brief moment, the frontiersman was buoyed by Johnny's enthusiastic attitude toward him. "Why thank you, son. That's mighty nice of you. Hope I can live up to your expectations. Seems like I'm not needed in Tennessee anymore. The voters have spoken and want me to leave. Like I said, if the voters didn't send me back to Washington, I was going to Texas and they could all go to hell."

He lowered his head and asked Johnny an unusual question. "Son, are you familiar with the gambling roulette wheel?"

Taken aback, Johnny answered, "Sir, I can't say as I'm an authority on the roulette wheel. When I was about fourteen there was one set up at the county fair, but the Sheriff shut it down after a couple of days. I did get to see them spinning the wheel and the little ball going round and round. That's 'bout all I know. Does this have to do with the evils of gambling? Is that what you are trying to tell me?"

"No son. I wanted to compare what I just experienced here today to standing and watching that little ball go round and round. That's my favorite part of the game; anticipation is high and when the game is over, you either wind up victorious or dejected. You know once the wheel of destiny is spinning, there is nothing one can do but wait. That is what waiting for votes to be tallied is like. But roulette wheels can be rigged and I have a strong suspicion this election was like a crooked roulette wheel. Blackhawk and Jackson rigged the election. There is no way I lost fair and square." The consummate politician suddenly thought it wise to change the direction of the conversation and extended his hand to the young man. "What's your name again?"

"Jonathan Satterwhite, Mr. Congressman Sir, but folks 'round here just call me Johnny. I'm from the Satterwhites that own the mill out on Brushy Creek down at the bottom of Muttonbluff. My pa is Bull Satterwhite. I think you know him."

David Crockett had started several mills himself, only to have two of them swept away by floodwaters. His father before him had also struggled in the mill business for many years. Not letting the young man see the painful failure the thought of running a mill brought into his mind, he answered, "I knew your pa. Fought alongside him in the Creek Indian war. A fine man. Didn't he die of consumption last winter?"

Johnny didn't want to dispute the great David Crockett, but the man the Congressman remembered was his uncle, Billy Satterwhite. Billy had fought the Creek Indians with the Congressman. Johnny's father, Bull, had left home when he was young and had never returned. Johnny heard rumors that he had taken up with the Indians and was living in Arkansas or Texas. Other stories had his father joining a freebooting pirate and sailing the waters of the Caribbean. Remembering his boyhood was painful. Johnny garnered all the courage he could muster and asked, "Sir, what makes you so darned fired up over going to Texas? That's not even the United States. I was told you gotta become a Meskin to live there."

"That's what Blackhawk Huntsman and Andy Jackson would have you think. I'm not like Huntsman; I don't have Jackson's dog collar around my neck. I'm my own man and don't listen to the likes of them. Besides, Governor Sam Houston was in Tennessee last year gathering up folks to go back to Texas. As I'm confident you know, I'm a good friend of Sam and was one who thought he should never have resigned after he got his divorce and then went off to live with them stinking Indians. No matter if he lived with the Cherokee, he is still a man of his word. You can hang your hat on anything he says. Anyway, he told me a man can get over 1,280 acres for just enlisting in the army for a year or, if he brings some other folks with him, he can get 11,000 acres for every ten families. I'm thinking I can own 100,000 acres of prime farmland in a few years. I won't have any problem getting a hundred families to follow me. You know a lot of folks here in this part of the country will listen to my promise of a better life. They know Jackson and his clan won't ever let the common man in Tennessee own land. Folks can come with me to Texas and own their own land, work their own farms. The ground is so fertile that all you have to do is toss a sprig on the dirt and watch the green shoot up. They tell me cotton gets as tall as a man and one stalk will produce a bale." The more Crockett talked, the more his common-man language came forward. "Ain't no way any man can get ahead like that here in this ironed-fisted state. Andy Jackson and his cronies like Blackhawk Huntsman have done messed things up here in the worst way."

Crockett wrapped both of his hands around Johnny's, pulling the young man in, holding his attention. David Crockett was taller than most, and used his stature to his advantage. Standing a solid six feet, he towered over the smaller Johnny. Looking down into Johnny's trusting eyes with practiced sincerity, Crockett continued, "I'd be much obliged if you and your family would join me as part of my group moving to Texas. I'll be leaving by horseback soon, but you can load a wagon and catch up with us on the trail. If you move with haste, you can catch up to us before we reach the Red River. I'm heading for San Antonio de Bexar soon and have several stops to make along the way to tie up some loose ends. If you don't catch up with us on the road, make sure you arrive by early spring. We have to be ready to plant when the soil turns warm. I'll give you the pick of my prime farmland allotment. You can have 1,280 acres, get your crops in the ground come spring, and harvest by fall. Since I knew your pa, your credit is good with me." David Crockett had no land to give and no agreement with Mexico allowing him to allot parcels. David wasn't lying in his mind; just bending the truth a little to fit his personal agenda. He was assembling followers so he could use them to demonstrate his ability to bring solid citizens into Texas and gain profitable favor with the Mexicans.

Johnny slapped his plow mule into a gallop and kept the pace until he could see the smoke rising from his one-room homestead. Johnny had built the log cabin with his own hands. The red clay floors were packed solid, the cracks between the logs filled with straw and red Tennessee mud. By the time he reached home, his dun mule with a black strip down the middle of her back was covered with lather, making her true color impossible to distinguish. He began shouting at the top of his lungs as he galloped up the dirt road. "Millie, Millie, Millie. Where are you Millie?" Dropping from his mount, he ran toward the cabin. Seeing the empty room, he instantly knew where they were. Leaving his exhausted mule panting in the dust, he ran full out the quarter mile down to the creek. Just before he topped the ridge above the waterhole, he heard his children's laughter. As his family came into view, he shouted, "Millie, you will never guess who shook my hand in town today. Not in a million years!"

The hot August summer made swimming too inviting to resist. Millie had allowed the children to coax her into delaying chores and joined them for a refreshing plunge in the cool creek water. Johnny's wife Millie had turned twenty-four the preceding week. For a mother of three, she had retained the girlish figure she possessed when Johnny married her just after she turned thirteen. Their oldest child, a rambunctious nine-year-old son would be ten on Christmas Day. They chose the name A.D. for the year of our Lord to honor his special birthday. Next was Ruthann, their eight-year-old chestnut-haired daughter. November 17th would be her ninth birthday. Ruthann was the apple of her pa's eye and the self-appointed boss of the homestead. Last was their baby son who they named David Crockett Satterwhite. Little Davy would be two the following April.

When Millie heard Johnny calling, she climbed from the cool spring water and was drying off next to the baby when her husband reached her. He grabbed her wet body, engulfing her with his embrace. "Millie, you will never guess in a million years who shook my hand today. Honest to God, he shook my hand and talked to me just like you and I are doin' now."

She smiled and leaned over, shaking her full auburn hair back and forth, forcing the excess water from her thick locks. As she ran her fingers through her hair, she responded, "From your excitement, it could only be one of two people: Jesus Christ Himself has returned or Congressman Crockett."

"Lord 'O Mercy gurl. You are not only the prettiest woman in all of Tennessee and the whole wide world, but about the smartest to ever live. You nailed it on the head. I shook the hand of Colonel David Crockett. I up and told him we named our youngest after him. Hot dang woman, gather the children and let's load the wagon. We are moving to Texas at the invite of David Crockett himself!"

Millie threw her long, thick hair up and over like an Andalusian horse in the wind. "What? Where did you say we are going? Have you lost your senses Jonathan?"

Johnny didn't mean to blurt out his plans so quickly, but wasn't able to restrain himself. He had never been an impulsive man, but he believed fervently that following Colonel Crockett to the land of opportunity was his destiny.

He continued, "Millie, Colonel David Crockett shook my hand and invited us to come with him to Texas. He wants us to help build a new nation, a place where we can be free to own a tract of fertile land and not be told what to plant or how much we can keep. We may never have such an opportunity again. Millie, if we stay in Tennessee, we are going to be sharecroppers for the rest of our days and our boys will follow if we don't make a better life. You know I'll never get out from under Hank Summers' grasp. He will never allow us to earn enough to buy our own land here in Tennessee."

"Jonathan William Satterwhite, I married you to be your faithful wife and to obey you as the head of our home. That's what I promised the preacher. I wonder if my obedience meant going half way 'round the world following a dreamer like Mr. Crockett. Johnny, you amaze me. In the depths of winter, you always have an invincible summer in your chest. I've never known anyone as determined as you. I see how you struggle to feed us on this little farm while at the end of every harvest we give most of the crop to

Mr. Summers. But I don't like the idea of leaving my kin and moving to a wilderness territory. I have heard the stories about savage Indians in Texas. Have you thought this through?"

Johnny was never a man to impose his will on his wife. Rather, he always carefully considered her opinion in larger matters. He could decide where to plant the corn, sugar cane or tobacco, but when it came to decisions like this, he did nothing without her involvement. Moving to Texas was different. The hopelessness of never owning his own land had weighed heavily in his heart for many years. Crockett told him that in Texas he could end up owning ten thousand acres of river bottomland. Crockett wouldn't lie. Millie would just have to listen to him. He felt the time was right for him to exert his God-given authority as the head of his family. He wrapped his strong arms around Millie's waist and pulled her close. "My darling, you are a wonderful wife and mother and have stood strong with me when things were goin' bad over the years. For that, I thank you. This is one time I have to take the leadership God granted me as man of the house. If we don't follow Congressman Crockett to Texas, we will die on this land that does not belong to us. You know I never ask for anything. Well, I am asking you now to go with me so we can build a better future for our children. Our daughter will have a chance to marry a man with money. I hear all the men in Texas are rich. Even boys no older than seventeen can own four hundred acres of land. We work forty acres for someone else and will never earn the righteous rewards of our labor only getting forty percent of what we grow. It is unjust."

Millie placed her head on Johnny's chest and could hear his heart beating wildly. They each paused silently as Johnny watched the oldest children splashing in the water while their youngest lay sleeping in the shade of a large hickory tree. Finally Millie spoke in a tender tone, quoting part of the Old Testament. "My husband, 'wherever thou leadest, I will follow.'" Then in her own words she added, "I will walk beside you. I want you to have your own farm and if that means moving to Texas, then know I will be at your side. No use standing here and talking. We have many things to tend to."

Not waiting for Johnny to respond, she called the children to get dressed and meet them back at the cabin. As her son A.D. reached the bank, Millie ordered, "Bring little Davy when you come. Your pa and I have important things to discuss."

While walking hand in hand, Millie suggested they not tell the children just yet. She was concerned they might tell a friend and the news would reach their landlord, Mr. Summers, a powerful man with strong political ties in the community. Summers would not be pleased at the prospect of them leaving and would use all means within his power to keep them in his debt.

There was much to be done. Johnny had crops to harvest, hogs to butcher, and a wagon to make ready for the long journey. The corn was ready to be pulled and shucked. They would not be able to carry their entire share of corn; however, he shucked and shelled several tow sacks full. One sack would be saved for planting, three others for bread and to feed their animals, and the rest would be sold. There was lead to melt and mold into shot for his guns and Johnny would need to secure a nice supply of DuPont black gunpowder. The family worked in unison like a swarm of bees. Johnny was lucky to catch three or four hours of sleep a night.

With the profits from the items they sold and loans of eight dollars from their family, Johnny and Millie had already accumulated just a little over forty dollars. That was not a great sum of money, but the most either of them had ever seen at one time.

David Crockett was slowly getting past the disappointment of his defeat. The more he thought about what Houston told him about Texas, the better he felt. Houston was confident that even if Van Buren became president, that wouldn't matter in Texas. Texas would become the twenty-eighth state and a man like Crockett would have no problem becoming a Senator. Houston had assured David of his support and guaranteed an easy victory for them both. Naturally Houston was planning on becoming a Senator once he helped free the land from Mexican rule and annexed Texas into the Union. Sam failed to mention that Mexico would not give up Texas without a fight. He knew Crockett would not come if there were a war to be fought.

With the chill of fall in the air and as the leaves started to blanket the Smokey Mountains with a cornucopia of reds, oranges, magentas and yellows, Crockett came out from under his depression. With the humiliating defeat behind him, Crockett decided to throw himself a going-away party at his Gibson County farm the first week of October. He sent word for Johnny, Millie and others to attend the celebration. He wanted one more shot at convincing all to join his migration.

Even shy Johnny joined in the logrolling once he had dipped his gourd a few times into the crock of homemade whiskey. The more gourds of moonshine Crockett drank, the more he talked about Texas. After several gourds full, the Congressman decided to join in the logrolling contest. Logrolling is the backwoodsmen sport where the bark is striped from a log and the cylinder then covered with hog lard. Once the log is sufficiently greased, the men stand atop the slippery logs and attempt to roll them downhill. The first few attempts tossed the big man flat on his back and left his friends red-faced with laughter. He then jumped onto a makeshift table and entertained the guests by playing his fiddle. Between songs, David gave speeches reiterating the glory that awaited them in Texas, imploring all to join him. He once more related what Sam Houston had promised, free land and fertile soil. He would be heading to Texas by the end of the month. Crockett told his half-drunken guests, "The sun won't see me in Tennessee in the month of November and that's a promise I'll make on my mama's grave…." *A promise he would miss by a week.*

Johnny knew he would be hard pressed to join the Crockett group before the end of November. But after spending the day with the man he revered, he was even more determined to pursue his dream. Millie, for the first time, had become enthused about the prospects of a new start in Texas as well.

At the gathering was another young admirer of David Crockett: Benjamin "Ben" McCullough. Ben was born in Rutherford County, Tennessee on November 11, 1811, the son of Alexander McCullough. His father had fought with Sam Houston and David Crockett in the Creek Indian wars. Ben's family was ardent Crockett supporters as he rose to the position of Congressman. Young Ben had known David all of his life, and in many ways was like his hero. Like Crockett, young Ben had an adventurous spirit; he loved hunting, fishing and spending months alone in the mountains. He learned to stalk and track as well as any man in Tennessee. One winter Ben McCullough killed eighty-four bears. Ben left home to fur hunt in the West, but when he arrived in St. Louis, the trappers had already gone. He tried to sign on a freight line to Santa Fe; however, all the jobs were filled. He went to Wisconsin to mine lead, only to find all the good claims taken. Ben finally returned home to Tennessee and followed David from town to town during his campaign, doing his best to garner support for the Congressman's re-election.

Ben promised Crockett that he and his brother Henry would meet him in Nacogdoches, Mississippi on Christmas Day, 1835. He pledged the pair would help David bring Texas into the Union. The brothers had to delay their trip by several weeks when Henry came down with fever. As a consequence, the McCulloughs were unable to meet Crockett on Christmas day and arrived in Texas too late to join the fight at the Alamo. Both Ben and Henry McCullough would later play an integral role in securing Texas' independence and taming the frontier. As Texas Rangers, their fame and daring would become legendary.

As Crockett headed west, Johnny still had a few loose ends to tie up. Millie's mother was gravely ill and landlord Summers was threatening to throw Johnny in jail should he move before spring. He demanded a new crop be put in the ground before he would relieve them of their obligation. As their departure date grew near, Johnny found Millie sitting and rocking little Davy, crying at the thought of leaving her brothers, sisters, and aging parents. Johnny offered Millie little comfort, fearing she would have a change of heart. He knew deep down that should Millie say no, he wouldn't force the issue. He also understood that if they remained in Tennessee, he would forever be a poor sharecropper in servitude to Mr. Summers.

In the ensuing week, Millie's mother took a turn for the better. By then, Johnny had completed covering the wagon with an oiled tarpaulin. A chicken coop was hung on the side for the eight hens and their sole red-combed rooster. Millie's stove clung to the opposite side, leaving room for them to sleep in the small wagon bed. Johnny secured the corn grinder to the wagon sideboard. Without the grinder, there would be no bread or means to break down the coffee beans. The family bible was wrapped in oilcloth to protect the soft leather and parchment pages from the elements. Secured in the holy bible was their birth information and marriage certificate. Johnny's biggest challenge was finding a place for his walking plow. He couldn't farm without tools. The shovel, rake, ax and hoe were no problem; he tied them to the belly of the wagon to prevent rain rusting the iron. Millie suggested removing the handles and fastening the plow blades under the front bench seat. Then he could tie the walking handles under the belly of his wagon. Johnny blurted out in his excitement, "Millie, what on earth would I ever do without you? You are the smartest women in the world and yet so humble."

The women of the Foursquare Baptist Church had held several quilting parties and made five blankets for the family. One was a thick, fluffy goose down quilt that would be used to sleep on. In the event of inclement weather, Johnny would drive bundled up on the seat in a quilt while Millie and the children could keep warm in the shelter of the covered wagon. Johnny spread a big tarpaulin for the wagon bed flooring, folding the fabric so the sides were covered as well. The tarpaulin would keep the cold wind from piercing the cracks in the floor and help keep the family warm.

One neighbor gave them an extra mule as a spare. Another gave them a bull so they could breed the two cows once they were settled on their new land. The bull would not wait to reach Texas; both cows become pregnant before the Satterwhites passed over the Mississippi River.

Family members and close friends gave them a few more small coins and the Foursquare Church passed a special plate for them as well. Johnny and Millie had more hard cash than at any time during their marriage and would leave Tennessee with more than one hundred dollars. Millie had heard the horror stories of men in Arkansas robbing those heading for Texas so she sewed almost a hundred dollars in gold coins into the lining of her and Johnny's clothes. She also placed a few in the children's clothing in the event highwaymen discovered the adult's gold.

Millie planned to travel with the pistol her brother had given her and would insist A.D. and Johnny keep the powder dry at all times. Friends rounded up extra powder and molded extra shot for their firearms so they had plenty of ammunition. In addition to two pistols for Johnny, he and A.D. each carried their Kentucky long rifles.

Millie's aunt prepared enough beeswax candles to last for several months. With the wagon covered, the floor sealed, and the end flaps closed, one large candle would keep the seeds from freezing and the family warm.

The most important gifts were cuttings from apple, pear, peach, plum, and grapevines. Each sprig was carefully wrapped in a burlap ball, ready to be planted once they arrived in Texas. Johnny tied the twigs to the rear of the wagon seat facing in toward the warm bed of the wagon. He included ten pounds of cotton, five of wheat, and several small bags of vegetable seeds; each carefully wrapped and tucked in the bed of the wagon. It was important to protect their start-up seeds from freezing or being crushed or they would not germinate and provide them with food come spring.

On November 30th, as soon as the sun set, Johnny finished filling two barrels of water from their cistern and lashed them securely to the wagon. The rickety wagon was loaded to capacity and the old iron rim wheels dug deep into the red Tennessee clay as they started down the narrow dirt road. Under cover of darkness, the family headed into the bright promise of their new life. Three miles into their journey, like a message from God, the sky illuminated with a ghostly brilliant streak of light. Gazing into the sky, they watched as Haley's Comet put on a display the likes of which none of them had ever seen; a massive ball of fire followed by a blazing tail spanned across the heavens. Young A.D. jumped from the moving wagon and ran beside the mules so he could get a better look. Johnny pulled back on the reins, halting the team so the entire family could enjoy the heavenly display. Millie put her arm around her husband's waist and whispered, "This is God pointing the way. Nothing else can explain this amazing sight. God has given our departure his heavenly approval." Johnny agreed. They bowed their heads and gave thanks to God for their blessings and His guidance.

Johnny knew he couldn't tarry, so he popped the reins and urged his mule team forward into the darkness. November nights in the Tennessee Mountains turn bitter cold, but this night was different, special. The temperature remained above seventy degrees. The family needed no covers or jackets, and the baby only a light blanket to keep him warm. With God's endorsement written across the sky, and the temperate weather, the Satterwhites were ecstatic to be following the great David Crockett. This was a night they would never forget.

Johnny drove the team until after two in the morning, needing to put as much distance between him and their angry landlord as possible. He found a clearing and pulled the team to a halt. Rather than unhitching the mules and staking the cattle to graze, he left them tied to the wagon. He hobbled the three mules and cattle. He didn't want something to spook them and have to deal with a runaway. He planned to sleep only an hour or two so they would be back on their way before daylight.

David Crockett and his men were watching the heavenly display less than five miles east of Memphis. Like the Satterwhites, Colonel Crockett also saw Haley's Comet as a sign of divine providence, a guiding light to the Promised Land. David was unable to sleep, contemplating the glories the Heavenly Father had in store for him once they reached Texas. He would be getting a fresh start with followers who would appreciate his talents. If there had been any doubt about going to Texas, all was erased by the brilliant comet streaking through the darkness of this night.

Once again underway before dawn, the Satterwhites trudged forward at a snail's pace. From time to time the big bull pulled back, putting an extra load on the mules. Well after daylight, the family stopped at the homestead of a close friend of David Crockett's, Calvin Jones. Calvin told them that Crockett and about fifteen men had spent the night with him two weeks earlier.

When Calvin learned they were trying to pull their load with two mules while leading a third, he made Johnny an offer that was impossible to decline. If Johnny would spend a week splitting logs for the winter, Mr. Jones would pay him with another mule. A four-team hitch would make pulling the wagon much easier. It was not that Mr. Jones needed the logs split, but he understood Johnny was a proud man and would not accept charity.

Millie and Mrs. Jones canned vegetables and made dill pickles. Young Ruthann helped with the canning while A. D. stacked the chopped wood into cords. The nights were filled with bible study and tall tales of David Crockett's adventures, each man exaggerating Crockett's escapades. The evening before they were to leave, Johnny fetched his fiddle and played some of his favorite mountain music. Before turning in for the night, Millie sang her most-loved Christian songs while her husband accompanied softly on his fiddle.

The young couple borrowed some red paint from the Jones and painted *G.T.T.* on each side of their wagon. They had wanted to tack a sign *G.T.T.* on their old log home before they left, letting all who stopped by know they had *Gone To Texas*, but didn't for fear Mr. Summers would prevent their departure. They were now truly on their way to Texas. This had indeed been a great week: A clean break without being harried by old man Summers, God had shown a sign in the sky, and now Calvin Jones had traded them a much-needed mule.

With the four-mule team, they were able to travel fifteen miles a day most days, and some days almost twenty. To their good fortune, the hens continued to lay eggs in their wobbly cage. Millie started breakfast before dawn and fed them scrambled eggs, flapjacks and bacon. They ate quickly and were on the trail before the rooster crowed.

Stocking up on salt, sugar, beans, and extra coffee beans in Memphis, they were waiting at the dock on Wolf Creek when Limus, the old ferryman showed up. Limus owned the ferry that would take them across the mighty Mississippi River. Fitting the mules and cattle on the ferry was not an easy task, even for a seasoned boatman like Limus. Once the wagon was secured, Limus slipped the dock ropes and pushed off into Wolf Creek and toward the swirling waters of the Mississippi.

Once across the Mississippi, the next 120 miles to Little Rock were uneventful. They stopped when Johnny found a nice pasture for the animals to graze and a stream so Millie could clean their clothes. Johnny greased the wagon wheels and put new shoes on the mules. Several men heading to Texas to fight in the impending war with Mexico passed them along the way and Johnny never missed an opportunity to let them know he and Colonel Crockett were friends. In Little Rock, Johnny was pleased to learn he was sharpening his ax on the same grindstone the Colonel used only sixteen days earlier. Each message let him know they were gaining a few days on the Colonel. Crockett had continued to stop along the way and barter or borrow funds while Johnny had pressed on, never wavering in his determination to catch up to Crockett and his followers.

A.D. took the responsibility of hunting for game. He was a crack shot with his curly-maple .50 caliber long rifle. Deer were in abundance and didn't fear man as they did back in the mountains of Tennessee. One morning young A.D. came running back to the wagon with their two coonhounds at his heels. He was shouting, "Buffalo, buffalo, I just saw ten thousand buffalo. Pa, it had to be more than that. The earth shook when they ran."

Johnny sternly popped the reins against the mule's rumps and pushed them forward so the entire family could get a glimpse of the herd. At the crest of a small ridge, he pulled the mules to a halt. Johnny estimated there were at least twenty-five thousand of these prehistoric giants of the prairie. They moved like the waves of an ocean, grazing in unison as they lumbered across the open plains. A.D. wanted to shoot one for the meat, but Johnny warned that one shot would start a stampede. Besides, Johnny guessed one shot wouldn't bring down one of these giants. He recalled a buffalo robe that a trapper had brought back to Tennessee from a trip West; the hide was almost half an inch thick. Millie was relieved to see the natural bounty. There would be plenty of meat to feed their family and hides to make warm clothing necessary for survival in the wilderness of Texas.

The days grew shorter and the nights colder as the second week of December brought torrential rain. The road became rocky and without warning, a large chug hole broke a spoke in their rear wagon wheel.

Johnny had carved hickory spokes before they left Tennessee, but in his haste forgot to put them in the wagon. To stabilize the broken spoke, they cut buckskin strips and soaked them in water. Then they stretched and wrapped the buckskin strips tightly around the spoke and let the sun shrink the leather taut. The wrapping was not a work of art, but the buckskin did keep the spoke together.

When the Satterwhites arrived in Lone Prairie, they met Isaac Jones who put them up for a week, and allowed the animals to graze on his winter grasses to regain their strength. He and Johnny replaced the broken spoke and made a few spares out of dried hickory. Jones showed them a pocket watch he purchased from Crockett weeks earlier. The watch was a twenty-five jeweled gold timepiece presented to the Congressman in 1834 by the city of Philadelphia. Isaac had paid David $30 for the watch because the Congressman was running a little short on cash; David Crockett was always short on funds.

Isaac warned the Satterwhites of the hostile Indians in the Texas territory and pointed out that lower Arkansas was not plagued with Indian raids. He encouraged them to stay in his area and offered them four hundred acres of prime bottomland on credit; Johnny could make annual payments after his crops were harvested. Four hundred acres was ten times the size of the parcel Johnny farmed in Tennessee and Millie was extremely tempted when she learned there was a church and school near the property. But nothing could sway Johnny from following his hero. He had given David Crockett his word he would arrive in Texas by spring. His word was his bond.

The family rolled into Clarksville, Texas the afternoon of January 15, 1836, not knowing there was another storm blowing in from Mexico in the form of General Santa Anna. That night they camped at the edge of town where Johnny chipped ice from a frozen creek bank and cranked out a container of vanilla ice cream. It was a victory celebration. They were finally in Texas. Johnny played some down home music on his fiddle. Even the coyotes seemed to enjoy the tunes, joining in from time to time, accompanied by a matching pair of great horned owls.

By January 23rd, they passed Bois d' Arc Creek near Choctaw Bayou on their way to the heart of Texas. Johnny missed the road to Nacogdoches and instead followed a seldom-used trapper's trail. This was a mistake that took them southwest and into the heart of Indian country. A week after the family crossed the Trinity River, a "blue norther" blew in, forcing them to stop and take shelter. As if by divine guidance, Johnny located a tall cliff about thirty miles east of Fort Parker. The chocolate cliff rose twenty feet from the ground and projected out over an enclosed ten-foot refuge. The south-facing overhang provided shelter and blocked the frigid northern winds. Johnny hobbled the animals behind the wagon and away from the freezing rain. The Jones' had warned them about the Texas blue northers but they never dreamed the entire landscape would become a solid block of ice.

Keeping a fire burning presented Johnny's biggest challenge. Dry wood was difficult to scurry up and wet, green wood wouldn't burn. Johnny's days were filled with gathering wood and hoping for a shot at some wild animal for food. Not many animals dared to brave the sub-zero temperatures, but when a rabbit did venture out and into the sights of Johnny's long rifle, their next meal was rabbit stew. One morning while looking for wood, Johnny spotted a rafter of wild turkey and managed to bag two before the rest scattered beyond the ice-covered trees. Millie roasted them over the open flame and the hungry family feasted.

Night after night, the family huddled against the cold wearing layers of clothing, blankets, and deerhide covers. Johnny slept very little, continuously stoking the fire. Each time he tossed a new log on the fire, sparks jumped into the air and it was a constant concern that a spark would ignite the wagon cover. Without a wagon cover, they would surely freeze.

Every night, a male mountain lion made the top of the cliff his resting place. His blood-curdling screams jolted them out of their sleep, causing the children to panic. His scream was not an unfamiliar sound. They knew the cry of the panther, but the silence of the night being penetrated by his close screams created fear, even in Johnny. The big cat kept them awake and unsettled for many nights.

Weakened by lack of sleep and the constant battle to stay warm and dry, stress was now severely affecting the mental and physical health of the Satterwhites. Johnny fought day and night to maintain the fire, leaving little time to console his distraught wife. Together, they had traveled so far and now it seemed they might perish only a couple of hundred miles from their dream. Millie's courage was slowly giving in to despair. Johnny had never seen Millie cry so profusely. Her mind drifted back to her mother running down the trail as they left Tennessee, begging them not to leave. Her mother kept saying she would never see them again. Now it appeared as if her mother might have been right. Unless there was a break in the weather, this spot would become their grave.

The winds created howling cries day and night. Millie began to believe she could hear words spoken by the winds, words of doom and despair. Johnny did his best to assure his wife the strong north wind only sounded like voices. It was the strain that was making her mind play evil tricks on her. He suggested they could find solace in reading the Holy Bible. Millie read out loud as best she could with what little light the candles produced. She believed their days on earth were drawing to an end and being right with God would ensure their eternal salvation.

Johnny also grew more despondent, knowing he might have made an unforgivable mistake that could mean the death of his family. The ninth night of the storm, Johnny wrote a short note to any who might find their bodies after the spring thaw:

To Whom it May Concern,

We are the Satterwhites of Tennessee and on our way to join Colonel David Crockett in San Antonio, Texas. In the event we do not survive our plight, please get our message to our friend and mentor. Let him know we did make Texas soil in January, 1836. Please see we are given a Christian burial.

May God have Mercy on our souls.

Johnny and Millie Satterwhite

He placed the crumpled note in his watch pocket. Then Johnny held Millie's weary body close and drifted into what he believed would surely be his final slumber.

Chapter Three
The Island

The ominous pair stood patiently as the Baron and Bud slowly descended the rickety gangplank. About half way down, Bastrop spotted the two strangers. He had an idea they might be waiting to speak with him. The Thompson brothers had come to Texas from New York a few weeks after San Jacinto and quickly established themselves as moneylenders. Their interest rates bordered on usury and their collection methods hovered around barbaric.

"Howdy boys. You are the two I was hoping to see today," the Baron growled with an air of confidence.

"Hope for your sake you have our money," the older of the two fired back.

"Let me get off this gangplank before the thing dumps me in the water. Boys, this ship is full of merchandise belonging to me. I will have the measly money I owe you and plenty more once I have an opportunity to start selling."

Again the older brother spoke. "What's that pile of rags you have there?"

"This pile of rags you so disparagingly refer to is Master Benjamin Miller. Young Miller is moving to Texas and will be my assistant. He's a bright boy and once I scrape the barnacles off, he will become a productive member of my organization and our great nation."

Finally the younger brother stepped on the first rung of the gangplank and grabbed the Baron's left arm. Bud's hand slid into his pocket, fumbling around for his pocketknife. He was not going to allow the brothers to harm the old man. Bud knew he could kill one man with a swift stroke of his knife and perhaps grab a pistol to shoot the second. Thinking quickly, the Baron smiled and in a jovial tone said, "Thank you. I was having a rough time getting down these steps. Now boys, don't get your dander up. You will see my merchandise unloaded shortly. You can rest assured the Baron has never cheated a man and I'm too old to start now. Your money will be paid along with your interest. First things first."

The older brother took the Baron's other arm and leaned over so no one could hear him speak. "Bastrop," he chided. "We don't care if you are old. We don't care if you are the reason Texas has white people. We want our money. Trust me, we cannot afford for people to know we let you stiff us."

"Gentlemen, gentlemen, you are dealing with the Baron de Bastrop. I am a man of honor. The purpose of my trip to New Orleans was to secure merchandise I can convert into hard cash. Do with me what you wish, but if you want your money, you will allow me the freedom to sell my wares."

"Sounds straight enough," quipped the younger brother.

"There is one thing I need from you. Since I already owe you five hundred plus interest, I will be in need of an additional loan. Spot me another hundred. I'm good for it. I need to get the boy some clothes and find us a place to rest."

Bud stood incredulous as the older brother released the old man and the younger brother opened his money pouch, handing the Baron five twenty-dollar gold coins.

"Thank you boys. Pleasure to see you," the Baron responded. With those parting words, and a hundred dollars richer, the Baron nodded for Bud to follow with the steamer trunks.

The Baron waved down a buggy and motioned Bud to load his trunks and other baggage in the back. The local newspaper editor, Gail Borden, was driving the buggy and recognized the Baron. After the luggage was loaded and Bud had joined them in the buggy, Borden asked, "Where do you need to go Mr. Bastrop?"

"We have one stop to make. If it's not too much trouble, the lad and I will stop at the dry goods store up near Main Street. Then, if you don't mind, we need for you to deliver our things to Mrs. Maxwell's boarding house. You can deliver my trunk and bags to the boarding house and advise Mrs. Maxwell that we shall be there shortly."

Bud couldn't believe how the Baron operated. How was the Baron so persuasive? Did people feel sorry for him, respect him, or fear him? Bud was puzzled by, and at the same time, impressed with the Baron's ability to get what he wanted.

Once in the dry goods store, the old man purchased the lad from Kentucky a pair of ready-made high top shoes, new flannel britches, a wool shirt, a broad-brimmed beaver hat, and a used wool topcoat. The storeowner tossed in a waterproof poncho after the Baron told him of Bud's pitiful circumstances. As always, the Baron put the clothes on credit, telling the storeowner young Bud would pay him once the lad found gainful employment.

December meant rain, rain, and more rain on the twenty-six-mile-long island. Galveston's streets turned into sand-laden swamps. As the two traversed the wooden plank sidewalks, now littered with chunks of mire, the Baron knew he would need to remain on the island until he could find a way to pay the consignment house. He knew Williams & McKinney would not release his merchandise without full payment and he needed that merchandise to secure his future. The Baron had accumulated a wealth of guns, powder, sugar, coffee, and bolts of cloth that represented his first real opportunity to earn cold hard cash. Trades, barters, deals, swindles and various larcenies had earned him either land or things he could find little use for in the past. Now at his advanced age, he was finally going to have gold and silver.

The Baron took Bud to the warehouse and selected a striped maple Kentucky long rifle with rich silver inlay for him. He also tossed in a ball mold, powder horn, gunpowder, wadding, lead balls and flint. The boy would now be armed with the most powerful and accurate firearm in the world. The showy long rifle shot a .43 caliber round and measured 52 inches long. Standing only 63 inches, Bud was not much taller than his newly acquired weapon. The Baron calculated the cost and then asked Bud to sign a promissory note. Bud didn't know the rifle's real value or that the Baron was charging him the full retail plus a 20% premium, but at that moment, he didn't care.

The Baron's trunks and luggage were neatly stacked in front of a sign that read: *"Mary Maxwell's Boarding House. Three hots and a cot, one dollar."*

"Grab my bags," the Baron directed.

Bud's hands were full with his rifle and accouterments; nevertheless, he did manage to pull the heavy trunks beyond the gate and through the front door.

Mary Maxwell was a rather large woman with a few missing teeth and ill-fitting spectacles. One earpiece was tied with sewing thread and the other dangled precariously on the edge of her left ear. Her thick ankles made her legs look like fence posts. Mary was aware that the old man was storing merchandise she could put a lien on should he try to skip town without paying her. Bastrop always found a way to procure credit even though everyone in the Republic knew his propensity not to pay. Perhaps it was because so many knew there might never have been an independent Texas without his intervention with the Mexicans for Moses Austin. In an odd way, many felt indebted to the old scoundrel and were willing to overlook his shortcomings.

Mary Maxwell's eyes opened wide when she saw young Miller. She seldom boarded youngsters. Most of her guests were adult men. Mary's son had been about Bud's age when he died of the black vomit. Yellow fever had also swept through Galveston that same year and Mary's sister and brother-in-law had died as well. Her husband had died in the battle of San Jacinto and his death had forced Mary to take in boarders. The thought of mothering young Bud delighted the lonely widow.

From the moment the pair moved in, Mary treated Bud like a son. Once she heard the story of how the two men came to know each other, she began lobbying for Bud to stay with her when the Baron left for Bastrop. Bud would be given free room and board in exchange for doing chores around the place. Her aggressive attitude toward keeping Bud didn't set well with the Baron.

At the boarding house, eight men shared one long room and were served three hearty meals a day for one dollar. Morning breakfast included coffee, eggs, grits with sugarcane molasses, and biscuits bigger than a man's fist. Mary's biscuits were not the typical hard as rock Texas variety, but rather possessed the delicate consistency of sweet, light cake. There were some days the supply of coffee dried up in Galveston and on those occasions, Mary served her guests bottomless cups of steaming hot ginseng tea. The cots were comfortable and larger than a normal bunk bed. Sleep was sporadic at best because of the snoring and frequent coughing. Men were up and about all hours of the night, slamming doors as they went out back to the two-hole privy.

Without question, the young Mexican senoritas were the most exquisite beauties Bud had ever laid his eyes upon. Walking the streets of Galveston, young Miller saw a sixteen-year-old Mexican girl who made his heart stutter. The Baron would never allow Bud to enter the *Brass Monkey Saloon* where the young girl applied her trade, but that didn't stop the boy from sneaking a look anytime he was on the streets. He made a point to pass the saloon several times a day in hopes she would venture out onto the sidewalk. The third time he walked past the saloon one morning, the stunning beauty was standing on the wood plank walkway. Her lips were painted fire red and her body moved with grace under her dress. Her raven hair shimmered as it streamed gently down her back. He wanted to stop and speak to her, but words would not come. He simply tipped his new broad-brim beaver hat and briskly walked on, spellbound.

Late-night chatter among the men at the boarding house aroused the young man's curiosity. The men told Bud how for one dollar he could have an older woman, and for a five dollar gold coin, the services of one of the three younger girls at the *Brass Monkey Saloon*. The Baron would not give Bud cash; he knew if he spent his only five dollars to be with the young girl, he would be destitute. He desperately tried to put the Mexican beauty out of his mind, but the girl haunted his thoughts day and night.

Once settled in at Mrs. Maxwell's place, the Baron immediately enrolled Bud in the local school so he could be taught to read and write. Bud refused to go until the Baron reminded him how Texas law dealt with runaway boys. Bastrop wove a fabricated tale of grave repercussions to frighten the boy, and his ploy worked. Bud did not dare risk getting in trouble with the law and agreed to attend school.

Bud felt uncomfortable sitting in the first grade classroom. Fortunately, there was one older boy and two adult men present as well. His teacher, Horace Weatherspoon was an odd-looking, tall man with a deep receding hairline and a hatchet chin. Weatherspoon, a Connecticut native, was a stickler for proper English. Horace's accent was crisp and precise, his manner, commanding. Immediately Mr. Weatherspoon began working to eliminate "ain't" and "kaint" from Bud's vocabulary.

Horace could see the young man was overflowing with promise. Besides, the teacher had other plans for the orphan boy. Horace lived alone and occasionally shared his bed with lonely seamen. Horace Weatherspoon went out of his way to be seen about town with two different widows. Ironically, some of the locals considered the schoolteacher to be a ladies man. He conscientiously maintained the appearance that he was a man's man and a rakish womanizer. He was acutely aware should his persuasion be revealed, he would be tarred, feathered, and carried off the island on a pole. Weatherspoon worked hard to suppress temptation. But from the first day that Bud walked through the schoolhouse door, Horace could think of nothing else but the handsome, pure boy who had wandered into his classroom.

In a casual conversation during recess, Horace asked, "Mr. Miller, do you have a girlfriend?" This was a safe, natural question to ask a teenager.

Bud's face flushed red. The teen directed his eyes away from his teacher while talking about the Mexican girl at the *Brass Monkey*. Horace's voice cracked as his breath shortened. "I don't have a problem with giving you private lessons in speech in the evenings, that is, if you like the sound of waves roaring through an open window. My cottage is on the beach and you can smell the salt water at night. I'd love to cook you a delicious dinner and give you some private instruction. How does that sound?"

The schoolmaster's true intentions passed over young Miller's head. Bud believed the offer would be of great value to him; he wanted to learn to read like the Baron. Without hesitation, Bud answered, "Sounds down right neighborly of you to do this fur me Mister Weatherspoon. I'd be much obliged to come to your house for sum grub and learnin'."

Horace's cheeks flushed cadmium red and his heart raced. The naive Benjamin Miller would be walking into his teacher's lair like a fly into a spider's web. He had no clue of the sticky trap Horace was laying out. Horace considered the danger he faced should he act out his plan and thought perhaps a few glasses of French wine or some laudanum mingled in cold milk would help break down the boy's resistance. Horace had no way of knowing what a volatile young man he had invited to dinner.

Each evening the Baron read aloud in his thick brogue two chapters of Fennimore Cooper's *The Last of the Mohicans*. The Baron wanted young Bud to be familiar with literature and know the importance of being able to read. The boarding house living room filled with men and women wanting to hear the gravel-voiced Baron bring the story to life. Bud sat entranced. He had never heard anyone read with such passion, painting such beautiful pictures with his words. Bud was in awe of the old man and became determined to learn to read as well as or better than the Baron.

Despondent New York immigrants assembled outside the Galveston immigration compound. Unethical land promoters in New York had sold the group of families land grants that were worth less than the ink used to sign the papers. There was no land available for such a ridiculously low amount as five cents per acre. Nevertheless, thirty-six families had purchased the worthless paper, chartered a ship and made the voyage to Texas. Once in Galveston, they soon discovered they had been defrauded. Ever the opportunist, the moment the Baron got word of their plight, he hastily made his way to the terminal and summoned a meeting with the group. For the next two days, the Baron de Bastrop worked tirelessly to convince the unfortunate families to move to Bastrop. He went from family to family presenting the opportunities that awaited them in his township. He told them how the farmers were growing cotton as tall as a man. With Mexico out of the picture, full slavery would be permitted in Texas. Now they could buy, sell or barter the slave labor they would need to establish profitable plantations. Men like Jim Bowie and James Taylor White had amassed fortunes in Texas through the slave trade, cotton plantations and cattle empires.

The Baron pulled out all the tricks he knew to convince the group to settle in Bastrop. He hammered over and over how unsafe and unsanitary living on Galveston Island would be, and how there were no jobs or places to live. Once the Baron saw the slightest twinge of fear cross their faces, he pounded home the dangers of settling on the isolated island. After all, the highest point on the island was only eight to ten feet above sea level, subjecting the island to endless flooding. Like a fire and brimstone preacher, he put the fear of God in them. Fear was an effective tool and he most certainly was not averse to using it to achieve his ends.

Of course, his motives were not entirely pure. In his offering to help improve their situation, they would be in his debt, and would surely vote for him when he challenged Sam Houston in the 1841 presidential election. Trade would be vital for the growth of the new Republic and should he be successful in moving the seat of government to Bastrop, the Baron would become a very wealthy and powerful man. He assured the group that Bastrop was ideally located on the Colorado River along the Camino Real. The Camino Real was the major travel route from Mexico City north through Saltillo, Coahuila, the Presidio de Rio Grande in Laredo, San Antonio, and New Braunfels, ending in Natchitoches, Louisiana. Thus, the township was strategically positioned to become a significant center of commerce along the trade route. Settling in Bastrop would provide them with endless opportunities.

On the western side of the Colorado River was a thirty thousand acre tract of land. Jim Bowie owned the land; however, there was suspicion his deed was forged. Jim had a propensity to forge documents. At the time of his death at the Alamo, Bowie "owned" over a quarter of a million acres in Texas. The Baron planned to sell the New Yorkers the Bowie parcel of land, allowing them to divide the acreage according to their needs. Each family would have around nine hundred acres. He would offer them the land for ten cents per acre and allow them to make payments. The arrangement would be extremely profitable for the Baron with the added benefit that the settlers would also purchase their supplies from his new general store. The small matter of not having clear title would not prevent the old swindler from issuing land certificates to this hapless group from New York.

Land speculation was nothing new to the Baron. He had done well for himself in Louisiana until Spain gave France full rule in 1800. As soon as the Union purchased Louisiana and Missouri in 1803, the Baron had fled to Texas, dumping his Louisiana holdings for bottom dollar prices. The move proved profitable until Santa Anna took control in Texas, making dealing in land almost impossible. Now, under the Lone Star, he could wheel and deal again. The Baron had not been a staunch supporter of the revolution, but now that Texas had won independence, he was moving at the speed of light to integrate into the new system. No one had the ability to reinvent himself better than the Baron. One factor in his favor was he knew the country as well as, if not better than, any man in Texas. He knew where spurious land titles were granted and how to circumvent the law.

Bastrop worked hard to make sure none of the two hundred immigrants became discouraged and decide to return to New York. The problem was there was no one person in charge of the group, and the Baron was encountering resistance. Bastrop decided to solicit the help of his friend, Jim Brown, who was originally from New York. Jim had left home when he was twelve and apprenticed with a brick mason. He worked on the Erie Canal project that linked Lake Erie in the west to the Hudson River in the east, which when completed in October 1825, was the engineering marvel of its day. Jim had earned a tidy sum of money working on the canal before finding his way to Galveston. Even though he had lived in Galveston only a short time, he had established himself as a leader on the island. If anyone could persuade the New Yorkers, it would be big Jim. As Jim Brown began to speak, the newcomers realized he was one of them, but even Jim found it difficult to gain a consensus; some wanted to return to New York while others wanted to remain in Galveston. After a long day of wrangling with the unruly group, Jim was finally able to persuade them to make the journey to Bastrop.

The Baron moved quickly to make the necessary arrangements. Unable to escort the group himself, he hastily solicited a young blacksmith by the name of Noah Smithwick to act as their guide. The Baron drew up a promissory note for five hundred dollars due upon the safe arrival of the immigrants in Bastrop. Noah didn't mind; he would have taken them for free because he never turned down an adventure.

As Noah organized the haggard group, several of the local townsfolk donated blankets, corn, sugar, salt, and beef jerky. Noah procured several handcarts to carry belongings and three wagons for the women with small children and babies. He then rounded up five friends with rifles to help escort the party westward. He was counting on the size of the group to keep hostile Indians at bay and deliver them all safety to Bastrop. The trip was four to five days by horse but Noah figured it would take them six weeks since many in the group were traveling on foot. After each settler signed a land certificate for lots plotted by Bastrop, they began their journey.

Many weeks had passed when Noah Smithwick returned with glowing news. The families from New York had decided to settle in Bastrop. They had claimed their plots and were beginning to build homesteads. One detail Noah failed to tell the Baron was that many in the group had spread west to Dripping Springs and Austin. Instead of a large cluster of homes in Bastrop, they were strung out like a string of beads for over fifty miles. Noah had done his best to tell them the land they selected was not part of the Bastrop plot and that some were settling too close to Indian territory, but a squatter mentality had taken over.

Bud spent the rest of the afternoon walking around in front of the *Brass Monkey*, hoping to catch a glimpse of the beautiful young Mexican girl. He had no way of knowing what he was about to encounter would change his life forever.

Chapter Four
Cold Country

January 1836

The morning sun melted the icy shroud clinging to the wagon's canvas cover. A large chunk slid free and crashed to the ground. Johnny sat bolt upright, and hurling back the front flap saw the sun shining triumphantly across the barren landscape. He bounded over the wagon seat and out toward the fire to stoke the dying embers back to life. Rousing his family, he raised his arms skyward and praised God for delivering them all safely through the storm.

It would be several days before the trail was passable. The family needed this time to regain their strength. As deer and wild boar emerged from their hiding places, Johnny and A.D. were able to provide the family with plenty of nourishing meat. Within days, the Satterwhites were strong enough to break camp and direct their team forward into the Texas wilderness. As their wagon jerked along the trail, the familiar clanging of Millie's black cast iron pots alerted the occasional fox or wild boar that the Satterwhites were once again underway.

The family was already two months behind schedule and Johnny feared Mr. Crockett would think ill of him, but no matter how loyal he was to David Crockett, they could not continue on to San Antonio. There was no doubt in his mind they must find a place to stop, build a shelter, and plant their seeds. On the morning of March 6, 1836, the mules pulled the wagon to the intersection of the Brazos and Little River (San Gabriel). Spread out before them was a field of bluebonnets sprinkled with crimson-red Indian paintbrushes. On the other side of the Brazos, waving strands of tall grass shimmering with early-morning dew beckoned the family to come across. The sight was so glorious, they knew instantly this was the spot God intended for them to settle. Once more, Johnny would construct a raft and ferry his family toward their future.

The young couple stood gazing at the abundance of rich farmland. There were no stumps to remove or rocks to clear. They saw Texas in all her glory on this plot of land awash with pink primrose, purple thistles, and bold yellow flowers turning their heads toward the sun. Giant pecan and persimmon trees lined the riverbanks, complementing the blanket of wildflowers that covered the rich bottomland. To the northwest, where the rivers intersected, the trees parted to reveal a stretch of open land covered with wild wheat. Johnny guessed the area to be between 300 and 350 acres of open pasture. He would need only to plow under the wild wheat and plant his seeds.

Behind the open area stood a fortress of giant oak trees with their arms dragging the ground as if picking flowers or sweeping the grass beneath them. A mangle of grapevines and scrub brush nestled in with the massive oaks created an impenetrable wall. Johnny stood on the pie-shaped property, thinking how well protected this swath of land was. He knew the only way Indians could attack was to cross the shallow waters of the Little River.

The couple knew they would need to obtain title for the property at some point, but for now this was the spot they would build their homestead. Unable to harness his excitement, Johnny tuned to Millie and exclaimed, "This is the best bottomland I have seen in all my days. In no time, I'll have our seeds in the ground. There is even more than enough timber to build our cabin and barns. We are home!"

As the Satterwhites surveyed the fertile land before them, they had no way of knowing the historic significance of this day or the tragedy that had befallen San Antonio. At dawn, Colonel David Crockett had been the last to die at the battle of the Alamo.

With only a few hours of daylight remaining, Johnny unloaded his plow and began assembling the handles and fastening the blades. He couldn't wait another day to start farming. He was accustomed to the thin rocky soil of Tennessee and the moment his plow dipped into the soft, Texas dirt, he was awestruck. Texas, unlike the Union states, was laced with strings of rivers running almost parallel from the interior into the Gulf of Mexico. Small creeks and springs supplied an abundance of fresh water and when the rivers overflowed, rich riverbottom soil was deposited several hundred yards inland, creating rich topsoil. This was not the case with the Mississippi, Delaware, Ohio, Missouri or other rivers in the east that carried their overflow for miles and miles downstream.

Johnny stopped plowing and insisted his family come and look. The moment A.D. saw the deep black-brown soil, he fell to his knees. Grabbing a hand full and raising the soil to his nose, he exclaimed, "Pa, I never smelled dirt so nice!"

Millie stood in disbelief. All the hardships they had endured getting to Texas were most assuredly worth the effort. She walked over to her husband, wrapped her arms around his waist and tenderly said, "My wonderful husband, this land will still be here in the morning. Let the mules rest and enjoy some of this wonderful grass. Come on and I'll finish cooking supper. Tomorrow will come soon enough."

In two weeks of dawn-to-dusk labor, Johnny had cleared over one hundred acres and planted corn, cotton and a vegetable garden as well, placed near the spot they had chosen for their future homestead. During planting time, everyone helped. One morning the family was in the field when they saw a massive dark object overhead, about two miles wide, zigging and zagging in their direction. The children began to cry, thinking the death angel was coming to take them, but Johnny explained the stories he had heard about the massive annual migration of pigeons in Texas.

The field darkened as the gigantic flock eclipsed the sun. Their ordure covered the ground as they passed. The wind from their wings fanned and cooled the air as the flock took more than four hours to pass over. A.D. wanted to get his shotgun and bring some down, but Johnny told his son to calm himself and enjoy the wonders of God. The Satterwhites had no way of knowing the fate that awaited these pigeons; relentless pursuit by greedy hunters would prevent the hens from nesting and reproducing, eventually pushing the passenger pigeon to extinction in the wild.

The family constructed a makeshift shelter from the canvas wagon cover and sealed three sides with upright poles. Millie and the two older children used mud and grass to fill in the cracks between the poles. On the front, Johnny constructed double doors from a long split log. The plank doors could be left open during the day and pulled closed at night to prevent a wolf, rattlesnake, or bear from entering. He hung a wooden whiskey barrel from one of the trees and it was A.D.'s chore to make sure the barrel was always full of drinking water and free of debris. Millie cleared the yard in front of the shelter while Johnny tilled the soil. He cleared and planted, then cleared and planted some more. The corn stalks seemed to jump out of the ground and his fruit tree sprigs quickly took root.

By May, he had finished planting all the seed they had brought from Tennessee and spent his days keeping the Johnson grass from invading his field. At night Johnny tied the two hounds at the edge of the garden rows nearest the Little River. Their barking would keep the deer, fox, and rabbits away from the tender garden leaves. To keep the cattle and mules from eating the corn and cotton, Johnny had no option but to tether them on long ropes made from strips of deerskin.

For their first dinner from the garden, Millie made new potatoes and snapped fresh peas. Indeed life was good. Schooling for the children became routine with the two oldest children setting aside three hours a day for study. Young A.D. was becoming a proficient hunter, killing two or three deer a week. Johnny tanned the hides and Millie learned to make clothes from the doeskins. They also used the deer hides to cover the roof; the canvas covers had rotted after a few months exposure to the Texas sun. Ruthann and A.D. mastered fishing and little Davy was dashing around exploring like any curious three year old. Mostly his vocabulary consisted of, "Why?" and "Why not?"

One June afternoon, as the summer sun blazed overhead, young A.D. decided to do some fishing in the Brazos. The river was brimming with giant catfish. As he neared the riverbank, he spotted a large grayish-black log lying across the path. He stopped a few feet away because the shape was unlike any piece of wood he had ever seen. Why would a log be on the river trail when there had been no flooding? He picked up a rock, slamming the stone into the middle of the log when suddenly the thinnest piece in the rear started to switch back and forth. Then the log turned toward A.D. on tiny tiny legs and opening its mouth, revealed a massive set of teeth. A.D. dropped his fishing pole and ran full tilt toward the field, shouting as he ran. "Pa, Pa, there is a log that walks down by the river."

Johnny wrapped the reins around the handle of his plow, picked up his long rifle and met his son at the edge of the field. He smiled as he answered, "Son, I do believe you spotted your first alligator. Ya know, folks back in Tennessee thought Davy Crockett was half man and half alligator. I ain't never seen one. Let's get your ma and the others. This is something special."

Millie stood well away from Johnny with little Ruthann and Davy hiding behind her skirt as A.D. ventured up a few feet in back of his father. The alligator opened his mouth once more to bare his teeth, warning the quintet what they would be up against should they move any closer. There was no question about him being angry; his tail flailed back and forth, kicking up sticks and stones with each wallop. Johnny raised his rifle into position but saw no reason for killing the creature. As they turned to leave, Johnny knew if there was one alligator, there were surely others lurking in the dark water of the Brazos. Texas was chock-full of strange and dangerous creatures the tenderfoot Satterwhites had never seen the likes of before. From now on, they would all need to be vigilant.

Johnny cut and notched logs for their new cabin. The mules made easy work of moving the logs to the new homestead's location on top of the knoll. Johnny laid the foundation logs, framed the door, and split the roof planks as Millie and Ruthann began the arduous task of packing the clay floor. They poured buckets of water on the red clay hauled from the banks of the Brazos and smoothed the surface forming the floor. They then packed the soil solid with their feet. Between each wetting and packing, the floor was left to dry. The process took several days.

It was early October before they had any visitors. Suddenly two men on horseback appeared at the edge of the forest, having just crossed the Little River. Johnny was notching logs for the cabin walls when he spotted them. The older man was dressed in buckskins, no longer the original soft yellow color, but a darkened well-worn brown. His younger companion wore a brace of pistols, carried a long rifle across the pommel of his saddle, and had a shotgun tucked in the scabbard under his right leg. A large hunting knife dangled from his side and an Arkansas tooth pick was visible sticking out of his boot top. A thick watch chain adorned with a small gold star fob dangled from his vest pocket and glistened in the sunlight. There was no question what the lone star stood for; he was a Texan. The younger man sat a saddle like he had been born on the back of a horse, his intense blue eyes cautiously scanning the treeline down to the river and back again, rarely glancing at the Satterwhites.

The two men had been following the old Ramon Road. In 1716, it had taken the Mexicans twelve days with knives, hatchets, axes and bare hands to forge the four miles of road from the Little River to the Brazos. In doing so, they were able to cross both rivers before they converged and deliver supplies to the early missions in east Texas for more than a century. Unknown to the Satterwhites, they had chosen a homesite only four miles from where the old Ramon Road cut a pathway through the mass thicket of trees. They would later learn that the Mexicans had named the forty-mile-deep forest Mount Grande, and the river, Brazos de Dios (Arms of God).

The pair of riders was surprised to come upon the settlers. As they approached, the older man tipped his hat to Millie and reached into his saddlebag for some rock candy. He always carried a few pieces of candy for the youngsters. Leaning over, he handed the candy to Millie and then spoke directly to Johnny. "We are Texas Rangers on a scouting mission. My name is Chuck Childress and this lad is Jack Coffee Hays. You can call him Coffee or Jack; he goes by either. The Comanches have been on the warpath since the Mexicans knocked down the Alamo and we are trying to pick up their trail and stop them before they kill again."

Johnny looked startled and confused. In almost a whisper he asked, "The Alamo? Sir, what do you mean 'knocked down' the Alamo?"

Chuck, puzzled, responded to Johnny's question with another. "You don't know about the fall of the Alamo and us crushing the Mexicans at San Jacinto? My friend, Texas now belongs to us."

It took a few moments for what Ranger Childress had said to soak in. Then, with even more urgency Johnny asked, "Sir, are you saying something happened at the Alamo? Was it torn down? I'm not sure what you are saying."

Young Coffee was not one to talk much. However, seeing the confusion on the Satterwhite's faces, he removed his flat-brimmed hat and continued, "Mrs. Millie and Mr. Johnny, I guess you haven't been apprised of what has taken place in Texas. I expect some time has passed since you received any news. Back on March 6th, the Mexican dictator Santa Anna and five or six thousand of his soldiers stormed the Alamo, killing 182 of our brave Texans. A few weeks later, Santa Anna massacred another 400 men down the river at Goliad. I only got to Texas after Sam Houston had turned the tide not far from Galveston Island at a place on the San Jacinto River. General Houston's men killed 640 Mexican soldiers and captured another 700, including the Napoleon of the West, General Santa Anna himself. Texas no longer belongs to Mexico. Let us be the first to welcome you to the Lone Star Republic of Texas."

Neither ranger was comfortable relating the gruesome details of the Alamo or Goliad massacres. Jack had helped to bury those murdered in Goliad and Chuck had lost several dear friends in both battles. Still in shock at the news, Johnny rushed over to Jack. His mouth opened, but words would not come. Millie moved closer to the mounted men and inquired, "Who died at the Alamo? Was Congressman Crockett among those who were killed?"

Captain Childress dismounted and walked toward Millie, holding the reins in his left hand. Keeping his right hand free was by force of habit in the event he needed to use his pistol. The tall middle-aged ranger took Millie by the hand. "I'm really sorry to be the one to tell you, but all except a few women and two black slaves were lost at the Alamo. They even killed Jim Bowie in his sick bed. Colonel Crockett fought to his last drop of blood."

Johnny looked at young Jack Hays and muttered in a barely audible voice, "Is it true what Ranger Childress said 'bout Colonel Crockett?"

Jack nodded his head affirmatively in the direction of Captain Childress. "Chuck has told you the God's honest truth."

Childress was afraid of no man or any living creature, but telling someone about the death of a loved one was something he dreaded. "Coffee, you were in San Anton' and spoke with folks who knew Colonel Crockett. Why don't you tell them what you know?"

Jack Hays dismounted his sorrel mustang mare. Walking around to Johnny he whispered in a soft tone, "I played a few rounds of cards with a fine bunch of Tennessee fighters. I'm from Tennessee myself. They told me about hearing the Colonel speak after the voters didn't send him back to Washington. He told them he was going to Texas and they could go to Hades."

Johnny was only able to mumble a correction, "Mr. Jack, he said Hell. He said those who didn't vote for him could go to Hell. I heard him give that speech." Johnny paused before questioning them again, "Colonel Crockett is dead? How can that be? We promised to meet him in San Antonio."

Chuck and Jack looked at each other. Jack deferred to his Captain with a nod as he removed his brown beaver hat with a braided hatband made of a Comanche brave's black hair. His forehead was stark white in contrast to his leathered brown face. Captain Childress continued, "Buck Travis' slave told how Davy Crockett was the last man to fall. Buck's man told of seeing Colonel Crockett kill two Mexicans with the butt of his rifle after he ran out of powder. David and six men took shelter in a barracks only to have the Mexicans blow the door off with an eighteen-pounder. David wrestled a rifle from a Mexican soldier and plunged the bayonet through his heart. That was when the Mexicans drug David and his men into the courtyard. David tackled one of the soldiers to the ground and was choking him with his powerful hands when another soldier rushed up from behind and stabbed the Colonel in the back with his bayonet. No man could have taken Crockett to his face. He died fighting for our independence with his bare hands. None will ever forget the Alamo or the legend of Colonel David Crockett."

Young Hays could clearly see how much Johnny loved and respected Colonel Crockett. He added, "Susannah Dickinson was in the compound for the duration of the battle. Susannah was the last to see Colonel Crockett's body. She says there were more dead Mexican soldiers piled near David Crockett than any other man at the Alamo. Even though none of those brave men lived to see the March 2nd Declaration signed, their valor created our new nation."

At first the Satterwhites stood motionless, like marble statues. Johnny's knees buckled as he fell to the ground. Screaming in anguish, he pleaded, "NO, NO, it can't be. He can't be dead. Say it ain't so, PLEASE."

Millie grabbed at Chuck, holding on in disbelief. "How could this be? Colonel Crockett had so many plans." She fell against the ranger and cried, staining his buckskin jacket with her tears. Johnny struggled to regain his composure. Once he was able to speak, he asked the rangers to stay and share all they knew.

He didn't have to ask because their intention was to stay, invited or not. They knew it was imperative to educate the young settlers on the very real dangers lurking in the wilderness.

A.D., now ten, was an accomplished hunter and that morning he had killed a young spike whitetail buck that ventured into a clearing. Jack Hays helped dig a firepit and set up roasting supports. He and A.D. took turns rotating the animal over the open flame. The venison meat was tender and the family and their guests ate their fill.

Jack then curried the horses as Chuck visited with the family. He didn't want to talk about the Alamo or Goliad; however, he explained that the Mexican dictator, Santa Anna, had been captured and jailed and would be held as insurance as long as Sam Houston deemed necessary. He told the Satterwhites they would need no Mexican land grant for their property ownership. He suggested they continue as squatters for the time being until the details could be worked out later. "I think you can get by on squatter's rights. I'm not a lawyer, but if I were you, I'd stay put. When the time comes, you can claim you homesteaded this place and made improvements on the land. Any court in Texas will side with you."

Suddenly little A.D. grabbed his long rifle, and raising the weapon he whispered, "There. Over close to pa's plow. See him? It's one of them savages on a painted horse. Do I kill him now or wait till he comes closer? I got my bead drawn down tight."

Jack Hays laughed as Chuck pushed the rifle barrel up. "Don't shoot, Son! That's Falcco, our Lipan-Apache scout. We surely need him. Falcco can smell a band of Comanches twenty miles away and can track a mountain lion over solid granite. Best of all, he is a great cook and a loyal friend. He and Coffee have been through some mighty tight scrapes together."

Falcco was the first Indian any of the Satterwhite family had ever seen in warrior dress. There were a few civilized Cherokee and Creek living in eastern Tennessee, but they dressed like the local white people. Falcco wore buckskin pants that he tied into his moccasins and a breastplate made of bones covered his chest. Around both arms were pure silver bracelets and a wide beaded belt held a quiver of arrows on his back. His hair was black, thick, and long, with an eagle feather dangling from the right side. The feather made circles in the wind as he rode his powerful tobiano paint stallion.

He sat tall on his mount and as he approached, they could see that Falcco's horse had five red hands painted along his left shoulder. Johnny and A.D. both wondered what the hands meant, but neither asked. Johnny assumed they represented kills in battle. Had he asked, he would have learned the hands represented those that Falcco had killed with his bare hands. On the opposite side of his prancing paint stallion hung fourteen Indian scalps. Johnny would later come to know just how exceptional a warrior Falcco was.

The two rangers and their trusted scout spent the next eighteen days with the Satterwhites. They helped raise the center pole for the cabin and one by one lifted the logs into place. Johnny made single saddle notches, the traditional way he learned back in Tennessee because the cut drained water well. The single saddle notch cabin was easier to construct when logs were left rounded and not hewn. The one room, eighteen-by-twenty-foot cabin went up in two days. It had no windows, just one solid front door. Johnny hand split logs for the roof and with the rangers' and Falcco's help, the cabin was rainproofed in less than a day.

They also constructed a split-rail fence around the farm to keep the cattle and mules from destroying the crops, and a picket fence around the garden to prevent rabbits or deer from eating the precious vegetables. There was no way the family could repay the rangers and Falcco for their help, but A.D. supplied fresh bear, deer, and rabbit, and Millie spent her days and nights cooking, while Johnny filled their evenings with fiddle music.

Johnny started to cut a defensive portal in the wall of the cabin when Chuck explained that if the holes to were too low, the Indians would use them to fire their arrows inside. The most effective protection would be to mark off an exterior perimeter and create a defensive fortress around the cabin. Chuck designed a fort with fourteen-foot log exterior walls that would encircle the cabin with a single gate facing south. The tops of the logs were sharpened to a razor point. Then gun ports were cut about eight feet off the ground; too high for an Indian to shoot an arrow through. They made sure each log placed along the perimeter had no notches that could be used as a ladder to scale the exterior walls. With the natural protection of the two rivers, only one side of the compound was vulnerable. Johnny and A.D. should be able to fend off an attack in the event they were discovered. The Captain told them that if they had time to inflict several casualties, the Indians would consider the risk was not worth their losses. Tribes were limited in the number of warriors they could afford to lose and usually retreated when faced with stiff opposition.

Even during the dry season, there were no places along the Brazos that could be forded so the four men worked for two days to construct a ferry that would move animals and supplies back and forth across the river. The ferry would also enable the family to earn a small fee by carrying newcomers across the rapid waters. Falcco taught A.D. and Millie how to make a seven-braid rope from strips of tanned deerskin. The seven-braid was then plaited into a five-strand rope, and the ends tied to trees on both sides of the river to keep the barge from drifting.

Even with all the improvements to the Satterwhite homestead, Ranger Childress still worried how vulnerable the young family was to Indian attack. The memory of the Fort Parker raid that left five men dead and several children captured in May of '36 was still fresh in his mind. Silas and Lucy Parker had led a group of missionaries from Clark County, Illinois to convert the Texas Catholics to their Baptist faith. The Parkers had built a compound similar to the one Chuck, Jack and Falcco helped Johnny erect, only much larger. Fort Parker had blockhouses set atop two corners, with the area around the fort cleared out for three hundred yards in all directions. The fort protected twenty family homes within the compound. Situated near the headwaters of the Navasota River, Fort Parker was built for its twenty-five men to withstand an assault by a band of two thousand Indians.

The month of May had been exceptionally hot at Fort Parker, so the women had left the gates open to allow a southerly breeze to cool the compound. Most of the men were in the fields, leaving only the women, three adult men, and two teen-aged boys to defend the fort. Had the gates been closed, the small group may have repelled the attack. With the gates open, an opportunistic war party of Kiowa, Kichai and Yamparika-Comanche charged through and killed all but the five older children. John Parker escaped weeks later and told of his sister Cynthia Ann's fate; she had been made the wife of Nocoma, a young Yamparika-Comanche Chief.

The rangers left Johnny a crude hand-drawn map marking the location of his property and where to find the nearest trading post. Johnny would need to follow the Brazos River south to Washington-on-the-Brazos where he could stock up on salt, sugar, coffee and other necessities. They also marked the location of the Groce Plantation and suggested the Satterwhites would be welcomed guests at the wealthy man's place anytime. Captain Childress felt they had done what they could to make things safer for the Satterwhites. The rangers must now continue their hunt for the renegade Comanches. As they prepared to leave, Millie gave them each a bag of beef jerky and a pound cake, and Johnny loaded them down with shelled corn. Just as suddenly as they had come out of the forest weeks earlier, they mounted and galloped off to resume their mission. Little A.D. tagged along on one of the mules until the rangers and Falcco reached the river. Jack Hays turned in his saddle, and looking over his shoulder, offered a stiff salute as he urged his mount into the shallow stream.

The day after the rangers left, one of the Satterwhite's cows dropped twins and the following week, the other birthed a nice healthy heifer. They now owned six head of cattle. The farm produced more than enough corn to last the winter and also provided them with an abundance to sell. Life was good and for the first time, Johnny could see being able to support his family. He was a rich man; three hundred acres of prime farmland had just yielded a banner crop of cotton and corn, they had healthy cattle and the family home was filled with love. He felt like a Baron.

Chapter Five
The Raven

The question is who was the most important man in the formation of the Lone Star Republic? Was it Moses Austin whose original vision made it all possible? Was it Stephen Fuller Austin, the sickly, yet obedient son who endured unimaginable hardship and danger to secure permission from Mexico for Anglo immigration? Could the Baron de Bastrop be the most important man? Without his interceding for Moses Austin, Texas may have remained part of Mexico. A case can be made for Jack Coffee Hays whose courage and cunning set the standard for all Texas Rangers. Was it young William "Buck" Travis who held the Alamo for thirteen days against impossible odds or the unknowns like Deaf Smith whose tireless efforts helped turn the tide against Mexico? Was it the steadfast Ben McCullough, Noah Smithwick or Samuel Walker, who helped revolutionize the revolver, who was the most important man in the formation of the Republic? Maybe it was Jared Groce who ran the *Bernardo Plantation* or an unknown dirt farmer like Johnny Satterwhite from Tennessee.

One man whose contribution cannot be debated is Samuel Houston. He was the tallest man in Texas, the most high profile man in the new Republic. Houston's stubbornness and determination, in spite of all objections, persevered until he set a trap for the more powerful, better-trained and well-equipped Mexican Army. Houston's level head prevented a second war with Mexico, which Texas was certain to lose. Houston would later be the man to save the Republic from bankruptcy after the spend, spend, spend administration of President Lamar. Not everyone was elated with Sam Houston. Interim President Burnet called him a coward. Many of his officers felt the same. When all is sifted through the sieve, Stephen Austin takes the prize. Sam Houston anointed Stephen F. Austin, *"The Father of Texas."*

Sam Houston was born on March 2, 1793 near Lexington, Kentucky. Stephen Austin was born the same year on November 3rd. Years later destiny would call the pair of leaders to Texas.

Sam Houston was destined to greatness in spite of his womanizing and attempts to drink himself to death. No matter which direction Houston walked, history was always waiting in front of him. He didn't need to seek fame and glory; those accolades sought out the man from Tennessee. Records indicate that he stood six-foot-six-inches tall when he defeated Santa Anna. Whatever his physical stature, Houston stands as a giant in the history of Texas.

Young Sam's great-grandfather John Houston, a Scotch-Irishman left Belfast and settled in the upper valley of Virginia. He made the voyage to the New World on a ship loaded with his valuable coin collection. Eight days offshore, he discovered the ship's crew was planning to rob him. John came from fighting stock; his ancestors were Scottish archers who led the way for Jeanne d'Arc from Orleans to Reims. John Houston and his men overpowered the Captain and crew and sailed the ship safely into Philadelphia harbor. Sam Houston's father married Elizabeth Paxton, the daughter of Squire Paxton, one of the wealthiest men in the state. The Houstons lived in Virginia on the stately plantation, *Timber Ridge*. Sam's four older brothers were Paxton, Robert, James and John, then came Sam, and four younger siblings; Willie, Mary, Isabelle, and Eliza Ann. Being stuck in the middle didn't stop Sam Houston from being a leader. When Sam was eight, his father gave him *The Manual of Arms*, the book used to train soldiers. Sam memorized the manual and could give orders as well as any officer by the time he was a young man of twelve. When the brothers played army, Sam always took command, assuming his father's name, Major Samuel Houston.

Major Houston died when Sam was fourteen. Before his death, the Major had purchased a tract of property south of Knoxville, near Maryville, Tennessee. Mrs. Houston decided the new property would be a good place for her and the children to start over. For the first time in his life, Sam faced uncertainty.

His oldest brother Paxton took charge of the family. Sam resented taking orders from Paxton, but out of respect to his mother, he obeyed. The entire trip to Tennessee, Sam dreamed of running away from the slavish discipline his older brother had imposed upon the younger children. Paxton pressed the family forward until they reached their tract of land, about ten miles from the town of Maryville. The boys needed to begin constructing a family home, but their mother made them wait to cut the logs in the dark phase of the moon to prevent bug infestation. They cut the logs into rough-hewn poles and flattened out two sides for a more finished look. Mrs. Houston insisted they secure the corners with a fairly complex half dovetail notch. Her insistence on perfection delayed the completion of the cabin and by the time the boys installed the roof, snow was falling across the hills of eastern Tennessee.

When spring arrived, the land was tilled and seeds planted. As soon as the sun made an appearance, corn shoots popped through the crusty ground. Fieldwork was not for Sam. Instead, he took a job working in Mr. Webber's store in Maryville. After a few months of weighing and bagging items for unappreciative customers, Sam became bored. The move to Tennessee had instilled wanderlust in Sam's heart and one day, he put some food, books, and his musket in a backpack and without a word to anyone, trekked westward into the woods.

After five days of wandering the hills of Tennessee, Sam came upon the Hiwasee River. In the middle of the river was an island inhabited by peaceful Cherokees who welcomed young Sam into their tribe. The young braves taught him their ancient tracking skills, how to master a bow and make arrows. The Cherokee gave him the name of Ci-lon-neh, their word for raven; a bird they considered to be a sign of good luck. For the remainder of his life, he would be known among the Cherokee as "The Raven."

After a two-year absence, Sam once again stepped through the doors of Mr. Webber's store. His shoulder-length braided hair, bronzed skin, bare chest and leather britches gave him the appearance of a native Indian. Five young Cherokee braves had come along to help him transport supplies back to the tribe. When Mr. Webber asked how he expected to pay for the supplies he had chosen, Sam answered, "I have two tanned deerskins."

"That's not sufficient to pay for what you have chosen. Is there any other way you can pay?"

Without hesitation, Sam confidently replied, "I'll sign an I.O.U."

Sam loaded his youthful associates with gifts and signed a $34 promissory note to Mr. Webber. He repeated the trips at three-month intervals until his bill reached almost one hundred dollars. Mr. Webber cut off his credit until he settled the past due account. Sam informed Chief Jolly he would need to leave the island, return to Maryville and earn the money to repay his debts. He placed his few possessions in his backpack and headed home. Upon his return, Sam faced ridicule from many of the townsfolk who taunted him for his appearance. Others assaulted him with racial slurs.

In the spring, Sam's little brother Willie's school held a party in which the students could choose a family member to participate in a spelling bee. To everyone's dismay, Willie's pick was his brother Sam. Willie chose well for when the contest was over, his Indian-looking brother was the last one standing. Sam won the spelling bee with ease, impressing the audience with his knowledge. There was a soft murmur among the audience as a male's voice shouted, "You should be a teacher."

Sam responded, "That's my plan. I will be opening a school in the fall. Anyone interested, see me before you leave."

Before the day was over, a classroom full of students had signed up. He rented a one-room cabin and when the school year began, his classroom was filled with eager children. Within a month, Sam was able to pay off his $100 I.O.U. to Mr. Webber. He intended to teach for one year, pay off his debt and return to the island to live with the Cherokee for the remainder of his life. Those plans would change in 1812 when the United States went to war with the Creek Indians.

In the battle of Horseshoe Bend, Sam took a Creek arrow through his leg. With no medical care available, Sam was faced with little chance of survival. It was his strong will to live and the care of a fellow soldier that allowed Sam to cling to life. Finally, Mrs. Houston was able to get her son to Knoxville, but the local doctor said he was too sick to survive, and refused to treat the wound. The doctor's refusal only made Sam more determined. His mother rented a room in Knoxville and after two months of rest and nourishment, Sam returned to the doctor and defiantly demanded, "I'm still kicking, now cut this arrow out."

Word of Sam Houston's bravery reached General Andrew "Old Hickory" Jackson. Jackson took a personal interest in Houston and the two men developed a bond that continued throughout their lives. Sam spent the next five years in the army where his leadership ability earned him the rank of first lieutenant. In the future, when President Jackson needed an accurate assessment of the situation in Texas, he would turn to the one man he could trust. That man was the Raven.

Sam wanted to study law; however, he was already twenty-six and considered too old. Once more his determination paid off as a lawyer friend told him: "If you bear down, you can pass the BAR exam in a couple of years. Here are my law books." Sam studied and within only five months passed the exam and established a practice that quickly became a high-profile law firm.

Sam's ambition grew to include politics and by the time Sam Houston turned thirty, he was a Tennessee Congressman. In 1827, he was elected Governor of Tennessee. He was poised for an easy second term victory when the Allens, a wealthy Tennessee family, started pushing for a marriage between Sam and their seventeen-year-old daughter. The Allen family insisted their daughter was mature enough to be the Governor's wife. There was no question in their minds that Sam would become the President of the United States within the decade. The Allens wanted their daughter to be first lady of the Union, giving their family the prestige they desperately sought.

Sam had little hesitation because Eliza was, without question, the most beautiful girl in Tennessee. The shy, beautiful girl with skin like alabaster, possessed a well-bred southern grace, and her charm won Sam's heart the first time they met. Sam fell in love, but Eliza was not so quick to come around to marrying a man many years her senior. In the end, Eliza would not defy her family's wishes and on January 16, 1829, the thirty-six-year-old Sam married the young Eliza Allen.

The marriage was frigid from the start. On their honeymoon night, Sam found her a reluctant bride; nevertheless, she obeyed her marriage vows and consummated the wedding obligations. Within a few months, speculation on the state of the Governor's marriage ran rampant through the community as rumors of infidelity spread like wildfire. Sam's friends caught Eliza in an embrace with her young lover and within days she departed out the rear door of the Governor's mansion, never to return. Sam never spoke of the divorce and neither did Eliza. The secret remained locked within the two families.

Sam was assured a second term, leading by a margin of four to one over his closest opponent when he abruptly resigned the governorship just weeks before the election. As he had done when he was a teen, Sam packed a few personal items, his favorite books, and boarded a riverboat headed for the Indian Territory of Arkansas.

When Sam arrived in Helena, Arkansas, a burly, sandy-haired man stood at the riverbank. The broad-shouldered man, with a wide knife dangling from his belt, extended his thick hand and introduced himself. "Sam Houston, I am Jim Bowie."

The two men spent the next couple of days drinking hard and talking about Texas. Sam had never considered moving to Texas until he fell under the spell of Jim Bowie, a master storyteller. Bowie talked of buried silver and hidden gold, but it was the land that Sam saw as an opportunity. But that would have to wait. Sam would first return to the Hiwasee Island Cherokee tribe where he remained for the next six years of his life. Chief Jolly helped Sam open a small trading post on the reservation and gave his daughter to the Governor as a common law wife. Chief Jolly's widowed daughter had six children. Sam became a husband and father. His Indian wife was a few pounds on the heavy side, but her extra weight didn't trouble Sam. He told an Anglo friend who visited the Indian camp, "She is shade in the summer and warmth in the winter." During his stay with the Cherokee, Sam became close with Chief Bowles, who went by the name, "The Bowl". When Chief Jolly died, The Bowl became the High Chief.

Unscrupulous Indian Agents under the orders of Major E.W. DuVal were robbing the Cherokee, Creek, and Choctaw tribes and forcing them to move from their fertile farmlands to worthless land in western Arkansas and eastern Oklahoma. Over the next few years, the remainder of Cherokee would also be forced from Georgia, a journey that would kill four thousand and go down in history as the *Trail of Tears*. Instead of giving the Indians gold coins, the Government issued paper, which was about 20% of the value of gold and had to be spent in the Indian agents' stores.

Sam finally had his craw full and planned a trip to Washington to see his former mentor, President Jackson. Along the way, he stopped to confront Major DuVal, telling him he was on his way to report his crimes to the president. With his eagle feather quill, Houston drew up a legal complaint against DuVal in duplicate and forced him to sign both copies. DuVal did his best to bribe Houston, offering a bounty of gold, a place to stay, and a soft featherbed to rest in. Houston flatly refused and chose to sleep under the stars with his Indian friends.

Sam's trip was successful in getting DuVal removed and during his visit with President Jackson, he was asked to grant the president a special favor. Jackson wanted Sam to assess the possibility of acquiring the enormous tract of Texas from Mexico. Jackson reminded Sam of the Manifest Destiny and that Texas was the linchpin to open the West for the Union. Jackson gave Sam a visa and provided him with a set of important looking papers that carried no real authority, but would offer official-looking documents should anyone question Sam's reasons for being in Texas.

Houston rode slowly toward Texas, always keeping the morning sun on his left and the setting sun on his right. After a few days on the trail, he met Elias Rector, U.S. Marshall for the Indian Territory. Elias asked permission to ride along and Sam agreed. Houston could not take his eyes off Elias' fine chestnut horse as his fire-red mane blew gracefully in the wind. The magnificent horse was a full hand- and-a-half taller than Sam's bobtailed mustang, Jack. The longer Sam looked at the large chestnut, the better he liked the idea of doing some horse swapping. Sam nonchalantly began pointing out Jack's virtues, telling the Marshall, "Jack can go a week on a mouthful of grass. Jack is extremely nimble and smart, and can run faster than any pony I ever saddled."

Elias didn't say a word, but listened intently as Sam continued to expound upon the virtues of old Jack. When the horse perked his ears, Sam pointed out his alertness. Should Elias' horse miss a step, Sam was all over the stumble, confidently mentioning that Jack was so sure-footed that not even a prairie dog hole would cause him to step wrong. Over the next two days, Jack became the most gifted, valuable horse in existence. At the end of the second day, Sam did admit one flaw. "Poor Jack is bobtailed and will be defenseless against those giant Texas horse flies. Why, Texas horseflies are the size of bumblebees. How can I take such a wonderful horse into a territory where he will be unable to swat the blood sucking horse flies? It's a shame to ride such a great horse to his death."

Elias could no longer restrain himself. Amid jerks of boisterous laughter he said, "Okay, you sold me, let's trade horses. I'd be a donkey to let Jack get eaten alive by those giant Texas horseflies. I'd never be able to sleep at night if we didn't make the trade. Go down there and take Texas away from Mexico. This Nation can use another great state and you are just the man to rope her in."

Sam would meet two other men on his way to Texas. One was a fur trapper who refused to speak and the other a bee hunter that wouldn't stop chattering. The old man's four pack mules were loaded down with beeswax and honey. He was on his way to San Antonio to trade with the churches. He explained to Sam that churches always need beeswax for candles and everyone could use honey because of the limited supply of brown sugar. The bee hunter told Sam to listen to the bees and they would prophesize the future. "When there is an abundance of honey, Indians take notice of the bee's extra activity and know that the white men are on their way from the north. That's why the white man can't sneak into Texas." The old man talked about bees from sunrise until the two drifted off to sleep at night.

When Sam arrived in Nacogdoches, Texas, he was surprised to find an old friend, Adolphus Sterns, was mayor of the town. The two Tennesseans talked of old times and the future of Texas. Adolphus tried to convince Sam to stay and set up a law firm, offering office space in a building he owned. Sam was impressed with the modern, thriving town of Nacogdoches, but was on an important mission for the president to gauge the chances of a successful operation against Mexico should the U.S. choose to take the land by force.

From Nacogdoches, Sam traveled south to San Felipe, hoping to meet with Stephen Austin. Austin was out of town, but he did run into Jim Bowie. After two days of hard drinking and storytelling, Jim accompanied Sam to San Antonio. After traveling five hundred miles and talking with a few hundred people on both sides of the issue, Sam came to the conclusion that Texas could be acquired from Mexico, if handled correctly. He knew bringing Texas into the Union would take a great deal of preparation. Texas needed to be stronger and the population increased to around fifty thousand before an attempted coup.

Upon arriving back in Nacogdoches, he wanted President Jackson to know Texas was worth fighting for and told him so in a letter:

Mr. President,

"I have traveled about five hundred miles across Texas and am now established to judge pretty near correctly of the soil, and the resources of the country. I have no hesitancy in pronouncing Texas is the finest country to its extent upon on the globe. For the greater portion of it is richer and more healthy, in my opinion, than West Tennessee. There can be no doubt the country can produce enough to feed ten million souls. It is probable that I shall make Texas my home. In adopting this course, I will never forget the country of my birth nor you, my President."

Your friend,
Samuel Houston

One evening Sam told his friend Bowie "in war, one doesn't always get to choose when the battle begins." Sam spoke as a seer because war would come before he was able to implement his plans for a peaceful takeover. History would forever link Houston and Texas with visions of blood, sweat and tears, the acrid stench of battle, the anguished sounds of wounded horses, and dying soldiers shouting above the blast of cannons. To this day, there is an axiom that one cannot speak of Texas without acknowledging Houston or speak of Houston without Texas.

By the fall of 1835, most of Texas could see the handwriting on the wall: Texas was going to war with Mexico. Governor Henry Smith promoted Houston to the rank of General, but did not give him power over the entire army. This would be a fatal mistake. Title without authority weakened Houston's ability to lead.

On January 17, 1836 Sam wrote Governor Henry Smith from Goliad:

Honorable Governor Smith,

Colonel James Bowie will leave here shortly for San Antonio with a detachment of between thirty and fifty men. I have ordered the fortifications in the town of Bexar to be demolished and if you should think well of it, I will move all the cannons and other munitions of war to Gonzales or Copano. I will blow up the Alamo and abandon the place, as it will be impossible to keep up the station with volunteers. The sooner I can be authorized, the better it will be for the country.

General Samuel Houston

After sending the letter to Governor Smith, Sam met with Jim Bowie. "The Mexicans have modeled their army after the French. Napoleon formed long lines and supported the foot soldiers with a skilled cavalry and Santa Anna has copied his idol Napoleon's battlefield tactics. Their mounted lancers can move through our men like a scythe cutting wheat. One thing in our favor is Santa Anna's center of operation is located 1,500 miles away, deep into the heart of Mexico. This means they must travel a great distance to Texas with their long line of supplies. Santa Anna has a lot of mouths to feed. The more we can stretch the battle, the thinner his supply lines will become. With well-executed attacks, we can stifle his war effort. Our only hope is to outwit and outmaneuver Santa Anna's forces. We have to wear them down with raids and forays, avoiding any direct confrontation. I hope to lead them to the forest around Nacogdoches where the advantage will go to our sharpshooters."

Jim sat and drank his whiskey for a few moments and then responded, "I see you have thought this through. You have been expecting this war for a long time haven't you? I tend to agree with you. I like your idea of stretching their supply lines, rendering them vulnerable. As long as we lure them into rifle battles, we can whip them ten to one."

Sam continued, "I wrote Fannin and told him all the things that happened at Gonzales, Goliad, Concepcion, San Antonio and driving Cos from the Alamo were just good luck on our part. We got the drop on 'em. This will not be the case when the 'Napoleon of the West' arrives with his six thousand professional soldiers. Governor Smith said we have been nicknamed 'The Texas Army, but in actuality, they are more like a mob.' He might be right. I know one thing we desperately need is artillery. We have no tents for the men, not enough rifles and, even if we did, not enough gunpowder. I think we need to keep just enough men to defend either Gonzales or Victoria." Jim didn't answer, but it was evident he knew Sam was correct.

Houston trusted Jim Bowie. The Louisiana knife fighter was calm under fire and followed orders. Texas was full of individuals who followed their own star and Sam had been disappointed dozens of times by men he trusted, but never once by Bowie.

Bowie and thirty men were dispatched to San Antonio where Jim met Lt. Colonel James Clinton Neill at the Alamo. Bowie carried a letter from Houston ordering the Alamo be destroyed and all the cannons brought to Gonzales. The twenty-one Alamo cannons would give the General the artillery he desperately needed. This stand at Gonzales was not the first: In 1832, an American changed his name from John to Juan and became Colonel Juan Bradburn in the Mexican army. Bradburn arrested William Travis and Patrick Jack. Their arrest brought on a conflict in which forty Mexican soldiers were killed and a large number wounded. Lt. Colonel Neill was in Gonzales when the Mexicans came for the old six-pound cannon. The defiance of Neill and those in Gonzales with their *"Come and Take IT"* flag flying had left Mexico no option but all-out war. But, the Texans were not finished; they went to Nacogdoches and defeated Colonel de las Peidras and his mounted cavalry, and lost only three men. Their marksmanship was too great for Peidras. He, like Bradburn before him, fled under the cover of darkness. These two victories gave the Texans confidence and convinced Travis and Bowie that the Texans were invincible.

Neill, a true Texas hero, was never given credit for all he accomplished. Family illness forced Neill to leave the Alamo. Some branded him a coward. The slander was not true. No one expected that Santa Anna would arrive in San Antonio until late March. Neill planned to return before that time, but never got the opportunity; Santa Anna surprised everyone, arriving in February.

Green Jameson, a lawyer turned engineer, mounted the cannons on the fort walls. After Jameson finished, the old Alamo looked like a real fort. Neill's enthusiasm had rubbed off on Jim Bowie, convincing him that the Alamo could be defended against the larger Mexican army. Jim understood that Houston had not seen the improvements. If he had, he would agree with Bowie and Neill that the fort could be held. Combined with Bowie's victory at Concepcion and the Texans' driving General Cos from the Alamo, Jim was confident his small army could defeat a much larger Mexican force from behind the Alamo walls. Jim Bowie, against Houston's orders, decided against destroying the Alamo. He called upon his local friends to supply extra food and horses. Within five days, he had filled the Alamo with supplies needed to mount a defense. He gathered his local Mexican friends and convinced them to spy on the movements of Santa Anna. On Sunday morning, Bowie spoke to the assembled men. He pointed out the possibility that the Mexican army might attack the Alamo. Santa Anna was still smarting from the early skirmishes at Anahuac and Nacogdoches back in 1832, and Gonzales and Concepcion where the Texans had soundly defeated his forces. Santa Anna's pride would not allow him to sit back and take one defeat after another. He would surely be coming to avenge those defeats.

To a man, the assembled fighters proclaimed they could hold the fort, and that Jim should send word to Governor Smith. Bowie's note to Smith simply stated:

Honorable Governor Smith,

Neill and I are agreed that we will die in these ditches rather than surrender this place. We have food, water, gunpowder and twenty cannons. We welcome the Mexican attack.

James Bowie

Meanwhile, Houston was faced with another potentially dangerous matter. Dr. James Grant, a physician and land baron had become Houston's chief protagonist and was challenging Sam's authority. Grant had mining interests and thousands of acres of land in Mexico. Wanting to reclaim his sizable amount of property, the doctor-turned-speculator was gaining support for his plan to invade Mexico. His proposal was to attack Matamoros, a city of over twelve thousand. Houston knew the Texans would be lucky to cross the Rio Grande in one unit.

In January 1836, Dr. Grant gained approval for his plan from the Texas Legislative Council. Grant and Colonel Francis Johnson stripped the Alamo and Goliad of most of the food, supplies, blankets, clothes, shoes, lead, and gunpowder. Then Grant and Johnson marched twenty-five miles south to Refugio. From Refugio, they would launch the Matamoros expedition.

Grant gave himself the title of Commander in Chief of the expedition. The Raven was too wise to challenge Grant's self-assigned title. Instead, Sam decided to ride along with the soldiers, moving from one to another, pretending to make small talk. His casual conversation always got around to pointing out, as only a Tennessee politician could, the lunacy of such a venture. Using his casual manner and noncombative attitude, he slowly planted seeds of doubt in the minds of the adventurous invaders. By the time they reached Refugio, Houston had managed to dampen the soldiers' enthusiasm.

Colonel Francis Johnson supported Grant's plan to invade Mexico, and like Grant, Colonel Johnson claimed he was the authorized leader of the campaign. He claimed the Commission had officially appointed Colonel Fannin to lead the Matamoros Expedition. He also presented Houston with stunning news; the Council had ousted Governor Henry Smith and stripped Houston of his rank. Sam smelled a rat. He knew better than to believe anything until he spoke directly with Governor Smith. He expressed to Johnson and Grant the folly of their incursion into Mexico before he left for Washington-on-the-Brazos to meet with Smith. Also before he left Refugio, Houston called the young soldiers together and gave them one of his famous stump speeches. He told them, "Boys, before you strike out on this insane expedition, I want to inform you of a few facts that Grant and Johnson have failed to disclose to you. Grant wants to go into Mexico because he has silver mines and a vast amount of property south of the Rio Grande. He wants you to fight to get his land back. This is not about Texas, but Grant's property. Johnson sees himself as some great leader and is willing to sacrifice your lives in his selfish pursuit of fame and glory. Follow Johnson and Grant and you will not live to see your next birthday. I ask you, how in the Hades do you think a handful of poorly armed boys can march twenty-one days without food and very little water and capture a city of twelve thousand? Did Grant and Johnson tell you that the Mexicans will consider you mercenaries? Did they tell you what Mexicans do to mercenaries? I plead with you not to let the greed of Grant and Johnson lead you to certain death. Boys, by all means take with a grain of salt what they are promising. If you are dead, the spoils of war will be of no value to you." Confident he had convinced the young men not to fight, Houston waved his hand in an exaggerated gesture to the crowd, whirled around as his spurs clanged against the platform, and quickly departed.

When Houston arrived in Washington-on-the-Brazos, Governor Smith confirmed there had been an attempt to install Lt. Governor Robinson as Governor, but Smith refused to step down and won the power struggle that followed. He was still in power and Sam was still his General. Smith encouraged Sam to go north and make peace with the Cherokee. Knowing Sam was an adopted member of the Cherokee Nation, Governor Smith felt he could persuade them and other tribes not to enter the war on Mexico's side. Should the Cherokee join Mexico, the war would prove a fatal blow for the Texans. They barely had enough men and supplies to fight on one front and they certainly did not have the men to fight on two.

Houston felt there was time to organize. Santa Anna was presently involved in an internal conflict with the state of Zacatecas. Houston knew as soon as that conflict was resolved, the Mexican dictator would turn his attention their way, but could never have predicted how quickly Santa Anna would squash the Zacatecas rebellion, killing two thousand.

Around this same time, the Texans intercepted a Mexican courier carrying papers that clearly stated the dictator's intention of either driving all Anglos from Texas or confiscating their guns. Without guns, they would be defenseless, and unable to hunt for food. The word spread like wildfire across Texas, prompting many to join the fight against Mexico. The only way Santa Anna would get their guns would be to pry them from their cold dead fingers.

On February 29th, the weather was warm and the sun blazed down on the twelve small buildings of Washington-on-the-Brazos. Fifty-nine men had come to work out a constitution and form a new Republic. One hundred miles to the north, in the village of Tyler, Sam Houston and his close friend George Hockley started back to Washington-on-the-Brazos after successfully signing a treaty with Chief Bowles and the Cherokee. The pair rode hard and steady, seldom stopping to rest. Houston felt the pressure to get to the convention. Hockley's mare started to limp, forcing him to lag behind. Houston pressed forward on a borrowed blaze-faced stallion, standing over seventeen hands tall. The powerful horse moved with grace and speed under the weight of the 235-pound Houston.

On March 1st the weather turned bitterly cold. Freezing rain and sleet plummeted the temperature to thirty-three degrees. The mood among the delegation had turned cold as well. Birds stopped singing, with the exception of a murder of crows perched on the leafless tree branches nearby, perhaps awaiting the arrival of the Raven himself.

The town of Washington-on-the-Brazos consisted of twelve buildings, six on each side of a muddy street. The thick black mud made crossing the street a slick and dangerous undertaking. Wagons could barely pass without getting stuck in the quagmire. Fifty-nine men crammed into a small room. There were no chairs or benches and the delegates were forced to lean against the walls or sit on the floor. Juan Seguin and Robert Potter scrounged up a table and a few cowhide straight-backed chairs for the leaders of the convention. There was no glass in the windows nor was there a door. Bedsheets and blankets were stretched over the openings in an effort to keep out the blustery March wind. Water in the drinking buckets froze. The men struggled to burn what wet wood they could find.

Covered with mud and ice, Houston arrived back in Washington-on-the-Brazos late in the afternoon on a horse so tired he refused to drink. He frankly didn't know what to expect, whether he would be welcomed enthusiastically or sent packing. To his surprise, he was received warmly; the delegates eagerly sought his guidance. All at the convention were aware of Sam's military background and were quick to overlook his Indian connection and penchant for heavy drinking. There was one problem; they had received correspondence from Travis relating the gravity of the situation at the Alamo:

Fellow Texans,

We have contended for ten days against an enemy whose numbers are variously estimated from fifteen hundred to six thousand men. I hope your honorable body will hasten on reinforcements, ammunitions and provisions to our aid and soon as possible…God and Texas — VICTORY OR DEATH.

William Barret Travis

The men wanted to leave the convention and go to Travis' aid. What they didn't know was by the time they could get to Travis, those in the Alamo would be dead and Santa Anna's men would be stacking wood to burn the bodies. Houston informed the delegation that for Texas to be recognized as a respectable government, they would need to create a Constitution. Without it, Texas would fail. Sam had no formal schooling, but Houston possessed something more important – a bushel of common sense and the foresight to see the bigger picture. Sam had a broad understanding of events, places, people, and governments. He could live with Indians or mingle with high society. To women his eyes were soft and kind; however, he had a steely-cold gaze that would freeze a man with one glance.

Juan Seguin jumped to his feet exclaiming, "The only way for us to defeat Santa Anna is for us to fight as one man. We need a single leader. That leader should be Sam Houston who has proved his worth in the past and will again if we give him our total support. I for one say we give the army to General Houston and let him lead us to victory over that maniacal dictator."

After Juan's fiery speech, the convention quickly appointed Sam to lead the army. Sam raised his voice, drowning out the screaming March wind and addressed the assembly. "I will leave at once for Gonzales. There, I will put together an army so we can help Travis, Bonham, Crockett and Bowie, and the other brave men who are holding out at the Alamo. Travis needs the 400 soldiers under Fannin's command. He is only a few miles to the south in Goliad and can move his men to the Alamo in a day's march. You gave me the authority to lead and by the power of the Almighty, that is what I intend to do. I will ensure Fannin's four hundred men leave immediately for San Antonio."

In spite of the bitter cold and meager accommodations, the group managed to have the documents ready for their signatures on March 2nd. Sam Houston was not only the first to sign, but his signature was by far the largest. Houston would later recall that day was the coldest he could ever remember. The freezing rain never gave the men an opportunity to dry out. Yet, in spite of all the hardships, no one complained.

After signing the document, Sam could see that some in the delegation still wanted to leave and join their friends in the fight. Juan Seguin made one final plea. "Let me go with you. I know the area. That is my home. I can help you find a way into the Alamo."

Sam rapped his walking stick on the plank floor to gain everyone's attention. Once more his voice rose to a thunderous volume. "Juan, my friend, I know you are right, but it is more important to Texas and our Republic that you remain here and not let anyone leave until we have a government. You are the one man who can hold this meeting together. I want to impress upon you all that your most valuable contribution will be to stay here and form a government that will be recognized by every country in the world."

With his speech ringing in their ears, Major General Houston strutted from the hall, his three-inch daisy rowels jingling as his spurs clanked against the wooden floorboards. He slung his mud-soaked Indian blanket over his shoulder in a dramatic gesture of authority and ducked through the doorway so the bald eagle feather in his hatband would not catch the mantel. Just as he slipped through the doorway, he turned and crooked his finger at his friend George Hockley. He paused for effect and then waved goodbye.

The bulk of the responsibility of drafting the declaration would fall to George C. Childress, a former Tennessee lawyer and a trusted friend of Houston and President Jackson. Alone in a freezing room, Childress drafted a document equal to the Constitution of the United States. He knew at any moment the Mexican army might arrive, driving a bayonet through his heart. Nevertheless, he continued to pen the words for a great Republic and compile a list of the Texan's grievances against the Mexican government.

Childress was not the only well educated man in the delegation nor was he the only one to have served in the Senate or Congress of the United States. Robert Potter, Samuel Carson, Richard Ellis, Martin Parker, Thomas Rusk, and James Collinsworth had all served. Men like Sam Maverick, a Yale graduate; Zavala and others were well trained in the law. Asa Bingham was a "cornstalk lawyer". Richard Ellis, the president of the convention, served as a Supreme Court justice in Alabama. And Sam Houston had served in both the United States Congress and as Governor.

Childress recommended the Republic adopt the pentagram, a five-pointed star, for their flag. He asked the group to consider being called the *Lone Star Republic*. There was some opposition because of the pentagram's association with devil worship, but George was able to quell the critics and the single five-pointed star became Texas' icon.

The Texas Constitution was a composite of the Constitutions of the Union and several southern states, with a few distinctive exceptions: Texas would be a unitary form of government in which one central authority, not a federal republic, would hold power. The president was to serve three years and could not succeed himself nor could he, without the consent of Congress, lead an army into battle. The Texans would not accept a dictator like Santa Anna. The president could not be a clergyman. Slavery was legal, but slave running would be considered piracy.

Childress began the Declaration of Independence:

"When a government has ceased to protect the lives, liberty and property of the people, from whom its legitimate powers are derived, and far from being a guarantee for the enjoyment of those inestimable rights, become an instrument in the hands of evil rulers for their oppression."

And he ended with the words:

"We do hereby resolve and declare that our political connection with the Mexican nation has forever ended; and that the people of Texas do now constitute a free and independent Republic."

By March 17th Childress and the delegation completed the Constitution. Reverend William Crawford, a circuit-riding Methodist Minister in his home state of Alabama, signed the document knowing he could never hold the office of president. Two other men who signed the final document lost loved ones at the Alamo; Benjamin Goodrich lost his brother, and Jesse Grimes, his oldest son.

An interim government was elected: David Burnet, President, Lorenzo d Zavala, Vice President and Thomas Rusk, Secretary of War. Sam Houston got what he wanted, Commander in Chief of the Armed Forces. The elected officials then fled to Harrisburg. From Harrisburg, they fled to Galveston Island. They knew full well any time they were exposed, they would be in danger of being attacked or captured by the brutal Mexican dictator.

Since the humiliating defeat Cos had suffered at San Antonio, Santa Anna had become a pot of water on a hot stove. Each bit of negative information only increased his anger and eventually he boiled over. The climate of vendetta was now deeply etched into Mexican culture as Santa Anna planned to show the upstart rebels the high cost of disobedience. He would make the stubborn Texans pay an even larger price than the rebels of Zacatecas. Santa Anna knew the total destruction of the Alamo would teach the cocky Anglos and rebel Mexicans a lesson they would never forget. He was correct.

Sam Houston knew defeating the superior Mexican army would be possible if he could thin their supply lines and lure them to a battlefield of his choosing. Superior strength could be defeated by leverage. Sam's skill in making Santa Anna think the Texas General was a sniveling coward bolstered the dictator's confidence. Houston ignored interim President Burnet and many of his officers who pled with him to stop and fight. Houston's first choice for a battlefield would be the piney woods near Nacogdoches where his marksmen would have a distinct advantage. With one final ace up his sleeve, Houston selected the perfect spot to fight in a place called San Jacinto. The Raven would draw the Eagle into his lair.

Chapter Six
A Visitor

Johnny Satterwhite was plowing the backside of his field when he saw movement near the pecan trees along the bank of the Little River. The Little River spread out to almost two hundred yards wide a half-mile west of the rivers' confluence, and the Brazos was too swift to be easily crossed without using his ferry. North and west, the denseness of the oak trees and undergrowth made passage impossible. He knew if trouble were to come, it would be from the south. The young farmer chided himself for not bringing his Kentucky long rifle into the field with him. With deep plowing to do, he had decided the gun would be too heavy for him to manage. Realizing he was too far from the homestead to warn Millie and the children, he stood frozen, watching the solo rider move closer and closer to the cabin.

Three months had passed since the rangers' visit and their stern warnings still resonated in Johnny's mind. Removing the reins from around his neck, he gently lowered the plow handles, letting them rest in the freshly tilled soil. He knew if he started running, the mounted figure would see his movement and gallop ahead toward Millie and the children. So remaining in a crouched position, Johnny moved quickly until he entered the corn rows. Once hidden amongst the corn stalks, he broke into an all out run for the cabin. Rushing into the open area near the vegetable garden, he saw he was too late. At the front gate of the compound was an imposing figure astride an ink-black horse. The man was tapping the hand-hewn porch planks with the barrel of his rifle. Out of breath from running in the freshly plowed ground, Johnny bent over, placed his hands on his knees and struggled to catch his breath. Then, up in the right corner of the compound, he spotted the barrel of his son's rifle poke menacingly through a porthole. His family had not been taken by surprise. The stranger was alive only because A.D. and Millie had determined he was friendly.

By the time Johnny reached the cabin, the man had dismounted and was speaking with Millie. Turning to greet Johnny, he said, "Hi, I'm Tom Green. Your wife says you folks are from Tennessee. That is my home and I'm heading back. My parents are there and I need to go home for a spell. You know how parents worry. I ran into Ranger Childress and he told me you folks might need me to take some letters back home."

Excited to meet another man from Tennessee, Johnny wiped his hands on his buckskin trousers and offered the stranger a firm handshake. As they vigorously shook hands, he inquired, "Tom Green. Are you kin to Judge Nathan Green?"

"So you know my crusty father? Then you know why I need to get back before he explodes or worse yet, sics my mama on me. They both can be steel on wheels when they get riled up. They didn't cotton to my comin' this far from home anyhow. I'm their youngest and I guess they don't think I can take care of myself."

Johnny quickly responded, "I'm not personally acquainted with your father. I just know of him. He has a fine reputation of being a firm but fair judge. Out where I come from, we don't get to meet many judges or rich men like your father. The only famous man I had the good fortune of knowin' was the great David Crockett, God rest his soul. Congressman Crockett told us about Texas." Johnny coughed to clear his throat and continued, "Awful shame. Colonel Crockett died the day we laid claim to this place. Don't seem fair does it?"

Tom sat silently for a few moments before responding. "David Crockett was the kind of man you would want covering your back in a scrape, that's for sure. I was told Colonel Crockett killed more Mexicans than any man in the Alamo battle. He made them pay dearly for his life."

Suddenly, as if stung by a bee, Johnny turned to his boy and commanded, "Son, take Mr. Green's horse, give him a good rubdown, some water and a bucket of shelled corn." Turning back to Tom, Johnny invited him to visit awhile. "You must be starved for some home cookin'. We would like to hear what you know 'bout this new Republic. When Chuck, Jack, and Falco stopped by, none of them wanted to say much. Chuck did say the Mexicans had 'bout 6,000 soldiers against our 180. To be honest, that's about all we know."

Tom gladly accepted the Satterwhite's invitation. He paused outside the doorway where he used a gourd dipper to fill a tin wash pan. Washing was customary before entering a home after a long, dusty ride. Tom washed his brown, chiseled face and powerful hands. When he finished, Millie handed him a towel. Tom then removed his spurs and clanged the rowels against the side of the cabin to dislodge any caked mud. "You have a nice compound here," he observed. "This is what I'm told is the best way to build a homestead when you are in Indian country. The extra fortifications will let the three of you hold off a fairly large group of Indians. Mind you, I've never been in an Indian fight, but I know many men who have. Texas Ranger Major Three-Legged-Willie Williamson says if you can kill their chief, you will end the fight. If anyone would know, it would surely be Major Williamson."

Johnny asked Ruthann to fetch the plow mules, and then replied, "Tom, I wish I could take credit for this compound. Chuck was the one who insisted we needed an outer set of walls should an attack come. The rangers stayed and helped us build our home and these outer walls."

Johnny just kept on chattering. Perhaps because it was unusual to have an adult male to speak with or he was nervous since Tom was from such a prominent family. His nervousness showed as he changed the subject. "What I find interesting is how those red-headed cranes eat. We have a pair of smoke-gray cranes with scarlet heads that have been here feeding in our field the past few weeks. I don't know what they are called, but when one is eating, the other always keeps its head raised. Never once have I seen both with their heads lowered at the same time. We got to be like those redheaded cranes; one of us has to always be looking to the south, lookin' for any trouble. You were on us before any of us saw ya. Had you been an Indian, we would be dead."

Tom finished drying his hands as he responded. "I think you are talking about the Sand Hill Crane. They stand about three and a half feet tall, gray with a crimson head. I remember as a boy seeing thousands of them in a marshland off the Gulf Coast when my father took me along with him to Mississippi. They were too pretty to shoot."

Johnny cocked his head to one side, looked at Tom for a moment, smiled and repeated, "Sand Hill Cranes. Sand Hill Cranes. Glad to know what they are called. Ruthann named ours Sam and Susie. There are so many different animals and birds down here in Texas, the children just make up names for them."

Tom Green had arrived in Nacogdoches on Christmas day, 1835. From there, he had made his way down to Gonzales, arriving March 11, the same day General Houston came to take command of the troops. Tom joined the army and immediately became part of the Runaway Scrape. Young, brash and bold, Tom Green wanted to fight. His bravado and youth made him feel invincible and his anger was past the boiling point as General Houston ordered the retreat.

Johnny and Tom walked into the cabin. Once inside, Tom's first words were: "General Houston made us abandon our horses because he wanted us to get accustomed to being a marching army. I'm here to tell you the thought of giving up my horse was the toughest thing I had ever done. It meant no way of quick escape. I didn't like the idea back then, but looking back, I realize Houston was right."

Johnny wasn't sure what Tom was talking about; nevertheless, he pointed to the handmade bench at the head of the table, indicating that was where Tom could sit down. As Tom lowered onto the bench, Millie said, "We want to hear about everything."

Tom didn't disappoint. "When news of the atrocities of the Alamo reached Gonzales, people panicked. Our retreat from the Mexicans was called the *Runaway Scrape*. We were aware of what Santa Anna had done to his own people in Zacatecas. If he would murder and let his men rape his own kind, we could expect no better. Torrential rains made pulling a wagon almost impossible and during our retreat, most abandoned their oxen and wagons, pushing hard to stay ahead of Santa Anna. Some of the cattle were slain for their meat and others put down.

For those fleeing, the rainy season in east Texas presented one of the biggest challenges. Rain poured from the sky in sheets like some giant monster was standing over the escape route and dumping buckets of water on the frightened settlers. The dozens of rivers and creeks were overflowing their banks. No bridges were passable and most ferries were unavailable to make the crossings. There was little opportunity to sleep. Finding high spots to make camp became nearly impossible. As you will learn, March can be one of Texas' coldest months."

Johnny and Millie smiled at each other. They said nothing. Tom didn't need to tell them about Texas weather. Tom didn't notice them giving each other a grin, and kept on talking. "At the start of the Runaway Scrape, many Texans burned their homes and filled their wells with rocks, timber, and furniture. They left no food or shelter for the enemy. They burned cribs of corn and removed their cattle, horses, mules and pigs when possible. When we reached the river, almost five thousand were stranded because the ferries were jammed. If the people didn't get across, Santa Anna would cut them down like wheat, but should they rush to cross, disaster would surely follow. In desperation, many did attempt to cross, only to drown in the violent river. Danger came not only from the angry water, but also from tree trunks shooting down the rapids like shrapnel from a cannon. Those rogue trees slammed into many who attempted to cross on their horses. We lost an officer when a tree broadsided his mount. He was tossed into the murky waters and vanished."

Johnny raised his elbows so Millie could set the table. Millie was rushing because she wanted to listen to Tom. She knew Johnny wouldn't remember all the details. Tom, an attorney by training, started building his case to the Satterwhites. Pulling his strong legs up under the table, his mood turned serious. "As I see it, the Anglos living in Texas never felt they were under the authority of Mexico. The original three hundred settlers just wanted to be left alone. They were not for war, that is, until the Alamo massacre.

Then, like the rest of us, they wanted Santa Anna's blood. The new Texans saw Mexico as an evil force that must be reckoned with. General Houston told us our only option was to defeat the Mexicans or be driven out of Texas. He had the confidence of a prizefighter that knows he can knock the opponent out with one solid punch. You could feel he was waiting for the right time to deliver the knock out blow."

Johnny plopped both elbows back on the hand hewn table, listening like a wide-eyed child, hanging on every word. He had questions by the basketful, but reckoned if he kept his mouth shut, Tom would answer most of them.

Tom didn't mind talking. He talked for a living. Suddenly, he switched topics, saying, "Once I planned to return to Tennessee, I decided to go by the way of Groce Point to check on his health. After leaving *Bernardo Plantation*, I remained on the western bank of the Brazos, stopping to purchase supplies in Washington. The people have rebuilt most of the town since Santa Anna burned his way through. When I got to the Little River, I instinctively followed an animal trail back west where I found the shallow water crossing right where Chuck and Jack said it would be. When I leave, I still have to cross that angry Brazos and I'm not looking forward to that swim."

Little A.D., who normally didn't speak when adults were talking, blurted out, "We can ferry you over. We got a ferry that Pa and them rangers built."

Tom whirled on his bench to make sure he heard the boy correctly. "Ferry, did you say ferry?"

Johnny couldn't contain his pride in his son or the new ferry as he responded, "He shore did. We got a good en. Our ferry can hold a large wagon and team of oxen. When yur ready, we will carry you across." Johnny then winked at A.D. to assure his son it was all right that he had spoken out.

Tom reached down, opened his saddlebag and lifted out a three-pound bag of coffee beans. His voice was clear and strong as he asked, "Millie, would you mind grinding some of these beans and brewing us up a pot of coffee? I could sure use a cup."

"Me too!" Johnny excitedly agreed.

Millie was more than delighted to fulfill Tom's request; coffee was a luxury the Satterwhites had not had since arriving in Texas. Ruthann ground the beans while her mother stoked the fire. Soon the aroma filled the small one-room cabin. Johnny had forgotten how wonderful freshly brewed coffee smelled. Life was good and having a friend from Tennessee in their home made things even better.

Johnny sipped his steaming cup of coffee slowly as Millie prepared a pot of venison stew, adding potatoes, corn and other vegetables from their garden. While they were enjoying the coffee, Tom told how he had been practicing law with his father for only a few weeks when he learned of the war in Texas. He persuaded his parents to let him go and join General Houston. His father chose the best horse on the farm and made sure young Tom was equipped with an ample supply of powder and balls for his Kentucky rifle. His older brother gave him a brace of pistols. His father also gave him four hundred dollars and one of the female slaves meticulously sewed the gold coins into the seams of his clothes. He was careful not to leave anything of value in his saddlebags. On his father's instruction, he did put a few coins inside his tapaderos (leather stirrup covers) expecting no one would search there in the event he was robbed.

Tom started talking as if the Satterwhites knew the recent history of Texas. Johnny interrupted, "Tom, I don't want to be rude, but Millie and I don't know any of the details of the battles. Locations of towns are hazy to us. We don't even have a Texas map. I can't tell you for sure where San Antonio or San Jacinto are from here."

Tom reached down and once more opening his saddlebag, pulled out a tattered map. Millie cleared the table so he would have room to unfold his well-worn map as Tom rose from his seat and started pointing out various rivers and towns. He moved his finger across the map, showing them a straight path to San Antonio. He then moved down to Goliad, pointing out Gonzales and Victoria along the way. He traced the circuitous route the army took when they left Gonzales.

Tom then addressed Johnny, saying, "If you have a piece of paper, I can make you a rough copy of this while I'm here."

Stepping on a chair to reach a high shelf, Millie retrieved a roll of brown butcher paper she had been saving to make dress patterns. She placed the roll next to Tom. "When you are ready, we would surely love to have a copy of your map."

Tom folded the paper and ripped off a piece about the size of his map. Then he drew the outline and added the rivers and towns. His drawing skills impressed the Satterwhites. Once the map was complete, Johnny pressed for information and Tom was more than willing to oblige. He constantly referred to the map as he spoke. "We camped at the Groce Plantation for two weeks, stuffing our bellies with beef and corn and marching everyday till we were blue in the face. We fought rain and mud and more rain and more mud. There was never any break in the clouds. I cannot remember being so wet in my life. General Houston told us he would kill any deserter and we believed him. A rumor quickly spread that Houston caught a man trying to swim to freedom and shot him in the back, letting his body sink into the murky water. I don't know if it was true, but I can testify that no one left the camp again after that story surfaced. Knowing the General, he probably planted the tall tale to scare us."

"Are you serious? Do you think Governor Houston really killed a deserter?" Millie asked.

"Danged if I know, but I do know that General Houston would tolerate no weakness in the group. General Houston is a student of history and I think he saw himself as George Washington. In the battle of San Jacinto, he patterned his actions after those of Washington. General Houston rode his horse between us and the Mexicans just like General Washington did when his troops were fighting the British. He kept us moving, causing the Mexican supply lines to thin the same as General Washington did to the British."

Johnny sat mesmerized. Tom was so smart. Finally Johnny said, "Dang, I've only heard one man to match you. That man was Colonel David Crockett."

Tom grinned like a cat that caught a mouse. He looked directly at the young couple and continued, "When we got word Santa Anna had four armies spread across Texas looking for us, things began to look very grim. General Houston turned us north where we were bivouacked and waited. He wanted Santa Anna to follow us so our sharpshooters could use the cover of the trees to their advantage. The General kept our scouts out scouring the countryside for information. We were prepared to run as soon as a scout brought word that Santa Anna was at Washington-on-the-Brazos, a half-day away. To be honest, we didn't want to retreat. We had plenty of food and a good place to make a stand, but General Houston ordered us to move on.

General Houston commandeered the *Yellow Stone* steamer and a yawl to get us across the Brazos. He immediately put us on a fast march heading due east. He didn't tell us where we were going. All we knew was there was an urgency to move as fast and as far as we could each day. We seldom rested. Houston ignored the letters from President Burnet urging him to stop and make a stand and sought advice from no one, as far as I could tell.

There were Union soldiers near the Texas border ready to join the fight. In fact, some two hundred did cross over and join us. If given a choice, most of us would have guessed General Houston was going to run across the Louisiana border. There were times we honestly didn't think he would stop and fight. He surprised us all when we came to a fork in the road and he directed us right, instead of left which led to the United States.

Houston then sent false messages into the Mexican camps through the Tejanos, who were Mexicans helping our side, relaying that we were down by Corpus Christi, near Richmond or north of Austin. Santa Anna bought Houston's ploy. Houston's plan divided the Mexican army and strung those pursuing us into a long thin line. Santa Anna outmarched his supplies. I remember as a boy seeing a fox run some of our dogs into the ground. He kept circling back and around until our hounds gave up the chase, exhausted. General Houston was the cunning fox and he wore down those Mexican hounds."

Millie interrupted, placing big bowls of steaming stew, a heaping plateful of biscuits, and a jar of wild honey in front of the men. Tom waited for Johnny to say grace, then punched a hole in a hot biscuit and poured the cavity full of sweet honey. When they finished eating, everyone agreed it was time to retire for the evening. Tom slept under a lean-to Johnny had built on the backside of the cabin in the hopes of one day having slaves to help tend to the farm. Heat from the cabin warmed the shelter and provided a comfortable place for Tom to rest for the night. As he drifted off to sleep, he realized that one day's visit was not going to satisfy the Satterwhites and decided to remain another day.

The next morning, Johnny and Millie were elated to learn Tom would not leave as originally planned, but would stay one more day to tell them all he knew. Millie prepared a hearty breakfast of fried eggs, ham, biscuits and gravy while the men worked on building a pen for the animals. She brewed a pot of coffee and then rang the cowbell, signaling breakfast was served. The Satterwhites were excited to learn they were only a day's ride from Washington-on-the-Brazos, the birthplace of the Republic of Texas.

"The village at Washington is where men like Sam Houston, Elijah Stapp, J. W. Burton, J. B. Woods, Rob Potter, Martin Parmer, Juan Seguin, Jose Navarro, Lorenzo de Zavala, George Smyth, Richard Ellis, Asa Bingham and Sam Maverick, fifty nine in all, created the Texas Constitution. In doing so, they were also signing their own death warrants on that freezing day in March. When you go there, you will be walking on sacred ground."

Johnny interrupted. "We almost ended up in Washington while those men were still there. We crossed the river to this side on March 6th. A few days earlier, and we could have ended up in Washington the day they signed the document."

"Fate. It had to be fate or divine guidance that brought you to this location. Otherwise, as you said, you would have ended up in Washington and perhaps been drawn into the army."

Millie wiped her hands on her apron before sitting down to breakfast. After Johnny gave thanks, curiosity got the best of her as she turned to Tom and said, "Tom Green, we want to know what happened at the Alamo and Goliad. We know so little. The rangers could not speak of it. Jack Hays did say he helped General Rusk bury the burned bones of the 340 that died."

Talking with his mouth full, Tom responded, "I don't know where to start. First, I guess I best ask if I'm keeping Johnny from his chores."

Johnny responded immediately. "My work can wait. I got the rest of my life to plant and reap crops. Like Millie said, we know almost nothing. We know Santa Anna killed everyone at the Alamo and Goliad. We understand he killed some others, even women and children along the way."

Tom stopped chewing and shook his head as tears welled up in his eyes. "Yes, the Mexican army killed, killed, and killed for no reason other than a vendetta. Before the Alamo and Goliad massacres, Captain Amon King, along with several others, set out to warn the settlers that the Mexican army was on its way. King and his men wet their powder crossing a creek and were unable to defend themselves when the Mexicans attacked them. They were outnumbered twenty to one and with no way to fight back, King was forced to surrender. The Mexicans tied Captain King and his men to trees and shot them like target practice. They also ambushed Dr. Grant and his Expedition. Some say they killed Grant because of his silver laden saddle. Others told me Grant had a lot of Mexican enemies because of some shady dealings.

I can only give you second-hand information on the Alamo and Goliad, but I do know about San Jacinto because I was there. The battle of San Jacinto started on the afternoon of April 21st. General Rusk later said the battle was over in eighteen minutes, but our men were so riled up, they kept on killing until dark. We ended up killing 640 Mexican soldiers and capturing another 700.

By the next day, Santa Anna was in the hands of a new republic. Houston was propped against a big oak tree with a perfect hanging-limb as the men delivered Santa Anna to him. Deaf Smith brought a rope as we all gathered around shouting, 'Hang him, hang him, hang him.' Several of us wanted to burn Santa Anna alive, but Houston interceded. He knew there were four Mexican armies still in Texas, five or six thousand strong with several cannons. General Urrea was in south Texas, General Ganoa was in the north around Bastrop and Austin, heading for Nacogdoches, and General Sesma was in the middle, following a little south of Santa Anna's route. Houston made Santa Anna write a letter to his second-in-command, General Filisola, ordering him to withdraw from Texas. Fortunately, Filisola did as he was commanded. We had little food and were very low on gunpowder; another battle would have been disastrous. President Burnet wanted us to chase the Mexican army. He called General Houston a yellow belly coward. General Houston knew we would be defeated if we attacked the Mexicans on flat ground. If their cannons didn't kill us, their lancers would."

Johnny spoke the moment Tom took a bite of food. "Jack said Santa Anna is still in a Texas prison."

"He was recently put on a ship to Washington. I don't have any idea why, other than to show the Union we were successful in defeating the best Mexico had to offer."

Millie pressed for more details. She didn't care if the information was second hand. Her husband's hero, Congressman David Crockett was one of the men killed. She asked kindly, "Tom, if it's too painful we understand, but if you don't mind, we would like to know a little more. Please!"

Tom turned toward Millie. He didn't have the courage to talk about David Crockett and look into Johnny's eyes. He knew Johnny worshiped Colonel Crockett. In stuttering jerks, Tom continued, "It was never, never the Texans' intention to set up a fort at the old Mission. I have seen the mission and there was far too much area to defend. Most felt Goliad would have been a better place to take a stand. The men called Goliad Fort Defiance. General Houston felt Gonzales was the place to make a stand. His intentions were to combine Fannin's army, the 180 men from the Alamo, and recruit another thousand. General Houston had fought in the Creek Indian War and had seen the Creeks try to defend a fort; their food supply lines were severed and they were not able to get new warriors into the compound. Houston told us forts were deathtraps and the Alamo was only a vulnerable compound made into a makeshift fort.

I believe that if Colonel Fannin had obeyed orders and joined the Alamo forces with his four or five hundred men, they could have beat the Mexican Army back until a larger force was organized."

Millie brought the coffee pot back, refilling everyone's cup, including little A.D. Tom delayed for a couple of moments to enjoy a sip of coffee and to grab another biscuit with gravy. "You know what amazed me the most?"

Simultaneously, Johnny and Millie asked, "What?"

"The physical size of the Mexican soldiers. Some barely reached my waist. I would say they stood only 4' 7" to 5' 6". Santa Anna was a giant compared to his men, standing almost 5' 10". No wonder he felt superior to the rest of his army. I recall standing next to some of the Mexicans who survived our attack in San Jacinto and marveled at how small they were. I swear A.D. is as big as many of those we fought. I tip my hat to the courage and bravery exhibited by those little brown people."

For no apparent reason, Tom shifted his conversation. "The name of the compound you know as the Alamo has an interesting origin. The word Alamo means cottonwood in Spanish, but there are no cottonwood trees anywhere near the *Alamo* so I asked Juan Seguin how the old church got its name. Juan would know, he is a Tejano and grew up around San Antonio. He told me how around 1800, Mexico sent a cavalry unit from *El Alamo de Parras* to command the old mission. The Spanish word 'El' was replaced with the English translation, 'the' and the name shortened to *The Alamo* in reference to the soldiers from *El Alamo de Parras*."

There was silence in the room. "But that's not the news you want to hear. You want to know the details of the battles and what happened to the men who gave their lives. Mind you, I'm just putting together bits and pieces. During the Runaway Scrape we had a lot of time to talk and men like Manuel Flores and Jesus Garcia gave their versions from the Tejanos' point of view. I guess I learned the most from Erastus 'Deaf' Smith. You spell it D-E-A-F but say it 'DEEF'. He moved to Texas back in 1821 and married a Mexican widow. He was almost completely deaf since he was a boy about the age of A.D., but I've never known anyone who could see or smell an Indian or Mexican like Deaf Smith. Anyway, Deaf didn't plan to get in the fight, but when General Cos captured San Antonio and refused to allow Deaf to go into town to see his wife and children, he decided to join General Houston. He turned out to be our best scout. I can say with full assurance that not one man in all of Texas knows the country better than Deaf Smith. He knows every creek, stream, and river like the back of his hand. His information was the most valuable of any scout during those trying days."

Tom stood and stretched saying, "Excuse me, I need to take a moment to visit the outhouse and then I'll give you my slant on things."

When Tom returned, he began his story like he was trying a case. "I see the conflict dating back to the time when Philip Nolan was hired as a filibuster to bring twenty armed men into Texas and round up mustangs. That would have been around the turn of the century. A United States General hired Nolan to round up the horses so he could lead an invasion from Louisiana; the General had plans to make Texas part of the Union. Do you know what I mean by the word *filibuster?*"

Johnny and Millie both acknowledged they had never heard the word. Tom assured them neither had he until he arrived in Texas. "Well, from what I understand, filibuster is a French word meaning mercenary, freebooter or pirate. The pirate Lafitte lived on Galveston Island for a decade; a filibuster in the purest sense of the word. We call him a pirate, but filibuster would apply as well.

Philip Nolan was not the first to hire a bunch of filibusters to try and take over Texas. Henry Perry, in about 1813, led an army of 850 men into Texas under a green flag. They were confronted by the Mexican General Joaquin de Arredondo and easily defeated. The green flag filibusters surrendered and General Arredondo ordered them slaughtered. One of Arredondo's men was a brash eighteen-year-old lieutenant named Santa Anna. Santa Anna learned when he was an impressionable young man that the best way to deal with filibusters was to kill them. That is exactly what he did at the Alamo and Goliad. He saw all

Americans as filibusters on Mexican soil, needing to be eradicated, just as General Arredondo had done with the green flag group."

Millie asked, "You are saying Santa Anna sees Texas settlers as being pirates who have come to take what is his?"

Tom grinned with one side of his mouth. "I would say you have made a good assessment of the situation. As any good lawyer does, I went after the facts. As I see it, Anglos are mostly English, Scotch, Irish or German, and we see things as our forefathers did. Like Deaf said, the core of the conflict is cultural. We Anglos see ourselves as more advanced and civilized than the Mexicans. The Mexicans see things from a more Spanish and French point of view. They see us as greedy barbarians who are trying to take what belongs to them.

Mind you, Spain has ruled most of the land from Florida to California for 250 years and only about 3,000 Mexicans lived in this vast area. Mexico was part of Spain until 1821 when on September 23, 1821 General Agustin Hurbide rode into Mexico City triumphantly declaring Mexico's independence from Spain. The next year, Hurbide joined Texas and Coahulia into one giant Mexican state called Texas y Coahulia. The Mexicans became like the possessive prairie dog; they dug a hole, stood on top patting the surface, barking, and keeping all others away. But you won't find any adventurous 'Satterwhites' coming up from Mexico to fight the hostile Indians, build homes and grow crops. Yet they want to keep people like you from coming and forging a place to raise your family.

Mexico was originally very hesitant to grant Moses Austin permission to bring Anglo settlers into the Mexican state of Texas. Then the Baron de Bastrop was able to convince Governor Antonio Martinez of the advantages of solid citizens building homes and growing crops verses the filibusters invading the state from time to time. He persuaded Governor Martinez that the Anglos could fight the Indians as well as help the economy of the vast territory. Moses Austin was given permission to immigrate three hundred families. After Moses died, his son Stephen continued to bring families into Texas."

Johnny slid his homemade spitting box across the floor. Most men in Texas used chewing tobacco and Tom had brought a rope of Texas-grown tobacco that he shared with Johnny. Tom talked as they chewed and spat. "Okay, let me see, what should I tell you next. Moses Austin was already fifty-nine and in poor health when he first came down here. Moses made his son Stephen promise on the old man's death bed that he would bring the three-hundred families to Texas. Stephen Austin went to Mexico City and spent almost two years down there working things out. First, he had to deal with the Federalists and then, when the Republicans won power, he had to start all over. Anyway, once the floodgates were opened to the three hundred, others came pouring in like the floodwaters of the mighty Mississippi. Stephen has brought in about fifteen hundred families. There are thirty-thousand Anglos living here now, and more coming everyday."

Tom looked out through the door and shaking his head he mumbled, "Stephen Austin was our first Empresario."

What did you call him?"

Johnny's question brought laughter from Tom. "That's a four-bit word the Mexicans use that means a contractor hired to settle a colony, and Stephen Austin was hired by Mexico to colonize Texas. Empresario."

"Was Colonel Crockett considered an Empresario?"

"Hardly. David just came the same way as you. He had no contract to bring in people. Austin was not the only man with an Empresario contract. For a while there was a whole host of them; I think there were about thirteen. There was Austin, of course. Then there was Robertson, Cameron, Burnet, Vehlin, Zavalla, DeWitt, Felisola, DeLeon, McMullin, McGloin, and Powers. I think Robertson and Austin were the most successful. The two Irishmen, James McGloin and John McMullen, received a land grant to settle two hundred families around 1828. The next year they brought Irish families from New York and established San Patricio on the north bank of Neuces River. Later, Irishman James Powers was given a grant and established Refugio. Those Irishmen are a fighting bunch. Men like Jackson, McGee, Nolan, McCafferty, Travis, and your own David Crockett. About forty of them died at the Alamo from the Refugio and San Patricio settlements."

Johnny spoke before Tom could continue. "It makes sense now that you mention the system. We were told there was so much land, a small parcel wouldn't be missed. Now I see, some men were hired to bring people in."

"Johnny, at first it was a good deal. I cannot remember the number of acres Austin was given, but it was something like two hundred thousand. He then sold land to people for twelve cents per acre. A family could buy six hundred and forty acres and another three hundred and twenty for each family member, plus an additional eighty per slave. The system was a good until Santa Anna changed the rules in 1824."

When the conversation paused, Millie asked, "Can I get you anything?"

"No thanks Millie, I'm fine." Then Tom's expression turned solemn, as if he had just been told he was going to be hanged. He took a deep breath, and with his words sorta seeping out, he continued, "Okay, I've delayed long enough. I know you want to hear about the Alamo and the other atrocities perpetrated by Santa Anna. The old Mission across the river from San Antonio, the Alamo compound, covered about two acres. When the Mexicans built it, they constructed the high walls to keep their Indian slaves in. The compound was more of a jail than a place of protection from the outside. The Mission's priests made slaves of the indigenous Indians, yet called us pagans for bringing in our black slaves. It was down right hypocritical. They talked about converting the natives to Christianity, but what they really wanted was free labor. Around all of the missions, you will find large clearings where the trees have been taken out and the soil turned into farmland. Who do you think did the work?" Tom answered his own question: "I'll tell you. It was the poor beaten-down natives. Eventually the priests worked them to death. I don't know how many thousands died working for the Church of Rome. When the priests ran out of Indian slaves, they closed up and went back to Mexico City. I could never be a Catholic for that reason."

Johnny jumped in, "We are Methodists and don't believe you have to ask Mary for blessings. We believe it's okay for us to read our bible and we can go straight to Jesus Christ without any go between. We don't understand how the Catholics can believe the Pope is like God."

Tom answered. "I agree with you. I attended a great Methodist camp meeting in Victoria this summer. The Reverend Frances Wilson preached and several dozen were converted at the consummation of his sermons. Brother Wilson said he has preached 7,000 sermons and ridden 15,000 miles bringing the good news of Christ to Texans."

Tom then lowered his head for a moment before continuing. "I'm getting off track. I won't win many cases if I don't learn to present my points better. Getting back to the Alamo, Lt. Colonel James Neill was in charge. He had around a hundred men when Grant and Johnson took all the powder, food, shoes, blankets, and clothes for their Matamoros expedition. Neill's entire family took ill so he was forced to go home. He planned to be gone twenty days and left the command to young Buck Travis. Now there was one tough guy. Buck was almost twenty-seven and had a wild streak, but understood what it took to lead and to be a good soldier. Loyalty, honor, and duty were at the top of his list. I hear Bowie was upset when Neill didn't make him the top man, but Neill knew he could not leave the responsibility to Jim because he was drunk or near drunk all the time."

Tom could see in their faces he was talking about people they didn't know, so he paused and explained, "You might not have heard of Jim Bowie. He was a knife-fighting braggart who came to Texas selling slaves. Back in Natchez, Jim was involved in a fight where he killed two or three men with his famous knife in what would become known as the Sandbar Incident. Some say he was a land cheat to boot. He won some Indian fights and gave the Mexicans a good licking at Mission Concepcion where he killed about seventy, and only lost one of his men. I give him credit; he feared no man. Joe told us that Bowie took ill right as Santa Anna got into town and was confined to his bed for the duration of the thirteen-day Alamo siege. In fact, he was covered with blankets to break chills when the Mexicans overran the walls. They shot him three times in the head as he lay defenseless in his sick bed.

I was told when Travis got word the Mexicans were charging the Alamo, he only gave one order: 'The Mexicans are upon us, give 'em Hell.' The Mexican soldiers marched in straight lines as their band blared the *Dequello*, a blood tune that goes back to the Moorish days. The song means no quarter to the enemy. Santa Anna was hoping the music would panic our boys, but the death song didn't faze the Texans. The Mexicans were met with a hail of lead as they moved forward. The first row fell, and then a second one took their place. The Mexican officers were the first to be killed because our boys were taught to look for their gold braids. Kinda like shooting turkeys, you pick the biggest gobbler.

Inside the walls, it was fire, pour powder, patch, shot, ram, splash the flash pan, aim, and fire again. The Mexicans had never seen such skilled weapon handling. Our boys were loading and firing several times a minute. Their officers must have thought we had a hundred men loading guns. They didn't realize we grow up learning to load fast and shoot straight. I'm sure young A.D. here can load his long rifle faster than a seasoned Mexican soldier can his musket."

Johnny and Millie were on the edge of their chairs, grabbing every word. They had only imagined what might have happened at the Alamo and Goliad since Jack and Chuck's visit. Now they were getting the real story.

Tom continued, "There are two versions of this story. Buck's slave Joe tells a story of Colonel Travis calling all the men into the courtyard and drawing a line in the dirt with his sword. He told them all who stayed would probably die. No man would be thought a coward if he did not step across the line. David Crockett was the first man to cross over. Crockett was heard to say 'We did not come to Texas to run. We will have Santa Anna's head on a stick.' James Bonham crossed over, and one by one, all except a single Frenchman crossed over. Jim Bowie asked his men to pick up his sickbed and carry him across the line in the sand. The Frenchman tucked tail and slipped over the wall in the darkness of the night. His name is not worth giving honor to by even mentioning it.

I spoke personally to Buck's slave Joe and he swears on the Holy Bible it's true that Travis drew a line in the sand. On the other hand, Mrs. Dickinson told me she never saw a line drawn. The first time she heard such a thing is when I asked her about it. For me, I believe Joe because he was always by the Colonel's side. This may be a point of debate years and years after we are all dead and gone. One thing I know for sure is that there was a lot of brave fighting spirit in that Alamo compound."

Tom had crossed his fingers behind his back when he told the fib about Crockett being the first to step over the line in the sand. Joe had said that it was Tarpley Holland from Anderson that was first to cross the line.

"I guess you know Travis and Crockett could have passed for brothers. They were about the same height. David was stronger built but they each had sandy red hair and fair complexions. From what I gather, they took to each other almost immediately. Travis was half the age of Colonel Crockett. I guess Crockett felt like Travis was like a son. When Buck asked Crockett to assume a leadership role, Davy flat out told him 'I just want to be a high private.'

Let me say that none of those men had to stay and fight. Santa Anna left a wide corridor open, hoping Houston would come to the Alamo. What Santa Anna didn't know was that General Houston and a group of other leaders were busy in Washington-on-the-Brazos writing a Texas Declaration of Independence.

The one hundred and eighty two men inside the Alamo knew no help was coming. Bonham had delivered word that Fannin refused to come. Those brave men at the Alamo stayed, knowing they were going to fight to their death for Texas."

Tom Green pressed back his tears and continued, "No one in Texas was expecting Santa Anna to make his appearance until late March. Neill thought he would be back from his furlough before Santa Anna arrived. Scouts alerted the Texans that the Mexicans were heading north, but expected that the snow and frigid cold would slow their arrival. Anyone in their right mind would have rested his men, but Santa Anna pushed his men onward without mercy. He fed them on eight ounces of food a day. They had to scrounge for water.

I understand on February 22nd, the Texans tossed a big fandango in celebration of President Washington's Birthday one day before the Mexicans got to town. A sudden blue norther had prevented General Filiosa and his men from reaching San Antonio until the 23rd. He could have caught our men in town without their guns and the battle would never have taken place. Is that not ironic?"

Johnny nodded an affirmative, but said nothing.

"When the Mexicans arrived, they immediately raised a big red flag on the San Fernando Church bell tower. Some say the flag bore a skull and cross bones. Whatever was on it, the flag signaled that no quarter would be given. Santa Anna sent a few men to offer our boys a chance to surrender and Travis answered with a cannon shot toward the bell tower. The Mexican army began bombarding the Alamo walls and would continue blasting away for twelve straight days."

Tom seemed not to tire of talking. He only paused for a moment before he continued, "Colonel Travis kept sending riders out to seek help. He never believed they would not have several hundred more men join the fight. His childhood friend and fellow lawyer, James Bonham made two trips to Goliad trying to get Walker Fannin to bring his men. Fannin was too wishy-washy. One lad told me Fannin buried his cannons, dug them up, buried them again, and then once more dug them up. He was incapable of making a decision. Fannin continued to disobey direct orders from General Houston and his refusal to join the battle left Crockett and Travis with only 150 men. Finally, Almeron Dickinson, a blacksmith from Gonzales, brought 31 men, raising the count to 182 to defend against the impending attack.

I was told when Fannin refused to help, James Butler Bonham got on his horse and returned to tell Travis no help was coming. Several tried to convince Bonham not to return to the Alamo, knowing he would be riding to his death. His answer was 'Buck deserves to know the truth. If I don't go tell them, then who will?' He spit on the ground, dug his spurs into the flanks of his horse and rode into history. If there was a special hero in that group, it has to be Bonham. He had the courage of a lion and was a loyal friend to his death. Bonham gave his life for others when he was in a position to be spared.

The Mexicans outnumbered us thirteen to one. We whittled down the odds. For a few days, men like David Crockett picked off soldiers who ventured within two hundred yards of the Mission." Tom paused, took a sip of coffee and continued, "Counting various battles, over sixteen hundred of Mexico's best soldiers had been lost. The battles had exacted a heavy toll on the Mexican Army, and their soldiers' morale was at an all time low when Santa Anna arrived at the Alamo.

It was Santa Anna's own ego that did him in. He could have waited one more day to charge the Alamo; there were two twelve-pound cannons on the way. He could have flattened the walls in two days and he would have saved several hundred of his men by waiting for the big guns. Against the advice of his officers, Santa Anna decided to attack on March 6th. There was a rumor the Texans were talking about surrendering, but I know that was not the case. Perhaps Santa Anna hoped they would. His officers told him if he attacked, the death toll would be heavy. It is said that Santa Anna replied coldly, 'So be it. They are worth no more than chickens.'"

Millie rose and began preparing lunch. When she got anxious, she liked to cook. Doing something with her hands relieved the tension.

"I don't want to get ahead of myself, but two men we felt were Mexias (Mexicans who only claim to be the Texan's friend) showed up in Gonzales to tell General Houston of the fall of the Alamo. Houston knew they were not Mexia spies; nevertheless, he had them locked up. He understood if our small army knew the truth about the defeat at the Alamo, many would have panicked and scattered in the middle of the night. Heck, I might have run if I had known the truth.

General Houston sent Deaf Smith to check out the Alamo story. He met up with Susannah Dickinson, her young daughter, Buck's slave, Joe and slave Ben on the road just a few miles outside of town. They confirmed the horrible news. The Alamo had fallen. Much of what we know is from Susannah Dickinson and Buck's slave, Joe.

Susannah and her young daughter had moved to San Antonio to be near her husband. When the scouts had spotted the Mexican army south of town, she and her daughter sought refuge in the Alamo and remained there for the 13-day siege. The night before the final assault, they said Crockett and a Scotsman named James McGregor, serenaded the men till almost midnight. The Scotsman played bagpipes and David, his fiddle. Santa Anna had a 230-piece band play Mozart and other German pieces each night, but on the night before the battle, the Mexicans neither played music nor bombarded the Alamo. The night was silent and our men finally were able to sleep. Unfortunately, even the three pickets on watch were asleep. The Mexicans slit the throats of the pickets as they slept. The Texans never saw the Mexican army move within one hundred yards of the Alamo. They didn't know the attack was underway until one overly anxious Mexican soldier shouted, 'Viva Santa Anna'. By then, it was too late. Like ants, the Mexicans swarmed the compound's walls. Crockett and a dozen Tennesseans were able to fend off those charging the south wall, but the numbers were too great for our boys on the north and west. Our cannons cut a wide swath through their lines as one blast killed forty. When the Mexicans raised ladders, the Texans shoved them off the walls, throwing them down onto the bayonets of the soldiers below.

Travis was the first to fall. He was on top of the wall with his double barrel shotgun, shooting down at the attacking soldiers when Joe saw him get shot between the eyes at the start of the battle. Buck fell at Joe's feet. Joe closed his master's eyes, then ran and hid.

Susannah told us David died like a true Tennessee hero, killing two Mexicans with the butt of his rifle after he ran out of powder. He fought to his last breath. She said the biggest pile of dead Mexicans was around Colonel Crockett. When the battle was over, Santa Anna instructed her to tell the rest of the Texans they would be next. He wanted her alive to put fear in us.

Susannah was so distraught that the Mexican General had refused to allow her husband to be given a proper Christian burial. Instead, he made three piles of the dead and had them burned like trash. Santa Anna's act of refusing to bury our dead was without question the most evil thing ever done on a battlefield. I still get sick to my stomach when I think of such an evil deed."

Johnny interrupted. "We agree. We believe we must be buried with our feet pointed east so when Christ returns and resurrects us, we will be facing him. That's the gospel truth."

Tom agreed and then tried to lighten the mood. He told them about one Texan who didn't want to be buried with his feet to the east. He was a reprobate. When he died, the community dug a seven-foot hole and dropped his body in feet first, his head facing to the west. The story brought some smiles. Johnny and Millie didn't know if it was true, but his story did break the somber mood.

To change the mood even further Tom asked, "You ever seen a Mexican flag?"

All heads shook no.

"A.D., I have one in my bedroll. Would you go and fetch it for me?"

The boy was back in flash. "This whut you lookin' for Mister Tom?"

Tom unfurled a small, tattered flag, speaking as he smoothed out the cloth. "Noah Smithwick captured this flag from a Mexican Colonel and gave it to me. Noah's explanation, and one I bet is correct is that the green banner on the left is for Mexico's independence from Spain, the white in the center represents the Church for purity, and the red on the right side is for the mixed blood of all Mexicans. Noah told me Santa Anna chose the Eagle holding a snake in one claw and the other on a cactus as a warning to Spain. The Eagle would crush them if they ever set foot on Mexican soil again. I cannot prove if Santa Anna designed the eagle, but I think the other part is true." Tom folded the flag and asked A.D. to place it back with his things.

Tom continued with another story to keep the mood light. "Seems an old Indian Chief was talking to his son. He told the boy, 'Outside this door are two hungry wolves. One is named Evil and the other Good. One of them will get you.'

The young brave asked, 'How can I know which one?'

The wise Chief answered, 'The one you choose to feed.'"

After the tale, Tom spoke seriously once again. "Goliad… Now there is another story. Some twenty-eight escaped so we have a pretty clear picture of what took place there. Well, let me back up. I think maybe only a dozen fighters escaped, but the rest were let go because they were doctors, interpreters, and children.

Like I said, Fannin had refused to join Travis and Crockett in the Alamo. He also delayed acting on Houston's orders to evacuate Goliad for five days. When he finally left, he waited until nine o'clock in the morning and then stopped an hour for breakfast. He said he wanted to let the oxen graze. But keep in mind, the Mexican soldiers were on the other side of the river. A mile or so short of Coleto Creek and the protection of a wooded area, Fannin set up his battleground. The Mexicans positioned their battle station on a hill overlooking the Texans' position. I can promise you General Houston or Davy Crockett would never have been caught in such a trap. Shortly into the battle, Fannin was wounded. He was in pain and constantly complaining, and quickly ordered his men to surrender. I heard that the Alabama Red Rovers, Georgia Brigade and the New Orleans Grays insisted they fight on; however, under pressure from Fannin and his supporters, they raised the white flag.

Fannin showed the Mexican commander Urrea a written agreement that allowed him and his men to go back to their home states. The agreement was as worthless as the paper it was written on. Nine days later, Santa Anna sent an order to the commander that the prisoners who were not injured were to be split into three groups. They were told they would be taken to Matamoras, and then shipped home. Each group marched out singing and in high spirits. After about three quarters of a mile, they came to an open area and were ordered to stop and kneel down. The singing stopped as most in the perplexed group followed orders. Some knew it was a trap and instantly made up their minds their only hope was to try to escape. They broke and ran while others obeyed and dropped to their knees. One brave man turned, opened his shirt and showed the Mexicans his bare chest. He was one of the first to die. The Mexicans then opened fire on the kneeling men.

Those who ran were chased down and stabbed with lances and bayonets. In the confusion and the heavy layers of black smoke, some did escape. The one I know of is Dillard Cooper. Dillard said the smoke gave him the chance to make a dash for the trees. He was almost there when a calvaryman came out of nowhere, wielding a saber. The cavalryman's saber slashed through Dillard's cape as he broke free of the garment. The saber pinned the cape to the ground while Dillard escaped into the trees. He and three others hid and moved toward freedom for twelve days, eating tree bark and whatever they could find. I for one am glad we didn't face Urrea. He won every battle he fought on Texas soil. He would not have been lured into the same ambush we set for Santa Anna.

Santa Anna ordered the Texans' bodies be burned, just like he did at the Alamo. If General Houston had listened to us, we would have rid the earth of that evil dictator once and for all and hung him from that big oak. Myself, I was for treating him like the Comanches do when they capture a white man. They take two saplings, bend them over and tie the man's arms and legs to each tree. Then they release the trees, slowly ripping him in half. But General Houston knew we needed to keep the skunk alive. As the General leaned against that big oak tree, wounded and near death, he negotiated peace with Satin Anna as we called him or the Emperor as he liked to be called."

Johnny and Millie could not believe what they were hearing; yet they knew every word was true. They sat horrified.

"Fannin and the other wounded were then carried or drug out and shot. They say the wounded Fannin was killed sitting in a chair with a blindfold over his eyes. His only request was they not shoot him in the face. Of course, the Mexicans put three muskets to the Colonel's head and blew his brains into splinters."

Tears flowed down the cheeks of all three adults. A.D. and Ruthann were crying. Tom took a deep breath. "The things I just told you are second-hand accounts. What I'm about to tell you now is the gospel truth. I know because I was there at San Jacinto. I marched every step from Gonzales to the battle. I was in Gonzales when General Houston gave the command to burn the town, leaving no shelter or food for the Mexican soldiers. The settlers fled like animals running from a wildfire, heading east as fast as they could. When their oxen got bogged down in the mud, they were shot rather than left behind for the Mexican army to eat. We butchered all we could and shot the rest. Everyone traveled light; taking only what was needed for survival. As we moved east, more and more men wanting to fight for freedom joined up with us.

We finally stopped at San Felipe for several days. Most of us wanted to fight there, but General Houston ordered the town burned and moved us up to Groce's Point. He wouldn't tell us a cotton pickin' thing. I think that was the biggest frustration, not knowing where we were going or if we would stop and fight. I do want to say we did respect that General Houston slept only about three hours a night and was subjected to the same living conditions as his men. Santa Anna, on the other hand, lived in a silk tent and was waited on hand-and-foot by an entourage of fifty."

The Satterwhites sat spellbound, leaving Tom no choice but to continue. Tom's voice grew louder. "It's my understanding Santa Anna thought we were finished after the Alamo and Goliad. He was preparing to go home when he learned of General Houston and our army. Rather than let another General have the glory, the little dictator made the mistake of staying to run the show. He could have sent his other Generals and probably won the war, but he wanted to be the one who killed Sam Houston.

Deaf Smith capturing two of Santa Anna's dispatchers. He found documents that told how Santa Anna had divided his forces. By dividing into smaller armies, he severely weakened his already depleted forces. Since so many of his best men were killed or wounded at the Alamo, he was traveling with less than his best. That's why General Houston always felt we could win.

Houston was the only one on our side with any real military understanding. He memorized the military training manual from his youth and knew the importance of having a disciplined army. His biggest problem was keeping an army together. Men needed to go take care of their wives and children. Mosley Baker broke down and cried as we watched the streams of terrified settlers fleeing the Mexicans while we were camped at Benson's Landing. I admit it was a horrific sight to behold. Their faces were gaunt and fear blanketed their countenance. This was the most horrifying event I have ever witnessed. I have never seen fear of death among such a mass of people. This escape was different because of Santa Anna's promise; women and children knew he would have no compunction about slaughtering them. Men were terrified for their families. Each time a rider from the west was spotted, we all feared they may be bringing news that the enemy was upon us. Terror hung heavy in the air.

We ran into three days of the most torrential rain and flooding you could ever imagine. We had to physically carry our wagons through the quagmire. I mean physically lift them up and carry them on our shoulders. For three terrible days, Houston drove our stumbling columns through the unrelenting rain, advancing only eighteen miles. On March 31st we halted by the Brazos River with nine hundred demoralized men. Mosley Baker and Wylie Martin refused to keep running. General Houston conferred with them and allowed Mosley, Martin, and a few others to make a stand at the river to delay Santa Anna's forces. The small group of sharpshooters killed several Mexican soldiers, including a Colonel, and never let any of the Mexicans cross over. It was a wise choice by General Houston not to make an issue of Mosley's insubordination, and allow him to engage the enemy."

Tom closed his eyes as he visualized the scene in his mind before continuing. "General Houston led us across the San Jacinto River by way of Vince's Bridge and picked the best ground to defend. The Mexicans got to the area not long after we set up camp. We could see them digging in about two miles to the east. We were ready to fight and so were the Mexicans. General Houston told us to eat, sleep and relax; we would not fight that day. I have to tip my hat to Houston. He waited and waited until he had things the way he wanted before he gave the order to attack. I think he learned this from the Indians. They will wait for weeks before attacking.

From time to time, our men would ride near the Mexicans' camp, making sure they were seen. The movement prevented the Mexicans from getting any rest. Houston wanted them to stay up all night worrying about us charging them at any moment. I woke up a couple times and could hear the Mexicans milling around and chattering among themselves. I didn't really understand then how Houston was methodically wearing the Mexicans' will down. He knew the rain and mud would break their spirit and thin out their supply lines. He knew we would be facing a dejected, tired and starving army. General Cos, Santa

Anna's brother-in-law was late in arriving to the battlefield after having force-marched his men all night in the worst conditions possible. Since we had left no food or shelter behind, by the time Cos and his men arrived, his soldiers were exhausted and demoralized.

We had the protection of the dense trees along the riverbank, leaving the Mexicans in an open field of tall grass. Santa Anna was poised for a traditional field battle. That was his style. Houston had studied the war strategies of Santa Anna's idol, Napoleon and knew Santa Anna would follow the same protocol. General Houston was an old Indian fighter with other plans.

The next morning we ate an early breakfast expecting to fight. General Houston slept until nine. When he awoke, he calmly went about as if nothing was going to happen. Finally around noon, he told us, 'Double check your guns and powder, sharpen your knives and play some cards. Just relax boys, your victory is near. You will get your revenge soon enough.' None of us could understand the delay and I know the Mexican army was just as confused. You could see the Mexicans lined up for battle as soon as the sun rose. Then around one or two in the afternoon, they started stacking their muskets and heading into their tents for siesta.

One thing none of us knew at the time was that General Houston had an ace up his sleeve. He had sent Emily Morgan to a spot where Santa Anna's men were sure to find her. Emily is a high yellow, a mulatto, who worked as a prostitute along the shores of Galveston. Knowing Santa Anna's penchant for pretty women, Houston knew the General would be unable to resist a beauty like Emily. I saw her and I have to tell you there are not many women in the world more beautiful. Our *Yellow Rose of Texas* was entertaining Santa Anna that afternoon. By three o'clock that afternoon, the Mexican soldiers were taking their siesta and Santa Anna was in his silk tent in the arms of Emily Morgan.

General Houston watched as we played cards and instructed our Tejano friends to place a big playing card in their hatbands. He didn't want us mistaking one of our own for Santa Anna's men. Juan Seguin wore the Ace of Spades, and I remember seeing those cards flashing in the late afternoon sun. As a result of Houston's idea, none of our Mexicans were killed by friendly fire.

When the sun was fully at our backs, General Houston asked if we were ready to fight. We shouted that we had been ready for weeks. Right about this time, Deaf Smith came galloping into camp, his horse lathered like he had been washed in soap foam. As he approached, his horse fell dead from the hard ten mile run to Vince's Bridge. General Houston had sent Deaf and four others to destroy the bridge so no more Mexican soldiers could join the fight and the ones we had cornered could not escape.

Deaf grabbed his saddle from his dead horse and was on another mount in moments as General Houston said 'Men, it is time to fight. We will win and in so doing, remember those slain at the Alamo and Goliad. Are you ready?'

In unison we shouted, 'YES!'

Then he told us, 'It's time to fight for Liberty.'

The ground was extremely soft because of the heavy rains. The cannon wheels sunk into the ground, making deep furrows in the fresh loam. There was no sound other than General Houston's loud whisper: 'Hold your fire, hold your fire men, hold your fire.' We marched up on the enemy with the stillness of death in the air. The wet grass muffled our footsteps while the blazing sun at our backs made it difficult for the enemy to see us approaching.

Our twin cannons were loaded with broken horseshoes, washers, nuts, bolts and some rocks. I was second in charge of one of our two six-pound cannons and Ben McCullough, a fellow Tennessean, was in charge of the other. Colonel James Neill was my commander. He is credited with firing the first shot of the Revolution. I guess I got a little excited and prematurely fired off a round when we got within two hundred yards of the enemy. Talk about ripping a hole in enemy lines! Our scatter shots did just that. That blast must have killed thirty soldiers. The Mexican soldiers who had taken up defensive frontline positions were blown to smithereens. I saw a splash of red shoot into the air with body parts flying.

The moment my cannon blasted, our men broke rank and charged the enemy. The fight was on. We could see the Mexican soldiers dashing confused from their tents, trying to find their guns. We were on them before they could figure out what was happening.

It was a rout from the git-go. Revenge was so thick; you could wipe it away from your face with your bare hands. We did remember the Alamo. We did remember Goliad. Many of the Mexicans there that day had fought at neither place. They pleaded, 'Me no Alamo, Me no Goliad.' That didn't matter to any of us. To us, they were all the same. They had to die. Nothing less would be satisfactory.

When the time came to play music, we had no band. All we had was a small black boy playing a drum and an old German on the fife. They didn't know any fight songs so General Houston suggested they play our favorite song, *Will you come to the Bower?*

General Houston was riding Saracen, an extraordinary white stallion given to him by Mr. Groce. The Mexicans shot Saracen right out from under him, shattering the General's leg. Not to be deterred, he grabbed a Mexican's horse and was back in action. I saw a second horse shot from under him and before I knew it, he was on a third, saber in his hand, shouting encouragement. Any doubt we had about his bravery vanished in a bat's breath. Talk about a leader! I feel like standing and saluting his courage right now." With those words, Tom quickly stood, gave a military salute and sat back down.

The Satterwhites were entranced by Tom's ability to spin a story. Johnny could hold back no longer saying, "I hated it when Governor Houston just up and resigned as Governor. Then running off to go live with the Indians in Arkansas. My folks felt he was a great Governor and someday would end up as president of the Union. It doesn't surprise me that he was courageous. Heck, General Houston is one of us. We Tennesseans are as hard as nails and twice as tough as buffalo hide."

Tom Green pushed his chest out as he leaned back and stretched his arms upward. With a shake of his head, he agreed. "You are right about men from Tennessee. We lost about thirty in the Alamo and it was Tennesseans that led the fight at San Jacinto. One of our Colonels tried to stop the killing when a fellow Tennessean was heard to say: 'If Jesus Christ came back this very minute and told me to stop, I'd keep on killing,' and then shouted, '*Remember the Alamo, Remember Goliad.*'

During the battle, some of the Mexican soldiers tried to swim across Peggy Lake and our men picked 'em off each time one raised his head for air. It was like shooting ducks in a pond. The lake turned red with the blood of the Mexican soldiers. I saw their bugler shot dead in the middle of a note. I don't know what he was signaling, but whatever it was, the men never heard it.

I guess one of the saddest things I remember about the battle was a young Mexican drummer with two broken legs who couldn't have been more than twelve, begging for his life. One of our men came up, looked at the child and shouted, '*Remember the Alamo*'. He then dismounted and slashed the boy's throat with his Bowie knife."

Tom's eyes filled with tears. His face blushed with anger. Retelling the story brought back the emotions he felt on April 21st. Removing a handkerchief from his vest, Tom blew his nose and wiped the tears from his eyes. Taking a deep breath, he continued. "When Deaf Smith ran out of powder, he grabbed a Mexican's saber and cut his head clean off. He then turned and broke the blade off in another soldier's chest. We stopped shooting and started beating Mexicans to death with the butts of our guns. The battle got so convoluted; I couldn't shoot for fear of hitting some of our men. Colonel Neill told me to forget the cannon and went to find some Mexicans to kill. I grabbed a pony and took off after those who were trying to escape. In their panic, many threw their guns and sabers to the ground. Looking back, I probably should have allowed them to surrender; however, at that moment, I could only think of avenging the deaths of our slaughtered men.

Santa Anna mounted the nearest horse and was long gone… So much for his bravery. We found him the next day sitting on a log trying to pass himself off as a lowly private. I have to tell you we all got a good laugh when the Mexican captives started bowing and saying, 'El Presidente, El Presidente'. You should have seen Santa Anna's face. He almost swallowed his tongue.

Houston flopped his massive body against a big oak tree, his boot filled with blood. He was asleep when some of our boys brought Santa Anna to the tree. The commotion woke General Houston and as he looked up, he motioned for Santa Anna to have a seat on an ammunition box. Some young boy, I don't remember his name, held our flag and stood next to the tree. You should have seen it: solid white silk with a beautiful painting of Liberty on it. Under Liberty, the words, *Ubi, Libertas, Habitat Ibi Nastra Patria Est*. That is a bunch of fancy words meaning *Where liberty lives, there is our homeland*.

We didn't burn their dead, but neither did we bury them. We felt God made buzzards for just such occasions. I'm not sure buzzards would even eat their flesh. That night the moon was full and the fragrance of the prairie wildflowers masked the smell of gunpowder. A soft southern breeze let us sleep in peace for the first time since we had arrived in Gonzales weeks earlier.

As I was leaving with General Rusk to bury the dead at Goliad, Jack Hays and his brother arrived. They accompanied us to Goliad. When we got there, most of the Texans' bodies had been burned and those who were not, the animals had devoured. We found only a few bones and relics to bury. After that, I decided I best go back and visit my family and get things in order. I had to go to San Antonio on business and then I stopped off at Mr. Groce's place. Then it was my good fortune to meet you all.

I know there is a lot more, but I have told you most of what I know. We can talk more and I will answer your questions, but I do have one request. If you don't mind, I'll stay with you long enough to help Johnny finish the pens and maybe build a shed for the animals. It does get pretty cold for them in the winter, and besides, I would like the opportunity to repay your hospitality."

Johnny and Millie glanced at each other and were getting ready to give their 'Amen' in unison when little A.D. screamed, "Yippee. Dang-nabbit, that will be better than rock candy."

Tom remained two more days. He whittled a spinning top and taught A.D. how to spin. On the last day, A.D. came home with a twelve-pound catfish and Millie fried catfish steaks in cornmeal batter, giving them a nice crispy crust. She opened a jar of homemade ketchup and everyone ate until their stomachs hurt.

With Tennessee on his mind, Tom rose early the next morning. He spent a little time with A.D. and Ruthann, telling them how fortunate they were to have such wonderful parents. The Satterwhite family then accompanied Tom to the river. As he was loading onto the ferry, Millie turned to him and said, "You are going to be a great lawyer and I know Texas will be proud to call you a son. We hope anytime you come back through this way, you will stay with us." Johnny then ferried him across the river. Tom waved back at the family as he rode off the ferry and headed into the dense woods. He was out of sight almost instantly.

Unknown to anyone that morning, some forty miles to the west, a band of one-hundred-and-fifty hostile Comanches were moving slowly toward the intersection of the Little River and the Brazos.

Tom Green would return eighteen months later only to find things had changed dramatically at the Satterwhites.

Chapter Seven
Turmoil

As young Bud Miller approached the *Brass Monkey Saloon*, the sounds of a heated argument across the street caught his attention. Was that the Baron de Bastrop in a screaming match with a younger, more powerful man? Bastrop's arms were flailing around like a wounded duck. Bud could see the Baron's face was flushed beet red as the younger man became more agitated with each verbal assault.

Hiking up the new pants he was wearing to Mr. Weatherspoon's, Bud crossed the muddy street and stepped onto the wooden walkway in front of the saloon. As he moved closer to the commotion, he could make out a few details of the argument. The burly young man with fierce black eyes and heavy dark mustache demanded in an unfamiliar accent, "Old man, you pay me or I'm gonna tear yur head off. I get my money or you don't leave this place in one piece."

Neither man noticed as Bud inched his way closer. As far as Bud could tell, the conversation was one sided. Trying in vain to distract his assailant, the Baron glanced over his right shoulder as if someone was approaching. The Baron shifted his attention back to the enraged man and with a barely controlled plea in his voice, he responded. "Sir, I am a man of honor. I can assure you there must be some mistake. I paid your friends the full amount required to transport my inventory from the docks to the warehouse. I suggest you take the matter up with those scoundrels instead of accusing me of larceny."

The Baron's words fell on deaf ears as the younger man reached out and grabbed him by his silk bow tie. Yanking the old man's wrinkled face forward, he looked the Baron dead in the eye as he threatened, "I already almost killed my cousin 'cause I thought he was lying to me. I cut off two of his fingers. I just left him squealing like a baby. Make no mistake old man, if you paid him, he would not have held back. You did not pay. You give me my money or die where you stand."

"Mercy me, I do hope you are not planning to do harm to an elderly gentleman like myself." Bastrop's words were those of a defenseless, desperate man. His face was no longer red with anger, but now sallow and growing paler by the second. Fear was obvious in his countenance. He had no doubt the assailant would follow through on his threat. The Baron had run out of options.

Bud could not stand by and watch his helpless old friend be slaughtered like a lamb. Young Bud Miller reached into his new pant's pocket and pulled out his "frog sticker". He flipped open the five-inch blade, honed sharp enough to split a hair. He was not going to allow this physically superior young bully to inflict harm on his old friend. Bud knew he must intercede quickly, or it would be too late.

The assassin's grip tightened as a defiant Bastrop screamed, "You dirty Mexican, let go of my tie before I call the authorities and have you locked up for attempted murder."

The assailant shot back. "Sheriff Maples? He's not gonna mess with Hector Garza."

At that moment, Bud realized the man threatening the Baron was of Mexican descent. That's why the stranger's speech was so broken and garbled. The thought of fighting a Mexican energized the sixteen-year-old Kentucky boy. His reason for coming to Texas was standing right in front of him.

Bud shouted at the top of his lungs, "You are a dirty Meskin that dun killed my pa. Yur gonna deal with me and leave Mr. Bastrop be. Turn 'round where I kan see yur face."

Still holding the Baron by his tie, the broad-shouldered aggressor glanced over his shoulder to see who was screaming racial slurs at him. When he saw the smaller boy, he smiled and shoved the Baron back into a horse hitching post, knocking the old man to the boardwalk. Then, with the quickness of a dancer, he whirled around to face the lad. The anger vanished from his face. He smiled. His gold tooth glistened as the sun bounced off the bright surface, giving him an even more menacing appearance. He realized one slap of his broad hand would send the boy flying into the muddy street. Like a cat with a mouse, he decided to toy with the boy before killing him. Hector Garza leaned back placing his hands on his hips and with an air of confidence, inquired, "What did ya call me? Who did you accuse me of killing?"

A defiant Bud pushed out his chest and answered the brick-solid man. "I called you a dirty Meskin and said you are one of them that dun killed my pa. I kaint stands by an' let you hurt my friend. If you think I'm scared of you, you are picked purdy green."

In a flash, a strong backhand sent Bud to the ground, causing him to see stars as his body bounced off the wooden surface of the walkway. The powerful Garza had addled young Miller. Bud knew he was in serious trouble unless he could shake the cobwebs. The Baron was no help. The old man was crumpled in a ball still struggling to raise himself off the ground. Bud knew he must get back on his feet or his fate would be that of his father. Fumbling around with his right hand, he found his knife.

The setting sun glanced off the bronze skin of the broad-shouldered Mexican, giving his face a strange iridescent glow. Simultaneously, the Baron was regaining his equilibrium and slowly struggling to his feet. He watched helplessly as his young friend was trying to clear his head. The Baron felt sadness for the boy he had rescued only a couple of months earlier.

Bud crawled to his knees. Before he could get to his feet, Garza reached down and grabbed the boy by the neck, lifting him off the boardwalk. The powerful grip cut off Bud's airflow. The Mexican killer made one fatal mistake, failing to secure Bud's hands. He didn't see the large open knife Bud was grasping in his hand. With one quick thrust upward of his left hand, Bud grabbed a mass of the Mexican's thick hair and yanked the assailant's face forward. Using the leverage, Bud quickly followed by an upper plunge with his right hand and drove the sharp blade into Garza's ribcage. The knife sliced through the bone and into the powerful man's heart. Instantaneously, blood began pouring from the corners of Garza's mouth. Releasing his grip on Bud's neck, the Mexican began tying to pull the long knife from his chest. As he yanked to free the knife from his body, the blade broke off in his sternum. The bloody, bladeless knife handle clanked onto the wooden planks, rolling in the direction of the Baron. Garza's eyes rolled back in his head as he staggered against the newspaper building. He looked skyward and pleaded, "Mary Mother of God, forgive me of my siiinnnnnnns." Those fading words would be his last as he slid to the ground choking on his own blood.

Bud stood frozen, gazing down at the Mexican man struggling to breathe. The man he had killed on his way to Texas had fallen into the water and was washed downstream. Bud never saw him die. Now he was forced to watch a man's last breath leave him. There was a deep emptiness in the pit of his stomach. While the lad stood frozen like a block of ice, the Baron grabbed the knife handle from the sidewalk and wiped the excess blood on the dying man's buckskin pants. He grasped Bud's arm and yanked hard to get the boy's attention. "Come on son. We gotta get you away from here right now. They will hang you for sure. There are several Mexicans in front of the *Brass Monkey* who saw you kill that man."

The Baron knew that he must move with alacrity. Bud was in a world of trouble. Within minutes, a crowd would gather and a lawman would be taking the boy away. If the Baron didn't get the lad to safety, he was sure to hang. Galveston had recently built a new gallows on the town square and the three-rope stand had already been used five times. Texas justice was faster than a greyhound chasing a rabbit.

The pair headed south down Main Street as fast as the Baron could move. Young Bud kept looking over his shoulder as Bastrop yanked him into an alley and out of sight. They could hear a girl's voice screaming in the distance. "Get the Sheriff, there's a dead man over there. He's been murdered. Help, help, help, somebody get some help." Then the voice repeated the same plea in Spanish. Bud realized the voice was Maria's, his dream girl from the *Brass Monkey*.

There would be no time to return to the boarding house and gather their belongings. There had been witnesses.

Everyone in town knew the Baron and the authorities would be looking for him and the boy in no time. Bastrop realized the fix they were in and for one brief moment wished he had not swindled the four workers out of their pay. He was almost willing to admit some responsibility for the dire straits Bud now found himself in. Breathlessly, the Baron said, "You are going to have to trust me. I am going to fetch a horse and buggy and as soon as it's hitched, I'll head for the ferry. I have a plan how I can slip you off the island and get you back to New Orleans. You won't like my plan, but you have no choice. It's either do what I say or swing from the gallows."

The pair stopped in front of a small rough-hewn log house not far from the warehouse where the Baron's merchandise was stored. In a firm tone, he instructed, "Wait over there under the myrtle bushes. I need to go and borrow some clothes from Mildred Garner."

Bud was still in a daze; he obediently followed the old man's orders. Slipping down to the ground behind a magenta crepe myrtle bush, he sat in silence on his haunches. As the Kentucky boy hunkered down, he heard a galloping horse coming in his direction. Pulling the limbs slightly apart, he saw the deputy sheriff rush past. He knew the lawman was looking for him. His body began to shiver. He felt like crying. Why would killing a Mexican get him in so much trouble? His Uncle Charlie taught him all Texans wanted to kill Mexicans. He was confused.

Bud could hear Sheriff Maples shouting to a group of men gathered around the murdered man. "Anybody seen a young boy with old man Bastrop? The boy just killed Hector Garza. Maria saw it all. I need to find that boy before he kills again. Come on, let's spread out and look for them. Don't try to apprehend him alone. I don't want any of you being his next victim. Shoot first and ask questions later."

Inside the tiny two room log house, the Baron bargained hard with Mildred Garner, a local seamstress who knew the old man only in passing. He wanted to purchase a used bonnet and calico dress.

Mildred queried, "Why?"

The Baron presented a reasonable explanation; he wanted to donate the dress and bonnet to a homeless lady. Lying was never a problem for the old swindler. Buying the bonnet and dress on credit presented a bigger challenge. Thinking fast, the Baron grabbed a writing tablet and pencil from her table and hastily wrote a promissory note for more than double the value of the worn clothing.

Bud almost fainted with shame when the Baron instructed him to slip the dress over his clothes. The Baron growled, "Stick your hat under your arm and pull on this dress! We must change your appearance."

Bud shook his head defiantly. "No sir, I kaint do that. I ain't no sissy Mr. Bastrop. Kaint wear no gurls clothes."

The Baron had faced too many close scrapes and he was not going to let a little mishap like the killing of Hector Garza corner him now. Bastrop replied angrily, "Listen to me young man. Shut up your sniveling disobedience and put on these clothes. I'm risking my life to save your skinny backside. Now do what I tell you or I'll turn you over to Sheriff Maples and collect the reward myself."

Bud held up the dress, not quite sure how to put it on. "Raise your arms," the old man scolded. Grabbing the garment from the boy's hands, he flopped open the bottom and pushed it over Bud's head, letting gravity do the rest. Once the dress was on, Bastrop made Bud roll up his trousers so they wouldn't dangle from under the dress. He then shoved the bonnet on and tied the strings under Bud's chin. Pausing for a moment, he pulled Bud's broken frog sticker from his pocket. Kicking a hole in the ground, he dropped the knife handle and kicked the dirt over it. Then he broke off several blossoms from an oleander bush, making a flower bouquet. Standing back, he looked at Bud and injected some levity into their dire situation. "Now you look mighty precious."

The Baron's voice once again lowered as he directed, "Now, I want you to head down to the bayou and go south to the ferry. I'm going to get a horse and buggy and meet you there. Now listen up, when you see me, if I remove my hat and rub my head you get on the ferry as if you were a lone foot passenger. This is important because they are looking for a man and boy together. Here's a dime. This will pay your passage on the ferry. If I get held up, you go ahead. Once you are safely on the other side, wait for me. I'll figure out what to do next." Grabbing Bud by his shoulders, he asked firmly, "Do you understand?"

"Sure Mr. Bastrop, I ain't no dummy. I don't want to git strung up for killin' a Meskin."

Bud's mind drifted from the task at hand as sadness overcame him. The dream girl of his life was the one who told the law about him stabbing Hector Garza. Surely she could see the Mexican was trying to kill the helpless old man. Now he would probably never see her again, and in all probability be hanged for murder. He wondered what his teacher would think when he didn't arrive for his lesson. His life floated past him in a panoramic blur of fear and uncertainty. Bud walked toward the bayou in a stupor, too dazed to think of anything except reaching the ferry.

A problem arose when the Baron got to the livery stable; he still owed a past due rental fee. The owner of the stable was not there and his Negro helper didn't think he should allow the Baron to rent a team of horses and a buggy until he cleared up his outstanding bill. Bastrop made it his business to know secrets about people. He knew the Negro was a runaway slave and not a free man as he had told the stable owner. Looking down into the slave's face, he shouted angrily, "Harness those damn horses to a wagon or you will force me to turn you over to Sheriff Maples. They pay a handsome reward for turning in men like you. I bet your Master back in Mississippi would dearly love to have you back where he could lash some obedience into your back. If I were not a caring person, I would turn you in myself for the one hundred dollar reward. What will it be? Do I get the rig or do you go back to the cotton fields?"

For the first time, Solomon realized someone knew the truth about him. He blanched with fear as he looked into the eyes of the desperate Baron. He knew Bastrop meant what he was saying. Solomon lowered his head and pleaded, "Massa Bastrop, sir please don't sends me backs. I done got me a family and everythin' here in Texas. It would kills my wife for them to takes me away from 'er and them chil'en. She ain't got nobody but me to care fur 'er. I git your rig right now, sir. Please don't tell my boss. You won't wills you if'n I git you hooked up in a hurry?"

"Solomon, I, the Baron de Bastrop, am a man of honor. No one has ever accused me of going back on my word. Toss in a bag of shelled corn, a jug of that whiskey you keep hidden behind the hay, and while you are at it, a rope of tobacco. Do that and your secret will go with me to my grave."

The best horses were already rented so Solomon hitched one mule and an older gray horse to the buggy. Popping the team's rumps with the reins, the Baron was quickly out into the street and pushing fast toward the ferry. Glancing in the back of the buggy to make sure the whiskey, corn and tobacco were there, Bastrop was satisfied when he spotted two gallon jugs.

Bud's trip was uneventful, other than a few ruffians whistling and yelling out catcalls. He wanted to yank the bonnet off and beat them up, but he walked on pretending not to hear. Their crude comments gave him pause to reflect on how a girl felt when boys made rude remarks. Walking in another person's shoes had taken on a whole new meaning. Once he reached the wharf, he turned south, breaking into a jog. He wanted to arrive at the ferry before the Baron.

Bastrop took an alternate route and was well on his way when he noticed one of the deputies up in front of him, stopping people in the middle of the street. The Baron turned left at the next intersection, went two blocks and then turned south again. Three blocks would have taken him past the lawman, but he took no chances and pushed on for seven. The street came to a dead end, forcing him to turn back toward the bayou. He passed the street where the deputy was questioning people and pressed on toward the water. Turning back north, he spotted Bud jogging in his direction. Luck was on the crusty old man's side; the ferry was just unloading a wagon and passenger as he pulled alongside the dock. The leather brown mule was lazy, forcing the Baron to continually pop him with the reins just to keep the traces tight. He nudged his team into place and waited to board.

Bastrop knew if they could reach the other shore, they would find refuge in San Felipe. After all, he had issued over a thousand land titles to the families who settled in the two Austin Colonies. Cow Milligan would take them in for sure. Bastrop couldn't remember Cow's given name. Like so many, William Milligan went by the nickname he was given because he made his living raising milk cows. Cow owed the Baron a rather large favor. The Baron had directed the uneducated man from Missouri to a splendid 4,600-acre plot of grazing land and extra rich farm soil in the Austin Colony. Unfortunately Cow was not much of a businessman and often talked of selling his operation should the price be right. The Baron hoped no one had taken his old friend up on the offer. He needed Cow more than ever for a place to hide until he could smuggle young Miller into the Union. The Baron had taken a liking to the boy and didn't want him to come to any harm.

Bud was sweating profusely when he arrived at the dock. He felt like he was suffocating. He clung to the bouquet of flowers like they were some magic talisman used to ward off evil. There was no one at the dock other than the Baron, a lone wagon-master preparing to disembark, and the elderly gray-haired black man who operated the ferry.

The Baron removed his hat, took his white handkerchief from his vest pocket and wiped his brow, brushing the cloth back through his thick dyed hair. This was his signal to Bud to not acknowledge they knew each other. He and Bud separately paid their fares. The ferryman then flipped the ropes free and was pulling away when a lone rider came galloping toward the dock. He was waving his arms and yelling, but the ferry driver was not about to return for another passenger. The anxious rider would just have to wait his turn.

Bud and the Baron had a pretty good idea the rider was not seeking passage. The Baron broke his silence and leaning down from his buggy seat said, "I think that rider spells serious trouble. We will be fine once we get across the bayou."

The flatbed ferry moved into the smooth bayou waters and was four hundred yards from shore by the time the man on horseback reached the shoreline. As the lone rider's bay mustang mare came to a sliding stop only inches from the water's edge, the stranger dismounted and fired a warning shot into the air.

Chapter Eight
Fame and Glory

August 4, 1836 was an unusually hot, muggy day. The Alabama humidity hung heavy in the air like the kudzu vines on the trees, and enveloped Tuscaloosa with a suffocating stillness. This was the day Samuel Maverick returned to marry the love of his life, Mary Ann Adams. He had lived in Texas long enough to see the raw, savage territory transform into a burgeoning Republic. Maverick participated in the battle that drove General Cos' army from his beloved San Antonio de Bexar and was one of the courageous few to sign the most important document in the history of Texas, the Declaration of Independence. The ties to his home state had been severed and the brash, young lawyer's loyalties had shifted to the Lone Star Republic.

After finalizing the Constitution, Maverick had become deathly ill and was not expected to live. Three friends carried the weak and dying Maverick to Nacogdoches where he received medical care, food, and much-needed rest. The news of Texas' victory against Mexico lifted his spirits, and when he regained his strength, Maverick's thoughts turned to marriage and the dream of building an empire for his family in the land he had come to love. As soon as he was able, he saddled his favorite horse, a chestnut stallion named Mex, and began the rugged trip east to Alabama. Mex stood seventeen-and-a-half hands tall and had the stamina and endurance of a mustang. Mex's tail almost brushed the ground if the stallion did not keep an arch in the crop. Mex possessed a smooth gait, making riding him like sitting in a rocking chair, Sam could ride all day without tiring.

Soon after arriving in Alabama, thirty-three-year-old Samuel Augustus "Gus" Maverick married eighteen-year-old Mary Ann Adams. The newlyweds spent the next six months visiting friends and family, making their last stop in South Carolina to visit the Maverick family plantation, *Montpelier*. *Montpelier* was one of the largest and most successful plantations in the country, growing cotton, fruit, and vegetables. The Maverick plantation was the most important operation in the state of South Carolina and required one hundred and forty male slaves to keep it running smoothly. Counting the women and children, Sam's father owned over three hundred and fifty slaves.

The newlyweds resided at *Montpelier* until Mary gave birth to their first child, Samuel Jr. No amount of pleas from Sam's father could change Maverick's mind about building his own empire in Texas. Since Gus, as the family called him, was the only son, *Montpelier* would be his when his father died. Even the promise of inheriting his father's enormous wealth could not sway Sam from taking his young family back west. Even Mary's ambivalence about leaving her family didn't dissuade him. He was taking his family back to Texas and nothing could stop him. His heart was tied to Texas.

Sam had a clear vision of his dream and had paid the price several months earlier to make it a reality. He had been working in his law office in early October of 1835 when the Mexican General Martin Pacifico de Cos marched his army into San Antonio and set up headquarters in the Alamo Mission across the river. Sam and John Smith, a client, rushed into the street to see what the commotion was all about. They froze in their tracks as they watched a thousand heavily armed Mexican foot soldiers flood into their peaceful little town. A third young man, seeing the hoards of armed men dressed in dirty white uniforms and wearing tall hats, dashed over to ask what was happening. Without warning, the three men were surrounded by several dozen soldiers. An arrogant Captain marched them at gunpoint to Sam's sister's home and informed them they would be killed if they left the premises. No explanation was given for their house arrest.

What became known as the *Anahuac Incident* had triggered the now escalating hostilities between Texas and Mexico. In 1831, a former Anglo filibuster and mercenary, John Davis Bradburn moved to Mexico and became a Mexican citizen. The Mexicans put the arrogant, self-centered Bradburn in charge of the garrison at Anahuac, Texas. His duties were to make sure taxes and duties were paid, but he had an unquenchable and dangerous desire for power. It was not long before he declared martial law, abolished the community of Liberty and seized the local citizens' property. His actions outraged the Texans, Anglo and Mexican alike. The Texans formed a militia and marched on Bradburn's garrison. After a brief battle, ten Texans and thirty-seven Mexicans were dead. Bradburn surrendered and then fled to New Orleans, leaving irreparable hostility in his wake. The rift had now grown into an immense chasm that could not be bridged, even if each side had been willing. Maverick suspected their arrests had to do with Santa Anna's retaliation for the rebellious incidents perpetrated by the Texans.

The new Mexican administration had given General Santa Anna supreme command, making him Dictator of all of Mexico, an enormous landmass reaching west to the Pacific Ocean, northwest to Oregon, north to Canada and east to Louisiana. There had been rumors among the local Mexicans that General Santa Anna was planning to teach the insubordinate Texas Anglos a lesson. Santa Anna viewed the settlers as disobedient for not paying taxes or duty on imports, and worse, as disloyal subjects rejecting his absolute power. Sam's suspicions were dead center accurate.

Santa Anna was a ruthless megalomaniac who wore linen shirts adorned with diamond studs worth $5,000 each and carried a $7,000 gold sword. He rode the most magnificent black stallion in all of Mexico, his saddle embellished with gold and silver. He traveled with his own ornate silk marquee, monogrammed china, crystal decanters and a silver chamber pot. A band of musicians accompanied his campaigns, playing his favorite Mozart or Bach on demand. Santa Anna was a notorious womanizer and gambled heavily on cockfights. Worst of all, he was addicted to opium. A Mexican Colonel told Austin that Santa Anna was heard to say, "If I were God, I would wish to be more."

Mexico had every reason to believe that suppressing the violence would be a simple task. Their highly trained soldiers outnumbered the Texans twenty to one, they had ample supplies, and most importantly, controlled the Gulf shoreline. The Mexican army marched into Texas like a schoolyard bully, hoping the ill-equipped and unorganized Texans would retreat in fear.

General Cos sent Lieutenant Francisco Castaneda to demand the return of a cannon the Mexican government had loaned the DeWitt colonists to protect Gonzales. Near the end of September 1835,

Lieutenant Castaneda and a hundred Mexican soldiers went to retrieve the old four-pound cannon. The Texans, under the command of Colonel John Henry Moore, crossed the river and by the next morning found themselves within three hundred yards of Castaneda and his men. James Neill set off the rusty old cannon the Mexican's had come to retrieve, firing the first shot of the war. After a brief battle, the Mexican troops withdrew. Two Mexicans were killed and several wounded. The Texans suffered no casualties. The day after the skirmish, Stephen Austin called an assembly and was elected commander of the Texas Army. Emboldened by their recent victory, the Texans were now prepared to organize their fight for independence.

General Cos then entered San Antonio, sending his soldiers from house to house confiscating all the weapons, powder and lead. He took possession of homes and converted them into mini-forts by cutting gun holes in the walls and blocking the windows and doors. He forced fifty local Mexican men to do manual labor without compensation. Not all were peons; some were the prominent leaders of the town. A peon was a pedestrian who couldn't afford to own a horse. His brutal actions also turned the Tejanos, who were previously Santa Anna supporters, against Mexico. General Cos then set up headquarters at the Alamo. The mission, originally built in 1744 had been neglected and left to crumble; Cos immediately began to transform the old mission into a fort. At the main gate, he had his men construct an earthen lunette. He added cannons, built firing ramps and fortified the walls. Stockade fences and cattle pens were repaired or newly built. They worked on the long barracks and spruced up the lower one. Cos made the local men clean out the two water wells inside the compound, ensuring a steady supply of fresh water should there be a long siege. On the roof, Cos installed an eighteen-pound cannon, the biggest in Texas, which could fire a half-mile past downtown; the same cannon William Travis would use against Santa Anna and his soldiers in the future.

Cos was careful to take no chances of an insurrection among the locals. He knew how unhappy many of the citizens were with the recent change of power in Mexico City and how a good percentage of the Tejanos and Americans who had converted to Mexican citizenship were still loyal to ex-president, Anastacio Bustamente. Bustamente had saved the Alamo when it was going to be torn down. He turned the old mission building into a hospital and had allowed American immigration, creating good will with the local citizens. What Santa Anna failed to capitalize on was that many Texans, in order to maintain peace, would have joined him in purging the Mexican state of the independent-minded rebels. Now Cos' invasion had awakened the sleeping kitten and prodded the Texans into becoming a raging lion. His actions prompted the two groups to merge into one united fighting force.

One of the men placed under house arrest with Maverick was John Smith, or as many called him, "El Colorado" because of his flaming red hair and beard that billowed in the breeze. John Smith arrived in Texas in 1831 and converted to Catholicism as he crossed over the Sabine River. A priest stationed on the border gave Smith the oath of conversion, sprinkled him with water and handed him a sheet of paper making him a Mexican citizen. Becoming a citizen and marrying a Mexican girl would also give him 4,600 acres of land and it was not long before he married Maria Curbelo, a beautiful twenty-three-year-old Mexican widow with two children. Once Smith had converted to the Church of Rome and married, he did his best to become a solid Mexican citizen. However, after seeing the way some were being treated by Mexico City, he joined with those talking of independence. A rebel at heart, there was not much persuasion needed to get Smith involved with the revolution.

The other man under house arrest was Robert Sullivan, a newcomer who had ridden into San Antonio only one day before the Mexican Captain caught him in casual conversation with Maverick and Smith. Robert was a pimple-faced young man with a cleft lip, just nineteen years old. Fighting was nothing new to the young man from West Virginia. He had fought his entire life because of folks making fun of his affliction. There was a deep-seated anger below the surface, just waiting to spring to the fore. The more Maverick talked about fighting for an independent Republic, the greater Robert's desire to participate became. He had never been part of anything. Now he had an opportunity to belong, and the best part was neither Sam nor John gave any indication they even noticed his impaired speech or deformed lip. They treated him as an equal and not like some freak of nature.

While Maverick was under house arrest, the Texas rebels outside the city were getting bolder. General Cos endured sporadic small raids on the perimeter of his command. The Texans were constantly taking pot shots at the General's men and stealing their horses. Twice, Jim Bowie's men defeated Cos in small skirmishes.

Austin ordered Bowie and James Fannin to search the missions fronting the Goliad road. It was rumored that the Missions Espada, San Juan, San Jose, and Concepcion were well stocked with corn, gunpowder and other supplies. Bowie and Fannin led some eighty men to the missions. No resistance was given; however, they soon discovered the supplies were not the property of General Cos, but owned by local men. Bowie, fluent in Spanish, was able to buy the much-needed corn and other supplies by giving the owners a promissory note signed by Stephen F. Austin. Most of the farmers knew if they didn't help Bowie, Santa Anna would confiscate their goods without any hope of compensation when he arrived.

Realizing the road from San Antonio to Goliad needed to be protected, Bowie set up camp along the San Antonio River in front of Mission Concepcion and sent Fannin downriver to protect his flank. Bowie and his men took shelter under the pecan trees that ran along the banks of the San Antonio River, leaving four hundred yards of open ground in front of their position. Only one day passed before the Mexicans came calling. The morning of November 1, 1835, Bowie awoke to discover they were surrounded by four hundred Mexican soldiers and mounted Calvary. The Mexicans had crossed the river during the night under the cover of thick fog and were in position to attack by dawn. Fortunately, the fog that had allowed the Mexicans to cross the river undetected was now impeding their ability to mount a charge. The delay allowed Bowie to rally his men and get them into defensive positions. He instructed them to clear out the underbrush so they could move freely up and down the riverbank. The embankment rose ten to twelve feet high and Bowie ordered his men to dig steps into the sides of the bank. The steps would enable half of the men to step up and fire, then drop down to reload while the other half assumed their position on the steps and fired.

As the fog lifted, one of Bowie's sharpshooters dropped a Mexican off his horse and the battle began. Bowie rushed up and down the line like a caged tiger, firmly instructing his men to remain calm and to make every shot count. Jim admonished, "Treat this like a turkey shoot back home. Only pull the trigger when you know you have a sure kill."

The Mexicans were shooting sporadically with their Brown Bess muskets, with few shots even coming near the Texans while Bowie's men stepped up on the dugout pedestals and took deadly aim. Each time the Mexicans charged, they were repelled by the accuracy of the Texans' Kentucky long rifles. With each repelled charge, Bowie moved his men down the riverbank closer to the cannons. Once he felt they were close enough, he and a dozen of his bravest men charged the cannons, killing the soldiers manning the weapons. The Texans then turned the cannons on the Mexicans. When the battle was over, more than seventy Mexican soldiers were dead and a large number wounded. Bowie lost only one of his men. Bowie's strategic battle position and his sharpshooter's marksmanship had achieved an important victory.

While under house arrest, Sam Maverick was compiling information. He filled his diary with vital statistics such as the size and movements of Cos' army, what times the soldiers ate, took siesta, changed shifts and performed other daily routines. With a spyglass his brother-in-law had given him, Sam was able to maintain surveillance on the Alamo and make copious notes on where each cannon was positioned.

On December 1, Sam, the other two captive Americans and one Tejano waited until siesta then escaped into the woods. Sam and the others quickly joined up with Colonel Edward Burleson, an old Indian-fighter, who had over four hundred men under his command. Maverick's notes provided valuable information to Burleson and the Texans planning to recapture the Alamo. Maverick estimated the number of fighting men under Cos' command was between thirteen and fifteen hundred. Sam's estimate would later be proven correct; Cos had an army of fourteen hundred soldiers. Sam told how the army was in disarray and morale extremely low after the two Bowie victories, and he believed there would be little resistance if a strong battle were taken to them.

Colonel Burleson split his small army into two groups: One group was led by Ben Milam, a veteran of several battles and the other by Francis Johnson. The two mounted columns slipped into the city from different directions, one from the north and the other from the south. They were able to sneak into town undetected until they were almost to the Military Plaza. The Mexicans spotted them, and in the ensuing confusion and black smoke, the Texans secured two houses facing the Military Plaza; the same Plaza where Bastrop had befriended Moses Austin sixteen years earlier and opened the Anglo immigration into Texas. Johnson's group took command of the De La Garza house for their assault center. Ben Milam and his men immediately moved into the Vernanendi mansion, the former home of Jim Bowie's father-in-law. House-to-house fighting continued for three days as the Texans made their way to the Military Plaza in the center of town.

When the Mexicans had seized control of the homes in the city, they had knocked portholes in walls and barricaded doors. The Texans used crowbars and sledgehammers to break open the doors after sticking their rifles through the portholes and shooting any Mexicans they could see. Hand-to-hand combat ensued, giving the advantage to the larger and more physically powerful Texans. Making their way to the bell tower, they seized a cannon and turned the weapon on the enemy.

On day four, a sniper gunned down Ben Milam. As soon as news spread of Milam's death, Francis Johnson immediately took full command as the Texans fought with a vengeance the likes of which the Mexican army had never seen. By the end of day four, the Texans had lost a dozen men while almost two hundred Mexican soldiers were dead and scores wounded.

The morning of the fifth day, General Cos awoke to discover that one hundred and seventy nine of his men and six officers had deserted during the night. Cos gave the order to raise the white flag and surrendered the Alamo and San Antonio to the Texans. Maverick drafted the terms for surrender in both languages and handed his turkey feather quill to the General. Under the terms of the document, Cos was permitted to take his men back across the Rio Grande with the promise to never return. By nightfall, San Antonio was under the control of the Texans. Unknown to the majority of overjoyed Texans, the real battle was still ahead. What many Texans perceived as victory was nothing more than a red flag in the face of an angry bull.

Sam Houston understood the vindictive Santa Anna would not stand still after getting his nose bloodied again by the Texans. Governor Anson Jones and Sam Maverick agreed. Maverick wanted to remain in San Antonio, but Houston insisted he participate in the Constitutional Convention. "Sam, few in Texas have your education and common sense. Your mind is needed at this crucial juncture."

Sam Maverick, a Yale Graduate and lawyer, joined the Constitutional Convention at Washington-on-the-Brazos on March 2, 1836. Had his education not been so valuable in the formation of a new Republic, he would have surely died in the Alamo along with the one hundred and eighty two gallant men.

Now that the battles were behind him and Texas was free, Sam Maverick was anxious to show his new bride the glorious opportunities that awaited them in his beloved Texas. He saw endless possibilities in the raw and rugged land. With enormous financial backing from his father and his knowledge of real estate law, Sam was confident he would become a very wealthy and powerful man.

Unlike the dirt-poor Satterwhites, Sam and Mary Maverick traveled in high style. The Mavericks had ten slaves and traveled in a large covered carriage with soft leather seats, accompanied by a nurse to help care for their new baby. Their cooks prepared several-course meals with each rest stop. Mary's sickly fifteen-year-old brother had also come along on their journey. Sam had been reluctant to bring the boy for fear he would die on the road, but Mary's mother had insisted.

Behind Sam and Mary's carriage followed a Kentucky Calistoga wagon driven by their male slave, Griffin. Accompanying Griffin on the wagon seat was "cook Jinny" who was given to Mary at birth. Griffin was a massive man with a physique resembling a Michelangelo sculpture. He was barely thirty-three and in the prime of his life. Jinny was a large woman, standing five-foot-eleven and weighing a solid 245 pounds. No one ran a kitchen like Jinny. When she spoke, all the slaves, including the men, listened. Jinny's wrath was something no one wanted to encounter. Yet, where Mary and the family were concerned, she was a humble, obedient servant. Mary and Sam cared deeply for Jinny and Griffin.

The Maverick entourage also included three extra saddle horses and one blooded filly. The Mavericks carried a six-month supply of provisions, and bedding and tents. A bed was set up in the tent each night for Sam, Mary, Sam Jr. and Mary's brother. Each morning, before the tent was disassembled, one of the female slaves swept the canvas floor of the dirt tracked in by the Mavericks. Sam and Mary were never in a rush to start early or drive late like Johnny and Millie Satterwhite had. Mary did no cooking and neither did she mend or wash clothes. Sam hitched no teams and carried no water. Sam spent his days reading and making notes in his diary. The contrast between the Satterwhite's and Maverick's journey to Texas was dramatic as daylight to darkness. Wealth vs. destitution. Privilege vs. poverty. Yet they each shared a common goal, establishing a new life in Texas.

The Mavericks crossed the Mississippi River at Rodney and the Red River at Alexandra. When they arrived at the Sabine River, it was a sluggish, muddy, narrow stream. They drove the carriage and wagons across, arriving on Texas soil January 1, 1838. Once in Nacogdoches, Sam purchased animal feed, corn and restocked their groceries. The Mavericks then stopped outside of town to spend a few days with Colonel John Durst, a close friend. Durst was a successful merchant who owned 36,000 acres. In 1835, Durst was serving as a Texas representative in the legislature of the Mexican state of Coahuila y Texas when he caught wind of the retaliatory attacks Santa Anna was planning against the Texans. He got on his horse and rode 960 miles to warn the settlers, earning him the title of "Texas' Paul Revere". While they rested with the Dursts, another dear friend of Sam's father, General Thomas Rusk, dropped in. General Rusk had taken command of the Texas Army when the wounded General Houston was taken to New Orleans for medical care. Houston's last orders before losing consciousness were to put Rusk in command. General Rusk was one of the leading founders of the new Republic.

The three men sipped whiskey at the family table under the amber light of an oil lamp and talked about the future of Texas. Mary knew Sam was well known in the area, but not until she saw the admiration he received from his fellow Texans did she fully comprehend his status in the new Republic. Nineteen-year-old Mary Ann's heart filled with pride upon seeing her husband in the company of these men of such greatness.

As the Maverick's resumed their journey, passage through the swamplands was slow going. Because of the inordinate amount of rain, traveling across the lowlands was extremely taxing. On one day, they were only able to travel a little over one mile. The slaves were forced to carry the load from the carriage and wagons across the deepwater areas. They let the carriage and wagons float as they walked beside and pushed them across.

The swarms of mosquitoes discouraged Mary. Baby Sam remained protected with only an occasional bite when his netting blew open. When a rogue mosquito slipped under the baby's covers, Jinny dipped some snuff and placed a brown dab on the bite. The old slave remedy stopped the itching and prevented the baby from scratching and spreading infection.

There was great elation among the Maverick caravan when they arrived at Springhill Farms on February 4. Even the quiet Jinny let out a yell, piercing the quiet and causing a covey of bobwhite quail to flutter into the air and vanish in a flash. There, the Mavericks met Captain Peck of the Louisiana Grays and Captain Sylvester, originally from Ohio, who had both stopped for a rest as well. Sylvester was the soldier who discovered the dejected Santa Anna sitting on a tree stump, dressed as a common soldier, after his defeat at San Jacinto. Mary quickly made friends with Fannie Menifee whose brother John was also one of the heroes at San Jacinto. The Mavericks enjoyed meeting new people and delighted in the fresh conversation after their long journey. Mary and Sam danced until the early morning hours four nights in a row. When Sam's legs grew tired of dancing, Captain Sylvester took Mary for a few spins, kicking up splinters with his heavy boots.

Mary was very well received among the locals and Sam felt comfortable leaving her and the slaves at Springhill Farms. He saddled up Mex, packed his bags and headed for San Antonio to make sure the city was safe. The last time he had been in San Antonio, he had taken part in the bitter fight that drove out General Cos. When he arrived this time, it was peaceful. He leased a house and gave notice to his sister and her husband that he would soon return with Mary and the baby. Since Sam's sister had never met Mary, there was joy in the anticipation of meeting Sam's new bride and infant son, Sam, Jr.

On June 12, 1838, the Mavericks arrived in the tranquil San Antonio valley. The town rested peacefully in the heart of a large valley framed by gradual hills that gently rose skyward. The next day, they traveled another sixteen miles to Marcelino Creek and on to Cantu's Ranch. Cantu's place was next to Erasmo Seguin's Ranch. Seguin's son Juan was a hero in the battle of San Jacinto. Each day seemed to grow longer and longer for the anxious couple. They could hardly contain themselves in anticipation of reaching San Antonio, especially Mary.

Once in San Antonio, the couple set up residence in the home Sam had leased from Don Casiano. The house fronted the Main Plaza, was bounded on the south by Dolorosa Street and extended halfway back to the Military Plaza. Mary was stunned with the size and quality of their new home. The limestone house was much larger than she had envisioned. The long room was filled with custom made furniture and fine kerosene lamps and was large enough to hold dances and parties. Her bedroom was furnished with a four-poster bed topped with a fluffy goose down mattress and there was also an elegant maple chifforobe for her clothing. The walnut dining room table would comfortably seat twelve, and the matching French-inspired high back chairs were covered in fine red velvet. Sam had spared no expense in furnishing their new home.

Soon after their arrival in San Antonio, Sam took Mary to the ruins of the Alamo so she could view first hand what remained of the centerfold of the Texas Republic. They were able to locate three piles of ashes where Santa Anna had burned the bodies of those slaughtered during the siege. Only a few graves were marked by a pile of rocks and crosses made from tree limbs or rough-hewn planks. The locals told them how a coffin maker had carved the four names of *Travis, Bowie, Crockett and Bonham* on the top of a coffin. Of course, the men had no way of knowing whose bones they were burying in that coffin, but wanted history to remember the names of the leaders who gave their lives for Texas' independence. Those four names represented the courage and character of all 182 men who died for freedom at the Alamo.

Several years later, Sam and Mary Maverick would build their ranch on the Alamo property, along the area known as the north wall. Their front porch covered the spot where William Travis was killed in the battle. To Sam, the Alamo was a sacred shrine. He wanted his house on the holy ground so he could protect the area. He wanted to be a guardian of the flame that had set a new nation ablaze. Sam Maverick had originally come to Texas for fame and fortune. He achieved both, but most importantly, he saw the Texas he loved grow into a strong, independent Nation.

His name did not enter into history as honorably as he had hoped. The name of *Maverick* would come to mean a rebel, rogue, or one who freely takes property belonging to others. This perversion of his good name was the complete opposite of what Sam stood for. The explanation is that Sam's ranch hands failed to brand his calves, and the neighbors, finding the unbranded cattle, called them "mavericks" and branded them as their own. Over time, any unbranded animal or freethinking man would be identified as a "maverick".

Chapter Nine
Cesarean Birth

Without the miscalculation of a sextant or the misdirection of a faulty compass, there is a possibility the indigenous Indian tribes could have remained Texas' only inhabitants. Mexico had no desire to settle the vast untamed land. With constant Indian depredations, very few Mexican families dared move to the wilderness area. The United States' interest was not in the rugged southwest, but west to the Pacific. Explorers like Zebulon Pike, and Louis and Clark focused their exploration on the mountains and streams of Colorado, Idaho, Wyoming, Oregon, or wherever beaver lived. Beaver was the cash crop, not land.

While trading with the Indians in Canada, Frenchman Sieur de La Salle learned of two great rivers in the southwest, the Mississippi and Ohio. After hearing many stories of the rivers and the Indians' belief that they flowed west, La Salle became convinced one or both of the rivers would be his route to the ocean. In 1669, he sold his land, hired a crew and set out to locate the rivers. After an initially unsuccessful exploration, he returned to France in 1674 where King Louis XIV gave him more land, including Fort Frontenac. La Salle returned to Canada and established a fur trading post and became one of the wealthiest men in Canada. Then, in 1677, he returned to France and King Louis granted him permission to once again search for the Mississippi and Ohio Rivers and hopefully discover the route to the Pacific Ocean.

In 1679, La Salle launched an expedition that gave France control of the Great Lakes region. The following year he founded the first European settlement on the Illinois River, naming the new outpost Fort Crevecoeur (Fort Heartbreak). La Salle and some of his crew once again returned to Canada for supplies and upon their return in late 1681, found the Fort had been destroyed by a rebellion among its occupants. The majority of people on both sides had been killed and any survivors had fled. The name Fort Heartbreak proved to be prophetic. La Salle buried the dead and then canoed down the Illinois River with a party of twenty Frenchmen and three-dozen Indians until they reached the Mississippi.

The expedition reached the Gulf of Mexico on April 9, 1682. Near the mouth of the river, La Salle erected a twenty-foot cross and a column bearing the French coat of arms as a landmark for future expeditions. In the name of King Louis, he claimed all the land and tributaries draining into the Mississippi as French territory and named his discovery Louisiana. This vast area extended from the Appalachian

Mountains on the east to the Rocky Mountains on the west, and from the Great Lakes south to the Gulf of Mexico.

La Salle's main goal was to establish a colony at the mouth of the Mississippi and in 1683, he once again returned to France to get the necessary supplies. One year later, with four ships and over three hundred colonists, La Salle headed for the Gulf of Mexico. He either misread his sextant or his compass was faulty and he sailed past the mouth of the Mississippi, completely missing his target and ending up in Texas. They began building Fort St. Louis at the mouth of the Lavaca River on the banks of Matagorda Bay, about 80 miles northeast of Corpus Christi.

Meanwhile, Spain mistook La Salle's navigational mistake as a French attempt to colonize Texas. Count of Monclova, Viceroy of Mexico reacted quickly on behalf of Spain and sent Alonzo de Leon, Governor of Coahuila, to destroy the French settlements. He was ordered to kill the French settlers, build forts and missions, and establish Spanish colonies. The Count could not have picked anyone more enthusiastic than de Leon. Perhaps Alonzo thought the blood of the Spanish Conquistador Ponce de Leon coursed through his veins one hundred years later as he zealously set out to locate and destroy the French forts along the Gulf Coast. On April 2, 1689, de Leon crossed the Rio Grande, and Texas became Spanish territory.

De Leon realized he was on an historic mission and kept extensive notes, measuring and recording the distance from river to river and landmark to landmark. His detailed maps and diaries would be invaluable for all who followed. He incorporated the surrounding topographical features in naming his discoveries as they moved across the land. As the expedition moved inland, they came to a grove of pecan trees along the banks of a river. De Leon named the river Nueces (pecan). His scouts returned, telling of meeting Indians who called the next river Frio (cold). Alonzo liked the name and noted in his diary the river would be called the Rio Frio. When they reached the next river, surrounded by tall bluffs, some as deep as thirty to forty feet, he named the river Rio Hondo (deep). Near the future home of Uvalde, they discovered a body of water, the bluest any of them had ever seen, and his men named it Rio Sarco (blue river). After seeing the magical blue water, Alonzo decided to name the rapid river Rio Leona. He would call the next river Rio Medina, whose name would be changed many years later when the residents of San Antonio renamed the river that ran from the middle of their city to the Gulf of Mexico, the Rio San Antonio.

De Leon's orders were to find and kill any Frenchmen still remaining on Texas soil. His expedition pressed on until they reached the river that local Indians called the Colorado (red) and finally located the empty Fort St. Louis. He found no Frenchmen alive, only bones of those killed by the Indians. De Leon ordered all the French structures destroyed.

De Leon was the first to reference the tall pines of Bastrop and noted them as natural markers for those trying to find his missions in the future. For the site of one of the missions, he chose the location where Texas' independence would be born, Washington-on-the-Brazos. After selecting several sites for future missions and forts, de Leon returned to Spain. His expedition had opened the gates of Texas.

The Spanish Crown realized that to successfully colonize an area the size of Texas, they would need to create a road system. Texas reached north to Colorado and west past Santa Fe. In 1716, Jose Domingo Ramon was given the task. Domingo's path would be given the name *The Ramon Road* though the trail he mapped out could hardly have been called a road. It was little more than an animal pathway; however, that was sufficient considering no wagons would be traveling over the international highway. Ramon began the road at Presidio San Juan Bautista, thirty miles east of Eagle Pass, the same starting point as de Leon. His road then followed de Leon's route past the first few rivers and cut off where San Antonio would be established. When his party reached San Antonio, Ramon remarked, "One day this spot will be an important place to establish a fort and mission." His words would prove to be prophetic; a hundred years later, that piece of land would be the home of the Alamo.

The Ramon Road crew met a huge setback when they reached an immense forest that spread fifty miles in every direction. They crossed the Little River and hacked through the dense jungle for twelve days just to cut a four-mile path before reaching the Brazos River. Ramon named the mass of trees Monte Grande and the crossing Brazos de Dios (Arms of God). The Ramon Road cut was located just a few miles from where Johnny and Millie Satterwhite would homestead more than a century later.

As Empire builders, the Spaniards conquered and displaced the native population and splashed a Spanish patina over their new territory. Once the natives were under the Spaniard's control, they were enslaved and taught to plow, plant, and harvest. The Spanish didn't call their method slavery, but rather "christianizing" of the heathens. The Spaniards had honed their conversion-slavery policy in Peru, the Caribbean, and Mexico, and they applied their method to the colonization of the Texas Territory.

In 1763, France turned Louisiana over to Spain. Though the French made no further intrusions into Texas, the Spaniards maintained their troops and missions in the piney woods of east Texas. Spain appointed the Marquis de Rubi to inspect the east Texas operations and after spending a month calculating the costs, he concluded there was no value in keeping soldiers posted or the missions open there. The Spanish immediately closed the missions, sending the priests, troops, and civilians either to San Antonio or Mexico.

Gil Ybarbo petitioned the King of Spain to allow him and his followers to remain and establish a permanent colony in east Texas. The King granted them permission; however, there would be no military protection. The group would be on their own. Gil led his group to the banks of the Trinity River in east Texas and named the town Bucareli. No sooner had Ybarbo's people settled, than out of the blue, Governor Manuel Munoz sent a regiment of troops to Nacogdoches. Ybarbo had mixed emotions about the uninvited troops. He needed the protection, but didn't want the government interference.

Once the troops were settled, communication became an issue. With the Ramon Road taking mail riders an extra two hundred miles out of their way, a shorter route was needed. A lower road was established which dipped down the rocky crossing over the Brazos River near the future town of San Felipe. The need for quicker movement of supplies then forced the Spanish to widen the road to accommodate oxen-pulled wagons. The road was named El Camino Real (King's Highway). The new, wider southern loop through San Antonio also brought Anglos from the United States, becoming an egress passage for the white man to move by wagon into Texas. Within a few decades, Texas' population grew from less than three thousand to over forty thousand.

Each attempt by the Spaniards to settle Texas failed miserably. The Spanish first sent priests to convert the natives. The conversion of the Coahuiltecan Indians to Christianity proved fatal for the enslaved Indians as sickness and depression plagued the captive Coahuiltecans. The Indians stopped reproducing in much the same manner as a caged animal, and the tribe's population slowly diminished.

When the Coahuiltecans died off, there was no one to do manual labor. The pompous Spanish soldiers refused to work in the fields, prompting Friar Morfi to write Spain for help. Without labor to plow the fields and harvest the crops, the settlement would be in jeopardy. In 1731, the King of Spain came to the Friar's rescue, realizing without a healthy population, Spain would not be able to hold the new land. His efforts to help the fledgling Texas colony were based on greed; he had heard the rumors that the hills around San Saba were laced with silver. The Monarch needed wealth to survive as surely as the Friar needed workers. The King gathered up fifty-six people who had been exiled to the Canary Islands for political reasons and sent them to assist the Friar. To entice the Canary Island families to immigrate, the King gave them the title of Hidalgo, a title usually reserved for those of high social status or pure Spanish blood. Once the King bestowed the elevated title, the new arrivals began believing they were indeed the descendents of importance. Awarding them titles had backfired; instead of helping the priests, the newcomers felt they were above manual labor. As a result of the Hidalgo's arrogance, starvation threatened the settlement.

The death of the Coahuiltecan Indians, the laziness of the soldiers, and the lofty title of those from the Canary Islands were too great a hurdle for the Friar to overcome. Out of frustration, the priest encouraged the soldiers to marry Indian women. The offspring from the mixed marriages were called Mesitzos. Slowly the Mesitzo community grew into a substantial group. The Indian women were hard workers and taught their children the same ethic. The industrious women compensated for their lazy husbands.

The settlement was surrounded by hostile Indian tribes. The Apache and Comanche were constantly raiding and stealing cattle and horses. Each time the Indians raided, the soldiers struck back. The killings were a never-ending vicious cycle. Bloodshed from both sides begat more bloodshed. Finally, the Lipan Apaches boldly entered the mission in San Antonio and demanded to speak with the "brown robes". The Apache told the padres they wanted a mission in their area near San Saba in the center of the rumored silver cache. The offer was only a ruse thought up by the intelligent Apache. The Apache's real plan was to lure the Spaniards past their territory and into the hunting grounds of the Comanche. The Apache plan set in motion a confrontation between their two enemies, the Spaniards and the Comanches.

Oblivious to the trap, five padres and a band of fifty soldiers headed out to build a presidio and mission in San Saba. Once construction was complete, the Apaches explained to the padres they would be on a long hunting trip and unable to attend the congregation until they returned. There was one excuse after another for not attending services at the mission. The patient padres waited and waited for the Apache to attend.

One warm day, a friendly Indian warned the padres of a horrible calamity soon to befall them. He warned they must close the mission and go back to San Antonio before Comanches attacked them. His passionate plea went unheeded. In spite of the warning, the padres kept an enthusiastic attitude and continued to establish their congregation.

Two years passed and nothing happened. Then, one day, as the rooster crowed, a soldier at the presidio heard shrieking screams. He rushed to the tower only to see sixty of their prime horses vanish into the morning mist. Colonel Parilla put his men on guard at the fort walls and sent word to the padres, instructing them to immediately come to the safety of the presidio.

After three days, the padres still had not heeded the warnings. As the sun rose over the horizon, Padre Terreros was conducting morning Mass when he was interrupted by a blood-chilling scream that shattered the silence outside the mission walls. He and Padre Molina rushed up the parapet and froze when they saw two thousand Comanches in war paint circling the mission. On their heads, the Comanche wore buffalo horns, deer antlers and eagle feathers. Molina was too scared to speak, but after his initial shock, Padre Terreros climbed down the ladder to greet a Comanche Chief. Believing there was good in all men, Terreros opened the gates of the mission and the war party stormed in. One of the Comanches grabbed Padre Terreros by his hair, dragged him from the mission grounds and was hauling him onto a horse when another savage put an arrow through his heart. Molina ran for cover, hiding in a small room in back of the mission along with three friendly Indians.

The Comanches killed seventeen soldiers and set fire to the mission. Providence smiled on Padre Molina and his small group. The room they had sought refuge in was recently constructed from green logs and didn't ignite along with the remainder of the mission. Once the Comanches were gone, the wounded Padre Molina made his way to the presidio and informed Colonel Parilla of the slaughter. The soldiers packed what supplies they could carry, set fire to the presidio and quickly headed back to San Antonio.

The Viceroy in Mexico City was not going to allow savages to intimidate him or the good name of Spain. He sent six hundred trained soldiers to San Antonio where two-hundred-and-fifty supportive Indians joined them. Well stocked with supplies, they also carried two four-pound cannons. Under the command of Colonel Parilla, they advanced north past the ruins of the old San Saba mission-presidio. Day after day, they moved onward with their scouts constantly searching for the savages. Finally, Colonel Parilla's best scout rode into camp, telling the Colonel that he had seen thousands of Comanche, Wichita, and Kickapoo camped along the river. The army made camp and awoke the next morning surrounded by thousands of Indians who had encircled them during the night. The Spaniards estimated their numbers exceeded ten thousand. Their only option was to break through the Indian lines and escape. With their cannons and muskets, they were able to penetrate the Indian's barricade and once through, Parilla ordered his men to shed all extraneous gear and flee for their lives. The Spaniards whipped their mustangs to the extreme of their endurance and retreated. The Indians, stunned by the cannon blasts, gathered their dead and allowed the Spaniards to escape.

Upon returning to Mexico City, Colonel Parilla reported the Indians had been carrying a French flag, and did his best to persuade the Viceroy his defeat was at the hands of the Europeans. To be defeated by Europeans was understandable, but to retreat from savages was a disgrace. Parilla was order to stand trial. In his defense, many of his men testified they also had seen the French flag on the battlefield. The men only participated in the falsehood to save their own necks. No evidence was ever produced to prove the French were involved.

The Spaniards finally ended all efforts to venture north of San Antonio. The Viceroy from Mexico City gave the edict to remove all settlers from outlying areas and bring them to either San Antonio de Bexar or La Bahia (Goliad).

Realizing it would be impossible to expand because of the Indians, the Mexican government decided to allow Americans to immigrate. At least the Anglos would provide the savages with horses and cattle to steal and places to raid besides the Mexican enclaves. Mexico did not take into consideration the huge number of Anglos willing to immigrate to the wilderness of Texas. The Anglos came in droves, many as filibusters, squatters, and as part of the Austin, De Witt and Robinson Empresario migrations. People like Johnny and Millie Satterwhite came as squatters. Sam and Mary Maverick came with the splendor of royalty.

Things drastically changed as soon as a third culture was added to the mix. Like a rifle hammer striking the flint, the Anglo presence set off an explosive shot in Texas. The Anglo filibusters and squatters were more adventurous and challenged the status quo with their expansionistic attitudes. Suddenly, cabins and farms were springing up like weeds, filling precious hunting grounds with farms and ranches, crops and cattle. Many came to Texas in search of a new beginning. Some came to escape past debts, a bad marriage or even greater crimes such as robbery or murder. In Texas, an individual's slate was wiped clean, offering newcomers a fresh start. One practice was to change one's surname to names like Smith, Jones, Miller, and White.

In the Anglo immigrants, the Indians found a resolute bunch willing to pursue them to the ends of the earth to extract revenge or find a stolen child; resolve they had never experienced with the Mexicans and Spaniards. Their boldness and expansionism philosophy angered the Indians who viewed the Anglo-Saxons as both the enemy and an opportunity. They were the enemy for killing bison and invading the Indians' hunting grounds, but brought the opportunity of new horses to steal, children to capture, women to take as slaves and young males to train as warriors.

This new breed of independent Texans were mainly of Scotch-Irish heritage. These immigrants were a mix of Danish, Gaelic, Saxon, and Teutonic Scottish. They had evolved as a tough, stubborn, dour people, conditioned to border war, having fought the English for generations. They burned their bridges with the Old World and came looking for the New Jerusalem carrying only an ax. Once ashore, they didn't plan to become sharecroppers or indentured servants to anyone. They wanted their own land to raise crops and build homes for their families. They rejected the whole mysterious panoply of the medieval world, along with the pageantry of the British life. With a broad broom, they swept the attic bare of Popes, prelates, and the concept of hierarchy. They were industrious and had a strong work ethic, following St. Paul's words "If a man won't work, he should not be allowed to eat," to the letter. Even if they earned a fortune, they never flaunted their wealth like the British.

The average Scotch-Irish family consisted of ten or more children. Their children were not ornaments for pleasure, but necessary to build up strong, populous communities. They needed boys to work the fields and be ready to fight the Indians and the girls were needed to bear children. Many of the girls married as young as thirteen. By marrying young, there were able to add many more children to the community.

These independent, rugged Scotch-Irish were ideal filibusters and squatters. Their very nature and free spirit gave them the inclination to go and take. Since most Texas filibusters came from Kentucky, Tennessee, Alabama, Mississippi, Georgia and Carolina, it is reasonable to assume a large number of those slipping across the state lines were Scotch-Irish.

These new inhabitants felt they were superior to the red and brown men and were ruthless in their intent to separate Texas from its mother, even if they had to violently cut her out.

Chapter Ten
Survival

While Stephen F. Austin was away in Mexico City, Baron de Bastrop finalized an agreement with the Governor of Texas y Coahuila that granted the Anglo empresario the authority to govern a new colony. Upon his return, Austin was pleased to discover the Baron's success in persuading Mexico to give him almost dictatorial power. Austin was also given the authority to form a band of men to protect those who immigrated to his 100,000-acre land grant. The early Indian defeats of the Spaniards had completely intimidated the Mexican military leadership and there was no will to protect the Anglos' expansion; the Anglos would have to survive the hostilities on their own.

Austin possessed neither a military nor the funds to form and support a fighting force. If he couldn't provide protection, recruitment of additional settlers would be impossible and the colony would fail. Being a brilliant man, Austin knew he would need to devise a radical approach to protect his new arrivals. Austin remembered Major Robert Rogers' Rangers of the American Revolution and chose to model his first band of fighters following Rogers' methods.

Unlike Rogers' group, Austin's citizen rangers would be regular, hard-working men who would spend time away from their farms and businesses to serve and protect. The rugged Scotch-Irish immigrants would have no problem fighting for the rich Texas soil that provided bountiful harvests for their families. The rangers' duties would include dealing with hostile Indians, arresting lawbreakers, and keeping the peace among the settlers. Austin would need men with courage and riding and shooting skills, who didn't know fear, and would commit to the job for little or no pay. He chose his rangers from lawyers, businessmen, farmers, and ranchers. What they lacked in manpower, the rangers would more than make up for with courage and skill. In May 1823, Austin chose ten men and called them *Texas Rangers*.

When the original empresario agreement had been made with Stephen's father, Bastrop convinced the Mexican Governor that the Americans would deal harshly with the hostile Indians. With the formation of the Texas Rangers, Stephen Austin was fulfilling his father's agreement to protect and defend against Indian depredations and provide security and stability in the territory. Little did he know that the Texas Rangers would become the most revered law enforcement organization in the world.

Austin was in charge of every aspect of the law, with the only exception being capital murder. Murder was dealt with in San Antonio by the Mexican authorities. The Texans would only have two murder cases resolved by the Mexicans before they decided to take matters into their own hands. San Antonio only gave a slap on the wrist to two murderers and set them free. The Texans wanted to exact their own brand of justice; a strong tree limb with a hangman's noose around the offender's neck.

In 1827, Moses Morrisson was given the rank of lieutenant and put in charge of assembling a group of ten new rangers. He selected John Croskey as his corporal and John Frazier as his private first class. Morrisson was promised a salary of forty dollars a month. Croskey was to get twenty-six dollars, and the remainder of the men were promised twenty-four. The pay was slow or never came. When Austin was unable to provide a monetary salary, he paid his rangers in land.

The rangers were required to own a horse, long rifle and pistol. Texas Rangers used Kentucky long rifles whenever possible, allowing them to shoot with accuracy at 250 to 300 yards, while Tennessee rifles were used for close-range shooting. The Texans felt the percussion cap was too unreliable. The self-contained percussion caps held mercury or another detonator on a nipple that when struck by the hammer, exploded and fired the main charge. The Texans preferred the flintlock. With a flintlock, the hammer, gripping a piece of flint, struck a metal shield and ignited powder poured into a priming pan; the flash carried through a vent hole and set off the main charge in the barrel. When a man's life was on the line, he needed a weapon that always fired. The Comanches and Mexicans used a smoothbore musket. The musket had the advantage of minimal loading time; the powder and ball charge was pre-wrapped in paper. Kentucky and Tennessee rifles took up to a minute to load because the powder charge and ball had to be rammed separately down the tight barrel of the rifle, and then the pan had to be primed with powder. This was the reason rangers fired only half of their guns; the other half would be ready to fire if they were charged upon while re-loading.

Nine of Morrisson's ten owned long rifles and one recruit owned only a musket, which was of little value, except at close range. These citizen rangers found themselves doing double duty; serving their community while trying to keep their farms going. Their largest challenge came from the Karankawa Indians. The Karankawa lived on the barrier islands along the Gulf between Galveston and Corpus Christi and completely controlled the inland waters, making importation of goods up the river from Matagorda Bay a dangerous proposition. The Karankawa would paddle alongside the vessel, kill the crew with their mighty longbows, and then help themselves to the cargo. In the 1700s, Karankawas had killed the Frenchmen left at Fort St. Louis at the Matagorda Bay entrance and captured twenty-five French women and baby girls, taking them as wives. By the time Stephen F. Austin and his three hundred families settled in Texas, the Karankawa's race was of mixed blood, having sired children with the captured French females. The new Texans believed the tribe's raging brutality was inherited from the modicum of French blood running through their veins.

Skirmishes and small battles were routine during the formative years of the Texas Rangers. By 1832, the need for more men forced Austin to expand the command into several groups. This time, Stephen Austin sought out the Scotch-Irish settlers, squatters, and filibusters. He needed their strong backbones to help his men stay the course. From time to time, the colony was able to supply the rangers with ammunition, but much of the time the gunpowder was either too coarse for the rifles or in very short supply. In spite of tremendous shortages, the rangers stood together and grew in numbers and strength. The decade following the formation of the Texas Rangers would see the original group of ten grow into a formidable force. Indians and outlaws alike learned to fear the Texas Rangers.

In August of 1833, J.C. Clark and four other men took a small boat down the Colorado to pick up coffee, salt, brown sugar and other supplies. On their return trip, they were waylaid just before sunset at the confluence of a stream and Skunk Creek; Karankawas were hiding in the thick underbrush at the bend of the river. Experts with their six-foot longbows, the Indians immediately killed all but Clark. He took an arrow in his leg, but managed to slip overboard and into the water. He removed the arrow and desperately swam into the canebrake. He hid there while the Indians gathered the supplies from his boat and left.

Earlier that same day, about fifteen miles upriver from where Clark was fighting for his life, forty-year-old Robert Brotherton encountered about twenty Indians coming down the trail in his direction. Thinking the Indians were friendly, he continued cautiously in their direction. In a blur, one of the Indians pulled a longbow and fired, severely wounding Robert in the left arm. He escaped into the scrub brush as the Indians stole his horse and rifle. They were the same band of Karankawas who would later attack Clark and his men. Brotherton was able to reach the ranger camp of Captain Robert Kuykendall. Kuykendall took a dozen citizen rangers on his mission to track down the Indians, with John Moore and Tom Strickland acting as scouts.

As darkness fell, Moore heard a repetitive thumping sound up ahead. Strickland thought the noise was wild turkeys, but Moore knew better. He was confident the sound was Indians preparing food, pounding briarroot into a starchy pulp. Then they heard a crying baby. The cry let them know without question they had stumbled upon the Indian's camp. Kuykendall moved his rangers down the banks and along the creek until they were standing at the edge of the Indian's camp. One of the rangers stepped on a dry branch, causing it to snap. The cracking sound alerted a Karankawa brave who leaped to his feet, his six-foot bow drawn into position. Kuykendall killed him before he could notch an arrow in his bow. The other rangers opened fire, killing seven, but the rest of the war party escaped into the scrub mesquite.

Still hiding near the riverbank, Clark heard the Texans shouting and managed to drag himself into camp. Piled in the middle of the camp were most of his stolen supplies. Kuykendall's men divided the supplies and carried them, along with the wounded Clark, back to the ranger's camp.

Then, on May 19, 1836, an event took place that would forever change the landscape of Texas. Silas and Daniel Parker had moved their families, along with several others to Texas to establish a religious compound. Silas Parker was the leader of the group of about thirty-five men, women, and children and was also the head minister. The Parker clan was Primitive Presbyterian Baptists, or more correctly, Independent Baptists who moved to Texas seeking a place to worship freely. They located their homestead about forty miles due east of Waco. Silas and his followers built a compound standing twelve-foot logs upright and cutting the tops into sharp points. The fort covered four acres with elevated blockhouses on the northeast and southwest corners, and shotgun portals eight feet off the ground cut into the walls. The cabins were built inside the compound and backed up against the protective log walls. The compound was built with two gates: One set of gates faced west and opened on a cleared out area that reached three to four hundred yards to the treeline. The other smaller gate provided a clear path to the springs where the community gathered their water. Silas' concept was very sound on how to survive in Indian country where the shadows were filled with hostile tribes waiting to kill, rob, or capture.

One fateful spring day, the temperature hovered around 100 degrees with humidity near 85 percent. Only the slightest breeze made its way through the trees surrounding the compound. To get some relief from the sweltering heat, one of the large front gates of the compound was left partially open. A large band of Comanche, Wichita, Kiowa and Caddo were lurking nearby when they observed the open gates of the Parker fort. Being opportunists, the Indians sent a group forward with a white flag of truce. As one of the Parker settlers attempted to communicate with them, a young brave smashed a tomahawk into his skull. In an instant, two hundred hostiles charged through the gate and swarmed the compound. Silas was killed before he could reach for his rifle. One Parker settler grabbed his long rifle and killed one brave, but as he was re-loading, a tomahawk split his skull. The Indians scooped up two women and three children and hauled them off. Among the captured group was Silas Parker's pretty blue-eyed, nine-year-old daughter, Cynthia Ann. A twenty-year-old brave named Peta Nocona was at the front of the group and the moment he spotted young Cynthia, he grabbed her and tossed her wafer-thin body behind him on his powerful paint. No one dared challenge Peta taking the young beauty as his wife. Peta and Cynthia would raise three children; Quanah, Pecos (peanuts) and Topsannah (Prairie Flower). Quanah Parker would become the Comanche Nation's supreme Chief. Quanah Parker was so important to the Comanche Nation that no other leader would ever be called Chief after he died.

Only seven men and women survived the Indian atrocities at the Parker compound. As surely as the Alamo battle had united the Texans against Mexico, so was the Parker slaughter the capstone of the Indian wars. Cynthia Ann Parker's name would be tacked to the walls of Texas history alongside those of Austin, Houston, Crockett, Bonham, Bowie and Travis. Her stunning beauty and innocence made men want to ride to the ends of the earth to rescue her. Traders were constantly on the lookout for a girl fitting her description. Cynthia, more than any other captive, became the child most families talked about when taking measures to protect their children from Indian capture. Her name would forever be woven like a delicate ribbon into the fabric of Texas history.

Anger and hatred for all Indians swept across Texas like a blast of cold wind in February. The Texas Rangers would be called upon to do what the French and Spaniards were never able to achieve: They would begin the expulsion of all hostile Indian tribes from the land they had called home for thousands of years.

The rage over Cynthia Ann Parker's capture solidified the Texas Rangers as men flocked to join the fierce force. One such man was Jack Coffee Hays. From Little Cedar Lick, Tennessee and of strong Scotch-Irish stock, Jack Hays knew no fear. Jack's baby face and fair complexion made him look younger than his age, but it was not long before people stopped noticing his youth and began praising his boldness, cunning, and bravery. He would set the standard for all other Texas Rangers to emulate. Indians feared him, Mexicans respected him, and Anglos loved and admired him.

Chapter Eleven
Trip Interrupted

As the ferry sloshed across the bayou, a forceful voice from the bank shouted, "Wait up! I need to talk with your two passengers. I don't want to shoot, but make no mistake, I will." The voice was that of Texas Ranger Jack Coffee Hays. In one fluid motion he jumped from his lathered mustang, grabbed his Kentucky long rifle and as his feet hit the ground, fired a warning shot. When the ferryman heard the rifle shot, he stopped forward progress and turned back to the island.

Jack Hays happened to be on Galveston Island to recruit a few new men for his San Antonio Ranger Company when Sheriff Maples asked for his assistance in locating Bud Miller and the Baron. He had figured correctly they would try to get off the island and that meant they would most likely head for the ferry.

The Baron whispered, "Youngan, looks to me like you are in a heap of trouble. You let me do the talking. I know how to handle these things. Don't worry son, I'll get you a good lawyer. After all, you did it to save my life. Now, whatever you say, never call Hector a dirty Mexican. There might be Mexicans on your jury. Are we clear?"

Bud was frightened. He had never been in a courtroom or jail. He didn't answer the Baron in words, but nodded affirmatively.

Jack was courteous, asking Bud to remove the bonnet and dress. Then Jack turned to the Baron. "Mr. Bastrop, I wish we could have seen each other again under different circumstances. Mrs. Garner told one of the deputies you purchased a dress and bonnet from her. I put two and two together and figured you would be trying to get the boy off the island."

Bud yanked the bonnet off and gave the Baron a look that said, "I knew this wouldn't work." He then pulled the dress over his head and threw both items of clothing into the buggy. As the Baron backed the buggy on to shore, Bud approached Jack and against Bastrop's orders to remain silent, asked, "Are you gonna hang me Mister?"

Jack's face showed no emotion as he answered young Bud's question. "Son, that's not my job. You and the judge will have to work that out. Now if you would please get in the buggy, I will follow you and Mr. Bastrop to the jailhouse. I am confident that Mr. Bastrop knows the way since he sold the city the steel bars for the jail cells."

Jack Hays knew the Baron well. Bastrop had given him and his brother title to land just south of San Felipe for their service in the army. The Baron had taken extra care to find adjoining properties with rich topsoil for the Hays' brothers. Jack felt he owed the Baron, but was in no position to grant leniency where murder was involved. He mounted his mustang and followed the buggy to the small one-cell jailhouse in the center of town.

The jail was a double-walled log cabin with rocks poured in between the interior and exterior logs. The structure had two rooms: A small office for the Sheriff and a cell partitioned off by a wall of bars. The cell contained a simple bunk bed, a straight-backed chair, and a chamber pot. A small table with a porcelain pitcher and washbasin was placed near the cell door, and a rustic gourd dipper hung on the lip of a wooden drinking water bucket. The office wall had a gun rack that held two shotguns, one Kentucky long rifle, and three waist pistols. The only furniture was a small desk, three cane-bottom chairs, and a cowhide rocking chair.

Sheriff Leland Maples was waiting in front of his office when the Baron tied the team to a hitching rail. Maples barked, "Howdy Mr. Bastrop. Would you and the boy mind hurrying inside? We don't want to call too much attention to your visit. You know how riled those Mexicans can get. They are a hot-blooded bunch and I don't need them storming in here and causin' a ruckus. Be a shame to let a lynchin' party hang this lad before he sees a judge. When he hangs, I want it to be legal."

The Baron, Bud, and Jack followed the Sheriff inside. Sheriff Maples was a rotund man, who stood about five-foot-eight and weighed almost three hundred pounds. He breathed heavily as he made his way behind the desk and plopped down in his cowhide rocking chair. Placing a hand on each knee, he studied his three guests. After catching his breath, he inquired, "Baron, what happened out there?"

To the Baron's dismay, Bud blurted out, "I killed that Meskin before he done it to Mr. Bastrop. It ain't Mr. Bastrop's fault. That dirty Meskin was gonna kill 'im if'n I hadn't got there in time. I heard that Meskin say he had cut his friend's fingers off and that he wuz gonna slit Mr. Bastrop's throat. Honest to God, on my ma's grave, that's what happen'. I'm like Mr. Bastrop. I don't never lie. I'm a truth teller Sir, and I'll swear that on a stack of bibles. It wuz either that dirty Meskin or Mr. Bastrop and everybody knows who is the best to save in a deal like that. Mr. Bastrop is a great man and one day will be president of this here Republic of Texas."

Bud had done the very thing he had been instructed not to. He was going to talk himself into worse trouble. The Baron stumbled back against the log wall, feeling for a chair. A cane-bottom chair found its way into his hand and the Baron slowly slid into the seat and paused before saying, "Sir, the killing was not premeditated. Young Bud here saw that my life was in peril and came to my rescue. I knew if we didn't get off the island, Hector's brothers and cousins would seek us out. You can believe me, as you know I'm a man of my word. We were not running from the law, but from a group of blood-thirsty killers."

Jack interjected, "That little Mexican girl over at the *Brass Monkey* pretty much collaborates the Baron's story. She said Hector came into the saloon looking for the Baron and told anyone who would listen that he was going to kill the fat old buzzard. From what I can tell, for a girl so young, she seems to have a good head on her shoulders and I don't see why she would lie to save a Caucasian stranger. It's your call Sheriff Maples. If it were my decision, I would let them go. I see no reason to charge the boy for riddin' the town of a bandit like Hector Garza. Well, I have to get goin' back to San Antonio with my new rangers. The Comanches are plundering again."

"Thanks for helping, Jack. I'll sort through this mess and make a decision today. Give the good folks back in San Anton' my best." Instead of standing, Sheriff Maples simply reached up his pudgy hand and gave Hays a soft handshake. Turning his attention to the frightened lad, the sheriff asked, "Boy, what's your name?"

Bud stood tall and proud as he answered, "James Benjamin Miller, but you kan call me Bud. Everybody else duz."

Not looking up, Leland scribbled the boy's name on a small card and dropped the notation in a tin box on the corner of his desk. Leland glanced back up, speaking to Bastrop. "Take the keys there on that nail, unlock the cell and let that feller that's in there out. He should be sobered up by now. Boy, you go on in and I'll have the Circuit Judge decide on what to do with you. I suspect, since you are fairly young, he will go easy on you. Don't think he will hang you. Then again, I could be wrong."

The slovenly Sheriff made Bastrop do his job as he mumbled, "Baron, that was a down right stupid thing for you to do. Trying to slip that kid off the island and all. I know you broke some law, but I don't rightly know what to charge ya with. Besides, the boy will need some outside help. Just between you and me and the fence post, Hector needed killin'. He has been bullyin' folks on this island for way too long. I guess I should have arrested him when word reached me he was talkin' of goin' after ya. But you can't arrest a man for talkin'."

Sheriff Maples' wife Janice brought Bud meals three times a day. Her cooking was without question the best the lad from Kentucky had ever tasted. Deputy John Holly took a liking to young Miller and enjoyed playing dominos with the boy. Bud was bright and learned the game quickly, and in no time was beating the deputy on a regular basis.

The second week of Bud's incarceration, Maria Varcinez, the pretty Mexican girl from the *Brass Monkey* showed up at the jail with a chocolate cake she had baked for the prisoner. As she entered the office, Bud and Deputy John were in a heated game of dominos. Maria paused meekly in the doorway and waited for the deputy to acknowledge her. John placed his dominos face down and turned his cane-bottom chair toward Maria. "What do we have here?"

"I bake cake for the boy," Maria answered as she motioned toward Bud.

"Hot dang! I ain't had any cake in a long time," John exclaimed as he jumped out of his chair, trying to grab the cake.

Maria put the cake behind her back as John reached for the plate. She shook her head back and forth. "I bake cake for brave boy, not for you Mr. John."

John was taken aback and was not sure how to respond. "Err ugh, I know. I was just gonna open the cell and hand the cake to the boy. But first I need to slice a piece. He just can't use his fingers and I don't dare let him have a knife. We all know what he does with a knife."

"It's okay you eat some. I want to be sure the brave boy gets all he can eat. Must be hard being in the jail for saving old man's life. It not boy's fault. Garza was a bad man and was going to kill the old man," Maria pleaded, trying to undo what she felt was her fault.

Bud gripped the steel bars with both hands and yelled, "Thank you, whut ever yur name is. Please don't feel bad 'bout me bein' caught. You dun right by telling the law whut you seen. It's the gospel truth I dun whut you said. I did jab my frog sticker in that feller. You wuz jut tellin' the truth. Mr. John, ask her name again fur me."

Maria had dealt with men since she was twelve and her mother started selling her to anyone with a few dollars in their pocket. But the young girl didn't know how to react in this situation. Here was a young man wanting to know her name. He didn't want to buy her. He was interested in her. No man had ever just wanted to know her name without offering to pay for an hour of her time. She glanced at Deputy John who was looking at her with equal amounts of curiosity and scorn. The beautiful young Mexican girl then answered in a whisper. "Maria. Maria Rose Varcinez."

"Whut did you say?" Bud asked, unable to hear her soft voice.

John took it upon himself to answer for the timid girl. "She said her name was Maria Varcinez. She is the *Brass Monkey* prostitute who told us you killed Hector." Maria suddenly felt ashamed. She handed the cake to John and quickly rushed out the door. As she was pulling the door closed, Bud shouted, "Thank you. Cum back pleeease! You don't have to brung a cake, I'd jus' like to get to know ya." He wanted to choke John for calling her a prostitute. Bud understood Maria was doing what she needed to do to survive. Bud knew all about survival.

Another surprise came when Bud's teacher Horace showed up at the jail one afternoon. Horace Weatherspoon had been very disappointed when the boy had failed to show up for dinner. Two days passed before he learned of Bud being locked up for stabbing the island bully. Horace brought a plate of steaming hot sugar cookies, fresh from his oven. Bud was standing on his cot looking through the bars covering a tiny window in the back of his cell when Horace entered. No one else was in the jailhouse as Horace sashayed through the door, balancing his cookies on one hand like a seasoned waiter. The slamming door startled Bud. He quickly jumped off his cot and rushed to the steel bars to see who was entering. "Mr. Weatherspoon? I didn't figure you'd be comin' here to see me. I jus' knowed you'd be mad 'cause I didn't show up or nothin'."

"Bud, Bud, mercy me. You should not use double negatives and I simply must teach you to finish your words. It's just, not jus. It's know, not knowed. Of course I'm not angry with you. I know all about the brave thing you did. I went to Mrs. Maxwell's boarding house and the Baron told me how you saved his life. You stood up to that bully Hector Garza and slashed his neck. I am so impressed with your strength and courage, young man."

"I thank you fur not being mad and all. I ain't talked to Bastrop since they dun locked me up. I gots to tell you I didn't slash that Meskin's neck. I gutted him and stuck my blade into his heart."

Horace pulled a chair near the bars and slid the plate of cookies through a small opening in the cell door. The teacher feasted his eyes on Bud before speaking. "Bud, dogs go mad, people get angry. Goodness gracious, there is so much I need to teach you. I guess I'll just have to come everyday until Mr. Bastrop finds a way to set you free. Trust me Bud that is going to happen. I spoke with the Baron and he assured me he is working to free you of all charges. I know he wants to visit, but he doesn't care to draw attention to himself. Sheriff Maples could still charge him with attempting to help a felon escape. He is more valuable to you on the outside and besides, locking up a man his age would kill him for sure."

John's mistreatment of Maria shamed her deeply. She would not return to visit Bud. Horace would be Bud's only guest. For the first time in his life, the young man desperately wanted to learn how to read and write. He could see the advantages of being able to write letters from his jail cell. He might even write a few words to the pretty Maria. Weatherspoon made him a little uncomfortable, but the opportunity to learn to read and write was worth the odd feeling the peculiar little man caused.

The next sixty days drug along slower than a plow behind a West Virginia mule. Playing dominos with John became boring. The two changed to checkers. John was so pathetic at checkers that beating him proved to be no challenge either. The Baron still hadn't visited. Maria had never returned. Bud had received no word on when the judge would be in town to hear his case. He started believing the Baron had deserted him and a judge might walk in one day and order him hung by the neck until he was dead.

There was one bright spot, Horace Weatherspoon. He visited every afternoon with reading and penmanship assignments and left books for Bud to read. There were so many big words; nevertheless, Bud trudged through each book until he fell asleep every night. If he was going to die, he wanted to write good-bye letters to his Uncle Charlie, the Baron, and Maria.

Horace continued to lift Bud's spirits with his daily visits. The teacher was as faithful as the winter snow in his hometown of Boston. Slowly the New England schoolmaster removed slang words from Bud's vocabulary. It took weeks of repetitive coaching to break him from saying kaint and ain't and to eliminate wuz, duz and several other Kentucky-backwoods pronunciations from his speech.

The third week, Horace brought a paper chart with the alphabet in both print and cursive script and gave the young man a slate to practice his penmanship. Bud grew tired of making circles and was angry with himself for not being able to make letters like Mr. Weatherspoon whose handwriting was as precise as a printing machine. When the young man became discouraged, Horace reminded him that it took years to learn his skills. The teacher bragged profusely about how well the lad was progressing, noting each tiny improvement. In spite of Horace's weakness, he was a Godsend for the uneducated boy. After a few weeks, Sheriff Maples left the front door unlocked after closing so Horace could stay until ten and teach young Miller.

Two months slipped into three before Bud received any outside visitors other than Sheriff Maples' faithful wife Janice and his teacher. Without warning, one day the Baron came through the jailhouse door and greeted Bud as if nothing had happened. Smiling like an egg-sucking skunk, the Baron said, "Good morning Mr. Miller. Do I ever have some great news for you! I have a lawyer lined up to take your case. It will cost me a pretty penny, but I'm confident he will get this mess cleared up as soon as Judge Harry P. Jones arrives in town to hear your case. There are two things that can be said about Baron de Bastrop. Number one, I am the best friend a man can have and number two, I am as faithful as the rising sun."

The look on Bastrop's face was worth a thousand words when Bud responded. Not only were his words different, but also his delivery was refined. Young Miller answered in perfect grammar, "I never doubted your standing with me. I do want you to know I feel badly about killing that Mexican man. I've had a lot of time to think about what happened. If I could do it over, I'd have run and let Deputy John or Sheriff Maples know what was happening. I made a mistake and now I have to be man enough to face my punishment. I just hope the price is not swinging on the end of a rope." Bud hesitated before adding, "But if that is God's will, then so be it. I am ready to meet my Maker."

Bastrop was speechless. Finally he blurted out, "What has happened to you lad? Your language is a thousand times better. You look great. I bet you have gained twenty pounds. It's difficult to understand how spending time in jail could be good for anyone, but you have changed my mind."

Bud rubbed the cell bars with the toe of his shoe, making a thumping sound. Sheriff Maples became irritated when the boy got nervous and made that annoying sound with his thick-soled shoes. Leland shouted, "Dat gum it, boy. If I've told you once I've told you a thousand times not to be kickin' them steel bars. I'll be glad when Judge Jones gets here and strings you up. Maybe then I can get some peace."

The Baron's eyes opened wide like a hoot owl at night. Whirling around, he shouted angrily, "What are you talking about? This boy doesn't deserve to be hanged; he deserves a medal for ridding this island of one of your biggest problems. A problem you were too afraid to rectify, I might add."

"Calm down Bastrop before I decide to charge you as an accomplice. I was just ragging the boy to get him to stop that darn kickin'. It grates on my nerves. I don't know what Judge Jones will do. He had a real bad reputation in Arkansas as a hang 'em first and ask questions later kinda judge. Maybe he will be lenient in the boy's case once he knows what a villain Garza was. Can't say for sure."

The front door flashed open and quickly closed again. Bud caught a glimpse of Maria, but was not quick enough to call out to her. She had returned to the jail knowing deputy John was over at the *Brass Monkey* drinking with a friend. Obviously she opted not to enter when she saw the Sheriff and Bastrop in the small office. Bud's life was bouncing up and down like a yo-yo. He went from euphoria to depression as events unfolded. Hanging his head in a dejected manner, he queried, "Mr. Bastrop would you please mind going over to the *Brass Monkey* and thanking Maria Varcinez for my cake? It was the best thing I've ever tasted. Don't worry about me. Alls, I know…" Correcting his miscue, he continued, "I mean all I know is that I did what I felt was right. I had to stop you from being killed. I wrote you a letter and was going to ask John to carry it over to you, but since you are here, I'd like to give it to you. It's a will. I'm leaving all I own to Maria and would like you to make sure she gets my five-dollar gold piece."

The Baron was stunned. "Son, did you say you wrote a letter? When on God's green earth did you learn to write?"

Bud smiled and replied, "Mr. Weatherspoon has been spending three or four hours with me every afternoon. He is teaching me to read, write, and speak proper. He has even been showing me how to do arithmetic. He gave me a printed copy of the Texas Constitution. I mostly read all day or practice my cursive. Mr. Weatherspoon is a nice man and a very good teacher."

Sheriff Maples had struck a raw nerve when he mentioned involving the old man in the killing of Hector. Making an excuse about needing to meet with Bud's lawyer, the Baron decided it would be in his best interest to make a quick exit. Promising to take care of Bud's will and go thank Maria, he reached through the bars and shook the boy's hand. "It is going to be okay." Then he whispered, "Don't let Maples get you down. I do want you to know I'm really proud of the way you have learned to speak and write so well. I have to tip my hat to Horace the next time we meet." With those parting words of encouragement, the Baron tipped the soft brim of his beaver hat to Sheriff Maples and quickly exited the jailhouse.

Maria was entertaining a customer when the Baron stopped in at the *Brass Monkey*. He decided to have a couple of shots of whiskey, assuring the bartender his credit was as solid as a rock. In his most sincere voice, the Baron gave assurances of his honesty. "Just run a tab for me. I'll be back to clear up the small bill tomorrow. No one has every accused me of welching on a debt. And I'm too old to begin now."

After downing three glasses of whiskey, the Baron watched as Maria came down the stairs looking somewhat disheveled. A burley man followed close behind her, a bright silver hook for a hand poking out from his shirtsleeve. Maria moved quickly out onto the boardwalk to get some fresh air. As the man rushed by him, the Baron knew immediately why Maria had rushed outside. He couldn't remember ever smelling body odor as rank. He then recognized the man. To the Baron's relief, the man did not recognize him in the dark saloon. The man who had been with Maria was Hector Garza's older brother, Ramon. The Baron motioned for the bartender to tally up his bill quickly so he could sign an IOU. Reluctantly the bartender complied, wondering if the money would eventually come out of his own pocket.

Maria's face was pale as she stood alone on the boardwalk. Looking up, she noticed Bastrop at her side. He tipped his hat and as only the Baron could, he softly reassured the young Maria, "My dear, fret not. The Baron de Bastrop has no illicit intentions where your honor is involved. I am a man of purity. No one in this great Nation has ever said otherwise. I bring you a message of good cheer, that is, if you are Maria Varcinez."

"I'm Maria," she answered, her words filled with inquisition.

Placing his hat back on his balding head, the Baron continued, "Young Bud Miller has asked me to personally deliver a message. His exact words were: 'Tell Maria I have never eaten a better cake. Tell her thank you, and would she please visit me again.' Bastrop did what he did best, embellishing the original message and adding the part about her visiting."

"I can't go smelling like this. That horrible man left his rancid odor all over me. I'll have to bathe and wash my dress before I can do anything." She hesitated. As her eyes filled with deep sadness, she reached over and placed her hand on Bastrop's arm. "Sir, Maria is not good enough for Mr. Bud. He is a nice boy and would not want me if he knew what I do."

Bastrop allowed her hand to rest on his arm and covered her dainty fingers with his strong grasp. "My child, young Miller knows your profession. He doesn't care about your past. He wants to rescue you from a life of degradation. You can trust me. I give my word to you in unwavering verse. Your occupation means nothing to the lad. If he escapes the hangman's noose, he will come courting. I know men of character and that young man has it stacked from the crown of his head to the tips of his toes. Now run back in, splash on some rosewater, put on a new dress and hurry over and spend a little time with my boy. He is mighty lonely locked in that cell."

Maria had every intention of visiting, but a boatload of Anglos pulled into port with their hearts filled with lust. She was not able to visit Bud that night and she would not get another opportunity to do so.

The following morning, Judge Harry P. Jones presented himself at the tiny Galveston jail wearing a tall black stovepipe hat and black coat with tails. His full white beard fanned out like an old broom, covering his collar. His demeanor was arrogant and patronizing as he entered the Sheriff's small office. Surprised, Leland jumped to his feet, knocking his chair back against the wall and with a bellowing voice, exclaimed, "Judge? I didn't expect you for a few more weeks. Won't you have a seat? I'll ring the bell and have Janice get you some coffee."

With his snobbish nose turned up, the Judge replied, "Coffee? It's past ten. What I'd like is a shot of good corn whiskey to clear the dust from my throat."

The Judge's sudden appearance was a chilling site. Bud could see why Jones was called the hanging judge; his appearance was that of an undertaker. He was not sure if he should speak or just sit and wait to be spoken to. Bud kept his head down and pretended to work on his script, but listened intensely to every word.

No sooner had the Sheriff poured the Judge a strong shot of whiskey than another man entered the office. Both the Sheriff and the judge stood to greet him.

"Why Sam Maverick, I heard you were killed by some Comanches a while back," exclaimed Sheriff Maples.

"Good morning Judge, good morning Leland. No, I guess my meat is too coarse for them to barbeque. Let's get down to business if you don't mind. I was on my way to New Orleans to find out why some of the furniture I paid for was not delivered. You cannot trust those Cajun merchants. Along the way, I stopped in Victoria to visit with my sister and ran into Ranger Jack Hays. He asked me to see if I could be of assistance to that young boy you have illegally locked up like a bear in a cage. The way he is being treated is unacceptable in any civilized nation. I arrived very late yesterday and have been interviewing the local citizens. The little girl Maria at the *Brass Monkey* is willing to testify that she saw the Mexican attack the boy, and only out of survival did he react to the situation. Even the Baron de Bastrop..." Sam paused. He was not sure if he should follow that line of defense, so he cut his sentence off in the middle.

The Judge came to his rescue. "Sam, good to see you. I didn't expect this case to have such distinguished representation. You can speak freely. We all know Bastrop and his ability to expand the truth."

"Good to see you as well, Harry. Give my regards to your lovely wife when you return to San Felipe." Then, back to the business at hand, Maverick continued, "Yes, the Baron does have a tendency to color things. However, we are talking about the life of a productive young citizen here. I spent most of the evening at the boarding house having the Baron tell me the story several times. Never once did he vary his statement regarding the incident.

Gentlemen, it comes down to this: If I miss my boat, I'm going to be mighty upset and I will certainly miss my boat if you two insist on going to trial. I'm a very busy man. My land acquisition is expanding and so is my family. I am well established in San Antonio and being pressured to participate in the legislature. If you insist on pursuing a trial, I will make it clear this boy is being denied justice because Leland here needs a conviction to get himself re-elected."

Sam Maverick was not only showing his anger with the situation, but also letting them know he was a man of power and would not hesitate to use it. If they bucked him, it could cost them both politically. Both men knew very well which way the wind blew, and Sam Maverick had a strong breeze at his back.

"Sam, I resent you implying I would keep this young man locked up for my own gain."

"Leland, resent all you want. I have no doubt that's what you are doing. Judge Jones here is just doing his duty or at least I hope that is his reason for coming. I know you are up for re-election. Jack Hays told me. He also told me you just might try to hang this boy to prove to the good people of Galveston you are tough on crime. If you were tough on crime, you would have locked up Hector Garza and his gang a long time ago. I hear from the locals you are afraid of the Garza gang."

Leland slumped back in his chair. He was not accustomed to being lectured. After all, he was the Sheriff, the highest office in the county. Judge Jones was not a man who lost his composure often, but Sam had also rattled him with his aggressive attitude. He wanted to challenge Sam, but thought better of it. Sam Maverick was one of the brave men who inked the Declaration of Independence and was also one of the wealthiest and most influential men in the Lone Star Republic.

It was Bud who spoke next. "Thank you sir. Mr. Bastrop told me he had someone coming to help me. I didn't mean to kill the Mexican. I just wanted him to not hurt my friend. When he grabbed me, I got scared. Before I could think, I shoved my frog sticker in his heart. That's the honest to God truth. I had no malice in my heart when I crossed that street. I will admit I came to Texas to extract revenge for the Mexicans who killed my pa at Goliad. I now understand there are good Mexicans as well as evil ones."

Sam didn't change his expression, but was laughing inside. The thought of the Baron telling the boy he had hired an attorney struck a funny cord with the big Texan. He was thinking how surprised Bastrop had been when he told him why he was in town and how profusely the Baron had thanked him for coming to the boy's rescue. Sam knew there was no defense lined up and had Jack Hays not taken an interest in justice, young Bud would have been tossed to the wolves. Judge Harry P. "Hangman" Jones and Sheriff Leland Maples would have dangled him from a rope within the week. Sam could also see how much the boy trusted Bastrop. Rather than disappoint him, Sam replied, "You have a good friend in Mr. Bastrop. He thinks a great deal of you, son. He says you will be a great asset to our Republic. If anyone should know Texas, it's the Baron. He has helped over three thousand families settle in our great Republic. A man needs friends in this world and you have two; the Baron and Texas Ranger Captain Jack Hays."

Leland blurted out, "Jack's a Captain? He didn't tell me so when I asked him to help us find the murderer."

Maverick glared down into Leland's soft face. Sam's cheeks flushed red, as he fired back, "This boy is not a murderer He acted in self-defense. If you want to go to court, then I'll stay here and I'll make sure you, Leland Maples, never work in law enforcement again. And you Harry. I want you to know that no matter what you may personally think of Baron de Bastrop, he has many friends in your area. Keep in mind; he handed out land titles to ninety-five percent of the people who voted you into office. If you want a political enemy, then you will be getting a bulldog in the Baron. I can promise you, not only will he campaign against you, but so will I."

Judge Harry P. Jones knew Sam was right. The Baron had given the judge the papers to his land when he arrived in Texas with the original three hundred immigrants. People may make fun of the Baron behind his back, but he still had powerful connections in Texas.

Judge Jones responded, "Sam, now don't go getting your dander up. I just came here to find justice for the lad. I'm sure we can work something out to save the good taxpayers of Galveston the cost of a lengthy trial. Sheriff Maples was just getting ready to tell me the facts when you arrived. Since you are so confident that this is a case of self-defense, then I see no reason to hold a trial. What do you say Leland?"

Sheepishly Leland Maples rose from his chair. He revealed his true self when he asked, "Do you honestly think it will not damage my re-election if I just up and let this kid walk outta here?"

"Blast you Leland, this is not about you getting re-elected. This is about justice. If Texas doesn't start administering true justice now, then we will be no better than Mexico. Corruption and avarice will dominate our Republic like it does south of the Rio Grande. This is about doing what is honorable and just, not that those qualities ever concerned you before. Now get over there and unlock the cell and let's do the right thing. My ship is at the dock. That whistle a few minutes ago was a signal for the first boarding."

Judge Jones took one final swig of whiskey as Leland waddled over and removed the cell key from a hook on the wall. As Leland paused before unlocking the cell door, the Judge quickly interjected, "Sam is right. We need to set this boy free and sentence him to time served."

As simple as that, Bud walked out of the cell that had been his home for five months. He immediately shook Sam Maverick's hand. "Mr. Maverick, sir, I'm not sure how to thank you. I don't have but one five-dollar gold piece I brought with me from Kentucky..." Sam cut him off in the middle of his statement. "No payment is necessary. Thank the Baron and Captain Hays. Thank the little Mexican girl who fought like a cat for your freedom. Me, I have a boat to catch."

Maverick then turned his attention to Judge Jones. "Harry, are we clear? Does this mean you have agreed to set the lad free for good? You won't try to renege on our deal after I leave?"

"No, no, I'm not like Bastrop. I really am a man of my word." The strong whiskey made the Judge a little tipsy, but not drunk enough to go back on his word after giving it to Sam Maverick.

Sheriff Leland understood as well. "Now go on and scoot boy. You can keep the extra clothes my wife sewed for you. You will need them. If I were you, I'd find a way to get off this island as fast as I could. Hector's brother and cousins won't cotton much to your killin' 'im, no matter the reason."

Sam shook neither of the men's hands as he left the jail. He was the last passenger to board as the boat made ready to set sail for New Orleans. As he walked up the gangway, he glanced back to the shore and saw the Baron and young Bud. Maverick got a warm feeling inside and hoped, should his son ever be in trouble, someone would do the same for him. Bud and the Baron watched silently as Sam's ship sailed out of sight around the end of the Bayou.

Walking toward the *Brass Monkey Saloon*, the Baron said, "I might need to borrow your five dollars to pay our boarding bill. I'm a little short on funds and it's definitely time we leave this island. I think I can trade some dry goods for a couple of horses. You need a good horse and my old mule is on his last leg. Son, there are only two things that scare a Texan: a decent woman and being forced to walk. Looks like you have your eyes set on Maria and have addressed the woman part, now all you need is a horse."

Bud squeezed the gold coin in his pocket, unsure of the prospect of giving up his only treasure. After all, he had already saved the Baron's life. Giving up his last dollar didn't seem fair. Bud changed the subject and asked the Baron about Jack Hays and Samuel Maverick.

As they made their way into town, neither Bud nor the Baron saw the six angry men hiding behind a watering trough. Two were Hector Garza's brothers and the other four, his cousins. Speaking in muffled Spanish, the six waited patiently to impose their own brand of justice on the sandy streets of Galveston.

Chapter Twelve
Manhood

Bud caught a flash of light as the sun reflected off the tip of a Bowie knife. Acting as if he had stepped on some debris in the road, Bud reached over and grabbed the Baron's arm to balance himself. He started to hop on one foot as if he were in pain. He spoke loud enough so the men behind the watering trough could hear as he pleaded, "Wait up, please. I jammed my foot on a piece of pig iron. I need to find a place to sit down."

Partially turning his back on the villainous group, Bud looked down as he continued to hop on one foot. Getting a firm grip on the Baron's arm, he leaned down and picked up a buggy spring from the dusty road. "Don't look back, but there are some men waiting for us up there behind the trough. I saw one has a knife. I bet it's the Garzas. Just act like you need to help me hobble over there to old Doc Wilson's. Don't say anything. I don't think they know I saw 'em." The two men struggled along at a labored pace toward the doctor's office.

Ramon Garza whispered to the others in Spanish, "It's okay. The boy jus' cut his foot. Looks like they're gonna get the doc to sew him up. Be patient. They'll be comin' back this way soon. Then we'll give the boy some new gashes. When we're done, Doc 'ill be sewin' him up for his funeral." Chuckles spread through the group until they almost laughed out loud.

Ramon Garza was known for his cruelty to both man and beast. He had killed many times, but no witnesses ever dared to come forward and the murders were never prosecuted. When Ramon was sixteen, he lost his left hand while attempting to plunder a merchant ship. His hand had been replaced with a silver hook he often used as a weapon. Across his left eye and down his cheek was a long, deep scar acquired during a drunken brawl in the Caribbean. As a young man, Ramon sailed with the buccaneer Jean Lafitte while he was hiding out on Galvez Island. After Lafitte was driven from the Island, Ramon remained there doing odd jobs, but mostly stealing from the new arrivals. All of the Garzas had been on the wrong side of the law most of their lives. Two of the cousins had fled Mexico to escape being hanged for murder. The oldest cousin worked in the slave trade for Jim Bowie and several other men like him. His job was to keep the slaves from escaping or impose harsh punishment if they attempted to do so. Beatings and killings were all in a day's work for this gang of six.

The streets of Galveston were now teeming with new arrivals buying supplies to travel inland. The new Texans purchased boots, tack, harnesses, saddles, leg wraps and liniment for their horses and mules as the Baron and Bud hobbled past them into Doc Wilson's office.

After an hour had passed, it became clear to the Garzas that Bud and Bastrop were not going to come back their way. The six men silently slipped away, knowing there would be another chance. They were confident they had not been spotted and would still have the element of surprise when the time came to carry out their vendetta.

When Bud and the Baron reached the saloon, the Baron planted himself on a rickety wooden bench just outside the door, breathing heavily. In the strongest voice he could muster, he said, "Bud, I can't keep up. Come sit a spell with me and let me catch my breath. You are about to walk an old man to death." Young Miller obediently returned to the Baron's side.

There was some truth in what the Baron was saying. He felt sharp pain shooting up his left arm and crushing pain in his chest, making it difficult for him to catch a full breath. With his right hand clutching his left forearm, he sat in silence and attempted to breathe deeply. He looked down the dusty street; still concerned the Garzas may be lurking about. The Baron then reached into his pocket and removed a small pad and pencil. As Bud cautiously sat down beside him, the Baron wrote:

To whom it may concern:

This is a letter of introduction for one Mr. Benjamin 'Bud' Miller, the son of Joshua 'Stump' Miller who gave his life as a hero at Goliad. Please act with all haste to help this heart stricken lad as he mourns his father's death...

He proceeded to explain Bud was the oldest son of Stump Miller and therefore, rightful heir to all property his father had acquired. The Baron had written the land title for Stump personally. At this moment, he was not able to remember the exact location, having written over three-thousand land titles, but he did remember that Miller had been given clear title to 4,428 acres in Goliad for his service in the Texas army. The local priest should be able to assist Bud in locating the land.

Fearing death may be imminent; the Baron found himself feeling grateful to the lad for saving his life and risking being hanged just to protect him. No one other than his own son had ever acted so bravely in his stead. The Baron's only son had died at the hands of villains in a botched robbery attempt in Natchez, Mississippi. On their way from Baltimore to New Orleans, he and his son had stopped in Natchez to earn traveling money, and allow his son to attend school. They lived in a makeshift shelter down by the river and one night a group of vagabonds attempted to rob them. The Baron and his boy put up a gallant fight, but when the struggle was over, his only son lay dead.

With a halting voice, the Baron said, "Son, take this letter to Padre Paul at Presidio La Bahia del Espiritu Santo in Goliad." The Baron thought for a moment and added more detail to his instructions. "Son, go to Goliad and there you will find a fort. Inside is a mission called Espiritu Santo and that is where you will find Padre Paul. He has a record of the Spanish land grants in that area and can help you locate your pa's land. I wrote the title myself and I know it's there. Padre Paul owes me. I helped him hide from hostile Indians and loaned him money for restoration after the Mexicans destroyed part of his mission. Not only does he owe me his life, but a nice stack of money as well and I want you to have it."

"Thank you Mr. Bastrop, I'm much obliged, but I understand Goliad is a long distance from here. With no gun and on foot, I'd be food for some of those Indians before I got fifty miles."

"I've already thought of that. North of town a few miles is a German gentleman I helped a while back. I found him some prime land and fixed it so he could become a Mexican citizen. He owes me. Without me, he would be back in Germany. He has offered to pay me and I think it's time we don't disappoint him any longer."

The Baron's heart calmed down. Fate seemed to smile on the pair that day. They had been saved by Bud's keen eye noticing the ambush in time to spare their lives, Maria seemed interested in Bud, and now the Baron was planning to help Bud claim his land. Bud and the Baron stood and moved slowly toward the saloon door. Before they could enter, fate was not finished blessing them. A voice shouted in a guttural German accent, "You too good to speak to your friend Mr. Bastrop?" To the Baron's astonishment, it was Helmut Treptow, the German he had just told Bud about.

"I need to speak with you Helmut," the Baron responded with urgency in his voice. The red-faced German with a smile as broad as his hat brim, pulled his buggy to an abrupt halt and asked, "What can I do for you on this glorious day Mr. Bastrop?"

"For one thing, you can give us a ride. Here, help me up into the seat. Bud, jump in the back." The robust German man was cat quick, leaping from his seat and lifting the Baron onto his buggy. The lever springs groaned under the weight. Still breathing heavily, the Baron wasted no time reminding Helmut of his debt. "I'll tell you what I'm going to do for you, Helmut. I'm going to set you free from your obligation. I know it has been a burden on you and one a man of your character should not have to carry. I have a way for you to be free from my shadow once and for all."

Helmut had dreaded the day when the Baron would come calling. He knew he did owe the old man something, so he inquired, "What's that Mr. Bastrop?"

Bud leaned up from the back seat of the buggy so as not to miss a word. The Baron didn't respond as the small bay mare trotted down the dusty street. He wanted Helmut to wonder what the request would be. Finally, the Baron answered, "This lad in the back lost his father in the massacre at Goliad. His brave father fought to his death against Santa Anna and his ten-thousand Mexican soldiers." Once more, the Baron exaggerated the numbers to make his case even more impressive. "The boy's mother is dead and he is alone in this massive country. No horse. No one to care for him. Fortunately providence brought him to me. You know me Helmut, I'm always one to help the downtrodden, never asking any favor in return. You know I wouldn't be asking if I didn't really need your help. What I did for you was out of the goodness of my heart. I never considered my keeping you in Texas as a debt, but as one Texan helping another. Nevertheless, I now need for you to pass my good deed on to this lonely lad."

Helmut glanced to the rear of the buggy and spoke to Bud with compassion. "I'm sorry for your loss young man. You will find Texas has as much heart as size. Our home is your home until you get on your feet. You are welcome to work on my ranch. I have no sons and my wife can no longer have children. It would be our pleasure and a blessing to provide you with food and shelter."

The Baron interrupted, "Here's my proposition to you. I'm willing to call it even in exchange for a fast horse and a fine saddle for the boy. The lad needs a fast horse because the Comanches and Lipan Apaches have been on the warpath for months. He will also need some good DuPont gunpowder, not the coarse cannon stuff the Mexicans use. Toss in a supply of lead, some beef jerky, and a warm blanket. Helmut, all this only amounts to about one third of what you would owe if I had charged for my services. Take care of my son and I'll call it even." The Baron didn't realize he had called Bud his son.

In the back of his mind, Helmut knew one day the Baron would come asking for a favor. From the looks of the lad, this might not be a bad time to settle the debt. The old German was quick to judge a man and was seldom wrong. Young Miller had a strong chin, sharp eyes and good teeth. His arms were strong and his manners good. Helmut could see young Miller making him a fine son-in-law and he wouldn't mind his daughter being married to a man who owned over four thousand acres. He could expand his horse operation with that much property at his disposal. With the extra acreage, he could end up with one of the largest horse operations this side of the Mississippi.

Located on the northern point of Galveston Island, Helmut Treptow's ranch had been spared the periodic Indians raids that many in the area had endured. The truth of the matter was he had never had a single horse stolen by a Mexican, American, or Indian. His remuda of horses had grown to almost three hundred animals. Men were always in need of a horse or mule and normally short on cash, allowing the shrewd German to acquire a large supply of guns and various items in trade. He had to admit that the Baron had allotted him a prime location for his operation. The only drawback to the expansion of his operation was his refusal to buy slaves. He had strong feelings about slavery and expressed his opinion openly. When Bud heard Helmut's views on slavery, he immediately liked the rugged, boisterous German. Bud's only complaint about the Baron was his acceptance of slavery. Bud knew one day Texas would be divided over the issue that was already splitting the Union. Horace had taught him of the division between the North and South over the issue of slavery.

Helmut agreed to the Baron's request. He smiled to himself, realizing the Baron never did a favor without strings attached. Anyone who dealt with Bastrop knew he never gave without expecting something in return.

The Baron sat quietly, pleased he could do something for the boy who had risked death to save him. The old charlatan finally relaxed as a tight-lipped smile slid across his face. He waited until the buggy got off the rub board road and onto the smooth beach and said, "You are a mighty fine man, my friend."

They followed the Gulf Coast along the broad sandy beach northeast for three-and-a-half miles. At the end of the road, there stood two towering posts with a long log beam running between them. On the horizontal log were painted three words: *Treptow's Horse Ranch*. The Treptow property reached from the gulf across to the inlet bay waters on the northwest side of the island. A six-foot tall split-rail fence bordered the land on the south side to prevent horses from wandering into the city and to keep a roving cowboy from "borrowing" one in the middle of the night.

The ranch house was a sprawling one-story log structure with five rooms, a dogtrot in the middle and a wide porch running the length of the home. From the porch, the Treptows could watch the ships sailing in and out of the bay as the wind blew the white foam back eastward. The exterior of the house was covered in mill-sawn planks, giving the appearance of an eastern home. Unlike most of the local homesteads, the Treptow home was whitewashed and sparkled in the bright island sun. The tranquil setting left the lad from Kentucky in awe. Without question, this was a wealthy family. As they neared the ranch house, Bud grew nervous. He had never been in a rich man's home.

Not far from the house, on a spit of land on the opposite side of the bay inlet, Bud spotted an old fort on Bolivar Point. "What's that?" he solicited. The Baron, feeling stronger, began to tell the story of Doctor James and Jane Long. Helmut knew part of the Long story; nevertheless, he knew he would enjoy hearing the rest of their story as only the Baron could embellish it. Helmut stopped the buggy to allow the Baron to complete the tale before they reached the ranch house.

"Bolivar Point is a fort that was established by Doctor James Long of Natchez, Mississippi. Dr. Long was wealthy beyond your wildest dreams. He was not satisfied with being rich. He wanted more. I think he wanted to own his own country. After his first wife died, Dr. Long met a fourteen-year-old orphan girl named Jane Wilkinson, married her and after the birth of their first child, moved to Texas.

The Longs immigrated to Nacogdoches, then down to San Antonio, and finally to Galveston Island. With the aid of the local Mexicans, he was successful in driving the Spaniards from Texas. Dr. Long also led an army of around eight hundred men into Texas to win freedom from Mexico. It wasn't long before his Mexican co-conspirators turned against him, forcing Dr. Long and his men to fight on two fronts. Many of his troubles were of his own doing. He failed to treat the Mexicans who helped him liberate Texas on equal terms. They began to resent his arrogance. I just thank God Helmut here still has his feet on the ground. Money tends to corrupt some folks."

"Thank you Baron," Helmut replied.

"Well deserved my friend. As I was saying, Dr. Long decided to build Bolivar Point in the belief that the location would be easy to defend against attack. Dr. Long then left for Mexico to look for silver or to drive the Spaniards deeper into Mexico; no one knows for sure. He was captured and later 'accidentally' killed by the Mexicans. His young wife Jane was left alone in Bolivar Point with a twelve-year-old slave girl, her young daughter and another child on the way. Jane gave birth to her second child at Bolivar Point, the first white child to be born in Texas, with only the help of her young slave. Their supplies eventually ran out and to survive, they scavenged fish and oysters from the bay. For two long years she awaited her husband's return and kept the hostile Indians at bay under the ruse that soldiers protected the fort. When they spotted Indians, she raised the flag and fired off a round from one of the cannons.

After two years of isolation, some Mexican friends of her husband came to see her. They told Jane of her husband's murder in Mexico and persuaded her to abandon Bolivar Point. The Mexicans escorted them safely to San Antonio. Once settled in San Antonio, Jane then left her children with her slave and traveled by horseback to Monterey, determined to seek justice for her husband's death. The Spaniards treated Mrs. Long with compassion, but the murder of Dr. Long was never solved and justice never served."

The Baron paused, taking a deep breath before he continued. "In my book, Jane Long is the Mother of Texas."

Bud was fascinated with her bravery asking, "Is that all?"

"No, that's not all. Jane is a friend of mine. I have stayed in her hotel in Bazoria, which was the primary port for new arrivals before Galveston assumed that role. Stephen Austin stayed with her when he was set free from a Mexican jail. I will say this: Many men pursued her affections, including me. She turned down Sam Houston, Buck Travis, Lamar and even old Ben Milam. Jane never got over her husband's murder. She dresses in black to this day, mourning her husband's death. I have never seen Jane Long laugh."

Bud began to truly comprehend the cruel price the original immigrants had paid for Texas' independence and became more determined to continue what those brave souls that came before him had begun.

Helmut tapped the bay mare's rump and she moved slowly toward the ranch house. The dogs alerted Mrs. Treptow and her daughter that the buggy was approaching and they were waiting out front to greet the trio as the buggy came to a halt.

"Mr. Bastrop, do you remember Frau Treptow and my lovely daughter Virginia?"

"Of course I remember your lovely wife. She is even more beautiful than I remembered. The salt air certainly agrees with her. And little Virginia is a full-grown woman. Her stunning beauty is only exceeded by her mother."

Virginia was indeed a full-grown woman with piercing blue eyes and soft blonde curls that dangled to the middle of her back. Her German heritage gave her full hips, strong legs and ample breasts. The string belt cinched around her waist accentuated her curves. Bud sat speechless. He had never seen a girl so perfectly built.

The introduction felt clumsy for both of the young people. "Pleased to meet you Mr. Miller," Virginia replied shyly.

Bud's answer was even briefer. "Same here," he mumbled.

Mrs. Treptow's round, plump face glowed red with excitement at the sight of young Miller. Almost ignoring Bastrop, she went straight to Bud, vigorously shaking his hand as if she was pumping water. Mrs. Treptow tipped the scales at well over two hundred pounds on a five-foot-six inch frame. Walking the incline leading to the porch, Mrs. Treptow's thick buttocks swished back and forth. Had Bud realized that pretty young Virginia could one day end up looking like her mother, he might not have been so thrilled with the meeting.

The men and Virginia followed Mr. Treptow while a Mexican ranch hand led the mare and buggy to the barn. As Bud glanced back over his shoulder at Virginia, he stepped on Mr. Treptow's heel, sending him sprawling to the ground. As Bud reached down to assist him, he exclaimed apologetically, "I'm sorry, I wasn't looking where I was going. I was looking at your beautiful…horses."

The Baron smiled and murmured to himself, "Horses my foot."

Virginia joined the men at the long dinner table. Mrs. Treptow poured hot coffee and served some of the most delicious pastries Bud had ever tasted. He was not familiar with the fruit-filled kolaches. As he reached for a second one, he realized why Mr. and Mrs. Treptow were so heavy. He would weigh two hundred pounds in no time if he ate her kolaches every day.

Mrs. Treptow could see that this was a new food experience for their guest. In a thick German accent she explained, "The kolaches are from my home country. My mother taught me how to make them when I was a young girl. Do you like them?"

With his mouth full, Bud replied, "I've never tasted anything so wonderful. Not even the food Sheriff Maples' wife brought me while I was in jail was this good."

The Baron coughed, realizing the slip of his friend's tongue. Bastrop felt an explanation was in order. The Baron spoke with eloquence about how his brave young friend had saved his life, facing down the vicious Hector Garza in a knife fight. Bud fully expected the Treptows and Virginia to think badly of him, but the opposite occurred. Mr. Treptow beamed and Mrs. Treptow removed another hot kolache from her stove, setting it in front of him. Bud glanced at Virginia to measure her reaction and to his surprise, she too was smiling. In Texas, valor was given high regard. After the Baron's explanation, Mr. Treptow was even more convinced that he had judged the boy correctly. Helmut was now even more hopeful that Bud would not leave without marrying his daughter.

The Baron and Bud bunked in the barn. The previous day's events had left the pair exhausted and they slept through the rooster's crow. As the morning sun bounced off the waters of the Gulf, the pair only awakened when Virginia delivered their breakfast, a huge plate of peach kolaches and a steaming pot of coffee.

Shortly after they finished eating, Mr. Treptow walked around the corner of the barn leading a prancing sorrel stallion. The stallion's face was adorned with a lightning bolt blaze that was set well between his eyes and ended at the tip of his nose. The tall, muscular stallion had a flaxen mane and his tail almost touched the ground. His three white stocking feet glistened in the morning sun as he reared into the air, whinnying his displeasure at being led.

Bud jumped to his feet. "Is he for me?" he shouted.

Mr. Treptow answered matter-of-factly. "If you are man enough to ride him. He is the fastest horse on the island and I suspect in all of Texas. It will take a strong man to handle him."

Bud had never walked away from a challenge and this magnificent animal was not going to be his first. Still stunned, he asked, "What's his name?"

"Whatever you want to call him," Helmut answered.

Virginia added, "Father doesn't do much naming because he'd rather not get too attached to any one horse."

"Lightning. I'll call him Lightning. His blaze ends like a bolt of lightning."

Bud was filled with excitement unlike anything the Baron had ever seen. The Baron knew the enthusiastic lad could not immediately ride a spirited animal like this one. They would first need to find a horse Bud could handle until he mastered the skill of riding. He would need to learn the ways and habits of the animal before attempting to ride a raw mount like Lightning. Bud was smart enough to know that riding a plow horse or passive mule was one thing, but the challenge of a horse with brio would be an entirely different matter.

Mr. Treptow made the suggestion that the Baron and Bud stay with them until spring. Helmut knew there were six angry gang members looking for the pair and he could offer them refuge and give the boy time to learn how to handle the high-powered horse. For being schooled in horsemanship, there was no better place in Texas than the Treptow Ranch. To sweeten the deal, Treptow offered to pay Bud a dollar a day. He would hold the money until it was time for the youngster to leave so he wouldn't be tempted to get into a card game or leave before he was ready.

The Baron liked the idea. The Garza gang wouldn't have a clue where they were and they could use the time to rest up. A loan he was counting on should be arriving within the next couple of months. Once his loan reached Galveston, he would be able to ship the merchandise to his new general store. Virginia loved the idea of having a handsome young man on the place and Bud didn't seem to mind the idea of a girl of her beauty being near.

One of Bud's daily chores was to spend five hours a day riding green horses and honing his riding skills. For a farm boy, whose experience was limited to riding sleepy mules or plow oxen, he took to being a horseman quickly. It didn't hurt that he was able to show off his skills to the pretty Virginia. He saw her sneaking peeks from inside the house as he went through his training.

Bud also spent two hours a day learning to become an excellent marksman, both with the long rifle and pistol. It was Bud's good fortune that Helmut employed a farmhand who had been a competitive shooter in Mexico City. He knew more about shooting than any man on Galveston Island and was eager to teach his enthusiastic pupil. After months of training, Bud was matching the old sharpshooter shot for shot at two hundred yards and gained a slight edge with pistols. At three hundred yards, he was besting the old Mexican sharpshooter in both speed and accuracy.

With the Baron's help, Bud also continued to read and further his education. He was feeling his oats and developing confidence and pride in himself. The fine German food, which was always in abundance, had transformed his boyish body into an impressive 172-pound physique. With the heavy workload on the ranch, Bud developed strong, muscular arms. When a green colt acted up, Bud simply flipped his lead rope over a post and physically subdued the animal. He was no longer the frail, uneducated boy who had stowed away on that riverboat to make his way to Texas.

Finally, it was time. Everyone on the ranch gathered in anticipation as Bud prepared to ride his spirited mount. Bud rounded the corner from behind the barn, leading the slender sorrel stallion. Lightning raised his feet in a prancing manner as he turned his body sideways following the lead rope. His mane flowed over his arched neck and his forelocks hung well below his eyes. What stood out was the distinctive blaze that ended in a lightning-flash twist at the tip of his nose. Lightning had the strut of a champion. He exuded brio and had the attentiveness of an eagle in his eyes. From the moment Mr. Treptow offered the stallion to him, Bud had watched Lightning in the pasture and dreamed of the day he would finally ride the high-spirited animal.

Helmut then spoke in a thick German accent. "This exceptional stallion is my pride and joy. He is without question my fastest horse. You won't have to worry about any Indian ponies catching you or wearing him out. He has just enough mustang blood to allow him to go all day and not tire. Now mind you, he is still young and you will need to keep a tight bit in his mouth. You might want to use the Spanish bit on him. I hear tell all the rangers use the Spanish bit. Gives 'em better control in a tight fight."

"No, no, I can't do that. Sir, it would kill me to see his mouth bleed. Don't worry Mr. Treptow. I can ride him with a hackamore if I have to. He is too extraordinary an animal to be yanked around with a Spanish bit. I'll teach him to respond to the touch of my knees. I'm not trying to be ungrateful. I just want you to know I'll treat him better than myself."

"I know that, lad. I wouldn't be giving you such a prized animal if I didn't trust your intentions."

"I guess now is the time to see if I'm man enough to own such a fine horse."

With those words, Bud gently placed the saddle blanket on the powerful stallion's back. Lightning shivered. Then Bud lifted the saddle into place. Lightning attempted to shake the weight off, wiggling his skin. Then, in one swift move, Bud pulled the cinch tight and let the key fall through the leather girth. Lightning hunched down on his hindquarters, but didn't buck. Bud grabbed a handful of Lightning's golden mane and with an agile leap was in the saddle. To everyone's surprise, Lightning stood still. Bud urged him forward with his knees and Lightning responded, breaking into a smooth trot.

The Baron proudly proclaimed, "Bravo lad. Looks like you own the finest horse in North America."

Suddenly the group's attention turned toward the beach road. In the distance, a rider was approaching at a full gallop. Helmut didn't recognize the horse as the rider dismounted to unlatch the gate. The stranger, riding a tobiano paint with only an Indian blanket for a saddle announced, "President Houston is in town and wants to meet with a Mr. Bud Miller, the son of Joshua. Any of you Mr. Miller?"

Bud turned Lightning back toward the group and raised his hand. "Why would President Houston want to see me?"

He glanced at Bastrop and then back at the young rider. Curiously, the stranger was wearing a three-piece suit and a brown derby hat. He sported a brace of briarwood-handled pistols and shoes polished so bright a man could comb his hair in their reflection.

"Please allow me to introduce myself. I'm Timmy Marcum. I'm a full-blood Cherokee who has come to learn the ways of the white man from my adopted uncle, the President of the Republic of Texas. President Houston lived in my village for six years when I was young, and he has brought me to Texas to get an education. One day I will go back and help my people."

Timmy's hair was coal black and his eyes were the deepest blue any of the group had ever seen. His movement was like a deer. Stepping in front of the stunned audience, he spoke again in perfect English. "Sam Maverick informed President Houston that Bud Miller was residing on the island. When we arrived in Galveston, I was dispatched to locate you. Sheriff Maples told me the last he knew, you and the Baron left town with Mr. Treptow. That was the best lead I had. I was hoping you were still out here."

Everyone was taken aback. Why would the president want to meet Bud? Bud inquired again, "What does an important man like President Houston want with me?"

Timmy answered, "I don't know the full story, but it seems that your father and President Houston fought together against the Creeks. Your father was the man who broke the arrow shaft off Mr. Houston's leg when he was wounded in the battle. He cared for him for two months before delivering him to his mother. I suspect he wants to shake your hand and tell you about your father saving his life. Don't know for sure, but that's my best guess."

Helmut hitched a team of his best horses to the buggy. This was going to be a day the entire family would remember. Virginia and Frau Treptow primped and put on their Sunday best. Then off they all went at a gallop. The smooth sand road made the buggy feel as if it was gliding on glass. Bud couldn't contain himself. He gave Lightning a loose rein and galloped a few hundred yards ahead of the buggy. Timmy dashed behind, but his black and white paint was no match for Lightning. Bud let Lightning run full out for about a mile before pulling him up.

A large crowd had gathered in front of the *Brass Monkey Saloon*. There was little doubt the president was inside. Bud all of a sudden felt uncomfortable knowing Maria would be in the saloon. What should he do? He was sure to run into her. He felt badly he had not made a better effort to make contact. After all, she was responsible for saving his life.

Finding an available hitching rail proved to be a problem. Helmut tied the horses several yards away from the saloon. As they walked, they passed the spot where only a few months earlier Bud had killed a man. They then noticed a group of older, overweight men preparing for a foot race. Their appearance was almost comical. As the plump men got into starting position, the walkway started to fill with spectators. Suddenly, the doors of the *Brass Monkey Saloon* swung open and a giant of a man stepped out. He had to duck to pass under the transom. There was no doubt this larger-than-life figure was the historic hero of Texas, and the current President, Samuel Houston. Bud was shocked to see how tall the President was and that he moved with a limp; nonetheless, stood as straight as a pine tree.

Everyone seemed to be waiting for the President to say something, and he didn't disappoint. "Let the games begin! I'll give a silver dollar to the winner."

As the race began, it became apparent that it was not so much a matter of who would win, but who would finish. Cow Williams stumbled across the finish line first, but hardly in Olympic form. President Houston presented Cow with his silver dollar and suggested they have a real race between some of the younger men. In a booming voice, the President commanded, "Listen up. I want to see about twenty of you young men give us a good show."

Bud slipped off his brogan shoes. He removed the pistol from his belt, handing the gun to the Baron. Bud hadn't been in a foot race since he was a child back in Kentucky. He questioned how well he would do. He just knew he didn't want to disappoint either Maria or Virginia. It was a strange feeling to be running to attract the attention of a girl. Mr. Weatherspoon was standing eagerly by the edge of the wooden walkway and Sheriff Maples leaned against the saloon door waiting for the race to begin.

The president shouted, "Someone walk off about a hundred meters. I'm going to give the lad that comes in first a brand new five-dollar gold piece. Now that should put some fire in your tails." Secretly, Sam felt young Timmy would win with ease. He had watched the Indian boy grow up and knew he was the fastest young man on the reservation.

Sixteen boys in all entered the race. Many were very young and stood no chance against the older and faster boys. Sheriff Maples was called upon to start the race. When he fired his pistol in the air, Bud stumbled and almost fell to the ground. Timmy broke away like a startled jackrabbit and was three steps ahead of the other boys at ten meters. Bud regained his balance and started to pick up speed but was in twelfth place in the sixteen man race. By the halfway point, Bud had managed to move into the top six. He was churning up dust and running step-for-step with Timmy and another tall boy. Bud was thinking the tall boy would take the prize when he heard a voice from the stands shouting, "Run young Miller run. You can do it." It was the booming voice of President Houston urging him on. Bud reached deep inside and found strength he was not aware he had. His stride increased and his legs moved faster and faster. Suddenly it was a three-man race. He moved within one stride of the tall boy and Timmy. With less than ten meters to go, he heard the booming voice again. "You can do it Miller." No doubt the president wanted him to win, and win he did. Bud leaned forward and shoved his chest through the finish-line ribbon.

Relying on his walking stick for support, Sam motioned for Bud to come over to him. Extending his large hand, he slipped a five-dollar gold coin into the winner's hand and exclaimed, "Boy, I knew your pa. He and I fought under General Jackson. I have never known a braver man than little Joshua Miller. You know he saved my life?" Not waiting for an answer, President Houston continued, "When we went over the wall, I took an arrow through my leg. Your father was the only one with courage enough to break the shaft off so I could move around. He remained with me, making sure I ate and treating my wound with ointment squeezed from leaves. I would have died then and there if he hadn't come to my rescue. He was not as big as you, but no man ever had a bigger heart. Sam Maverick told me you were here and had been in a little trouble. When I realized we would be passing through Galveston, I wanted to tell you face to face you are the son of a brave man you can be very proud of."

Bud had never spoken to anyone of such importance. The President made small talk and made Bud comfortable in his presence. Bud recalled the Baron's dislike of Houston from their night on the deck of the *Destiny*, but drew his own measure of the man and concluded he was a man to be respected.

As people gathered to listen to President Houston tell stories, an unwanted guest joined the group. Ramon Garza pushed his way through the crowd to where the President and Bud stood. "I challenge you to a duel at daybreak down by the water, boy. If you are not a coward, you will oblige me the honor of avenging my brother's death."

Duel??? Bud knew nothing about a duel. His first thought was to jump on Lightning and head out of town as fast as he could. Before he could respond to Garza's challenge, President Houston responded, "Sir, from what I understand, Miller here killed your brother in a fair fight; however, it is the law of the land. If young Miller has the courage to face you, then I see no reason we shouldn't carry out your wishes. I have a brace of matching pistols in my carriage you and the boy will use. In fact, young Miller, I'll be your second to ensure a fair fight."

With a scold on his face, President Houston admonished, "This is something you should have left alone Garza. This young man has a future in Texas and yours is brief. It's just a matter of time until you are swinging from a tree with a rope around your neck. I think dueling is a most archaic means of settling a vendetta. Yes, I have engaged in more than one myself and as you can see, came out the better man, but that does not mean I condone this. Why don't you let the past be the past? You cannot bring your brother back by killing this boy."

No words changed the angry brother's mind. Garza stormed away shouting, "Sunrise at the beach. Down where they are building the new seawall. I'll be there. Just make sure you bring that fast-runnin' yellow belly."

Within only a matter of minutes, Bud had gone from the height of pride for his father's bravery and the privilege of meeting President Houston to the depths of despair, fearing yet again for his life. Young Miller struggled to hide his fear. His bravado did not fool the wise Houston as Sam placed his arm around Bud's shoulder and led him into the *Brass Monkey*. Sam gulped down a shot of whiskey and then addressed Bud. "We will need to draw up a will in the event things don't turn out positive tomorrow."

With a flip of his wrist, the president summoned for a writing quill and paper. Being a lawyer, it was the least he could do for the young man. "Now boy, who do you want to get your land in the event you don't come out of this mess?"

"Golly Sir, I never thought about that. The Baron has all he needs. The Treptows are rich. There is a young girl who works here in the saloon. She helped save me from hangin'. I left her my gold-piece when I wrote a will in jail. Yes, maybe I ought to leave the land to her."

The bartender, who was listening intently, interrupted, "Son, that little Mexican gal and some of the other girls went to San Antonio. If you want my two cents worth, I'd leave it to some newly arriving couple that come to Texas with only hope and a prayer. Let them have a place they can call home."

"Bud, he does have a good point. I'll make myself the executor of your will and should you not make it tomorrow, I'll find a deserving new couple from Kentucky. Is that acceptable to you?"

Bud didn't have much to say. He signed the paper and then listened to the president talk about the Indian war. The more Houston drank, the more he repeated the same stories. But along around midnight, the President did offer Bud a piece of timely advice. "Son, it's not the man who shoots first, but rather the man who remains calm that wins these things. General Andrew Jackson, 'Old Hickory' himself told me when I was in my first duel to put a bullet between my teeth to steady my jitters and my aim. Not to whirl and fire blindly, but to make sure my shot counted.

Just remember, your opponent is as afraid as you are, if not more. Garza acted brave in front of his friends, but he knows you have already proven you are willing to kill and will do it again if he gives you the smallest advantage. I plan to make sure you have that advantage."

Sam removed a round from his purse and made two X's on the shot with his belt knife. He handed it to Bud, saying, "This is an Indian sign of good luck. Trust me, this shot will be the one that takes the day. Now go on home and get some rest."

The ranch was silent when Bud arrived back at the Treptows. He knew he should be very afraid, but President Houston's calming words let him sleep soundly until an hour before daylight. Shortly after he awoke, Frau Treptow knocked on the barn door and delivered a piping hot cup of coffee. She softly requested, "Son, we want you to get dressed and meet us at the big house for a prayer breakfast. We feel you need Christ Jesus our Lord on your side this morning, and Virginia has a good luck piece for you that belonged to her grandfather."

Prayer and breakfast were accomplished before the sun rose over the Gulf of Mexico. One of the hands saddled Lightning and had him waiting for Bud. The Baron gave Bud a firm handshake. Virginia, unable to contain her emotion, grabbed him and squeezed tight as if it were the last time she would ever see him. Then she slipped her grandfather's well-worn New Testament into his vest pocket saying, "May this bible protect you as it did Pa-Pa when he went to war."

Lightning moved with grace along the sand. As they neared the duel site, there was already a large group of men waiting. A man in a white hat, an eagle feather in the hatband, stood the tallest and Bud felt relieved the president would be with him. He was not afraid of dying, but did not want to die alone.

A local newspaperman rushed up wanting to interview each man, but Bud had little to say, and Garza even less. Garza was quietly confident that his opponent would freeze in fear as he launched his deadly lead into the boy's heart.

Garza's reputation as a cold-blooded killer floated around the island like a dense morning fog. As the betting line formed, the odds stood at 100 to 1 in favor of Garza. The talk among the locals was that one of the seconds would end up shooting Bud as he tried to make a run for it. It was fairly common for young men to run in such circumstances.

There was a little commotion when it came time to establish the ground rules. The rising sun was not an issue as it would be off the shoulder of each man. Then there was the discussion of how many steps would be taken before they could turn and fire. Garza wanted twelve, but Houston said the standard was ten, and ten it would be. Houston knew how gentlemen fought duels.

Bud kissed the shot President Houston had marked for him, double-checked his flint, and making sure his powder was dry, packed an extra heavy load. The two men then stood back to back. Garza was a pro and had witnessed dozens of deadly duels. He wanted every advantage he could get and understood fear was the major factor in determining who lived and who died. He pushed hard against the boy and whispered, "Say your Hail Mary's while there is time. In a few minutes I'll put a round of lead in your heart." Bud's heartbeat pounded in his head as the threatening Garza pushed against his back.

President Houston chose to be the counter. Appreciating the drama of the moment, he paused before saying, "Men, when I start the count, you take a step with each count. If either of you turns or fires early, I have two men with long rifles ready to take you down. Make no mistake; there will be no cheating in this fight. Are your ready?"

Bud grunted, "I guess."

Garza let out a maniacal laugh that would have intimidated even the most seasoned fighter as he answered, "Ready, I stay ready. Let's get this done so I can meet up with me amigos and celebrate."

Sam began the count: "One." Each man took one step forward. "Two." They moved forward once more. Time seemed to stand still between each count. Three…Four…Five…Six. In an even more somber tone, Houston counted, "Seven." Both men took their seventh step, their pistols extended in the air, trigger fingers at the ready. Bud's heart pounded uncontrollably. Garza belched and the smell of garlic permeated the morning air. Even in the tenseness of the moment, he blasted out another maniacal laugh. This was something he learned watching the old salts of the sea in duels to the death; instill fear in the hope that your opponent will falter. All he needed was for Bud to miss by a hair's breath.

President Houston shouted out, "Eight," followed by a quick, "Nine."

Both men knew the next time they heard President Houston speak, one of them would die. The shoreline crowd became deathly silent. The betting had stopped, but not before the Baron de Bastrop used Bud's five-dollar gold coin to make a small wager.

Houston then blasted out, "TEN!"

As quick as a cat, Garza turned and fired off his round before Bud could even take aim. The lead smashed into the young boy's chest, knocking him backwards. From the position of impact, it appeared as if the shot hit Bud directly in the heart. That was where Garza had aimed. But one thing neither Bud nor Garza had figured on...Virginia Treptow. The cover on the New Testament she had slipped into Bud's pocket was made of polished brass and Garza's shot had not penetrated the metal cover. Bud was stunned, but quickly realized he was not wounded.

Garza stood frozen, holding his spent weapon. He started to run, but realized the long rifles were fixed on him and would drop him before he could take a step. Slowly Bud raised his pistol, bit down on the bullet between his teeth and took aim. He pulled the trigger. His lead shot true, smashing through the only good hand Garza had. General Houston looked at the young man and understood what he had just done. Instead of killing Garza like one would a sick dog, Bud had rendered him useless as a killer.

The Baron was quick to collect his five hundred dollars before the other gamblers made a hasty exit. No one had expected to pay out on such large odds, and the Baron had been the only one to place a bet on Bud. In the Baron's way of thinking, he would keep four hundred and give Bud his five-dollar gold piece along with a hundred in winnings. That should be enough for the lad.

The smell of black powder hung in the air as the crowd dispersed. Bud knew he owed a huge 'thank you' to Virginia. As he grabbed his saddle horn to mount Lightning, young Timmy Marcum shouted, "President Houston would like for you to meet him in front of the *Brass Monkey*. I think he wants you to ride to Gonzales with us. That will put you near Goliad."

Timmy's words brought mixed emotions. Finally discovering the truth about his father's death was something Bud definitely wanted, but leaving the Treptows would be bittersweet. While pondering what to do next, a voice from behind him whispered, "I'm proud of you for not killing that weasel of a man. I must tell you I am surprised how big and strong you have become."

Bud pivoted around to see his teacher standing close behind him. "Mr. Weatherspoon. I didn't know you were here."

Chapter Thirteen
Party Time

San Antonio de Bexar was blessed with four waterways, and in addition, two man-made canals built by Indian "converts" provided irrigation for the fields and an abundance of water for the town. Running parallel from north to south, the trees that bordered the canals provided a lush green canopy in the summer and lent color and charm to the city in the fall. The better homes were clustered near the rivers whereas the poor farmers lived to the west along the sloping mountainside. Longevity for those living in the shadow of the city was short, Indian raids frequent, and the labor hard; yet, the desire to own a piece of land outweighed the dangers.

The Mavericks leased a San Antonio house for only a short time and then purchased the Huisar home. The Huisars were a prominent family known for their exceptional woodworking craftsmanship. Mr. Huisar's father was the artist who carved the massive wooden doors and embellished the interior woodwork for the Mission San Jose. The Mission project was an enormous undertaking, which took several years to complete and employed a large number of the local population. The Huisar sons inherited their father's reputation, but not his skill. They were never able to match his ability, originality, or level of success.

The home, constructed of solid native white Texas limestone, was centrally located at the northeast corner of Commerce and Soledad, in a corner of the Main Plaza. The walls were almost two feet thick, making the home cooler in the summer and warmer in the winter. The Spanish-style home was built with nine vigas (log beams that support the roof and protrude from the exterior walls) extending out over the large porch along the front of the home. Considered large by the standard of the day, the Maverick home had three rooms; one long room fronted south onto Main Street, and the others faced west onto Soledad. Along the eastern side of the home stood a forty foot by ten-foot adobe brick shed which served as a kitchen and servants quarters. The shed provided far superior living quarters than the shanty shacks the Maverick's slaves had lived in back east.

The slaves began constructing a limestone master bedroom adjoining the main house, and a stable with locks on every door, over near the river. Sam Maverick knew the value of good horses, and the tendency of the Indians to steal if given the slightest opportunity. The slaves also built a decorative whitewash picket fence around the front yard and another to separate the garden. A well-protected garden was essential. Much of their food was produced in the garden, and a stray deer or pesky rabbit could wipe it out in one night. As added protection, dogs were chained to the trees at night along the edge of the garden to ward off hungry intruders.

The garden was not just for growing vegetables, but also nurtured sixteen large fig trees and several rows of pomegranates. Chinaberry trees filled the front yard, along with sweet-smelling magenta myrtles, and purple mountain laurels. Nearby, along the river, massive cypress trees reached inland. If left unchecked, the intrusive cypress roots would sap the garden soil. The chore of keeping the roots at bay fell to the capable hands of Sam's slave, Griff.

The original owners built nine deep niches into the exterior walls along the porch for displaying colorful flowerpots. Mary's slaves planted and carefully pruned the bright red geraniums she brought from Alabama. In the spring, there were brightly colored ivy geraniums hanging from the vigas, and in the winter months, chili ristras. No one in San Antonio displayed a more beautiful home and garden than Mary Maverick.

One of the Maverick's neighbors was a Greek by the name of Roque Catahdie. Roque's shop was on the street side of his home and he and his young wife lived in the rear. Roque was industrious; his shop opened early and did not close until long after dark. He was married to a pretty, bright-eyed fourteen-year-old Mexican girl. Roque purchased a piano for her so he did not have to worry as long as he could hear his wife playing. The piano allowed the jealous Greek to keep an eye on her even when she was out of his sight. If the music stopped, Roque would immediately leave the store to check on his young wife. He even did all the cooking so she could practice well into the evening. Eventually, she became such an accomplished pianist, the townsfolk would gather in the street outside the Cathadie home to listen to her play.

The Maverick home became the showplace of San Antonio and the center of dazzling social gatherings. When they received word that President Houston would soon visit San Antonio, Mary planned a party to celebrate his glorious victory over Santa Anna, but that would have to wait…

Chapter Fourteen
Aftermath

Black smoke lingered in the morning air. The confrontation was over, but Ramon Garza now held a double vendetta against Bud Miller. He was in no position to present any immediate threat; his right wrist shattered by Bud's perfect shot. The beach was now empty, with the exception of Garza's friends trying to console him. He was inconsolable and bewildered as he insisted repeatedly, "I hit him. I hit his heart with my shot. I know I did not miss. That Miller boy is a dead man walking."

After gathering some supplies at the Treptows and spending a few moments with Virginia, Bud was ready to join the President's entourage. He wanted to kiss Virginia on the cheek, but hesitated, knowing someone might be watching. Then in a bold move, he closed his eyes and leaned forward to place his lips against her cheek when, to his shock, he felt her warm moist lips meet his. Virginia grabbed the back of his head with her right hand and pulled his face tight against hers. Her full lips lit a fire that resonated throughout his body. This was his first kiss and Bud surely liked the way it felt. When she released her grip, Virginia asked, "You will return, won't you?"

Bud stammered, "Do geese fly south in the winter? Sure as they do, that is how confident you can be of seeing me again."

The Baron bargained Helmut out of a horse for himself and was down by the bayou when Bud arrived at the dock. Seeing Bud galloping toward the group, President Houston moved his white stallion over to greet him. "Nice shooting young man. I suspect you planned to hit his wrist."

"That's correct, Sir. I did not want to kill him. He ain't, err, I mean he has never done anything to me. I didn't see any need to kill him to defeat him."

Sam smiled at Bud's answer. "You are going to make one fine Texas Ranger. I will introduce you to Captain Jack Hays when we arrive in San Antonio. He can use a man like you."

"That would be mighty nice of you, Sir." Excusing himself, Bud nudged Lightning in the flank and moved toward where the Baron was holding court, trying to sell President Houston's aides on the advantages of moving the State Capital to Bastrop. Standing in the group was Ben McCullough. Ben and his brother Henry made their living rafting logs and flat-boating cargo down the Mississippi to New Orleans when, upon their return to Tennessee in 1835, the brothers found their hero David Crockett in a tight race for his Congressional seat. They became active in his campaign, and after his defeat, Davy convinced them to follow him to Texas. The brothers followed a few weeks later once Henry recovered from a sudden illness, and arrived in time to help defeat Santa Anna at San Jacinto. Houston was so impressed with the stout, sandy-haired Ben McCullough that he promoted him to lieutenant. Not long after the battle, Ben and Henry returned to Tennessee, but the fire had started to flicker; Texas was in Ben's blood. So too was leadership; Ben was elected to Congress in his home state and now often traveled with President Houston. Sam was delighted to have a fellow Tennessean along, but more than that, he appreciated the proven courage and fighting skill Ben McCullough brought to the table.

Another man in the group stood out for his size, with only President Houston being taller. Thirty-three-year-old Craig Winborn, a Georgian, had originally come to Texas as a land speculator. Craig was on a trip to raise capital for a land purchase when he read a recruitment pamphlet Travis had penned. Upon reading the message, he immediately joined the fight. There was only one problem; the pamphlet was six weeks old. By the time Craig reached Texas, independence had already been won. After settling in Texas, Craig became a trusted friend of Sam Houston and now served as President Houston's protector. At six-foot-three and 230 pounds of solid steel, Craig used his size and strength to intimidate those who might consider doing harm to the president.

Houston had penned the agreement with the Mexican dictator, Santa Anna, in exchange for his life and in doing so secured Texas' independence:

1. *Santa Anna swore never again to take up arms against Texas.*
2. *All hostilities between the two nations would cease immediately.*
3. *All Americans would be released from Mexican jails.*
4. *All lands north of the Rio Grande would belong to Texas.*

Mexico was still embarrassed that a rag tag group of Texans had defeated their greatest General. The Mexicans did not accept Santa Anna's agreement and there was always the possibility they might retaliate against President Houston. Most of the 27-man entourage rode to protect the president from Indian attack or a group of angry Mexicans sympathetic to Santa Anna.

When President Houston's entourage arrived at the rebuilt city of San Felipe, Bud was pleasantly surprised. The city streets bustled with stores and other businesses, and the citizens treated the Baron like a King; men tipped their hats and women curtsied as he passed by. The citizens exhibited more reverence for the Baron than for the President. Many of the locals did not appreciate that Houston, an outsider, had "stolen" the presidency out from under their hero, Stephen F. Austin.

The group remained in San Felipe for three days. The president drank heavily, and Bud listened intently as Houston expounded on his vision for the future of Texas. Young Miller watched in awe as Houston's imposing manner compelled men to listen. At times, the big man spoke in almost a whisper and the room would hush so all could hear.

After spending four nights sleeping under the stars, the president's group made Gonzales before dark on the fifth day. This brave little town had given her best for Texas, and the widows of Gonzales greeted the president with despondent tears. The memory of the Alamo and Goliad were more than the president could bear. Being in Gonzales brought it all back, and Houston got dog dead drunk their first night in town. Timmy Marcum knew he must get the president to move on or he would likely stay in a drunken depression for days. He had watched Houston try to drown his troubles in whiskey many times, yet the wise young man understood troubles couldn't drown; they float. Timmy enlisted Bud's help, suggesting they cook up a credible reason for the group to leave Gonzales. Bud thought for a moment and then replied, "The Baron! Trust me. If anyone can concoct a story, the Baron can. I suspect he is hiding from creditors over at the Gonzales Hotel."

Sure enough, the Baron was sitting in a hand-hewn rocking chair reading from a Spanish bible when the boys knocked on the door. At first, he was reluctant to answer, but then recognized Bud's voice. Bud and Timmy explained the problem, and the Baron, not missing a beat, responded, "Indians, that's it. A Comanche raid on Cibolo Creek. We must go and save a family in need. That will sober him up if anything will. I would not mind getting out of here myself. Let me grab my things and we'll go talk to the General, err, I mean the President."

Houston instantly sobered up when the Baron came rushing into the saloon shouting, "Mr. President, Mr. President. There has been an Indian raid over on Cibolo Creek, not far from San Antonio. Bud and Timmy are saddling the horses at this very moment. There is no time to waste. If we hurry, we may be able to save the children."

Houston grabbed his hat, crammed the eagle feather deep into his hatband and said, "Let's get the Hades outta here." He directed the bartender to quickly total his tab. The tall, thin man played with his handlebar mustache for a moment before answering, "I don't want your money, Mr. President. I would like to have something of yours as payment. That would mean more to me than your money. I'd love to have your pocketknife."

Sam reached down, removed one of his daisy rowel spurs and tossed it to the bartender. "I can't part with the pocket knife. Chief Jolly gave it to me, but here is my favorite spur. Give it to your boy and tell him Sam Houston wore it at the battle of San Jacinto."

Before mounting to leave, the Baron pulled Bud aside and told him he would not continue traveling on with the group. He needed to return to Galveston and arrange to have his merchandise delivered to his new store. Bud understood. He reached out and gave the Baron a bear hug, and thanked him for all he had done. Choking back tears, Bud whispered, "Mr. Bastrop, Sir, I'm going to make you mighty proud of me here in Texas. You can bet your boots, your best boots on that."

That night, the group camped under the stars, listening to a group of coyotes howl at the full moon. Since the Baron had raised the alarm about hostile Indians in the area, President Houston insisted on posting pickets. As luck would have it, Bud and Timmy pulled the early morning watch, one of the disadvantages of being the youngest in the group. The two talked and eventually the subject got around to girls. Bud quickly learned that Timmy was much more experienced where girls were concerned and decided to ask for some advice. "This girl back in Galveston kissed me on the mouth before we left. What do you think that means?"

"Depends on why. What made her kiss you on the mouth?"

"Well, she gave me this little bible." Bud fumbled in his pocket and retrieved the New Testament; lead ball still embedded in the cover, and handed it to Timmy. "This is what saved my life. That Mexican shot me dead center, but the bullet hit this bible, and here I am today. Well, before we left, I wanted to thank her for saving my life and all, so I reached over to kiss her on her cheek. I'll be darned if she didn't just up and kiss me right on the mouth."

Timmy tried to conceal his laughter, but snickering slipped out anyway.

Bud shot back angrily, "It's not funny."

"No, no, no, I wasn't laughing at you. I was just thinking about how surprised you must have been when she kissed you on the mouth. I saw the way Virginia looked at you the day I was at the Treptow ranch. Make no mistake; she is looking for a husband, and you are her choice. She was trying to let you know she is in love with you. Any blind hog could see that."

"I'll be danged. I never thought of her as a wife. I really like her. I think she is pretty. I suspect you may be correct. Why else would Mr. Treptow give me such a fine horse? Well, I have to say I could do a lot worse. The Treptows are a God-fearing family." Then Bud leaned back against a tree, smiling as he pondered what Timmy had said.

Before the sun broke over the treetops, coffee was brewing and two of the men were busy preparing breakfast. As they prepared to break camp, not knowing the Baron's information had been a ruse, the men saddled their horses quietly and moved toward Cibolo Creek, rifles at the ready across their saddle pommels. As they neared the creek, no one was more shocked than Bud and Timmy when they saw a smoldering wagon on the other side. Putting spurs to the flanks, the rangers pressed into the creek, splashed across and climbed the opposite bank. The sight was dreadful: Two men scalped and tied to a tree with buckskin.

Houston was the first to reach the wounded men and quickly pulling out his pocketknife, cut them free. As he lowered the men to the ground, he realized one of them was still breathing. Sam bent down and asked the man what had happened. In a thin voice, the injured man answered, "Hank and I were haulin' merchandise from Galveston to San Antonio when a group of about thirty Comanche surrounded us. We killed three, but before we could reload, they were on us. Hank has a weak heart and I suspect when they scalped him, he gave up the ghost. I acted like I passed out. I could feel them cutting my skin, but it didn't hurt as much as you would think. Hurts worse now… Do you have annny whiskeeey?"

Houston motioned to Doctor Dave Wagonvoord and shouted, "Doc, bring some morphine or laudanum. We need to ease this man's pain."

Doctor Wagonvoord rushed over and knelt down beside the scalped man. Looking through his wire-rimmed glasses, he inquired, "What's your name, lad?" The doctor spoke so calmly and casually, it seemed as if it were just another day at the office.

"Michael Mitchell, but everyone calls me Mitch," the wounded man answered.

"Here, drink this," Dr. Wagonvoord ordered. In moments, the pain eased and Mitch's eyes closed. Turning to the group, Dr. Wagonvoord said, "As odd as it may seem, I think he's gonna make it. We need to make a travois and get him into San Antonio immediately."

Ben McCullough and another man scouted ahead of the group. Houston trusted Ben to make sure the trail was safe before the group proceeded. The unshod hoof prints offered evidence of a large war party; however, no one expected an attack because the President's group was rather large. Comanche were more likely to attack small groups of stragglers that are easier to overcome without risking too many casualties. Only freelancers like Mitch and his friend risked their lives for a few fast dollars. Most suppliers and individuals had learned to travel in caravans with armed escorts.

San Antonio was abuzz with anticipation as word spread that President Houston would be arriving soon. Mary Maverick had been busy planning a party to end all parties in his honor. She had enlisted many of the local women to help and the slaves had spruced up her home from top to bottom. Mary even convinced Roque Catahdie to allow his wife to perform at the party. There would be food and drink, and music for dancing. Unfortunately, when the president pulled into town with Mitch on a travois, the mood turned somber. Everyone realized the Comanche were once again on the warpath. Instead of celebrating, it was time to fortify the town's defenses. They needed to warn the farmers on the outskirts of town. A ranger force needed to be organized.

Houston learned that Jack Hays and several others were surveying property fifty miles south of town. He immediately dispatched two riders to bring Hays back with all haste. President Houston knew the importance of tracking down the band before they killed again, and that Captain Jack Coffee Hays would be invaluable in achieving that end.

After two days of organizing the town's defenses, Sam decided it was time to party, and party they did. The president danced and drank into the early morning hours. Timmy and Bud stayed in the shadows: Bud, so no one would ask him to dance and Timmy, to conceal his Indian heritage.

Chapter Fifteen
Change

Houston ordered three of his most capable men to locate Jack Hays and bring him back to San Antonio. Congressman Ben McCullough, was a skilled communicator who could be counted on to convey the urgency of the situation, Craig Winborn was a superior marksman with fearless fighting skills, and Deaf Smith was one of the most experienced scouts to ever travel the hill country of Texas. On the second day out, the scouts came upon an enormous flock of mud swallows. None had ever witnessed such a spectacle as thousands of split-tailed swallows dove into the crystal clear creek and carried the mud back to their overhanging nests. The trio stopped for a few minutes to watch the tiny birds work. Ben removed a note pad from his saddlebags and made a few sketches to show folks back in San Antonio. Deaf had heard of the birds, but in all of his travels had never seen them building their mud shelters. It was an impressive sight.

The rangers finally arrived at Camp Wood, abandoned when Mexico withdrew their troops and missionaries after the debacle in San Saba. As Ben, Craig, and Deaf neared the Camp, there was an older man cooking lunch. The javelina roasting over an open pit was indeed a welcome sight for the three hungry riders. The cook was Thom Webber, a drifter who arrived in Texas before the Alamo. Thom was an excellent marksman and a skilled rider, but he was unable to think clearly, having had been kicked in the head by a mule when he was young. As long as he had someone to tell him what to do, he was a great man to have in an Indian fight. When Thom spotted the three men, he started clanging a big brass cowbell. Hearing the warning signal, Jack and his men dropped their surveying instruments, grabbed their rifles, and were mounted and on their way back to camp faster than a mud swallow could dip down for a beak of water. The six men were in defensive positions by the time the president's scouts came within voice distance. Ben waved his beaver hat and shouted, "Jack Hays, it's Ben McCullough. We have urgent news from President Houston."

This was not a message Jack wanted to hear. He needed three more days to complete his survey. At twenty-two, Jack "Coffee" Hays was mature beyond his years, yet still possessed the impatience of youth. Jack's appearance was deceptively unthreatening. His sandy brown hair seemed always to be a few days late of a haircut. He stood barely five-foot-eight and weighed not much more than 150 pounds, leading his fellow Texans to describe him as being "thin as a bed slat." There was no man President Houston trusted more than Jack Hays to track down the menacing band of renegades.

After casual greetings were exchanged, Deaf Smith lamented, "There's another dat blamed war party doin' mischief. Who's to say how many there are for sure? You know how they don't show their hand and keep a large band of braves hid back till they need 'em."

Jack motioned for two of his men to return to the survey site and retrieve their equipment. He turned back toward the trio and suggested, "Might as well take care of this javelina before we start back to San Antonio."

Thom made cornbread and cooked up a pot of red beans, and the men ate as if they hadn't eaten in weeks. As they stuffed down their meals, no one spoke. There would be time to talk on their way back to town.

When they arrived in San Antonio, President Houston quickly apprised them of the situation, and then introduced Captain Hays to young Bud Miller. "Jack, I think this lad can be of some assistance to you as a ranger. I have seen his courage and shooting skills with my own eyes. Take my word for it. This boy has what it takes. Reminds me of you when you were his age."

Jack smiled. "I've not seen his shooting skills, but I know of his courage. I had to arrest him in Galveston for killing one of the meanest men in town. That was a job I didn't cotton to in the least. I heard later from Sam Maverick that the charges had been dismissed."

Puzzled, Houston inquired, "So you know each other?"

Bud answered, "I wouldn't say we know each other. Jack here hauled me to jail when the Baron and I were trying to get off the island. I know who he is, that's for sure."

Jack turned to Bud and asked, "Got a good horse?"

"Yeah, I got one of the fastest in the country. That's him right over there," Bud responded proudly as he pointed to his sorrel stallion. "He was given to me by Mr. Treptow before I left Galveston." Then without thinking, Bud blurted out, "Today is October 4th, my birthday. I'm a full seventeen."

Sam and Jack smiled and simultaneously said, "Happy birthday, Miller. You got a long way to go." Then the president added, "Age doesn't make the man. It's what is inside that matters, and I have seen what you are made of, Miller. You are the kind of man we need to build our great nation. One day we old codgers will have to hang up our spurs and turn things over to youngsters like you and Jack."

Captain Hays then posed a direct question. "How well armed are you?"

"I got a Kentucky Long Rifle, a pair of new pistols and a decent supply of powder and lead. I reckon I'm fairly well armed. Could use a shotgun, but that's about it."

"You are correct. Most of our action will be up-close. You will need a short rifle or shotgun to carry across your saddle and a Kentucky rifle for long-range shooting. I recommend two pistols hanging from your saddle horn and another pair in your belt. You'll also need at least two hundred rounds of shot and powder, extra horseshoes and nails, and a rain poncho and wool blanket."

Bud nodded in agreement and asked, "Anything else?"

Before Jack could answer, Noah Smithwick rode up and dismounted. Jack made the introduction. "Bud, this is Noah. He will teach you to ride like a vaquero. No one sits a horse better than the Mexican vaqueros. Noah is a blacksmith by trade and he will teach you how to shoe your horse. Can't have your horse going lame 'cause he throws a shoe. You will also need a set of Spanish bits. I know they are brutal if not used correctly, but they are necessary to control the animal in tight situations. In an Indian fight, we need every advantage. Noah can teach you how to use the bit without doing damage to your sorrel's mouth."

Turning to Noah, Jack instructed, "Noah, take Miller over to Juan Lucas and have him make Bud some high-heeled boots." Hays turned back to Bud and emphasized, "I insist all my men wear them. If knocked off your mount, with your foot slipped too deep into the stirrup, you can be dragged to your death. Noah will need to teach you to shoot while at a dead run. If your horse spooks at the sound of gunfire, you will need to get him used to that."

Jack glanced down at Bud's high-topped shoes and instructed, "Also pick him up a pair of spurs with a set of daisy rowels like President Houston's."

Noah reached over and shook Bud's hand. "There are a few things you need to know about Indians," he said. "They take no prisoners. They don't have jails so they always kill all the adult men. They keep the younger women and girls as wives or workers. They kill babies three and under, so you better get your gut in shape to see a baby with an arrow through its body. When fightin' Indians, it's kill or be killed."

President Houston interrupted the long-winded Noah. "Bud, we have a saying here in Texas that 'A Ranger must ride like a Mexican, track like an Indian, shoot like a Tennessean, and fight like the devil.' If you will listen to Noah, he can teach you to ride, and Deaf can teach you to track. The rest will be up to you."

Before daybreak, Thom Webber, Deaf Smith, Noah Smithwick, George Erath and the handpicked group of sixteen men headed out to track down the renegade Indians. Bud was proud to be traveling with the rangers. He was surprised there were so few pursuing such a large group of savages, but kept his thoughts to himself.

They rode hard the first day, only stopping occasionally to let the horses drink. About an hour before sunset, Jack pulled the men to a halt. Bud started to unsaddle his horse when Noah said, "We will do our cooking here and then Jack will take us at least two miles north to set up camp for the night, just in case the Indians have seen our cooking smoke. He always does this. You will learn a lot from Jack Hays. He is a clever young man and the best Indian fighter to ever pull a trigger."

Thom did the cooking as the men checked their gear and rested from their hard ride. They had traveled forty miles since daylight and would do the same tomorrow.

Three weeks had passed since the attack on the shipping wagon and Jack surmised the Indians would still be scouting for another easy mark, and in no rush to return to their main camp. Bud did little talking, but listened as the men speculated on which direction to proceed. Austrian-born Ranger George Bernard Erath suggested, "What about the compound that Captain Coleman's Ranger Company built on Walnut Creek south of Austin? We can use the old blockade as our base. It will provide us a safe, warm place at night and allow us to scout the surrounding area during the day."

Jack quickly responded, "George has come up with a great idea. I had forgotten about the blockhouses. They will shelter us from this early norther that blew in last night."

One of the men, speaking with a mouthful of red beans, garbled, "It seems a little early for such a cold spell." Small talk continued until the men finished eating.

It was almost as bright as day under the full moon as they rode another few miles north before making camp for the night. Each man hobbled his horse and fed them a ration of corn. They then busied themselves, gathering twigs. Bud was uncertain what they were doing when Deaf, noticing his confusion, explained the twigs would elevate their bodies off the damp earth and give them a modicum of cushioning.

The next afternoon, the rangers reached the blockhouses. That evening during supper, the conversation turned to the savagery of hostile Indians. Each man told a story, but none could top Craig Winborn's experience. Craig had been working with the friendly Tonkawa Indians, who had a special interest in helping the Anglos because the Comanche had driven them from their homeland. On one occasion, the Tonkawas joined Craig and a group of settlers in tracking down some Comanches who stole twenty of their horses. They caught up with the Indians and killed all three. The Tonkawas then field dressed the dead Comanche braves and tossed them in a kettle with some corn and potatoes. When the stew was cooked and cooled, they used their hands as ladles and slurped up the human stew. Craig was invited to partake, but thinking fast, he told them he had just eaten a large rattlesnake and was too full to eat another bite. No one in the group even tried to top Craig's story.

The next morning, the group moved down the Colorado in the direction of Bastrop. Traveling was slow because they tracked out two or three miles on each side of the bank searching for any sign of the war party. Just before dark, they set up camp to cook and then moved downriver another couple of miles. Sleeping on the ground, using his saddle as a pillow, was a new experience for Bud. He discovered that pulling his hat down over his face and tucking the blanket over his ears muffled most of the loud snoring that surrounded him. The night was extremely cold and keeping a fire burning was not an option. He was pleased he had listened to Noah and had purchased himself a set of wool long johns. Bud, like the rest of the men, drifted off to sleep with his boots on.

Around four o'clock in the morning, there was a rustling in the bushes. Jack was the first to hear the noise, followed by Deaf Smith. Even though Deaf had lost most of his hearing when he was young, he had an uncanny ability to hear out-of-place noises. It was as if he possessed a sixth sense. A gun in each hand, Jack slipped into the bushes near where the noise had come from. He was taking aim when the clouds parted and the moon illuminated the outline of a woman. Jack realized he had discovered a white woman in desperate need of help. In a soft, comforting voice, he said, "We are Texas Rangers and are here to help you. Please don't be afraid."

Battered and bruised, and shivering uncontrollably, the woman slowly limped toward him. Blood seeped from the scratches and cuts that covered her frail body and her dress had been torn into strings by thorn bushes and tree limbs. Jack moved forward as she collapsed to the ground. Gently picking her up, he carried her into camp. With a quick motion of his head, he signaled Noah to stir the coals and bring the fire to life. Noah responded immediately, stoking the embers into flames. Bud grabbed his new wool blanket to wrap her battered body as George rushed over with a mixture of whiskey and honey, telling her to take a few sips. Jack held her close to his body, whispering, "Ma'am, please drink. It will help warm and calm you. Then you can tell us what has happened."

The men gathered around her, curious as to how a white woman could stumble into their camp miles from the nearest farm or compound. With the courage of a lioness, the battered woman began to speak. "My husband wanted to see the Alamo where David Crockett was killed. He made several gallons of corn whiskey we hoped to barter for supplies in San Antonio. We loaded our wagon and headed west, then southwest. About three or four days out, as we drove through a grove of pecan trees along the riverbank, my husband Johnny spotted the Indians."

It was when she said the name Johnny that Jack suddenly recalled where he had seen her face. She was so bruised and battered; Jack was unable to recognize her at first. He moved over and put his arms around her. "Millie, Millie Satterwhite? You are Millie aren't you?" He didn't wait for her to respond as he continued, "I'm Ranger Jack Hays. Remember me? Ranger Childress and I visited you and Johnny." Looking up at his men, Jack said, "This brave woman is Millie Satterwhite from Tennessee. She and her husband Johnny and their three children have a farm not too far north of Jared Groce's place at the fork of the Little River and Brazos."

Millie's face was pale and her lips pursed tightly together as she responded, "Jack, I'm sorry for not recognizing you. I guess I'm a little numb from all that has happened." She then painfully continued, "Johnny was right about it being dangerous to visit the Alamo, but the children and I talked him into taking us along. The first few days were wonderful. We laughed and sang. Johnny played his fiddle. Suddenly, Indians in war paint surrounded us, making frightening screaming noises. I had never heard anything like that. Johnny killed one and A.D. shot another before they charged us. Johnny was able to kill a third with his knife as they swarmed around us. Before my dear husband could reload his gun, five braves pulled him from our wagon and cut his scalp. It was the most horrible thing you can imagine. I can still hear him screaming… and the blood. Then two braves drug me from the wagon by my hair as I clung to my baby with all my strength. I saw them wrap our oldest son, A.D. in a blanket and tie him to our brown mule. Then they put baby Davy and me on to another one of our mules as one of the Indians—I think he was the Chief—placed Ruthann in front of him, and we rode away. I remember turning and seeing our wagon burning and Johnny on the ground as we disappeared into the trees. I shouted to Johnny and told him I loved him. I'm not sure if he heard me."

George insisted she take another sip of the honey and whisky mixture. Millie did just that; in fact, she took two. Even though this was her first time drinking alcohol, she ignored the burning as it went down.

Jack, his arms still around her to keep her warm, gently asked, "How did you get away?"

She sat in a daze looking into the fire before answering. "It was bitter cold. A norther had just blown in so the Indians took us into a clump of scrub cedars to escape the wind. They built a big fire and left A.D. tied to the mule not far from the fire. My baby Davy was freezing and scared and he wouldn't stop crying. I was rocking him in my arms and trying to keep him silent when one of the savages yanked him out of my arms, jabbed a hole under his chin with his knife and hung him on a dead tree limb like a piece of meat. His cries became whimpers and then… only silence. That Indian killed my baby in cold blood because I couldn't stop him from crying."

Even after giving such a vivid account of the horrors she had just endured, Millie was unable to change her expression or cry. She sat almost catatonic, sipping whiskey and honey from the gourd dipper. She rested her weary head against Jack's chest and continued, "They didn't tie me up. I guess they didn't think I'd leave the children. I pretended to go to sleep. With my eyes barely open, I could see one of the braves had my daughter wrapped in his blanket. I could hear her weeping and I wanted to kill him with my bare hands, but there were too many of them. They were too strong. I was powerless."

Millie did not mention the multiple times she too had been defiled. She had already made up her mind she would carry the secret to her grave. Millie was painfully aware of the many white women rescued from the Indians having to then face being forever ostracized by the Anglo community. Some churches refused to allow a woman raped by Indians to attend services. Their own families refused them shelter. No white man would ever marry a defiled woman. Millie suddenly regretted telling them about little Ruthann and quickly changed the subject.

"I knew if they took us any further north, we would be too far from help and would never be rescued. I listened until I could hear them breathing deep or snoring. When I was certain they were all asleep, I got up and slipped into the cedars. As I was running, I stumbled into one of their ponies. One Indian rose up on his elbow and looked around, but lay back down and pulled his blanket over his head. God was on my side and I escaped."

Bud felt tears flowing down his cheeks. Her story was horrifying, her pain palpable, and Bud's desire for revenge was to the boiling point when Jack asked, "How did you find us?"

Millie remained stoic as she answered, "I remembered we were close to the Colorado and thought that if I followed the river far enough south, I'd find a farm. I made it to the river and stepped into the dark water. It was freezing cold, but I knew if I stayed in the water, they could not track me. The next morning I got up onto the bank and walked along the granite stone so I would leave no tracks. I followed the river all day yesterday and today. Tonight, as I walked along the riverbank, I heard a mule bray. Then I heard a man talking in his sleep in English and knew I was safe. That's how I found you."

Jack offered Millie some dry buckskin clothes. Four of the men held up a blanket, creating makeshift privacy so she could change into the warm, dry clothing. Captain Hays then instructed the men to break camp, adding, "We're going to rescue her children and take care of some Comanches."

The rangers answered with muffled approval. In less than ten minutes, the group and Millie were mounted and riding toward the Comanche camp. They proceeded at a hard gallop for several miles until Jack signaled for the group to slow down. He then sent Deaf and Noah ahead to locate the grove of cedars Millie had described. He felt certain the Indians would still be there since there had been no break in the weather. He knew they were not concerned with Millie's escape, knowing she would not get far in the cold, and if she did, a panther or pack of timber wolves would find her. The Indians had what they wanted: The two younger children, a warm campfire, and plenty of Johnny's whiskey.

Noah located the Indians' ponies as he crept through the cedar grove. The startled horses began to move about, nickering and snorting, alerting the braves. Realizing they had been discovered, Noah and Deaf rushed the camp with guns blazing. When Jack and the others heard the shots, they broke into a dead run, crashing through the small cedar scrub brush and into the Comanche camp. The braves had armed themselves and were now firing back. One ranger was shot from his horse, but not seriously wounded. Robert Hall shot an Indian and believed he was dead, but his shot had only wounded the savage who then rose up and shot another ranger in the back, killing him instantly. Robert raced back to the wounded Indian and with the butt of his rifle smashed the Indian's skull. George Erath spotted someone running away on one of the mules. He raised his rifle to take dead aim. Just before he could pull the trigger, Bud shoved the barrel up, screaming, "That's the woman's son. He's a white boy." Bud plowed his daisy rowel spurs into Lightning's flanks and the stallion lurched forward as if shot from a cannon, tossing Bud back against the cantle. In a flash, he caught up with little A.D. He snared the mule's bridle and brought him to a gentle halt, and as calmly as he knew how, said, "It's okay. We are Texas Rangers and we are here to help you." Bud felt a shiver of pride move through him as he said he was a Texas Ranger. Using his belt knife to cut the boy free, Bud reassured young A.D., "Your mother is with us. Be brave for your mama. Everything is okay now."

When the fighting was over, the rangers had killed eleven Comanche, but many more escaped. When suffering heavy casualties, the Comanche would never stand and fight. Some early settlers mistook Comanche retreats for cowardice. That was never the case. While Anglos and Mexicans seemed to have an endless pool of young males to draw from, the Indians would have to wait years for a boy to grow into a man before they could replace a fallen brave.

Jack made the decision to care for the Satterwhites rather than pursue the escaping savages. The rangers found little Ruthann cowering under a tree, so traumatized she was unable to speak. Millie pulled her daughter into her arms, rocking her back and forth. As Bud delivered A.D. to his mother's side, Jack took his men aside and instructed them to never discuss the violation of little Ruthann at the hand of the savages. Knowing the social stigma that followed a woman defiled by Indians, to a man they vowed to protect the secret.

Some of the rangers dug a small grave for baby Davy while Noah read passages from his New Testament. George carved into a tree next to the grave: 'Here lies little Davy Satterwhite.' The men then covered the tiny grave with rocks to prevent wolves from digging up the body. Millie watched, but shed no tears. Tears would come, but much later.

Jack instructed Craig and two others to search for Johnny. If the body was in too gruesome of condition, he told them to bury him where he fell and make a cross that could be seen from a distance to mark the grave. He knew one day Millie and her children would want to visit his gravesite.

A day's ride outside of San Antonio, the three rangers caught up with the rest of the group. Craig Winborn rode into camp carrying an injured hound dog across his saddle, followed by a second dog trotting behind. A.D.'s face lit up. He thought he would never see his dogs again. He dashed over to Craig, grabbing the wounded dog and hugging the animal as one would a dear friend. The second hound stood up on his hindquarters and licked A.D.'s face. It was difficult to tell who was the happiest, the boy or the dogs. The dogs had almost starved to death, but had stayed faithfully with Johnny. One hound had tried to fight off a wild hog to protect his master's body. He was no match for the tusked swine, yet did his best to protect Johnny from becoming a meal for the predator, sustaining a nasty wound for his effort. In the end, the dogs were no match for the hogs and eventually became too weak to scare off the buzzards. One of the rangers sewed the gash with a needle and thread, a staple every Ranger carried in their saddlebag for suturing a wounded horse or ranger.

Craig pulled Jack aside and told him what they had found. Buzzards had eaten the flesh off Johnny's body and it appeared as if feral hogs had chewed his bones. What few bones they could find, they placed in a grave. On one of the wagon sideboards that had not completely burned, they chiseled the date and Johnny's name and erected a wooden cross that could be seen for a mile or more.

Jack colored the truth as he informed Millie that Johnny's body had been discovered intact and it appeared as if he had died quickly. He explained that his men had given Johnny a Christian burial. Craig Winborn then reached behind his saddle, and slowly unwrapping his slicker, pulled out Johnny's fiddle and bow. Millie softly smiled as he handed Johnny's favorite possession to her. They told her they found it not far from the wagon. It was their guess the Comanches had no use for it and had tossed it away before setting fire to the wagon.

The group made good time on their return to San Antonio. Millie spoke infrequently, while little Ruthann remained mute. Not even her mother was able to get her to speak. When the rescue party reached the hill overlooking the tranquil San Antonio valley, the evening camouflaged the bitterness of bloodshed that haunted the city's streets. Topping the ridge, Jack pointed the Alamo out to Millie and her children. They paused to reflect on the brave men who had given their lives for Texas' freedom. Travis, Bonham, Crockett, Bowie and 178 others had made the incision. Sam Houston had completed the operation at San Jacinto, cutting Texas from the belly of Mexico.

Chapter Sixteen
Divided

Sam Houston had no interest in running for president. He wrote an encouraging letter to his friend General Thomas Jefferson Rusk, suggesting he enter the race. Rusk wrote back, telling Sam he was not old enough nor experienced enough to lead the new Republic. Even though Rusk was a very popular general, he was only thirty years old and was not confident he was qualified to manage a government. He felt Sam would be the better man for the job. Eleven days before the election, friends finally persuaded Houston to toss his hat into the ring. The Raven's campaign took wings and he won by a landslide. When the votes were tallied, Houston received a whopping 5,119 to 743 for Smith and only 587 for Stephen F. Austin.

Sam Houston became President of the Republic of Texas in September 1836. Martin Van Buren became President of the Union ten months later. President Houston's presidency would sit directly in the middle of a chasm: Mexico refused to recognize Texas' independence, and the Union was not ready to embrace Texas as the twenty-eighth state. Even Houston's closest friend Andrew Jackson, the man responsible for Van Buren being elected, was not powerful enough to persuade the Union president to support annexation of a slave state. Texas was in a catch twenty-two: The northern states were staunchly against another slave state being added to the Union, yet without its Negro slaves, Texas' main source of income, cotton, would vanish.

On his inauguration day in Columbus, Houston stood in front of a table covered with an Indian blanket. He raised the sword he used at San Jacinto, saying, "We are only in the outset of liberty." Then he raised the sword high above his head, touching the ceiling with his knuckles, and continued, "It now has become my duty to make a presentation of this sword, this emblem of my past office. I have worn this weapon with some humble pretensions in defense of my country; and should the danger again call for my services, I expect to resume and respond to the call. If needful with my blood and life." There was no state seal, so Houston used his gold cuff link. Engraved with the head of a dog and rooster and the words *'Try Me'* embossed in the metal, Houston dipped his cuff link into the hot wax and made his mark.

Mirabeau B. Lamar was elected vice president in spite of Sam Houston's strong opposition. Mirabeau Bonaparte Lamar and Samuel Houston held polar opposite views when it came to important issues of the day, including slavery, war, annexation, expansion, and how to deal with Indian depredations.

Upon first visiting Texas, Lamar knew the new frontier was the place for him to seek his fame and fortune. He returned to Georgia to get his affairs in order when he received the news of the fall of the Alamo and the battle of Goliad. He immediately returned to Texas to seize the opportunity to fulfill his ambitions. He joined up with Houston's army at Groce's Point. The thirty-eight-year-old Lamar entered the army as a private, but it was not long before he caught Houston's eye. Promotions came almost daily for the brash and arrogant Georgian. He showed great promise as a leader and gave notice he was a brave warrior. Just before the fight got underway at San Jacinto, General Houston made him a Colonel and put him in command of a cavalry unit. Ten days after the battle, Lamar was promoted to secretary of war in President David Burnet's cabinet and within weeks, to Major General of the Texas army.

Lamar came into the fray too late and rose to power too quickly. Perhaps if he had marched through the muck and the mire, endured the brutal elements and faced starvation with the soldiers, they may have been willing to follow him, but the independent-minded Texans refused to accept his pompous and haughty attitude. They put down their arms and refused to serve under his command. Lamar blamed Houston, when in reality Lamar simply did not possess Houston's leadership ability or charisma. Men followed Houston without him speaking a word, while the insecure Lamar demanded loyalty.

Shortly after taking office, President Houston put down an attempt by Vice President Lamar to seize control of the government. Inside information alerted Houston to the coup and he was able to squelch the takeover before the poorly planned movement materialized. From that time forward, Houston never trusted Lamar. To get Lamar out of his hair, Houston suggested his nemesis go on an extended trip to the Union. Immediately and enthusiastically, Lamar accepted. The thought of returning to Georgia, holding such an elevated position in the government, was a close second to being sent to heaven for the egotistical Lamar. He spent most of his second year as vice president in his home state of Georgia, parading himself around like a distinguished hero.

The first year of Houston's presidency endured many other difficult obstacles as well. General Felix Huston from Mississippi was one of the latecomers to Texas and, like Lamar, had arrived with ambition and power at the top of his agenda. Huston had swiftly worked his way up the ranks into a position of commanding a 2,500-man army; three times the number Houston commanded when he won Texas' independence at San Jacinto. Eager for glory, General Huston became edgy for another campaign against Mexico. He missed the action against Santa Anna and desperately craved recognition as a great leader. War with Mexico could achieve that goal. Huston was aching for a war so he could prove his leadership while war was the one thing President Houston intended to avoid, knowing Texas had neither the money nor the weapons for a sustained confrontation. This was something General Huston never considered.

When word reached the president of General Huston's planned invasion, Houston sent his secretary of war with orders to furlough all but six hundred of Huston's men, effectively reducing the army to a small fraction of its effective fighting strength. When General Huston returned to camp, the majority of his army had scattered to the four winds. With no army to command and no war to fight, General Felix Huston resigned and returned in disgust to Mississippi.

In spite of Lamar's attempted coup and General Huston's push for war, Sam Houston was able to achieve important goals for the growing Republic. Government officers were paid a small salary, veterans of war received their land grants, mail was delivered on a regular basis, and custom duties were collected on imports. The population grew steadily as settlers came in droves from the Union and foreign countries. President Houston's leadership stabilized the fledgling Republic.

By law, President Houston could only serve one three-year term in succession. Lamar, who had his sights on the presidency, would not have to run against the Texas hero. Instead, Lamar's opposition would be Peter W. Grayson, who wrote most of the brilliant Texas Constitution single-handedly, and James Collinsworth, Chief Justice of the Supreme Court. In the polls, Collinsworth was well ahead, followed by Grayson, and Lamar, a distant third.

Six weeks before the election, James Collinsworth leapt to his death from a steamer in Galveston Bay. He was known to have periods of depression and it may have been that the thought of being president was more than he could handle. Whatever the reason, Texas lost a valuable son and one of the great minds of the day. This unfortunate turn of events cleared the way for Peter Grayson, a lawyer of considerable ability, and a man who led an exemplary life, to take the lead. Grayson was in the United States when he received the news of Collinsworth's death. He left immediately for Texas, realizing his victory was all but guaranteed. Stopping in Nashville, he took a room in a tavern for the night. Like Collinsworth, Grayson had suffered from depression since his youth, and in his solitary tavern room, he penned a note to his supporters asking for forgiveness. He then placed a pistol to his head and pulled the trigger. The coincidence of the two most popular presidential candidates taking their own lives on the verge of the election was a statistical long shot. There were rumors that Lamar or his supporters were somehow behind the dual "suicides", but no evidence was ever brought forth.

When Lamar returned to Texas, he discovered Sam Houston had organized a considerable movement opposing his candidacy. Lamar quickly aligned himself with an anti-Houston group and persuaded them to support his bid for the presidency. Houston desperately tried to find a suitable replacement to challenge his nemesis, Lamar, but time ran out. Lamar won the presidency.

Sam Houston didn't go out like a lamb. On December 10, 1839, the day of Lamar's inauguration, Sam dressed in slender black pants, shinny silver buckles on his shoes, a topcoat, and white wig. He could have passed for his hero, General George Washington. He took the floor and made a three-hour speech, pulling out all of his oratory tricks. The audience was spellbound and Lamar was livid.

Once Lamar took office, he moved the capital out of Houston to a pimple of a town called Waterloo and changed its name to Austin. Austin was located in the middle of nowhere on the edge of Indian country. Congressmen were reluctant to visit the new State Capital or move their families to the edge of the frontier for fear of Indian attacks, but Lamar saw locating the capital that far west as an opportunity for westward expansion.

Lamar rejected Houston's conciliatory approach toward the Indians and immediately enacted a policy of aggression and force. Unlike Houston, Lamar wanted all Indians dead. When it came to Indians, friendly or hostile made no difference to President Lamar. He believed the natural order of man in Texas was Caucasian first, then Mexican, then Negro, with Indians at the bottom of the barrel. His failure to recognize the difference between friendly and hostile Indians was dangerous and short sighted. With an alliance of friendly Indians, Texas would have been able to cope with Mexican invasions.

Before Lamar's forced Indian extraction, Sam desperately tried to convince his Indian friends to leave willingly, to no avail. Chief Jolly told him: "It's not up to me. This is my peoples' home. Our young women are carrying babies and our crops are growing in the fields. My people will not leave. I know I will die and so will many of my people, but we cannot walk away from the place we have planted our roots. We moved from Tennessee when you asked us to, and in exchange, were given inferior land. Now you want us to move again? My old friend, they will have to climb over my dead body if they want to evict us."

With a heavy heart, Houston left his peaceful Cherokee friends and went to visit his old friend, Andrew Jackson. He then traveled down to Mobile, Alabama to purchase horses and raise capital for his new town. Once in Alabama, he met with horse breeder William Bledsoe who invited the General to stay in his stately country home, *Spring Hill*. Sam accepted the invitation and the warm Sunday afternoon in May was the perfect setting for Mrs. Bledsoe's strawberry festival. Beautiful eighteen-year-old Emily Antoinette was given the honor of being the General's hostess for the event. During the festivities, Sam inquired about a beautiful brown-haired girl with violet eyes, who turned out to be Emily's older sister. Having married at eighteen, Emily was concerned her twenty-two-year-old sister Margaret would end up an old maid, and decided to become a matchmaker. She arranged for her sister to bring strawberries for the General and when Margaret offered him the plate, Emily would introduce them. As Sam and Emily strolled through the rose garden, the lovely Margaret approached, carrying a dish of strawberries.

"General Houston, my sister Miss Margaret Lea," Emily acknowledged with pride.

Sam bowed his tall frame exceptionally low as he responded, "I'm charmed."

Houston was not just being polite. He had never seen a woman so beautiful as Miss Margaret Lea. Her features were delicate; her complexion fair, and her placid violet eyes mesmerized Houston. It was love at first sight for Sam. He plucked a rose from the garden and gently placed it in Margaret's hair, and from that day forward, Sam found time on several occasions to be alone with her. They took long walks together as Sam spoke of his beloved Texas and recounted the battle of San Jacinto. Margaret shared how she had been in the crowd of 5,000 on Sunday, May 22, 1836 when the wounded hero arrived in New Orleans. She recalled how weak and pale he was as he had to be assisted from his cot to the gunwale to address the crowd. Margaret related his comments word for word: "My kind physicians say I should not speak, yet I must thank you for your sympathy for Texas. But fellow citizens, remember while Texas has conquered Santa Anna and his bloody soldiers, she has another grander victory to gain before she is really free and great; she must conquer herself, her passions, and her sins. And in this second greater battle, Texas needs to recruit great numbers of pious women and ministers of the gospel." He then collapsed and was carried unconscious to the coach of his friend, William Christy. No one expected he would survive his wounds. With tearful emotion, Margaret recalled how, as she had watched him carried off that morning in May, she had a premonition she would one day see him again.

Before Sam left Mobile, he asked the brown-haired beauty to be his wife and she accepted. The night before he was to return to Texas, Major Towns held a barbeque in Houston's honor. The gathering took place in an oak grove adjoining the graveyard of the Siloam Baptist Church. As "President of the Day", it was Major Towns' responsibility to offer a toast. When he stood to speak, he focused his attention on young Margaret, the daughter of his dear friend, Temple Lea. Raising his glass, he said, "To the Conqueress of the Conqueror." No one in the audience, not even Margaret could possibly have known how prophetic the Major's words were. Margaret had already made it clear to Houston that his drinking would cease once they were married, and her deep Christian faith would become Sam's source of strength in defeating the demon of whiskey.

As Sam left Mobile, his heart was overflowing with joy. Unfortunately, his return to Texas would not be a happy one as tragedy more deplorable than he could have ever imagined was awaiting his return. Lamar sent troops to slaughter all the Cherokee who did not voluntarily relocate outside of Texas, and eighty-four-year-old Chief Bowles was shot and killed in cold blood. When Houston went to the site, he found Chief Bowles still clutching the sword Sam had given him as a birthday present. The man who gave him the name "The Raven" had been killed because he would not move off of his land, which, by all rights, was more his than Lamar's. The Raven wept bitter tears for the inhumane slaughter of his Cherokee family. He later gave an impassioned speech in Nacogdoches stating that, without any doubt "the Bowl was a better man than those who murdered him." White men were not accustomed to hearing such outrageous thoughts and Sam infuriated the audience. Even his close friends, Adolph Sterns and Henry Ragruet were extremely angered by his speech, but Sam stood by his statements. Sam Houston was not a man to abandon his moral convictions to pander to prevailing sentiment.

During his campaign, President Lamar had been in favor of annexation. One month after his election, the Union pulled the offer of statehood off the table. Their action angered the insecure Lamar and caused him to feel shunned by the Union. After that, he vehemently opposed annexation and started to push an agenda of Texas remaining an independent Republic. Like his namesake, expansionism became Mirabeau Bonaparte Lamar's agenda. He developed a grand vision that Texas would control more land than the United States by ultimately expanding its boundaries to the Pacific Ocean. There was one small problem standing between him and his dreams of expansion—money. When Lamar had taken office, the Republic's debt was only 190-thousand dollars. With his ambitious schemes and wild spending, the debt swelled to over 5-million dollars, coins disappeared from circulation, and everyone lost confidence in Texas currency. Without Houston's stability standing behind investments in Texas' future, potential investors dried up and the economy became dangerously weakened.

Lamar began squabbling with Mexico. His poking and jabbing was pushing Mexico to the verge of coming back across the Rio Grande. Shortly after Lamar became president, Houston became a member of Congress and was well aware that Lamar's actions were putting Texas in jeopardy. Sam could not stand by and let him destroy the Republic, so he joined forces with Anson Jones and brokered a settlement with Mexico, keeping Texas out of another war. Had not Houston and Jones moved with alacrity, the Mexicans would have poured across the Rio Grande in unstoppable numbers.

It must be said that not all of Lamar's term was negative. He enticed Britain and France to take an interest in investing in Texas. During Houston's tenure, the Europeans had not been aggressive in dealing with the Republic. Foreign governments viewed President Houston's Texas as an extension of *Jacksonian* policy, whereas Lamar made it very clear that he was not about to suddenly take Texas into the Union. The British helped with Mexico, and the French talked of colonizing nine thousand settlers along the shores of Corpus Christi. France was considering a very large loan to the Republic; a loan Houston would not have been able to secure because of his ties to the Union.

Congressman Houston stayed in the capital in Austin more than Lamar did. He knew the struggling Republic needed men like himself, Maverick, and Jones. They would hold the Republic together until Sam could regain control of the presidency and finish the job he had begun in his first term. That is, if they could keep a lid on Lamar.

The clash of wills between Houston and Lamar was blowing divisively across Texas. Could the Republic survive a bitter battle between the current and former presidents? Would the debate be settled in a duel? Would civil war erupt between the pro-Houston and pro-Lamar factions? The Republic was split down the middle like a ripe watermelon.

Chapter Seventeen
Together

As the sun sank below the horizon, Hays motioned to proceed into the city. San Antonio was already in shadow as lantern light guided the weary group toward the Military Plaza. The locals came out to greet them as they rode into town. When Millie dismounted, it was Mary Maverick who embraced her first, saying, "I will have it no other way. You and the children are staying with us."

Millie was taken aback by the hospitality. A total stranger was reaching out to her with arms full of love. "I don't know what to say," Millie responded softly.

"Say nothing," Mary answered. "Our home is yours. We will get you and the children fixed up with some new clothes, and we'll clean and dress your cuts and scratches. You don't have to say anything, unless you feel like talking. I can only imagine the ordeal you have endured. I am so sorry, Millie." Mary stomped the ground in a gesture of deep disgust. "I hate those redskins. They are not human; they are animals."

Millie turned to Jack Hays and said, "Jack, thank you and please thank your men for all the kindness you have shown us. Please thank Craig and the others for giving my sweet Johnny a proper Christian burial."

"No thanks needed Ma'am. Just wish we could have reached the Comanches before they found your family. I'll be in town if you need anything. I have some business to do before I go back to Uvalde and should be here for most of next week."

With that said, the family was scurried off to the warmth and safety of the Maverick's home where Mary's slaves drew a hot bath for Millie. This was the first time in her life she had bathed in a four-legged tub and she marveled at the luxury. By the time Millie finished soaking, Mary had laid out new clothes and a new pair of shoes for her and each of the children.

Young Bud Miller was the talk of the town, a rising star among the citizens of San Antonio. They admired his courage and willingness to fight so fiercely at his young age. One man was heard to say, "I hear young Miller is another Jack Hays." An older ranger told everyone what a great shot Bud was, having witnessed Bud take down an Indian brave at 150 yards at a dead run. Jack Hays added, "That boy can cover my back any day." Ranger Noah Smithwick said, "Bud Miller was as cool as the underside of a pillow during the battle. He's a keeper."

Bud rented a small room at Juanita Salinas' home. The ebony-haired Juanita was a widow in her mid-forties, known throughout the city for her warm, eager smile. Santa Anna had killed Juanita's husband Poncho for sympathizing with the Texans' cause. Her family in Mexico had disowned her. To survive, she rented out a room, took in laundry, sold eggs, milk, butter and homemade bread. The room she rented to Bud was actually a shed built on the back of her little stone house. Juanita had two rules: The room kept clean, and no female guests allowed at any time. Juanita was very firm about her rules. One morning Bud started to leave with his bed unmade, but after Juanita finished lecturing him, he never made that mistake again.

Bud took a job at the local livery stable mucking stalls and currying the horses. Noah taught him the farrier trade and Bud was able to pick up extra money shoeing horses. The pay was minimal, but working at the livery provided shelter for Lightning and gave Bud time to practice his shooting skills every day. Each afternoon, across the river near the Alamo, one could find young Miller shooting at tree stumps while spurring Lightning to a dead run.

Noah set up logs forty yards apart for Bud to practice, and within a month, he was able to ride full out and shoot the logs dead center. Noah increased the difficulty by placing small white dots on each log. Soon Bud was hitting the dots dead center. Next, Noah taught him how to drop down to the side of his horse, only one foot and hand exposed, and fire his pistol or short rifle from under the neck of his mount. Bud practiced this maneuver from both sides of his horse until ambidextrous shooting became natural. His final challenge was to develop the ability to reach to the ground and pick up a hat, coat, gun, and finally, a silver dollar while at a dead run on horseback. This skill could mean the difference between life and death. In a battle, it could be necessary to reach to the ground and grab a knife or gun without stopping.

Maria Varcinez was working at the *Buckhorn Saloon* when she overheard someone mention the name Bud Miller. Her heart skipped a beat. Her mind raced. Could it be Bud was in San Antonio? If so, would she see him? Maybe he would not want to see her. Maria was now seventeen and still strikingly beautiful. Her job had not made her bitter or haggard in her appearance like so many of the young girls in her profession. She held tightly to the dream that someone like Bud Miller would rescue her from her life of degradation. When she spotted Noah Smithwick standing at the bar, knowing he was a ranger, she approached him and asked, "Do you know a young man named Bud Miller?"

"Know him, sure as God made little green apples, I know him. Frankly, I don't see Bud as the type to hang out in a saloon though. As long as I've been around the boy, I've never heard one word of profanity from his lips nor seen him take strong drink. He is a rare breed, bright as a new dollar and sharper than a barber's razor. Why do you ask?"

Maria shrugged her shoulders. "I knew him in Galveston. Well, I didn't really *know* him. I baked him a cake while he was in jail for killing Hector Garza. I didn't know what happened to him after he got out of jail. Then I moved here because things were getting pretty rough in Galveston; too many rowdy and filthy seamen coming to the island." She paused, as if trying to figure out what to say next, and continued, "I honestly didn't think I'd ever see Bud again. Then I heard people talking about what a hero he was in the recent fight with the Comanches. I saw his bravery with my own eyes in Galveston."

Noah smiled. He didn't know about the Hector Garza incident or anything about Bud being in jail. Maybe he had misjudged the boy after all. "I'll run him down and tell him you are wanting him to drop in," Noah assured her. "But first, tell me more about this Hector Garza and about Bud being in jail."

Maria felt she had opened her mouth foolishly, and replied, "Oh, it's nothing. Really."

Noah shot back with fire in his voice. "Nothing my boots! They don't just throw a man in jail for nothin'. What's the story?"

Maria sat down on a barstool next to Noah so she could speak in a hushed voice. "Hector was one of the meanest Mexicans to walk the streets of Galveston. He was trying to kill old Baron de Bastrop and Bud stepped between them. Bud pulled out his pocketknife and jabbed it in Hector's heart. It was self-defense. I was standing across the street and saw it all. Garza would have killed them both if Bud had not stopped him. Sometime later, a friend from Galveston told me that Bud and Hector's brother were in a duel. Ramon Garza shot first, but missed. Bud could have killed Garza, but spared his life and instead, only shot his hand. I can tell you this: Bud Miller is no killer. I just wish he would notice me. He will make some lucky girl a wonderful husband."

Noah had just learned more in five minutes with Maria than he had in all the time he spent training Bud and going on the Indian campaigns with him. Noah had heard what a villain Hector Garza was. For young Bud to kill him in a hand-to-hand fight had to have been worth the price of admission. Then defeating Ramon Garza in a duel? Noah now had a better understanding of the gallantry Bud displayed in battle and why the President had recommended a boy so young for ranger service.

Several of the children in town came to play with A.D. and Ruthann. Ruthann played, but never said a word and only occasionally did a faint smile cross her dispirited face. One day, a young playmate gave Ruthann a tattered rag doll and from that moment on, she clung to it everywhere she went, even bringing the frayed toy to the dinner table. Mary Maverick made sure Millie also stayed active, understanding that her mind was sure to focus on horrendous memories if she had too much time to think. Three months had passed when Mary felt it was time for Millie to meet some of her friends. The group included Mrs. Higginbotham, Mrs. Smith, Mrs. Jacques, and Mrs. Elliott. Mrs. Higginbotham was Mary Maverick's closest friend and each night they would listen to the Greek man's wife play the piano or take strolls together. The two insisted that Millie join them. Millie was grateful for the love and acceptance Mary and her friends showed her, and slowly began to regain her equilibrium.

James "Dog" Willingham was a tall man, standing over six-foot-two with strong arms and a handsome rugged face. The nickname "Dog" had been given to him as a youngster when his father bragged to friends that when they went hunting, Jim could smell deer tracks. Jim was a rare individual for Texas; he didn't drink and he attended church whenever he was in town. He was aware of Millie Satterwhite and knew her husband had died in a brutal Indian attack. Being single was not the life for Jim and he finally got the nerve to ask Mary Maverick to introduce him to Millie. Mary came alive when Jim approached her about an introduction. Sam had raved about what an honorable man Dog Willingham was on many occasions, and Mary was sure the decent, God-fearing man from Tennessee would be a wonderful match for Millie. Millie had spoken often of returning to her farm, and Mary knew having a man on the place would make it safer, and especially young A.D. would benefit greatly from having a man around.

Mary planned a dinner for twelve. She made sure that Millie and Jim were the only two unmarried guests and seated them across from each other at the dinner table. Mary set it up ahead of time that once they were seated, Sam should bring up the subject of Millie's land. Right on cue, Sam said, "Millie, as soon as Jack Hays can go survey your land, I can record the title. How does that sound to you?"

Millie was speechless. Her stunned expression told the story. Finally, she was able to respond with a question. "Is that possible? I thought Johnny had to fight in the war for the land to be ours."

"Yes, and he did, in a way. He was fighting Indians when he was killed and thus, he died fighting the enemy. It's just a matter of the way I worded things for the court. Since the judge is a good friend, he was easily persuaded. Texas needs people like you. We need framers who love the land and will raise families and help us build our great Nation."

"Well, we didn't start out to fight Indians, but Johnny did kill two."

Sam grinned. "Good enough. As an Indian fighter, he is entitled to 460 acres. From what Mary tells me, you have about that much land with a house and barn already on it. It sounds like I did the right thing. I'll get Jack Hays to set your boundaries. You can trust him to pick the very best."

Jim sat silently, glancing at Millie as much as he could during dinner without being too obvious. Finally, he offered, "I'd be happy to go along. With the Comanches on the prowl, Jack can always use an extra gun."

Millie had noticed Jim when he first entered the Maverick home. She thought how handsome he was when he took his seat at the table and had felt a tinge of guilt. Mary understood Millie would be reluctant to get into a relationship so soon; however, men like Jim Willingham didn't grow on trees. It wasn't easy for a widow to find a good husband, especially if Indians had defiled her. It took a real man to understand Indian torture was no reason to shun a woman. Jim Willingham was just such a man.

Mary winked at Mr. and Mrs. Elliott, signaling it was time for them to say goodnight. Shortly after they excused themselves, the Jacques' got a wink, and they too made apologies for leaving early. The Smiths then followed them. This left only the Mavericks, the Higginbothams, and Millie and Jim. Mary suggested they go into the long room where the seating was more comfortable and Jinny would serve them steaming coffee and teacakes.

Jim was shy, but Sam gently nudged him into conversation about why he came to Texas and what were his hopes and dreams for the future. Sam, being a great lawyer, had no trouble getting the young man to open up. Jim started out making small talk, but before he knew it, he was sharing with everyone his dream of having a farmstead and a family. He talked about how his folks were sharecroppers back in Tennessee and how he believed that if a man worked hard, he could succeed and even prosper in the vast Republic of Texas. Millie listened intently as Jim spoke. He made several statements that verified to her that he understood and loved farming and possessed a strong work ethic, just as her Johnny had. He spoke eloquently about his love for children, bringing tears to Millie's eyes. She slipped her handkerchief to her nose and discreetly wiped a tear from her cheek.

Breaking into the conversation, Mary said, "Millie has some of the best land in the state. With Sam getting her title, the property will soon be hers, free and clear. I bet she could use a good hand to work the farm."

Millie blushed as it became obvious what Mary was doing. "But Mrs. Maverick, I don't have any money to pay a gentleman like Mr. Willingham," she responded.

Not to be deterred, Mary continued, "I'm sure Jim would be willing to work the farm as a sharecropper, right Jim?"

Jim had not expected things to progress so rapidly. His answer came in short breaths. "I'd be pleased to do anything I can to help Mrs. Satterwhite and her children. I've gotten to know little A.D. and he is a fine lad. I could live in the barn. I don't know what people would say about it and all, but as long as we know in God's eyes we are moral people, I can see no reason not to."

The speed at which Mary moved things along stunned the Higginbothams and even Sam. He had seen his wife in action before, but this might be a record.

Mary turned to Millie and bluntly asked, "What are your thoughts about having a worker like Jim come and help with the place?"

"I, I, well, errr, I can't see why it wouldn't work. Mr. Willingham might not like my cooking. I can't cook like Jinny." The room filled with laughter.

Mrs. Higginbotham replied, "Honey, no one cooks like Jinny. Cooking won't be the problem. The question is can you allow yourself to let another man live on the land you and Johnny picked out?" Knowing how close Millie and Johnny had been, what Mrs. Higginbotham was really wondering was if Millie could allow herself to care for another man.

Sam finally broke into the conversation. "Johnny, God rest his soul, is gone. It's time Millie dear that you think about yourself and the children. I have to be honest. It would not be possible for you and A.D. to manage the farm alone. You will need a good man, and honest men like Jim here are not in abundance. I suggest my dear friends the Higginbothams go home and get a good night's rest. Mary and I plan to do the same because I have to be up very early. Millie, you and Jim can sit in the parlor and get to know each other. It just might be that the two of you will be able to come to a working agreement."

Once everyone had left the long room, Millie and Jim sat, neither saying a word. Jinny came in to refill their coffee and asked, "Whut da madder? Da cat done got yur tongue? Honey child, you ain't gonna do no good tills ya open yur mouth."

Jim spoke first. "Mrs. Satterwhite, I know this has put you in an awkward position, and I apologize. I'm afraid this is entirely my fault. I told Mary that I was very interested in meeting you. The first time I saw you, I knew I wanted to meet you. Then later I learned of your ordeal and my heart was deeply touched. Mrs. Satterwhite, I would love to come and work your farm. If you never come to love me, I would be content being your farmhand. Seeing you every day would satisfy me for the remainder of my days."

Millie interrupted, "I hope you don't mind, but I need to talk with my son and daughter and see what they think of this arrangement. As for me, I would be honored to have you help us work our farm. I know you are a gentleman by the way Mary and Sam Maverick respect you."

Jim "Dog" Willingham made sure he was at Church thirty minutes early each Sunday so when Millie and her children arrived, he could sit with them. A.D. had become very fond of Jim and so had his mother. Millie loved Jim's tender way with the children. Little Ruthann continued to have problems from the abuse she had suffered at the hands of the Comanches. She refused to speak until one day after church when Jim asked if they would like some homemade ice cream. Little Ruthann smiled, and to the astonishment of everyone, replied with a soft "yes." Millie and the children hadn't eaten ice cream since Johnny had chipped ice from a frozen creek and fashioned ice cream to celebrate their arrival on Texas soil.

Jim continued, "At the edge of town, there is a doctor from Russia. The Emperor sent Dr. Weideman to Texas to do research. Well, last winter he had several wagonloads of ice hauled down from a lake near Austin. You know, up where the weather gets mighty cold. He stored the ice in his cellar and still has some left. Last week he needed some work done on his place and I agreed to do the job for the payment of one block of ice. I borrowed Mary Maverick's ice cream freezer and it's at my place right now. What do you say, A.D. and I go pick up the ice and you girls meet us at my cabin?"

Millie made a mixture using rich cream verging on butter, several eggs, sugar and vanilla extract. Jim and A.D. took turns sitting on the freezer while the other cranked the handle. Jim continually added salt to the ice and in about twenty minutes, they had some of the most magnificent vanilla ice cream any of them had ever tasted. After two huge helpings, Ruthann spoke again, saying, "Mr. Willingham, thank you for letting me know what real ice cream tastes like. Now I know why my pa was always talking 'bout how good it is."

Millie broke down and cried at hearing Ruthann speak. Jim moved to her side and placed his massive arms around her. In front of the children he said, "I would love to have you as my family. I know I should wait a few more months, but I am overcome with the desire to care for you. I know I can never replace Johnny and I won't try, but I'll care for the children like they were my own." Jim turned and spoke directly to the children. "I promise to love, honor and protect your beautiful mother and both of you." He then looked back at Millie and softly asked, "Will you three marry me?"

Millie looked at the children for their approval. Ruthann answered by rushing to Jim, grabbing his leg and squeezing with all her might. A.D. gave a broad grin of approval. Turning to Jim, Millie gave a warm smile and answered, "Jim, I would love to be Mrs. James Willingham. It would be an honor to share the remainder of my life by your side."

As the days passed waiting for Jack Hays to survey the land, Jim became a regular guest at the Mavericks, spending the evenings talking about the farm and the improvements Millie felt needed to be made. Finally one night Millie brought up the subject about a marriage date and expressed some concern. "Jim, what do you think people will say when we get married? You know they will talk because I was captured by the savages."

Jim leaned over, and placing his hands on her knees, he strongly answered her question. "Who cares what people think! What you and the children think is all that matters. I would marry you tonight. Why don't we find a minister tomorrow and start the tongues really wagging?"

Millie reached down and squeezed Jim's powerful hand as her eyes filled with tears. "My dear Jim, I want nothing more than to be your wife. You know Mary and everything she has done for the children and me. It would break her heart if she did not get to host our wedding."

From that evening forward, Millie glowed. A smile never left her face. Mary Maverick took charge of all the wedding arrangements, and made sure Millie had a fine new dress to wear and the children were properly attired. The Ladies Club supplied the flowers and several of the local ladies prepared food for the reception.

Finally, the day arrived. The wedding was attended by almost all of San Antonio. A.D. gave his mother away, and Ruthann and Millie each carried a bouquet of roses cut from Mary Maverick's garden. Mary and the women cried and even the minister's eyes filled with tears of joy. Weddings were common, but this was not an ordinary ceremony.

Mary Maverick made a list of things Millie had mentioned needing and passed it around to all the locals. As the new family prepared to leave San Antonio, their wagon was brimming with sugar, flour, seeds, coffee, gunpowder and lead. Mary gave bolts of cloth and an abundant supply of needles and thread to Millie. A local dry goods store gave each child a new pair of shoes. As they pulled out onto the Camino Real, townsfolk lined the streets to bid the family farewell. An Army unit, headed to Nacogdoches to quell a feud, escorted the family most of the way to their farm. If not for the military escort, Millie would have seen Indians behind every bend in the road.

Jim and Millie left the army unit and took a small trail north to the farm. After they crossed the Little River, Jim looked at the survey plot for the first time. To his amazement, the parcel actually measured 563.4 acres. The land reached from both riverbanks to the edge of the heavy woods. At that moment, he knew he could earn a living for his new family and have plenty of corn and cotton to barter.

As they neared the farmhouse, the hounds sprang from the wagon and took off after a jackrabbit. To everyone's surprise, the cattle were still on the farm and a baby heifer had been added to the herd. The chickens had also survived by roosting in the barn, and there were several new chicks. Millie could not hold back the tears as they pulled up in front of the farmhouse that she and Johnny had built. Jim placed his strong arms around her and pulling her close, whispered, "Darlin', it's alright to cry. I understand your sadness at arriving back at your homestead. I know your loss and your deep love for Johnny and I want you to take all the time you need to grieve. He was a great man and one I don't expect to replace. What you and I have is different. I'll not try to replace Johnny. I'm just plain ol' Jim, 'Dog' Willingham from out near Memphis, Tennessee."

To Jim's astonishment, the place was even better than he could have imagined. Johnny had chosen a prime tract of land. He was either extremely lucky or wise beyond his years in choosing the property. There was no way Indians could fight their way through the mass of trees that surrounded the farm, and the Brazos River to the east was too swift to cross. The only easy access was from the San Gabriel River to the south.

Jim quickly went to work building a split-rail fence around the field and a bigger barn. One of their wedding gifts was a well pump with extra leather washers and two hundred feet of pipe. Jim and A.D. dug a well so Millie wouldn't have to trudge down to the river for water.

Contentment seemed certain and prosperity locked down tight as the family settled in, but a darkening storm was gathering south of the Rio Grande that would threaten to tear their peaceful life asunder.

Chapter Eighteen
Murder

Lonely and tired, the Baron de Bastrop made several stops on his return trip to Galveston Island. Not having young Bud to talk to left an unfamiliar void in the old man's heart. He wasn't expecting such a reaction. Why should he? For so many years, no one had been able to penetrate his thick shell. Young Bud Miller had worked his way into the Baron's hardened old heart, a heart now weary and causing him to contemplate his mortality. Fainting spells and shortness of breath were becoming more frequent now. He knew his days were getting shorter and it was time to make things right with his Maker.

Stopping in the community of Heartright, the Baron collected twelve hundred dollars owed him from a land transaction. This gave him the currency he needed to pay the storage fees and hire a wagon to transport his merchandise to Bastrop. He would pay off the *Brass Monkey* and Mrs. Garner at the boarding house. He would send a messenger to find young Miller and alert the boy to his inheritance. Perhaps Bud would work with him in the store and learn the business before he was summoned home. That night by the campfire, the Baron removed a small pad from his pocket and jotted down what he would bequeath to Bud. He would leave his land to the boy who had become like a son to him. He willed his books to Mrs. Garner and his horsehide satchel to Mr. Treptow.

The next day, the Baron stopped in Houston to pick up supplies and have attorney Jack Patrick formally draw up his will. He turned down an invitation for female company, but did treat himself to a hearty dinner, and indulged in a hot bath and a good night's sleep at the Mann Hotel. No bed in Texas was more comfortable than the goose down featherbeds provided by Pamela Mann.

When the ferry docked at Galveston wharf, the Baron was the first one off and he headed straight for Mildred Garner's place at a gallop. Mildred was standing at the front door with both hands on her hips as she watched the Baron enter her front gate. She was ready to blast him when he beat her to the punch, saying, "Greetings Mrs. Garner. I indeed have wonderful news for you. In my pocket is sufficient capital to retire my past due bill and pay for a month's boarding in advance."

Mildred Garner was floored. Not knowing exactly how to react, she answered, "Why thank you. It is wonderful to have you as my guest again. Please come in. I'm making dinner and I do believe it's your favorite, country fried ham with brown gravy, and German chocolate cake for dessert."

While the will was fresh on his mind, the Baron asked Mrs. Garner to hold a copy just in case something happened to him. He assured her that he was in perfect health, but instructed her to make sure Bud received the document in the event of his untimely demise.

At the boarding house dinner table that evening, all the faces were unfamiliar to the Baron. He noticed the accent of one of the men as being Dutch. Though it had been many years since he had fled his native country, the Baron was a bit paranoid and anxious to find out if the man had been sent to locate him. Like a cat, his curiosity got the best of him. In his best "Texan", the Baron addressed the Dutchman asking, "Whut brung you to this neck of the woods?"

The stranger stood and removed his pistol from his belt and placed it on the table before speaking. "Please forgive my rudeness, Mrs. Garner. I had been unaware that you didn't allow firearms at your dining table. I just noticed the sign attached to the door." Then he turned to the Baron and answered, "You ask a fair question. I am here looking for a man wanted in my country."

The Baron's appetite waned and he even turned down a slice of Mildred's German chocolate cake. He had opened the door and now he wished he hadn't.

The Dutchman posed a question. "You lived in Texas long?"

Mildred, pouring more coffee in one of the guest's cups, answered for the Baron. "He has been here longer than anyone you will meet." Turning to the Baron, she asked, "When did you come, 1817?"

The Baron coughed and quickly answered, "1820, I didn't get here 'til 1820."

The Dutchman inquired further. "So you have been here forty years or almost that long? You must know everyone in Texas. How fortunate for me to meet you so quickly after my arrival."

The Baron decided to end the suspense and see if he could find out who the big Dutchman was looking for. "If I can help you locate this fugitive, I'd be happy to do so," he offered.

"You might just be able to do that," the Dutchman replied.

The Baron turned white as he wondered: Had he been tracked down? Would the Republic allow him to be extradited? Had there even been time for Texas to draw up extradition documents with other countries?

The Dutchman continued, "I'm looking for a man who murdered the King's favorite nephew, his sister's only son. He is a tall blonde-haired man with a thick beard and ice-blue eyes. I would guess he is twenty-two or twenty-three years old. I tracked him to New Orleans, and based on reliable sources there, I was informed he had moved to Texas."

"I think the young man you are looking for was a guest of mine two weeks ago," Mildred answered. "He acted nervous and asked if anyone had been in town looking for a stranger. I knew he must be in some trouble, but we Texans try to mind our own business. Live and let live, you know."

The Dutchman solicited, "Do you have any idea where he may have gone? It's my job to bring him back home either alive or with his ears in my baggage. From my point of view, dead would be easier."

After discovering the stranger was not looking for him, the Baron decided he would take a piece of Mildred's German chocolate cake after all. For the moment, he was blissfully unaware that much larger problems were looming in his future. There had been three men at the ferry looking for odd jobs when the Baron disembarked. The trio followed him to Mrs. Garner's and waited outside until they were sure he rented a room, then quickly left to notify their associate, Ramon Garza.

Ramon blamed his brother's death on the Baron. Had the Baron paid Hector, there would never have been a confrontation and Bud would not have interceded. Had Bud not interceded, Hector would not be dead, there would have been no duel, and Ramon would still have his right hand. In Ramon's mind, culpability for everything that had happened laid squarely at the doorstep of the Baron de Bastrop. Ramon had a score to settle and now was the time, and Galveston Island the place.

After dinner, most of the men retired to the long room to warm by the fire and have a smoke. No sooner had the Baron pulled out his Cuban cigar than he noticed a first edition copy of *Oliver Twist* lying on the table. How would such a new book find its way from England to Texas in less than a year? He assumed the book must belong to the Dutchman. The Baron picked up the book and, as was his custom when he stayed in a boarding house, began reading aloud. Soon, all the men pulled their chairs in closer to listen to him read.

Ramon's limp, blackened hand dangled from his wrist. The skin had dried and darkened from lack of blood reaching the phalanges. Rather than remove the hand and wear a second hook, Ramon chose to let it hang lifelessly at the end of his arm as a reminder of the vendetta he needed to settle. Ramon was not thankful for Bud's gesture of sparing his life; nothing short of killing the Baron and Bud would satisfy him. Bud would have to wait, but they did have the Baron in their sights and that was a very good start.

Ramon and the other thugs didn't sleep; they drank Mescal and smoked hemp until almost daylight. They finally passed out and didn't wake up until after ten in the morning. They hastily checked their guns and made sure their powder was dry while Ramon, no longer able to use a gun, sharpened his hook on a grindstone before heading out to go "Baron hunting". They assumed the old man had left the boarding house by this time of the day, so they went to the storage warehouse to look for him. No one there had seen him. Next, they went to the livery stable and got lucky. The Baron had requested the attendant shoe his horse and told the stable hand he was going to the *Brass Monkey* and would return around noon.

The Baron crossed the street and was at about the exact location where Bud had killed Hector Garza when he heard footsteps clomping down the plank sidewalk behind him. He turned to see a half-dozen angry Mexicans running toward him. He knew he wouldn't stand a chance if he tried to make a run for it. Quickly pulling his pistol from his belt, he stood tall and slightly sideways to steady his aim. Raton the Rat was at the front of the group and Bastrop's shot hit him square between the eyes. He instantly fell to the ground. Instead of jumping over the "Rat" to pursue him, the group bent over to check their fallen friend, allowing the Baron time to reload his flintlock. When they stood up, he took one of them down with a single shot to the heart. He was attempting to reload for a third time when Snake's belt knife ripped into the old man's chest. As the Baron slumped over, Ramon took a swing at him with his sharpened hook, ripping the Baron's eyeball from its socket. Like a pack of wolves, they continued stabbing the Baron long after he had taken his last breath. The ghoulish gang then stood over his lifeless body and gloated. Ramon, noticing several people coming out onto the street, shouted, "We need to get off this island pronto."

Snake answered in Spanish, "Calm down. The Sheriff is scared of his own shadow. He will talk big, but won't dare arrest us. He never has and I don't expect him to have a sudden shot of courage."

Several locals quickly notified Sheriff Maples of the Baron's murder. They told the Sheriff they would be willing to testify in court as to what they had seen, but the Snake was totally correct about the Sheriff; he was a coward and had no intention of hunting down the ruthless killers himself. Instead, he wrote a letter to Sam Houston requesting the Texas Rangers be sent to Galveston to bring the men to justice. Meanwhile, Ramon and his gang walked the streets of Galveston with impunity. Some residents were outraged, while others believed Maples was correct in waiting for the rangers. After all, they were trained to handle such dangerous cases as this.

As the messenger was dispatched to deliver Sheriff Maples' letter to Sam Houston, the townsfolk planned a funeral for the Baron. Despite the fact that the Baron had swindled most of the townspeople in one way or another, there was still a great deal of affection for the old man. His charm had worked its way into the hearts of many of the citizens of Galveston.

Sheriff Maples found over $950 in gold coins in the Baron's waistband, more than enough to pay for a proper burial. As was his custom, Maples would pay $20 for a pine box, $5 for a plot of land, $2 for the gravedigger, and keep the rest of the money for himself. He also found a small notebook with several pages of instructions, which caused him to wonder if the Baron knew he was facing death. The pages were filled with information outlining his will. The notebook had lists of the properties the Baron owned, who he owed money to, and who owed money to him. One entry jumped out at the Sheriff. The page read:

> *"I bequeath my estate to Bud Miller. I need to draw up a will leaving my Bastrop home and land, new merchandise and money to this Kentucky lad, Benjamin Miller. He has captured my heart and replaced my dead son. This is the least I can do for the joy he has delivered to me since, by God's providence, he was placed in my care."*

In the Baron's side pocket, Maples also found a blood-soaked document drawn up by attorney Patrick Jack. The pages were stuck together; nevertheless, the intent of the will was legible.

By the time Sheriff Maples' letter reached Congressman Houston, the Baron had been laid to rest. Sam forwarded the message to Captain Jack Hays in San Antonio by way of his trusted helper, Timmy Marcum. Houston's note read:

Jack,

Muster you a group of rangers and go find Ramon Garza and his rubbish and rid the Republic of them once and for all. We don't need to go to the expense of a trial. Without the dear Baron de Bastrop, there would never have been a Republic. Moses Austin would never have been allowed to come here in the first place if not for the old man. He had his faults, but they are forgivable. Justice for his cold-blooded murder needs to be administered in haste. Sheriff Maples is a disgrace to the good people of Galveston, and unfortunately, he has made it necessary that you must go and do his job.

With his usual hefty signature, he signed the letter,

"Your friend, Samuel Houston"

Jack Hays was out of town on a survey job, but his landlady promised Timmy she would give him the letter as soon as he returned. Jack was gone for almost three weeks. Upon his return, tired and ready to sleep in a real bed for a few weeks, Jack found himself once again pressed into service. He felt eight men would be sufficient in tracking down and bringing the outlaws to justice and that Bud Miller would be a valuable addition because he could identify Garza. He also gathered up his brother William, Samuel Walker, "Big Foot" Wallace, Richard Gillespie and three other men.

"Big Foot" Wallace was a six-foot-two Virginian who tipped the scales at well over 230 pounds, and got his nickname because of his size 17 shoes. He was a seasoned Indian fighter with the strength of two men and the bravery of a lion. Jack wanted the cream of the crop for this mission. He felt indebted to the Baron. The Baron had given him many surveying jobs and assisted him in choosing a prime piece of property as payment for his service to the Republic.

Each ranger carried an assortment of guns and most had one form or another of a Bowie knife. Each kept a boot knife secreted away near their ankle. Their saddlebags were stuffed with gunpowder, lead, parched corn, tobacco, coffee, salt, sugar, a blanket and rain slicker, and a necessary staple, beef jerky. Jerky would not spoil and a traveler could carry a month's supply in his saddlebag without fear of the meat going bad. Each ranger also carried two ropes: a leather-plaited macate used by the Mexicans, and a hemp rope for catching horses. The ranger's motto was to travel light and fast.

On their third day out, Big Foot raised his hand and put his finger to his lips for the men to be silent. He listened for a moment, then dismounted and knelt down. Placing his ear to the ground, he listened for a few moments and then stood back up, saying, "Someone is approaching in a hurry from not too far behind. I suspect they are in trouble to be pushing a horse that hard. We need to go back and intercept them and find out what's going on."

Without hesitation, Jack shouted an order to William and Big Foot: "You two go back and find out why this rider is in such a hurry."

By the time William Hays and Big Foot backtracked to where the rider would cross their trail, he was within a hundred yards of them.

Earlier that morning, Peter and Agnes Pieper's two daughters had been playing on a swing Peter built for them under a massive oak tree when a band of Comanche slipped into the yard and kidnapped them. Their mother Agnes looked out the window just in time to see two Comanche snatch the girls, ages seven and nine and hand them to two other braves on horseback. Then they mounted in a flash, and were gone. She could only watch helplessly as her girls disappeared into the thickness of the forest.

Peter Pieper had arrived in Texas too late to fight in the Alamo or Goliad, but participated in the battle at San Jacinto. For his service to the Republic, he was allotted 320 acres of land. He later married Agnes, a widow with two baby daughters. Peter was a brick mason by trade and was getting more work than he could possibly handle. This morning, he was laying bricks on the Robert Lay Plantation.

Agnes waited until she was sure the Indians were gone, then saddled their fastest mule and galloped to the plantation. Peter was devastated by the news. The girls' capture could not have been more painful if they were his flesh and blood. How could lightning strike twice? The Comanches had massacred his first wife only weeks after they had moved into the little log cabin. Now the savages had returned and captured his girls.

He knew his only hope was to rescue his babies before they went deep into the hill country. He also knew the Indians would not ford a river unless necessary, but would remain between the Navidad and Lavaca Rivers until they had passed the headwaters. The Lay Plantation was located between the Lavaca and Navidad Rivers, about halfway from the headwaters north of Gonzales and Linnville, and the location worked to Peter's advantage. The Indians would be forced to travel a narrow path northward until they passed the rivers, making their tracks easier to follow.

Peter made ready for the ride of his life. Mr. Lay provided a superior horse, food, a blanket and a shotgun. Bobby then prayed, sending Peter off with God's blessings. Everyone knew he would need a miracle as he set out for La Grange to enlist the help of the Texas Rangers. Riding at a nice lope, so as not to wear out the big bay mare, Peter hoped to reach La Grange by the next morning. He knew he would be traveling faster than the Indians were. If he could reach La Grange in time, he and the rangers could cut them off before they reached the rocky mountain ranges of the hill country.

When Big Foot and William spotted Peter, William shouted, "Hey wait up."

Peter shouted back, "Thank God I found someone! I was praying for a miracle and you look like angels from the Almighty."

Stopping in front of the two rangers, with tears streaming down his cheeks, Peter poured his heart out, telling them what happened.

"Come with us and let's see what we can do about your situation. You can fill us in as we go join the others," Big Foot assured him.

After hearing Peter's story, Jack said, "Mr. Pieper, time is all we have on our side. Once the Comanches leave the corridor between the two rivers, they will move northwest into no-man's land. It's my guess we are up ahead of them or we would have crossed their tracks coming this way. Perhaps they haven't crossed our path and are still east of us."

"What if they hadn't reached us by the time we went past?" asked Bud. "Mr. Pieper said his wife was on a fast mule and he is riding a strong mount. I have a gut feeling they are still behind us."

Big Foot contributed to the discussion. "The boy makes a good point. They wouldn't go east. It would be out of their territory. I think they would work their way more northwest. I'd bet my skinnin' knife they are lingering behind somewhere south of our path. We need to backtrack and if we don't pick up their trail, camp and wait."

Jack thought for a moment. "It's a gamble," he responded. "If we're wrong, then we lose several hours. But I'm inclined to agree with you both." Swirling around in his saddle, he asked the others, "Men, what to you think?"

Only Samuel Walker offered his opinion. "Like Big Foot said, Mrs. Pieper rode as fast as she could to give Mr. Pieper the news, and Peter wasted little time in getting on the road. I have no doubt we have passed ahead of 'em." He looked at Peter and asked, "On which side of your place in the Lay Plantation?"

Peter answered, "About twenty miles to the northeast."

Jack dug his spurs into his horse and waved his hand for the men to follow. They were going back in the direction of San Antonio. As he dashed out, he shouted, "Come on men, let's pray to God we are going in the right direction. We need to find their tracks while it's still light."

After covering almost twenty miles, they were beginning to doubt they had made the right decision when Samuel Walker, who had taken the lead, yelled, "Hallelujah. There they are, bigger than life."

When they examined the tracks, there was no doubt. The hooves were shoeless and to everyone's guess, the band numbered between sixty to seventy-five riders. The fresh dung told the rangers they were less than an hour behind them. From past experience in dealing with the Comanches, everyone agreed there were too many for the small ranger force to confront head on. Even if the number were only fifty, it still would be a formidable force for eight rangers. Since Peter was armed only with a shotgun, he would be of little help in a firefight. Besides, his mare was too tired to engage warriors on fresh mounts.

Bud asked, "Why can't we catch up with them, and after they fall asleep, sneak into their camp and steal the girls back? I've heard tell of rangers doing that."

"Other than being scalped alive, I can see no reason why it wouldn't be a good idea," William Hays said, laughing. Then he turned and pointed to Big Foot. "My friend, here is the ranger you heard about. He crawled in on his belly and rescued a young boy last year."

"No wait a minute," Jack interjected. "Bud's idea just might work. After a successful raid, the Comanche always have a celebration. I suspect they feel secure, thinking they have made a clean getaway. There is a good chance they will be drunk on mescal or drugged out on hemp and will be dead to the world by midnight."

Big Foot agreed, and turning to the others, asked, "Is it unanimous then?"

None of the men answered aloud, but all turned their horses in unison to follow the Comanche's trail. God smiled upon them as they tracked the Indians; the moon was full and the clouds dissipated and illuminated their path. Their plan was to catch up to the Indians an hour or so before midnight and free the girls after the band retired for the night. It was imperative they catch up to them and be in place when the last Indian fell asleep.

Jack kept the pressure on. He didn't want to wear the horses out because they would be needed for the escape, but speed was essential nonetheless. Peter's mare was growing tired so Samuel Walker suggested he cut back his pace. "We will catch up with them and hopefully have your daughters by the time you catch up to us. This mission won't depend on a gunfight. We either steal them tonight or wait until we amass a larger force. Rest assured Peter. We will get your babies back. Keep the faith and we will see you in a few hours."

Peter knew Samuel was right. If he didn't slow the mare down, she would give out and he would be on foot. Being a religious man, he prayed continuously, but could not suppress his intermittent bouts of anger: Anger at himself for not buying property closer to a community, anger that he had not hired a couple of male slaves to work his farm. They could have protected his family when he was away. He continued to be tormented by the "what ifs" as he watched the rangers' silhouettes grow smaller and smaller until they were completely out of sight.

Around midnight, Big Foot was riding point when he spotted a campfire. He slowed down so the others could catch up. He pointed up ahead and whispered, "That's them."

Richard Gillespie pitched in, "Yes, Yes. We have 'em! That's them shore as shootin'! They don't know they're being followed or they would not have a blazing campfire."

The rangers dismounted about a mile from the Indian camp and led their horses with their free hand ready to quiet them should one smell the Indians' ponies and begin to nicker. They were still a half-mile away when they heard the whooping and shouting of braves chanting victory songs as they circled the campfire. Leaving one ranger with the horses with instructions to keep them silent, Jack and the others moved to the edge of the bluff overlooking the Indian camp. They spotted the girls tied to a small Spanish oak located at the outer perimeter. Big Foot estimated the Indians numbered over sixty.

As the flames subsided, the braves drifted off to sleep, some on blankets and others on the bare ground. Jack whispered, "Men, I cannot command any of you to go down with me. That choice is yours to make. If just one brave awakens, there is no way we can escape. Our horses are too tired to run and we don't have the firepower to repel a serious charge." Looking at Bud, he continued, "Son, no one will think less of you if you remain on the bluff."

In a voice almost too loud, Bud answered, "Sir, if you don't mind, I'd like to accompany you. Let's face it. I'm the fastest of all of you. If anyone should go, it has to be me."

"Then it's settled," Gillespie interjected. "When Jack thinks it's safe, they will make their way down the side of the bluff. The five of us will stand guard on the ledge with our guns primed to take down any who might charge Jack and Miller."

About three in the morning, the last brave dropped off to sleep. Samuel Walker requested, "Men, let's pause for a minute to ask Christ our Lord to give us safe and successful passage."

All Peter could think of was reaching his babies. Ranger Tommy Jones spotted him and slipped out from behind the trees, waving his arms in the air. Peter saw him and slowed to a soft walk. Tommy whispered what was happening and suggested he dismount and give his mare a rest; she would be needed shortly. The two waited for a couple of hours, which seemed like an eternity. Peter wanted to check what was going on, but Tommy restrained him, knowing the stricken father might stumble or make a sound. With a mission of this nature, the element of surprise was the only thing the rangers had in their favor.

Jack Hays led the way as he and Bud slid quietly down the bank to level ground. Samuel Walker moved a long tree limb to the edge of the bluff and silently indicated that Jack and Bud could use the limb as a ladder. All of their communication was through signs. They were so close to the camp, they could not even risk a whisper.

The braves continued to snore, then suddenly one stirred just as they reached the sleeping girls. Jack and Bud froze with their hands on their pistols. The brave turned over and started to snore once more. With cat-like quickness, Jack pulled his clasp knife from his pocket. Jack and Bud simultaneously put their hands over the girls' mouths to muffle any sound they might make. Jack whispered, "Kate, Alice, we are friends of your mother and father, Peter and Agnes. We are here to take you home. Nod your head if you understand. Don't speak a word or we may all be killed."

Kate, the oldest, immediately nodded that she understood. Alice was too frozen with fear to react, but finally gave a faint nod up and down. In two swipes, Jack used his razor-sharp knife to slice through the main rawhide ties that held the girls together. Cutting the ties from their hands and legs would have to wait until they were on safe ground. Samuel scrambled to a firm spot on the clay bank as Jack and Bud tiptoed through the underbrush to the tree-limb ladder. The other rangers stood vigilant, guns primed, in the event the braves discovered what was taking place. Bud and Alice were sent up first and then Jack and Kate. Inside, each man was shouting, "Praise the Lord"; however, none uttered a word.

Once safely on the bluff, they ran with all their speed back to the horses. Peter grabbed the girls, holding them as if they were still one and three, the ages they were when he married their mother. God had protected the girls from harm; the savages had molested neither of them. They were two very lucky girls. Unfortunately, most females captured by Indians were not so fortunate.

Jack knew it could be only a matter of minutes before a brave might awaken and discover the girls were missing. "Mount up and follow the trail back south," he whispered. "Bud, you and William come with me. You have the fastest mounts. We are going to the north rim and fire into the camp. I want them to give chase northward in the direction of Austin and the hill country. We'll ride north just far enough to get them moving in that direction. Once we have them hot on our northbound trail, we will double back."

Jack then turned to Peter. "I know you want to carry the girls with you, but your mare cannot bear the burden. You will need to explain to them that they will have to ride with Richard and Samuel. Each has stronger and more rested mounts."

With those words, Jack swung his leg over his saddle and started in the direction of the north rim. Bud and William followed. The three walked their horses around the Comanche camp and slowly removed their Kentucky long rifles from their saddle scabbards. Each placed their guns in the seat of their saddles and took aim. "On the count of *three*, pick you out one and don't miss. We want them to have to deal with three dead redskins," Jack ordered.

On the count of three, their rifles belched fire, screaming in unison. Three braves were dead with a ball of lead in their brains. Quickly, the three rangers fired rounds from both of their belt pistols. Six direct hits, two fatal. In the wink of an eye, the rangers were mounted and on a dead run, shouting at the top of their lungs. They wanted the sound of their horses and their screams to be as loud as possible so the shocked Indians might think a larger group had ambushed them. Jack, Bud, and William kept the spurs to their horses and ran all out for about four hundred yards, then pulled back to a lope. After about a mile or so, they turned east for another two miles and then back down southwest to intersect with the Comanche's original trail. About an hour after the sun rose above the treetops, the three spotted fresh tracks. William's elation was obvious as he said, "We are not more than twenty minutes behind them, if that." It was another hour before the three made up the twenty minutes they were behind, and caught up with the extremely happy Peter Pieper and the other rangers.

Dealing with Indians for so long made Jack Hays a very cautious man. When the group reached a small creek, Jack instructed the men to veer off course and enter the water heading back north. He led the group about a hundred yards upstream and climbed out on the opposite bank. The group traveled two hundred yards and re-entered the water, this time turning south for almost two miles before exiting the creek again. Jack never took anything for granted. His motto: Always consider the impossible and the improbable and you will never be surprised.

When Jack felt it was safe to stop, he asked Walker to seek out a deer to eat. Samuel was gone less than twenty minutes when he returned with a nice young doe. They stuffed themselves then moved on another ten miles before finding a spot to sleep. The sun was just sinking below the horizon when they bedded down for the night. No one had difficulty going to sleep. Walker pulled the first watch. At midnight, he shook Big Foot awake, letting him know it was his turn. Bud slept until three, and then Big Foot woke him to stand guard.

In the morning, they ate parched corn and beef jerky for breakfast, and mounted up before daylight. Bobby, Norma Lee and Agnes were standing in the yard when the rangers, along with Peter and the girls, came trotting up the gravel road. The girls broke into tears when they saw their mother. Peter joined them, with tears pouring from his soulful eyes. Joy abounded at the Lay Plantation.

The rangers spent the night bedded down on the Lay's porch. After an early breakfast and many 'Thank yous' were exchanged, the rangers continued on to Galveston. They reached the Colorado River early in the afternoon. After crossing, Samuel and Richard went fishing. Richard always carried fishing line and fishhooks. The two were lucky enough to find a shallow wash where Samuel used his big hands to splash minnows to the shore and grab them before they could flounder back into the water. Using the minnows as bait, the two returned to camp with thirty big mouth perch, some weighing over a pound. After eating, the group moved about two miles from the river and made camp for the night. The horses grazed as the men organized their gear and made ready for a long ride the next day. Jack knew it would be a push, but once they crossed the Brazos at Thompson's ferry, the route to Galveston Bay would be easy going. With an early start, they should arrive in Galveston before nightfall.

Clear skies and rested horses allowed the group to make excellent time and they reached Galveston Bay at sunset. Big Foot yanked the bell for the ferry, to no avail. The ferry operator had gone home for the evening, so the men pitched camp and spent the night on the west bank of the Bay. The next morning, Big Foot swore two mosquitoes had tried to carry him off during the night. Bud had a good laugh. He had lived on the island long enough to be well acquainted with the size and abundance of mosquitoes in the area. Most of the men had wisely pulled their hats down tight over their faces and used their blankets to shield themselves. Big Foot had foolishly failed to cover his face, and when he awoke was covered with bites; the bloodsuckers had added him to their food supply. He learned an excruciating lesson about sleeping near the bay.

As they saddled up, the ferry pulled up to the dock. Once across the bay, Jack headed straight for Sheriff Maples' office. There he found a very angry Mayor Allen chastising the Sheriff for not apprehending the Baron's killers. The Mayor expressed his disgust that a coward like Maples could get himself elected sheriff. One of the major reasons Maples was able to become sheriff was because big Jim Brown had backed him. Jim was a very persuasive and influential man and was not averse to using his influence to get "his" people elected. He was known to brag: "It's just good business to own a Sheriff."

John M. Allen, no relation to the John Allen that settled the city of Houston, was a war hero at San Jacinto. He settled in Galveston and became Mayor despite Jim Brown's efforts to the contrary. No one could have been more pleased than Mayor Allen when Jack walked through the jailhouse door. He knew Jack Hays. They had both helped bury the men at Goliad, and traveling from San Jacinto to Goliad, John came to know and respect Jack and his brother, William.

"We have a situation here and we could use your help," Maples exclaimed.

"How many are we looking for and where might we find them?"

Mayor Allen sarcastically answered, "Walking the streets with no fear of being arrested by our dear Sheriff here. It's shameful. Thanks to our Sheriff, they will not be difficult to locate. They may just walk past here at any moment, without fear of being apprehended."

Not wanting to waste any more time with the cowardly Sheriff, Jack said, "I have young Bud Miller with me. He can identify this Ramon Garza fellow, and I suspect the other three will be with him."

Maples brightened up. "Bud's with you? Bring him in. I know my wife will want to see him. He is really a great boy. Too bad I had to lock him up."

Then reaching into his desk drawer, Sheriff Maples pulled out a small notebook and a gold watch. "This is stuff that I found on the Baron. In this book, he wrote that he wants Bud to have this watch and it appears he left Bud his house and small farm in Bastrop."

Jack reached over, took the watch and notebook, and grunted, "I'll make sure Bud gets the watch and we will have Sam Maverick represent the boy in court to convey the land deed. This is a good start for a deserving young man."

Jack pulled the stem and set the big hand to twelve on the 18k gold timepiece. Placing the notebook and watch in his pocket, Jack made the decision not to tell Bud about the Baron's death until after they apprehended the Garza gang.

"By the way Sheriff, did the Baron have any money on his body?"

Sheriff Maples lied. "Not that I could find. I also searched his room. It looks like to me he used his last dollar to pay Mrs. Garner. We all pitched in to bury him. I gave twenty dollars myself."

Mayor Allen entered the conversation. "That's strange. It's difficult to imagine the Baron not keeping some funds on his person. It's not like him to use his last dollar to retire a debt. I knew him well and he would rather owe than pay."

Maples stammered, "My thinking too. I figure those Mexicans robbed him."

Jack, William and Big Foot shook Mayor Allen's hand, ignoring the Sheriff as they exited the jail. Maples followed them to the door, he shouted, "Good to see you Bud."

Bud crossed his fingers behind his back and replied, "Same to you Sheriff." Then he uncrossed his fingers and added, "Please give my best to Mrs. Maples."

Mayor Allen had told Jack that the Garza gang normally hung out at a small bar on the Gulf patronized by riff-raff and sailors. The place was on Ocean Boulevard and appropriately called *The Hole in the Wall*.

With only one window, the saloon was dark and dank, smelling of unbathed men and whiskey. As the rangers entered, Jack asked, "Bud, do you see them?"

"Can't be sure. It's so dark in here."

As they moved through the bar, each ranger kept their hands on the handles of both belt pistols. Jack gave the order to shoot first and ask questions later. After checking every man in the place, Bud told his companions, "They are not in here."

Jack walked over to the bartender and looking at the burly man with his steel blue eyes, demanded, "Where can I find Ramon Garza?"

"Don't think I know the gent," the bartender answered coldly.

In a dizzying blur, Big Foot reached over, grabbed the bartender's shirt collar and slammed his face down hard onto the bar. "Try him again, Jack. And this time say pretty please," he bellowed.

Jack smiled, appreciating how effectively Big Foot could intimidate a man. "Please, pretty please. Tell me where I can find Ramon Garza and his gang. If you don't, I'm afraid I won't be able to control Big Foot. He just loves to kill and today may be shaping up to be your last one on earth. He might just pull you over the bar and beat you to death with his bare hands before I can stop him."

The bartender looked into Jack's eyes and could see he was not bluffing. Trying to squeeze out his answer while his neck was in the vice-like grip of Big Foot was not easy, but he finally squealed, "They were in here earlier. I heard one of 'em say a ship was comin' in with new arrivals. I suspect they are at the docks seein' who they can rob. I know they're short on funds 'cause I've had to carry their drinks on my books for the past couple a weeks."

Jack turned to Bud. "Know where the docks are?"

"Yep, sure do."

"Then let the gentleman go Wallace and let's go find what we came for."

The bartender's statement about the gang being broke validated Jack's suspicions that Sheriff Maples had robbed the Baron. Otherwise, Ramon and his men would not be seeking whiskey money.

As they headed out the door, the bartender hollered, "If they come in, can I tell 'em who was asking for 'em?"

Big Foot stuck his head back in the door and answered, "Yeah, the men who are arranging a meeting for them to meet their Maker, sooner rather than later."

There were more than a hundred people waiting at the dock as Garza and his men fixated on the ship, scanning the decks for an easy mark. The rangers moved slowly and discreetly through the crowd. Suddenly Bud punched Jack on the arm. "That's Ramon right over there. He's the one with the black hat and dark brown coat standing in between the big man with the black sock cap and the hump-shouldered thug in the raccoon hat."

Jack raised his hand, halting his men. He motioned for them to come in closer. "Here is what we are going to do. We are going to take a page out of the Comanche's book. We are going to overpower them. Bud, I want you in the middle, at Ramon's back. I don't want him to see you. We will use our horses to push the bystanders out of the way. If we are lucky, we can isolate them and never give 'em an opportunity to react."

Jack's plan worked to perfection. Some people were irritated to have a horse shove them away from the railing, but not after seeing the eight well-armed rangers. Samuel Walker moved up near the railing on the right side of Ramon as William Hays closed in on the left. They pushed their way up to where the muzzles of their horses were less than a meter from Ramon and his men. Sitting beside Walker was Big Foot and next to William was Richard. The other rangers filled in next to Bud and Jack behind Ramon. Suddenly, the four suspects were isolated from the rest of the crowd. Feeling closed in, Ramon turned and saw the eight men on horseback. Before he could say a word, he heard sixteen pistols cock. "What's this about? You want my hook in your horse's face?"

Jack heatedly replied, "I'm Texas Ranger Captain Jack Coffee Hays and we are here to arrest you for the murder of a true Texas hero, the Baron de Bastrop."

When Bud heard Jack's words, he turned ashen. His stomach clenched as his heart sank. How could this be?

Ramon gave Jack an arrogant look and snarled, "You planning to arrest us on murder charges?"

Big Foot answered his question with another. "Is a frog's butt water tight? Clean out your ears, Garza. We are not planning to arrest you; we are GOING to arrest you or carry you across our saddles deader than a doornail. I suggest all of you raise your hands and put them on top of your heads. Rest assured. None of us misses when we shoot. If my math is correct, we have sixteen pistols anxious to fire. I think that rounds out to four balls apiece for each of you boys."

Snake was the first to comply, followed by Ramon placing his hook and floppy hand on top of his brown felt hat. Big Ears thought for a moment about jumping the railing and trying to swim away. Then he noticed they were all carrying long rifles. Even if he could escape out of pistol range, they would kill him with their big guns. He too placed his hands on his head. Juan was the last to surrender.

Early the next morning, Sheriff Maples was making sure the gallows were in proper working order. He knew the locals would not wait for a judge to hand down a verdict for Garza and his men. A mob was already gathered outside the jail, wanting to take justice into their own hands. As Maples checked the gallows' trap doors, about forty men stormed the jail and dragged the four killers into the street. Someone in the mob shouted, "Welcome to the sunrise necktie party."

Maples started to protest, but backed off as the four men were dragged to the gallows. Ramon protested, "We are a nation of laws. You men are breaking the law. Sheriff Maples, tell this band of thugs they cannot hang us without a trial. This is anarchy."

Maples shot back, "I'm sure your words will have as much power as mine. They saw your pack of wolves kill the old man and now they want you to pay."

Once the hangman's noose was in place, someone in the crowd yelled, "Pull the lever! Pull it hard!"

As the undertaker moved his wagon into place, the quartet simultaneously disappeared through the floor hatches and jerked to a stop under the platform. The thirteen-loop hangman's knot, placed behind the left ear, violently snapped their necks to the right, breaking their cervical vertebrae instantly. Texas justice was swift for Ramon and his cohorts.

Ramon Garza's three sons and Hector's five children helplessly watched the execution as they clustered in the shadows. The oldest of the group related his thoughts to the others, saying,

"I say we don't sit back and let them kill our family without paying. Who do those Gringos think they are? They didn't even have the decency to have a priest present. We will take a blood oath to extract revenge."

Ramon's son made a suggestion. "We'll call our group 'The Blades'. This town thinks they know what fear is? They haven't seen anything yet. We will avenge what has happened here today."

Chapter Nineteen
Unraveling

President Sam Houston found himself busier than a barefoot boy on a fire-ant hill. Forming a new country was extremely complex, especially under such raw circumstances. Texas was flat broke. The infant Republic had no credit and no prospect to repay should some country miraculously grant them a loan. Houston's only hope was to get his friend President Andrew Jackson to annex Texas into the Union. Like a drowning man reaching for a straw in the middle of the ocean, Sam Houston was splashing with both arms, hoping to grab onto a miracle. He found himself at a carrefour with one road passing through President Jackson and the other through ex-president Adams. Andrew Jackson's term was about to expire, and with the departure of his mentor, Houston's chances of accomplishing annexation were about as slim as a snowstorm in Hades. In addition, Adams was now bitterly against Texas achieving statehood.

President John Quincy Adams, son of John Adams had been prepared to buy Texas from Spain in 1820. Serving under President Monroe, John Q. Adams was one of America's great Secretaries of State. He arranged with England for the joint occupation of Oregon, and obtained the cession of Florida from Spain. He was the driving force in formulating the Monroe Doctrine. Adams felt Texas would be the next prize, but when his efforts failed, he treated Texas like a spurned lover. Instead of continuing to work toward gaining another state, Adams became obsessed with preventing annexation and bellowed the slavery issue from steps and lecterns all over the northeast.

In the political tradition of the early 19th century, as Secretary of State, Adams was considered the political heir to the presidency. There was a clamor to change the way the president was elected to popular choice. With only one party, Republican factions developed, with each section nominating their own candidate. The northern candidate, Adams, received more votes than William Crawford or Henry Clay, but fell far behind General Andrew Jackson in both popular and electoral votes. With no candidate receiving a majority of electoral votes, the final decision went to the House of Representatives, where Henry Clay, whose views paralleled Adams', threw his support behind the New Englander. Jackson and his outraged followers charged corruption. Jackson's point of anger was justified; he was clearly the peoples' choice and the leader by a wide margin in the Electoral College, nevertheless, backroom wrangling had wrestled the presidency away from him.

Knowing he would face hostility in Congress, Adams confidently proclaimed in his first annual message a bold new national program. He proposed the Federal Government bring the states together with a network of highways, canals, using funds from the sale of public lands. Yet, he was no longer inclined to attempt to purchase Texas from Mexico. Texas annexation, the project near and dear to his heart only a few years earlier became an unwanted stray dog covered in ticks. Adams' hatred for Jackson spilled over into the annexation issue: If Jackson was for it, Adams was determined to be even more against it.

The fight between Adams and Jackson took on a personal tone of bitterness unparalleled in Washington. Normally, Adams was a passive, soft-spoken old man who walked with a cane and a small set of glasses on his nose. When he talked of Texas, his soft-spoken ways changed and spiked with hatred and vitriolic rage. His voice cracked as he ranted and raved. Friends were concerned about his mental health and Andrew Jackson sought ways to silence the vociferous ex-president. There was no law to prevent his outrage and it seemed no urging from friend or foe could get him to leave Washington. Adams was an elitist in the purest form, while Jackson, on the opposite end of the spectrum, was a backwoods country boy.

Shortly after the battle of San Jacinto, the news spread faster than a prairie fire with a tail wind. People in Washington spontaneously burst into thunderous celebration. Petitions began to surge in seeking recognition of Texas. Not long after the request for statehood emerged, John Adams rushed to the floor to denounce the Texas Revolution, venting, "The entire purpose of the revolution was to re-establish slavery in the territory where it had already been abolished through Mexican law." Then he bitterly attacked President Jackson for sending General Gains to the Texas border. "It was in defense of slavery Jackson sent Gains. Jackson is a slave monger and so is Gains."

One of Adams' most skillful moves was linking Texas annexation to Negro slavery. His spin on the annexation issue took hold and with each revolution, the knot tightened. Texas and slavery cemented together as surely as wine and grapes. The northern states refused to consider Texas annexation, placing a seemingly insurmountable roadblock squarely in front of President Houston's path. No one person did more to divide the Union than the elderly, embittered John Q. Adams. Adams shuttled slavery to the forefront and eventually his message brought on the bloody Civil War between the North and South. His greatness as a leader was rendered null and void by his splitting the Union.

John Adams and the north viewed the vastness of Texas on Mexican maps and wrongly assumed the entire area was suitable for cotton plantations. He believed if Texas were to become a state, there would be a hundred thousand Negro slaves working the cotton fields. What he did not know was the best farmland was already under cultivation, and without irrigation, nothing but cacti and rattlesnakes would grow west of Austin. Those who knew the topography and vast climate differences of Texas tried to educate the old curmudgeon, but he turned a deaf ear. The truth didn't stop Adams' frequent outbursts against annexation.

Slavery was, in fact, only a secondary issue; the core of the bitter division was a political struggle to control Congress. The southern states wanted Texas annexation to strengthen their representation in Congress, while on the other hand, the North wanted to retain their political power and it was in their best interest to keep Texas out of the Union.

Houston and Jackson could not understand the rationale for the Union's rejection of such a vast area of land. The two leaders saw slavery as an economic problem, with the most important issue being expansion and the power of the white race. Houston and Jackson possessed equal disdain for the northern abolitionists and the southern nullifiers and believed, in time, the moral issue of slavery would be resolved.

Oddly enough, the abolitionist movement started in the South around 1820 and worked its way north. There were many in the North who owned slaves, but just not in the large numbers of the southern plantations. The northerners didn't have vast amounts of land under cultivation; therefore, the slave trade was not as pervasive. In the South, a plantation may have as many as three hundred slaves while four to eight was considered a large group in the North. While the South had trading blocks where slaves were auctioned off like cattle, the North purchased their slaves from dealers. Slaves were purchased and sold with the same vigor as in the South, only in a microcosm. The issue was never *if*, but rather how many slaves each side owned.

Confusion reigned on all sides. It was like a room full of blind people playing Texas Hold 'em. The Union was confused about what to do with Texas. The Mexicans were confused about the Union's intentions. The Texans were not clear about their boundaries, or if the Republic could even survive. The Texans claimed their boundaries reached to the Rio Grande. Spain set the Nueces River as the northern boundary and the Rio Grande as the southern tip of the state of Nuevo Santander. When Mexico won independence form Spain, they changed the name of the area in question to Tamaulipas. As part of his surrender, Santa Anna gave Tamaulipas to Texas. In a brilliant move to resolve the boundary issue once and for all, Sam Houston and Stephen F. Austin persuaded Santa Anna to travel to Washington to settle the dispute. No one knows how Houston and Austin were able to get the dictator to make the trip; nevertheless, he did, and he confirmed the Rio Grande was the southern boundary of Texas.

Senator Robert Walker of Mississippi shrewdly added a last-minute resolution to a bill recognizing Texas as a Republic. The bill tied 24-24 and the vice president cast the tiebreaker in favor of Texas. The bill was sent to President Jackson with only a few hours left in his term. He signed the bill and acknowledged Texas' independence. He invited Texas agents Memucan Hunt and William Horton to his office and before the stroke of midnight, in his last moments in office, the tall chiseled-faced Tennessee Indian fighter raised his wine glass and toasted, "Gentlemen, to the Republic of Texas." As the clock struck midnight, he raised his glass once more and gave one final drink to the health and honor of his old friend: "To Sam Houston, the President of the Republic of Texas."

Even as euphoria was spilling over into the streets and everyone celebrated, Houston stayed focused. He was fully aware the Mexican Government did not accept Santa Anna's promise of Texas independence. He was also acutely aware of the weakness of his army. The Texans who had defeated the Mexicans had left the service and returned to their farms and businesses, happy as a dog with two tails. All that remained was a mish-mash of inexperienced volunteers and a few misfits from the original army. With extraordinary skill, Houston managed to keep the Republic afloat and hold off war with Mexico. Just as he was getting a handle on how to keep Texas solvent and fend off Mexican confrontation, his three-year presidential term expired.

In Lamar's presidential inaugural address, he stated, "If peace can be obtained only by the sword, then let the sword do its work." He was agreeable to peace with Mexico; however, if the Mexicans didn't see things his way, he had no apprehension in knocking them to their knees. Lamar did not seem to comprehend that Texas would be a 120-pound featherweight in the ring with a 220-pound heavyweight Mexico. He loved to gather a group of friends and tell them what he would have done to Santa Anna. Unlike Houston's peaceful resolution, he would have made an example of the Mexicans not soon to be forgotten. Texans wanted to fight and many agreed Houston had been too soft on Santa Anna and the captured Mexicans. Lamar seized upon the desire of Texans to challenge Mexico and wage all-out war against the Indians.

Lamar's hatred of Indians was well defined. The irony was that those who opposed Lamar had no compunction about the eradication of the Indians. The hypocrisy of their stance stood out like a sore thumb. They were the descendants of the Plymouth Puritans who had killed or shipped off into slavery one third of the native population within fifty-five years of the Mayflower's arrival. The killing fields, which began along the Massachusetts shore, painted a crimson swath across Texas and eventually extended the blood trail all the way to the Pacific Ocean.

The Texans were completely misunderstood throughout much of the Union. Many failed to comprehend that fiercely independent individuals were required to build the Republic. The first Texans, and all who followed, made "courage" their middle name; their boundless fighting spirit borne out of their horrific struggle. Each new farm was in danger of a Comanche raid. The Comanches numbered only about five thousand yet dominated the Southern Plains. What made them such a terrifying enemy was their lack of discrimination. They raped, pillaged, tortured and killed infants and children, the elderly, women, Mexicans and other Indians with unthinkable brutality. Nowhere in the history of the United States was every square inch of land so thoroughly washed in blood. Each mile toward the Rio Grande and every yard west up the endless rocky plateaus, the Texans left their blood and raw bones to bleach in the blistering sun. Unlike Kentucky, Tennessee and other states, where the frontier only took a brief time to establish, the Texans had to fight for every inch, with untold numbers paying the ultimate price. Only because of superior firepower and the vast numbers of men willing to fight and die, did the Texans finally capture Quanah Parker, the last Comanche Chief, in 1874.

Texas pride passed from generation to generation. No other part of the world has ever equaled the attitude and boasting associated with being a "Texan." To this day, when someone proclaims, "I'm a Texan," it has meaning that runs deeper than the Red River during flood season. "All for one, one for all" was more than a slogan, it was a way of life.

When President Lamar selected Waterloo (Austin) as the sight of the new Texas Capital, he knew the move would outrage Sam Houston. The city of Austin was not a wise choice for the seat of government; the hills surrounding the town provided a perfect escape route for a band of Comanche after a lightning-fast raid. When construction began on the new capital, Indian attacks were so frequent that riflemen stood guard day and night. The Baron de Bastrop's argument for his town being a better location for the capital was a valid one. All old and new roads passed by the township. Located along the banks of the Colorado River and surrounded by tall pine trees, only the eastern side of the community would need protection. The pines, which had no reason to be located so far inland from east Texas, could produce plenty of timber for future expansion. The one thing the town of Bastrop could not offer was a burr under Houston's saddle, making the choice of Austin a pleasure for Lamar.

The Republic was growing deeper in debt and President Lamar's administration couldn't borrow or earn the money needed to keep the Republic solvent. Texas needed trade, and Lamar decided Santa Fe appeared to be the ideal place to start. Mexico City was already doing a booming business hauling merchandise up the Santa Fe Trail and on to St Louis, and Lamar desperately wanted part of the Mexico City/St. Louis trade revenue for Texas' coffers. He assumed the residents of Santa Fe would greet the Texans as those in San Antonio had. Setting his sights on Santa Fe, without sending an emissary to see if his plan would be mutually acceptable, would prove to be disastrous.

Lamar did have a good template for trade with Santa Fe. Missouri was doing a thriving business between the two countries. Their wagons didn't stop at Santa Fe, but went all the way to Mexico City. President Lamar knew the amount of income being generated from the traders in Missouri, and on the surface, it appeared he had good reason to think Texas could do even better because, in his mind, Santa

Fe was already part of the Republic. On the maps, Texas reached west to the Rio Grande and Santa Fe rested on the east side of the river.

As he mulled over the pros and cons of the "Santa Fe Expedition", good fortune came his way. William G. Dryden, a citizen of Santa Fe visited Austin, and Lamar invited him to dinner and laid out his plan for the expedition. Excited about the proposal, Dryden agreed to carry the message back to the citizens of Santa Fe. Two other Santa Fe citizens, John Rowland and William Workman also stopped in Austin for supplies and the President summoned them to his office as well. Neither was as enthusiastic as Dryden was, but each gave Lamar the impression that the Texans would be welcomed with open arms in Santa Fe. Lamar immediately made the three Santa Fe men an integral part of his venture, appointing them as Commissioners. Lamar also appointed Texans William Cooke, Richard Brenham, Jose Navarro, and George Van Ness as Texas Civil Commissioners who would answer any questions the citizens of Santa Fe might have.

Lamar promoted 24-year-old Hugh McLeod to Lt. General and commander of the expedition. Responsibility for assembling a three-hundred-man army fell to Colonel George Thomas Howard, second in command. Then, General McLeod became ill, and the expedition delayed for three months. As well educated as Lamar was, he didn't have the common sense to realize they were flirting with disaster in getting underway so late in the season. With the critical loss of time, the sun dried out the spring grasses and dried up water sources. A more experienced leader would have recognized the deadly folly of the delayed departure.

With the Baron de Bastrop dead, Lamar attempted to confiscate the old man's merchandise from the Galveston warehouse, but the commodities were secured by a lien and prevented him from taking what, by law, belonged to Bud Miller via the Baron's will. Unsuccessful in gaining the Bastrop property, President Lamar approached Sam Maverick to supply his expedition with wagons of trade goods. Maverick laughed, answering, "Have you lost your mind? We don't even know the way or the dangers that are out there. I'm not sending my wagons or merchandise on a wild goose chase. If the men don't die along the way, the Mexicans will cut them down the moment they step on Santa Fe soil."

A zealous Lamar then presented his plan to Congress. Sam Houston took the floor, berating the idea and garnered enough support from Maverick and a few others to defeat Lamar's proposed expedition. Lamar crowed Houston was just jealous because it was not his idea. In the cloister of his office, Lamar called Houston a shortsighted sniveling coward.

One of Lamar's strongest supporters was William Cooke from Fredericksburg, Virginia. He was trained to run his family's drug business, but wanted adventure and moved to New Orleans in 1835. Shortly after he arrived, he joined the New Orleans Grays. From there, he went to Texas, where he took part in defeating General Cos in the siege of San Antonio. Cooke, promoted to Captain during the battle, received General Cos' white flag of surrender. In 1838, Cooke rejoined the army as Quartermaster General of the Republic. Caught up in Texas expansionism, he chose to join Lamar's expedition. Even his old friend, Sam Houston was unable to convince him of the folly of the expedition.

Jose Antonio Navarro was one of the brave men who signed the Declaration of Independence and felt strongly that Houston was wrong-minded regarding the Santa Fe venture. He was convinced there were golden opportunities waiting in Santa Fe, and his heavy lobbying helped make Lamar's dream a reality. In actuality, many who supported the expedition did so for the opportunity to siphon off some of the Mexican silver finding its way to Missouri. Greed has a way of blinding otherwise brilliant men.

Even though Lamar's plan was soundly defeated in Congress, the President was not about to give up without a fight. Lamar sent a rider to New Orleans and had a large sum of worthless Texas money printed. He would use the fresh currency to purchase what was needed for the venture. He was able to fill twenty-one ox-drawn wagons with well over $200,000 worth of merchandise. Utilizing his new money, he purchased mules, ordered flashy new uniforms for the army, and hired three Mexican guides who swore on their mother's graves they knew every inch of land between Austin and Santa Fe. There was one small problem. The guides were not being truthful.

On June 19, 1841, the officially designated "Santa Fe Pioneers" launched their expedition from Kenny's Fort on Brushy Creek, about twenty miles north of Austin. Traveling was extremely slow. The oxen moved at only two paces: slow and slower. Teamsters walked beside them with bullwhips, cracking the plaited lashes in the air, but the cadence of the oxen never changed. The group made camp each day an hour before sunset and did not get back on the trail until an hour after sunrise, further impeding their travel time.

One day, one of the Mexican guides rushed into camp announcing he had located the Red River. They had indeed reached a river, but it was the Wichita, located at least thirty miles to the south. The next morning General McLeod awoke early and turned the wagon train westward, following the Wichita Valley. Now all he had to do was follow the river until it stopped and they would be close to Santa Fe. After sixteen days, the river narrowed and became so shallow a man could cross without getting his boots wet. McLeod knew enough to realize the Red River would not get that shallow so rapidly. That night he had a long talk with his three Mexican guides. After the confrontation, the guides vanished into the darkness, fearing the angry men might hang them. The wagon train was lost. McLeod immediately sent a scouting party north to see if they could locate the Red River, and after two days, they did.

Provisions soon grew sparse and discontent spread among the soldiers. The August weather was exceptionally hot, with temperatures reaching well over 100 degrees. Humidity hung heavy in the valley, increasing the misery among the already discouraged group. Their uniforms, which were made for winter travel, added to their discomfort. McLeod allowed the soldiers to remove their jackets and travel in shirtsleeves, but that didn't stop the sweltering heat from taking its toll. Almost daily, one or two men fell dead from heat stroke. Adding to the tension, a small band of Comanche shadowed them from the Wichita to the Red River, occasionally charging the convoy, shooting off a few arrows, and then dashing back out of rifle range.

The expedition traveled northwest until they came to an area called the Caprock, a natural wall rising straight up from 200 to 800 feet onto the Llano Estacado. In some places, the wall rose a thousand feet straight up for miles along the Panhandle of Texas. Llano Estacado, Spanish for *staked plains*, was a relatively flat mesa (tableland) dotted with numerous small lakes. The Llano Estacado elevation rose from 2500' in the east to over 5000' in the west. Forming deep crevasses, rivers cut their way through the surface to make the Palo Duro (hardwood) Canyon, which refers to the tough scrubs and trees found in the bed of the canyon. The steep walls of the canyon rose to form numerous pinnacles, buttes, and mesas, each protected by a cap to prevent erosion. The canyon floor was covered with several varieties of grasses and other vegetation such as prickly, yucca, mesquite, juniper, cottonwood, willow, and salt cedar. General McLeod was stunned by the beauty, and at the same time realized they would never be able to get the twenty-one heavy wagons to the top of the rim. They would be forced to follow the canyon bottom until it gradually came to level ground.

A student of history, McLeod realized he was on the same ground Coronado may have walked in the late spring of 1541 while searching for Quivira and the gold the area was reported to contain. That evening around the campfire, he recalled to his senior officers and the merchants what he remembered of Coronado and his search for the Seven Cities of Gold. He explained how Coronado was misdirected by a lying guide the same as they had been. His best guess was they were camped at the foot of the vast

Llano Estacado. Coronado had written that the land was as flat as a tabletop and covered the area from the Canadian River several hundred miles south to the Big Spring. He continued, "Francisco Vazaquez de Coronado lived from 1515 to 1554. He came from Spain and married into a wealthy family similar to what our James Bowie did when he immigrated to Texas. For many years, there had been rumors of Seven Cities of Gold in North America, and Coronado, a small man of considerable wealth and tremendous ambition, used his money to fund the expedition. He brought with him three-hundred Spanish soldiers, over a thousand Tlaxcalan Indians, an enormous number of livestock, and a supply train of mules."

A young lieutenant Robert Allen Terrell asked, "Is that where the Comanche and other Indians got their horses? Did they steal them from Coronado?"

The General puffed on his pipe and contemplated the answer before speaking. "I'd have to give you an affirmative on that, with some qualification. Coronado never came into contact with the Apache or the Comanche. He only encountered the friendly tribes of the Zuni, Hopi, and Pueblos. He ran into trouble on his way back when he tried to convert the Pueblos to Christianity. It is my belief that the Pueblos then captured several hundred of his horses and learned to ride. Then the Comanches raided the Pueblos and stole their horses. Once the Comanches saw the benefits of the horse, they did what they still do today; they stole them. They went deep into Mexico and raided horse ranches there. Why wait and raise a colt when you can steal one that is fat and mature?"

It was evident that the cocky General had a fascination with the explorer and, in some ways, considered he was the same type of bold adventurer that Coronado had been. That is why he had lobbied so hard to head up the Santa Fe Expedition. He felt history would recognize his exploits the same as it had recorded the discoveries of Coronado centuries earlier.

Standing, letting the men know it was time to call it a day, McLeod said, "Tomorrow a few of you will get to ride into history. Captain William Lewis, I am placing you in charge to take some men and parlay with the New Mexicans. It'll take some time for us to find our way out of this canyon or to build a jig to lift the wagons to the top of those cliffs."

Captain Lewis and his men followed a trail made by bison, deer and Indians up an embankment that was so steep, the men walked and led their mounts to the top. On their way, Indians attacked them several times. Not serious fights, but enough to wear them down. Food became in short supply because game on the Llano Estacado was very sparse. Even the rivers did not yield the abundance of fish they were accustomed to in Texas. After crossing the Quitaque and Tule canyons, they met a small group of Mexican travelers who willingly shared their food and water with the half-starved and thirsty Texans and agreed to take them to Las Vegas, a small community and trading post about forty miles east of Santa Fe.

The Texans were still expecting to be greeted with open arms in Santa Fe. No one had mentioned Governor Manuel Armijo, who had risen to power by physically driving the duly elected Governor from office, ruled the area like a dictator, and was dead set against any Texas interference. Upon learning of the Texans' impending arrival, Armijo sent an army of a few hundred men to greet them. The greeting was not a welcome call, but one of confrontation. Captain William Lewis turned into a petrified coward when he saw the Mexican army. He immediately surrendered without resistance even though the Mexicans were poorly armed, carrying only broken guns, sticks, knives, bows and arrows, and makeshift lances. The Texans, with their deadly long rifles, could have easily killed thirty or forty and sent the rag-tag army running for a chaparral bush.

The remainder of the expedition was camped at Laguna, Colorado near the small community of Tucumcari when, on October 5, Captain Lewis led the Mexican troops into the encampment under a flag of truce. His ploy kept the Texas soldiers off guard until the Mexican forces surrounded them. Lewis made the surrender sound as if the Texans would be allowed to trade, enjoy the company of their western friends, and within eight days be sold supplies. Then their guns would be returned and they would be free to return to Texas. McCloud felt safe in surrendering under such generous conditions. Texas was built on heroes, but one coward could unravel bravery and sacrifice in an instant. Without one shot fired, Captain Lewis helped Governor Armijo defeat an army of 300 Texans.

Lewis would find himself isolated and soon realized he would be given no preferential treatment for his traitorous actions. The American merchants visiting Santa Fe never spoke to him. The local Mexicans treated him like a stray dog. After two months, he moved deep into Mexico. Even in Mexico, word of his cowardice preceded him and he was rejected and ostracized. Out of desperation, he changed his name and caught a freighter to South America, never to be heard from again.

General McLeod was deeply hurt knowing one of his handpicked men had turned on his fellow Texans. General George Washington must have felt similar emotions of betrayal when General Benedict Arnold tried to give up West Point to the British.

The Texas prisoners, roped together into groups of six to eight, marched two thousand miles from Santa Fe to Mexico City. Since they were tied together, when one man fell, the impact was felt all the way down the line. A Mexican cavalryman was always near with a lance or whip to force the fallen to rise to their feet quickly. If one could not, he was shot, his ears cut off, and he was abandoned where he fell. A few bold Texans who protested the inhumane treatment were murdered in cold blood. None received a Christian burial. The Texans were deprived of any nourishment, and on one leg of the journey, were force-marched through a dry lakebed for ninety miles with no water. Snow covered them as them made the grueling death march. The Texans suffered many indignities on the two thousand mile trip, but nothing compared to what they would face once they reached Mexico. The men were first housed in a leper colony, and then transferred to rat-infested jail cells. The food was no better than slop fed to pigs. There was no medical care. The Texans were forced to work on the roads and dig ditches from daylight until nightfall. Always present was a Mexican on horseback, carrying a bullwhip. Should a man stumble, he could expect lashes across his back. He then would be forced to keep working with blood flowing from the open wounds.

Diplomatic rhetoric heated up on both sides and after strong pressure from the United States, the prisoners were released almost two years after they left Brushy Creek. After their release, those who survived made their way back to Texas consumed with anger and resentment toward President Lamar. George Kendall wrote an eight-hundred-page book on the Santa Fe Expedition that sold more than forty thousand copies. His brutal account of the severe treatment of the captured Texans fanned the flames of war with Mexico yet again. George Kendall became a Texas Ranger in Ben McCullough's Company and a staunch advocate for annexation. In 1845, Jose Navarro escaped from a Mexican jail and arrived back in Texas in time to participate in the annexation process as well. Texas distinguished Navarro by naming a county in his honor.

The Santa Fe Expedition was a dismal failure. Skating on thin ice under a blazing sun would most aptly describe the conditions under which Sam Houston assumed the office of President of the Republic for the second time.

Chapter Twenty
Harassment

Back in Galveston, Jack Hays knew Bud was stunned over the death of the Baron and wanted to stay more than a few hours with the Treptows. In ten days, a seven-wagon caravan would carry merchandise to San Antonio under the protection of fifteen heavily armed men. Rather than giving his new recruit an option, Jack ordered Bud to wait and help escort the wagons. He knew Bud would jump at the chance to stay a few days in Galveston with the Treptows.

Captain Hays was aware of the brewing problems with Mexico. The week prior to Jack and his rangers leaving for San Antonio, Lieutenant James Rice and seventeen rangers from Captain Andrews' Company attacked thirty Indians and Mexicans about fifty miles due west of the Satterwhite farm along the old Camino Real Road. Three of the men killed were Mexican, one being Manuel Flores (not to be confused with the Texas hero by the same name), who was carrying secret papers which revealed a plot to unite Texas Indians with the Mexican army. Their plan was to eradicate all gringos from Texas, scaring off the weak and killing the brave. The letter highlighted the constant problem facing the new Republic: It was not enough that Texas soundly defeated the Mexicans and signed a peace agreement with their dictator. Once a rival group took power south of the Rio Grande, they were itching to invade the Republic and re-take the land.

The Texans were confident the concept would not succeed because those crossing the border into Texas erased the word fear from their dictionaries. Few cowards moved to Texas, and any who might venture in were quickly weeded out. Captain Lewis of the failed Santa Fe Expedition was the exception, not the rule. Rather, Texas was built by men like Peter Pieper, who didn't even like to kill a deer for food; yet, when the safety of his daughters was in jeopardy, demonstrated bravery beyond measure. There was a standard joke told to all who arrived in Texas: "Stepping on rich Texas soil sucks the yellow streak from your spine."

The Indian-Mexican coalition would be the first organized act of terror on American soil. None of the kidnappings or "random" killings was accidental, but part of a well-organized plan to instill terror in the hearts and minds of new arrivals, as well as keep the "old timers" in a state of confusion. Men were fearful of working in the fields and leaving their families unprotected. No man plowed his fields without his long rifle and many carried a brace of pistols in their belt. Women honed up on their shooting skills, and most homes hung a warning bell by the front door. There was an ever-ready attitude among Texans.

Nevertheless, life went on amidst the chaos and depredations; babies were born, new cattle birthed, crops planted and fields harvested.

Not long after the fall of the Alamo, and the Texans' defeat of Santa Anna in San Jacinto, a group of high-ranking Comanche Chiefs made a trip to Matamoros to negotiate the re-conquest of Texas. According to the papers found on Manuel Flores, Valentine Canalizo of Matamoros was the mastermind of the plot that guaranteed the Indians' retention of their hunting grounds once the Anglos were driven out. Mexico would then set up a buffer state between the Indians and the United States. In 1837, the plan moved forward from discussion to implementation: Participating tribes would rendezvous north of San Antonio and south of Nacogdoches along the El Camino Real as soon as the leaves put out in the spring. The Mexicans promised to bring 5,000 men across the Rio Grande and meet up with the council of Indians. Once united, they would march across Texas, methodically exterminating or expelling Anglos and unfriendly Mexicans from the territory. Once the Texans were eradicated, Texas would be divided up among the tribes. This promise made fighting alongside the Comanche and Mexicans enticing for all tribes, even friendly ones. Each Indian Nation wanted to make sure they got their fair share, and knew if they didn't join the fight, they risked expulsion as well.

The plan evolved from its original concept, and under the new plan, the Indians were to create a ruckus that forced the Texans to put a large army together. Canalizo knew if a large body of Texans concentrated to fight, the Indians could hang on their flank and rear, and hold them at bay for weeks. He didn't want the Indians to engage the Texas Army, but rather hang on the border and harass them like a feisty dog nipping at their heels. While the men were away from their homes, other bands would move in on the helpless women and children, burn their homes, and divide the spoils. The plan was brilliant; however, it didn't take into consideration how effective the Texas Rangers were when it came to fighting and out-maneuvering an enemy. Instead of an Army of a thousand men, the rangers only needed a force between fifteen and forty to take care of most any threats the Indians posed. Rangers always overpowered the initial force sent against them, forcing the enemy to tuck tail and run.

The Comanches had done more than their share to harass the Texans with acts of terrorism. They were unsuccessful in getting other tribes to join them, but if they would have, it would have been impossible for Texas to expand. The obstacle facing the Comanche coalition was each tribe had its own agenda. Some wanted to farm and possessed disdain for the nomadic life, some were constantly moving and on the warpath, while others hated other Indian tribes more than they did the Texans.

Realizing the need to move the frontier, Congress authorized the formation of new ranger units to expel the Indians. The outrage became so great in Brazos, Colorado, and Trinity counties that a group of fifty rangers from Austin and Ft. Bend were sent to build Fort Milam. Captain John Bird led the company. Bird was a capable man, but didn't have the native instincts of Jack Hays. Neither did he have the experience in fighting Indians. After they made Fort Milam battle ready, Captain Bird set out for another fort up the Little River, deeper into Indian country. One morning, the Indians ran a herd of buffalo through the ranger camp. Acting quickly, the men were able to save their mounts and most of their supplies. Bird immediately led thirty-five rangers in pursuit of the Comanches, leaving the rest to guard the camp. They soon came in sight of twenty-seven Indians and chased them for three miles. Bird, realizing they would not be able to catch the well-mounted Indians, ordered a retreat. The Indians gave chase and the rangers soon found themselves surrounded. The Indians drew their battle line and shouted out war whoops, holding the rangers at bay for two hours. Then, 250 Kickapoo and Caddo joined the band, raising their numbers to over three hundred warriors. After blood curdling war cries, they charged the rangers' position. A fierce battle ensued. Fighting furiously, the rangers inflicted several causalities, beating the Indians a little further back with each charge. After incurring a significant loss of life, the Indians retreated to the hilltop. After dark, they tossed something in the air that resembled lightning, which was a sign of retreat. As the defeated Indians rode away, the rangers could hear the guttural howling that followed the death of a warrior.

The rangers gathered their four wounded and three dead, Captain Bird among them, and slipped down the draw headed for Fort Smith. Captain Nathan Brookshire assumed command, and after reaching the fort and gathering the remaining rangers, moved to Fort Nashville. Even though the battle was often referred to as Bird's victory, it only added fuel to the fire of Indian depredations on the frontier. The Indians perceived they had beaten back the white intruders. On the other side, the Texans were inexorable where Indian efforts to expel them were concerned. Neither side would concede defeat. It came down to who was the most determined and the short side of the fulcrum tilted heavily in favor of the Texans.

West of San Antonio, Captain Juan Seguin and his company of fifteen Texas Rangers pursued a large group of Comanche into Canyon de Uvalde. Some speculated they were part of the bold group who kept venturing to the edge of town and harassing the citizens of San Antonio. Juan located their deserted camp and destroyed it. They didn't engage any Indians in a fight, but reported seeing large numbers crawling above his men in the scrub cedar. After ten days, Juan, along with Sam Maverick and the other rangers, returned tired and dejected. The realization that such a large band of Comanche could be that near San Antonio and they were unable to catch up with them made the rangers realize the futility of the conflict. The Comanche presence kept everyone in and around San Antonio on edge. Sam would no longer allow Mary to stroll with her lady friends in the evenings for fear a small band of Comanche might slip in undetected.

Galveston Island was more like a city of sanctuary. Bud slapped Lighting on the rump with his hat shouting, "Yippie." Dust trailed his path all the way to the front gate of the Treptow ranch. It was difficult to tell who was more excited to see Lighting coming down the road: Mr. Treptow, Mrs. Treptow, Virginia, or the Mexican workers. The closer Bud got to the ranch, the faster his blood surged into his heart. He had forgotten how much he missed living on the ranch and of course, being with Virginia. The time spent away had made him realize how much the family meant to him. When they were together, there was much laughter, conversation, and thanks to God.

A storm was forming out in the Gulf of Mexico. Mr. Treptow had seen those ominous skies before and knew the danger, but wouldn't let the impending storm prevent him from enjoying the arrival of a young man he had learned to love like a son. Bud dismounted and made a dash through the small gate and onto the porch where the family was waiting. He wanted to hug Virginia, but felt he must pay attention to her parents first. He gave Mrs. Treptow a big hug and shook Mr. Treptow's hand, saying to each, "It's so good to see you." He caught a glimpse from the corner of his eye and noticed Virginia was starting to get a long face. Pulling his hand free of Mr. Treptow's steel-grip handshake, Bud turned to Virginia. He took both her hands gently in his, saying, "I brought you a gift from San Antonio. It's in my saddlebag."

Virginia squeezed his hands and looked up into his face without saying a word. She realized Bud was no longer a boy. He had left a smooth-faced teen and had returned a man. He was even more handsome than she remembered. Finally, Virginia smiled and whispered, "We have all missed you. Even the men working the horses have asked when you would return. I missed you most of all. I miss our moonlight horseback rides along the beach and talking on the porch swing after dinner. We prayed daily for angels to hover over you and keep you safe."

Mr. Treptow had heard the news that Bud was now a Texas Ranger and riding with Captain John "Jack" Hays' Company. He had so many questions, but restrained himself, allowing the young couple to have a few moments alone. Mrs. Treptow was not so considerate. She spoke with her usual volume, asking, "How long will you get to stay with us this time? We hope you don't just dash in and out."

Bud didn't release Virginia's hands as he turned and replied, "Captain Hays assigned me to travel back to San Antonio with a wagon train in about ten days. The Baron, God rest his soul, left me a house and some land up in Bastrop. I'll need to go see about that. Sheriff Maples told me Mildred Garner has a copy of the Baron's will and I'll go pick it up in the next few days. Some of the rangers have visited the Bastrop place and if they are not jerkin' my leg, it's a wonderful home. I guess I'm getting ahead of myself. I'd like to bunk in the barn, if that's okay with you."

"No, you cannot stay in my barn!" Helmut answered firmly.

Bud's face flushed. He was unsure what to say. The family had seemed so happy to have him return. What was going on?

Helmut was not able to keep his stern expression for long. Looking at his wife and then back to the young couple, he finally said, "The reason you will not be staying in the barn is because my wife and Virginia had me build an extra bedroom. Now you have your own room in the main house. How does that sound?"

"Sir, I don't know what to say. You didn't have to go to all that trouble for me. The barn was plenty nice."

Virginia tugged his hand and in a mellow tone inquired, "Wanna come into the house and see your new room?"

"Yeah, sure, let me grab my saddlebags. I want to get your gift."

A thick buffalo rug covered the floor next to the ornate cast iron bed. In one corner of the room was a small table with a cane bottom chair resting alongside, and next to the table and chair, a tall chifforobe for his clothes. On the opposite side of the room was a wood-burning fireplace with a stack of fresh cut logs piled near the hearth. The pine floor was highly varnished and the young couple could see their reflections on its surface. Virginia placed her hands on the curtains and giving a gentle yank, said, "I sewed these for you."

Bud fumbled to open his saddlebags, digging his hands around until he found the small box, then handed it to Virginia. "I hope you like it. I bought it from Mrs. Maverick. She said it belonged to one of her aunts. I had to do some pretty fast talking to get Mrs. Maverick to sell it, but the moment I saw it, I envisioned how beautiful it would look around your graceful neck."

Virginia slowly opened the box and carefully pulled the cotton padding away, revealing a broach with small diamonds encircling an opal and an outer ring of alternating rubies and emeralds. "I love it. I love it. This is the most beautiful piece of jewelry I have ever seen. Mama, look." As she handed the broach to her mother, Virginia's enthusiasm got the best of her. She threw her arms around Bud's neck and planted a kiss on his cheek.

Mr. Treptow waited impatiently in the long-room. When Bud stepped into the room, Helmut commanded, "Let's go look at the new foals. We got a good crop of young horses and mules since you were last here."

Before they could make their way outside, one of the Mexican horse trainers rushed to the front door screaming in Spanish that a tornado was heading toward the ranch. Everyone dashed out onto the front porch. A huge thunderstorm blackened the sky, leaving layers of clouds floating like dirty fleece hanging from an old sheep. There was definitely a tail dangling from the cloud's base. Bud's Uncle Charlie had told him tornadoes were like a grizzly bear; you were safe as long it was on the opposite side of the river. Mr. Treptow instructed the helper to go round up the men, women, and children and meet them at the storm cellar. Then he turned to his family and Bud and shouted, "Follow me! We need to get in the cellar ourselves. That storm looks like a nasty fellow and he's heading right for us."

Rain spit down on them as they ran to the back of the ranch house and into the storm shelter. Some of the ranch hands had already opened the door and had lit a kerosene lantern. A set of creaky wooden steps led down into a dark, dank room with shelves on three sides where Mrs. Treptow stored her preserves. The shelter door was never left open for fear a rattlesnake might take up residence, and the cellar smelled very musty.

Sand flowed across the ground like liquid waves. Gusts popped Bud's jacket as he spread his legs apart, bracing against the wind. Everyone had entered the shelter, but Bud wanted to catch a glimpse of the tornado. He watched in awe as the twister's tail dipped onto the beach, ripping a wide hole in the sand. The tornado lifted up and jumped across the road, then kissed the earth again, throwing sod like a high-pressure waterspout. Bud thought he saw full-grown trees swirling around in the center of the funnel. He then noticed his prized horse, Lightning struggling to get free from his tie rope. He felt Lightning was safe tied to the hitching post in the middle of the roping lot. Unless the tornado made an acute turn, Bud felt it would miss the ranch.

The tornado wind gusts were over 270 miles-per-hour, ripping gashes in the earth each time its tail touched down. Small pellets of hail began to assault Bud. After a few stinging shots of ice, he decided to go into the cellar with the others. He pulled the heavy doors closed behind him and the Mexican men tied them down. The room was crammed full of people, but he was able to squirm his way over to Virginia. She snuggled against his chest as hail pounded the wooden doors in a frightening rhythm. "Don't be afraid. Unless it makes a harsh turn, it will miss us completely. It looked like the tornado was moving across the island and out into the bay."

It was not difficult for Virginia to appear afraid, for indeed she was. Two years earlier, a tornado had touched down in Galveston's shantytown, killing five and totally destroying all the houses in its path. She knew the devastation a tornado could inflict.

When the hail stopped, one of the farmhands cracked open the shelter doors to check the conditions. He hollered back down in Spanish that the storm had passed and it was safe to leave the shelter. Bud was soaking wet and the air the storm left behind was ice cold. Virginia insisted that he go into his room and put on a set of dry clothes. That was when Bud had to confess he had only brought the clothes on his back. Mrs. Treptow interrupted, "You can wear some of Helmut's things. They may be a little large around the waist, but you can wear your belt tighter. I still have some of his old things before he got so…" She paused, and then finished her sentence with a laugh, "fat." Looking down at his muddy boots, she continued, "Leave your boots on the front porch. Virginia can clean the mud off while you change into dry clothes. We cannot have you getting sick on us, now can we?"

The next few days seemed to fly by while Bud and Virginia took long horseback rides along the Gulf shore, letting their horses splash in the gentle surf. He spoke with obvious pride about being part of the elite Rangers. He talked of anything that could steer his mind away from the death of his mentor, the Baron de Bastrop. He never anticipated his mind could be so grief wracked. He had been taught grown men don't cry. That sounded good in theory, but it was not working. He pulled Lightning to an abrupt stop and turned his face from her.

Virginia's woman's instinct knew he was in angst. She asked, "What's wrong?"

Bud froze with fear. If he spoke he would break down and bawl like a baby. He knew the next words that came out of his mouth would be the unbearable pain gushing forth. Tears began to flow freely, even though he was doing all in his power to be a man about the death of his friend. He pulled his hat down over his face to conceal his hurt.

Virginia could see through his brave facade, "Bud, it's okay to experience grief over the loss of someone as close as the Baron. He was like a father to you."

He choked out hurting words, "I should have been here to defend him. He was old and helpless. The Baron had his faults, but to me he was a true saint. Without him I'd never met you and your family. Without him I wouldn't be able to read and write. Without the Baron I wouldn't be a Texas Ranger. He was an amazing man. I hurt so much right now. I miss him and his gruff ways so badly."

She pushed her horse closer to her anguish-ridden friend and placed her arms around his thick shoulders. They sat in silence for a long time. Then Bud's mind drifted to his own father. He was able to transfer some of the sadness thinking what his father did with the land he acquired from the Republic. Had Stump Miller gambled the inheritance away or was it waiting for him?

One thing for sure, Bud would be careful not to imply he would need a wife to help him take care of the property the Baron left him. There was no doubt Virginia and her parents had marriage on their mind. His sudden wealth would bring more pressure from her mother and father. Mr. Treptow was the boldest of the group. When any opening presented itself, he never missed an opportunity to point out what a great cook their daughter was, how she could sew like a professional seamstress, sing like a bird and how her Christian ways were unparalleled. Maybe when the pain subsided he would consider marriage, but for now all he wanted to do was get on Lightning and run far, far away.

Early mornings found Bud at the corral breaking young horses, and in the afternoon, riding the green stock. Everyone on the ranch could see the dramatic improvement in his horsemanship skills. Bud did love to show off his talent. Dropping over the side of his mount, he would shoot a fence post dead center while at a dead run. The Mexican helpers started placing cantaloupes on the top of the posts for him to shoot. To everyone's amazement, Bud never missed, splattering each cantaloupe while riding full out. Each time another helper came in from the pasture or Mr. and Mrs. Treptow ventured out, he repeated his performance. They applauded and Bud showed off even more. With one final "Hey look at me," Bud dropped a coin on the ground, and riding a young colt all out, leaned over in the saddle at the last moment and plucked the shiny coin, holding it high above his head for all to see.

On his last evening before joining the wagon train, Virginia and Bud went riding on the beach. After a few miles, they dismounted and led their horses as they walked barefoot in the wet sand. The clouds to the east were a delicate soft pink, while the setting sun on the bayside was a blaze of hot red. Romance was in the air. Bud took her hand as they walked. After walking a mile or so, Bud stopped. Wiping his dry lips on his shirtsleeve and placing his right hand behind Virginia's head, he pulled her face into his. The kiss was earthshaking. His voice cracked as he said, "I hope I didn't offend you. I was caught up by how beautiful you look tonight. Come daylight, I'll be gone. I don't know how long it will be before I'll be back this way, but I promise I will return."

"You didn't offend me. I have been hoping for days that you would kiss me, but I didn't feel right asking you to. I wanted the kiss to come from you."

Silence became a third party as they sauntered down the beach, listening to the crashing waves. Virginia knew the large waves meant another storm was forming out in the Gulf. They walked and walked and did not arrive back home until almost ten. Bud apologized profusely, taking full responsibility for them being late. Helmut replied, "I have a strong feeling my daughter is equally responsible. Trust me young man, I'm more concerned about the Indians you will be facing soon than the romance of the evening causing you to lose track of time."

Mrs. Treptow said nothing, but smiled as she served warm food to Bud and Virginia. At the table, she presented Bud with a new pair of pants, shirt, and some socks she and Virginia had made for him, using his old clothes as their pattern. Virginia wanted to make sure Bud knew she knitted the socks. She desperately wanted his approval. She didn't have to wait long. As soon as he received them, he excused himself from the table and went to his room. He came back out dressed head-to-toe in his new clothes, and hiked up his pant leg to show off his newly knitted socks.

At daybreak, Bud was tossing his saddle blanket over Lightning when he glanced up to see Virginia holding out a steaming cup of black coffee. Leading his horse to the front hitching rail, he tossed the neck rope over the railing and entered the house for one last breakfast. Mr. Treptow was reading *The Daily Gazette*, published by Dennis and Lib Kirk, newcomers from the Kansas Territory. The Kirks had been in the printing business back in Kansas when they sold everything they owned and moved to Texas. The paper was thin, but the only source of information on the island.

As Bud swung his right leg over the cantle, he glanced down and saw the broach he had given to Virginia pinned to her dress, squarely over her heart. There were no good-bye kisses. Bud tipped the brim of his hat and nudged Lightning with his knees. As he galloped down the dirt road, he turned in his saddle and waved with his left hand in a large sweeping motion to make sure everyone would see. He didn't dare turn and look again or he might not leave.

The wagon train was at the ferry when Bud arrived, but most of the wagons and many of the men had already crossed. Everyone was a stranger to Bud, so he asked who was in charge. A burly red-haired man in his fifties spoke up. "I'm Robert McCombs, but everyone calls me Red. I guess I'm in charge of this outfit. You must be the boy Hays was tellin' me 'bout. Jack says you are a good hand, and a crack shot. We can surely use both on this trip. The Comanche are on the prowl and the Mexican cowboys are always looking for trouble. It won't surprise me if we get hit by 'em after we cross the Brazos."

Bud reached over and extended his right hand in a gesture of friendship. "Glad to be riding with you, Sir."

"Hays tells me you got you a redskin scalp. Is that right?"

Bud reached into his saddlebag and pulled out a wad of long black hair attached to a dried scalp. "I didn't do the scalping. Noah Smithwick is the one who cut the hair off and dried the skin. I feel sorta funny about showing it off, but it was my first kill and Noah went to so much trouble."

Once all the wagons were across Galveston Bay, Red gathered the men and told them they would need to be more vigilant than on any prior trip. The number of Indian raids was on the rise and they must not let down their guard for one moment.

Meanwhile, spies in Galveston had sent word to Mexico that the wagon train had crossed the Bay. An army of two hundred of Santa Anna's finest crossed the Rio Grande, heading north. Their mission was to capture the wagons at the Brazos River intersection, confiscate a ship and transport the merchandise to Mexico. Their orders were to take no prisoners. While McCombs was looking west for Comanche, the real threat was steadily approaching from the south.

Chapter Twenty-One
Peace

The wagon train's main obstacle became the relentless rain. Sheets and sheets of rain fell day and night. In two days, they had traveled only four miles. The oxen were unable to pull the heavy wagons through the muck and mire of thick clay. The wheels stuck in the mud and would only release when forced free with manual effort. Because of the heavy rain, the wagon train was ten days late making the Brazos River crossing. The Mexican renegades from south of the Rio Grande waited nine days and on the morning of the tenth, decided to head home. When the Mexicans gave the bugle sound to retreat, the caravan's advance scout heard the call. He was puzzled as to why Mexicans would be so far north, and figuring he had misheard the sound, he passed it off as a false alarm. By the providence of God opening the heavens and drenching the way, the group had avoided certain death at the hands of two hundred well-armed Mexicans set on robbing the caravan.

The tired group made the rest of the trip in record time. All of San Antonio spilled onto the streets welcoming them. There was dancing and jubilation throughout the city. Mary Maverick was at the head of the welcoming committee. She was expecting a large bolt of cloth and a set of twelve high back oak chairs that Sam ordered from New Orleans. Various merchants gathered around, waiting to find what wagon contained their merchandise.

Bud excused himself to Captain McCombs, thanking the wagon master for including him, and then galloped off to see if his room was still available. Fortunately, no one was renting his little nook at Juanita's house. Digging into his pockets for loose change before turning his clothes over to be washed, he discovered a $50 gold piece. He realized Mr. Treptow must have put the coin in the new pants as payment for breaking the green horses. Bud rubbed the shiny coin, kissed it, and then placed it in his vest pocket, buttoning the flap.

The morning was Tuesday March 19th, 1840, *"Dia de San Jose"* (the Day of St. Joseph) as Bud left for the township of Bastrop, Texas. Lightning pranced sideways as they made their way up the hill north of San Antonio. About two miles out, he met a band of about sixty Comanche coming down the Camino Real. He started to turn his powerful stallion and run for help when one of the Chiefs raised his right hand, demonstrating they had come in peace. Even though he didn't completely trust them, he really had no choice. Bud returned the friendly gesture and continued to ride in their direction. He kept his right hand free as his eyes scanned the group. His horse brushed against a brave's horse, and as the animals touched, each man gave the other a strong glare. Bud thought he noticed a young white girl in the group, but was not confident he was right. Just after he passed, the majority of the group stopped, and only a few continued on to San Antonio. Bud would not find out the reason for their visit for many weeks.

Seven Penateka Comanche Chiefs strolled into San Antonio, each of their horses adorned with a number of painted hands signifying the white men they had killed. One Chief's horse displayed nine hands. A few displayed white men's scalps draped boldly over their horses. One older warrior displayed a scalp of scarlet red. The Chiefs stated their intention was to discuss a peace treaty. They had Matilda Lockhart, whom they had kidnapped two years earlier, a small Mexican girl, and several more children held just outside of town. Their intention was to barter their captives, a few at a time, to extract the largest ransom possible. The plan was disgusting to the Anglos, but a cunning move on the part of the Indians. If they brought all of their captives at once, they would diminish their bargaining power.

It was agreed that city officials and military leaders would meet with the Chiefs in a council at the Court House. The Chiefs who remained in the plaza pranced their horses around the square with arrogance, making sure to ride through any gathering of three or more residents and brush them aside.

The five Chiefs at the council meeting demanded a large ransom for the return of Matilda and the Mexican girl. News spread like a wildfire in a windstorm that Matilda Lockhart was one of the two captives. Matilda was now fifteen, and everyone was anxious to see her. Maverick sent word for her parents to come into town and get their daughter.

Some people barricaded themselves in their homes, while the curious Mary Maverick and her friend Maude Higginbotham found a safe spot near the plaza to watch events unfold. Everyone waited with anticipation as the Indians holding the girls were summoned into town.

Word of the council reached Secretary of War William Cooke. He immediately moved two Companies into the vicinity under the command of Lt. Colonel Fisher. Cooke wanted to make sure he had the manpower to handle any situation that might arise. No one trusted the Comanche, and for good reason. The Comanche had no friends, and furthermore, wanted none. They even found themselves feuding with each other from time to time. Fighting was in their blood and defined who they were. The Comanche lived for war, and used any stratagem available to gain the advantage. The one rule the Comanche followed: All is fair in war.

Meanwhile, Bud kept a steady pace, riding with his head on a swivel, looking in every direction for an Indian trap. He followed the Camino Real to Bastrop without encountering any more Indians. As the evening sun brushed the tops of the oak trees, Bud arrived, surprised to find how small the town was. The way the Baron had described it to the two hundred settlers from New York, he had the impression Bastrop was almost as large as Galveston. He counted ten houses and four businesses. The sign over the general store had part of the name whitewashed out, but Bud could see the sign originally read: "*Bastrop and Patton, Merchandise Emporium*". The front door was locked, but Bud knocked anyway. He could see a man at the rear of the store working on his books under lamplight. The portly man in his late fifties or early sixties opened the door and barked, "What kan I do fur ya, yung feller?"

"I am in need of a place to sleep and a stable to board my horse."

"Are you the boy the Baron done left his place to?"

"Yes Sir. I'm Benjamin Miller, but most folks call me Bud."

The storeowner had been in partnership with the Baron, but since the Baron had died and had no relatives, he made himself sole proprietor of the business. So far, no one had challenged his claim. He wondered if Bud might do so.

The older man's name was Robert Patton and he had known Bastrop back in Baltimore, more than thirty years earlier. Robert only had one good eye and was deaf in his left ear. His wife had grabbed a fireplace poker and jabbed the white-hot iron into his right cornea one night when the pair was doing some heavy drinking. His hearing loss was the result of a shotgun blast that destroyed his eardrum. Robert was an angry man, moody, and often depressed. Back in Baltimore, the Pattons routinely became embroiled in drunken fights with each other. After Robert lost his eye, they both gave up drinking and took a vow of sobriety. He never blamed her; however, the citizens of Baltimore made remaining in the city difficult. Robert was constantly ridiculed for being a wimp and allowing his tiny wife to blind him. His wife, Lola, was a wisp of a woman, less than five feet tall and weighing no more than ninety pounds. Living in Baltimore became unbearable for Robert and the couple moved to Nashville. It was in Nashville that the Pattons caught "Texas Fever." They read an ad in the local newspaper written by the Baron de Bastrop promising the opportunity of a lifetime for those who would immigrate to Bastrop, Texas. Since Robert already knew the Baron, he felt they would have a leg up, and the Pattons joined a group of thirty-eight who moved from Nashville to Bastrop. The Baron was more than willing to have the chubby man and his skinny wife join him in opening a general store, especially when Robert showed his stash of gold coins.

The Pattons had hoped to get the merchandise stored in Galveston, but were told the inventory was willed to young Miller. Robert felt God had smiled on him by letting Bud stop at his store. He was confident he would have no problem getting the naive young man to consign the merchandise or perhaps see the goods were rightfully his.

"Lola, git this boy sum grub. Looks hungry as a lobo. Bet he's starved."

Robert's inflection let his wife know there was some urgency to feeding their young visitor and taking care of his needs. She guessed, by Robert's demeanor, that Bud's arrival had something to do with several wagons of much-needed merchandise. Her thoughts were correct.

Robert and Bud chatted for a while. After some small talk, Robert wanted to know how Bud got so close to the old land promoter and had inherited such a large amount of property. He also wanted to know about the Baron's murder and the men who killed him. Bud obliged Mr. Patton with the intriguing story of how they met, killing Hector Garza to protect the Baron, and the capture of the gang.

Lola Patton came back into the store with a tray of food. "Eat your fill. There is plenty more where this came from."

Bud thanked her and immediately grabbed a stick of venison sausage and a cold biscuit. While he was eating, Robert suggested Bud could stable his horse behind the store. There was corn in the silo and water could be fetched from the well. Lola recommended Bud bunk down in back of the store on a stack of new saddle blankets.

Several roosters tried to out-crow each other just before the crack of dawn. Bud started to pull his hat tight over his face when he heard the door unlatch. He jumped up, waiting with his hand on his gun as Robert stuck his head in. After a cup of black coffee and a couple of fried eggs, Bud saddled Lightning and was off to see his new home. The house was located about a mile and half from the center of town on 720 acres of choice bottomland. Adjoining the bottomland was a stand of tall pines that filled the other 1,900 acres. Along one edge of the property coursed the powerful Colorado, and on the other, Willow Creek provided an endless supply of crystal-clear spring water. The Baron had placed a small dam across Willow Creek to form a lake where the bend came closest to the house. Bud assumed the Baron wanted to make sure he always had drinking water, and the little lake made a nice fishing hole. Having fish nearby was important in the event game became scarce.

The house was impressive. The structure was much larger than the Baron had described. To understate was rare for his old friend. The typical dogtrot floor plan home was built with square-hewn logs and a double-notch corner locking system. There were two large rooms on each side of an open porch and a lean-to kitchen on the north side. The two large rooms had limestone fireplaces on the outer wall and the floors were white pine varnished in a clear coat. Only the better homes had varnished floors. The kitchen ran the full length of the house, was built over the water well, and came complete with a freestanding sink. Another water pump was located on the exterior of the kitchen for washing or getting a cool drink without entering the house. Noticing a bucket filled with water next to the kitchen sink, he realized the bucket was there to prime the pump. He couldn't resist trying out his indoor Pluming. Sure enough, after he wet the washers and gave a few pulls on the handle, water began to flow. He lowered his head and drank a mouth full of the ice-cold deep-well water. Indeed the Baron had left him a wonderful place to raise a family. Since living with the Treptows, Bud had dreamed of owning a horse ranch. There was always a need for good horses, and with proper breeding, his animals would bring in top dollar. Lightning would sire amazing foals and in time, he could build a nice herd.

Bud rode Lightning up and down Willow Creek. He stopped to examine the dam and then led his horse across the open area and into a grove of massive old oak trees. The lad from Kentucky could hardly believe all of this belonged to him. As he walked slowly through the live oaks, Lightning following a few paces behind, a seventeen-point whitetail buck stepped into a clearing up ahead. Sun bouncing off his majestic antlers, the buck froze, looking straight at them. Bud slowly stepped back to where Lightning was grazing. He gingerly pulled his long rifle from the saddle scabbard and in one motion, raised his weapon to his shoulder and squeezed the trigger. Two-hundred-and-fifty yards away, the big buck dropped to his knees and then slumped to the ground.

Bud looped a rope around the antlers and dragged the buck back to the house. Tossing the rope over a limb, Bud lifted the dead animal off the ground so he could field dress his kill. He proceeded to cut strips of meat to be jerked, and then tacked the hide to the side of the house to tan. He hung a few prime cuts on the limb to prevent a bear or wolf from stealing his food, then tied the remainder of the meat to the back of his saddle and carried it into town. The Pattons were grateful to get fresh venison. Robert was unable to hunt and, as a result, they were only treated to deer meat through occasional bartering. Bud joined the Pattons for supper. Lola was more than willing to cook and Robert wanted the opportunity to persuade their young visitor on the wisdom of consigning the Baron's merchandise to him. Robert Patton was a rank amateur compared to the Baron. Bud was trained by the best, and Roberts's clumsy attempts at manipulation amused the young ranger.

On the third day, Bud brought a fresh batch of catfish and the next two, wild turkey. During the day, Bud cleaned up around his new house. Cobwebs had grown in thick masses and large rats occupied the attic. Robert gave Bud three cats. Bud worried the cats might go hungry if left alone, but Lola assured him that with the abundance of rats and mice scurrying around his home, he would return to a pastel of fat cats. While he cleaned debris, his three cats were hot on the trail of the rats, stampeding in and out of his new home.

The day Bud had left San Antonio for Bastrop was a day that would never be forgotten in the small town. To many, the events equaled the fall of the Alamo. About an hour after Bud had passed the band of Indians, the citizens of San Antonio watched as Comanche Chief Muguara and six other Chieftains strutted into the Military Plaza and demanded a meeting with the man in charge. San Antonio had no man in charge. There was no elected mayor in power. At the time, the highest-ranking official was Captain Tom Howard, the Company Commander in the Alamo. After brief conversation, the Chiefs told him they wanted to barter for two captive girls. Howard told them to bring the girls and he would personally make certain they were treated fairly. In less than two hours, the two other Chiefs returned with the two captives, and a band of sixty-five braves, women, and children. Howard instructed the Indian women and children to remain in the public square while he invited the Chiefs and the older braves for a pow-wow in the Court House Hall. True to their word, the Indians did have Matilda Lockhart and a young Mexican girl with them. They turned the girls over to Howard and then recited a list of items they wanted in exchange. The list was enormous, but rather than haggle, Howard told them he felt most of their requests could be met.

Young Matilda Lockhart was in a horrible condition. Her head, arms, and face were full of bruises and sores. She had burn marks all over her emaciated body, and parts of her nose had been seared off with fire sticks. Her hair was a wad of tangled knots and crawling with lice. Matilda's five-foot-eight-inch frame barely weighed seventy-five pounds. She was a walking skeleton. The younger Mexican girl was in a better shape because she had only been a captive for a short time. No one in San Antonio had ever witnessed anything like the inhumane treatment of Matilda. She told horrific tales of how the Indians had raped and beaten her daily. They would wake her by sticking a chunk of fire to her flesh, especially her nose. With tears running down her cheeks, she described how they shouted and laughed like fiends when she cried in pain. Seeing young Matilda made grown men cry, and enraged any who saw her.

Matilda had become adept at understanding the Comanche language and related to Captain Howard that the Indians were holding back fifteen to sixteen children to negotiate for later. They wanted to dole them out slowly as they needed more supplies.

Mary Maverick was present when Matilda and the little Mexican girl arrived. She took the girls to her home, bathed and dressed them in fresh new clothing. Mary was appalled at their utterly degraded condition. She told friends that Matilda would never be able to hold up her head up again. Her face, arms, and legs were covered with bruises and sores, and her nose had been burned to the bone. Both nostrils were wide open and denuded of flesh. Matilda never did recover from her experience. Once back with her family, she kept her face covered with a white cloth. Not even her mother was allowed to see her uncovered. The fragile child died in less than three years, a broken soul.

The young Indian boys entertained the local citizens by showing off their skills with a bow and arrow. The Texans placed coins on fence posts and the young braves shot them off with deadly accuracy. The young boys left no doubt as to why braves were so accomplished with a bow and arrow; they were taught to shoot as soon as they were big enough to pull a string.

This was actually the third such peace mission the Comanches had brought to the Texans in as many years. The two earlier attempts to negotiate the release of captives had ended in disaster. In one instance, the Texans agreed to trade flannel, gunpowder, blankets, paint, and other valuables in exchange for the release of several white children. A trader was dispatched with the goods; however, while he was at the Indian camp, a chickenpox epidemic broke out and several Indians died. They thought it was a white-man trick, so they killed the trader and kept his wares. Captain Howard was determined not to let history repeat itself.

Howard suspected this was a Comanche trick to extract a ransom with no intention of giving up the other captives. Howard made it clear he was interested in the other fifteen to sixteen children the Comanche Nation was holding captive. The Chiefs conferred among themselves and agreed they would be willing to trade for what amounted to an obscene amount of supplies. The Captain didn't split hairs over the amount of supplies; his goal was to get the children home without risking more bloodshed.

The Chiefs were quick to point out that they freely returned the two girls as a gesture of good faith. Chief Muguara appeared to be in charge of the negotiations as the others deferred to his opinion. Howard directed his statements to the elder Chief. "Chief Muguara, four or five of your Chiefs shall remain here while the rest of you return to the Nation and bring all the captives to us, unharmed. Then, and only then, will we be happy to pay you everything you have asked for. You have my word as an officer; your demands will be met. The Chiefs that remain here will be treated as our brothers. Not one hair on their heads will be harmed. This, we have determined, is the only fair way to address this matter. If you fight, our soldiers will shoot you down where you stand."

The moment Captain Howard's words were translated, the Comanches instantly and in unison, let out a terrifying war cry that resonated throughout the limestone walls of the meeting hall. When the shrill war cry sounded, it was so loud, so inexplicably horrible that, for a moment, no one could comprehend what was happening. The Chiefs drew their arrows and commenced firing as they retreated from the room. Howard's voice could be heard over the shrill war cries, giving a command: "Fire." His men instantly began shooting into the crowd of retreating Comanches. Their first volley killed several Indians and friendly fire dropped two Texans. The Indians rushed the doorway, pushing through the guards and out into the public square. As the Indians spilled onto the street, the soldiers pursued them, guns blazing. Some of the Indians made for the river, while others ran up Soledad Street or east on Commerce. Citizens and soldiers overtook the Indians at all points. Fierce fighting continued in the streets and alleyways as some Indians took refuge in rock houses, securing the doors from the inside.

Inside the Court House Hall, Sheriff Julian Jones, Judge Thomson, advocate from South Carolina, G. W. Cayce, one Army officer, and two privates lay dead. The wounded included Lieutenant Thompson, younger brother of the judge, Captain Howard, Matthew (Old Paint) Caldwell, Judge Robinson, Mr. Morgan, Mr. Higginbotham, and two Army privates.

Mary Maverick and Maude Higginbotham were standing behind a fence watching the young Indian boys' skills when they heard the screams. Mary saw the young braves freeze as she and they recognized the meaning of the shrill whoops. Grabbing Maude by the arm, Mary made a run for her house. They needed to reach Sam and Andrew. As the women started to cross the street, two wild Indian braves ran past them. One turned and gave chase. The women rushed toward the hand-carved front door as a brave grabbed at Maude's dress. Mary shoved her through the door, pulling her free from the warrior. The two braced themselves against the thick wood slab from the inside. The brave was on the outside pushing to get in, but Maude's robust 180-pound body thrust against the door was just enough resistance for the brave to give up and run to save his own hide.

Mary talked as rapidly as a woodpecker banging on a tree. In a frantic burst of words, she apprised Sam and Andrew of what was happening on the street. Both men jumped to their feet, grabbed their guns, which were always loaded and primed. Sam went out the front door and Andrew dashed into the backyard.

Mary shouted at the top of her voice, "Indians are here! Indians are at our house!"

Three braves had come through the gate on Soledad Street and were heading for the river. One stopped near Jinny the cook. Jinny stood strong with the Maverick children and her own tucked safely behind her. She held a large rock over her head with both hands, screaming at the top of her lungs, "If you dos, I'll mash yo head in wift dis here rock. You hears me?"

One brave paused for a moment, pondering the idea of trying to grab one of the children as a hostage or as ransom to save his life. He looked again into Jinny's face and realized she was not going to give up the little ones without a fight. He gave up and ran on. His later choice didn't work out so well. Andrew watched him descend the riverbank and when he started to climb out on the other side, Andrew raised his long rifle and killed the fleeing brave with one perfect shot to the back of his head.

Mary grabbed Jinny and the children, then like a mother hen shooed them into the main house. With them safe, Mary slipped open the front door so she could see what was going on. She didn't have to look far; a dying Indian was in her front yard, less than twenty meters from her door. He lay stretched out upon the ground, moaning in pain. Only seconds after Mary opened the door, an apprentice to Mr. Higginbotham came up the street and spotted the dying Indian. He lowered his pistol over the Indian's head and was ready to pull the trigger when Mary shouted, "Oh, don't. He is almost dead."

The big Texan let out a strong laugh, showing his missing front tooth before answering, "To please you, I won't, but it's the humane thang to do. I need to put him out of his misery. No need to let him suffer just 'cause he's a redskin."

Mary realized he was right and nodded an affirmative with her head. The snaggle-toothed Texan didn't hesitate and fired a round into the center of the Indian's forehead. The body bounced slightly, released a sickening quiver, and then was silent. Two more Indians were on the ground near him with spears protruding from their bodies. Death covered the landscape as a painter's brush does a masterpiece.

Captain Lysander Wells rode past the Maverick's house, headed north on Soledad Street. He was elegantly dressed and riding a small, gaited horse whose hooves flopped outward as he moved. Captain Well's saddle, bridle, and breastplate were laden with silver. As he reached the Verimendi house, an Indian jumped from behind a crepe myrtle bush. He lunged up onto the horse, behind Wells, and wrapped his arms around the captain, trying to wrestle the reins away. The two struggled, bending back and forth, swaying side to side. Finally, Wells was able to grab the Indian with his left hand, leaving his right free to draw his pistol. Wells managed to turn enough to fire a point-blank round into the Indian's stomach. The dying brave clung to Wells for a brief moment and then slid off the rear of the horse. Wells glanced down at the dead Indian, fired one more round into his chest, and then continued on down the street. Mary was so caught up in the death struggle that her fascination had carried her into the middle of the street. She was standing breathless when Lieutenant Chavallier hollered, "Are you crazy, woman? Get back in the house before you get killed." Before she obeyed, Mary took one last look down Commerce Street, where she counted five more dead Indians sprawled on the ground.

Darkness was falling on the city by the time Maverick and Andrew returned home. Neither man was even scratched in the fracas. The children and slaves were safe as well. Even with the good news, Mary didn't feel like celebrating. There were so many dead bodies lining the streets of San Antonio.

Captain Mat Caldwell or "Old Paint" as most folks called him was in from Gonzales visiting the Mavericks. He was one of the most famous Indian fighters in all of Texas. Caldwell fought with Jackson in the Creek Indian War and never stopped. He just kept on fighting. Anyone who had been in the new Republic for a short amount of time knew the story of "Old Paint." His nickname came from a red malformation on his forehead that extended down the side of his cheek. When he heard the Indians would be meeting at the Court House Hall, he decided to mosey over and get in on the conversation. Not expecting trouble, he left his pistol back in his room at the Mavericks. At the first war cry, Caldwell wrestled a gun from an older Chief, killing him on the spot. Using the butt of the gun, he killed another. Then one of the braves shot him in the right leg, breaking the bone.

One of those killed at the Courthouse was young G. W. Cayce, who had called on the Mavericks that morning with a letter of introduction from his father. G. W. was in town to marry Gertrude Navarro, the daughter of a prominent San Antonio family. After visiting with Sam, he decided to go over to the Court House Hall and see what was happening at the council meeting. The truth of the matter was that young Cayce had never seen an Indian and thought this was his best opportunity. He was extremely excited about rubbing shoulders with the savages in a safe environment. Something he could tell his grandchildren about. Cayce walked part of the way to the Courthouse with Mary and Maude. When the women stopped to watch the young Indian boys put on a shooting display, he continued on to the Hall. He had just stepped in the front door when the Chief screamed the signal of war. He was the first to fall in the initial barrage of arrows. He died in the doorway, at the feet of Captain Caldwell.

The injured Captain Caldwell was carried to the Maverick's home, where one of the male slaves was sent to get Dr. Weideman. Dr. Weideman was a surgeon and research scientist from Russia. He could communicate fluently in seven languages and hold his own in five more. His young wife had died giving birth to a stillborn son back in Russia. He became restless and sought employment from the Russian Government. The Emperor sent the young doctor on a research mission to Texas to study animal, vegetable, and flora and fauna specimens. The Emperor could not have picked a better man. Dr. Weideman was tireless in his efforts and completely devoted to his research. He developed a deep affection for Texas, with its temperate climate, gracious people, and spirit of independence. He especially loved San Antonio because, unlike his rugged homeland, snow was an anomaly. He was a regular on Texas Ranger maneuvers and often accompanied Sam Maverick, Jack Hays, and other surveying parties. He wanted to be with them as they explored the frontier, and his medical expertise saved many lives after Indian battles.

Dr. Weideman cut off Captain Caldwell's boot and discovered the bullet had passed clear through his leg. When he pulled off the boot and flipped it over, the bullet came rolling out. The wound was extremely painful, but not dangerous, as long as gangrene could be prevented. The crusty "Old Paint" was not going to let a little thing like a bullet hole through his leg and a shattered bone keep him down. Within a week, he was walking around with a snake stick, a limb with a fork on the end to hold a rattlesnake's head to the ground until one could either cut his head off or shoot him. The more adventurous would pick the snake up by its tail, popping the head off like a leather tassel on the end of a bullwhip. The bullwhip technique was Caldwell's favorite way to dispose of the poisonous reptile. He loved nothing more than grabbing a six-footer by its rattlers, drawing it up, giving it a pop and watching as the head splattered, especially if greenhorns were present.

Mary Maverick waited until Captain Caldwell's wounds were dressed and then ran across the street to the Higginbothams. Mr. Higginbotham had been an invited guest at the Courthouse and became an unwilling participant in the fighting. He received only a surface wound, which Maude cleaned and dressed. Shortly after her arrival, a male slave rushed in and told Maude that two Indians had taken refuge in the Higginbotham's kitchen and refused to surrender. After several attempts by an interpreter to coax them out, a group of young men came up with a plan. A little after midnight, Anton Lockmar went home and brought back a roll of candlewick. Candlewicks were rolled into a ball where it was cut off to dip into the boiling wax. Anton and Steve Wall climbed onto the roof and unrolled part of the ball, and soaked the remainder in turpentine. They located a hole in the roof large enough to drop the ball through. Anton set the candlewick ball on fire, dropped it through the hole and started swinging the flaming sphere around. After a few passes, he was able to place the blazing ball on top of one of the Indian's head. The Indian became terrified and without thinking, exited the back door, followed closely by his companion. The frightened duo rushed out of the kitchen and into the arms of death. Homer Sims was waiting with his ax and split the first Indian's head down the middle like a ripe watermelon. His comrade was shot as he leaped over the fallen body. The standoff was over.

Lieutenant Rubin Thompson was found with an arrow through his lung and taken to Madam Santita's home on Soledad Street, next door to the Higginbothams. He vomited blood and begged to die. The lieutenant's agonizing cries reverberated throughout the city, unnerving even the most seasoned soldiers. Dr. Weideman remained at the lieutenant's bedside the entire night. No one expected the young lieutenant would survive, but Dr. Weideman's competence as a surgeon was unparalleled, and Thompson pulled through. Within ten days, he was able to walk several feet without assistance.

The captured Indians were placed in chains, and housed in the long barracks at the Alamo. The less aggressive women, along with the children, were marched to Mission Concepcion under heavy guard. After a three-hour pow-wow, the two sides agreed to a twelve-day truce. The widow of one of the slain Chiefs was chosen to deliver a message back to the Comanche: The Texans were willing to trade the Indian prisoners for the children held in the Comanche Nation. The squaw seemed more than eager to convey the message and gave assurances she would be successful in returning the captive children in exchange for the thirty-one Indian prisoners. She promised to travel day and night to reach the Nation. The Texans provided her with a horse, blankets, and plenty of food for the journey. Captain Howard warned, "If you are not back by the 28th of this month, all thirty-one Indian prisoners will be killed. Do I make myself clear?"

She answered through an interpreter: "I understand and I will not let you or my people down."

The citizens stood in the street and watched her ascend the hill and disappear over the horizon. Confidence reigned. No one could conceive the Indians would allow their own to be killed just to keep a handful of frail children. Days passed and no sign of the squaw or the children. After a month, all hope was lost.

Several years later, the Texans would learn what happened through the words of young Billy Lee Webster. Billy Lee had been kidnapped and adopted by an Indian family. He was spared the fate of the other captive children. When he was rescued, he told the story of what had happened when the squaw came in to the Comanche Nation. Upon learning of the deaths of the Chiefs, the Indians began to howl and cry, cutting themselves with knives. Then they turned their wrath on the thirteen captive children, brutally torturing and mutilating them before killing them. They would bring a child to the brink of death and then revive them so they could continue torturing them. When one died, the braves roasted their carcass over an open flame and ate the cooked flesh while the other children watched in horror.

When the squaw did not return, the Texans chose not to kill the captive Indians. People demanded an eye for an eye, but Captain Howard refused to stoop to the level of the savages. The Indian prisoners fully expected they would be killed after the twelve-day deadline had passed. They couldn't understand the kindness shown by the Texans. Slowly, the strictness was relaxed, and they were allowed to escape and return to their tribe. A few of the less aggressive Indians were taken in as domestics by the families of San Antonio.

The San Antonio Courthouse fight had the same effect on the Comanche as the Alamo and Goliad had on the Texans. The bitter memory of several Chiefs' deaths remained with the Comanche for decades. In their minds, the Texans had lured them into a trap and murdered a peace-loving group. On the other side of the coin, the Texans had the proof they needed that no Comanche could ever be trusted. The distrust on both sides widened like the mouth of an angry alligator.

The afternoon of the Courthouse Hall fight, Mary and Maude noticed Dr. Weideman walking toward the front window. The two women were sitting in the long room and couldn't figure out what the doctor was holding in his hands. To their amazement, he was carrying the severed head of an Indian woman. He bowed courteously, and in his thick Russian accent asked, "With your permission, Madam?" Without waiting for approval, he placed the severed head on the windowsill and disappeared. Shortly, he returned with the bloody head of a man and perched his trophy next to the female head. Once more, he smiled graciously and addressed the stunned ladies, "I have been exceedingly anxious to secure such human specimens. Now my dears, I must hurry and get my cart to gather the cadavers. Not to worry, I'll be back to fetch the heads."

The doctor grinned and turned the male head facing the inside of the home. The death stare from the open eyes turned Maude's stomach. She rushed out the backdoor just in time to avoid upchucking on the floor. Mary sat and looked, but appeared unfazed. Her thoughts were on the senseless brutality each side exhibited during the battle. Ever since she had arrived in Texas, there had been a constant flow of blood. "When would the killing stop? Why could there be no peace?" she wondered.

The doctor returned around dark to retrieve the heads, carefully wrapping them in oilcloth and placing them in his cart, along with several bodies. Waving vigorously at the two ladies, he rushed off with his treasures. When he arrived home, he instructed his Mexican workman to put the bodies in a large soap boiler down near the bank of the ditch. The ditch ran alongside his home and provided drinking water for the families with no wells. At least eighty percent of those living in the San Antonio depended on the ditch for their drinking and cooking water. A city ordinance prohibited dumping any rubbish into the ditch because it was important to keep the drinking water clean and pure. Anyone in violation was subject to heavy fines. The thought of a fine didn't deter Dr. Weideman. In the darkness of night, he emptied the cooked flesh and blood from the soap pot into the ditch. The blood and flesh made a wide brown-red sickening strip as the current carried the carnage downstream.

The next morning, a Mexican housewife went to fetch a bucket of drinking water and was horrified when she recognized the floating debris as a bloody glob of human flesh. She followed the glob up the ditch toward the doctor's home and observed more of the same ghoulish body parts. Anger shot through her veins as she sounded the alarm for help. Men rushed to her aid and traced the starting point to Weideman's property. The cooking pot was still on its edge, perched next to the ditch. Rage exploded with the residents and there was some talk of a lynching party. The citizens crowded around the Mayor's office, cursing and screaming obscenities. Women cried. Some vomited on the Mayor's steps. Those who drank the water thought they had been poisoned, and would die. Panic surged up and down the ditch along with the belief the crazy doctor wanted to kill them. Dr. Weideman was arrested and brought to trial. He acted as his own attorney. Each day he was overwhelmed with verbal abuse from those in the courtroom calling him "El Diablo", (the devil). No matter what they called him, the doctor remained calm. Speaking in a soft voice, he told those in attendance they would not be harmed, that the Indian poison ran off with the water before daylight. He paid a hefty fine of $500 and left the Courthouse, laughing.

The doctor employed seven Mexican men to care for his string of horses and his menagerie of wild animals. One of his workers, Jose had worked and lived with the doctor for two years. Jose seemed to have one problem: a propensity to steal. One day he stole the doctor's valuable gold pocket watch. Dr. Weideman made several inquiries about his missing watch and waited four weeks, hoping in vain the thief would return his heirloom. He was determined to get his watch back, even if it meant he had to perform some magic. His father had been a professional magician and Weideman had learned several tricks from him.

After a month, convinced that Jose had stolen his pocket watch, Dr. Weideman came up with a plan to get a confession and put a stop to the constant stealing. He waited until there was a full moon before summoning all of his Mexican workers together. He instructed a few of the men to build a fire on the dirt floor in the middle of the room. Then he placed a pot of liquid over the fire and brought his employees and several visitors into the room. Weideman was dressed in a long flowing robe covered with stars and moons, and wore a tall, pointed hat that rested mysteriously on his head. In his hands, he held a twisted stick with which to stir the liquid while uttering strange words in an unknown tongue. Finally, he told the assembled group in both English and in Spanish that he would douse the fire and let the magical liquid cool before having each person dip their hand into the pot. If one were innocent, his hand would be clean when removed from the liquid. If he were the thief, his hand would turn black. Everyone lined up and proceeded to dip their hand into the pot. One by one, they pulled out a clean hand. After each person dipped their hand in and pulled it out, the doctor would mumble unintelligible words as he stirred the pot for the next suspect. When everyone else present had passed his test, it was Jose's turn. Again, the doctor recited some magical words, stirring the liquid. Sure enough, when Jose removed his hand, it was black. Jose fell to his knees. He started begging the doctor not to kill him. He admitted he had stolen the doctor's watch and would return the timepiece immediately if his life would be spared. The doctor let him wallow in his shame in front of the others before saying, "Go get my watch and all other items you have taken from me and all will be forgiven."

The watch was the last item stolen from the doctor. He had used his father's old magic trick to get his watch back and make an honest group out of his workers. No one in Texas employed a more honest group of men than the Russian doctor. From that day on, when the local Mexicans saw the doctor on the street, they would make a Christian sign of the cross and say the "Hail Mary".

Doctor Weideman would not live to see Texas become the twenty-eighth state. One year before the Lone Star was lowered and the Stars and Stripes rose over Texas, he and another man drowned while attempting to cross a flooded creek near Gonzales. Neither of the men's bodies was ever recovered. The Mexicans back in San Antonio felt the devil took the doctor's body in water since he had polluted theirs. They believed his death delivered just retribution for the doctor's evil acts. The Anglos deeply missed Dr. Weideman, but the Mexicans shed no tears.

Bud Miller reached San Antonio around four in the afternoon. He was full of life and floating with joy until he ran into the cheerless face of Noah Smithwick. After Noah told him of the council battle, his countenance dropped. He knew rangers would be summoned to protect the citizens of San Antonio from Comanche retaliation, and went directly to the trading post to stock up on powder and lead.

Texas was heading into an even more tumultuous time. No family living on the fringes would be secure. No travelers would be safe. Dark days and stormy nights were in the future of the Lone Star Republic and young Ranger Miller would be riding point. Bud could never have imagined just how dark the future would become. Challenges beyond his comprehension waited around every bend in the road as Texas fought mightily for her right to exist.

Chapter Twenty-Two
Fear

Few people understood the Comanche. Certainly not the second-term President Samuel Houston. He thought a peace agreement could be drawn up with the Comanche as he had with the Tonkawas, Lipan, and his beloved Cherokee, but the Comanche were different from the other plains tribes. They had no formal leadership or High Chief to rule the Nation. They created no set of laws and observed few customs. They performed no yearly Sundance, no unison parlays where the Nation came together, like other tribes. The Comanche observed no sacred dogma, ceremonial rites, obligations or taboos. They did share one commonality of purpose: the pursuit of warrior superiority. They were vigilant opportunists, always looking for an opportunity to assault any and all. Although they numbered only about five thousand, they terrorized the plains from the Arkansas River down into northern Mexico. They were so ruthless that no other tribe dared challenge their supremacy. Fear was their standard-bearer, and no other group rivaled their ability to terrorize an entire country with just the mention of their name.

There was an attitude among Texans that they should step up their efforts to find and destroy all the Comanches they could before the Indians struck again. Several new companies of Texas Rangers were formed. Jack Hays, being such a solid leader, had his pick of skilled Texans wanting to eradicate the Comanche. Bud Miller made a beeline to Jack's office. Bursting through the door, he shouted, "Count me in to go with you."

Jack smiled and replied, "I already have your name down. Go get your things together because we will be gone by daybreak. We are going to be scouting areas where Comanche have been seen lately. Just yesterday, a Mexican spotted a large number of Indians northeast of us. He suspected they were Comanche by the markings on their horses."

Bud knew if it were Comanche, they were not hunting for buffalo that far east, but looking for horses or scalps. In many ways, horses were more important to the Comanches than killing their enemy. They didn't feed and nurture their horses like the white man or Mexican. They rode their horses into the ground, then slit their throats and cooked the meat. They constantly needed fresh mounts and the easiest way to accomplish that was to steal them.

Ben McGee was new to Texas. His parents had moved from Georgia to Louisiana and he later migrated alone to Texas. Bud met the new man at the stable. Each was admiring the other's horse when Bud extended his hand. "My name is Benjamin Miller, but folks call me Bud."

The new lad answered, "My name is Sampson Benjamin McGee and folks mostly call me McGee. I'm here to join the Texas Rangers and I here tell this is the town where I can sign up."

Bud smiled. "Welcome McGee. Have you spoken to Jack Hays? He is the one to give you the go-ahead. I have no authority in hiring you, but I'll testify that you have the best lookin' mount I've ever seen."

"Yep, he can run all day and never break a sweat. Ain't no Indian gonna catch me on Pretty Boy. Pretty Boy belonged to my grandpa. When he learned I was coming to Texas, he insisted I take his best mount. He said a fast horse will save a man's life quicker than a gun."

Bud knew that before Jack would sign McGee up, he would have to prove his shooting skills. With Bud's help, Ben passed the test, and then introduced to Jack. Based on Bud vouching for him, Jack instructed the young McGee: "We ride on the third bell in the morning. Be in the Military Plaza ready to go by then or we'll leave without you."

Since McGee and Bud were the youngest, they rode together and talked for the next two days. Hays could feel the lack of fear in the newcomer; however, he also knew courage and common sense were two different things. He had seen too many good men die in the name of being fearless. Jack wanted men with courage, but he also wanted them to understand fear. A dead ranger is of no use to anyone.

Also in Hays' Company were big Craig Winborn, Ben and Henry McCollough, Jack's brother William, Noah Smithwick, Big Foot Wallace, Samuel Walker, and Clark Owens. All were heavily armed and riding exceptional horses. Jack required that all of his men's horses could outrun and outlast even the best Indian ponies.

The Ranger Company traveled a few miles to the south of the El Camino Real, knowing the Indians would not be so dumb as to ride down the middle of the road in broad daylight. From time to time, Jack would lead the men to the north side of the road, constantly looking for any sign of fresh Indian tracks.

Ben McCullough knew the wilderness better than any ranger in the company. He learned his skills as a youngster traveling the backwoods of Tennessee with David Crockett. It was at one of Crockett's gatherings that he had met Johnny Satterwhite. He knew of Johnny's tragic death and wanted to pay his respects to Millie. He would be the second man that had manned a "Twin Sister" cannon at San Jacinto to visit the Satterwhite home. Tom Green was the first. He knew of her marriage to Jim Willingham, who he had been a friend with in San Antonio. Ben asked Jack if it would be possible for them drop in on Millie and the children. Jack thought the suggestion was sound. He told the men they were less than a day's ride from James and Millie's place and thought it was a grand idea to drop in and check on them. He worried about their isolation. His one consolation was that they were near the Groce Plantation and Washington. The Comanche knew Jared Groce owned over 150 healthy male slaves and could produce a sizeable army with the ring of a bell. The Comanche stayed clear of the Groce Plantation and consequently, the Satterwhite homestead. The rangers pushed northward until they reached the Little River, then traveled east until Jack spotted the low water point he and Ranger Childress had crossed a few years earlier.

Jim was working on the roof of his second house when he saw the horses and riders enter the water. Putting two fingers in his mouth, he let out a shrill whistle that blasted A.D.'s ears and put him on notice to get the guns. In a flash, A.D. handed Jim his Kentucky Long Rifle and got the Tennessee rifles for his mother and sister. He joined his mother, Ruthann, and the new baby inside the house while Jim stayed on the roof. When the riders cleared the riverbank, Jim recognized several in the group. He climbed down from the roof and shouted, "What brings you into this neck of the woods?"

Ben McCollough laughingly answered, "Free food."

"Well you thought wrong. We don't take in freeloaders out here. That's what the city folk do."

Jim's big smile gave him away. He couldn't contain his joy in seeing the group of old friends and meeting the new rangers. After being introduced to Bud, he solicited, "Are you Stump Miller's boy? Heard a lot about you."

"Yes Sir," Bud answered with a smile.

Millie came out of the house holding the new baby, followed by a much-taller A.D. and the pretty Ruthann.

"My word," Jack said. "You didn't let the grass grow under your feet. What's the baby's name?"

Jim pushed out his chest and with great pride, exclaimed, "We named him Johnny. The only problem is he won't be a Satterwhite, he's stuck with being a Willingham."

There was a lot of catching up to do and each man was able to shed some light on what was taking place throughout the Republic. Jim and Millie were saddened to learn of the Courthouse fight. The Matilda Lockhart story broke their hearts. Millie bowed her head and said a soft prayer, knowing but for the Grace of God, that could have been her Ruthann.

Jack looked around and noticed that Jim had added two rooms onto the main house and had another house almost completed some fifty yards from the original residence. "What's with the other house? You plannin' a large family?"

"Naw, I'm building a rental house for people using our ferry. We get a good amount of people using our crossing, and we thought it might be nice to have a place for them to rest after being on the road. We have already had two families stay in there, and I don't even have the roof completed. We are not getting rich, but we are earning a little money from the ferry and lodging. As you know, there's lots of bartering, but not much hard cash. The ferry and our guesthouse will give us gold and silver to buy the things Millie and the children need."

Millie knew of Ben McCullough because Johnny had spoken often of their friendship. It didn't take her long to start asking Ben questions. She named about twenty women from San Antonio and wanted to know about their welfare. She even asked about the children, slaves, and Mexicans. Ben was pleased to see, from all appearances, Millie, Ruthann and A.D. seemed happy and full of life. Jim refused to allow the torment of the past to tarnish their future and worked very hard to keep them in the present. His wit and charm soothed Millie and the children and helped them to forget the hardships, and eliminate the night terrors. Jim was devoted to making up for all the hurt his family had endured, and to healing their wounds.

Each mile Jack and his men had traveled eastward had actually taken them further away from the Comanche. After spending two days with the Willinghams, Jack decided he had been given false information. They would head back southwest to pick up the Comanche's trail.

The real reason Jack had been unable to pick up a trail was that the Indians were not moving. The Comanche were hiding along the Blanco River at the confluence of Cedar Creek, not far from the future township of Wimberley. This was no ordinary assemblage, but an enormous group of 650 to 700 Comanche warriors, Chiefs, and women and children. Chief Buffalo Hump brought together the Penatekas, Taminas,

Tenawas, Kiowas, and other southern Comanches to hold council deep into the Comancheria. Buffalo Hump, a charismatic leader, managed to unite the tribes for a great battle against the white man. At night around the campfire, the wise old Chief kept up his rantings against the untrustworthy Texans. He reminded them how the Texans treated the peace mission in San Antonio. He built up a frenzy to kill. Once the warriors' anger reached a fever pitch, they headed out of the hill country near the head of the San Marcos River and skirted along the low divide between the Guadalupe and Lavaca rivers.

For two days, the Comanches circled the city of Victoria, taking pot shots at anyone daring to show their face. The savages held the citizens of Victoria hostage in their homes, in utter fear. On the second day of their siege, a band of cocky young braves rode through the center of town, killing fifteen people, including two women, a blind man, several unarmed slaves, and a schoolteacher. The new schoolteacher, Andrew Johns carried a white flag, seeking a parlay. A hotheaded young brave answered his request with the deadly aim of his tomahawk, killing Johns instantly.

The Indians stole over two thousand horses and mules and drove the stolen animals south. The massive war party proceeded southeast another twenty miles to the Bay of Lavaca, pushing down Peach Creek under a Comanche moon, and finally made camp three miles outside the town of Linnville. The two thousand horses and mules were gold to the Comanche; however, they would prove to be Buffalo Hump's undoing. Traveling with so many horses under the crescent moon made it easy for ranger scouts to track them.

As soon as the Victoria citizens were out of danger, several riders were sent in various directions seeking help and warning everyone they saw about the size and viciousness of the band of savages. Cole Young ran into Jack Hays. Knowing his ten men could not defend against such a massive fighting force, Jack immediately dismissed Ben McCullough and Big Foot Wallace, instructing them to assemble a large company of rangers. Jack figured the Indians would make a dash into the hill country around San Marcos. Once in the hill country, they would be untouchable. If the savages were to be stopped, there would need to be a large force in place before they reached the turning off point. He sent Ben McGee and Bud Miller to the area he expected his seasoned fighters to make a stand. The remainder of the rangers would accompany him and merge with those attacking from the rear.

The following morning, the Comanche swooped down on Linnville, a small bayside community consisting of mostly warehouses, a customs house, and a smattering of log homes. The alarm was sounded in plenty of time for the residents to reach the boats and head out into the bay, where they would be safe. Not all moved with alacrity. Why people didn't immediately flee became a mystery to be debated for decades. Each had some reason to linger. Newlyweds Eli and Daphne Watts started running to the boats when she realized she had left her wedding gift from her husband, an inexpensive lapel watch with a gold-plated chain behind. After picking up the watch at the house, they were halfway back to the boats when the Indians caught up with them. One of the young braves rammed his lance through Eli's chest and then took Daphne captive.

As the Indians raided Linnville, Judge Jack Hays (no relation to Texas Ranger Jack Hays) became outraged with their barbaric ways. He waded to the shore with an empty shotgun and stood his ground, cursing the savages. Indians on horseback swarmed around the old judge, who seemed oblivious to them. It's unclear if they respected his courage or thought he was insane (Indians were known to spare crazy people). Whatever the reason, the braves watched him rant and rave and then just rode off, leaving the judge up to his belly in water.

From Gonzales, Victoria, Cuero, and every community between Linnville and Austin, men were organizing to track down the savages and hold them at bay until sufficient help arrived. Angry Texans gathered from the Colorado to the Guadalupe and beyond. Volunteers came rushing in to fight under the commands of Mathew Caldwell, Ed Burleson, John Moore and other seasoned leaders. The fighters' ages ranged between thirteen and seventy-two. All came with a full supply of food, lead, and powder.

The Comanches were not difficult to track after they left Linnville. Bolts of ribbons, muslin, and calico streamed from their horses and dropped along their trail. Buffalo Hump had loaded up twenty-seven mules with as much merchandise as the animals could carry. The band was in no hurry. Because of their overwhelming numbers, they were confident that when Anglos saw their massive assemblage of warriors, they would tuck their tails and run for cover.

In the early stages of the retreat, the Comanches had plenty of fresh horses and easily out-distanced the rangers. The Indians kept switching to fresh mounts, while the Anglos in pursuit were forced to ride the same horses. The problem facing the Indians was not fresh horses, but carrying their loot. The overloaded mules were unable to keep up, forcing the entire group to slow down and giving the rangers and Army time to build a considerable fighting force to pursue them. Jack Hays, Sam Maverick, Big Foot Wallace, and Ben McCullough, each leading a force of rangers, soon joined veterans like Tumlinson, Mathew "Old Paint" Caldwell and Ed Burleson. Two days ride from Linnville, the seasoned Indian fighters picked up the band's trail.

Buffalo Hump made a critical mistake in not turning west just south of San Antonio. Once in the canyons of Uvalde, they could have escaped into the hill country unmolested. Instead, he arrogantly decided to travel northwest, adjacent to the Colorado. His over-confidence and greed kept him on a direct path northward, allowing those in pursuit to catch up to them before they reached Balcones.

James Bird and John Moore's companies were able to position themselves in front of the Indians, heading them off at Plum Creek. Bud Miller, Ben McGee, and Noah Smithwick managed to catch up with Bird and Moore prior to the encounter. On an exceedingly hot August day, General Felix Huston of the regular Army arrived on the scene, and in spite of protests, assumed command. The next day, another 112 rangers under Maverick, Wallace, and McCullough made their way into camp. Jack Hays and his men were still to the south trailing the Indians, while reinforcements joined his group hourly.

The Texans on the front dismounted and waited. When the main Comanche cavalcade moved into the open prairie next to Plum Creek, the Texans mounted up and rode out to greet them. Burleson, Caldwell, and Huston were at the front as the men cleared the cedar breaks. The trio moved forward at a slow walk. Two large lines of horsemen approached each other, ready for battle.

John Jenkins, a Bastrop volunteer described the Indians in a letter to his wife: "The savages pranced in front of us on magnificent mounts, challenging our blockage of their path. Arrayed in all the splendor one can imagine, they seemed to dare us to a fight. Their horses were decorated with feathers and brilliant-colored ribbons and the braves brightly painted, and many wore feather war bonnets. Their shields, made of thick buffalo hide to repel our bullets were decorated with signs to ward off evil. The Indians rode in and out of the battle lines, exhibiting feats of horsemanship and daring so spectacular that no one but a Comanche could perform. I was in awe of their arrogance and poise."

The Comanche created an unforgettable spectacle while the experienced ranger captains were trying to delay combat until the Comanches pushed the enormous herd of horses and mules past them. Rather than split his main unit, Buffalo Hump unwisely chose to keep the band together. As the horses and over-burdened mules passed by, McCullough, Burleson, and Caldwell wanted to press the attack. Caldwell angrily demanded they fight, but Felix Huston hesitated. The old Indian fighters knew if they stampeded the horses, the resulting pandemonium would give them the upper hand. Felix Huston thought otherwise; he was accustomed to normal wars. Mathew Caldwell decided to challenge Huston's authority. He knew if they were going to have any chance, they must use the horses to distract the warriors. The Indians were too many in number to fight without an advantage.

As Caldwell and Huston argued, a Comanche chief in a magnificent feathered headdress broke rank and began to perform in front of the Texans, challenging their leader to individual combat. Young Bud Miller watched the Indian flaunting himself as long as he could stand. He realized Captain Caldwell and the much wiser ranger captains were trying to persuade Huston to act, and he decided it was time to take action. He steadied his Kentucky long rifle on a low branch and implored Lightning to remain still. Then he took careful aim and squeezed the trigger. His shot hit the target squarely between the eyes, knocking the warrior off his horse. He was dead by the time he hit the ground.

"Now General, now!" Caldwell bellowed, "Charge 'em! Give 'em lead!"

General Huston reluctantly gave the order to attack. Their charge stampeded the massive herd and the Comanches dispersed, trying to control their animals, rather than prepare for battle. Caldwell's strategy was proving correct. Horses and mules piled up in the boggy creek bed as they rushed into Plum Creek. The Comanches were scattering from their battle positions. Those unfortunate enough to be caught up in the stampede were picked off one by one by the Texans using their precise long rifles. Caldwell took his rangers to the left flank, methodically killing every Indian in their path. The running fight went on for fifteen miles. The combat was close and brutal.

A massive pile of gold and silver, cloth, clothing, whiskey, gunpowder, and tobacco were recovered, but it was the nineteen hundred horses and mules that were the most painful loss for the Comanche. Reminiscent of the white man's lust for gold, the horse was the Comanche's passion. It was not uncommon for a brave to own two hundred horses. He only rode a few, and the others were representative of his wealth. Instead of the white man's gold, horses were the Indians' currency.

After the battle, one Texan commented in reference to the Comanche skills on a horse: "They are like the fabled Thessalian Centaur—half horse, half man. The brave is so closely joined and dexterous on his horse they appear to be one animal, both fast and furious."

Old Paint Caldwell offered his thoughts to Bud, commenting, "Texas is like an open grave waiting patiently to be filled with corpses."

Peace was a foreign word to the raw-boned Texas frontiersmen.

Chapter Twenty-Three
Maturity

After the Plum Creek mêlée, the rangers and volunteers began dividing up the items retrieved from the Comanches. The pieces with clear ownership were returned to their rightful owners, while the rest became the spoils of war, with the victors grabbing what they wanted. Some of the men were mercenaries that only joined the fight for the spoils of gold and silver, a realization young Miller found disgusting. Bud didn't feel comfortable taking the property the Indians had looted from defenseless settlers, and had more to worry about than squabbling over a few stolen possessions. During the fight, an arrow had ripped into Lightning's throat, leaving a wide gash in his flesh. Blood was gushing out, washing the powerful stallion's white stockings in crimson. Bud was standing with cotton rag against the cut, trying to stop the bleeding when Tom Arnold, an old ranger rode up. "See ya got a problem, boy."

"Yes Sir. The Comaches cut a gash that I can put my hand into."

Tom dismounted and ambled over carrying a small pouch in his hand. "I think I can fix it. Git a good grip on his bridle and hold 'im still. It's just a flesh wound. I'll sew it together and that should stop the bleeding. He'll be fine."

Lightning pulled his head back and tried to rear up. Two other men stepped in and helped Bud control his horse as the pot-bellied old man went about his business as if he were a skilled surgeon. Seasoned Indian fighters always carried a large needle and wax thread in their kit in the event a horse or man needed stitching up. "Don't worry 'bout these stitches; they will rot out in time. It may leave a small scar, but once his hair grows back, you won't be able to notice it."

Bud thanked Tom asking, "How much do I owe you?"

The old ranger paused, giving Bud a strange look. "Owe? Son, we are Texans. 'All for one and one for all.' There will come a time when you can pass the favor on." He strode back to his horse. As he mounted, his weight pulled the saddle over slightly as he swung his right leg over the cantle. Adjusting the saddle back in place, he was off at a gallop to get his share of the loot.

Bud asked Ben McGee, "Would you like to ride with me back to San Antonio?"

"Sure, my folks don't know where I am. Alls they know is I went redskin huntin'. They are down in a community called Belmont. Ever heard of it?"

Bud thought for a few moments, trying to recall where Belmont was before he spoke. Then he said with candor, "Can't say as I know. Where is it?"

"East of San Anton'. It ain't really a town. Just a few families who built their homes close together, with their fields going out in five directions. Sorta like a star with the houses in the center and the land going out like a piece of pie. We thought if we kept close together, we would be better able to fight off the redskins if they showed up. My Pa, Sampson McGee got in a little trouble back in Georgia, so we moved to Louisiana. He heard how a man could get land cheap in Texas, so he upped and moved us over to Belmont."

"At least you got a Pa. The Mexicans under Santa Anna killed mine at Goliad. I came here to kill Mexicans, but since found out the Indians are the real problem."

The two didn't talk for the next two hours as they made their way through the blood-soaked killing fields, awash with the dead and dying. Bud glanced back over his shoulder to see buzzards descending from the sky to feed on the corpses.

When the two young men came to a small creek, they made camp. Bud led Lightning into the water and washed the dried blood off to prevent flies from clustering around his wound. The cool water felt good and Lightning responded by nuzzling against Bud's chest as he was being bathed.

The following day, Bud and Ben caught up with Colonel Edward Burleson and about two dozen regular army troops who were scouting for stray Comanche that may have escaped the battle. The Colonel invited the young rangers to ride along with them. After coming to Texas in 1830, Burleson made a reputation for himself as a fearless Indian fighter and leader of men. Burleson then served as a Texas Ranger for a brief time, but at President Lamar's request, became a Brigadier General in the Texas Army. Unknown to Bud, he and General Burleson were neighbors, with Burleson's farm only a few miles north of Bud's.

About three o'clock that afternoon, they came upon a fresh trail of horses and cattle heading south. The General knew no new settlers would be bringing so many cattle into the region, and besides, none of the horses was shod. This gave the old Indian fighter a strong indication that the tracks must have been left by Indians. They followed the trail until dark and made camp. Unlike Jack Hays, they didn't move to a secondary location after supper. Neither did the General post a picket.

Bud approached Burleson timidly. "Sir, Cap'n Hays always has us move camp again after we eat, so if any Indians see our smoke, we will be gone when they arrive."

"Young man," the older man gruffly responded, "I don't need a boy still wet behind the ears lecturing me on fighting savages. I was fighting those red barbarians before Jack Hays could tie his shoes. Consider it a favor that I'm letting you ride with me and don't come here trying to tell me how to run my business."

Bud's face flushed with anger. He bit down on his lower lip, taking deep breaths as the Baron had taught him to do before speaking in anger. "Sir, if I may ask you a question."

Burleson's eyes were thin slits, like an alligator pretending to be asleep. He glared at Bud before grunting, "I guess now you plan to tell me where to post the night watch. Well, let me tell you something boy. My men are tired, I'm tired, and if there are any Indians, they are darn sure tuckered out. They won't come charging in here tonight. I strongly recommend you retire early. We will hit the road before the rooster's crow. He never allowed Bud to ask his question. Burleson removed his bible from his saddlebag and began reading, and refused further acknowledgement of Bud's presence.

The following morning Burleson was true to his word. The men finished eating, were mounted and following the fresh trail before the sun rose. Burleson pushed the men hard all morning, not stopping to eat. They relied on shelled corn and beef jerky for sustenance. Bud rode with the front three scouts. They were almost a mile ahead of the group when they spotted a camp on the banks of the Blanco River. Bud noticed three Indians riding out to meet them, carrying a white piece of cloth tied to a stick, signaling they came in peace. Two were dressed in traditional white man's clothes and the other wore buckskin. Bud spurred Lightning into a full gallop and was the first to greet the three friendly Indians. He was shocked to hear the older Indian speak English. With his right hand raised, showing his open palm, the gray-haired Chief greeted them with a roaring voice. "Me Chief Running Water, we friend of Great Raven. You know him as General Houston."

"Chief, then you must be Cherokee. I knew a Cherokee back in Kentucky where I'm from. He was a good man," Bud answered as he relaxed in his saddle. Chief Running Water remained stoned-faced, nodding that Bud was correct.

"Why are you going south?"

Bud's question was a valid one. The old Chief answered with a tinge of sadness. "We go to Mexico because the man who took The Raven's place is killing all Indians. We want no war with anyone. We are people of peace."

By now, the others were in the mix. Burleson took over. "Who in the deuce are you?"

The old Chief pointed to the youngest of the three answering, "That's John Bowles, son of Chief Bowles, friend of General Houston." Then he pointed to the other man saying, "That's the Egg."

Before the old Chief could tell his own name, Burleson gave the order to open fire. Bud whirled Lightning around and pulled back to Burleson's side. He was too late. Bud turned back just in time to see Chief Running Water fall from the back of his horse, his body full of bullets.

"But Sir, they are friendly. These are the people General Houston lived with. Please, for God's sake, have mercy," Bud implored.

"They can get mercy from their god, if they have one. Personally, I don't believe these savages have a soul."

Bud witnessed three Indians murdered in cold blood without raising a hand of resistance. When Burleson was finished, the total death count was seven adult men along with all of their horses and cattle. There remained one old man, five women and nineteen children, stranded with no means of travel. Among the survivors was the mother of John Bowles who treated a young Sam Houston as her own when he first came to their village, and welcomed him back again when he lived with them for six years in the Oklahoma Territory.

Bud refused to continue on with Burleson. Before the army departed, Bud told him, "You may be considered a brave man by some in Texas, but I think you are a sniveling coward."

Fully expecting the seasoned Indian fighter to challenge him to a duel, he waited, but no response came. Burleson knew Bud had defeated the man many considered one of the top duelers in the Republic. He mumbled something and motioned for his men to proceed. Ben McGee didn't say a word. He tucked his hat low over his face and followed, leaving Bud with the grieving Cherokee.

Six-foot platforms were erected, the dead hoisted to the top and covered with twigs and the hides of the freshly butchered animals. For the remainder of the day, the surviving Indians sang and danced around their dead. Bud had never seen an Indian burial, and his heart was heavy as he tried to deal with the senseless pain inflicted by Ed Burleson. He stayed with the Cherokee, doing his best to console the survivors. Knowing they would need food for the long journey, he helped them butcher the dead horses and cattle. While helping them butcher and jerk the meat, he discovered some hidden bags of corn the women had stashed when they saw Burleson kill their men. He knew with the meat and corn, they would be able to survive. He recommended they turn back north and settle in Oklahoma. They trusted that Bud was correct, thanked him and began to load their supplies on travois for their dogs and three surviving horses to haul for them.

As he prepared to leave, Bud gave Mrs. Bowles his short rifle and a nice supply of lead and powder. He knew they would need to kill game if they were to have enough food to reach the Red River. Then, wheeling Lightning around, Bud dashed as fast as he could from the killing field. He could feel the pit of his belly begin to rumble. He knew he was getting ready to vomit. Riding parallel to a small stream, he suddenly pulled Lightning to a sliding stop and made a beeline for the water. He fell to his knees and vomited until it hurt, then splashed cold water onto his thick brown hair and over his face. Using his fingers as a comb, he pushed his long locks back off his forehead, and looking skyward, he yelled, "Dear God, how could you let that happen? If you are a God of love and mercy, then why do you allow such evil?" No answer came as he remained on his knees and suffered in silence for those left behind. He wondered how General Houston would react to the news that his Cherokee brother was shot down like a dog for no reason whatsoever, other than the color of his skin. For years to come, the young man from the backwoods of Kentucky would have nightmares, seeing Chief Running Water blown off his horse, a hole the size of a silver dollar in his forehead, and hearing the chilling screams of the women and children as they stood helpless and horrified. Bud would have been pleased to learn that the remaining Cherokee made their way back into the Oklahoma Territory safely.

Another group of Texas Rangers led by Ben McCullough was heading back to San Antonio when the lead scout spotted Bud's horse, then Bud kneeling beside the creek, hat in hand. Bud glanced back when he heard the scout's horse nicker. The scout bellowed, "What in all get out is goin' on here?"

Bud stood and pulled his hat down tight over his wet head. He looked up with the broad brim shielding his eyes and answered, "Burleson and his men just murdered seven peaceful Cherokee in cold blood. They are the family that General Houston lived with all those years ago. One of them was John Bowles, the son of Chief Bowles. Heck, it's like they murdered the General's brother. I'm here to tell you it was uncalled for. I was talking with Chief Running Water, Bowles, and The Egg when Burleson rode up. In a flash, he ordered his men to open fire. All the Cherokee wanted was to get to Mexico so they could live in peace." When referring to Colonel Burleson, Bud purposefully dropped the military title. To him, Burleson was nothing but a murderer.

Ben McCullough sat on his sweating horse in disbelief. His jaw tightened as he asked, "Are you sure the Indians didn't make an aggressive move?"

Bud's anger showed in his voice as he answered, "There was no danger coming from any of them. The Indians did nothing to provoke being shot down in cold blood. All they wanted was permission to move through Texas into Mexico. I don't mind killing murderous redskins. I've shot my share of Comanche, but these people were seeking peace."

"Any need for us to go down there?"

"Yeah, go arrest that murdering Burleson. Trust me, the word will spread and Indians will never try to parlay again with Texans. I did my best to make sure the women and children had a way to feed themselves and strongly suggested they go back to Oklahoma."

The rangers dismounted and led their horses over to the creek, allowing them to drink. McCullough spoke to Bud. "We are on our way back to San Antonio. You wanna ride with us?"

"Might as well. I need to catch up with Jack."

Ben slowly breathed out, saying, "God bless their souls."

Some of the men were surprised to hear McCullough say the Indians had souls. Many white men didn't believe Indians had souls. None challenged Ben because, even though he was soft spoken, he was anything but supple. Few men in Texas were as brave or possessed more courage than Ben McCullough.

As they traveled south, Bud didn't speak. He was thinking of the irresponsible actions of Edward Burleson. Ben McCullough and the rangers could see Bud's grief and allowed him solitude as the group moved toward home.

Early the following morning, Don Cheek, one of the rangers scouting ahead, topped a ridge and couldn't believe his eyes. There, on the next hilltop, stood the mystical white stallion. Don had heard many stories of the magical horse, but never believed they were true. Very few men had ever seen him, yet the stallion was a legend in Texas lore. There he stood, like a noble white statue, watching over his mares and foals in the viridian valley below. The wind was blowing from the south, preventing the white stallion from smelling Don's horse as he sat motionless, awestruck. Don desperately wanted to stand up in his stirrups and wave his hat for the others to come see, but knew the slightest movement would spook the stallion, and he would be gone like a puff of smoke.

Just as the other rangers were coming up the ridge, Don watched in awe as the stallion reared up on his hind legs, kicking his front hooves in the air as he broke through the silence with a powerful nicker. The south wind blew his neighing toward Don, allowing the ranger to hear the stallion's signal to his mares, and then, with a brilliant white flash, he raised his tail in an arch and was gone. When the rangers got near, Don shouted, "I saw him. Honest to God, I really did see him!"

"Saw who?" asked Ben.

"I saw the Pacing White Stallion. I swear on my mama's grave. I really did. He was right over on that ridge," he answered breathlessly, pointing toward the now-empty hilltop. Don had a propensity to stretch the truth a little. No one believed he had seen the fabled White Stallion even though every man, woman and child in Texas had heard the stories of the mystical white horse. There was evidence that a dominant stallion recently was on the ridge as steam was still swilling up from the fresh dung. In the valley, they found the tracks of the remuda. Ben estimated the number of horses to be about fifty, a rather large remuda for any stallion. Silently, he believed perhaps Don had seen the legendary white horse, but no one except Bud expressed belief in Don.

Texas boys fell asleep and dreamed of being the one to capture the powerful magician of the plains. Many reported seeing him or trying to run him down, but no one had ever been successful. Even the Baron de Bastrop filled Bud's mind with visions of the snow white horse with a mane reaching to his knees, and an arched tail that swept the mesquite grass as he paced. One thing about the white stallion that stood above all others was that no matter how fast he was chased, the horse never broke out of his pace. He changed leads, but refused to gallop or run, and still no one could catch him. The Baron de Bastrop told Bud the Ghost Horse, as the Indians called him, was known for his blazing speed; the stallion had been timed pacing a mile in under two minutes. If the tales were true, the Pacing White Stallion was the fastest horse to have ever lived. Perhaps he was, and that was the reason no one was able to get a rope around his neck.

Bud tried to remember the landscape and some notable markers so he could return and perhaps catch the wild mustang. He knew Lightning had the speed to run down most any horse, and his skills with a lasso rivaled those of the Mexican charros. He urged Ben McCullough to follow the tracks, but Ben realized how exhausted their horses were and, having heard the tales of the white stallion running good horses into the ground, he knew their mounts were in no condition to be chasing a wild mustang that could run all day without stopping.

Don pouted all the way back to San Antonio, trying in vain to convince the others he really had seen the Pacing White Stallion of the Plains. Finally, Don reached Bud, and to his delight, discovered a believer. He rode alongside young Miller the rest of the way home. According to Don, The White Stallion of the Plains embodied grace, fire, speed, and incredible beauty. He told Bud of an article written by George Kendall for the *New Orleans Picayune* relating his encounter with the Pacing White Stallion. Kendall's heading read: *"Magical White Mustang Hightailed out of Sight."* Kendall had been camped with a group of seasoned hunters when a drove of mustangs galloped up near them. The wild horses stood with heads raised, then wheeled around and were gone as quickly as they had arrived. George wrote the leader was the white mustang of lore; however, he never galloped or trotted, but paced 150 yards in front of his mares, with his tail arched.

Unknown to Bud, large sums had been offered to anyone capturing The Pacing White Stallion. A doctor in San Antonio offered a thousand dollars in gold to the man who could bring the mythical horse to him. A man named J. T. Roundtree had taken three men, four pack-mules and a dozen hunting dogs to try to capture the stallion and collect the gold. One of the men Roundtree brought along was a Mexican who rode what was said to be the fastest horse in Texas. The Mexican man was an expert with a lariat and knew the area like the back of his hand. When the hunting party located the Pacing White Stallion, they gave chase. With their mounts running all out, they were unable to gain any ground on the stallion or his mares. Eventually the hunting party's horses gave out. They, like so many before them, gave up their quest to capture the elusive stallion and returned to San Antonio, dejected.

When Bud arrived back in San Antonio, he took Lightning to the livery stable and headed for his rented room. The young ranger's mind was filled with visions of being the only man in Texas to track down and capture the Pacing White Stallion. He pondered what he might name this glorious horse; it would have to be something special. Perhaps, White Cloud, Flash or Silver. When he arrived home, his landlady Juanita gave him a letter and a folded note. The letter smelled of mountain laurel. The note, folded four times to prevent anyone from reading its contents was from Timmy Marcum, whom many felt was the son of Sam Houston, a rumor that had never been denied or confirmed by the General. One thing for sure, Houston loved young Timmy as if he were his own flesh and blood.

Bud unfolded the note…

Bud,

President Houston is on his way to Nacogdoches after visiting the Union and wants you to give him an honest appraisal of the Plum Creek Comanche fight. Word has reached the President of the Burleson massacre. He wants you to tell him the truth. When you return, you can find me residing with the Higginbothams.

Your friend, Tim

After reading Timmy's note, Bud raised Virginia's letter to his nose, smelling the sweet laurel scent. He could visualize the row of laurel trees growing on the south side of the Treptow ranch, and recalled the evenings spent with Virginia, letting the wind bathe them with the aroma. The envelope was addressed to:

Mr. Benjamin "Bud" Miller,
Texas Ranger
San Antonio de Bexar
Republic of Texas

The return address:
Miss Virginia Mary Treptow
C/o The Treptow Horse Ranch
Galveston Island
Republic of Texas

Bud didn't want the landlady watching him read Virginia's letter, so as he left for his room he tipped the brim of his hat, a gesture he had seen the Baron do on many occasions when leaving the company of a lady. "Please excuse me. I have business to attend to for General Houston." It felt good to speak Houston's name as if the great General needed him. Rushing toward his small room, he was all thumbs trying to open the letter without tearing the envelope. Closing the door behind him, he sat on the edge of the bed and slit the envelope open with his pocketknife.

My dearest Benjamin,

May the Grace of our Lord Christ Jesus find you in good heath and prosperous in all of your endeavors. My mare dropped another colt that is the spitting image of Lightning. I named him Bolt.

Mama and daddy wanted me to extend you a personal invitation to attend my 18th birthday party. In the event you have forgotten my birthday, it is December 2nd. I'm writing early so you will have ample time to adjust your schedule. I will be heartbroken if you are not here to help me celebrate.

With deep affection,

Ginny

Pulling the letter again to his nose and closing his eyes, Bud visualized Virginia's vivacious smile. Folding the paper carefully and placing it back in the envelope with the loose laurel blossoms, he slid the letter under his pillow.

Bud's thoughts then turned back to General Houston's request, wondering why he wanted to hear his version of the story when there were several seasoned rangers present when the incident occurred. Why not ask the more experienced men like Jack Hays or Ben McCullough? Why not question Sam Maverick, who could also do a much better job of explaining what had transpired? After all, Maverick was extremely well educated and articulate. What could he tell the General that the older and wiser men could not?

As he approached the Higginbothams, he saw Timmy in the front yard pitching horseshoes with their teenage son. A large block of time had passed since they had seen each other. Bud didn't remember Timmy's ponytail being so long. He didn't want to disturb the game, so he leaned casually against the big oak tree in the front yard. On Timmy's last toss, he hit a "leaner" and that gave him the winning toss. He let out a victory shout, turning to make sure anyone watching knew he had just beaten one of the best horseshoe pitchers in all of San Antonio. As he turned, he spotted Bud leaning against the ancient oak with a big smile on his face.

"See you got my note."

"Sure as a bee makes honey," Bud answered.

Timmy Marcum was without challenge, the best-dressed young man Bud had ever met. Even pitching horseshoes did not ruffle his starched white shirt or his velvet jacket. Timmy approached Bud, saying, "I guess you are wondering why the General is so anxious for you to come to Nacogdoches."

Bud's grin remained on his face as he reached out to shake Timmy's hand. "I sorta had something like that in mind. Can't imagine what I can tell that others can't."

"The General has great respect for you and Jack Hays. Jack is out on a surveying job, so I left the note for you. General Houston knows you are just like Jack Hays; you will not lie no matter how damaging the truth may be. I told the General you had a better viewpoint than Jack because you were at the front when the battle started."

"We best get going. I have an appointment I don't want to be late for," said Bud.

"Then let's ride like we stole something," Timmy answered as he winked a good-bye to the Higginbotham boy.

The two young men left immediately, following the lower Camino Real to the Brazos River that ran about halfway between San Antonio and Nacogdoches. Bud and Timmy rode two of the fastest horses in Texas and were both well armed as they traveled cautiously toward Nacogdoches, aware that highway robbers or rogue Indians could be around any bend. The Mexican outlaws had not ventured as far north as the new road, but that was no insurance that they wouldn't. The two remained vigilant. Bud rode on the right side, scanning to the south and Timmy on the left, looking north to northwest. At night, they used Jack Hays' procedure of eating, and then moving to a different location to camp for the night.

Arriving in Nacogdoches, Bud was surprised at the humble house General Houston occupied. The construction was new, but the two rooms were small in comparison to other homes in town. The giant of a man was standing out front, talking with his finger in the faces of two frightened men. His anger had not subsided since the insult was sent to him in the form of Chief Bowles' hat. Sam's strident defense of the Cherokee was splitting his local support into splinters. Already his friendship with Mayor Adolphus Sterns and Henry Raguet of the United States had cooled because of the heated speech Houston had given after learning his mentor had been murdered in cold blood. Both were his close friends and loyal supporters, but his outrage at the treatment of his beloved Cherokee was causing even his closest friends to grow distant. They both pulled away rather than engage Houston in defense of the Texan's actions. They, like Lamar, made no distinction between the "good" and "bad" Indians. Henry Raguet's beautiful 19-year-old daughter, Anna, was the only one to support Houston's outrage. To her, he was a hero with few flaws. She treasured the laurel wreath he plaited while propped up against a tree after the battle of San Jacinto. Even though in immense pain, Houston had managed to pen a note and send the wreath to her. The romance was one-sided; nevertheless, Anna held Houston in very high esteem. His efforts to woo her failed and she went on to marry his dear friend, Dr. Irions.

"The ex-President appears not infrequently carried away by bursts of tumultuous, uncontrolled passion…to be fairly beside himself on many occasions. The killing of The Bowl and so many civilized Cherokee has embittered him. I understand his passion; however, cannot embrace his love for the Indians," Ashbel Smith wrote a friend.

Without question, Timmy and Bud were witnessing one of those outbursts. Sam never glanced in the boys' direction as they dismounted. The General spoke without raising his voice; nevertheless, his words may as well have been shouted because they were making a solid impact on the men on the receiving end.

As soon as Houston noticed the boys, he summarily dismissed the men and a broad smile filled his face. He waited for the boys to come to him before extending his hand to Bud. Once the two men clasped hands, Sam took his left hand and covered their grip with his right. He pulled Bud in close, asking, "Tell me lad, did you have a safe journey?"

Bud was too petrified to speak, so Timmy answered, "Yes Sir. The only people we saw were two new families heading in the opposite direction."

As Sam released Bud, he commanded, "Come on in the house and my male servant will fix you some grub. You must be famished."

For three days, Sam kept Bud and Timmy engaged in conversation on a variety of subjects. However, the topic always ended up coming back to the atrocities committed against his beloved Cherokee. He was unable to shake the pain and anger against those who had slaughtered the tribe that had adopted him as one of their own. Sometimes he spoke in anger, and other times with sadness, tears running down his cheeks. During their lengthy talks, Houston told the boys he planned to sell his new Nacogdoches home and move back to the town named in his honor. He no longer felt welcome in the east Texas town where he had originally chosen to settle. Perhaps it was because the town was so near the killing fields of his Cherokee brothers, or because his embittered speeches had alienated him from many of the townspeople. Whatever the reason, Houston was no longer comfortable in Nacogdoches and needed to move on.

Despite being rejected by those in Nacogdoches, Houston fully expected to be elected President of the Republic for a second term. Once re-elected, perhaps then he could prompt action by the Union. What Sam failed to mention to the boys was the fact that almost every newspaper in the Republic was writing editorials opposing his re-election. The newspapers' constant criticism did not dampen Sam's confidence nor lower his expectation of winning back the presidency.

As Bud related the details of Burleson's actions, Houston became even more determined to win back the presidency. The thing that galled Houston the most was Burleson's bible waving and preaching about living a good Christian life, while at the same time murdering unarmed Indians. Only taking power again could assuage his pain.

Sam asked Bud to escort him to Houston in two days and Bud jumped at the opportunity to ride with the General and his wife. Sam sent Timmy ahead with a letter to his supporters in San Augustine. He would need their support when he threw his hat into the presidential race.

Bud helped pack and run errands for the General as final preparations for the move to Houston were made. Two days stretched into ten before they were finally on their way. Before leaving Nacogdoches, Sam patched up his differences with Sterne and Raguet; however, he would never forgive or forget the evil deeds of Rusk and Burleson.

When they reached Houston, Sam suggested Bud return to San Antonio and aid Jack Hays in dealing with the Mexican bandits raiding the no-man's land south of Corpus Christi. Those were welcome words to the young ranger. He thanked the general and was packed and on the road within the hour.

Sam allowed his mind to remember better times. He would sit and daydream about the day he and Margaret arrived in Galveston. She brought with her three dresses and her rosewood piano. One dress was white satin, one purple silk, and the other, blue muslin. Sam closed his eyes and visualized how beautiful his new bride was, her charm and grace, but even Margaret's soft manner and loving spirit was unable to diminish Sam's anger toward Lamar. At every opportunity, he leveled an all out verbal assault on the president.

Sam's letter was well received in San Augustine. Philip Sublett threw a bash for the newlyweds at his home. Sam seized the opportunity to gather the fine citizens together, and proceeded to cut Lamar from limb from limb. When they were lathered up and on the verge of being drunk, he announced his intention of being President of the Republic again. His announcement was received with a standing ovation.

Behind Sam's back, all of Texas was making wagers on how long his marriage would last, and the debate soon turned into an opportunity for gambling. How long would Margaret stay with General Houston? How long could she put up with his philandering and heavy drinking? How could such a sweet, naive young beauty from Alabama tame the hardest-drinking womanizer to hit Texas since Buck Travis? No one who knew Sam personally or even marginally believed the tall stallion from Tennessee's wild spirit could ever be quelled. What most did not figure into the equation was the strength of young Margaret. She knew exactly what she was getting into when she agreed to marry Sam. In their time together, he opened his heart to her. Margaret cast a spell so powerful that even when they were separated for long periods, Sam never strayed. Her power came from a pure heart, filled with an abiding love. A catharsis took place; Sam's future quest for recognition and approval would reside in the political arena. He no longer felt the need to prove his manhood by how many women he could be with or whom he could drink under the table. Sam and his beloved Margaret became a world of two until they increased their family, having nine children together.

Sam sat in the back of the chamber as the debate over the Santa Fe Expedition raged on the floor of Congress. Twenty-seven-year-old Isaac Van Zandt stood to speak. Van Zandt's superior oratory skills were well suited for politics and had carried the young man from Tennessee to a Congressional seat. Sam listened attentively as Van Zandt expounded on the virtues of the expedition. When Isaac finished speaking, Sam took the lectern and paused for a full three minutes before bellowing at the assembly, "You are about to send a column of soldiers more than seven hundred miles across unexplored territory to a city that will receive them as enemies. Those in Santa Fe have given no indication they want us. Your actions will provoke Mexico into new hostilities. You, young Van Zandt, are too full of idealism to see the folly of proceeding on this course. I must tell you a story: A Tennessee neighbor of yours and mine once sent his slave to set up watch on a deer trail and told him to shoot when the deer broke cover. The deer sprang out, but the slave's rifle made no sound. When his master cursed him for not shooting, the slave replied, 'Lord a mighty, Massa, dat buck done jumped so high, I think he done broke his neck.' So it is with my young fellow Tennessean, Mr. Van Zandt. He jumped so high in his speech that he broke his own neck."

Laughter erupted, the bill was defeated and Houston was able to shake hands with Van Zandt and remain friends. The battle had been won in Congress, but President Lamar was determined to proceed with the expedition one way or another. He would proceed independently to obtain support for his venture through private resources.

In April, Houston entered the race with his eyes wide open; understanding he would be faced with the daunting task of bringing the bankrupt Republic back from the brink. His challenger was the first provisional president, David Burnet. The people of Texas were expecting the campaign to be a vicious one and they were not disappointed. Burnet started the mud slinging, calling Houston a blasphemous drunk. In turn, Sam referred to Burnet by the Indian name of Wetumpka, which meant "Hog Thief." When Burnet accused Sam of being a coward that crossed the line. Sam took great pleasure in asking where Burnet had been during the battle of San Jacinto, knowing full well that the interim president was on a boat, safe from the fighting. Sam would puff out his large chest and chide, "Look who's calling the kettle black."

San Augustine cast 100% of their votes in favor of Sam Houston, jump-starting his campaign. Knowing how important the votes in Nacogdoches were, Sam returned there with his beautiful wife, hoping she could help him regain favor with those he had alienated in the past. Margaret prevailed. Mayor Sterns held an event in their honor. Sam's close friend Nat Walling was in attendance. He waited for the right moment and asked, "Margaret, have you ever been to Shelly County?"

Margaret answered, "No."

Nat grew a wide smile. "Too bad because Sam has forty children in that county."

The crowd was scandalized, Sam was angered, and Margaret flushed with embarrassment. Nat began laughing so uncontrollably, he couldn't speak. Finally, he gained some composure and answered, "Sam is so popular in Shelly County that at least forty families have named their sons after him!"

Everyone erupted with laughter, including Margaret. However, Sam was not amused. "Nat, my dear friend," he snarled. "I will thank you to connect your sentences more closely in the future."

Meanwhile David Burnet continued to call the General a disgrace and wrote scores of scurrilous letters to the newspapers, signing them with the alias, Davy. His slanderous rhetoric was so transparent that anyone with an ounce of brains knew who the author was. Finally, Houston had his fill and decided to strike back. Sam wrote his own letters exposing Burnet's hypocrisy. He sent the letters through his trusted friend, Ashbel Smith, asking him to ensure the letters be published anonymously. Ashbel made sure all of Houston's letters to "Davy" were published in the same papers that so liberally ran Burnet's letters. Sam's first letter read:

"Will you judge Burnet, or will your friends deny that after you went to Galveston onboard the steamboat Yellow Stone, (the color of the stripe down your back?) you were so deeply inebriated, that though you attempted to make a speech abusive of General Houston to the soldiers and spectators present, you failed, but not until the soldiers gave you the devil for lying.

Nor will you deny that at Austin, during the first session of Congress. . . you were so deeply intoxicated that you went sound asleep in your seat and snored away your time until you were awakened by Mr. McLeod, Secretary of the Senate, by order of the members? When you were disturbed by being well shaken, you raised yourself up with an ineffably idiotic smile and hiccupped out saying, "Gentlemen, I believe—hic—I was in a doze—hic." Now, Sir, you are the man who prates about sobriety, morality and religion. Oh, shame, where is thy blush. . .you hypocrite.

You political brawler and canting hypocrite, whom the waters of Jordan could never cleanse from your political and moral leprosy, may the God of heaven have mercy on your soul for you shall need it in the end."

Even when it appeared Burnet was sure to be swept into office, Houston remained confident and ordered a plantagenet green velvet suit and a French hat for his inauguration. After the clothes arrived and Margaret saw them, it was decided he dress in something more appropriate for the occasion. Houston was the head of the household, but Margaret was the neck, turning the head in whatever direction she felt it needed to go. Sam let his wife choose his inaugural attire.

The election was held on September 6. When the votes were tallied, Houston received a massive 7,508 and Burnet, a measly 2,574. Memucan Hunt, a Lamar man, was soundly defeated by the Houston-backed Edward Winfield for the office of vice president.

The first couple returned to Houston where the newly elected second-term president addressed a large group. The trip had been tiring for Margaret, due to poor health, and she was not in attendance as her husband electrified the audience. After remaining overnight with friends, the victorious couple was off to their Cedar Point retreat. Houston needed time alone with his beloved Margaret to build strength for the difficult challenges that lay ahead. The challenges would be even more demanding than Houston could possibly imagine. His will and patience would be tested to the extreme limit.

Chapter Twenty-Four
Conflict

Stephen Fuller Austin was not the first American to settle in Texas/Mexico. Long before Austin arrived, squatters were slipping across the border. Aylett Buckner, a veteran of the Gutierrez Expedition, was the first American to build a cabin with the intention of making Texas his home. He settled along the banks of the Colorado in an area that later became part of the allotment given to Stephen Austin for his original three hundred families. According to his agreement with Mexico, Austin could sell the land for twelve-and-a-half cents per acre, and he strongly resented Buckner and others "squatting" on his land without paying. In one of their many heated arguments, Buckner told Austin: "I have never asked the first cent for a man to eat under my roof and I have fed as many and I believe more than any man in this Colony. I have lost as much, if not more, property to Indian depredations than any other man on this river. I have paid ten times over for that on which I now abide."

Buckner was a man who asked for nothing but equal treatment. Steven F. Austin, on the other hand, had a propensity to treat some families better than others. Not all of the settlers paid him for their property. In many, many cases, Austin allowed new arrivals to barter horses, cows, chickens, bee's wax, whiskey, pelts, or anything of value for their land. Others, he let take three to five years to pay. If he liked a new arrival, he instructed the Baron de Bastrop to find them a choice riverfront piece of land with good topsoil.

Dissention grew among the settlers because of the presence of squatters who were not part of the Austin colony. The conflict reached San Antonio where the political chief of Texas/Mexico, Jose Antonio Saucedo, sent an order for the colony to obey Austin. After all, Austin had been granted almost dictatorial power over his colony. The orders from Saucedo were ignored with the same vigor with which the colonists had rejected Austin's authority. The grumbling and complaints kept rolling back to Saucedo in San Antonio. He grew tired of his words being ignored and finally suspended Austin's fee schedule and introduced one of his own. The fee for a league was reduced to $192, with $127 going to the land commissioner, the Baron de Bastrop, $27 to the land surveyor, and $38 to the government, leaving Austin out in the cold. Austin pouted for several weeks, then exploded and went to visit with his colonists, telling them the sacrifices he had made so they could have the opportunity to live in Texas. Austin reminded them his fee was established before they immigrated to Texas. More than half of the colony sided with Austin's position. The tension in the community was coming mostly from a handful of squatters. Buckner was not among those who grumbled. He just went about the business of raising his family and trying to survive on the frontier.

Finally, Austin took his case to Jose Antonio Saucedo in person. After a long conversation, Saucedo decided to let Austin receive $47 of the $127 going to Baron de Bastrop.

Austin understood that in order to attract colonists to Texas, he would need to accept slavery as an unavoidable evil and set aside his personal ideology for the broader picture. He understood that no serious farmers like Jared Groce or Bobby Lay would risk everything to move to an unknown frontier without slaves. Slave ownership was essential to the success and prosperity of a plantation, and Austin needed men like Jared Groce and Bobby Lay to settle in his colony and persuade others to follow. He never imagined his beloved Texas and the issue of slavery would be the catalyst that divided the United States. Texas was like a kettle of water on a stove. The water first simmers and when the heat is turned up high enough, it boils over. Slavery became the boiling point.

In the north, former President John Quincy Adams had never given slavery much thought until Andrew Jackson sent him home with his tail tucked between his legs. Adams detested the fact that a country bumpkin could send him back to Massachusetts. Even worse, Adam's beloved alma mater awarded an honorary doctorate degree to Jackson. Adams told his cousin, who happened to be the President of Harvard: "I could not be present to see my darling Harvard disgrace herself by conferring a Doctor's degree upon a barbarian and savage who could scarcely spell his own name." Adams could have remained at home and enjoyed his old age; however, he accepted a seat in the House of Representatives just so he could place a burr under Jackson's saddle.

Adams never forgave "Old Hickory" and became determined to wage war against Jackson and his partisans, including Sam Houston. Houston's attempts to convince the Congress to consider Texas statehood were met head on by the crusty old Adams. Adams never missed an opportunity to slander Houston; therefore, throwing mud at Texas and stoking the slavery issue to the boiling point at the same time. Adams didn't care if Houston was vocally against slavery; Houston, like Austin, tolerated the practice for the formation of a sovereign Texas. John Quincy Adams was tireless in his resolve to defeat Texas annexation and keep the slavery debate in the forefront. He viewed the Texans' victory over Santa Anna as a conspiracy to foster slavery and push the United States into war with Mexico.

During the ten years Texas was a Republic, there was never peace. There was conflict in every direction: Texas vs. Mexico, Texas vs. Indians, Houston supporters vs. those who vehemently opposed his policies, and Texans wanting statehood vs. those wanting to remain an independent Republic. Lamar wanted all Indians dead, while Houston wanted to pursue a peaceful resolution. The northern states wanted to count each southern slave as only one-third of a person. In other words, it would take three slaves to count as one person, diminishing the Texas population and restricting the Republic's representation in Congress. The South angrily demanded they be granted Congressional seats based on their entire population, including slaves. There was continual conflict over property ownership, where the capital should be located, and the taxation and importation of goods. Sam Houston confided to a friend, "What doesn't kill us will make us stronger. Dang, I wonder how much stronger we can get." Eventually these and other bitter disagreements between the North and South would contribute to the onset of the most deadly war in the history of the United States; pitting brother against brother, father against son, and mother against daughter, in a struggle to the death.

1839 began with personal tragedy for Sam Houston. One week after Lamar took office as President of the Republic, Houston's closest friend, John A. Wharton, died of yellow fever. Two weeks later, Sam's brother William died, accidentally shooting himself while dismounting his horse. As in the past, heavy drinking accompanied Sam's despair. This time, Sam did some serious thinking on his personal weakness. Once more, he made an attempt to reform and attended the first temperance meeting ever held in the Republic capital bearing his name. The town of Houston was a frontier town where the residents were known to bend an elbow with something approaching ferocity. Sam, never forgetting the importance of "the vote", spoke so long at the meeting that the preacher who was supposed to follow him was forced to cancel his sermon altogether.

Meanwhile, Lamar cleaned the capital of all Houston supporters and replaced them with his own. Lamar divided the Republic into two camps: the Houston and Anti-Houston parties, though not single-handedly; Sam did his share to contribute to the rancor. Lamar was like a bull in a china closet in his term as president. He didn't have a clue how to run a nation, and quickly ran up the national debt. He did achieve one very significant success: the Public School Act. Lamar's vision for a quality public education system created the foundation of his legacy as the "Father of Texas Education."

The major difference between the two Presidents was experience. Houston was an established public servant and a skilled politician, having served as Governor of Tennessee and as a victorious General in the Texas Army. Lamar only held a minor position in the state of Georgia and was not experienced in making the hard choices necessary to run a burgeoning nation.

Houston didn't have to wait long before a new; intriguing issue arose in his life. As a Congressman, he was in the position to know about France's decision to send a representative to scout the possibility of investing in Texas. In the fall of 1839, France decided to recognize Texas as a Republic. A spy was dispatched to assess the new Republic and send his findings back to Paris. A Frenchman by the name of Jean Peter Isidore Alphonse Du Bois, Count de Saliguy was selected to make the journey to Texas. The truth of the matter was Du Bois was no count. Like the Baron de Bastrop, he anointed himself with the pompous title.

As soon as the Count established a good relationship with the Texans, he was appointed charge-d'-affaires. He landed at Galveston, and then took a barge up to Houston and from there, traveled by horseback to Austin. Once in Austin, he was appalled by the crudeness of the town and its residents. Coming from Paris, the most advanced city in the world at the time, he was aghast to see such squalor. Du Bois rented a room in the Bullock Hotel at the corner of Congress and Pecan Streets until he contracted to have a home built overlooking the city. It was not long before the Count would further the discord between himself and the citizens of Austin, neglecting to pay his bill at the Bullock Hotel. The Count was not impressed with Austin, and to say the least, the animosity was mutual.

Du Bois was no fool. He gave Lamar token respect; however, he knew who the *real* power in Texas was. There was only one man to impress, and that was Samuel Houston. When Du Bois obtained permission to meet with Houston, the Frenchman arrived wearing an ostentatious sash around his waist and an array of colorful, "prestigious" medals on his jacket. Sam knew what a clotheshorse the Count was and decided to disarm the Frenchman. Houston wrapped an Indian blanket around his bare shoulders and opened the door. Once the Frenchman stepped inside, Sam slowly let the blanket slide from his back, turning so Du Bois could see his scars from the Creek Indian War. Then he turned back around toward Du Bois and proclaimed, "Here in Texas we wear our medals like this." Houston made his point and effectively disarmed the Count's pretension.

After having his fun with the Count, Houston figured out a way to use the Frenchman against his nemesis, Lamar. He knew Du Bois was promoting a project, which came to be known as the "Franco-Texiene Bill". The terms of the proposed agreement were that France would be granted the right to send eight thousand French settlers to Texas, and in return, the Texans would build a line of fortifications to protect them. The immigrants would also be granted twenty years of tax abatement. Houston knew President Lamar and Vice President Burnet were both opposed to the project. That was reason enough for Sam to throw his weight behind Du Bois' proposal. No one was better than Sam Houston at fast tracking a pork barrel project, and in January 1841, eleven days later, the "Franco-Texiene Bill" passed the House and Senate.

President Lamar was in Georgia, showing off to the people back home how important he was, and had left Texas in the incapable hands of his vice president, David Burnet. Just as Sam figured, Burnet vetoed the bill, and the Senate, knowing they couldn't muster a two-thirds majority to overturn the veto, let the bill die. Houston had no doubt the bill would fail; his primary purpose had been to build up substantial good will with the French. Lamar and Burnet had unwittingly provided Sam with political capital he would cash in at a later date. Houston knew when he became president again, and started the annexation process; he would need France's friendship. He saw the entire annexation process as a card game: It was not always the man with the winning hand, but the one who could bluff the best, that walked away with the money. When the international cards were laid on the table in the future, the tall man from Tennessee would be holding all the chips.

Frank Bullock grew more and more frustrated trying to collect the substantial debt the Count refused to pay the hotel. Bullock took matters into his own hands, turning his hogs loose in Du Bois' beautifully appointed new home. The rambunctious filthy swine made a shambles of the place, chewing up furniture, shredding fine bed linens and defecating on the highly polished floors. This was more than the Frenchman could endure. He challenged Bullock to a fistfight. Unfortunately for Du Bois, Bullock was much larger and more powerful. With a few well-placed punches, Bullock beat the smaller Du Bois into the ground, breaking his nose. Blood covered the Count's velvet jacket and pantaloons. Incensed, the Frenchman took Bullock to court. The judge laughed when Du Bois presented his complaint and tossed the case out with the crack of his gavel.

The judge and the citizens of Austin were unaware that Du Bois' brother-in-law was the finance minister of France. The courtroom antics cost Texas five million dollars, money that France had already authorized to loan the fledgling Republic. With that five million dollars, there would never have been a need for Texas to join the Union. Who would have ever dreamed that a bloody nose would prevent Texas from remaining a self-sustaining Nation? Houston, aware of the loan, had considered defending the Count, but decided against it, believing he could revive the loan once he became President again.

J. Pinckney Henderson was acting as Houston's eyes and ears in Paris. He corresponded frequently, keeping Sam fully informed on all the diplomatic maneuvering. In one letter, Henderson wrote:

"I am now daily expecting this Government to recognize Texas. I have, since the receipt of Saliney's report, been urging the matter in the strongest terms. All of France is waiting for word from Admiral Bodon. As soon as they get a positive report from him, they will give us full recognition."

Learning his mother-in-law, Nancy Lea and others were on a ship heading for Galveston, Sam raced to greet them. He was waiting on the docks when the schooner arrived and as the first passenger stepped on deck, he ordered a three-cannon salute fired over the bow. After greeting Mrs. Lea, he inquired about Margaret. Mrs. Lea let Sam know the kind of woman he was about to marry when she chided, "General Houston, my daughter is in Alabama. She goes forth in the world to marry no man. The one who receives her hand will take it in my home and not elsewhere." Nancy Lea made it very clear there would be no wilderness wedding for her daughter and she expected her request to be honored.

Houston obeyed his future mother-in-law and soon returned to Alabama for the wedding. The day of the wedding, one of Margaret's male family members approached him. Shivering in his boots, he looked up into the eyes of the tall Texan and asked, "If I may inquire what happened to cause your first wife to leave?"

Houston answered in a commanding voice, "Sir, I'm marrying Margaret, not the whole family. If this wedding depends on me telling everything about my first marriage, then stop the fiddlers now. Come with me and we can settle this mess right now!" The family member backed down, slipping into the crowd as quickly as his feet would carry him. Sam and Margaret were married in Marion, Alabama on May 9, 1840.

Lamar's term expired just as the Texas economy was listing precariously and getting ready to sink. On December 13, 1841, Samuel Houston returned to his position as President of the Republic of Texas. In less than two weeks, Secretary of State Dr. Anson Jones, would stand before a joint session of the House and Senate and admonish the group with a blistering speech: "The country is absolutely without present means of any kind. Her resources are large and prospective, but her credit is utterly prostrate. The entire annual revenue would not be sufficient to pay the interest on the national debt. My policy regarding Mexico is to remain defensive with no overt actions or plundering moves toward our neighbors to the south. As soon as she finds we are willing to let her alone, she will leave us alone. We have no choice but to shut down the Army, cut back on the Navy, and let the Texas Rangers take care of the outlaws, ruffians, and Indian depredations. President Houston's attitude toward the Indian problem is this: We feel it is cheaper to buy them than fight them. If we will take these dramatic and drastic moves Texas might have an opportunity to recover from her present and utter prostration. Without such dire actions, we will surely perish."

Noah Smithwick, who knew the ways of the Comanche better than any white man, explained to President Houston that the Comanche felt all the land from Bastrop west was their "Comancheria", or "Land of the Comanche". Chief Muguara and his people wanted to draw a line in the sand that no white man would cross. Houston responded to Noah with sadness, "Even if I could build a wall from the Red River to the Rio Grande so high that no Indian could scale it, the white man would drive themselves crazy trying to devise a means to get beyond it. Conflict is inevitable. Thank you for your advance warning, Noah. I have long expected as much since their aggressive nature seems to expand when we break the barrier line you mention."

The Lamar presidency had been like the mythical blood-sucking Chupacabra, draining Texas of her life's blood of growth, prosperity, and peace. Perhaps the word "politics" better explains the climate Lamar created: *poli* in Latin means many, and *tics* are bloodsucking creatures. Depression and despondency loomed over the Republic like pea-soup fog draped over an Old World graveyard.

In Sam Houston's second term as president of the Republic, two things were certain: Mexico was coming and Texas was bankrupt. Shortly after taking office, Sam wrote to Margaret. "Our chances for invasion once more by Mexico are far greater today than it has been since 1836." Deeper in the letter, he asked Margaret to pack an emergency travel trunk and be ready to escape over the border into Louisiana at a moment's notice.

Only quick, decisive action, with no political strings attached, would save the drowning Republic. Houston made drastic cuts in the national budget, consolidated all government departments, and ordered the navy returned from the Yucatan and placed in dry dock. He was not concerned about his popularity or his place in history. The goal of his presidency would be to pump life back into the anemic territory so it could gain strength, and thrive. He would do everything in his power to save the Republic he had fought so hard to build and protect and defend.

Chapter Twenty-Five
Mustangin'

Nacogdoches was much larger than Bud had imagined. The most noticeable difference between the east-Texas piney woods town and San Antonio was the absence of Mexican citizens. There was a mixture of Anglos and Negro slaves, but only a handful of Mexicans.

Waiting to accompany General Houston on his move to Houston, always in the back of his mind were visions of the great Pacing White Stallion. Most of the rangers had not believed Don Cheek, but Bud did. He had seen the flush of excitement in Don's face that would have been difficult to fake. Bud dreamed of returning to the area where the magnificent stallion had been seen while the location was still fresh in his mind.

While shaving one morning, Bud looked at himself in the polished metal mirror. The thought of turning twenty on his next birthday caused him to laugh aloud. If he were still living in Kentucky, he would be married and have four children by now. His father had married at sixteen, and his sister, at thirteen. Here he was a Texas Ranger, and the owner of a fine home on a large tract of property tucked in amongst the lost pines of Bastrop, Texas. Still, something was missing; he had no wife with which to share his good fortune.

After a hearty breakfast, he decided to take a stroll through town. When he passed the saloon, he glanced inside and saw a large round table with nine men huddled in deep conversation. He recognized one man to be Charles Grimland, a ranger from down near San Felipe. Charles was a big man, and his broad shoulders made him stand out in the group. Bud decided to slip inside and perhaps join in the conversation. As he approached the table, Charles jumped to his feet and extended his hand. Turning back toward the table, Charles said, "Gentlemen, this is a friend of mine, Ranger Bud Miller. Bud is a young Jack Hays if I've ever seen one."

Looking back at his young friend, Charles asked, "Will you join us?"

Bud spotted an empty chair, walked around the table, and stood behind it, grasping the straight back with both hands. This placed him next to a pot-bellied man dressed in black, wearing an undersized black hat and tiny thin-rimmed glasses. Bud instantly realized he was standing next to the Mayor of Nacogdoches, Adolphus Sterns. Bud heard Sterns was Jewish, and to his knowledge, he had never met a Jew before. He knew they were God's chosen people or that is what his preacher said. He was feeling pretty good until Sterns spoke, asking in a sarcastic tone, "I hear you are Sam Houston's boy. I guess that makes you an Indian lover." Sterns didn't realize the kind of young man he was scolding.

Bud shot back, "Mr. Sterns, I beg your pardon Sir, I am no man's lapdog. As far as the Indians are concerned, they are not all bad. I saw several Tonkawas run more than thirty miles over rugged rock-laden land following us into the Plum Creek Battle. They fought as hard as any soldier or ranger. Captain Jack Hays relies respectfully upon the assistance and skill of Falcco, a Lipan Apache with whom he has survived many scrapes. As far as General Houston is concerned, I can see why he would be upset. I suspect you would be insulted as well, if a fellow Texan had sent you the bloodied hat of a man you loved like a father. All of you at this table know President Houston loved The Bowl and lived with his family for several years. When it comes to Indians, I make up my own mind. I do not rely upon Mr. Houston, or you Sir, to tell me what to think."

Sterns had not become Mayor by being feeble-minded. He realized he had just stirred up a hornet's nest, unwisely letting his disappointment in one of his dearest friends overflow onto the young ranger. Sterns quickly responded, "No offense intended Mr. Miller. Let's shake hands and not let my disappointments with my old friend Sam Houston cause a rift between us. What's your plan, young man?"

Bud didn't want to fight either and accepted Sterns' apology. "While we were making our way back to San Antonio after the Plum Creek fight and the slaughter of several peaceful Cherokee, Don Cheek spotted the famous Pacing White Stallion. I have been giving some thought to getting me that mustang. I guess all of you here know Noah Smithwick."

Most of the men only nodded. One man spoke up, answering, "Noah and I served together as Texas Rangers."

"What might your name be, Sir?" Bud asked.

Sterns jumped in, saying, "That's Senator Isaac Burton, the leader of the 'Horse Marines'."

Burton interjected, "We were not Marines. We were Texas Rangers who just happened to capture three ships."

Grabbing the straight-backed chair, Bud spun it around and sat down, straddling it like a saddle. He couldn't believe his good fortune. He was meeting Isaac Burton; a hero who many said saved the Republic. A man who should stand beside heroes like Stephen Austin, Baron de Bastrop, Buck Travis, General Houston, Jim Bowie, Juan Seguin, Davy Crockett, and all the brave men at the Alamo.

"I am sure you have grown tired of telling the story, but I would like to hear it directly from you, Sir. I first learned of your bravery when I was a small boy back in Tennessee. Our preacher was one of a few people in the area who could read and I remember him reading a newspaper story about you that someone had carried back to Kentucky. I cannot believe I'm sitting at the table with Ranger Isaac Burton."

Isaac really didn't like to talk about the event because it addressed his insubordination of General Rusk's orders. He tried to push the request aside, but several of the men at the table began prodding him to speak. Charles Grimland was the most vocal. It was his urging that prompted the Senator and former ranger to relate his story.

"I grew up in Georgia, and from there I went on to attend West Point. West Point was not for me, so I returned home and fell in love with the woman of my dreams. No sooner than I was preparing to ask for her hand in marriage, her family up and followed Lamar to Texas. Didn't leave me much choice but to tag along after them. I started a law practice, but soon found myself in the Texas Rangers. As most of you know, if you can shoot and ride, the rangers have a way of finding you. By the time of the Alamo, I was elevated to Captain and we were fighting Indians on all fronts. We caught up with General Houston at the Groce Plantation and stayed with the army through the victory at San Jacinto. After Santa Anna sent his letter to that Italian General, Vicente Filisola, telling him to high tail it out of Texas, I retuned to my job as a ranger captain. I don't want to bore you with all this."

Grimland was quick to say, "You are not boring us. Most of us have heard the story only second-hand. We would love to hear the truth directly from you."

Another man at the table said, "I second that motion. Everybody in favor say aye."

The table answered in unison, "Aye."

Burton didn't want to make himself sound like a hero, yet he knew the importance of setting the record straight, once and for all. He had remained silent about the event since 1836. Now was as good a time as any to tell the truth. "Gentlemen, you asked for it, so, if I get long-winded, it's your fault. As you all know, Houston sent General Rusk to give the men murdered at Goliad a Christian burial. General Rusk and about 350 men dug a grave on the tallest hill they could find and buried what remains were left. I'm not exactly sure when our provisional President Burnet and General Filisola met and signed the Treaty of Velasco. All I know is the army and we rangers were not allowed to get within a league (thirteen miles) of the Mexicans, making it very difficult to travel. The landscape was blanketed with tired, hungry, and I'm sure, confused Mexican soldiers. We found out the government in Mexico City told Filisola to stay and finish the job or he would be replaced. If General Filisola stayed, we knew we would be no match for his large army. We estimated he could muster an army of six to seven thousand. We also knew, from our Mexican spies, that his men were starving. In his retreat, Filisola chose to turn south toward Victoria instead of going to San Antonio as Santa Anna had ordered, expecting to find supplies and food. That would not be the case. The Texans fleeing Santa Anna had taken all their cattle with them, burned their homes and poisoned their wells so as not to leave any sustenance behind for the enemy.

Rusk asked me to take my corps of twenty men and scout the area for the Mexican army. I guess it was our fourth day out when Tom Harris came hell-bent into our camp shouting he had spotted a strange ship anchored in Copano Bay. We were at Refugio, not all that far away. That night, I moved my men down near the bay. We dismounted and left four men behind to care for our mounts. When day broke, we saw a black schooner with no flag moored in the bay. With my spyglass, I was able to read the lettering on the side, *The Watchman*. Obviously, an English name. Yet, we didn't fully trust the name, so I headed into plain sight, taking three men with me. We concealed our guns behind our backs and started waving at the ship. Finally, one of the sailors spotted us and shortly thereafter, raised an American flag. I just had a gut feeling it was a trap. I didn't have to wait long to be proven correct as they lowered the Stars and Stripes and raised Mexican colors. We acted excited, jumping up and down, waving our arms. Can you believe the fools bought our deception? The next thing we knew, they lowered a boat and were on their way to pick us up. Once aboard, we pulled our guns and captured the eight-man crew.

We discovered the ship was loaded down with replacement supplies for the Mexican army. I sent a letter to General Rusk telling him what we had found. He was not happy with me. He sent a letter back demanding we leave the ship because our action was in violation of the treaty Burnet had signed. I came to two conclusions: Rusk was young, and could not possibly understand the impact the supplies would have on our independence, and two; the Mexican General was on his way to pick up that cargo. I made the choice to maintain control of the ship. Before the wind picked up so we could travel upriver, we spotted two more ships coming our way. As they pulled alongside, we signaled their captains to come aboard *The Watchman*. To our surprise, they boarded immediately. By then, I had sixteen of my men on the ship. We boarded the other two boats with their respective captains at gunpoint and seized control of their vessels as well. I made the decision to sail the three ships to Galveston Island and turn them over to the Texas government. We had confiscated over 120-thousand dollars worth of goods, was ten times as much as we got from the battle of San Jacinto.

How the 'Horse Marine' thing started was a fluke. Sid Clay, one of my rangers from Kentucky, sent a letter back home, which was published in his local newspaper. Bud, I suspect that is the article that your preacher read to your congregation. The story took legs and someone in a New York paper dubbed us the 'Horse Marines'. To be honest, we didn't expect our capture of those ships to be considered such a big story. We were just doing our job. I know I ticked General Rusk off, but it didn't matter to me. I had to keep the supplies out of the Mexican Army's hands. I honestly think if General Filisola had taken control of the goods on those three ships, there would be no Texas as we know it. He would have rallied his troops and counter-attacked. We would have been no match for a re-stocked, well-fed Mexican army.

After arriving in Galveston, it was discovered American businessmen leased the ships to Mexico. President Burnet sent the ships back to the American owners. How he justified his actions, I will never know. I don't care if General Houston did speak out of line for the Indians, I will walk across Texas to prevent Burnet from becoming President."

After Isaac finished his story, Bud spoke up. "Thank you, Sir. I have to say the way you tell the story is a lot different than it was told to me. I was told you swam your horses out to the boat and rode them up a ramp of some sort. It never made sense to me, but who was I to question what a ranger and his horse are capable of doing. I've seen some pretty amazing things."

One of the men asked, "You want to go mustangin'? I know a little 'bout them there critters. Back a long time ago, when the Comanche were not as hostile toward us white folks; I was at Fort Smith, Arkansas when a band came in to do some tradin'. The Major, I can't recall his name, wanted to have some fun so he challenged the main Chief to a horse race. The Major had a pureblood mare that ran like greased lightning; she easily out-ran all the horses at the fort. He goaded the Indians, and to our surprise, a redskin, weighing at least 175 pounds was picked to ride their horse. He was short and fat, and Lord O' mercy, his nag was a runt, barely fourteen-hands tall. The pony's head drooped like a dog and his knees was nothin' but skin over bone. The Indian's pony looked more like a big sheep than a horse. You could count every rib from forty paces." The lumbering giant of a man knew he had the table spellbound. He picked up the spittoon and hurled a shot of chewing tobacco into the brass pot as he continued, "The Major, he done started feelin' sorry for the Indians, and told his man to bring out his third-best horse so as not to shame the Indians too much. He didn't want to insult the Indians 'cause we needed to keep tradin' with 'em. It was agreed the race would be 400 yards. Well, the big Indian sorta stepped over onto his horse and our soldier, who weighed about 120 pounds soakin' wet, jumped onto his mount.

At the firing of a gun, they were off. The Indian had a big stick to beat that little horse, and managed to stay a nose-length ahead of our army horse. It was the darndest thing I ever saw. As they neared the finish line, the soldier yanked out his quirt and began urging his mare on, to no avail; the Indian won by at least a half-length. The Major was infuriated he had lost a parcel of sugar, coffee, and blankets, and challenged the Indians to a second race. This time, the Major brought out a big bay gelding, while the same big fat Comanche jumped back on his lathered up little mustang. Once more, the Indian started beating the poor little mustang. You wouldn't believe it, but it was a mirror image of the first race. As the mustang barely kept his nose ahead of the seventeen-hand gelding, the big Indian beat the stuffing out of the sheep-sized pony and edged out the bay by a half-length. The Major was furious. He had been too kind. The Indian Chief agreed to double the bet, so the Major instructed his men to bring out his special mare and a real beauty she was. With a coat that shined like polished copper, she strutted confidently; she knew she was fast and was chomping at the bit to run. By then, every man, woman, and child at the fort had come out to see the mare walk away with the prize. The same Indian mounted the same little pony that had just run two hard races. I admit, if I would've had anything to bet on that race, I would have jumped in on some of the action. I honestly felt sorry for the tiny mustang. The starting-pistol fired and the horses lunged forward. I saw the Indian toss his stick to one of his tribe members and give his mustang freedom to run, never touching the shaggy little horse. The mustang started to open the gap in the first fifty yards and was ten lengths ahead by the time they reached the halfway mark. About three-quarters through the race, the Indian swirled around on his horse, facing the soldier on the mare and started waving his arms, laughing and taunting his opponent to run faster. The Indian's mustang beat our mare by at least ten lengths. That cunning Indian had baited the Major into thinking he was forced to whip the skinny little mustang to victory in the first two races. That fat Indian knew the Major was holding back and made sure he only won the first two races by a nose. I swear on my mama's grave that's a true story 'cause I seen it with my own two eyes. You know what the Mexicans say. 'Praise the tall, saddle the small.'"

The story perked Bud's interest. He was almost breathless as he spoke, "Golly, that's another amazing story. I know they are fast 'cause I saw them at the Plum Creek fight. Can I ask you all a question?" Bud waited for permission.

His permission came from Mayor Sterns. "Fire away, we may get another tall Texas tale before we have to go do our chores." Sterns realized what he had implied, and quickly corrected his statement. "I didn't mean to imply my colleagues were stretching the truth. Please excuse my slip of the tongue."

The thought of capturing the magical white horse had Bud sitting on pins and needles as he posed his question to the group. "Does anyone here think Don Cheek actually saw that white stallion or did he just make up the story to impress us? None of us that day ever got so much as a glimpse of the Pacing White Stallion."

One man, John C. Duval, had been sitting and listening with his chin on his clenched fist. He had not said a word as the others had told their stories of mustangs and horse races. Duval was one of a handful to escape the Goliad Massacre. Bud had no idea he was sitting with a man who had been with his father as the massacre unfolded. When the men at Goliad were instructed to kneel down in that killing field, John knew something was not right. He had studied Spanish back in Kentucky and understood the orders shouted by the Mexican officer. Before the first volley of shots, he was running like a deer. Staying low and running as fast as his legs could carry him, John made a wild dash for the river, and the swift current carried him safely downriver. Now he was sitting across the table from the son of a man he saw killed by the cold, calculated orders of Santa Anna. "Son," he said as George Minton, who had a propensity to interrupt, butted in. "I guess you all know I once was a mustanger. I know a lot about mustangs…"

Mayor Sterns reached across the round table and tapped George's hand, smiled and said, "George, let John finish. I'm sure Bud would like to hear what he has to say."

Once more, Duval's face tightened as he continued, "Bud, your pa and I served together. I cannot in truth say I saw your father fall. I was scared to death and running with my head down as fast as my legs would take me. I was praying as I ran. I promised God if He would let me live, I would devote my life to Him. He answered my prayers and I've done my best to keep my end of the bargain. I can tell you this about your father: There was no braver soldier in our army than Stump Miller. He did have a weakness for cards. All men have a weakness. For Travis and President Houston, it appears to be women. Your pa's weakness for gambling didn't make him a bad man…" John's voice froze. He found the pain too excruciating and suddenly excused himself from the table, wiping tears from his eyes. His voice cracked as he uttered, "Sorry men. I must be going." Before he left the table, he squeezed Bud's hand, looked deep into his eyes and with a heavy heart advised, "Wear the name Miller proudly It was paid for in blood."

No one questioned Duval's sudden departure. They all saw the pain in his face and empathized with his not wanting to open an old wound. That didn't stop the talkative George Minton. From his side of the table, he held court, explaining, "I have done my share of huntin' mustangs. I'm here to tell you they are as slippery as chewed elm bark. Them stallions can spot a hunter better than a deer. I've been told the first thing the Indian does when he snares a wild one is to breathe into the colt's nostrils. Horses want to smell what's strange to them. I've never seen it myself, but I'm told the colt will follow the Indian like a dog after that. About that fast pony you were telling about. I bet the redskin slit his nostrils. You know that is what the Indians do. They take a knife and split the nostrils so the horse can get more air. I'd bet my saddle that's what that Indian did back at Fort Smith."

Burton added, "That is why I say they are not human. No human would be that cruel to his horse. How in the deuce can a human slit his horse's nostrils? I don't even wear spurs. You don't have to hurt a horse to get him to respond to a command."

"I don't know about that," Sterns broke in. "Have you seen the spur rowels the Mexicans use or the spade bit they have on their horses? Many times I've seen them almost cut a horse's tongue off."

Burton fumed, "Far as I'm concerned, the Meskins are in the same boat as the Indians. Both are a few steps below human."

Some of the men squirmed. They knew, without the aid of some Mexicans fighting alongside the Anglos, there would be no Texas independence. Even Bud, who came to Texas to kill Mexicans, realized the value of Mexican friendship.

Minton jumped back into the conversation, wanting to talk about mustangs, not the merits of what Indians did or didn't do to their horses or the humanity of Mexicans. He looked only at Bud since he was fresh meat to listen to his stories. He asked questions he knew he was going to answer. "Do you know how we got so many wild horses?" Before Bud could respond, George answered, "I'll tell you. Some say they are descended from the horses that broke free from the Spanish explorers. That ain't true. What the Spaniards didn't ride to death, they killed and ate. What they didn't eat, the Indians did. Especially the Apache. No, what happened was the Indians realized that they could ride horses into the ground the same as the Spaniards, and then replace them by stealing more."

Bud raised his hand as if asking permission to speak.

George asked, "What is it?"

"Listening to you talk, you act like we didn't always have horses in Texas."

The table broke up with laughter. George began beating the table with his fist. He was laughing too hard to speak, motioning with his other hand for Senator Burton to answer. Isaac was also laughing, but managed to respond. "Bud there were no horses on the North American continent until the Spaniards brought them over three hundred years ago. Once they conquered Mexico, the rulers established horse ranches around the capital city. The horse ranches spread north, and when they did, the filthy thievin' Indians began to steal 'em. It was not long before all the plains tribes were riding horses. They were not satisfied just to get one horse. They got it in their minds that the more horses they owned, the richer they were. Several tribes owned as many as ten to fifteen thousand horses. Naturally, stallions would steal a few mares and off they would go. Breaking free from domestication, they become feral horses. The more horses the

Indians stole, the more they lost, and in time, the feral population exploded. Some estimate the numbers at a million wild horses now roaming the southwest. I suspect that count is low. Big Foot Wallace told me of once seeing a herd of between thirty and forty thousand mustangs. He said the horizon seemed to be moving like waves on the ocean. Gee, I've talked too long. George, finish what you were saying."

George Minton was honored the Senator wanted him to continue. Placing his elbows on the table, he leaned closer to Bud explaining, "It ain't easy to snag a wild one. They're as smart as a fox and faster than a deer. It helps if there are several men doin' the ropin'. You can surround them and rope the ones you want as they break through the line."

Bud answered, "I see your point. Unfortunately, I don't have a group of men. It's just me and my horse, Lightning."

One by one, the men excused themselves from the table, leaving only Bud and George Minton. The two men sat and talked until mid-afternoon. That night, Bud tossed and turned, not getting much sleep. He kept having a nightmare in which the Pacing White Stallion was rearing up on his hind legs as Bud lay helplessly on the ground beneath him. The stallion was getting ready to pound him into mush when Bud awoke, dripping in sweat. Each time he fell back to sleep, he would have the same dream.

The next morning he awoke to Juanita's voice calling him to breakfast. "Bacon in the pan, coffee in the pot. Get up an' get it. Get it while it's hot!"

Sitting and eating, Bud kept wondering if the dream had a special meaning. Could the white stallion be the devil? Didn't the Bible say something about the devil in sheep's clothing?

On his way to saddle Lightning and make preparations to escort the General and Mrs. Houston to their new home, Bud couldn't help but envision the great White Stallion. Charles Grimland came over and stopped to talk. Charles wanted to know if Bud needed a companion to help him capture the stallion. Bud didn't want to lie, but neither did he want to be hooked up with anyone else in his quest for the mythical horse. He crossed his fingers before answering. "I have to help General Houston move. Don't know when I can go searching." He shook Grimland's hand and thanked him for the offer, then swirled around on his heels to continue saddling Lightning.

After accompanying Sam and Margaret to Houston and helping them unload their wagon, Bud purchased a pack mule, several long ropes, a small ax and enough supplies for his hunt. Two days out, he arrived at the Brazos River and followed the stream north until he reached James and Millie's ferry. He yanked the rope attached to a big brass cowbell and it was not long before A.D. descended the riverbank and brought the ferry across. Bud could not believe how much A.D. had grown. On the other hand, A.D. could not believe how much Bud had grown. Bud was now a solid six-foot-one with broad shoulders and sat a saddle as if he had been born on a horse. The two exchanged greetings and made small talk as A.D. worked the ferry to the west bank.

Bud was invited to stay for two days. Jim and Millie would have it no other way. During the day, he helped A.D and Jim pick cotton. It was his first time picking cotton, and he was a bit careless. The burrs from the cotton balls split the ends of his fingers, causing them to bleed. After the first day, he learned to gently pull the cotton out rather than grab at the sharp burrs.

Jim and Millie were isolated on their farm and were always interested in what was happening throughout Texas. In the evenings, Bud would fill them in on what news he could. Jim was especially interested in the prospects of General Houston being re-elected as president. Bud was honest when he told them he had his doubts. General Houston had stirred up a hornet's nest with his stand to protect the Indians. Jim, in turn, assured Bud never to underestimate The Raven. "You have never seen General Houston campaign. They might be angry now, but once he starts talking, they will forget the past. Everyone knows Houston *is* Texas."

The most amazing transformation was Ruthann. She had begun to develop a woman's figure and her face was no longer that of a frightened child. She laughed and sang as Jim played Johnny's fiddle. Before Bud realized it, he was on his feet dancing with Ruthann. He could see the happy expression on Jim and Millie's faces. They were elated he was showing interest in their daughter.

When the time came for Bud to leave, Millie stuffed his right saddlebag full of bread, cookies, and sugar cane candy. A.D. rode with him to the low water crossing on the Little River. Deep down, the young boy wanted to go with Bud and help him capture the white stallion, but knew Jim needed him to finish picking the cotton before the rains came.

On his search for the Pacing White Stallion, a ballad that the old black stableman back in San Antonio had sung for him, kept coursing through Bud's mind like the wind through the trees:

Fleet barb of the prairie, in vain they prepare.
For thy neck, arched in beauty, the treacherous snare.
Thou wilt toss thy proud head, and with nostrils stretched wide.
Defy them again, and as still hast defiled.
Not the team of the Sun, as in fable portrayed.
Through firmament rushing in glory arrayed, could match,
In wild majesty, beauty and speed.
That tireless, magnificent snowy-white steed.

Bud knew one secret about the Pacing White Stallion he had shared with no one. A San Antonio stable hand had told him an interesting story about a man named John Young who said he knew where to find the mystery horse. Young had raised racehorses back in his native Kentucky before relocating about eight miles south of Austin on Onion Creek. He told the old man how one day he looked down by the creek and saw a snow white stallion with fifty to sixty mares. The stallion was pure white with ebony eyes and two black ears. Young followed the band of horses across the Blanco, San Marcos, and Guadalupe Rivers. He observed the stallion kept his mares clear of clumps of trees and never crossed the Colorado on the east or entered the cedar laden hill country to the west. Young had disclosed to the old stable hand one more vital piece of information; the best spot to view the stallion was a place called Pilot Knob, about four miles from McKinney Falls and about eight miles southeast of Austin. With the coordinates of Don Cheeks' site, and John Young's information, Bud felt confident he would be able to narrow his search enough to locate the White Stallion of the Plains.

Bud chose an ideal camping area on high ground near Onion Creek. He cut some small trees and built a lean-to facing south for protection from the wind and blowing rain. In the event someone stumbled upon his camp, Bud camouflaged his long and short rifles by wrapping them in oilcloth, placing them on top of his lean-to and covering them with grass and branches. He then tied his supplies and meat to a high Spanish oak tree limb. He would need to be riding with a light load if he wanted to capture the white stallion.

From his camp, Bud went out daily in search of the prized stallion. On the third day, he heard the pounding of hooves approaching from the rear. Wheeling around in his saddle, he saw the flashing cascade of a black stallion's mane and his curving comet tail as he led a remuda of twenty-five to thirty mares and foals. The drove of mares was a mixture of bay, sorrel, brown, grullo, roan, dun, gray, and pinto, with a few blacks tossed in. They were running in a direct line and then suddenly fanned out into a sinuous curve. As they got closer, they formed a long, straight line and stopped abruptly about 150 yards from Bud and Lighting, heads tossed high, nostrils flared. As the group stood in formation, the magnificent black stallion positioned himself at the forefront. The bright morning sun transformed his ebony black coat into shaded hues of deep-blue purples. The bold stallion's muscled chest, slender legs, and glowing presence conveyed the most powerful site Bud had ever seen. As Bud and Lightning stood motionless, fixed on the marvelous creature, the stallion reared up and boxed the air with his front hooves. Bud was not sure what the body language meant. He could only imagine the stallion was warning him to leave his territory. As the black stallion's ebony eyes remained fixed on the pair, he pawed the ground with his right hoof. Suddenly, he released an impudent snort, and tossing his long black mane to the wind, he raised his tail and dashed away, his mares following closely behind. Bud finally exhaled, and dreamed of the moment he would capture the magnificent Pacing White Stallion.

Each evening, Bud marked the days off his calendar to keep track of time so as not to miss the trip to Galveston for Virginia's birthday. After five grueling weeks, he had seen several herds and thousands of wild mustangs. One day he came upon what he estimated was around five thousand in one drove, but no white stallion. He had searched from Knobs Point to where Don Cheek reported seeing the steed several times, only to return to camp disappointed.

Finally he knew he had stayed as long as he dared. The nights were turning cold and the leaves on the Spanish oaks were turning from green to crimson red, cadmium orange and lemon yellow. The sumac trees were turning from sea foam green to scarlet red. The skies were filled with flocks of wild geese headed south in formation. He would try one more time and if he didn't find the Pacing White Stallion, he would accept defeat and head for Galveston.

As he marked an X through the calendar date, suddenly the date jumped out as if printed in bold text. Today was October 4, 1841, his twenty-first birthday! He didn't look a year older; however, he loved the idea of being twenty-one. Living alone at the edge of the frontier had afforded him plenty of time to think, dream, and plot his future. He could see why a man would want a wife to share things with. None of the men he rode with was interested in his adventures or the narrow escapes he encountered fighting Indians, but a wife would be waiting with an open heart to let him share with her his glorious adventures.

Bud found sleeping difficult, tossing around most of the night. Well before daylight, he mounted Lightning and was on his way to make one final effort. As he topped a small ridge, he came upon a band of about seventy horses gathered at a watering hole along Onion Creek. His heart began to race. On a distant hill, overlooking the landscape, like a marble sentry, stood the prize of all prizes. Lightning even seemed to sense the importance of the moment as his flesh quivered under the saddle. His response was the same as his master. Was this the day?

Chapter Twenty-Six
The Revolver

President Mirabeau Bonaparte Lamar had no idea how to make the most of his leaders' talents and abilities. He assigned Jack Hays to the Army during the Plum Creek fight when clearly Jack was the model for a Texas Ranger. Hays was accustomed to charging forward, asking his men to follow. The Army told him where to go and what to do, and officers stayed behind the lines as opposed to the "follow me" attitude of a ranger captain. Jack was extremely frustrated. The army was too structured for a freelancer like Jack Hays and prevented him from getting in on as much of the action as he craved. By the time his group was organized and reached the battle, the fight was mostly over. They did kill a few stray warriors, but were mainly responsible for rounding up horses and transporting the animals back to their owners. Jack felt anyone could transport animals. He let his position be known to Lamar and resigned his army post. As Jack prepared to return to the United States, Lamar realized the value a man like Jack Coffee Hays brought to the fledgling Republic. Rather than allow a man of Hays' proven valor and stalwart character to move back to the United States, in January 1841, Lamar promoted him to the rank of Major in the Texas Rangers.

Before his presidential term expired, Lamar also appointed a local Mexican and fierce enemy of Santa Anna, Antonio Perez, George Erath, a hero in the battle of San Jacinto, and John Price to the positions of Ranger Captain. Antonio Perez was the first to assemble his men. Living in San Antonio, he mustered a roll of fourteen local Mexicans and one Anglo, John Trueheart. Trueheart's brother chose to ride with Jack Hays and so did Bud Miller. As soon as Jack signed on his thirteen men, he and Perez headed out to search for Mexican outlaws (cowboys) or enemy soldiers who may have crossed the Rio Grande. After riding for about fifty miles, the groups split, with Perez heading toward Corpus Christi, and Jack, in the direction of the Frio River. They each returned home tired and low on rations. The meanest thing either group had encountered on their foray was an angry longhorn protecting her calf.

In January of 1841 Captain George Erath, a no-nonsense Austrian immigrant, led 140 men, consisting of more than 125 Texans and the rest Tonkawa and Lipan scouts on an expedition against the eastern Indians. The group followed the Brazos River as far as Comanche Peak, then crossed over to the Trinity River and back, finding no sign of any hostiles. Erath was extremely disappointed and felt the mission had been a waste of time and manpower. He resigned, saying he had better things to do than go on long rides with a bunch of men. George Erath was much better suited for the structure of the military.

Captain John Price's first assignment was to respond to a letter written by rancher Phillip Dimmitt. The letter informed the Republic about the suspicious activities of a man named Henry Lawrence Kinney who ran the first trading post north of Matamoros on the Gulf of Mexico. Kinney had purchased his land for his trading post from Colonel Canales, a Mexican officer. This transaction alone made Dimmitt suspicious, but aside from that, Dimmitt had learned Kinney was acquiring guns and ammunition, and possibly a cannon. Captain Price assembled his unit and headed out to investigate. When the rangers arrived at the Kinney trading post, Price realized Phillip Dimmitt had indeed been telling the truth. Kinney possessed an exceptionally large supply of guns, powder and lead, as well as a four-pound cannon. Kinney explained that he was just providing protection from Indians, and Mexican and Anglo bandit attacks. Kinney was either telling the truth or he was a darn good liar. The small cannon appeared to pose no real threat, and Captain Price understood Kinney needed to maintain an adequate supply of guns and powder for protection. He could see the tightrope Kinney was walking, and decided to cut him some slack. Unknown to Captain Price, three weeks earlier, Kinney had provided a Mexican officer with a supply of lead and powder. Kinney was a cunning man who swayed with the wind.

Price did request a fresh supply of dry powder, flint and five good horses. Kinney reluctantly obliged, knowing unless he gave an eager response to the Captain's request, he may raise suspicion. Price and his men were preparing to leave when a small group of "cowboys" operating in no-man's land sauntered in to the trading post. Price recognized one of the cowboys. When the Captain ordered him to surrender his gun, the bandit refused. In a flash, guns blazed. Instantly four of the bandits were dead and one ranger slightly wounded. John Price gave Kinney a stern warning: If the rangers had to return, he would order the trading post burned to the ground with Kinney inside. Kinney knew the Captain was not making an idle threat.

President Lamar didn't appoint all the ranger captains in 1841; some like Ben McCullough were promoted locally. The citizens of Gonzales unanimously elected Ben Captain. In the winter of 1841, Comanches hit Gonzales hard, stealing over 150 of the town's best horses. Most raids were in warmer weather, so this one took everyone by surprise. Ben selected sixteen men to ride out with him the next morning; he had learned from riding with Jack Hays to allow the Indians to believe they had escaped safely. Once the band felt secure, they would camp, celebrate and sleep. Ben hoped to surprise the band when they were drunk and tired from a vigorous victory dance. Before noon, the rangers picked up a trail. Ben tracked them at a judicious pace; he didn't want to wear the horses out in the event of a running battle. He adopted a Jack Hays ploy, dismounting and asking his men to wait while he proceeded on foot to locate the camp. As he suspected, the Indians were huddled around the campfire, fast asleep, secure in the knowledge they had made a clean get away. Ben returned and told his men how they would attack, and they trailed him back to the edge of the Indian camp on foot. The Indians' belief of security was shattered with the first gunshot at the hand of Ben McCullough. The initial volley of gunfire killed five Comanches in their sleep and wounded several others. The remaining Indians grabbed their weapons and vanished into the darkness. Ben ordered no pursuit. He didn't want to risk getting any rangers being killed just to eliminate a few more Comanche. The rangers left the wounded. Ben didn't like the idea of killing a wounded man, even if he was an Indian. He also forbid any of his rangers to scalp those killed. They rounded up the stolen horses as well as those belonging to the Indians. If anyone in Gonzales had questions about Ben's leadership, those ideas vanished into the cold winter air.

All men who served as ranger captains were brave beyond description, but none stood taller than Jack Hays. Jack's protocol was one that all succeeding ranger captains adopted: "Follow me." His bravery and heroism set the bar so high that it was almost impossible for any ranger to rival his courage. That didn't prevent men like Big Foot Wallace, Ben McCullough or Samuel Walker from trying to surpass his reputation. Nelson Lee, a veteran ranger, had been on several missions with Jack Hays. When asked what he thought of Hays, he replied, "He is a smooth-faced boy, slim build, weighing no more than 185 pounds and standing less than five foot ten. His manner unassuming to the extreme, he is a man of few words. His bravery and courage have no equal among mortal men."

One ranger said, "Jack Hays is a lamb in peace and a lion in battle."

Because of Hays' daring, his fellow rangers and the citizens of the Republic came up with a saying when they saw the enemy fleeing: "They are running as if Jack Hays himself were after them."

John Lockhart (Matilda's father) told an eastern reporter: "Jack Hays is the best Indian fighter and skilled tracker to ever draw a breath. In the dry and rocky portions of west Texas, a squad of fifteen to twenty Indians can move through the country without turning over a pebble. Jack Hays can spot a bent blade of grass. He can judge the time the Indians passed through by the maturity of their horse's manure. His ability is instinctive. He can ride along at a trot and notice signs when even the most experienced trackers can see nothing. I have seen him dismount, observe one small pebble and because of its displacement, know an Indian pony had just passed and in what direction he was heading. I have never known an Indian or white man who was equal to Jack Hays as a tracker."

Two hundred Comanche slipped into an area several miles west of San Antonio and stole a large number of horses and mules. One of the Mexican ranchers rushed to Leon Springs where Jack was living and woke the ranger, who had just returned from a grueling trip. He was sleeping in his buckskins and only needed to slip on his boots, and grab his hat and gun. Jack sent the Mexican to the Military Plaza to ring the bell. He didn't have to wait long before several of his men, including Henry McCullough and Bud Miller arrived, ready to ride. As dawn broke, the group galloped northwest for about twenty-five miles before Jack picked up the Indians' tracks. Jack appointed Henry and Bud to scout ahead. They returned in short order, informing Jack the trail was getting warmer; there was fresh horse manure just ahead. Jack then dashed out in front of his men about thirty yards. As he came to a clearing, he spotted the marauders camped along the Guadalupe River. He sat on his horse with one leg over the saddle horn, and waited for his men to catch up. Jack then dropped his leg back over into the stirrup and said, "Boys, yonder are those horse thieves and over there are the stolen animals. Looks to me we are outnumbered ten to one. Don't be concerned. I know we can whip 'em. What do you say we give them a welcoming party?"

In unison their voices rang out, "Let's get 'em. You lead and we will be right behind you."

Jack slid off his horse, saying, "Dismount, tighten your saddle girths, and check your guns. We are going to show 'em not to mess with Texas."

Hays grabbed his saddle horn and in one fluid motion, swung back up into his saddle. In a flash, he was running at full speed in the direction of the warriors. He turned in his saddle and shouted, "Come on, boys, shoot to kill." Then he turned back, facing the much larger Indian force, whipping his horse with the reins. As soon as they were close enough, Jack began shooting and his men followed his action. The rangers were riding so fast, the momentum propelled them through the Indian lines. They startled the Indians' horses, causing them to rear and lunge in different directions, making them impossible to control. Jack wheeled around and again his men followed. They dashed back through the Indian line, killing on either side as they passed through the camp. The warriors tumbled off their mounts from the blast of the rangers' rifles. Their Chief, mounted on an ebony stallion decorated with ribbons and other colorful trimmings, let out a blood-curdling battle cry to rally his warriors. Jack Hays headed straight for the Chief and when he dropped his shield for a moment, the ranger captain's shot was true. As soon as the warriors saw their leader fall, they scattered into the scrub brush.

One of the men recognized a chestnut stallion as Sam Maverick's prized horse, Mex. The rangers gathered up the horses, including Sam Maverick's treasured stallion. Big Foot Wallace picked up the Chief's shield and later gave the trophy to President Lamar who displayed the prize in the capital.

Seeing Hays lead his men, the Comanches wanted to know his name. When they learned it, they called him "Captain Yack." From that battle on, Jack Hays would be known by his enemies as Captain Yack or Devil Yack. A handsome reward was offered to any Indian who killed Devil Yack, and the Mexican cowboys south of the Nueces had their own five thousand dollar bounty placed on his head. Captain Jack Hays became enemy number one to both hostile Indians and Mexican outlaws.

Hays was assigned to deliver a message to any who may be considering invading Texas. He and his men rode into Laredo, captured several dozen of their best horses, making sure to intimidate the Mexican soldiers. Jack and his unit stopped about five miles from town, posted pickets, and set up camp along a small stream so the stolen horses could drink and eat their fill of tall Texas grass. The following day, Jack waited until the Mexicans were taking their siesta before returning to town. He called the Mexican leaders together and told them he had not taken their horses with the intent of stealing them. His intention was to impress upon them that rangers could and would retaliate should the Mexicans choose to inflict their larceny on Texas citizens. He was given blood-oath promises, some swore on Saints and others on their mother's graves that they would not make any further raids or robberies on Texas soil.

Trade between Mexico and Texas was on the rise, especially along the border with San Antonio. The Mexicans brought beans, flower, sugar, leather, shoes and saddles to trade for the Texans' calico, tobacco, and American hardware. This was a good arrangement for both sides. Then, in April of 1841, the robbery and murder of two Mexican traders required swift Texas justice. About seventy-five miles south of town, their string of pack mules were stolen and the two traders shot by a group of cowboys under the Mexican leader, Agaton. One of the traders lived long enough to tell the name of the bandits' leader. Word was sent to Jack Hays. He chose eleven rangers for the mission, including Big Foot Wallace, Ben McCullough, Samuel Walker, five regulars, plus three new men. The twelve rangers joined forces with thirteen Texas-Mexicans under the command of the distinguished Indian fighter, Captain Antonio Parez of San Antonio. Not long after bedding down for the night after their third day, an express rider passed their camp, riding full out. Unknown to Jack and Parez, the rider was carrying news of their impending arrival to the Mexican Army. The Mexican Captain in Laredo hastily assembled an army of thirty-five men to ambush Hays and Parez about ten miles north of town.

Early the next morning, Samuel Walker and a Texas-Mexican from the Parez group, scouting a mile or so ahead, spotted a cloud of dust rising over the tops of the rugged huisache trees. Walker asked, "Do you think that's a group of hostile riders?"

The Mexican didn't answer. He was on the ground, listening to the pounding hooves, trying to estimate the size of the group when Sam said, "Let's get out of here and warn the men we have company."

His Mexican companion answered, "Best I can tell, there must be at least forty."

As the two scouts turned to run, Sam glanced back over his shoulder and saw a large force topping the ridge about two miles away. Sam had no doubt the group was on their way to kill some gringos. As Walker and his companion reached Jack, they could hear the Mexican Army sounding their bugle. The ranger group dismounted and waited. As the army got within voice range, the Mexican Captain shouted in broken English, "Surrender or we will overrun you." Captain Garcia was full of confidence, but that would soon change.

He was about to meet Texas' best. Captain Jack Hays was about to introduce the Mexicans to the five-shot Samuel Colt Paterson revolver with a revolutionary five-spout powder flask. Garcia ordered his men to fire a volley of lead over the heads of the rangers, demanding surrender. To his shock, Jack answered with three rounds from all of his rangers who carried five shooters. The three rapid shots from several guns caused alarm and the Mexicans threw their guns to the ground and their hands into the air. Captain Garcia and two others yanked their horses around and made a run for Laredo. The rest of the Mexican soldiers raised a white flag, asking for quarter. Hays spared their lives.

Captain Garcia carried the news of the humiliating defeat back to Laredo. The Mayor went to speak with the rangers, waving a white flag. He begged Jack to spare his town and not burn it to the ground. He remembered the last time Jack Hays visited Laredo, he promised that if he had to return, he would leave nothing but ashes behind. Hays negotiated to spare Laredo if the Mayor delivered Agaton and guaranteed future protection of all traders traveling to and from San Antonio. The Mayor agreed and took the rangers to Agaton's tiny one room house on the south side of town. Jack stationed eight men between the house and the river before having Big Foot Wallace kick the door down. Agaton was found hiding under his cot, crying like a baby. He came out begging for his life. Jack's men said nothing as they tied him to his horse and escorted him back to San Antonio to stand trial. Once in San Antonio, Texas justice was swift. Agaton was hanged within one week after being tried and convicted of the murder and robbery of the two Mexican traders. A large crowd gathered to watch the hanging. Even small children were often in the crowd. Public hangings sent a strong message: This is what happens if one does not respect the laws of society. No doubt seeing the black hood placed over a begging man's head was enough to scare many young boys to choose to become respectable members of society. Outlaws were not glorified, but shown as despicable people that no one should emulate.

Hays and the rangers would have little time to rest. No sooner had they unsaddled their horses than word reached San Antonio that the Comanche were active again. The Plum Creek victory had calmed the Comanches down for a while, but only until they regrouped and altered their strategy. The resumption of hostilities was no surprise to the rangers. They had fully expected the Comanche would start raiding small ranches and isolated farms once they re-established a band of warriors.

The news of the Comanche activity came from a Mexican peon, whose farm had been raided, and his wife and four children captured. He had been plowing his field and all he could do was watch in horror as his family was kidnapped. His feet were bloody, as his tattered shoes had fallen apart on his several mile walk to reach the rangers. At first, he was too overwrought to speak. All he could do was cry. One of Captain Perez's men was able to console him in Spanish and finally drew out the story of what had happened.

The following morning, Jack rang the bell in the center of the Military Plaza to signal his men they had fifteen minutes to ride. He didn't have to ring the bell. Most of Hays' fourteen and Captain Perez's twenty-two men were saddled and ready long before sunrise. By the time the rangers reached the entrance to Uvalde Canyon, the day was reaching the end. Samuel Walker and a Mexican scout were riding point when suddenly they spotted a group of ten Comanche heading in their direction. Standing up in his stirrups, Walker grabbed his hat and began making a circling motion to alert Jack and the others there was trouble ahead. The Indians didn't hesitate, and letting out a shrill scream, they headed for a large thicket grove. The scream was one any veteran had come to recognize as a cry of their willingness to fight to the end. Jack had the men surround the thicket and selected two rangers, Big Foot Wallace and Ben McCullough, to dismount and follow him into the thicket. The moment the fighting broke out, Sam Walker rushed in to join the firefight. Ben McCullough sustained a small arrow wound, but fortunately, it was not poisonous. The four rangers killed eight braves, wounded one, and took a squaw prisoner. Hays knew it would be useless to interrogate the captives. Many had tried in the past, only to find Comanche captives were prepared to die rather than disclose the location of their camp.

As night fell, the rangers stopped and ate, then as always, relocated their camp. Jack felt they were within two or three miles of the main band of Comanche, but the following day they failed to locate the Comanche camp. Jack saw how tired his men and their horses were and ordered they return to San Antonio. Once back in the Alamo city, Hays allowed the horses to rest for a week and then headed out again. Sam Maverick joined them for their return mission. This time, Jack took fifty men, including ten Lipan scouts and his trusted Indian scout, Chief Falcco. The group pressed on to the mouth of Uvalde Canyon, exploring deeper than any white man, other than Jim Bowie, had. The Indians would not be expecting the rangers to venture that far into the frontier, but Jack Hays would have tracked them to the ends of the earth.

As the rangers neared the Comanche's main camp, a hunting party of seven braves met them. Seeing the rangers and Lipan scouts, the small band turned their horses and made a mad dash to warn the rest of their camp. As the rangers broke over a small hilltop, they saw a number of warriors heading toward them. Suddenly, in choreographed unison, the Indians made a sharp right angle west. Jack called out twenty-five men and gave chase. This was exactly what the Indians were counting on. Jack's actions would allow the main camp to start moving deeper into the hill country; Comanche could break down and move camp in under five minutes. Hays and his twenty-five rangers drew close enough to engage the warriors in a running fight which lasted for over two hours. Then the Comanches broke off into a line and circled the rangers, shrieking and shooting arrows at the mounted men. Hays realized the predicament they were in. Instead of dismounting, as the Indians expected, he shouted, "CHARGE!" The rangers were on top of the shocked Indians before they could react. They had fully expected Hays and his men to do what all white men had in the past: dismount and fort up so they could use their long rifles as they hid behind their horses. Jack Hays was as unpredictable as Texas weather. He shouted at the top of his voice, "Powder burn 'em boys. Powder burn the red devils."

The rangers crashed through the Indians' ranks, knocking them down on either side. Realizing they were being defeated with guns that never stopped shooting, the Indians broke rank and scattered in every direction. Jack and his men once more gave chase. As if on cue, braves began throwing their lances and shields to the ground to lighten their load as they retreated. The Indians were on fresher mounts and began to open a wide gap between the rangers. Hays realized the rangers' horses were exhausted and reluctantly abandoned the chase. Several rangers were wounded, fortunately none mortally. Jack was unable to ascertain how many Indians were killed or wounded. Even in the heat of battle, warriors recovered their fallen from the killing field.

The search for the Comanches took the rangers several miles deeper into the hill country than anyone expected. The rangers did not have enough provisions for such a long excursion and had to finally resort to killing the weaker horses for food. None of their horses were in any condition to travel any further until they were able to find water and nourishment. The journey back to Uvalde Canyon would take the rangers seven miserable days. The first three days, the barren landscape was covered with only rocks and prickly pear cactus. Then they came to cedar trees so thick it was impossible for them to kill any wild game. A deer only needed to move two steps and viridian shrubs hid them from view. Not even a jackrabbit strayed into view long enough for a clean shot. There was no water, no wild turkeys, only prickly pears. Once they reached the Canyon, they found Sam Maverick and the other men waiting along the banks of a creek. Sam had anticipated the rangers would be low on food and had sent three riders to San Antonio for fresh supplies. Hays' rangers grabbed hands full of corn and began to eat like starved animals. The wounded were treated and their famished horses ate their fill on the lush grass.

Their mission was highly successful. Never again would the Comanche penetrate in or around San Antonio. One of the Comanche Chiefs would later say he lost half of his men in the fight with Hays. Many of the wounded died on the hundred-mile trip back to their camp at Devil River. The old Chief vowed, "I will never again fight Jack Hays who has a shot for every finger on his hands."

One of Jack's rangers, Samuel Walker had participated in the development of the five-shot Samuel Colt Paterson revolver that had so successfully intimidated the Indians. In 1831, a lad of sixteen by the name of Samuel Colt was working as a sailor on a ship heading for Calcutta. His days were filled with doing the grunt work adults were inclined to avoid. At night, by the light of a dim candle, he whittled. One night he came up with an idea for a revolving pistol. Right then, he began to carve out a revolving handgun. During the five-year voyage, young Sam Colt carved and carved until he perfected a wooden model of his revolving pistol.

When his ship returned to the United States, he took out a patent on his new invention in the United States and England. On February 26, 1836, twenty-one-year-old Samuel Colt held his new American patent, signed by President Andrew Jackson and Benjamin Butler, in his hands. Now all he needed was money to produce his invention. He figured he would only need to put his invention before a few men with capital and they would see the value of such a revolutionary weapon. The next day, Samuel Colt was on his way to New York City, where he started selling stock to finance the manufacture of his five-shot pistol. He quickly generated enough cash to open a gun factory in Patterson, New Jersey. With lightning speed, his lathes and drills began humming as he turned out his first four-and-a-half inch, octagonal barrel .34 caliber, five-shot revolver. As superior as his invention was, he had trouble marketing the new pistol until word drifted down to Sam Houston. After seeing a sample, President Houston ordered 180 of the revolvers for the Texas Navy. When the Navy folded, an alert Jack Hays talked Houston into giving the guns to the rangers. On the black market, the guns were bringing $200 apiece. Only about four-dozen could be rounded up, so only veteran Indian fighters were able to own one of the new revolving pistols. Jack Hays kept two, and made sure Big Foot Wallace, Ben McCullough and Sam Walker each received a pair. Bud Miller was able to trade one of the older rangers out of his revolver. The ranger had an arrow wound turn gangrene, forcing him to have his leg amputated and he was no longer able to fight. With the old ranger's revolver and the one Jack had given him, Bud ended up with a matching pair.

The five-shot revolvers were a tremendous upgrade for the rangers because they were ideal for fighting on horseback. Shooting five times without having to reload was a noted advantage. The rapid-fire gun sent cold chills through the Indians. Seeing fire spitting from a ranger's fingers was effective enough for the Indians to be more selective about where they plundered.

Colt was doing his best to get the Federal Government to purchase his weapon, without much success. While Colt kept meeting with failure after failure in the north, the Texas Rangers were cutting a wide swipe across the Republic with his new guns. Because of the success the rangers were having Colt changed the name from "The Patterson Colt" to "The Texas Revolver."

The rangers identified flaws and limitations in the weapon under battlefield conditions and sat around their campfires under the scrub oaks and huisache of south Texas, discussing ways to improve the gun. It was decided that Samuel Walker would carry the rangers' suggestions to Samuel Colt. Walker and Colt met in the store of Samuel Hall. Colt, the master gun maker; Hall, a leading gunsmith and arms dealer; and Walker, the wise Indian fighter, hit it off from the first handshake. Ranger Walker explained the revolver was the best on the market; however, there were flaws that limited the weapon's effectiveness in battlefield conditions. The biggest problem for the rangers was reloading; they not only had to remove the barrel, but the cylinder as well. Breaking the gun into three parts was not an easy task, especially when riding full out while being chased by men intent on killing. One slip and the barrel could tumble to the ground. The rangers also suggested the gun have a longer barrel. The extra weight and longer barrel would serve as a club in the event a ranger needed to coldcock the enemy in close-up fighting.

The veteran Walker mesmerized young Samuel Colt and Sam Hall. Colt invited the ranger to his manufacturing plant in Patterson. After six weeks, Walker returned to Texas with a matching pair of the new and improved handgun called the "Walker Colt." The grip was more compatible with a man's hand and much easier to hold. The disappearing trigger of the first pistol had been replaced with a visible one protected by a guard. The cylinder was longer and heavier to accommodate a .44 caliber charge. The new gun weighed almost four pounds. The feature Walker was most proud to have inspired was the fast rammer, which attached below the barrel and seated the bullets in the revolving chamber without either being removed. The gun was perfectly suited to the needs of the Texas Rangers. Colt's output of the new weapon was limited; however, Walker placed a nice order so each ranger could own at least one. Samuel Colt's revolving handgun defined the Texas Rangers, and in turn, the rangers elevated Colt Firearms' status as respected master gun makers. Quid Pro Quo.

Chapter Twenty-Seven
The Reunion

In 1827, empresario Sterling Robertson purchased a colonization contract from Robert Leftwick who had an agreement with the Mexican government to settle 800 families. Robertson located his colony along the Brazos River, northwest of the land granted to Moses and Stephen F. Austin. In the twelve years before the Texas revolution, Robertson settled more than six hundred families in his colony. Only Austin would bring more families to Texas.

No one could expound upon the virtues of Texas with more passion than Sterling Robertson. He possessed superior oratory skills and spoke as passionately as a fire-and-brimstone preacher about the rich Texas soil, the expansion opportunities, and the adventure offered in the new frontier. Preaching about the glory waiting any and all in Texas, Robertson's words mesmerized the young Noah Smithwick. Noah was ready to leave the next morning, but his two older brothers wouldn't go with him. Finally, after a year of dreaming and planning, the nineteen-year-old Smithwick left Hopkinsville, Kentucky and set out for the "Garden of Eden" Robertson had described. He took his long rifle, a few dollars, a change of clothes, and the small hand tools necessary to find work as a gunsmith, blacksmith and farrier. Noah possessed skills in all three trades in a time when a man's survival depended on his gun and his horse.

For a young man like Noah, the mundane daily grind was not what he came looking for. He wanted excitement, action, and adventure. He would discover all three when he started smuggling tobacco into northern Mexico. The young adventurer thrived on the danger. Using his backwoods skills as a hunter saved his life on several occasions when Mexican authorities or Indians were on his trail. Smuggling turned into seeking the riches of silver. Like James Bowie before him, young Smithwick caught "silver fever" and combed the mountains of Mexico looking for the elusive treasure. He followed rumors and myths until he exhausted his resources and was forced to return to Texas, disillusioned and broke. With his money supply down to zero, Noah headed for Nacogdoches to do some serious gambling. This first city in Texas was known as a wide-open town where gaming rooms and women of the night were in abundance. Noah grew up with a gambling father who taught his boys to deal from the bottom of the deck before they could read and write. He was skilled at marking cards and could read his competition's body language like an open book. Not a day passed that a few greenhorns didn't drift into town and fall into his lair as Noah relieved newcomers of what few dollars they had. One autumn day, Noah got careless and was caught dealing from the bottom of the deck. The man being cheated went for his pistol, but damp powder caused his handgun to misfire, allowing young Noah to escape out the rear door.

After his near-death experience in Nacogdoches, Noah decided to settle down in San Felipe. The town welcomed having a blacksmith-farrier-gunsmith and soon he had more work than he could handle. He hired a helper, paying the man per job. He advanced his helper money to chop wood for his forge furnace. When Noah returned, the man had cut no wood. He asked Noah for more money and the young man from Kentucky refused. The angry helper grabbed his ax and headed for Noah, only to whack at the thin air. The much quicker and more agile Smithwick vaulted aside, planting his blacksmith hammer between the angry helper's eyes. The big man fell at Noah's feet. Austin felt Noah had acted in self-defense and dismissed the charges.

Later that month, one of Smithwick's dearest friends killed the Mayor of Gonzales in a dispute over a woman. Austin asked Noah to make a set of shackles and chains to transport the prisoner to Mexico City to stand trial. Standing trial in Mexico only meant one thing, and it was not good. Noah knew his friend would be hanged as sure as the sun rises. Before the group left with his friend in chains, Noah met with the prisoner and gave him a pistol and file, providing explicit instructions on how to file the shackles off. All he would need to do was file the head of the rivet holding the cuffs. Once the friend was free, he was to leave Texas and never return. Noah made it clear that staying in Texas was not an option. The friend did as instructed, with the exception of leaving Texas. As soon he broke free of the shackles, he went back to San Felipe. This was the last place in the world he should have gone. Austin had him arrested again, and this time he was escorted under heavy guard to Mexico. He was dead by hanging within two weeks.

Stephen Austin then turned his anger on Noah Smithwick, banning him from living in his colony. Selling his blacksmith tools to a fellow Kentuckian, Noah left for New Orleans. Once there, he met an older version of himself, James Bowie. Perhaps more ruthless, with his slave trading and land swindles, nevertheless, the two men became close friends.

In 1835, Bowie persuaded Noah to return to Texas. With the news of a large Mexican army gathering along the Rio Grande, Austin decided Noah was his kind of man after all, and welcomed the young man back with open arms. Austin knew Texas was on the verge of war with Mexico and men like Jim Bowie and Noah Smithwick were essential if Texas were to have a prayer of survival.

Perhaps Smithwick, now thirty-three, saw a youthful version of himself in young Bud Miller. They both were from Kentucky and had arrived in Texas full of sky-high dreams. Each had become a Texas Ranger when they were very young. Noah had come to respect his young companion's brio and maturity, and steered his young protégé away from bad habits like drinking, gambling, and risk-taking.

Maybe it was mere chance or perhaps the providence of God when Noah and seven rangers stumbled upon Bud Miller's makeshift camp. No sooner had the men dismounted than a dejected Bud came into view. Bud had found no Pacing White Stallion. Noah knew by Bud's long face that something was amiss. He asked, "What's the matter, good buddy?"

"Ah nothin'," Bud replied.

"I won't buy that story. Your face tells me you are one dejected young man."

Bud recognized all but one of the men accompanying Noah. After some hellos and handshakes, Bud answered, "I've been camped here for six weeks and one day searching for the Pacing White Stallion."

Noah didn't want to crush Bud's dreams; yet, neither did he want to perpetrate a lie. He spit a wad of chewing tobacco into the creek before answering, "I'm not too sure there is this Pacing White Stallion.

The Reunion

I have crisscrossed Texas as much as anyone, except maybe Ben Milam and the late Jim Bowie, and neither of them or myself has ever seen the mystery stallion. Mind you, I'm not calling those who say they have seen the stallion, liars. I'm just sayin' there's a possibility he is not out there to be found." Noah couldn't help but see the correlation between his own quest for the elusive silver, the silver white stallion, the white buffalo, and a new book *Moby Dick,* telling the story of a white whale.

Bud was so disappointed. He didn't want to discuss the white stallion. He asked, "What brings you to this neck of the woods?"

Noah replied, "We are on our way to Galveston Island. We have to escort the Ambassador from England back to Austin."

Bud's face brightened up and he started to laugh. He was thrilled to know he would have company on his return trip. Noah knew all about living solo for extended periods. He could remember how lonely he had felt when he searched in vain for silver, only to come home with empty pockets.

The eight rangers drifted off to sleep while Bud jabbered away until well past midnight, not realizing his audience had been sleeping for two hours. It didn't matter. Bud needed to empty out his head, if only to the hoot owls, coyotes, and thin air. The group was up early and on the road by the time the sun made its appearance the next morning. Bud moved from ranger to ranger, engaging in conversation. He had not realized how much he missed being in the company of people.

After sleeping under the stars and fighting off chiggers for several nights, the group was delighted to see smoke rising like a twisting cloud from Saul and Betsy Hempstead's chimney. Saul, like many farmers, rented his barn to travelers. The barn loft rented for fifty cents and a bed on the floor was one dollar. Betsy cooked a hot meal for supper and another for breakfast. The Hempsteads found an eager group with the rangers as the nights had turned bitter cold and any relief was greatly appreciated. Bud was especially pleased at the thought of some home cooking and a roof over his head.

Saul and Betsy Hempstead were part of the original three hundred families who settled with Stephen Austin. They owned a four-room house and an exceptional barn. Their property was on the road that linked Galveston, Houston, San Felipe and the capital, Austin. Seldom did a week pass they didn't have several houseguests. They were making more money boarding and feeding road-worn travelers than their farm could ever generate.

Among their regular guests were Sam Houston and his entourage. Saul Hempstead was a staunch Lamar supporter and had vowed to kill Houston on sight. Since Saul had never seen Houston, he didn't know Sam had rented his barn on several occasions. During one such stay with the Hempsteads, everyone was seated for dinner when Sam raised his hand and asked if they owned a bible. One of the children brought Sam the bible, which he opened to the twenty-third Psalm. In his polished voice, he slowly read the Psalm and then gave thanks for the food they were preparing to eat. The next morning after breakfast, Sam formally introduced himself to Mr. Hempstead. Saul was stunned. This could not be the vulgar barbarian of a man he had vowed to kill. No man could read the scriptures and give thanks to the Lord the way General Houston had without being a strong Christian. Saul told Sam that he had planned to kill him, and apologized for how wrong his assessment had been. From that day on, Houston had no stronger supporter in all of Texas than Saul Hempstead. President Lamar learned of Saul's conversion to Houston and never darkened the Hempstead doorway again.

Since moving to Texas, Saul and Betsy had actively built a family; they arrived in Texas with four children, and quickly added eight more. The children ranged in age from three to eighteen. Saul Jr. was eighteen, pushing nineteen, and their daughter Charm was seventeen. Bud could not believe his eyes when he first saw Charm. She was beautiful. Her deep auburn hair complemented her jewel-green eyes, accentuating their brilliance. When she smiled, two tiny dimples pressed gently into her rosy cheeks. Her parents had aptly named her, he thought to himself. She was the personification of charm in her manner, speech, and appearance.

Only the two eldest children, Saul Jr. and Charm were allowed to dine with visitors and Mrs. Hempstead seated Bud next to Charm at the dinner table. Bud had not expected to be drawn to another girl; his thoughts these past few months had been focused exclusively on Virginia. He was blindsided by Charm and could tell she found him attractive as well by the way she blushed when she took her seat next to him. She looked straight into Bud's eyes when they talked, letting him know she was interested in getting to know him better.

The Hempsteads had never received a houseguest as robust and handsome as Bud Miller. He was now twenty-one years old, a property owner, and a respected Texas Ranger. They were pleased and surprised to discover he owned a house and large tract of land in Bastrop. Being a Texas Ranger afforded Bud honor and respect. Owning his own home demonstrated stability. Betsy Hempstead knew he would be a prize catch for her daughter. Texas had a significantly larger number of single men than women; however, few would make a suitable husband for their little Charm. She was so bight and headstrong that not just any man would do. The man to capture Charm's heart would have to be extra special. Thus far, the only men who had shown an interest in Charm had been much older or young and immature. Betsy, like a protective mother hen, would allow no man to come calling unless she felt he measured up to her high standards. He must be moral, not use gutter language, and be of the Christian faith. Both Saul and Betsy took an instant liking to Bud.

One by one, the rangers excused themselves from the table and made their way to the barn. As the rangers exited, the benches filled with the ten younger Hempstead boys. Bud lingered behind, pretending to visit with Saul, while at the same time making sure to include Charm in the conversation. Bud learned from the Baron to ask questions and let the other person talk about them self if you want to make a good impression. Bud inquired what books she had read lately. This was a gamble. What if she couldn't read? When he asked that question, the floodgates opened. To his pleasure, Charm was a prolific reader. She explained how the circuit preacher brought books from other families and took the ones they finished reading and passed them on. Not only did he preach the gospel, but he also served as the community's traveling librarian.

Charm told Bud she had read all of Fennimore Cooper's works as well as several other contemporary authors. *The Life of George Washington* was one of her favorites. Bud sat mesmerized by her enthusiasm as she discussed why she preferred one author's style to another. Since learning to read, Bud enjoyed a good book as much as anyone, but had never thought about writing styles, voice, or character development. She stunned him with her literary knowledge. Her brother Charlie mentioned that their mother taught school before they moved to Texas and insisted each of her children receive the best education she could offer them.

Bud, Charlie and Charm talked until almost midnight. Finally, Bud excused himself and headed for the hayloft. After finding a spot to toss his bed, he soon discovered two of the rangers blasting his ears with horrific snores. The barn roof lifted a little with each snort, or so it seemed. He drifted in and out of sleep, tossing and turning. Finally, he pulled the blanket over his head to muffle the sounds. What he was not able to muffle were his thoughts. Charm had invaded his head like Santa Anna storming the Alamo. When he had arrived at the Hempsteads, he was one hundred percent certain he would ask Virginia to marry him. Now, after five hours talking with Charm, he was unsure. He had never entertained the thought of another girl entering his heart, mainly because he never dreamed one so beautiful, soft and serene existed. He had traveled across the Republic several times and had never been tempted, but all of a sudden, his life felt very complicated.

The next morning, the rangers were up before daylight. So were the Hempsteads. Betsy had a marvelous breakfast on the stove when the men came into the house. She served black coffee, ham, eggs with gravy, and flour biscuits the size of a man's fist. Charm was wearing her best muslin dress and helping her mother set the food on the table when Bud entered. Her hair was pulled back and tied with a soft, green bow. Bud even noticed a hint of rouge on her cheeks. His heart began to pound. Bud felt bad he had not shaved. He had planned to, but could not find any water in the dark barn. He rubbed his chin, feeling suddenly insecure about the stubble. Charm was accustomed to seeing her father and brothers unshaven and didn't even notice. Charm stopped and looked at Bud as he took his seat. Her eyes locked on his. For a brief moment, the young couple was the only people in the big kitchen.

Conversation was light. Bud didn't want the other rangers seeing him paying special attention to Charm because he had already expressed his interest in Virginia to them. He didn't have to say a word. Not a man in the group missed the sparks flying back and forth between the two young people.

As the rangers excused themselves, Charm approached Bud. She didn't want to appear bold; nevertheless, she was not going to allow him to leave without knowing she wanted to see him again. She had tatted a border around a small, white, pocket handkerchief with her name embroidered along one corner. The handkerchief had been in her cedar potpourri box, filled with a mixture of rose, sage, and scented salvia. She slipped the handkerchief in his hand and said, "We do hope you will stay with us when you come back this way. Charlie and I truly enjoyed the conversation last night. You are so smart and well read. Most of the men who stop by are old and boring or young and silly."

Bud carefully folded the soft handkerchief and placed the gift in his vest pocket, saying, "The pleasure was mine."

He wanted to kiss her full pink lips, but Mrs. Hempstead was washing the morning dishes only a few steps away. Then tossing caution to the wind, Bud placed his strong arms around Charm's slender body and gave her a gentle squeeze. Mrs. Hempstead pretended not to notice. She was delighted that the well-mannered young man was paying attention to her only daughter. Too many of the young men coming to Texas were on an adventure quest. Bud gave the impression Texas was his home for life and he would be starting a horse ranch on his Bastrop property. Those things were music to Betsy's ears and Charm's heart.

Charlie had Lightning saddled and was feeding him shelled corn when Bud and Charm stepped from the lighted doorway into the darkness of the early morning. Bud thanked Charlie and said goodbye to him and Charm. Each made Bud promise to stop and visit on his way back. Bud didn't want them to know he would not be part of the escort team returning with the group from England. His return route would be taking him to San Antonio where he could again join Jack Hays and his company of rangers. That news could be told later in a letter.

There was not a day on the trip that some of the men didn't tease Bud about Charm and threaten to tell Virginia. He had to take the ribbing because he didn't want Virginia to know about Charm. One day his life was a clear path and the next, he stopped at the Hempstead farm and everything changed. Now he was not so sure Virginia was his choice. Yet, how could he not marry her after all the nice things the Treptows had done for him? His honor was at risk. He knew his letters and the kisses were almost the same as a marriage proposal.

Noah pushed the men onward, not stopping at any other farms. Once they got past San Felipe, they stopped to eat and then moved camp for the night. The next day, the group stopped in Houston for supplies and a round of whiskey at the local watering hole. Bud was surprised how much the town had grown since he came through with the president. Businesses were bursting out in all directions and several very large two-story homes were under construction on the higher ground.

By the time the group arrived at Galveston Bay, the ocean breezes were warm and the skies were sunny. The new ferry was double the size of the old one and more than adequate to accommodate all eight men and their mounts at once. The fee had also doubled since the last time Bud had crossed. On the way over to Galveston, his mind drifted back to the time Jack Hays arrested him and the Baron. Even though only a few years had passed, it seemed like a lifetime ago. So much had changed. Even Galveston had grown. Several new brick buildings had popped up since Bud was last on the island. Two big church steeples reached skyward, and another livery stable had been built. Bud took a quick ride through town, passing the jail and the old boarding house, then down to the seashore where he fought his duel. Bud delayed his visit to the Treptows. He didn't know how he felt. How could a short visit have so deeply affected his life? He waited in town as long as he could and still reach the Treptow ranch before dark.

Once through the Treptow Ranch gate, he touched Lightning with his spurs, making an all out sprint for the house. Several of the Mexican horse trainers spotted him and recognized the blazing red stallion with the flaxen mane, tossing his head as he ran. They knew it was young Miller and alerted the Treptows. Virginia was folding freshly washed clothes and didn't have time to change or fix her hair. She was the first to greet Bud after Lightning came to a sliding halt at the yard gate. Virginia ran and grabbed him around the waist, stunned at how much taller and thicker his body was. Bud returned the hug. Mrs. Treptow stood on the porch as Helmut delayed getting too close. He wanted the two young people to have a moment together. As Virginia released her embrace, her left hand accidentally rubbed across Bud's vest pocket, her bracelet catching the handkerchief Charm had given him. The feminine piece of white cloth floated to the ground and a puff of wind carried it a meter or so away. Virginia, thinking the handkerchief was a gift, rushed to pick it up. Bud watched her face drop as she read the name "Charm" embroidered on the handkerchief and caught a whiff of its lingering fragrance. Virginia realized this was no gift, but the possession of another girl. She slowly picked up the scented handkerchief and stuffed the thin fabric back into Bud's vest pocket.

Bud was caught. Did he admit meeting Charm or say the handkerchief was something he found? Would this be the time he broke the vow of honesty he had made to his dying mother? Could he stand to see Virginia crushed by the truth? He could tell by the fire in her eyes she was surely going to demand an explanation.

Meanwhile back in San Antonio Samuel Maverick was preparing for another exploratory expedition into an unmapped region of Texas. He had an eye for profit and like a bloodhound, could smell a land deal when others saw nothing. Sam never dabbled in any venture without expecting a handsome reward for his efforts. He was constantly exploring the landscape of Texas for a hidden valley, a tract of open rich soil, creeks that supplied water all year long, or the best climate for raising cattle or growing crops. He made several exploratory trips each year, traveling for as long as two months at a stretch. In every case, he returned with glowing words and praises about his great discoveries to any and all who would listen and twice to those with money.

Sam Maverick was many things: Husband, father, lawyer, trader, rancher, ranger, but above all else, he was a land speculator. He endeavored to buy cheap and sell at a great profit. Searching for land meant being away from home quite often. With his father's enormous wealth, Sam had unlimited borrowing power. This allowed him to take advantage of those who were forced to sell their land to feed their family, or soldiers who wanted the cash more than their land allotment for their service to the Republic. Mary Maverick gave her blessing on his endless forays into the wilderness and took on all the responsibilities of the home. Slowly, the Mavericks built a Texas dynasty.

The area west of Bastrop was still largely unexplored and Sam felt would offer a grand opportunity to make a killing, selling to people from Europe. Sam's dream was that once Europeans learned of the vast riches of Texas, they would flood the landscape like the buffalo and wild horses.

As he was packing for his latest expedition, Mary entered the room, prompting her husband, "Sam, I need your promise that you will return by December 12th. You do know that is a day of celebration and we are expected to be present."

Sam stopped packing his saddlebags, walked over to his diminutive wife and holding her tightly answered, "You know I always keep my word. My dear, dear, wife what would I ever do without you? You are the sun that lights my days and my shining star at night. Of course I will return by December 12th whether the job is complete or not."

Sam took eight Mexican helpers and his assistant surveyor, Vernon Laphan with him and rode two days into the cedar-laden hill country. First, they traveled to New Braunfels, then turned northwest and made camp along the Llano River. The soil was healthy, there were plenty of superb plots to survey, and certificates to be written. Sam realized the enormity of the project would cause him to miss keeping his promise to Mary. He had never lied to his wife and didn't plan to start now. Two days before he was to return home, he put Vernon in charge and returned to San Antonio on December 12, with a few hours to spare.

December 12th was the day the Mexican families celebrated *Dia de Nuestra Senora de Guadalupe*, the Patroness Saint of Mexico, whom the priest identified as the Virgin Mary. Sam and Mary found an excellent spot on Military Plaza to view the parade. The first to pass by was the local priest, followed by twelve young girls dressed in white, carrying a platform with a statue of the ornately dressed saint placed on top. Each girl placed one hand on the platform and held a lighted beeswax candle in the other. Following the girls were several men playing violins, and following behind them, a procession of devout local Catholics. Every now and then, the procession stopped and everyone kneeled and said a small prayer. They repeated this ritual every few yards, either praying the "Ave Maria" or the "Pater Noster." The final destination was the Cathedral of San Fernando on the Main Plaza, where a long ceremony took place. Afterwards, the prominent families took the Patroness along with them to Mr. and Mrs. Jose Flores' home on the west side of the Plaza. Some of the families in attendance were the Sotos, Garzas, Navarros, Zambranos, Seguins, Veramendis (Jim Bowie's in-laws), and the Yturris. The Mavericks were the only non-Mexican family at the celebration.

While Sam and Mary were enjoying the gaiety of the *Dia de Nuestra*, up on the Llano River a horrific event was taking place. The very day Sam had left his surveying team, a band of twenty-eight renegade Comanche had discovered Vernon and the Mexicans. They waited patiently for two days and on the evening of December 12th, the Comanche moved against the surveying party. Catching Vernon and the Mexicans totally off guard, the fight was over before it started. In less than five minutes, Sam's crew was dead and scalped.

The lone survivor, Jesus Rios, was lucky because he was gathering wood at the edge of an area hidden by large oak trees when the attack began. An arrow ripped the flesh from his leg, but didn't penetrate or remain intact. In the confusion, he was able to climb up a low-hanging limb and hide in the shelter of a giant oak. His position in the hundred-foot diameter tree obscured his view of the massacre and protected him from the Indians' view as well. When the siege was over, he bandaged his leg, gathered some food and began walking back to San Antonio. The Comanches had taken their pack mules and horses, but not the wounded Mexican man's will to live. Eight days later, the wounded Jesus Rios stumbled into town and made his way to Sam Maverick, blurting out the horrific news. After being awakened in the middle of the night, a stunned Maverick froze for a moment to grasp the horror. Then he turned to Mary, who had awakened from the pounding on their front door and kissed her on the forehead. He didn't have to say a word; his wife knew what he had to do.

Guilt and sadness flooded Sam's heart like a raging river. It was two o'clock in the morning when Maverick pulled the warning bell at the Military Plaza three times, sounding the alarm. Jack Hays was the first to arrive. In the next fifteen minutes, Ben McCullough and twelve more rangers assembled, bringing the total to fifteen. Once Sam told them of the savage attack, the rangers' anger was so thick it could be cut with a knife. Every ranger knew the mild-mannered Vernon, and was anxious to extract revenge on the Comanche. No one wanted to wait until daylight. To a man, they were ready to ride immediately.

Major Jack Hays was the highest-ranking ranger in San Antonio; therefore, he took charge of the unit. Jack sent Henry McCullough to notify his Indian friend Falcco and four other Lipan Apaches scouts they would be needed. The Indians lived at the north edge of town in tee-pees and were not close enough to hear the bell's rallying call. Once Henry woke the Lipans, they were ready to ride almost instantly.

By daylight, the rescue party had reached New Braunfels and turned northwest, where Jack asked Maverick to lead the way since he was the only one to know the survey camp's exact location. After a hard day's ride, they camped for the night and by noon the next day reached the camp. When they arrived at the site, it was evident the surveying party had not fired a single defensive shot. Some of their rifles were found under their bodies, primed and ready. The sight was traumatic for even the most battle-hardened veterans in the group. The bodies were bloated, and wolves or mountain lions had eaten parts of their extremities. Rather than taking the dead back to their families, Jack felt it best to bury them where they were killed. Mounds of dirt and rocks covered the bodies and crude crosses placed atop the graves. Jack felt the least they could do was give them a Christian burial. He asked Henry McCullough to read a passage from his New Testament as they held a brief service for the fallen.

Once the bodies were buried, Sam Maverick was hell-bent to track down and kill the Indians who had perpetrated the massacre. Jack Hays knew Sam was speaking out of rage and not taking into consideration the Indians already had more than a two-week head start on them, and early winter rains had washed away their tracks. Even Jack Hays could not track after flooding. He knew the Indians could be 150 miles into the wilderness of no-man's land by now. Rather than pull rank, Jack suggested the rangers could use a cup of coffee before moving on. He did his best to calm his friend and fellow ranger. He told Maverick that the war with the Indians was a two-way street. Jack understood the white men were slowly chipping away at Comancheria, an area the Indians had roamed freely for generations. Even though Jack Hays was, without question, the most fearless Indian fighter in Texas, he understood the Comanche's anger and frustration with the white man's steady encroachment into their sacred hunting grounds. He equated the Indians with a bumblebee hive. Punch the hive with a stick and all thunder will break out. He failed to convince Maverick. Sam's blood boiled. When would the senseless murder of the innocents stop? Sam Maverick did not have the same perspective as Jack. His attitude was more closely aligned to President Lamar's on the Indian-eradication issue, but parted company with Lamar in regards to the Mexicans. Maverick lived in a city dominated by Mexicans and knew them to be hard working, honest, loving and caring people with strong traditions and religious beliefs.

Sam argued that once they penetrated the wilderness, they would be able to track the Indian's path. Armed with their Samuel Walker Colts, they would be able to take care of a large band of Indians with not much effort. Jack, not wanting to fuss with his grieving friend, suggested they let the men drink their coffee and settle their nerves after seeing such a horrific site. He told Sam they needed to give the plan serious consideration before acting too quickly.

Once the coffee was ready and everyone filled their cup, Jack poured his. Hunching down on his legs, he blew the steam as it rose into the chilled air. "Sam," he said, "We don't have enough supplies to follow those killers. You remember what we went through in the Uvalde Canyon episode. We had to eat some of the horses to get back home. If the Comanche don't waylay us, we will surely starve. My dear friend, if we follow them deeper into the unknown, another party of rangers will have to come bury our bones."

Sam lowered his head and solemnly responded, "Jack, you are right. I want you to know I appreciate you not pulling rank on me in front of the men."

Jack stood up and extended his hand. Once Sam extended his, Jack said, "Let's start home. You will need to take Vernon's glasses and pocket watch to his widow. We will pass the hat and raise some funds for her and the children."

Sunset ran them down like a greyhound after a rabbit and forced the group to stop for the day. Sadness and gloom weighed so heavily on the men, none felt like eating. They nibbled only a few bites and retired for the night.

Back in Galveston another tense situation was playing out. Her face flushed, what should she do? Was Bud trying to tell her he had found someone else, or had he forgotten to hide the evidence of another woman? Virginia was not accustomed to confrontation. As she replaced the dainty handkerchief, she asked, "Who is Charm?"

Bud stood speechless. He had totally forgotten about the handkerchief. He had planned to put it in his saddlebag, but with all the conversation on the road, Charm's gift moved out of his memory, only brought forth when Virginia accidentally pulled it free. When he didn't immediately answer, Virginia repeated her question with more force and a tinge of anger. "Who is Charm?"

From Bud's point of view, he was not experiencing one of life's most treasured moments. He didn't want to lie. He moved from one foot to another and crossed his arms. He was getting ready to break his promise as his hand moved slowly up to his chin. Then he dropped his hands and showed Virginia his open palms in a subconscious body language gesture of openness. He was going to tell the truth and let the chips fall where they may. "Virginia, Virginia, this is not what your imagination has conjured up. The story is long, but the ending is one you will be pleased with. Please, no tears of anger. If the handkerchief were anything to concern you, I would have hidden it in my saddlebags. I do hope you know I'm telling you the truth."

Virginia realized Bud could have hidden the handkerchief before he arrived at the ranch. She felt a tinge of relief and calmed down. She wiped the tears from her cheeks and gave Bud a hug. She wanted to kiss him, but her mother and father had walked off the front porch to greet their visitor. Virginia didn't want to push the issue any further with her parents present, but would most assuredly take up the conversation at a later time. Bud shook Mr. Treptow's hand and then gave Mrs. Treptow a hug. She was like hugging a soft barrel. Forcing a smile, Virginia turned to her parents saying, "Isn't it wonderful to have Bud home?"

Mrs. Treptow was eager to jump in with her thoughts. She crashed a smile across her plump cheeks and answered, "Oh my yes. We have longed for the day of his return." Then, to Bud's embarrassment, she continued, "My dear young man, we agree that you have matured into a handsome adult…so very tall and strong…and handsome!"

Bud lowered his head, kicked the brown dirt with the toe of his boot and answered, "Ah, I've not grown all that much."

Virginia countered, "Yes you have, Benjamin Bud Miller. You are a full two, maybe three inches taller."

Her words didn't reduce the red glow covering Bud's face nor cause him to raise his head. Finally, he answered, "Dang, if I'd had a clue you were going to be so generous in your assessment of me, I would have returned the day after I left."

Helmut only had one question. "Have you been to Goliad to claim your father's property?"

Bud straightened up, replying, "No Sir, not yet. My ranger duties and an errand I had to do for General Houston tied me up. I chose to come here for Virginia's birthday rather than make the trip to Goliad. I plan to go down on my way back to San Antonio and see what the padre has on file."

When the Treptows finished greeting him, some of the Mexican ranch hands made their way over to welcome Bud home. One of the boys took Lightning and began to lead him to the barn when Bud shouted, "Ride him if you wish."

The fourteen-year-old boy could not believe what he was hearing. As he put his foot in the stirrup, Lightning shivered, making his skin roll on his back and moved a step or two to the right. It was then Bud realized that no other person had ever mounted his horse. Placing two fingers in his mouth, Bud let out a shrill whistle. As soon as Lightning heard Bud's whistle, he came running and stopped within inches of Bud's face. Bud reached up, softy rubbed his horse's muzzle and whispered, "It's okay, big fella. The boy only wants to take the saddle off and curry you down."

Lightning seemed to understand. With Bud holding the reins, the Mexican lad had no problem getting in the saddle. The leather squeaked as he seated himself. Bud handed him the reins and gave a nod that all was well. So, off the happy youngster went, riding the great Lightning. The stallion had matured dramatically, along with his master.

The four went into the house where Mrs. Treptow immediately asked Bud if he wanted some plum kolaches. Bud glanced over to Mr. Treptow, realizing for the first time how fat Virginia's father was. With two overweight parents, what chance did Virginia have of staying at her ideal size? Currently she was the perfect size of about five foot seven and around 140 pounds. For a moment, his mind drifted back to Charm. She too was around five foot seven, but only weighed 120 pounds. Finally, he answered Mrs. Treptow. "Yes Ma'am, I'd love some. Let me put my saddlebags and guns in the bedroom and wash the road dust off my face."

Mr. Treptow knew Bud would return for his daughter's birthday and had saved up his unbroken horses for him. For the next three days, Bud was up early breaking green horses, gobbling up Mrs. Treptow's home cooking like a starving dog at lunch, and returning to the roping pen until suppertime. Virginia was down at the roping pen the moment Bud tossed a rope over the first wide-eyed green horse every morning. She sat on the fence rail, not missing one ounce of the action until Bud finished for the day. At the end of each day, the most appealing thing to Bud would have been to soak his feet in a pan of hot water and flop down on the bed, but Virginia had other plans. She insisted they take long, romantic horseback rides on the beach. Once alone with Bud, her intentions were to broach the subject of Charm. She came close to asking the first two days, but their conversation never drifted toward their relationship as it had in the past. Bud had not kissed her or told her how pretty she was. He seemed distant. Was it Charm or the killings that had changed her man?

As Lightning splashed through the white foam of the Gulf, Bud spoke. "My dearest, pure, beautiful Virginia, there is much I need to tell you. I have killed a man protecting Mr. Bastrop, three Comanche in the Plum Creek battle, and several Mexican bandits. I have blood on my hands; only with God's grace will I be permitted into heaven. If I remain a ranger, I will be asked to kill again. Nothing leaves a man emptier than taking the life of another. I was sick to my stomach for several nights after each killing. I still have nightmares, but this is not what I need to tell you. I need to explain Charm. The reason I have delayed addressing your question is there really is not much to tell. On our way from Austin, we stopped at a poor farmer's house and paid for lodging in his barn. The Hempsteads have a large family, eleven boys and one daughter. Junior, the oldest boy, is a little older than you are, and Charm is a few months younger. Both are bright, but sheltered young people. Neither of them has been off the farm since the family moved to Texas seven years ago. After supper, I remained to visit with Junior. He was interested in one day becoming a ranger and I told him about the skills required. Once the dishes were washed, Charm removed her apron and sat down to listen to Junior and me talk. After a bit, she got involved in the conversation. I must tell you she was extremely well read for being so isolated in such a backwoods location. Even though her family is poor and her dress was common, it was clean and ironed. You, on the other hand, are a girl of privilege and your family has a prominent position in the Republic. Your clothes are made of the finest cloth and you are not required to do chores. You have Mexicans taking care of the daily chores. I guess I felt sorry for them and ended up visiting until bedtime."

Bud was suddenly interrupted by a blast of anger from Virginia. She yanked back too hard on her reins, cutting her mare's tongue. Her mare stopped in the wet sand, almost sitting down as her rear feet slipped from under her. Virginia waited to speak. She didn't want the horse's heavy breathing to cause Bud to miss a word she was about to say. Finally, she shouted at the top of her lungs, "How am I to interpret what you are saying? Do you imply that your interest in me is to gain access to my father's wealth?"

Bud was stunned. The thought of the Treptow's money had never entered his mind. Her curt question angered him. He shot back, "Whoa, wait a minute girl, let's get this straight. What do you take me for? The only thing the Treptow family has that I've ever been interested in is you. I don't want your father's money, land or horses. I do appreciate Lightning, but by now, I have done enough work to pay for him several times over. I have the blisters on my backside and calluses on my hands as proof of my payment. If you think breaking young horses is a cakewalk, then you have been picked pretty green. I am grateful for your mother and father's generosity, but I don't need their money. I don't need your father's property. I own a new house and more land than he does in Bastrop. I'm young and have an opportunity to be part of this new nation or follow her into the Union. I will make my own mark in Texas and not be branded by any."

He abruptly stopped his diatribe as quickly as it had started, remembering what the Baron had taught him: Speak in anger, repent in solitude. Lightning was getting impatient. The big red stallion had come to run and was chomping at the bit, beginning an uneasy prance around in the water. Bud touched the reins and the powerful animal responded to his command by quieting down. He threw his leg over the saddle horn so he could sit facing Virginia. With calmness, he told her: "I rode through inclement weather, fought mosquitoes the size of my thumb, and slept on the ground on a pile of twigs to be here for your birthday. I get here, and you have the audacity to suggest I am courting you to gain access to your father's wealth? When I take a wife, it will be because I love her, and for no other reason."

Virginia was shattered to hear Bud speak so firmly, his voice tainted with anger. He had never talked at such length or so deeply in all their time together. What had she done? Was her jealously pushing him away? Her mother had taught her to hold a man was like handling a small bird. If she griped too tightly, it would die; too loosely, the bird would fly away. Had she squeezed Bud too tightly and irreparably damaged his affection toward her?

Both horses were getting impatient, so Bud gave Lightning his freedom and Virginia followed at a gallop. As they rode, she wished she had not spoken with such jealousy and possessiveness. When they slowed their horses to a walk, Bud forced a smile and let Virginia speak. Her response was conciliatory in tone. "I'm sorry, I'm so sorry, I'm so SORRY for not trusting you. It is just that I became confused. I had visions of you leaving me. I know how much mother and father want me to be with you. I don't know what to say."

Bud cut her off. "Virginia, then say nothing. I should have tossed the handkerchief along the trail. The only reason I didn't was because I suspected it was the only nice thing that young girl owned and I could not just throw it to the wind."

As if Bud had not spoken, Virginia repeated her apology. "I'm sorry, I'm so sorry for my actions. My father will be angry with me." As if Bud was not there, Virginia started talking into the air. "They want me to have a husband who will live in the ranch house. That is why they made the room for you. They want that to be my wedding room. That's what daddy said when he had it built."

This was the first time she had mentioned marriage. There was no doubt in young Miller's mind that the entire family had already earmarked him to marry Virginia. It was not until this moment that he fully comprehended that Mr. Treptow expected him to stay on the ranch and become his full time bronc-buster and eventually take over the operation. Bud made up his mind long before this conversation that the girl he would marry would help him raise a family in Bastrop. If he had any land left around Goliad, then he would either sell or trade it, and add to the tract he already owned in Bastrop.

Bud had heard the two words Virginia had just spoken a thousand times, but it was not until this moment that he really heard them. She constantly used the words, 'I'm sorry'. For some reason, perhaps divine intervention, this time the words stuck in his mind. It suddenly occurred to him the foundation of those words. He responded by saying, "My dearest little Virginia, you are not a sorry person. The Baron, God rest his soul, said if we tell ourselves we are sorry, then we will end up that way. I tell my mind that I am a good person and I want to be part of this great Republic. Who knows, I might be a Senator or something. I've seen Senators and they don't look all that special to me. My concern is for you. I want you to promise me that you will never use those two words again. Will you promise me that?"

Her head dropped and she was unable to look him in the eyes. No one had ever spoken to her with such passion or caring. There was an intimacy in his voice she had never heard before. She knew he was being earnest. She also knew she had a deep, dark secret that, if he found out, he would never marry her. She promised to try and never say she was sorry again, and thanked Bud for caring.

The two made small talk and listened to the waves. The tide was now crashing on to the shore; it looked as if another storm was blowing in. Bud motioned with his head they should head back to the ranch, while at the same time saying, "The size of those waves tells me there is some nasty weather coming this way. We need to get in and let your father know. He will want to barn some of his stock."

Virginia agreed. These were some of the biggest waves in her memory. The two spoke no more as they galloped back to the ranch.

After telling the Treptows what they had seen, everyone on the ranch got involved, bringing the top stallions and pregnant mares into the shelter of the two barns. The doors were bolted shut with three long, thick boards. Just as they were returning to the house, the heavens lit up with lightning bolts from every direction. They paused on the porch to watch the chains of fire dancing across the darkness of the night sky.

Bud spent a few hours on the porch watching the raindrops splattering on the dusty ground. He knew the importance of rain, yet at the same time, he wished the bad weather had waited one more day. Virginia had so looked forward to her birthday party. That evening, the four enjoyed food and conversation. Bud gobbled down Mrs. Treptow's German chocolate cake as the rain blasted against the tin roof, making the sound of a woodpecker during mating season. Then Helmut posed a question that caused Bud to stop eating. "Did the Baron leave you the merchandise he had stored at Williams and McKinney?"

Bud flushed as he swallowed wrong and started choking on his cake. Virginia slapped him hard on the back and the cake went down his throat. His head shot around and looking Helmut into the eyes, he answered, "It never occurred to me what the Baron meant by all his possessions. I was just thinking about his watch, books, and the property in Bastrop. Of course that would include the merchandise he consigned when we landed in Texas. I'm sure there is a hefty storage bill, but I guess that won't matter because the Baron said it was $100,000 worth of dry goods, whiskey, gun powder, and rifles."

Bud then laughed out loud, causing him to cough again. After a sip of coffee, he continued to smile, and in almost a giggle, he finished his thoughts. "The Baron did have a propensity to expand the truth just a little. I know there was a lot of merchandise because I was there when the goods were unloaded, but I can't be sure the dollar amount is anywhere near what the Baron said it was. Bless his soul, he had a vivid imagination."

Helmut interrupted, "We need to go investigate. You might be surprised to find how much you inherited."

"What do I need to do to claim it?"

Mr. Treptow lit up his pipe, drew a long puff and sat back in his chair as if in deep contemplation. Everyone waited for him to answer. "I think it's time we made a trip into town and had a talk with the good people at Williams and McKinney. I don't think you are aware about their new competition. That fellow Mills from Kentucky has opened a warehouse that dwarfs everyone in town. Several of the smaller consignment houses have already closed, and I hear Williams and McKinney is hanging on by their fingernails. If they didn't own the biggest bank in town, they would already be out of business."

Bud cocked his head with a puzzled expression. "Is that the same Robert Mills from down in Brazoria? I heard he was trading with the Mexicans and bringing back so many bars of silver that his donkeys were breaking their backs trying to haul his loot."

Helmut moved his chair back so the Mexican maid could pick up his plate before answering. "That is the one. Robert Mills became a very wealthy man trading with the enemy, and now he is here, wanting to drive our little people out so he can monopolize the consignment house business. Not only that, but he has gone into cotton and sugar as well. I understand he owns around 200,000 acres of raw land and has over 3,000 acres in cultivation. He owns a hundred or more Negro slaves and some say he is the richest man in the Republic. What do you say we get up early tomorrow morning and go check out what is yours? I don't think Williams and McKinney have the assets to buy your goods, but Robert Mills does. I hate to do business with the devil, but in your case, he may be the only one in town with pockets deep enough to pay you a fair sum for your merchandise."

Virginia anxiously waited for her father to finish, then asked, "May I tag along?"

Her father nodded yes and replied, "You know you are always welcome, my little Princess."

The following morning after a hearty breakfast, the trio put on their raincoats and headed to the big barn. The Mexican workers harnessed a big black stallion to the single-hitch buggy. The rain made it impossible for the three to carry on a conversation on the way into town. Finally, there was a break in the weather as they arrived at the warehouse. McKinney was gone, but Williams greeted them with a warm handshake. Samuel Williams was a diminutive man with big black eyes glaring out from under a pair of brushy eyebrows. His voice was deep and words rolled from his tongue as if he were warming up for an opera as he said, "So you are young Miller? The old Baron sure loved you. I have a note from him stating that if anything happened to him before he could round up the money to release his goods, I should arrange for you to have his merchandise. We have also been informed he included the same wish in his will."

He motioned for the three to follow as he continued, "We want to be as benevolent as we can in order to accommodate you, Mr. Miller, or I guess I should say Texas Ranger Miller. We here in Galveston know of your bravery, your duel with Garza, and your courage in fighting the savages. Galveston is proud of you and I am sure all of Texas is as well."

Helmut came expecting an argument and was pleasantly surprised to find Williams so agreeable. Instead of letting Bud respond, Helmut felt he needed to be the spokesman, inquiring, "Mr. Williams, we understand there is a tariff to be paid. How much would that be, with interest?"

Williams didn't answer, but motioned for them to follow. Virginia placed her hand on Bud's shoulder as they followed Helmut and the little warehouse owner. They reached a tiny room lined with shelves of dusty, leather-bound ledgers. Using a stepladder, Williams reached up and pulled a ledger down and started flipping through the pages. Finally, he stopped, took his pencil and scribbled some numbers on a small notepad. When he spoke, it was not about the Baron or the debt, but to berate Robert Mills. "Mills came into town like a tidal wave, sweeping most of the small companies under. He dramatically undercut the local storage prices. He doesn't care if he makes a profit; he wants to push all the others out and then he can jack the prices sky high. If we weren't so well established and treated our clients fairly, we would be gone as well."

Bud, anxious to find out how to retrieve the forgotten treasure, interrupted, "What do I owe?"

Henry raised his head and answered, "Please excuse my diatribe about that scoundrel, Mills. I don't care if he is the richest man in the Republic. He doesn't have to flaunt his wealth. Jared Groce has money and he is as common as your everyday house cat. There is that cattle rancher not far from here, named White. He is overflowing in money, but as common as a shoe. Anyway, we have given you a special dispensation to help you retrieve the merchandise and get you a good start in our new Republic. Your storage bill comes to a little over $4,000, $4,127.34 to be exact. I think this is a fair and reasonable sum considering the original bill was almost $9,000. We have only charged you for the time spent stocking the merchandise on the shelves and the interest on the storage."

Williams dusted the pages as he motioned for the three to take a look at the ledger. Bud couldn't believe what he was seeing. There were five pages filled with descriptions of the Baron's merchandise. Henry tore two small pieces of paper to mark the pages and said, "Son, if you will take this to my partner Thomas McKinney over at our new hotel, the Tremont House, he will know what to do. He and I own the Commercial and Agricultural Bank and if I may say so, the first legal bank established in Texas. This note instructs Thomas to loan you the money for the storage. Then, when you sell the goods, you will be able to pay the bank and be a very wealthy young man. This load of merchandise was probably never paid for back in New Orleans; nevertheless, since we didn't have the bills of lading, we didn't know where to return it. This was going to be the venture that gave the old man money to retire. Too bad he did not live long enough to enjoy the fruits of his labor."

"Thank you, Sir. Do you have any idea the value of the Baron's inventory?"

"If my memory is correct, there was close to $48,000 worth of dry goods, powder and guns sitting on my shelves collecting dust. The flour and some of the other things got moldy or river rats chewed into the boxes. I would conservatively say you have $45,000 worth, give or take a few dollars."

The three looked at each other in disbelief. Bud was rich beyond his wildest dreams. Helmut was astonished and Virginia could see herself in a big, white, two-story plantation home with slaves and a private seamstress. Bud's vision was very different. He wanted to buy more land, establish a home so he could raise a family, and be part of building the Republic's future. He was not comfortable growing cotton and had no stomach for buying slaves.

Samuel Williams was correct. His partner, McKinney was more than willing to put a lien on the merchandise, loan Bud the money to pay the warehouse fees and hire wagons to deliver the goods to wherever they needed to go. After consulting with McKinney, an overwhelmed young man from Kentucky knew his next stop would be to meet with Robert Mills. When in town, Mills stayed at the Tremont House Hotel, renting five rooms for him and his escorts, while his ten slaves bunked at the livery stable. They found Mills in the lobby of the hotel, sitting at a large wooden table with a land plat in front of him. He was a small, red-faced man with protruding hambone sideburns and a thick brownish-red beard that covered a tomahawk scar acquired in a dispute with a Lipan.

Helmut wanted to be part of Bud's life now more than ever and approached Mills first, saying, "Good Morning Robert, my young friend has a business proposition to discuss with you."

Mills' belly showed his wealth. The years of sitting, counting money and eating the best food had expanded his waistline to over fifty inches. He was dressed in a velvet jacket and the finest black leather riding boots Bud had ever seen. His manner was brusque as he responded, "I'm not loaning or hiring."

Bud responded, "I too am from the blue grasses of Kentucky. My name is Benjamin Miller and I am a Texas Ranger. I don't need a job. I have something to sell at a very reasonable price. I have over $40,000 worth of merchandise sitting in the consignment house of Williams and McKinney. These goods will save you the transport costs from New Orleans. I came by them because the Baron de Bastrop left me a considerable fortune in his will."

Mills struggled to get out of his chair. One of his men jumped to his feet and gave his boss a lift. His attitude changed like the Texas weather as he said, "Well, my fellow Kentuckian, I know of the merchandise you are speaking of. My auditor put the worth at $43,346.87, so your number is fair and accurate. Of course, the product still has to be taken to market and sold. That can cost a considerable sum. I'm in the business to sell what you own and frankly, you are not. Tell you what I'm willing to do because I like the fact you didn't come to me lying. I have no patience with men who lie. I'm going to make you a rich young man."

Virginia didn't let him finish. "Mr. Mills, Bud Miller never told a lie in his life." She stopped abruptly, suddenly remembering it was not proper for a woman to get involved in a business discussion.

Mills ignored her. Turning his attention to Bud, he continued, "Young man, you do have something that I want and am prepared to pay a fair sum for. I also know I am the only man in the Republic that has the money to purchase your goods."

Bud stood tall, as if he had a board in his back. "With all due respect to you Sir, I beg to disagree. I know for a fact James Taylor White over at Liberty has more than enough money in the Commercial and Agricultural Bank to purchase what I have stored and more. Mr. White is a friend of Noah Smithwick, a fellow ranger. Noah also told me Mr. White is one of the richest men in the Republic."

Bud never implied that White was remotely interested; he just wanted to spark the crusty old man's fertile imagination. Robert Mills' greed immediately conjured up visions of White buying the merchandise and getting the taste of what he was doing. He knew of White's power and wealth and that James was in fact capable of generating strong competition in the marketplace. White could join forces with Williams and McKinney. He could not allow that. "Tell you what I'm going to do. I will give you $5,000 in silver bars for the Baron's merchandise, sight unseen." Mills was not being honest. He had already visited the warehouse and knew exactly what was in those wooden crates collecting dust.

Bud never flinched, stepping closer so he could look down into the face of the much shorter Robert Mills. He responded without hesitation, "Sir, add twenty in front of your five and we may have something to shake hands on."

After Bud spoke, he smiled and began to move his head up and down ever so slightly. He learned from the Baron, the first man to speak loses. Bud waited for Mills' response. The air in the room became thick. Mills' brow formed sweat beads. He grabbed the back of his chair to remain steady. Bud waited. Time hung in the air. Finally, Mills responded, "$25,000 is an enormous sum of money."

"You are correct Sir, but so is the value of my merchandise. You just said I have almost $44,000 stored in those crates."

Mills didn't want to offend and drive his fellow Kentuckian to strike a deal with Taylor White. He was on a slippery slope. Finally, he extended his hand and said firmly, "$21,000 and we have a deal."

Bud remained confident, offering a firm rebuttal. "Add another thousand and we can walk over to the bank right now. Thomas McKinney is waiting to draft your account."

Mills could see by looking into Bud's eyes he was not bluffing. After a pause to inhale a short breath, he extended his pudgy hand to consummate the deal. "Consider it done." Quickly turning his attention to the men seated at his table Mills said, "Gentlemen, please excuse me for a few minutes. I need to attend to this urgent business."

Once at the bank, Mills requested the transfer of $22,000 worth of silver into Bud's account. Thomas made a bank draft to Williams and McKinney for their fee while Bud signed the documents transferring Bastrop's merchandise to Mills. After paying storage fees to Williams and McKinney, almost $16,000 was deposited into Bud's account. Then McKinney cashed a bank draft for Bud, giving him $2,000 in gold coins.

The reality of having so much money didn't soak in until Bud was on the way back to the ranch. Heavy rain prevented the trio from talking very much on the way back, but that didn't stop Helmut from trying. He wanted Bud as a son-in-law more now than ever. He envisioned expanding his operation and exporting horses on a major scale. There were still several million wild mustangs roaming the hills and meadows of Texas, just ripe for the taking. He could hire vaqueros and round them up, domesticate them, and take them back east to sell. Virginia dreamed of being on Bud's arm as he introduced her to General Houston, Sam Maverick, and Jack Hays. As darkness fell, the fireplace sparks shooting from the chimney offered a welcoming beacon as the trio neared the ranch.

Virginia shook Bud from a deep sleep. The trip into town the day before had exhausted him more than chasing Indians for days at a time. Virginia left the room to allow Bud to get dressed. He dressed and sleepily made his way to the breakfast table. As daylight broke, the sun returned and brought with it warm, clear air. Bud felt that he could follow the storm as it moved west, staying dry all the way to Goliad. After all that had transpired he felt compelled to see where his father was killed and talk to the padre about the status of his land inheritance. Perhaps he would look up Dillard Cooper, who had survived the battle that took his pa's life.

Virginia was disappointed that Bud had failed to ask her father's permission for them to marry. Bud, on the other hand, was not as sure about marriage as he had been. Money had not changed the raw-boned ranger, but a country girl named Charm was working her spell on his heart.

As he saddled Lightning, Virginia came to the barn and leaned against the door. This was her last effort to get Bud to change his mind and ask her to be his wife. Bud smiled and kept preparing for his journey. When he was finished, he walked to her and put his arms around her waist, pulling her near. For a brief moment, the desire to ask her to be his wife almost drew the words from his lips, but the young ranger took her waist and slowly moved her body away from his. He looked deep into her turquoise eyes, now pooled with tears, and with tenderness said, "The temptation to stay is strong. I know if I don't leave now, I will linger too long. I would regret my actions. If I am going to serve as a ranger, I must be the best I can be one hundred percent of the time. My responsibilities are constant and my duties ever present."

Virginia's faced flushed pink as her words seemed locked in her throat. Suddenly, she felt confused. Bud was rejecting her. She didn't know how to respond. She spoke hesitantly. "I'm sorry. I'm sorry. Bud, I'm sorry I've been difficult."

Placing his right forefinger over her full lips, he cautioned, "My dear sweet one, you are not sorry and I will not allow you to demean yourself. I hold you in the highest esteem. Trust me. I would love to stay here. If I did, I wouldn't be the honorable person Major Hays believes I am. My unit is depending on me."

Virginia flung her head against his chest, crying and sobbing. "Please don't go. I don't want to be here without you. Take me to Bastrop. I'll go pack right now if you will let me go with you. I promise I will never ask to come back here again. Bud, I want to be with you."

This was not the reply Bud expected. He didn't know how to handle her tearful plea. The Baron had taught him many things, but not how to handle a desperate, lovesick girl. He knew it was impossible to take her without her parents' consent, even if she was of age. He knew it might mean a gunfight with her father or several of the men in his employ. How could he live with himself if he killed the parent of the girl he married? What would they tell their children? Yet, how could he tell her no? He knew if he turned her down, it would be the ultimate rejection. Finally, he lifted her chin so he could look into her eyes before consoling her. "Shush your crying Virginia. Here we are, standing in Helmut's barn, talking about taking you to the edge of the frontier without a proper marriage. I would disgrace your honor and shame your parents if we acted so irresponsibly."

Virginia continued to sob. He paused. Then a plausible solution came to him. "If I take you now, that would be kidnapping. In Texas, they hang people for kidnapping. You and I know your father is very possessive and he would most assuredly report me to Sheriff Maples."

"I know," she mumbled, her voice cracking under the emotional strain. Taking deep breaths and using a calmer voice, she responded to his logic. "Bud, I do understand. I could not live if I were responsible for you being hanged. I'm ashamed of the way you were treated this visit. Pa worked you like one of his vaqueros. I made it impossible for you to say no to our evening horseback rides. I didn't take into account that you were sore and tired from breaking young horses all day. Then I accused you of giving your affections to another girl. Please do write. I'll have a stack of letters waiting for you in San Antonio when you get there."

She could not stay and watch Bud leave. As she walked toward the house, she turned and said, "Be safe."

Bud mounted, spurred his burnt sienna stallion through the gate, and out onto the road. Hard choices lay ahead as neither death nor danger could be ransomed with his newly acquired riches.

Chapter Twenty-Eight
Taylor White

Noah Smithwick handed Bud a letter to deliver to James Taylor White. Now that young Miller owned a large tract of property, all he needed was the know-how to start up his cattle business, and Noah knew the most qualified man in Texas to provide that knowledge was Taylor White. Knowing Mr. White was illiterate, he instructed Bud to read the letter to him.

The temperature remained warm, even though Christmas was only two weeks away. Lightning was fresher and stronger than on any of their previous rides because, while at the ranch, the powerful stallion was fed all the corn and alfalfa hay he could safely devour. Bud was not in the same robust shape; his legs and buttocks were bruised and sore from the thrusts and jerks of breaking thirty-seven green horses in his two weeks at the Treptows.

James Taylor White was a poor cattle rancher who was near starvation in 1828 when he slipped his sickly wife, Sarah Cade White, five small children, three cows, two skinny horses, and a pack of coonhounds across the swamps of Louisiana and over the Sabine River into Texas. He made his way to a plot of land near Anahuac just across from Galveston Island, constructed a crude shelter for his family and began planting. One day, while cutting logs for his cabin, he spotted a large herd of wild longhorn cattle with strong legs and robust attitudes, the bulls' horns extending eight feet in width. Taylor asked his neighbors if it was okay to capture some of the nearly one million rugged animals that roamed freely over the plains. The locals told him the longhorns were abandoned when Mexican ranchers fled south across the Rio Grande because of constant Indian depredations, and everyone gave him the same answer: "If you can catch 'em, they're yours."

Taylor originally planned to move deeper into Texas, but his wife fell ill and forced them to stop. They squatted along Turtle Bay on a tract of prime flatland with grass as tall as a man's waist. Providence had led White to the ideal place to begin a cattle business; the land had abundant water and more grass than cows could ever eat.

Taylor knew cattle. His father, Jack White raised cattle in Carolina before moving his family to Louisiana. By the time he was five years old, he knew how to milk and was assisting in birthing calves. He had a deep fascination with the longhorns and began to capture and brand them. He preferred the longhorns because they had adapted to life in the diverse and oftentimes harsh landscape of Texas. They could go for days without water; when drought came, they ate brush and cacti. Their massive hooves allowed them to maneuver effortlessly over rugged Texas terrain. Their razor-sharp horns prevented predators from grabbing a newborn calf, allowing the herd to multiply rapidly. Along with their good traits came an ugly attitude. They were lean and mean, with the ferocity of a cornered rattlesnake. Taylor began rounding up the cattle and started the *JTW* brand, later switching to the *Cross W* willed to him by his father.

Taylor observed how, after a lightning fire, the grasses returned fuller and more verdant, and from then on, he periodically burned large sections of his pastures. Healthier pastures meant larger, healthier herds. As his herd grew, he sold more cattle, and purchased more slaves. With more slaves, he could run a larger operation. The cycle continued and within three years, White rounded up and branded almost three thousand head of longhorn cattle.

Having grown up around New Orleans, Taylor White understood the demand for beef in Louisiana and up along the Mississippi River. He knew that if he could find a way to deliver his cattle to New Orleans, he could provide very well for his family. There were no railroads and shipping the rowdy animals by boat was not practical, so Taylor chose to move them overland, driving small herds of yearlings through the swamps and alligator-infested rivers of Louisiana to New Orleans. He was the first rancher to drive cattle to market out of Texas to the east and north. Years earlier, the Mexicans drove large herds over the Rio Grande to the south, but no one had ever taken them to market back in the Union. James Taylor White set the paradigm for others to follow.

Bud rode past a thousand or more of Taylor's thirty thousand longhorns on his way to the main ranch house. He had seen longhorns in the wild, but had never been close enough to see just how massive and menacing the bulls' horns were. When Bud arrived at the front gate, Taylor and a pack of coonhounds were waiting to greet him. Taylor White was a small man with a big belly and graying hambone sideburns that puffed out like the fur on a scared cat. Sam Maverick had told Taylor of Bud's bravery and he was pleased to have him drop in, and surprised to receive a letter from Noah Smithwick. Instead of Bud reading the letter, Taylor handed the envelope to his son, thirty-five-year-old Tom. Taylor made sure his children were literate; all seven learned reading, writing and arithmetic. Noah's letter offered best wishes to the family, reminisced about the time he and Taylor spent together in New Orleans, and thanked Taylor for introducing him to the late Jim Bowie.

The letter ended with the postscript: *"You will like young Miller."*

Taylor was proud to tell his visitor they had recently driven 1,100 steers, each weighing over 1,000 pounds, to market in New Orleans, and had purchased five more stout Negro slaves. On their way to the main house, White mentioned that in the spring he branded around 3,700 calves. Bud was amazed to learn Taylor owned 40,000 acres of land. What Bud didn't know was that Taylor had over $60,000 in the banks of New Orleans and his wealth of cattle waiting for market pushed his net worth close to $500,000. He owned 100 male slaves and 60 Negro women and children.

The White home was an extremely large brick structure, which stood two stories tall. Six massive columns spread across the entire width of the front porch, and the huge entrance doors were embellished with leaded-glass panels and shiny brass hardware. At 52, James Taylor White was clearly the first cattle baron of the Lone Star Republic; his was an inspiring rags-to-riches story.

Since it was almost dark when Bud arrived at the ranch, Taylor told him to wash up and join the family at the supper table. One of the slaves led Lightning to the barn, and unsaddled and curried him down. He noticed one of the shoes was loose, so he replaced it. He then fed the big sorrel stallion a trough full of corn and fresh water from a half whisky barrel.

All seven of the White children, along with the spouses of the two sons and one daughter, were waiting when Bud entered the dining room. The three married children lived in smaller homes on the ranch property, but Taylor insisted the entire family eat together in the big house. The table seated sixteen and was the largest dining table Bud had ever seen. China was set for their special guest as well as genuine polished silverware to show off Taylor's wealth. As soon as Bud was seated, Taylor gave thanks. When the "Amens" were spoken, Jim's oldest son Tom asked, "What's it like to be Texas Ranger? If pa would let me, I'd leave in a heartbeat and join you in killing those deplorable redskins."

Bud was uncomfortable with the perception that all Texas Rangers did was kill Indians. He didn't want to offend his host, but felt he needed to set the record straight. He leaned forward, answering, "We do more than just fight Indians. We are commissioned to keep the peace. This means we take an oath to enforce all the laws of Texas. We still have a problem with Mexicans slipping over, and from time to time, bandits to deal with. The cowboys operating in the no-man's land between Texas and Mexico can be a menacing bunch of criminals. Make no mistake, I'm not saying Indians are not a problem; they are just not the only problem on our plate."

After Tom's question, the floodgates opened and everyone began speaking at once. Like a group of hungry reporters, they hammered Bud with questions. He could hardly eat for having to answer the barrage of questions. If he thought the Hempsteads were hungry for news from the outside, this group was on the verge of starvation. Taylor and his wife excused themselves from the table, but not before asking Bud to consider employment with the *Cross W* brand. The cattle business was on the verge of being bigger than cotton and Taylor wanted to expand west to acquire more wild longhorns. He was aware that Sam Maverick was preparing to emulate his ranching technique and he needed to be in position, ready to compete for the wild cattle.

Upon realizing how profitable the cattle business was, Bud's mind began to reel with the potential of having his own spread. He would need a larger place than the Baron's land. He would also need vaqueros to manage the herd. He now had money, and in his area of the Republic, no one was attempting to capture the multitude of free-roaming cattle. Sitting at Mr. White's dinner table that evening, Bud discovered his destiny. If Taylor White, a man who could not even read and write, was able to amass such a fortune in a brief amount of time, Bud was confident he could reap the same rewards. He saw the future was northern cattle drives, supplying the American Army as it moved west to fulfill America's Manifest Destiny, and Bud wanted to be part of that future.

The house slaves prepared a pallet for Bud in the long room. Even with just a quilt between him and the floor, he slept like a baby. His weary body needed the rest and not even the rooster's crows stirred him from his deep sleep. It was only after a few shakes from a slave that he opened his eyes.

Once again, the twelve family members assembled for breakfast. The questions began before Bud could even sit down at the table and continued until he had finished breakfast. Taylor was impressed with Bud's vocabulary and his self-assured manner. Before they finished eating, Taylor extended an invitation for Bud to stay a few weeks on the ranch. Through the Baron's generosity, Bud had the capital to invest in the cattle business and it was obvious the White Ranch would be the best place for him to get an education. Before he could respond to Taylor's invitation, Tom asked, "Would you stay with my wife and me? We built a second room on the house for our children. So far, we have no babies so the room is empty. You won't be any trouble since we all eat at pop's house."

Bud answered, "That sounds fine to me, if you don't mind."

Taylor further explained the cattle business to young Bud as they sat around the breakfast table. "Sam Maverick spent two weeks with us studying my cattle operation. I will freely admit there are more wild longhorns than ten Taylor Whites, ten Sam Mavericks, and twenty Noah Smithwicks could round up in a lifetime. On the other side of the San Antonio River and up where you have your place in Bastrop, wild longhorns are as thick as fleas. They are so wild, it is impossible for us to drive them all the way back down here. I can see in your eyes you are thinking of getting your own stock. Son, you will need help, and that costs money." He paused and then added, "*Lots* of money. A good slave doesn't come cheap. No need buying the runts and haggard old men; you need the ones who can do a full day's work."

Bud was unsure how to answer. Finally, he replied, "Yes Sir, I know. I was thinking of not buying slaves, but using vaqueros. No one works cattle better. I've never seen anyone rope the way they can."

Taylor gruffly responded, "Those greasers cost money to hire and are about as reliable as Texas weather."

Bud didn't dispute, but simply answered, "I have some money. I know some hardworking Mexican men in San Antonio. I think I can hire all the men I need."

Taylor pressed harder. "You do know it will take a nice nest egg to buy land, build pens, and pay your men?"

Bud didn't dare tell them about the two thousand in gold he was carrying in his saddlebags or the substantial sum deposited in the Galveston bank. The Baron had taught him to trust no one when money was involved. It was always better to remain silent and be safe, rather than to speak and regret in leisure.

He simply answered, "In Texas, all things are possible. I know your story and have a great admiration for your accomplishments. May I ask you a question, Mr. White?"

"Of course. Ask away."

"I have been told there were no horses or cows in Texas until the Spaniards brought them over. I don't know if that's true or if someone was just jerkin' my leg."

Cocking his head to one side and smiling, Taylor replied, "That is correct. When Columbus arrived to the Caribbean Islands in 1492, there were no horses or cows on the North American Continent. Difficult to believe, isn't it? 'Tis true. When he returned in 1493 with a colony, and horses and cows, he deposited them at Santo Domingo. As the ships came, they spread seed stock to the West Indies. When Cortez sailed from Cuba in 1519, he brought the first horses to North America and began the conquest of Mexico. Two years later, some of Cortez's followers brought cattle. One of the things I find most interesting is how rapidly those few horses and cattle multiplied. Twenty years later, Coronado gathered five hundred horses and three hundred head of cattle for his New Mexico expedition. Think about what I just said. Coronado went up into New Mexico and as far as Kansas in 1540 with hundreds of horses and cattle born and raised in Mexico. This has to be where he got the animals. It would have been impossible to transport that many by ship."

"Sir, that is amazing. Then, if I may ask, how did so many longhorns end up in Texas? Did they wander this far north from Mexico City?"

"The Spaniards seemed to grasp ranching like it was in their blood. Some of the wealthier Spaniards owned as many as ten ranches around Mexico City. As Mexico grew, they moved north into Texas, building some very large cattle ranches. They prospered until the Comanche and Apache decided they no longer wanted anyone living in their hunting grounds. The Indians forced the ranchers to leave their cattle and horses and flee Texas or be murdered. The cattle and horses left behind began to multiply in the wild. One thing in the longhorns' favor was that the Indians didn't like beef; they preferred buffalo meat. The buffalo followed the plains, leaving the rest of Texas for the wild horses and longhorns. It is my understanding that the original Spanish cattle didn't have those massive horns when they were imported; when they began to multiply in the wild, their horns started to grow. In a few generations, their horns extended wider and wider until they were like the ones we have today. I suspect panthers or wolves killed the cattle with short horns and the ones with larger horns survived and bred. It was nature's form of selective breeding. Seldom does a cow lose a calf to a predator. We have observed a pack of wolves circling a newborn only to turn into complete cowards when the mama rolls her eyes and lowers her head. No wolf wants to be on the receiving end of one of those massive horns."

"Sir, how well do the longhorns mix with domestic cattle?"

Tom answered, "They don't. A longhorn can smell the human odor on a domestic and will not associate whatsoever, and like pa said, they know how to use those horns. Just last year, an angry bull charged one of the slaves and rammed a horn through his body before anyone could shout a warning. He tossed the 190-pound man into the air like he was a rag doll. If you plan on longhorning, then you best keep your head on a swivel."

Bud's two-week stay stretched into six. Suddenly it was February. Taylor had a batch of early births in February and Bud got his first experience with branding and castrating calves. He felt a little squeamish at the thought of sticking a white-hot iron to a young calf, but watched attentively as the Negro slaves placed several branding irons in a fire and waited until they became white-hot. At first, the stench of burning flesh made his stomach turn, but after a while, he grew accustomed to the smell. He was smart enough to know if he planned to raise cattle, this was part of the business. Bud had the unenviable task of hocking the calves. Once he wrestled the animal to the ground, he sat at the rear end, grabbing one leg with both hands while placing his boots on the other, and then a slave burned the *Cross W* brand onto the right side of the calf.

In his time on the ranch, Bud learned valuable tricks in handling longhorns, but when the March winds came howling in, he knew it was time to leave. Soon the spring wild flowers would paint the landscape brilliant yellow and scarlet red, mingled with purple and blue as far as the eye could see. Taylor White also realized it was time for Bud to leave and would not ask the hard-working young man to remain any longer. The wise old man could see his visitor would never be satisfied working for anyone else, no matter how well he was treated.

The entire family and most of the slaves were at the barn as Bud mounted Lightning for the first time in several weeks. His big red stallion was chomping at the bit to run. Bud had to hold the reins taut in order to say goodbye and thank the Whites for their hospitality. Then someone mentioned the day being March 6th. Taylor removed his hat and bowed his head, saying, "Six years ago today, our brave men lost their lives in the Alamo. Let us pray we will never have war with Mexico again." The pause brought back some painful memories. Taylor's eyes filled with tears as he prayed silently. He had no way of knowing what was happening at that same moment back in San Antonio.

Before Bud could leave, Taylor approached and motioned for him to lean down in the saddle. Cupping his hands together and whispering so no one could hear, Taylor asked, "Son, do you need a loan to get you started?"

"Thank you for your kindness, I will be just fine. I've saved some gold coins," Bud replied, a little too loudly.

Bud's comment confirmed what the three visitors at the White ranch suspected. Marvin O'Reilly and his cohorts lived on the edge of the law, having escaped the hangman's noose in Missouri before fleeing to

Texas. Once in Texas, they moved south of the Nueces River into no-man's land and joined the cowboy gangs. The vast majority of Irish immigrants who settled around San Patricio were honest, hard-working folks, friendly with their Mexican neighbors and loyal to the Republic, but Marvin O'Reilly and his two companions were the exception. Before Bud released Lightning, Marvin stepped from the crowd and asked, "Where are you heading? Maybe we can ride with you."

Tom answered for Bud. "He is on his way to Goliad to visit his pa's grave. His father was murdered at the Goliad massacre."

That was the very information Bud was trying to avoid disclosing to the suspicious trio. He recognized their type and suspected they spelled nothing but trouble. "I'll be traveling light and fast. Unless you have rested mounts, you won't be able to keep up. Much obliged for your offer."

Marvin O'Reilly and his men had not stopped at the White ranch by chance. They had been in Galveston when word spread like spilled marbles that young Miller had suddenly become a rich man, and the three malcontents set their sites on robbing him. Shortly after Bud had left Galveston, O'Reilly confirmed the rumors with a visit to Helmut Treptow, implying he was delivering a message from Major Hays in order to gain information. Helmut freely told him Bud was on his way to visit his father's grave in Goliad. Marvin and the other two wasted no time in going after Bud and his gold.

Once in Goliad, they waited for Bud to arrive. Marvin bribed one of the priests to let them know if their prey came seeking information on his father. After two months, Marvin knew Bud must have stopped along the way. Perhaps he was buying land, or had a lady friend. Maybe someone else had learned of the gold, and followed and killed him. The three zigzagged back and forth toward Galveston, going from farm to farm and town to town asking if anyone had seen a tall, broad-shouldered young ranger riding a deep sorrel stallion. They were ready to give up when Marvin remembered James Taylor White's place. His hunch paid off. They found Bud branding calves along with a host of Negro slaves. O'Reilly and his friends asked to rent a place to sleep and rest their horses in the White's barn. Taylor would not take their money, but gave them free lodging in one of his barns.

Bud waved goodbye and nudged Lightning. His fresh mount responded and they were off. Marvin knew not to immediately follow him, or Taylor might suspect something was amiss. When O'Reilly and his two comrades left the White ranch, he implied they were going to Galveston, asking if they could deliver any letters. Two miles south of the ranch, the three cowboys turned west to track their prey. They counted on Bud not pushing his horse too hard and Marvin planned to reach the Goliad trail by noon and catch up to him the following day. His plan was to make their mark think they wanted to ride along with him, and then, at the opportune moment, shoot him in the back and take his horse and gold or perhaps wait until he was sleeping and put a shotgun to his head.

Marvin and his men picked up Bud's trail the next day and kept him in their sights as he traveled westward. Marvin decided they would wait until he camped for the night and the rest would be simple; kill and take. The thirst for blood and gold moved like electric sparks between the three outlaws. All of their effort was about to pay off.

Unknown to Bud, death followed him like a hungry wolf tracking a wounded deer. He was careless, believing the true danger was ahead of him in the Indian hunting grounds.

Chapter Twenty-Nine
Unrest

In his second term, President Houston faced the difficult task of sweeping the government clean with a wide broom. He brought "planter types" into Congress so he could turn off the public tap. He abolished several dozen offices and cut salaries to a token honorarium. He all but eliminated the Texas army, depending on the rangers to deal with cowboy invaders and Indian depredations. He shut down the Texas navy and planned to auction off the vessels, stirring up a hornet's nest. When he attempted to sell the ships docked in Galveston, Commodore Moore, who had been in charge of the Texas navy, began holding meetings expounding the virtues of having the Lone Star of Texas flying on the high seas. His pleas moved the citizens of Galveston to action. They responded by forming a wall around the ships and refused to allow anyone near. Their will was so strong Sam Houston was not able to break down their barrier without killing Texans.

The original navy ships, *Brutus, Independence, Liberty,* and *Invincible* were all lost due to various reasons. Creditors seized the *Liberty*. The Mexican Navy captured the *Independence*, the *Invincible* ran aground in Galveston Bay and the *Brutus* was lost in a storm. Texas then commissioned the construction of seven more ships: *Archer, Austin, San Jacinto, San Antonio, San Bernard, Wharton* and *Zavalla*. Six were sailing ships, and the seventh was steam-powered. The *San Jacinto* and *San Antonio* met the fate of earlier ships destroyed at sea, and the *Zavalla* deteriorated to the point she had to be dismantled. One positive result of shutting down the Navy was that their Colt pistols were given to Jack Hays and the Texas Rangers. The revolver shifted the tide, allowing fifteen rangers to defeat one hundred Indians.

Houston's new Congress repealed all of President Lamar's currency and banking laws. Houston kept tight control over the printing of money, allowing only about $200,000 to be printed. The new currency, "exchequer bills", was used to pay taxes and custom duties. Houston cut his own annual salary from $10,000 to $5,000. It was not a comfortable matter to cut the budget and he faced a barrage of heavy lobbying on all sides. Each Congressman had a pork-barrel project that needed funding, but Houston learned the power of "NO" and used the word daily. In the three years of his second term, Houston's administration spent less than $600,000 and borrowed only $350,000, using public land as collateral. His frugal efforts saved the Republic from bankruptcy.

Houston created a political firestorm when he reached out to save his beloved Cherokee. His efforts stirred anger in many Texans, but gained him the respect and trust of several hostile Indian tribes. Tribes like the Waco, Tawakoni, and even some of the southern Comanche, agreed to a peace treaty. Houston's peace agreements saved hundreds of lives on both sides.

One of the more controversial regulations President Houston instituted was the requirement that anyone trading with the Indians must obtain a license. His action initially caused an uproar among traders; however, the fuss died down once they realized there was no use protesting. Sam Houston had spoken, and his would be the last word on the matter. The trade-licensing requirement prevented the Republic's enemies from inciting further Indian hostilities. Houston built trading posts at San Marcus and Waco as a step toward establishing peace and meeting the needs of each side.

There were many fences to mend. The second-term president was like a man standing in the middle of a grass fire with a wet tow sack. There were still Northern Plains Indian attacks, the Mexicans were still riled up over the Santa Fe Expedition, and a feud was brewing in the old neutral zone of east Texas. The "Regulators" and "Moderators" were squabbling when they left Appalachia, and had brought their feud with them. By the time word reached the president, the hostility had escalated to the boiling point and the factions were killing each other in the streets.

President Houston proclaimed March 2nd as Texas Independence Day, which also happened to be his birthday. He was acutely aware of the importance of having Independence Day fall on his birthday; few, if any, world leaders had such an honor. He invited several members of Congress and even extended a tongue-in-cheek invitation to ex-president Lamar, knowing full well Lamar was out of the Republic. Houston was determined to make Independence Day one of joy and fun. He danced with the ladies and toasted a sarsaparilla with the men as they lifted an elbow of beer or whisky. He didn't forget the love of his life was sick back in the city of Houston. That night, he knelt at his bedside and prayed for divine guidance in dealing with the multitude of problems facing the Republic and for his beloved Margaret. The day was over and tomorrow he would face more problems than any three men should be expected to deal with. March came in like a lamb, but went out like a lion for the second-term President.

The following day, President Houston stayed in bed two hours past daylight. When he awoke, his first matter of business was to write a memo to Congress imploring restraint in their actions toward Mexico. The brutal treatment of the Texas prisoners by Mexico enraged the hawkish element in Congress and they passed an obscene bill, claiming one-third of Mexico south of the Rio Grande and all land west to the Pacific Ocean, making Texas larger than the United States. Houston called the bill a "legislative jest" and vetoed it. Before Congress adjourned, a hawkish faction rallied enough support to overthrow Houston's veto, making the annexation law. In response, Houston wrote: "In the true interest of Texas, we must maintain peace with all Nations and cultivate our own soil."

The Texans kept waving red flags in front of Santa Anna as if he were an angry bull facing a Matador. The "Napoleon of the West" regained power and was anxious to extract revenge. Still smarting from the humiliating defeat at the hand of General Houston, the annexation bill just added one more slap in Mexico's face.

General Vincente Filisola, military commander of Matamoros, contacted Vincente Cordova from Nacogdoches, who opposed breaking away from Mexico. Cordova was ripe, and Filisola knew it. He easily persuaded Cordova to attempt a coup against the Houston administration. Filisola encouraged Cordova to put together a force of Tejanos (Texas Mexicans) and Indians, and drive the Anglos from "their" land. Word of the plan reached President Houston, who issued a proclamation against unlawful assembly of large groups. Mexico sent insurgents into the fray and some Indian tribes joined forces with the angry Cordova. In a brief time, the rebels assembled seven hundred men who proceeded to inflict frequent raids against the Anglos. Houston sent General Rusk with a thousand-man militia to quell the uprising. Most of the insurgents went back south across the Rio Grande, and the Indians tribes retreated. Cordova realized resistance was futile and he too returned to Mexico.

President Houston did his best to protect the misguided Texas-Mexicans who associated with Cordova, but couldn't protect all of them. Many Tejano men were arrested and their families suffered because there was no one to protect them. The racial prejudice against Tejanos in east Texas increased a thousand fold as Anglos saw each Tejano as a potential "Cordova", even though only a few had actually taken part in the uprising.

President Houston's biggest threat was getting ready to explode like a Texas sunset across the Republic; Santa Anna was again in power and preparing to strike. Word reached San Antonio that a large Mexican Army was assembling south of Laredo. Jack Hays had heard so many cry wolf so often that he felt this was just another false alarm; he and about forty men went to survey property for the families of men who died in the war with Santa Anna. The survey party camped on the bank of the Medina River when someone noticed a long log floating in the water. They began throwing rocks at the log when suddenly a pair of eyes opened; the log turned out to be an enormous alligator. One new recruit was Earl Davis. Earl, wanting to prove his manhood, removed his boots and guns, dove into the frigid swirling water and made an all out dash for the alligator. In a flash, he was on the back of the big reptile. No sooner than Earl mounted the twelve-foot king of the river, the alligator's tail slapped the water and swished around, knocking Davis off his back. Unfazed, he jumped back on top of the angry alligator. This time Earl locked his legs around the gator's belly and managed to get his hands into a vice grip around the jaws of the reptile. The pair tumbled over and over in the water, churning up mud and debris. It became impossible to distinguish between the gator and Earl as they tossed haphazardly in the water, the alligator trying its best to shake free of his passenger. The rangers were laughing so hard they could hardly stand. Some collapsed into a ball on the ground, holding their stomachs. Finally, Earl gained control and slowly moved the giant to shore. Once on the bank, he let his strong body fall on the back of the monster. Then he released the furious alligator and braced himself for the ribbing and jokes of his fellow rangers. He had accomplished what he intended; he had demonstrated his courage. "Alligator" became his nickname for the remainder of his life. From that day forward, few even knew his first name was Earl.

The fun and frolicking ceased when a rider came into camp on a dead run. As his horse slid to a halt, the scout dismounted shouting that the Mexicans had crossed the Rio Grande. "They are heading for San Antonio. This time it's for real!"

Jack and his men left immediately for San Antonio. Ninety percent of San Antonio's population was Mexican, with the vast majority in favor of Texas becoming an independent Republic; however, there were spies who were more than willing to aid Santa Anna in Mexico's quest to drive the Anglos out. Distrust in the city was as thick as cold molasses, with no one knowing for sure whom to trust. When Jack arrived, he sent Mike Chevaille and James Dunn toward the Rio Grande to see if they could determine the true strength of the invaders. He dispatched his loyal Mexican friend Antonio Coy down on the Rio Frio to see if any were approaching along the old De Leon route. Antonio, being Mexican, could integrate himself into the enemy camp, pretending to be a Santa Anna supporter. Ben McCullough and A.S. Miller were sent back to Gonzales; Jack suspected a division of the Mexican Army might come up through Goliad. A.S. had followed his brother "Stump" to Texas, spent six months in the Army, and then started farming on the land granted to him for his brief service. After his brother's murder at Goliad, A.S. re-joined the Army. When the president serrated the military budget, he was discharged, and returned to his farm and became a part-time Texas Ranger. A.S. Miller had no idea his brother's son Bud was a Texas Ranger.

Big Foot returned from Laredo with chilling news. He estimated the number of troops marching toward San Antonio to be between 1,350 and 1,500 men. Jack consulted with Mayor Juan Seguin and other city leaders. The Alamo and Goliad massacres had shattered the myth of Texans being invincible, and only a handful wanted to remain in the city; Sam Maverick was the only Anglo who voted to stand and fight. With only a measly 107 men willing to fight, Jack had no choice but to order the immediate evacuation of all non-Mexicans from the city. He implored the Tejanos to leave as well. Sam Maverick spoke to the residents assembled at the Military Plaza, urging them to pack their possessions in haste and leave within the hour. For some, the situation brought back the horrible memories of the Runaway Scrape.

Hays then dispatched riders to San Felipe, Houston, and Galveston warning the citizens along the way of the impending invasion. He put Keno Edwards in charge of a group of scouts, sending them out to monitor the movements of the Mexican Army. Keno and his men made a circle around the Mexican camp and as they were returning to town, saw a rider approaching holding a white flag. The rider was Colonel J. M. Carrasco. He assured Keno he was authorized to extend the terms of surrender from General Rafael Vasquez. After a very brief conversation, Keno ordered the Mexican Colonel blindfolded, and then escorted him to Jack Hays. The Colonel told Jack they wanted an unconditional surrender or they were prepared to flatten the city with their cannons. He lied and said two thousand reinforcements were joining their force in the next two days. Jack told the Colonel he would have an answer by the afternoon and ordered his men to make the Colonel comfortable. Jack soon returned and gave his response, telling the officer they would abandon San Antonio immediately. Conceding the city to the Mexican Army was the most difficult decision Jack Hays had ever faced; giving up without a fight went against every fiber of his being.

The Texans hitched their artillery behind teams of oxen, removing the armaments first. Then, with rangers and volunteers leading the way, the group left the city by three in the afternoon. As the exodus began, crying spiked with fear wafted from the retreating line of wagons. Jack and his rangers were angry they were not able to defend the city. He could relate to Travis' emotions as the command to surrender reached the Alamo. Those at the Alamo knew they would die, but chose death rather than retreat. Jack contemplated the thought of returning and fighting. His emotions yo-yoed back and forth until the caravan reached the Cibalo River.

On the evening of March 6th, the anniversary of the fall of the Alamo, Jack and the San Antonio refugees pitched camp. That same evening, General Rafael Vasquez led his forces into the city of San Antonio, reclaiming her. Rafael, using the same church flagpole that Santa Anna used to raise his red flag of death during the siege of the Alamo, hoisted his banner. The General chose Sam Maverick's home for his headquarters and let his officers select from several other homes left abandoned by the evacuation. One officer chose Commander Moore's home and found himself face-to-face with a defiant Anglo woman holding a shotgun. Rather than risking death or having to shoot a woman, the Mexican told her he would find lodging elsewhere.

Jack Hays was determined to raise a substantial fighting force and return to San Antonio as soon as possible. Once the caravan made camp, he sent an urgent message to President Houston alerting him to the gravity of their situation. He also dispatched messengers to locate more rangers and round up more fighting men. Many of Jack's top rangers, like Bud Miller, Noah Smithwick, Henry McCullough, and Deaf Smith were scattered throughout the Republic.

The second night, the refugees camped on the bank of the Guadalupe River. About midnight, one of the lookouts heard two horses approaching and woke Jack. He was relieved to discover it was Ben McCullough and A.S. Miller. Ben told him the good news that on the morning of March 8th, General Vasquez had lowered the Mexican flag and departed San Antonio heading south back to Mexico. Jack immediately dispatched two spies to trail the retreating army and make sure they had crossed the Rio Grande.

The following morning, Hays was as busy as a short-tail mare in fly season, calming the citizens and deciding his next course of action. He called everyone together and told the group of the Mexicans' departure and issued a caveat that the citizens not return to San Antonio. Hays was concerned that the show of force by General Rafael Vasquez was only to test the will of the Texans, and believed the next assault would be a greater force returning to finish what Santa Anna started.

Fear flowed through the ranks of those camped along the riverbank. Confusion and concern laced with terror as families debated whether they would return to their homes or continue their flight eastward. A few decided to return, but the majority felt it was not safe to go back. Sam Maverick took Mary and the children on to Richmond. Others went to stay with friends or set up camp once they reached the San Felipe area.

Jack Hays and Ben McCullough consoled each other that night, trying to justify leaving the city without a fight. The Texans had made things too easy for the General, and Vasquez would report to Mexico City that he found nothing but cowards. The thought of being called a coward galled Jack Hays to the core. Around midnight, the two rangers made a promise to each other to fight to the death to protect the Republic from any future invasion. The pair would get another opportunity to do so.

Chapter Thirty
Reality

After leaving the White ranch, Bud was unaware that three men, intent on killing him for his gold, now followed his trail. On the spur of the moment, he decided to stop in Houston to purchase new clothes and perhaps a better saddle, similar to the one Jack Hays used. As he rode through town, he spotted a sign offering lodging and board. Tossing Lightning's neck rope over the hitching rail and securing the knot, he stepped inside the elegant Mansion House Hotel where a plump young girl took his money and gave him the key to a second floor room. Bud put his things away and was on his way to find boarding for Lightning when he met Mrs. Pamela Mann, the woman who stood toe-to-toe with General Houston demanding her oxen back, forcing the army to pull the twin cannons by hand. She stood at the bottom of the stairs with her hands on her hips as Bud descended the staircase. "How long do you plan to hang around? I'm Mrs. Mann, the owner of this here establishment. If you want anything, look me up." Then she paused, grinned, and continued, "Sonny boy, I do mean anything."

Cool as the underside of a pillow, Bud tipped the broad brim of his beaver hat and answered, "Thanks Ma'am. I'm not here to enjoy the pleasures of your establishment. I need to purchase supplies and a new saddle. I have a long ride ahead of me." Before he walked away, he posed one request. "Mrs. Mann, I do need some help. I need a place to board my horse for the night."

"Tom Williams runs a good stable and has a barn if you want to pay extra for your horse to stay there overnight. He feeds plenty and grooms well. Yep, I'd say Tommy is the best for a young whippersnapper like you."

As Bud worked Lightning's knot loose, an older man was leaning against the hitching rail, his buckskins almost black from many years of wear. The old man inquired, "Enjoying the necessities Mrs. Mann dishes out?"

Bud stood erect, answering, "No Sir. I'm only stopping for a saddle and supplies. Can't tarry long. I'm afraid Mrs. Mann is a little on the untamed side for me."

Those words brought an immediate response. "Son, do you know Mrs. Mann took Almeron Dickinson's wife Susannah and her baby in and gave them a place to stay after San Jacinto. She didn't charge them a red cent either. I guess you know Susannah was in the Alamo when her husband and the others were killed."

As Bud started to answer, a pair of dogs started fighting in the middle of the street, startling Lightning and causing the stallion to pull on the reins, rolling his eyes so he could see the disturbance. Bud gave a yank and calmed his stallion down as he replied, "Sir, I have heard the story of how Mrs. Dickinson, Buck Travis' slave Joe, and little Angelina stopped at John and Sarah Bruno's house after they were set free by Santa Anna. I understand they rode in the Bruno's oxcart in their escape as Santa Anna swept across Texas. They lived for a long spell with the Brunos at their home on Nash Creek. I was not aware of Mrs. Dickinson and Angelina coming to Houston."

The old man's buckskin leggings drug the ground as he moved away from the railing and spit a slug of tobacco juice on the dirt, making a splatter pattern the size of a dinner plate. He straightened up, pulled up his pants, and snapped, "You seem to be a bright feller. Not all youngens know what you do 'bout the Alamo and our fight with Santa Anna. I wuz there. I fought in San Jacinto. I took my revenge for them killed at the Alamo and Goliad."

Before either man could speak again, a rider came galloping down the street screaming, "The Mexicans have taken San Antonio. Thousands of Mexicans occupied the town on March 6th. People are fleeing. We need fighting men. I have a letter from Jack Hays. Who will go with me?"

Bud mounted without saying another word to the old man, and galloped to catch the rider. When the rider stopped, Bud was at his side. "Sir, did you say Jack Hays wants all the rangers to return? We're going to be fighting the Mexicans?"

Breathlessly, the rider answered, "Rangers, farmers, blacksmiths, doctors, lawyers, saloonkeepers, anyone who can fire a gun. We need men. When I left, there were over three thousand Mexicans in San Antonio. I hear five thousand more are coming. We have to make a stand now."

This was news Bud had been waiting for. He could now kill his father's murderers. His heart was pumping as he asked, "Where are they camped?"

The rider's answer was brief. "The men are on the bank of the Guadalupe, close to Seguin."

Three riders tied up in front of the Mansion House Hotel. Marvin O'Reilly and his two associates had wanted to catch Bud on open ground, but his capricious stop in Houston had foiled their plan. They had observed the ranger and the old man talking when the rider came rushing into town. The trio had no idea Bud would immediately head west, so they entered the hotel and ordered three whiskeys.

Bud never returned to his hotel room. He stopped at the general store and purchased extra powder, lead, and a bag of corn for Lightning. He asked the storekeeper for a writing pad and pencil. Leaning on the counter, he wrote a brief letter to Charm:

My Dearest Charm,

I pen this letter to let you know the Mexicans have attacked our great Republic again. Please forgive my having been tardy in writing. There is no justifiable excuse I can think of, other than my own laziness. My intentions have been often to write; however, somehow I was never prompted to execute the note. Now that I will be facing death, I must tell you, should I survive the war, I plan to come your way for another visit. I enjoyed our conversations together. I want to return to my farm, walk among the tall pine trees and ride my horse in the open fields. God willing, perhaps you and your brother can accompany me when I return. The beauty is unparalleled. I pray God will look over me that I might one day show you the beautiful home left me by the Baron de Bastrop.

I must ride and ride hard to join Major Jack Hays and fight for the freedom of Texas.

With much admiration and affection,

Benjamin "Bud" Miller

P.S. I will always treasure the handkerchief you gave me. It remains in my vest pocket where you placed it.

Bud folded the note and stuck it in an envelope. After writing a general address, he gave the storekeeper a dollar and told the elderly man, "Please, Sir. It is urgent this letter be delivered post haste. The Mexicans have taken San Antonio. I must join the fight. We cannot allow them to occupy our city and live."

The young ranger's spur rowels clanged against the pine floor as he exited. The storekeeper stood with the letter in his hand, thinking who might be going to Austin and could deliver the letter. He was impressed with the young ranger and wanted to oblige his wishes if possible.

By the time the trio of cowboys had gulped down their second shot of whiskey, Bud and Lightning were on their way to join Jack Hays. Chatting with Pamela Mann, Marvin inquired about Bud, pretending to be the ranger's uncle. Pamela didn't just fall off a turnip wagon; running the Mansion House gave her great insight into the character of men. Pamela didn't mind lying as she curtly answered their inquiry. "The boy is in town waiting for several of his fellow Texas Rangers. I have rooms set aside for them. Jack Hays and Ben McCullough are coming with fifteen men to meet the young ranger. Seems the young man discovered he was being followed and sent for help. He asked me if I'd seen men fitting your description when he checked in. I don't think you are his uncle or you would have called him by his name. I suspect you are the three cowboys the rangers are on their way to apprehend."

None of the three dared get near Jack Hays or Ben McCullough. The two rangers would recognize them for sure, and before they could say, "jackrabbit", there would be a necktie party in their honor. Marvin didn't think they had followed close enough for Bud to detect them, but paranoia prevailed. Believing their cover was blown, Marvin decided they might as well spend some time fulfilling their carnal hunger, and leave before the rangers arrived.

Lightning slung his head from side to side, chewing on his bit, wanting to run, but Bud knew not to wear his horse out and kept Lightning reined in. If he were a day late on a fresh mount, it was better than arriving earlier on a mount too tired to fight. His second day on the road, he encountered the first wave of refugees fleeing San Antonio. A Mexican couple, speaking in broken English, told him it looked like there was going to be another war with Mexico. They heard there was a large army heading to San Antonio intent on murdering all Texans. Bud thanked him for the information and quickly headed toward Bexar County.

As he rode, he started thinking about James Bonham and his bravery, knowing Fannin was not coming to aid his fellow Texans in the Alamo. What must have been going through Bonham's mind as he headed back into the Alamo knowing he would surely die? Bud had moments of doubt and fear as he and Lightning kept a steady pace, only stopping for a few hours sleep each night. Lightning ate and rested, then woke Bud by nuzzling his nose against the sleeping ranger's face. He never hobbled Lightning, but rather used a long tie rope so he would be able to mount and ride at a moment's notice.

It was midday when Bud arrived in San Felipe. The remains of the buildings burned in the Runaway Scrape were testimony to the fear those escaping Santa Anna must have felt six years earlier. Only a few homes had been rebuilt; piles of debris overgrown with weeds were all that remained where most buildings once stood. One of the few shops still standing was Noah Smithwick's old blacksmith shop. Bud took time to ride down the empty main street and ponder the loss. He thought of the Baron, knowing the old man had been part of seeing this town grow into a thriving community, only to be reduced to cinders. His anger welled up, and any doubt he may have had about joining the fight vanished.

Bud saw no one until he got to the edge of Gonzales. There he noticed a campfire in the center of the city and was not sure if it was friend or foe. Riding north, opposite the direction of the wind, he maneuvered near the camp. When he got close enough to see the canvas-covered wagons, he realized they were Texas citizens fleeing the Mexican army. He kicked Lightning in the flanks and galloped toward the camp. As he drew near, he shouted, "I'm a Texas Ranger on my way to join the battle."

Mary Maverick was the first to greet him. Her words were a mixture of relief and concern. "Welcome to our humble camp. We have stopped here in Gonzales to decide what to do next. There is plenty of food for you and your horse. The Mexican army that occupied San Antonio left, but my husband thinks a larger group will return. Jack Hays and my Sam wanted to go after the Mexicans as they were retreating, but couldn't assemble a large enough force to challenge them." Then she asked, "Did you know the Mexicans also invaded Goliad and Refugio?"

Bud was shocked. Had he not stopped in Houston for supplies, the young ranger would have been in Goliad when the Mexicans arrived. Bud was anxious for news, but got more than he bargained for and the shock showed in his voice as he answered, "I had no idea. All I heard was that San Antonio was under siege. I knew something like this would happen when I heard of the Santa Fe Expedition debacle."

Bud had his own idea of why the Mexicans attacked. They had to be angry that Lamar sent an army of almost three hundred men into Santa Fe without permission, and ordered the Texas Navy to assist the Yucatan rebels. Whomever or whatever was to blame, one thing was now certain: Bud Miller would get his wish to kill Mexicans.

Mary continued, "We think they were sent to test the strength of our defenses in the three towns. I feel, even if we had put up a fight, they would have left no sooner than they did anyway. They didn't come prepared to stay. They just rode in, spent a couple of nights, and then returned to Mexico. Had my husband and Jack been able to muster an army, there would have been fireworks. The Mexicans would have run back to Mexico carrying their dead. The next group will come to stay, and we must be ready. Sam, Jack, and Ben McCullough are gathering an army so we will have the men to defend against their next assault. I so dislike leaving my dear husband and brothers, but Sam insisted I get the children to a safe place. I'll be taking them to Richmond and staying at Jane Long's place."

Mary then told him of a scare the group had experienced that created a panic. A rider told them two thousand Mexican soldiers were right behind them. "We were caught in a torrential rain storm and expected to be surrounded the next morning, only to find the rider was just crazy with fear. I think half of Texas is crazy."

Mary Maverick was not much older than Bud. She was only twenty-four, but acted as if she was a mature woman. He was amazed at her calmness and take-charge attitude. Bud noticed the pistol stuck in Mary's belt, and at that moment, decided he wanted a wife with the spunk of Mary Maverick. He couldn't help comparing Virginia and Charm being in the same situation. He felt Virginia would not be able to cope with living in a tent, fleeing for her life. She would want the comforts of home. On the other hand, Charm would be more like Mary Maverick, facing down any situation. If he had to go to war and leave a wife behind, Charm would be the better choice. She had the attitude of a Texas woman; unspoiled and self-assured, able to endure any challenge.

"Where are the men gathered?" Bud asked.

"Sam and my brothers are in San Antonio, trying to estimate the damage. They are going to be returning to Gonzales in a day or so."

Bud's heart went out for those leaving their homes and possessions in San Antonio, not knowing if they could ever return. He thought of the futility of war and wondered why Mexico felt compelled to return. Trade between Mexico and Texas was flourishing, and General Houston was president again and making no aggressive gestures. Bud found himself blaming President Lamar for the Mexican invasion. He knew for certain Lamar had instigated war with the Indians. Timmy Marcum had told him Lamar had worked for the Georgia Governor as an aide back in 1828 and drafted the bill to have all Cherokee and Creek removed from their land. Lamar certainly bore some of the responsibility for the "Trail of Tears". Even though Lamar was President of Texas at the time of the incident, his bill instigated the action years earlier. The Indians were living in peace, had their own schools, and lived in brick houses, the same as their white neighbors; yet, in his bill, Lamar called them "Red Barbarians."

Suddenly, Bud was overcome with sadness as he reminisced about his friend Timmy Marcum. After the Cordova revolt, intense hatred toward local Indians had overflowed to the point where no Indian was safe. Bud was out mustanging when a group of angry newcomers realized Timmy was part Indian, and before the sheriff could stop them, the mob hanged Timmy near downtown Nacogdoches. Timmy's refusal to cut his long, black hair and look more white than Indian, cost him his life. In Bud's mind, Lamar's heroics at San Jacinto were completely overshadowed by his hate-mongering presidential policies, even though his racism against Indians did not exist in isolation; the majority of Texans felt the same way. Likewise, Lamar's desire for war with Mexico was not an aberration; at least half the population supported southward expansion. Beyond expansion of the territory, most Texans wanted to avenge the massacres at the Alamo and Goliad and the way their fellow Texans were denied any dignity in death, burned like rubbish by Santa Anna's Army.

After feeding Lightning, Bud talked with some of the displaced families, and then received directions to Jack and Ben's camp, a hard day's ride away. As he rode, the displaced families' plight weighed heavily on the thoughtful young ranger. Some were frightened, while others were angry and more determined than ever not to give up the fight. He thought that if all the Texas women had the spunk of Mary Maverick, the Mexican army would be in trouble. Mary reminded him of Charm Hempstead, not so much in appearance, but in attitude. Charm knew what it took to survive on the frontier. Like Mary, Charm was always happy and full of energy. As he rode west, his mind was occupied with Charm, and not Virginia. Perhaps the crisis of war and seeing Mary Maverick's calmness had brought the country girl to the front of his mind. He recalled how his Uncle Charlie had often used a phrase that never meant anything to him until now; "Under pressure, cream will rise to the top."

Suddenly, from the east bank of the Guadalupe River, he spotted a blazing campfire as a voice from the darkness shouted, "Who goes there?"

Bud squinted as he tried to identify the shadowy figure tucked behind the trees. He turned his stallion in the direction of the voice and answered, "Texas Ranger Benjamin Miller reporting for duty, Sir!"

The voice from the thicket answered, "I've heard of you." The dark figure emerged and approached Bud, introducing himself, "I'm Simon Bateman, originally from Mississippi, here to join the fight."

"Glad to meet you, Simon. Are you also called Bull Bateman?"

"Sure as flies swarm to watermelon rind."

Simon "Bull" Bateman owned a small plantation in Mississippi before moving to Texas. He raised cotton in his home state, but had a yearning to own a cattle ranch, so he brought his slaves and purchased land southeast of Gonzales. He soon built up a sizable herd. He earned the nickname "Bull" when one day his slaves were driving some wild longhorns into a pen and one bull became especially cantankerous. Simon had a good laugh and then climbed over the rail and dropped down into the corral on his hands and knees. The bull bellowed, and Simon snarled back. Then the bull started pawing the ground, and Simon copied the angry animal's actions, kicking up as much dust as the bull. When the bull started swinging his head from side to side, Simon did the same. The bull then charged, and Simon rolled safely to one side. The bull charged again, and once more, the agile Bateman was able to evade the bull's assault. His final charge was too quick for Simon. The bull's massive horns lifted Bateman and flung him over the railing and onto the ground. Simon Bateman spent four months in bed recuperating from his injuries. His new Texas friends were quick to tag him with the nickname, "Bull".

Bull was not a big man, and to bear such a nickname seemed odd to Bud. He had expected Bull to equal the size of someone like Big Foot Wallace. Bud inquired, "How is the army coming together?"

Bull spoke with the same confidence he had displayed in the corral with the angry longhorn. "I think the greasers got word we are assembling and cut tail and ran. I don't think they cotton too much to tanglin' with the likes of us."

Bud knew the real reason the first group left; however, he didn't argue with the older man. He simply nodded an affirmative and then asked, "Where do we cross the river?"

"Follow me."

The two forded the river about five hundred yards to the south. When they reached camp, Bud learned that Jack Hays and Ben McCullough were away on scouting missions; he would have to wait until they returned to get his orders.

A few weeks before the invasion Big Foot noticed fifteen to twenty Mexicans milling around in San Antonio. He knew all of the locals, and thought it odd so many unfamiliar Mexican men were in town spending money on lead and powder. He assumed they were in search of the silver mines reportedly near Llano and San Saba. What he didn't know was those men had systematically purchased the entire local supply of ammunition. Others were doing the same in Goliad and Refugio, assisted by local Mexicans sympathetic to the dictator. Santa Anna had out-maneuvered the Texans.

Santa Anna's spies informed him that Dr. Anson Jones, the secretary of state in the second Houston administration had advocated shutting down the military, telling his cabinet, "Texas is a country absolutely without present means of any kind. Her resources are large, though prospective, but her credit is utterly prostrate. We cannot afford to maintain a standing army."

The dictator also learned of Jones' stance that Texas should act solely in defense. His position was that if Mexico saw Texans being friendly, they in turn would do the same for the Lone Star Republic. Santa Anna saw Jones' conciliatory remarks as a sign of weakness. Two things were in place: Texas was weak, and Sam Houston was back in power. Defeating President Lamar would not have satisfied the dictator; he wanted to make Houston feel the same humiliation and shame he experienced in defeat. Santa Anna had patiently waited for Sam Houston to become the supreme leader of Texas once again so when he reclaimed Texas, it would be over the dead body of his sworn enemy. Everything was falling perfectly into place for the vengeful Mexican dictator.

The second day in camp, Bud's old friend Noah Smithwick and twenty more Texans arrived. To Bud's surprise, Noah handed him a letter from Charm. About the time he had been writing her a letter in Houston, she was penning a note to him. Her penmanship was letter perfect, and the wording cautious:

Mr. Benjamin Miller,

With quill in hand, I write to inquire of your health and well being. We had hoped for a visit or correspondence. I trust you will not think of me as a forward woman for writing. I am doing so only because of my concern. Please do send word when you have time and let us know if you are in good health.

With admiration and grand respect,

Charm Hempstead

Chapter Thirty-One
War

Millie was hanging clothes on the line when she saw a rider splashing across the Little River. By the speed at which the rider pushed his horse up the riverbank, Millie sensed he was delivering an urgent message. Placing the wooden homemade clothespins in her apron, she sat down near the clothesbasket and waited. As he neared, the rider's demeanor told the story. Then his words confirmed her fears. He removed his hat as he dismounted and spoke before his boots touched the ground. "Where's Jim?" he hastily asked.

Millie quickly answered, "He and our son are hunting on the other side of the Brazos. I expect them home shortly. Will you let me make you some food?"

His hands nervously rolled the brim of his hat as he shuffled from one foot to the other. He didn't want to look Millie in the eye. He coughed to clear his throat and replied, "No thank you, Ma'am. I have miles to ride and people to warn. The Mexicans have taken San Antonio, Goliad, and some other cities. It looks like we are at war with Mexico again. Captain Ben McCullough from Gonzales wanted me to tell Jim to come as quickly as he can. We need to put an army together or the Mexicans will run us over. We gotta make a stand."

Millie stood speechless. She had hoped the victory at San Jacinto settled the dispute between Mexico and Texas once and for all. Millie sank to the ground, clasping a wet shirt in her hands but she had no tears.

The rider needed an answer, but was reluctant to press. He had been in San Antonio when Millie was rescued. She never saw him, but he had seen her terror then. Now he watched helplessly as dread overcame her. Finally, he muttered, "If it wuz up to me, I wouldn't ask for Jim, knowin' how you done lost one husband. Don't seem fair," he said clumsily.

Like a true Texas woman, Millie stood, hung the wet shirt on the clothesline and offered a stoic reply. "James will need a change of clothes. Where does Ben want him to meet up?"

The rider was relieved to see her resolve and answered, "Along the Guadloop River. Bunch a men are camped out not far from Seguin. He'll need his best horse and plenty lead and powder. No telling how long this will take. I'd stick in some corn and jerky if'n it wuz me."

Millie understood his mispronunciation of the Guadalupe River and knew the area where the army was camped. She mustered a smile. "Let me grab a small bag of corn for your horse and some venison jerky for you. I think I still have a slice of pecan pie as well. You both need food or you won't have the strength to alert the others."

The rider seemed hesitant to impose as he asked, "Would you mind if I filled my canteen from the well?"

Millie nodded and went into the house, returning with a large slice of pecan pie. Without saying a word, she hastily went to the barn for the shelled corn and jerky. By the time she returned, the pie was gone and the rider was licking his fingers. Once she gave him the horse feed and dried meat, he tipped his hat and was gone as quickly as he had arrived. He never mentioned his name and Millie had not asked.

Millie, Ruthann, and the baby went to the ferry to wait for Jim and A.D. It was almost dark before she saw the two emerge from the area Tom Green passed through six years earlier. Her little boy was now sixteen, a man. He sat his horse well and was almost as tall as James. Millie knew long before the two crossed the river that A.D. would want to join the fight. She also knew she couldn't refuse; she must allow him to fight for freedom or he would never forgive her. She was counting on James to come up with a solution.

Millie was wringing her hands in her apron as the men rode off the ferry. James knew something was wrong. He kicked his bay mare in the flanks, arriving ahead of A.D. The mare's hindquarters dipped to the ground from the sliding stop. James dismounted and rushed to his wife, wrapping his powerful arms around her. The moment he touched her, tears began to flow. He asked in a gentle voice, "Millie, what's wrong?"

Millie reached up, placing her hands on each side of his chiseled jaw and replied, "War! James, we are at war again with the Mexico. A young man came earlier today. He said Ben McCullough wants you to join the fight."

A.D. arrived in time to hear his mother mention war and the need for men. He shouted, "Praise the Lord, I'm gonna get to fight those devils that took the life of David Crockett."

James continued to squeeze Millie tightly as he turned to his stepson. "I know you are old enough to fight and can shoot better than most. I also know I cannot in good conscience, allow you to leave your mother and the children unprotected. Son, there is as great a danger here at home as I will face. One of us must stay here. Your mother needs you to protect her and your brother and sister. I am going, and you are staying. That is my final word."

A.D. hung his head, knowing James was saying what he thought was best. He muttered back, "Yes sir, I understand. I was just hoping." He then continued, "Sir, which horse do you want to take? The black stallion or the bay mare?"

James didn't hesitate. "I'll take the mare. She has a better gait and is lot less temperamental."

Ruthann walked up behind Jim and placed her arms around him and her mother. The three embraced while A.D. led the horses to the barn and removed the slain pig from the pack mule. The baby, now three, tagged along behind him, not understanding the reason for everyone being so solemn.

James wanted to spend the night with his family; however, both he and Millie knew there was only one choice. As soon as his supplies were ready, he kissed Ruthann on her forehead, picked up the baby and cradled him tight while shaking A.D.'s hand. As he was mounting, he looked at A.D. and said, "Son, you are now the man of the house. The family is yours to protect. I'm very proud of you. It is my fervent prayer that I return safe and in good speed."

Millie watched as her man went to join the scores of other men leaving everything behind to join the fight. All across Texas, women were left to tend to the farms, birth the animals, take care of the children, and defend their homes. The call to arms opened old wounds as fear and heartache swept across the Republic once again.

Santa Anna's return to power was the result of a French blockade of the port of Vera Cruz in April 1838. The action was in retaliation for Mexico's failure to pay damages claimed by French citizens. The blockade and ensuing battle earned the name of "The Pastry War" because the xenophobic participants in an 1828 anti-Spanish Parisian Market riot had looted a French bakery. By November 1838, no satisfactory settlement had been reached so the French fleet started shelling Vera Cruz. The Pastry War opened the door for Santa Anna to emerge from his exile from the San Jacinto debacle; Santa Anna left his estate and offered his leadership to drive the French from Mexican soil. He was readily welcomed because the French were getting the upper hand in the conflict. Upon the Eagle's arrival, almost immediately the tide turned in favor of Mexico. To demonstrate his bravery, Santa Anna moved to the front of the battle line as he had seen The Raven do at San Jacinto. Just as he reached a small hilltop on his gleaming black stallion, a cannonball slammed into the side of his horse and severed his leg just below the knee. He was not as fortunate as General Houston; Santa Anna's leg had to be amputated on the battlefield. The Mexican people saw the loss of Santa Anna's leg as a supreme sacrifice. By the time his leg healed, Santa Anna had returned to the pantheon of Mexico heroes and, in 1839, regained his position as President of Mexico.

The word of war rumbled across the rivers into the United States like the aftershocks of a powerful earthquake. Images of a raven and eagle began to appear in newspapers and artists renderings. One small town newspaper wrote a story about the Raven and the Eagle, pointing out the superior power of the latter. Another editorial contrasted the cunning and brilliance of the raven, indicating that Houston was the superior warrior. The writer pointed out the Raven had conquered the Eagle once, and he would do it again. Houston didn't share the same confidence. With no money and no prospects of acquiring capital, Sam knew Texas was vulnerable. Houston studied ancient history and employed the tactics of Roman General Quintus Fabius Maximus when he defeated Santa Anna. Maximus defeated Carthaginian Hannibal by retreating until Hannibal's men were exhausted, and then led them to terrain favorable to the Roman forces. Maximus' battle wisdom became known as the *Fabian Tactics*: avoidance of direct confrontation in order to gain the advantage and claim the final victory. Fool me once, shame on you; fool me twice, shame on me. Houston knew Santa Anna was no fool.

Ironically, as the riders raced throughout the Republic warning the citizens of war, they saw dozens of crows perched on trees, as if awaiting the arrival of The Eagle. One rider swore a murder of crows followed him across the Republic, waking him at the slightest sign of danger with their piercing cries. Perhaps it was purely coincidental, but Texans started looking for the big black ravens as a good omen.

By the time riders reached smaller communities and isolated farms, word had already spread that the Mexicans retreated after only two days of occupation. Many mistakenly thought the hostilities were over and the Mexican army would not return. Those who believed the Mexicans were gone for good made no preparations and carried on as if the threat of war was over, but the Raven knew the Eagle would return. Santa Anna did nothing without purpose. The vindictive dictator would not rest until the Texans' heads were on the end of a pole. How dare they have the audacity to oppose him?

Houston was cautiously optimistic that Santa Anna did not want a sustained fight; Mexico was in turmoil and had higher priorities than punishing the wayward Texans. The dictator was dealing with rebel uprisings throughout Mexico. Like a giant hurricane, the Texas Revolution sent squalls over northern Mexico, with rebellions breaking out in several states. One of the leaders of a peasant uprising was

Antonio Zapata. Zapata was born around 1800 in Guerrero, Tamaulipas. He spent the early part of his life as a sheepherder, and eventually made a fortune as a horse and cattle rancher. Zapata distinguished himself as a cavalry officer fighting the Comanche and Lipan Indians. The Indians called him "Sombrero de Manteca" because he used hair oil, which made his raven hair glisten under the blazing sun. He joined with other northern leaders in armed resistance against Santa Anna's Centralist subversion of the Mexican Constitution of 1824. Commissioned as a Colonel, the gifted cavalry officer was compared by the Texans to Stonewall Jackson. Zapata became a major leader in an insurrection organized at Guerrero against Santa Anna's government and led various military campaigns against the Centralist forces at Mier. In January 1840, a convention of Mexican delegates met at Laredo, proclaiming the Republic of the Rio Grande and selected Laredo as the capital. The convention named Zapata as military commandant and Zapata's cavalry took Laredo and other Rio Grande towns in rapid succession. Canales' forces took the field against Monterrey, but as the battle got underway almost half of his forces deserted to the enemy. Colonel Zapata's cavalry and Texan auxiliaries formed the rear guard, and after heavy losses, returned to the Rio Grande. Canales then sent Zapata with forty men, including twelve Texans, on a foraging expedition. They were captured at Santa Rita. Zapata and twenty-two of his men were tried by a military council, convicted of treason, and executed. Zapata's head was carried to Guerrero and exhibited on a pole for three days as a warning to any would-be conspirators. This ended the republic's first stirrings, but the conflict would be periodically revived over the next few decades. The following year, sentiment against the symbolic public display of Zapata's head prompted rebellion in several Mexican states. In the wake of Texas winning its freedom from Mexico City, Mexican Federalists wanted the same autonomy.

The disputed area known as Tamaulipas, situated between the Nueces River and to fifty miles below the Rio Grande remained the central source of conflict between Mexico and Texas. Houston was willing to give Mexico the flat, dry land south of the Nueces River in exchange for peace while the Lamar hawk faction wanted to extend the border another two-hundred miles south. This unsettled strip of land became a bitter flash point. The Raven and the Eagle would meet again, with the spoils going to the victor.

The conflict between the Eagle and the Raven involved man-sized egos cloaked in inferiority complexes. Sam Houston was over six feet tall before he was fourteen. Girls shunned him and men mocked him, saying he walked like a stork in shallow water. Only after he became a powerful leader did he find success with women, and even then believed that women only sought his company because of his lofty position. Margaret was the first to make him know she loved Sam, the man, not the leader of the new Republic. Houston came from humble beginnings, yet reached the highest levels of military and political power. The United States had only two class divisions: Anglo, and Indian and Negro. No matter where a white man was born, or who his family was he could reach the highest office in the land. On the other hand, Santa Anna had to overcome the unyielding class system of Mexican society where one's family lineage had more to do with success than any abilities one possessed. He was a *Creole*, suspended in between the *Mestzo* and the *Peninsular* classes. Mexico had four distinct class groups, starting with those called Peninsulars at the apex of the social ladder. A Peninsular was born in Spain from a family of distinction with pure Spanish blood. The local Mexicans gave the Peninsulars the nickname of "roosters" because they preferred wearing spurs reminiscent of those found on fighting cocks. The arrogant Peninsulars stole as much power and wealth as they could safely get away with and then dashed back to Spain, only to be replaced by someone even more corrupt. Just below the Peninsular class was the Creoles. The Creoles were of the same pure Spanish blood, but suffered one small indignity; they were not born in Spain. This misfortune did not impede their education or opportunity in business, but did prevent their appointment to positions of leadership; top leadership positions were reserved for the Peninsular class, no matter if a

Creole was more than doubly qualified. A much larger percentage of Mexico's population was the half-castes or mixed breeds. They were given the less-than-flattering title of *Mestzos*. For a Mestzo to reach any position of power, they would have to be extraordinary, and even then, faced almost impossible odds in the 1800s. At the bottom of the pecking order were the local Indians or *Indios*. Denied any hope of social recognition, wealth or power, they received no education and had no option but to obey those in authority. Indios were peons, walking for transportation, never having funds to purchase a donkey or mule. It would be decades before the exceptional Benito Juarez, an Indio, would eventually break through the rigid class barrier and attain the presidency.

Santa Anna lived in Xalapa, where the wealthy citizens of Vera Cruz fled in the sweltering summer months, and where yellow fever killed thousands each year. The life expectancy of those who stayed in the city during the summer months was less than thirty years of age. In spite of the plagues and health dangers, Vera Cruz was the most important port in Mexico; customs duties were collected, and Mexico's treasures were housed there. Each new revolution began by capturing Vera Cruz. The party who controlled Vera Cruz held power over Mexico.

As a young man, Santa Anna walked the streets along the white bluffs and pastel painted houses of Xalapa in the shadow of San Juan de Ultia, a massive structure that towered into the sky along the bay. San Juan de Ultia housed the most deplorable prison in the world, much worse than the Bastille of Paris, the hellholes of Constantinople or the dreaded dungeons of Newgate in London. Each summer, Santa Anna's family moved into the mountains, the Pico de Orizaba peaks rising 18,858 feet above the grasp of yellow death. The cone-shaped volcano remained snow covered all year long, contrasted with the emerald green jungle and the azure blue-green bay of Vera Cruz below. In all probability, no view had more grandeur in all of Mexico or perhaps the world, than Santa Anna's boyhood home. He had everything, except status by birth.

Santa Anna and Sam Houston each had a chip on their shoulder; only power could feed the hunger in the pit of their stomachs. The two men were similar in many ways. Each was taller than the men they led. Each had a leg damaged in battle. Houston had a flair for dressing on occasions. Santa Anna was the epitome of a clotheshorse, wearing custom-made pants and boots. After he lost a leg, he wore a different one for every occasion. He used the loss of his leg to propel himself back into power. Houston shunned using a walking stick, not wanting pity for his war wounds. No man other than Santa Anna could have turned a battle as insignificant as the Pastry War to his advantage the way the dictator did.

Corruption is where any comparison between Houston and Santa Anna ends. Santa Anna used government funds to purchase several hundred thousand acres of land near Vera Cruz, and army personnel to build a palatial second home and one of the largest cattle ranches in Mexico. Santa Anna set the standard all other Mexican Generals would follow. Mexico's military power suffered because of the siphoning of military funds by its leaders. On the opposite side of the spectrum, Houston cut his salary in half during his second term, and lived in a very modest home. When he traveled, he slept under the stars with his men, unless there was shelter for all.

When Bud Miller and Bull Bateman joined the camp, the news of General Vasquez's retreat was on the lips of all the men. With Jack Hays and Ben McCullough away, many of the men felt they could leave for home. There was no money to pay a standing army and considering most of the volunteers were poor farmers, they couldn't afford to wait around now that the imminent danger was gone. New arrivals drifted in daily, while at night, recruits saddled their horses and slipped away into the darkness. "Three-Leg Willie" Williamson encouraged the men to wait for a report from Jack and Ben before disbanding, but as the days passed, more men were leaving than arriving. James Willingham was one such volunteer who heard the news of the Mexicans' retreat. After exchanging small talk with some friends in the camp, he too mounted up and headed back to his family.

Spring grass sprouted from the ground almost overnight, giving ample food for the horses. The new leaves on the trees gave the men a feeling of new life and growth. Flowers covered the hillsides and valleys with a full spectrum of color. Those still in camp used the time to tend to their gear, shoe their horses, and clean and repair their guns. Jack returned on March 15th and Ben, on the 16th. Both were satisfied the Mexicans were across the river and would not immediately return. Ben addressed the men, explaining the damage done in San Antonio and with a sad heart told them that Juan Seguin, the former hero of San Jacinto and Mayor of San Antonio, was seen in the company of the enemy. He explained how recent immigrants made living in Texas almost impossible for Juan because he was Mexican. Many Anglos just saw the color of his skin and seemed not to care that he, on many occasions, had risked his life for Texas freedom. "Judge not Juan Seguin. If the country I fought for turned on me and caused me to fear for my life, I might have done the same thing. I suspect Juan slipped into Mexico and feigned to be on their side to protect his family. Who among us can fault a man for wanting to save his wife and children? Though I have neither, I can empathize with him." Ben concluded his statements, saying, "Make no mistake in thinking this is the last time we will see the Mexicans. They are going to regroup and gather an army to return. We made it too easy on them this time. Trust me gentlemen, we must be ready. Go home and tend to your crops, and make your families safe. I will need fifteen of my men to stay. We need to keep a vigilant eye on the border."

Then he turned to Jack Hays, "I think Jack has a few words for you."

A few words indeed were all Jack had to say. His face flushed with anger as he spoke. "Men, I have never seen such crude behavior as what I witnessed in San Antonio. The destruction of our citizens' homes and property was deplorable. The town is full of spies and robbers and I plan to rid San Antonio of these undesirables. I need twelve to eighteen men to go with me."

Bud stepped out from the crowd shouting, "I'm with you sir!"

Quickly, Jack had seventeen men, and Ben, the same number.

Ben addressed his small group, asking, "Those of you with families raise your hands." Two raised their hands. Ben gave them instructions to go home.

Jack knew the seventeen men in his group, and knew the ones who had families. One was Josh Johnson, an older man with a large family. Josh used every excuse that came along to get away from his nagging wife. He would tell anyone who would listen that no Comanche or Mexican was equal to his wife when it came to fighting. The other man was a tall thin, red-haired Irishman, Jake McCain. Jake had a wife and five children at home. Jack simply nodded to them, indicating they should go home. Ironically, A.S. Miller left with the married men, never knowing his nephew Bud was in the ranger group. Bud didn't know his uncle A.S. was even in Texas. The two would never have an opportunity to meet again. A few months later, A.S. was chasing a stray calf when his horse stepped in a prairie dog hole. The horse threw him and he died instantly from a broken neck. Serendipity placed the two in the same camp, and then fate stepped in, never letting them meet.

Jack and Ben divided duties. Ben would take a scouting party down through Goliad, then across the flat lands to Laredo, and back up to Crow's Creek. Their mission was to scout the valley and report any movement or capture any spies. Jack and his men went looking for Agaton and Christopher Rubio. Needing a new man unfamiliar to the spies in the city, and one who could pass for a bandit himself, Jack sent Keno

Elliott into San Antonio to do some spying. Keno grew up in a Spanish-speaking neighborhood in New Orleans and spoke the language as well as the locals. His gruff, dark exterior made him look sinister; a man a bandit would instantly trust. Keno had no difficulty integrating into the community of outlaws.

Keno quickly learned that Agaton was living in a house by the river and Rubio had taken over the Mission San Jose for his headquarters. Keno also learned there was a large group of pro-Santa Anna Mexicans in the town and after two days, he rode back to camp and gave Jack an assessment. Jack didn't hesitate; he and his men entered the city and went straight for Agaton's hiding place. Once Agaton and his men were apprehended, the rangers headed south for the old Mission, and Rubio. Word that Jack Hays was in town and had arrested Agaton reached Rubio moments before the rangers arrived. Four men managed to flee, but several, including Rubio, did not escape and were trapped inside the mission. When the rangers arrived, they found the mission doors locked. Jack quickly found a priest around back pretending to be working. He didn't ask, he ordered, "Open these doors or I'll burn them down. I know Rubio is in there and I intend to arrest him."

The padre picked up his robe with one hand so he could move faster, and hastened to the massive front doors. Without saying a word, he unlocked the heavy doors, allowing Jack, Bud and Keno to enter. Bud discovered Rubio hiding beneath some blankets. He nudged Lightning with the toe of his boot and the well-trained horse kicked the pile beneath the blanket. In a flash, Rubio was up and running. He made it to the water ditch and started across, but in his haste, he fell. Jack picked up a stick and waded into the water. He took the stick and forced Rubio's head under for a minute or so at a time while Bud waited with his lariat. After Jack had his fun, Bud dropped a loop around Rubio's shoulders and, wrapping the rope around his saddle horn, pulled the bandit to shore.

Jack called the leaders of San Antonio together and issued a "no immigration" decree. He made it clear that no further Mexican immigrants would be allowed into the city, reminding them that Juan Seguin was now riding with Santa Anna, and that many residents in the city were also pro-Santa Anna. There would be no more groups of Mexican men entering the city and buying up the ammunition and supplies. He told them that if he had to instill martial law, he would, and promised a necktie party for anyone discovered slipping information to the enemy. He never raised his voice; nevertheless, everyone heard his message. Jack's reputation was so intimidating that no one wanted to risk reprisal; his warnings caused many to flee south of the Rio Grande.

When Jack announced he was taking Agaton and Rubio to Seguin for trial, there was an outcry among the locals. They didn't want the rangers to remove the bandits, swearing on their mother's graves they could judge them fairly. Hays stood his ground and demanded, "These men have committed egregious crimes against the good citizens of Seguin and there is where they will stand trial. I will leave at daylight with the prisoners and a heavy guard of rangers. If any of you attempt to stop us, you will be shot or added to the group of prisoners."

A large contingent of local men gathered near the jail around nine o'clock that night. Henry McCullough, one of the men guarding the jail, walked directly into the middle of the mob with a revolving pistol in each hand, stating, "If you have come here with the thought of helping these men we have under arrest, then I want you to also be prepared to die tonight. We have been instructed to shoot to kill any sympathizers who even hint they have intentions of setting these cowboys free." One by one, the men slipped into the darkness.

Just before dark the next day, Jack and fourteen rangers left San Antonio for Seguin with the felons bound and tied to their mounts. Jack's rangers rode on all sides of the bandits, giving the impression of them being under heavy guard. About three miles outside of town, Jack ordered Keno Elliott and Henry

McCullough to escort the prisoners on to Seguin, confident the two could carry out the mission. His last words were in Spanish, "Shoot Agaton and Rubio first if anyone tries to make a run for it. Shoot first and ask questions later." Agaton quickly instructed the other bandits not to attempt escape. He knew Jack Hays was a man of his word and would not have selected Keno and Henry if they were not extremely adept with their weapons.

Once in the custody of the Seguin sheriff, the trial took place quickly and the verdict was death by hanging. The sentence was harsh for just the Seguin crimes; however, their reputation and other acts of violence were taken into consideration when determining their fate. Texas-brand justice was swift and final for the leaders and painfully exacted on their followers as well. Within ten days, the two leaders were hanged, and the other eleven prisoners, stripped of their horses and shoes, were set free to return to Mexico. Only two would survive the harsh journey.

Jack gave his horse some rein and pulled alongside Bud. "Good to see you back with us. Where in the heck have you been?"

Bud was ready to talk. He told Jack of his wild scheme to capture the Pacing White Stallion and his good fortune of the Baron de Bastrop leaving him such a generous inheritance. He talked about Taylor White and Pamela Mann. After talking back and forth for a couple of hours, Jack confessed to Bud that he too had hunted the elusive Pacing White Stallion, with similar results. They both had a good laugh. Bud had seldom seen his friend laugh.

After the group stopped for lunch, Jack chose to ride once more with Bud. They made small talk as Jack occasionally pointed out tricks of tracking. After a few hours, Bud asked about his job as a surveyor and Jack explained how he got into the business and the fine points of laying out parcels of land. Then, out of the blue, Bud asked, "What really happened at Enchanted Rock?"

Bud's question caught Jack off guard. His exploits had been written about in newspapers as far away as New York City, and clearly, the Enchanted Rock story was one that implied he had done something of extreme importance.

"Might as well tell you what really happened rather than you latch on to some of those wild stories floatin' around. Back about this time last year, I took my surveying crew around ninety miles north of San Antonio, up the Pedernales River, deep into Comanche territory. I had heard stories of the 'Enchanted Rock', but had never seen the stone monolith. I don't know how to begin to describe Enchanted Rock. It's round like a river stone, only a gigantic mass of granite rising up from the ground over five hundred feet. The boulder is three miles around at the base and the summit is smooth, like a rock that had tumbled in a river for centuries, and can't be more than thirty to forty feet wide.

We camped in the area for two days, and had not seen any sign of Indians, so I foolishly decided to go check it out alone. Some of the sides proved too difficult to climb, in fact downright impossible. While riding around the base, I spotted a large band of Comanche. They had me cut off from my men. I had only one choice and that was get to the top of that rock. Here is where stupid comes in. When I'm surveying, I sometimes loop my pouch and powder horn over my saddle horn, figuring if push comes to shove, I'll be on my horse fighting anyway. Well, I tied up my horse, and in my haste, forgot my lead and powder. I was on the top before I discovered my mistake. How dumb is that?"

Bud was not one to call Jack Hays dumb. He defended Jack's choice, saying, "I'd have done the same thing. You get accustomed to it always being on your body so when you leave it for convenience, it's easy to forget."

Jack appreciated Bud's attempt to make him feel better, but still recognized he had made a mistake that almost cost him his life. He shook his head and started talking, anxious to tell someone the real story, not the newspaper version. "I had no difficulty reaching the top, even carrying my long rifle, shotgun, two pistols and my knife. I cannot think of a more exhilarating feeling than walking around the apex of that enormous granite rock. From the top, you can see forever. You can see the Texas hills for a hundred miles in every direction with cotton ball Texas clouds floating back in perspective on all sides. I got so engrossed looking into the distance, I almost forgot the Comanche at the base of the rock. The moment they discovered my horse, they started that high-pitched war cry that rose from the ground in amplification and echoed all around me. I immediately looked for a place to hide. I know the newspaper stories said there was a large indentation that I was able to take refuge in. I want you to know the top of that rock is a smooth as a baby's backside. There was no place to hide. When I heard them call me 'White Devil' in Spanish, I knew they realized the figure on top of the rock was none other than 'Captain Yack'. That's what the Comanche call me."

Bud interrupted, "Why didn't you fire off a few rounds so your men could hear you were in trouble?"

"That was my first thought, but I realized I was upwind from the survey site. Sound carries up, like the Indians' chants, but I was not sure a gunshot would carry down and did not want to waste any shots. If the Comanche were going to kill me, I wanted to inflict heavy casualties on them. I walked around the edge and tried to see if there was more than one way to the top; I surmised the attack would come from one direction. I squatted down on my haunches for a spell, and nothing happened. Then I remembered the Indians believe the Enchanted Rock to be some sort of spiritual ground and that only the pure of heart could climb the rock. That became my solace for a while. I knew eventually their desire to kill me would cause them to overcome their superstitions and one of the younger braves would take a chance so he could say he killed 'Devil Jack'."

"Were you scared?"

Jack didn't hesitate. "Dang right. I figured they had me in a trap, and I only had a limited number of shots. Each one had to take a life. My only hope was that if I could kill a few, the rest might back off. My fear increased as I began to think about my limited options. I realized if my men hadn't heard the screaming of the Indians, chances were they wouldn't hear my gunshots."

Bud butted in again. "Why didn't they use their bows and drop arrows on top of you?"

Jack gave Bud his characteristic half grin, and answered, "They tried. The rock was too tall and the position they were forced to shoot from increased the distance considerably. I saw several arrows fall short. That is when I realized they would have to climb up if they wanted to kill me. I guess they must have waited two or three hours before one stuck his head over the edge. The minute I saw him, I dropped on my belly. There was a very shallow indentation, perhaps eight inches deep. Even eight inches helped reduce my exposure a little. He ducked back down before I could get my rifle in position to fire. Moments later, his head bobbed up again like at a turkey shoot. He kept this up, hoping to draw my fire. My mama didn't raise no fool. I knew they would have to expose themselves to get a shot at me. I just waited, and finally one of them with less brains than guts made the mistake of coming over the edge. He raised his bow and I put a ball in the center of his heart. The blast from my rifle sent him back down the side of the rock. There was a lot of hollering and shouting as they called me every evil name they could think of. I was just hoping my men had heard the shot."

Jack's storytelling reminded Bud of the nights the Baron read from James Fennimore Cooper novels. Each element of Jack's story brought on more questions. Bud asked, "I wonder why they didn't rush you all at once?"

"I thought the same thing myself. I suspect their Chief told them to draw my fire and get me to use up my shots, and then rush me while I was reloading. They didn't know I had no way to reload. I guess thirty minutes passed, maybe longer. I was spread eagle on my belly, waiting. Several braves kept peeking their heads over the edge, and then ducking back down. By then, there had to be fifteen all along the edge. Two or three at a time would jump up and then duck back down. They didn't want to stay up long enough for me to shoot. What they didn't realize was their tactic saved my life. I would threaten them with my empty rifle and bluff them back down. Just when I was beginning to think they would never risk charging me, I heard a war cry that signaled they were on their way over the rim. I waited until five of them were fully on top of the rock and heading toward me at a dead run."

Bud pulled Lightning to a halt. He could tell Jack was getting to the most exciting part of the story and he didn't want to miss a word. "Major, please continue. The wind was blowing and I was missing a few words."

Jack thought for a moment as if he was trying to remember the events exactly as they unfolded. Jack had never told the story to anyone, other than the men present that day. Finally, he began again. "I remember the first one was heavily painted. He was carrying a tomahawk and had it ready to strike when I pulled the trigger. He fell to one side into one of the others as I pulled off another round. The second shot was as deadly as the first. Then I fired the other three rounds with the pistol in my right hand. Five Indians piled up in front of me, providing me some protection. The first one fell within a meter from where I lay. I crawled on my belly and placed my empty rifle across his limp body. The others stopped looking over the rim for a while, screams of anger and profanities spewing from their mouths. I knew I had to be ready for another assault. I shoot better with my right hand, so I switched the loaded pistol for the one I just emptied."

Jack paused and took a drink of water, passing his canteen to Bud. Bud took a deep drink of water and replaced the cork in the gourd. Then he turned in his saddle so he could look into Jack's eyes as he exclaimed, "That's pretty darn amazing!"

"I honestly thought that was going to be my demise. I was sure others would be behind the first five. One brave started to poke his head up, and then ducked back down. I knew he was trying to get the courage to see if he could get up on the top and fire before I could. He was carrying a rifle and each time he would jump up, I'd fake like I was drawing a bead on him with my rifle. Finally, after we played cat and mouse for a while, I noticed a second brave way over to my right. He was doing the same thing. I realized they were dividing and getting ready to rush me from opposite directions. I got up on one knee and waited for them to give a war cry. Sure as flowers bloom in the spring, the war cry sounded and over the periphery came two braves, about thirty yards apart. They each were carrying British muskets. I took a chance and shot the one on my right. I hit him high and the lead shattered his shoulder blade. I didn't kill him right then. He fell backwards down the incline. I then put a round in the pit of the other brave's stomach. He crumpled to the granite surface. I wanted to crawl over and grab his rifle, but didn't know how many others might be waiting at the edge."

Bud again jumped ahead by asking, "How many Comanche were there?"

"I never got a good count, but from what my men tell me, between sixty and seventy five. Contrary to the myths that have floated around, I still had three rounds and my knife when I heard my men shooting at the base of the rock, surprising the Comanche who had their attention focused on me. That was the sweetest sound I ever heard. Finally, after about fifteen minutes, Henry McCullough hollered up, 'You okay?' By the time I got to the base of Enchanted Rock, one of the men had retrieved my horse. I'll never be caught without my ammunition again, and that's a promise. One stupid mistake is more than enough.

If God had not been looking out for me, my scalp would be dangling from some Comanche's belt. I am indeed a lucky man to have survived the ordeal on top of the Enchanted Rock."

Bud couldn't help but recount Big Foot Wallace sharing his impression of Jack Hays. "Jack would fight a rattlesnake with one hand tied behind his back and spot the snake three bites." After viewing his leader's face when he spoke of being isolated on that rock, with no way to escape, he could see how Big Foot would come to that opinion.

They scouted for six weeks before returning to San Antonio for supplies and rest. While there, President Houston sent word that he wanted to raise a force of about 150 men to patrol the border. Jack knew that number was impossible to assemble. The Republic had no money. Most of the men were too poor to leave their farms or businesses for extended periods. Jack knew if he could get fifty men, it would be a miracle. He would have to depend on new volunteers. He wrote a few letters asking local men in various cities and towns to spread the word. He felt there was no urgency, assuming it would take a few months for Santa Anna to regroup and mount another invasion. His immediate problem was the large band of cowboy bandits spread across the lower part of Texas in Tamulipas. The strip of land was a safe haven for outlaws, both Mexican and Anglo. They posed an even larger threat to the citizens than the Comanche.

Hays, eighteen rangers and Falcco headed for Cuero. From there, they traveled down to Corpus Christi. The second day out, Jack was riding point when he topped a hill and spotted a single rider on the opposite ridge. He surmised the rider was a lookout for the bandits and motioned for Miller to take one flank and McCullough the other. He instructed them to pretend to be trying to catch the bandit, but hold back. Jack was hoping if they frightened the rider just enough, he would believe he could get away and when he retreated, he would lead them to the bandits' camp. Jack's plan worked like a Swiss watch; the picket took off like a scared antelope with Jack, Bud, and Henry pretending to be spurring and whipping their horses in hot pursuit. When the bandit felt he could shake them, he made a forty-five degree turn to his left. Jack knew he was now on his way to the main camp. That's when Hays gave the signal for the men to spur their mounts into an all-out charge. The three were closing ground fast when from their right came Falcco on his mustang, flashing ahead of them. "Shoot him," shouted Jack. Falcco, at a dead run, pulled his rifle to his shoulder and knocked the fleeing rider from his saddle. The momentum carried the four through a thicket and into the middle of the bandits' camp. The cowboys were startled and began running for their horses, stumbling, jumping back up, stumbling, and struggling back up again. Jack, Bud, Henry and Falcco didn't wait for the other rangers. They began killing bandits right and left. Fourteen cowboy bandits were killed or captured, while miraculously, no rangers were wounded in the fight. Falcco hung four new scalps on his waistband. Jack was frustrated the leader of the gang had escaped or perhaps had not been in the camp.

For the next two months, the rangers scoured the territory without any further incident. At night, the men sang songs and told stories. Bud spent much of his free time reading, and so did Jack. Each carried a bible and at least one book. One night, Bud found Jack sitting by the campfire reading a large, well-worn book. When Bud asked what he was reading, Jack replied, "Alexander the Great. He was the most brilliant general the world has ever known. He always used a smaller army to defeat almost impossible odds by out-thinking the enemy. I have employed some of his battle tactics when dealing with our enemies."

Bud ribbed Jack by saying, "I guess you lured the Comanche into a trap on top of the Enchanted Rock."

Without any change of expression, Hays answered, "Truer words have never been spoken. When I saw them at the base of the rock, I thought to myself, now I have them where I want them." He could only carry the charade so far, as he laughed and said, "Alexander would never have gained the title of the Great doing dumb things like that. He was great because no leader before or after him has matched his strategic vision and superior intellect on the battlefield. Santa Anna could have learned from Alexander. When Alexander captured a country, he spared the defeated leaders and invited the conquered soldiers to join his army. If Santa Anna had not slaughtered the men at the Alamo or Goliad, he would still be in control of Texas. Especially Goliad. I would bet my pistols many Anglos would have joined his army to secure peace in the territory. Too bad Alexander died so young and Santa Anna has lived so long. Alexander was only thirty-three when he had conquered the entire known world. Jesus Christ was also thirty-three when He captured the hearts of millions without firing a shot."

Bud was surprised at the depth of Jack's analysis. He was determined to learn more, and now that he had money, Bud planned to buy the great books of the world. The two men spent more time together and dreamed of what they would do after Mexico calmed down and the Indians expelled. Jack admitted that adventure was in his blood. He would probably seek new frontiers. Bud told of wanting to marry, have children, and establish a cattle ranch in Bastrop. He shared that he had not come to Texas seeking fame and glory, but revenge, and had found the taste very bitter. He met too many brown people who were the backbone of Texas and could no longer toss everyone with brown skin in the same group with Santa Anna.

The mention of Bastrop aroused some interest in Jack. He asked Bud if he knew the Jennings family.

"I cannot say I've met them, but I know of the family. I understand Gordon Jennings was the oldest man to die in the Alamo. His widow and children live not all that far from my place. Gordon's brother Charles was killed with my pa in Goliad. I know of the brave little Catherine Jennings who rode to warn the families along the river that the Mexicans were coming. I heard she was ten at the time. Katy is now about seventeen." Bud grinned before he finished his thoughts, "I guess I should be more neighborly."

Jack laughed and told Bud how the Jennings family had a long history of heroics dating back to the American Revolution. Bud made a mental note to go by and personally thank little Katy for her brave ride and tell her mother he was proud to be their neighbor.

Bud's heart was content. He now had a good friend in Jack. Likewise, Jack trusted Bud and respected his discretion. The two bonded as if they were brothers.

Chapter Thirty-Two
Disaster

Mary Maverick and the children stayed in Richmond with Jane Long until Sam felt confident the Mexicans would not immediately return; however, with the reality of the enemy's probable return to San Antonio, he relocated his family to La Grange. He purchased a home there and quickly had his slaves build a shed for the kitchen and a separate side room for the children. The slaves' quarters were located in a log barn about fifty yards from the main house.

Mary, in her typical fashion, immediately made friends and became involved in the community. Her first week in La Grange, she was invited to a quilting party. The women brought any old cloth they could find. Mary's cloth was back in San Antonio; however, she brought one of Sam's colored shirts to contribute to the quilt. There was a wooden rack suspended from the ceiling with broadcloth stretched from edge to edge. Each lady chose a section and began stitching pieces onto the broadcloth. The pattern of the day was "the butterfly" because of the variations of color and the shape of the patches. The finished quilt was a conglomeration of cloth, from wool to linen and cotton; yet, when all the scraps were put together, the result was a stunning work of art.

Once his family was secure and the house complete, Sam left for Alabama at the end of April 1842. He needed to collect money owed him in Tuscaloosa and bring Mary's sister Lizzie to Texas. Lizzie was nineteen, single, and deeply lonely for her brothers and sister. Sam rode his favorite horse Mex to Galveston, left him in the livery stable, and boarded a ship for Mobile. Once in Alabama, he took care of his business, and then helped Lizzie pack, and purchased a fine mare for her to ride once they arrived in Texas.

Once back in La Grange, Sam worked on his books and sealed up some pressing business deals. Then, near the end of August, a rider approached the farmhouse telling Sam court would be in session on August 22nd and he was requested to attend. Sam had Griff and two other slaves hitch a wagon and accompany him to San Antonio so they could transport some household goods back to La Grange. Sam especially wanted the beds for Mary and their baby daughter.

Mary, Lizzie, and a friend, Colonel Dancy, rode along with Sam and Griff for about seven miles. Mary felt a strong premonition that Sam should not go on to San Antonio. She had an uncanny ability to sense danger. During the resettling trip after the March 6th invasion, they came upon a vacant log cabin that travelers often used for a night's lodging. When Sam had wanted to stop, Mary insisted evil lurked inside and refused to spend the night in the old cabin. Sam knew not to argue with Mary so they moved on and set up camp under a giant oak tree about a half-mile away. That night, the heavens put on a fireworks display as lightning flashed and thunder roared. Rain poured from the sky most of the night like water rolling over a waterfall. Sam became irritated with Mary for not letting them seek shelter in the old log house. The next morning, when they passed the cabin again, they were stunned to see smoldering logs where the cabin had stood. Lightning struck the old log cabin, burning it to the ground while they were asleep under the spreading oak. Even though she sensed danger, Mary did not express her concerns for Sam's return to San Antonio. She would later berate herself for not telling her husband of her premonition.

On September 9th Sam ate dinner with his old friend Jack Hays at a local cantina. They talked about defending the city against marauding cowboy bandits and possible Indian depredations. The recent predatory attacks by the Comanche were causing concern among the locals. Jack had the area blanketed with his scouts and spies and should any undesirables approach the city, he would notify Sam and the court well ahead of their arrival. Jack didn't have to wait long. Around 4:00 AM the next morning, two of his spies came banging on his door; they had spotted a band of undesirables nearby and feared they were planning to enter the city. Jack quickly dressed and rousted Henry McCullough, Bud, and two other rangers. He wanted to check out the situation for himself, having learned from experience not to totally trust some of his secret agents. He stopped to relay the information to Sam Maverick so the court would be aware of the possible threat. The five men then headed southwest to scout for signs of any bandits.

Sunday morning, fifty-three Texans were conducting court as usual, giving little thought to the report of bandits. They knew if danger lurked nearby, Jack Hays would locate and dispose of the threat in plenty of time. The court proceeded in a normal fashion, secure in knowing the best men in Texas would stand between them and any rogue cowboys.

Santa Anna had an aversion to hiring Mexicans as Generals. His paranoia was so pervasive that he would not allow anyone of Mexican heritage to gain significant power, for fear of a coup. Only two of his generals with him when he defeated the men at the Alamo and murdered those at Goliad were native born: Urrea and Sesma Ampudia; Tolsa and Gaona were of Cuban descent; Filisola was Italian, and Woll, French.

Adrián Woll was born on December 2nd, 1795 in a small French town near Paris. Educated for the military profession, he served as a lieutenant in a lancer regiment of the Imperial Guard. In 1815, he was a captain adjutant major in the Tenth Legion of the National Guard of the Seine. Then, seeking adventure, Woll sailed to America carrying letters of introduction to General Winfield Scott, headquartered in Baltimore, Maryland. Scott told the young French officer of the opportunities in the Mexican revolutionary movement against Spain and advised him that a young man like himself, so highly skilled in the military arts, would have no difficulty finding use for his services in a country riddled with strife. Woll followed Scott's advice and joined the staff of General Francisco Mina as a lieutenant colonel. He landed with Mina near the mouth of the Santander River on April 15th, 1817. When the Mina expedition failed, Woll looked for ways to participate in the Mexican War of Independence. General Santa Anna soon hired him. After Mexico achieved independence from Spain, Woll became a naturalized citizen, married a local girl and started a family. Promoted to colonel in 1828, he served as Santa Anna's aide-de-camp during the capture of Tampico from the Spaniards in 1829. Woll was promoted to brigadier general in 1832, and was awarded the prestigious Cross of Tampico. He then participated in Santa Anna's coup against President Anastasio Bustamante, which successfully propelled General M. Gómez Pedraza into the presidency.

From Guadalajara, Woll led a small, well-organized force, which then defeated Lt. Col. Joaquín Solórzano at Taxinastla. On November 15th, he entered Colima and placed President Pedraza's people in office. Once things settled down, Woll moved his family to Morelos. In 1835, he served as quartermaster general during Santa Anna's campaign to squelch the Federalist uprising led by a pureblooded Indian, Juan Álvarez. After his victory over Alvarez, Woll turned south of Mexico City and defeated an army led by Francisco Zacatecas. His string of quick victories caught the attention of Santa Anna. In 1836, he was appointed quartermaster general of the army for Santa Anna's invasion of Texas. On March 8th, he reached San Antonio and reported to General Vicente Filisola, second in command of the Mexican forces. After the battle of the Alamo, Santa Anna ordered Woll to join General Joaquín Sesma and march his 720 men to Gonzales, and from there, over to San Felipe. Finding the towns vacated, they marched to Harrisburg and on to Anahuac. General Sesma confronted some of General Sam Houston's men on the opposite bank of the Colorado River at Beeson's Ferry near Columbus. The Texans were able to hold their position while General Houston moved his main forces in retreat to Groce Point.

In April, Santa Anna reached Atascosito Pass on the Colorado, finding the waters too strong for them to cross. Woll assigned a battalion to construct rafts to ferry across the remainder of the army arriving under Filisola while Santa Anna moved a division to the east, where he was soundly defeated at the battle of San Jacinto. During the chase, Woll became Filisola's chief of staff. When a messenger brought news of Santa Anna's surrender, Filisola dispatched Woll to the Texans' camp as an emissary. On April 30th, Woll rode into the Texans' camp under the pretext of establishing the terms of an armistice, but actually came only to gain information on the manpower, armaments, and resources of the enemy. The injured Houston was in New Orleans, so thirty-three-year-old General Thomas Rusk was in charge. Rusk saw the transparence of Woll's visit and placed him under arrest. After a few weeks in custody, Woll was released and provided safe passage to Goliad. From Goliad, he joined the retreating Mexican army and returned home.

Woll became second in command and head of the Department of Coahuila in June of 1842. During the summer, he received orders from Santa Anna to invade Texas; a mission he had waited to perform. Finally, he would get to retaliate for his capture while under a white flag. Woll was told to capture San Antonio, then move down the Guadalupe River to Gonzales and across to Goliad. Santa Anna gave him thirty days to accomplish his mission. To avoid Texas scouts, General Woll crossed the Rio Grande at Presidio, a tiny fort about three hundred miles west of Laredo, along the banks of the Rio Grande River. The fort was so remote, no one considered the outpost to have any value and it was unoccupied at the time the army passed. Woll knew the Texans would have spies watching the southern and western roads into San Antonio, so he took a page out of Jack Hays' book: Come at the enemy from an unexpected location. Jack and his men scouted from Uvalde south to Goliad, crisscrossing back and forth, never imagining the Mexican forces would invade from the north. The mountains on the north side of San Antonio near Boerne gave perfect cover until the French General was ready to attack. He was able to move a large army undetected in to the valley of Leon Spring until he was ready to attack. As the sun rose on Sunday, September 11, 1842, General Woll was ready to make his move. He was confident no one had spotted his army and slowly began his parade down the mountainside into the heart of San Antonio.

About ten miles south of town, the sun was just tipping the tops of the mesquite trees as Jack Hays finished his cup of coffee. He and his four men had seen no signs of trouble and would return to San Antonio and report that, once again, the spies had given false information. As the Mexican general moved his forces into the San Antonio valley, Jack and his rangers were mounted and on their way for the three hour ride north.

As the first wave of Woll's soldiers entered the outskirts of town, they passed a small Mexican farmer's home. A lad of thirteen saw the army and ran to warn the town. Following a deer trail, he outran the army, and reaching the Military Plaza in total exhaustion, he fell on the rope, tugging with all his strength to ring the warning bell. General Woll heard the bell, but since it was Sunday, he assumed the sound was a call to church services. The locals knew differently. Sam Maverick and those assembled in court wasted no time in getting to the Plaza. Thinking the boy mistook bandits to be soldiers, Sam suggested they gather at his house to make their stand. Sam opened the massive front doors and closed them quickly after fifty-two Texans rushed in. The two-and-a-half foot parapet, which encircled the perimeter of his house, created an ideal place from which to take a good shot at the enemy. When the first wave of Mexican soldiers entered the Military Plaza, the Texans opened fire, killing eight. Only John Twohig suffered any injury, a smashed wrist, in the first round of gunfire.

The moment General Woll realized there was armed resistance he summoned a parley. Sam Maverick was chosen to represent the Texans. Woll was courteous and soft spoken, but exuded the confidence of a man who had his opponent outnumbered almost thirty-to-one. The general promised the Texans they would be treated as prisoners of war should they put down their arms. He told Sam they could remain under house arrest without shackles, and would be provided food and water. Since Sam was an honorable man and his word as solid as the Ten Commandments, he felt hopeful the Mexicans would treat their captives with respect. He thanked the General for his offer, telling him he needed to confer with the rest of the men and would give him an answer shortly. Maverick knew it would be an impossible battle to win; all Woll had to do was knock his house walls down with a cannon blast. Sam also knew Jack Hays would see the Mexican Army and summon additional help. When he explained his rationale to the others, they were in full agreement to lay down their arms and await rescue.

Woll was true to his word and even allowed Mrs. Elliott to visit the captured Texans, supplying them with food and necessities. Sam entrusted Mrs. Elliott to smuggle twenty gold doubloons, along with an encouraging letter to Mary. He assured his wife that he was healthy and in good spirits and expected the situation to be resolved by the time she read his letter. No one knew how long the general would occupy the city, but the Texans fully expected to be released when Woll pulled out.

By the time Jack and his rangers reached the edge of town, they found all the roads leading into the city blocked by Mexican soldiers. Jack felt a knot in the pit of his stomach as he realized they had been tricked. He knew there was nothing the five of them could do, so they rode west to Seguin to regroup. Jack fumed. Realizing several of his dear friends had been captured, he wanted to take full blame, but Henry and Bud would hear nothing of it. There was no reason to expect that the Mexicans would invade from the north. The circuitous route made them march an additional six hundred miles to reach San Antonio. No one could have predicted the Mexican army would go that far out of the way to avoid detection.

When Henry asked, "How did they get around us? How did they muster the effort?"

Jack shot back, "Alexander the Great had his men scale a seven-hundred foot wall, in ice and snow, to give them the advantage. A smart General always does the unexpected. I got us into this mess and now I have to find a way to get us out."

The rangers desperately needed food and supplies. The help they considered necessary came quickly as Ben McCullough was waiting for them with an abundance of fresh beef, salt, sugar, corn and coffee. After a brief conference, the two leaders decided to set up camp at Cibolo Creek, about six miles from San Antonio. The creek provided an ample supply of fresh water and the bank provided shelter.

Jack wrote a letter to the Secretary of War:

I immediately made the best possible arrangements and started with five Rangers to spy out the approach and get a count of the number, but not able to find them on any public road. However, the next morning, I discovered they came down through the mountains on the north into the city. Once we reached the city, we tried to enter, but found it surrounded and impossible to impregnate. What followed is communicated by the prisoners that surrendered. Woll commands the Mexican Army. I stayed around town all day of the 11th and have spies watching the city. If I can, I will try to watch their approach to the river.

The Mexicans attacked the place and the citizens made a slight resistance, killing eight. When they realized the army was too strong, they surrendered 53 in number. I examined the company and found it to contain 1,300 men, mostly regulars, and 2 pieces of artillery. I shall continue to watch their movement and would like a few well-mounted men to join me as quickly as possible for the purpose of spying. Then we need to assemble a respectable force and free our citizens.

Respectfully,

John C. Hays

While Jack was writing the Secretary of War, President Houston was in the process of moving the capital from Austin to Washington-on-the-Brazos. The City Fathers had offered furnished buildings for the Congress to hold sessions, free of charge. The Lockharts would provide free lodging for Sam and Margaret, and a local lawyer offered the use of his offices to administer the Republic's business. The Republic was almost bankrupt and the move would save the government $5,000 a year. President Houston saw the opportunity as a sign from God and the result of the fervent prayers of his wife.

Houston sent Thomas "Peg Leg" Ward and William "Uncle Buck" Pettus to remove the archives from Austin and deliver them to Washington-on-the-Brazos. They did not trust making the trip in a wagon for fear of being spotted by Indians, and traveled by horseback instead. Once in Austin, they rented wagons and started loading the documents. The townspeople, seeing what was taking place, surrounded the wagons and refused to let pair leave town. One woman, Angelina Eberley, was especially passionate. Rushing into the street, she began waving her pistol, promising to kill any man who moved a wagon. When her pistol did not stop their departure, she commandeered a cannon and fired at them. Missing the wagon, the blast knocked a hole in side of the Congressional building. One shot is all it took; there would be no removal of papers that day. Houston would try again at the end of the year.

After the incident, T.W. "Peg Leg" Ward had remained in Austin and suffered daily verbal abuse by the citizens of Austin for trying to move the Republic's archives. Houston wrote Ward:

"Though I have not written often, there is seldom a day that passes that you are not in my thoughts and prayers. I know your unpleasant position, surrounded as you are by so many difficulties and disagreeable circumstances. I will soon send you help."

Your friend,

Sam

Houston called on two old Texas Ranger friends whom he knew he could trust: Eli Chandler and Thomas Smith. Both were men of courage, having proved their worth dozens of times, starting at the battle of San Jacinto. Their assignment was to bring the archives from Austin to Washington-on-the-Brazos. He told them, "Do not be thwarted in this undertaking. You are acquainted with the conditions of things in Austin and the exasperation of feeling pervading by those who are directly interested in that God-forsaken place. You will govern your movements so as to suffer no detriment to either yourselves or the property you may have in your charge. Be prepared to act with efficiency."

Sam estimated it would take fifteen wagons to carry the archives and made sure Eli and Thomas recruited a sufficient number of men to handle the team and protect themselves from the citizens of Austin. Houston issued a Presidential proclamation making their actions legal. His proclamation read: "All persons are hereby enjoined and especially commanded in the name of the Constitution of the Republic, to in no way to interfere with, obstruct or impede the removal of the archives from Austin and moving them to the current capital of the Republic in Washington-on-the-Brazos."

It took two weeks for the Eli and Thomas to assemble the number of wagons and men needed for the mission. Peg Leg Ward was secretly notified of the plan. Just past midnight, with a new moon showing a faint sliver of light, the expedition rolled into Austin and began loading the wagons. As they were loading the last wagon, the roosters began to crow. The Austin alarm clock caused a stir among the citizens, especially Miss Angelina Eberley. She hurried to the cannon the moment she saw the wagon train in front of the Congressional building. Angelina knew if the papers were removed from Austin, her business in the Lubbock Hotel would die. She took matters into her own hands and once more fired off a round from the cannon. Eli and Thomas knew it was time to leave even though some papers would be left behind. They headed out of Austin, taking the old road up through Brushy Creek instead of south via Bastrop, feeling that to be the safest route.

It didn't take Angelina long to organize a substantial posse and catch up to the slow-moving wagons. A few shots were fired when Eli called the caravan to a halt. He felt the papers were not worth killing a bunch of his fellow Texans over; he told the men to turn the wagons around and return to Austin. Once back in Austin, they decided to keep the archives in the Lubbock Hotel. Angelina won.

It took a week for Ward's letter to reach the President. After Houston read the news, he penned a letter to Ward commending him for his efforts and told his friend that should the archives be destroyed, it would not be the blame of the executive office. Houston was disappointed he did not retrieve the papers, but was impressed with the Texans' spirit. He was governing a special breed of independent people. No place on the earth had such a freethinking, self-assured group come together to build a nation. Not even those settling the United States possessed the same fire and determination as those who chose to settle in the Republic of Texas.

When the folks of Austin learned how easily San Antonio had fallen and Judge Hightower and fifty-two lawyers and court officials captured, they softened their position on keeping the capital in Austin. They realized how damaging it would be to the Republic if the Mexicans captured the archives. That didn't mean they would let the papers go; they opted to bury the archives under a city building. The citizens remained confident that one day the Mexican problem would be resolved and the capital would move back to Austin.

Sam knew the San Antonio hostage crisis was in the capable hands of Jack Hays and Mathew Caldwell. He also knew the people of Texas were going to be calling for blood; they would want to invade Mexico in retaliation. He would have to juggle with superior skill to make it appear he was willing to go after the Mexicans, while at the same time, making sure there was no overt action taken to force an all-out confrontation.

Meanwhile back at Cibolo Creek, Jack and Bud were able to capture a Mexican spy who told them reinforcements were coming to support Woll. Bud could tell he was making up the story. He told Jack, "He is lying. I can tell by the way he keeps covering his mouth with his hands when he is talking." The Baron had taught Bud to read a man's body actions rather than rely only on his words. Jack agreed, and they returned to camp with their captive in tow. Then they asked him for information again, this time with one end of a rope around his neck and the other end tossed over an oak tree limb. The spy admitted that it would be several months before Woll would receive more troops. This invasion was not like the two-day incursion; the Mexican army would occupy San Antonio until a larger force arrived, and then march clear across Texas. Jack knew immediate action had to be conducted before Woll got entrenched in his position. If they could defeat Woll before any reinforcements arrived, it might put a stop to the Mexicans' attempts to re-take Texas.

Mexicans loyal to Texas were slipping in and out of the city, giving reports that substantiated Jack's assumptions. Jack, Bud, and three other rangers captured a second Mexican rider carrying a message that when translated, read: *"The second campaign against Texas has been opened to eradicate all those who are enemies of Santa Anna."* This confirmed what the Texans knew: Woll would have to be driven out soon or his forces would grow too large for the Texans to deal with. The survival of the Republic lay in the balance. Word spread quickly and soon men began arriving from across Texas to join the fight. The army grew daily and the Texans started devising a plan to extract the enemy and rescue their fellow citizens.

Colonel "Old-Paint" Mathew Caldwell brought 120 men from Gonzales, and others joined along the way. Caldwell had only been home a few weeks since being in a Mexican prison for eighteen months after the failed Santa Fe Expedition. The memory of the Mexicans fixing ropes around the necks of the Texans and leading them like animals to Juarez was still fresh in his mind. When the Mexican government released the Santa Fe prisoners, they had to swear they would never again bear arms against Mexico. Caldwell regarded the oath taken under duress as meaningless and made a vow of his own never to surrender to a Mexican soldier again.

In the Caldwell group were two free Negro slaves. One was Samuel McCullough Jr. whose father was a white plantation owner and his mother a slave. After he was born, his father gave the child his name, and freed him and his mother. Samuel came to Texas in 1835 and earned the distinction of being the first man to shed blood in the Texas Revolution. He was one of sixty-three men to fight under Collinsworth and capture the fortress at Goliad. He was also the only man wounded in the fight. Although Congress passed a law prohibiting free slaves from living in the Republic, an exception was made for Sam McCullough Jr. and he was granted a half league of land for his service to the Republic. The other free slave was Hendrick Arnold who had moved to Texas and participated in the battle for San Antonio. Deaf Smith and Hendrick became friends and after General Cos was driven out, Deaf invited Hendrick to his home. Smith's eldest stepdaughter fell madly in love with Hendrick, and he with her, and they wed.

Jack and Mathew Caldwell needed information. No white man could enter the city and all Mexicans sympathetic to the Anglos were known to the San Antonio Mexican community; the task of spying fell on the backs of the two free black men. They both spoke Spanish, and if caught, were to say they were free slaves trying to get to Mexico. Their risk was minimal, yet any information they could obtain would be of immeasurable value to the Texans. The pair entered San Antonio and moved about the city with freedom.

News reached La Grange that fighting forces were gathering on Salado Creek under Colonel Caldwell and Jack Hays and preparing to drive the invaders from Texas soil. Captain Nicholas M. Dawson, Caldwell's friend, immediately raised an army of fifty-three men. Mary Maverick seized the opportunity to send assistance to her husband, requesting that Griff go to see if he could help his master. Mary promised Griff his freedom if he would go to Sam's aid. He replied, "I is already free. My Massa treats me like a brother. You ain't got to do nothin' for Ol' Griff. He loves Massa and will do what he cans to heps."

Mary had Jinny sew some coins into Griff's clothes, and gave him supplies and a rifle. Mary instructed him to pretend to be a runaway slave, knowing Mexico would protect a runaway. There were screams of pain as big Griff climbed on a mule, waved goodbye, and was on his way to meet the La Grange group. Jinny cried all day after Griff left and the other slaves moped around in a somber mood. Griff had never been away before and the other slaves were scared because he was their leader.

Mary feared for Griff's safety and for her brothers, William and Andrew, who were with Caldwell and Hays. The twenty-four-year-old Mary feared she might lose her husband, top slave, and two brothers. She kept a brave face in front of her sister, the slaves, children and friends, but at night, she wept bitterly. Being a woman during the early years of Texas took more backbone and courage than can possibly be imagined.

Santa Anna lost the war of 1836 because he underestimated the resolve of the Texans, and did not understand the climate or topography of east Texas. He never considered that snowmelt eight hundred miles to the west would affect the streams in east Texas. Houston had counted on the flooding to impede Santa Anna's advance as he led his dispirited forces from one swollen river to another. This time, Santa Anna gave Woll explicit instructions not to invade during the spring flooding season.

When the two black scouts returned, they reported that Woll had two large cannons; the Texans had only pistols and rifles. They estimated the Mexican forces numbered over 1,300; the Texans had only 257 men. No one expected Woll would leave the city willingly, but if the Texans could kill a hundred of his men, he might be forced to leave his secure place and seek revenge. Jack Hays and Ben McCullough conferred with Matt Caldwell and they agreed they would have to lure the Mexicans out of San Antonio. Hays had an idea, explaining to the group, "I need men whose horses can make the ride to the Alamo and back. I know many of your horses cannot make the trip, especially on the way back when we will be running for our lives. Only those of you with truly exceptional horses step forward."

Thirty-six men responded. Jack eliminated five because he knew their horses couldn't make the grueling ride. One more stepped back, knowing he acted in haste. With Caldwell's soldiers using the creek bank as a breastwork, Jack knew it was up to him to lure the Mexicans to Caldwell.

A group of thirty-one rode to within two hundred yards of the large Mexican camp near the Alamo. Bud and Ben McCullough were at Jack's side waiting to see what their leader was going to do. Suddenly Jack slapped his warhorse's rump with his reins, gave a shout and charged the enemy. The rangers followed, shouting insults in Spanish and firing into the crowd; 13 Mexican soldiers were killed or wounded in a matter of seconds. Then, as quickly as their assault had begun, the group whirled their horses around and retreated as though their pants were on fire. The Mexicans fell for the trap. About 400 mounted lancers gave chase, enraged at the rangers' brazen and deadly attack. The Mexicans on fresh mounts were gaining on the rangers who turned in their saddles and started shooting to keep them at bay. When the rangers got to Salado Creek, they spilled over the bank and through Caldwell's men with Jack shouting, "We brought you a present!"

Caldwell, as thin as a fence post from starvation, screamed, "Boys, ever since I spent those months in a Mexican hell hole, I have longed for the chance to fight these rascals. The time is now. Do not shoot 'til you see the whiskers on their chins. We don't have the means to take any prisoners, so shoot to kill. Huzza, huzza for Texas, give the barbarians hot lead!"

The first charge cost the Mexicans thirty-seven men. They regrouped and charged again. Once more, the Texans, hiding beneath the creek bank, killed another twenty-three. Woll, hearing of Jack's attack on his army, made an unwise move. Revenge provoked him to order the remainder of his army to the battle scene. He found a mountain about a mile from the fight so he could observe the action. He then set up his cannons from another hilltop closer to the creek and began shelling the Texans with grapeshot. The only damage done was to tree limbs being shattered. From Woll's position, he was unable to see the Texans; only his men falling like matchsticks in a strong wind. Charge after charge was repelled with the deadly accuracy of the Texans' long rifles.

While the Texans were succeeding at the battle of Salado Creek, only a mile and a half away, a calamity was occurring. In response to Caldwell's call for volunteers, Captain Nicholas Dawson and fifty-three men, including Griff, marched down from La Grange. Believing Caldwell's forces to be in grave danger, Dawson chose not to wait for Captain Jesse Billingsley's company and decided his men should fight their way to the Salado camp. Near Caldwell's embattled line, around 3:30 in the afternoon, 500 Mexicans intercepted Dawson's company, two 6-pound cannons supporting their efforts. Dawson and his men dismounted in a mesquite thicket where Fort Sam Houston now stands. Dawson threatened, "I'll shoot the first man who runs."

The Texans were quickly surrounded, but repelled the first cavalry charge and killed nineteen of the enemy. The Mexicans retreated out of the Texans' rifle range and opened fire with their cannons. Unlike Caldwell, Dawson's group was not protected. Billingsley's company, which arrived while the fight was in progress, was too weak to go to Dawson's aid and Caldwell's men on Salado Creek remained heavily engaged. The Texans put up a vigorous resistance, but seeing they were defeated, the badly wounded Dawson reluctantly raised a white bloodied shirt taken off the lifeless body of sixteen-year-old Thomas Riggins. The Mexicans continued firing. Lead balls ripped through Dawson several more times. Seeing surrender was impossible, he gasped out, "Let victory be purchased with blood." A.S. Miller, Bud's uncle, grabbed the white shirt clutched in Dawson's dead hand and in token surrender, waved the banner as he rode toward the Mexican lines. Holding the bloody shirt high in the air, he spurred his horse forward. Miraculously, Miller galloped straight through the enemy line and headed unscathed for Seguin. Henry Woods, after witnessing the death of his father and the mortal wounding of his brother Norman, turned in fear and escaped into the black gun smoke. Some Texans continued to resist, while others laid down their arms. Heroic in the fight was Grifffin, Sam Maverick's slave. When he had no more powder, he killed two Mexicans with the butt of his rifle. When his rifle shattered over the head of a Mexican soldier, he then grabbed a mesquite limb and bludgeoned a third soldier to death. Griff died with the mesquite club in his hand after being shot nine times. Dawson's group killed ninety Mexicans and severely wounded scores more. Among those killed by Dawson's men was Vincente Cordova, who started the rebellion in Nacogdoches two years earlier, and eleven of his Cherokee. Thirty-six Texans lay dead on the battlefield; fifteen were taken prisoner, with Miller and Woods escaping. Of the fifteen Texans captured, only nine survived to return to Texas. Dawson and his men were buried in shallow graves in the mesquite thicket where they fell, Grifffin buried next to Dawson in honor of his brave end. Later, Dawson and his fallen men would be moved to La Grange and buried at Monument Hill overlooking the city.

James Willingham rejoined the fight in the last hours before Woll ordered retreat. He worried about Millie and the children, but knew if Woll achieved victory, they would have to leave their home. Only one Texan, Roger York, died and seven were wounded; York was killed by one of Cordova's Cherokee. Bud spotted the puff of smoke from the Cherokee's rifle shot and motioned for James to take the opposite bank. The two crawled toward the Cherokee's position and James let out a war cry. When the brave jumped to his feet to shoot, Bud put a rifle ball into his heart. He staggered against a tree and remained standing momentarily, even though he was dead. James took no chances, putting another chunk of lead in the middle of the Cherokee's forehead, splattering his brains against the moss covered bark.

At dark, Woll sounded the retreat, collected the three hundred dead, and left the battlefield, dejected. The Texans allowed the Mexicans to remove their dead without fear of being killed. The next day General Woll gave those killed in battle a military funeral, burying them near the Alamo.

Mary Maverick's two brothers had escaped injury, but when she heard the news of how courageously Griff had fought and died, her weeping became uncontrollable. The slaves mourned, knowing they would never hear him sing songs of their heritage again. Griff was a special man and left a void too deep to fill in the Maverick household. Mary also knew her dear Sam would have to endure without the aid of the man who had been by his side since they were boys.

Jack Hays' scouts, Sam McCullough and Hendrick Arnold slipped back into San Antonio to find out what Woll's plans were. While in town, Hendrick slipped into his house to assure his wife he was fine, and he and Sam ended up spending the night. Before going to bed, they watched ninety to a hundred locals preparing to leave the city. They had plundered the empty homes and gathered around five hundred head of cattle and horses. Then, during the night, the Mexicans and several hundred soldiers departed. The next morning, they saw General Woll gather his prisoners and head north. As soon as they were sure General Woll was leaving the city, Sam and Hendrick rushed to inform Caldwell and Hays.

President Houston called Edwin Morehouse into service. Morehouse, along with one hundred New York recruits, arrived a few hours late to the battle in San Jacinto, but later, Morehouse earned the rank of Brigadier General in response to Rafael Vásquez's attack on San Antonio. Now he was being pressed into service again to respond to the Woll invasion.

Margaret feared her husband would be on the Rio Grande fighting Mexico. Houston had no such plans, but didn't dare let anyone know; not even his wife knew his bravado was only a tactic. He had to feign retaliation without an actual invasion. When the Mexicans left so quickly, Houston sent General Morehouse to inform the troops who had so bravely rallied in defense of Texas to go home.

Jack, Ben, Bud, and several other rangers rode to a hilltop and watched the crippled Mexican army heading home in defeat. Jack could smell vulnerability like a wolf tracking a wounded animal, and he felt it was time to attack while the enemy was dejected and depressed. He found plenty of the younger men on his side; however, Mathew Caldwell and several of his older men felt it unwise to give chase, considering the enemy was armed with cannons. Their cannons' range was significantly longer than the Texans' rifles. After a heated debate, the leaders agreed to pursue and destroy the remainder of Woll's army and free the captured Texans.

Jack felt an urgency to catch up with Woll's forces before they reached the high banks of the Median River. There was no question the Mexicans would follow the De Leon Road toward Eagle Pass and cross the river just south of Crow's Creek. Jack pressed hard to catch them before they crossed the Medina, knowing the opposite bank would give them an advantage, but by the time the Texas army reached the Medina, the Mexicans were already safely on the opposite side. Hays' next goal was to catch them before they got to the banks of the Hondo River. Jack knew the area well, having surveyed there several times. On the opposite side of the Hondo, the Mexicans would be shooting down on the Texans. Hays and about a hundred men were a full mile in front of the regular army when Jack spotted the Mexican army's rear guard. He sent Bud back to inform Caldwell that the enemy was just ahead. Suddenly, a rifle cracked and Judge Jason "Storyteller" Lucky, tumbled from his horse. Blood gushed from the wound in his skull, but Lucky had indeed been lucky; the bullet had only grazed his forehead. Jack handed him a clean cloth and said, "Better hurry up and get that blood stopped 'cause we're getting ready to take some revenge."

Jack then dashed off toward the puff of smoke from the rifle shot as Bud and four other rangers followed. When they reached the area, they saw an Indian disappear into the thick brush. Everyone believed the bullet had Hays' name on it because while in San Antonio, Sam and Hendrick learned that Woll had placed a five hundred dollar bounty on Jack's head. Jack didn't want to risk following the Indian into an ambush, so the rangers turned back.

Jack again made his case to pursue the retreating army, but met with dissension among the leaders as to who would make the decision. J.H. Moore was the ranking officer, but Caldwell had just won the second most significant battle in the history of the Republic. Squabbling like chicken-pen roosters, each tried to establish their position in the pecking order. Meanwhile, the enemy was escaping. Since it was almost dark, Jack knew they could do nothing until the next day. He would take advantage of the darkness to collect information, knowing he needed more knowledge if he planned to persuade the older officers to fight. He asked Ben McCullough to go with him into the Mexicans' camp and find out what the enemy was up to. Ben warned Jack of the bounty Woll had put on his head. Jack gave a rare laugh, and answered, "They won't know it's me. I'll tell them my name is Ben McCullough."

The pair draped serapes over themselves, put on large rowel Mexican spurs and sombreros, stuck hand-rolled cigarettes in their mouths, and then asked a young soldier to accompany them. Once the three reached the edge of the camp, Jack asked the frightened soldier to hold their horses. Jack and Ben then entered the Mexican camp undetected. They ambled through as if they were attached to the unit, finding men sleeping from total exhaustion and others chatting by the campfire. Knowing how the Mexicans treated prisoners of war, Jack wanted to linger until they located Maverick and the other captives, but Ben insisted they not push their luck; their disguises would not stand up to scrutiny in the daylight. Ben finally gave in, but after two hours, even Jack realized their effort was futile. There was little doubt the general had sent the captured Texans up ahead of the main forces.

After picking up what information they could, the pair casually sauntered out of the camp. This time they noticed a guard on the road in front of them. He thought they were Mexican and asked in a cheerful voice, "Why aren't you sleeping?"

Hays replied in Spanish, "We are Texans and don't need the sleep you yellow-bellies do."

The guard lowered his musket, pointing it at the rangers. Ben nudged Jack, "Let's be careful. That fella will shoot us."

"Not a chance in heaven. You heard the fear in his voice. You keep your shotgun on him and I'll take his musket," Jack replied with confidence.

Jack walked over to the frightened Mexican, grabbed the musket and tied the soldier's hands behind his back. Then he and Ben shoved the Mexican along in front of them until they reached their horses. Jack put the captured Mexican behind the young soldier and led the way back to camp, where they delivered the captured picket to Caldwell. The captive told Caldwell that Woll was very angry about having over three hundred of his men killed and told his captains their goal was to get out of Texas without losing any more. Jack's assumptions were confirmed. He turned to Caldwell, Mayfield, Moore and Morehead, and said, "Now is the time to finish them off." His request was met with the argument that the mission was too risky, but Jack knew the root of the problem lay with Moore's ego. Moore was the ranking officer and definitely did not want Caldwell to have a say in the matter. On the other hand, Caldwell's men would not follow Moore, Mayfield or Morehead.

When daylight came, Jack was the first up and once more demanded they finish the job. Finally, a significant number of the men confessed they didn't want to go against the Mexicans' cannons. They saw what Woll's cannons had done to Dawson, and they were reluctant to face the grapeshot. Jack responded, "Give me a hundred good men and we will take those cannons." He was not a very persuasive speaker. Only eighteen rode forward. At the front of the line was Bud Miller.

Major James Mayfield then stepped up and made a rousing appeal for one hundred men to accompany Major Hays. Mayfield's results were more successful than Jack's, but they still needed more men. Caldwell requested Reverend John Morrell to make a plea. Slowly men started riding out from the group. When enough men had come forward, Jack gave an inspection, making sure each was on a capable mount. His mood was somber as he stood up in his stirrups, waved his arm, and shouted, "Follow my lead. We are going to take their cannons. The rest of you, get ready to mop up. When we finish, there won't be anything but cactus between you and victory."

The dispute over who would lead was still not settled when Jack and his men left camp, but he assumed they would get the issue worked out and be ready to take the fight to the Mexicans once his group captured the cannons. Jack didn't look back and failed to realize that only about 30 of the original 150 volunteers were following him. He pressed on and when he was within four hundred yards of the cannon, he yelled, "Give 'em your best boys. Shoot to kill." Then he gave his horse the reins and charged forward. The Texans were screaming at the top of their lungs when the Mexicans fired their cannon, grapeshot sailing harmlessly over their heads. Jack was counting on the Mexicans shooting high; their first shots always were. As the Mexicans were frantically reloading, Jack and his men were closing in fast. Realizing there would not be time to reload, those around the cannons opened fire with their muskets. The speed of Jack's push brought the rangers within shotgun and pistol range. Jack felt something rip into his leg, and his horse lunged to the right. He knew his warhorse had been hit, but the bullet didn't keep him from running. Beside him was Big Foot Wallace on a mule, braying with each lunge forward. On the other side was Bud Miller, urging Lightning on with speed to match his name. The Mexicans were gunned down before they could reload their muskets. Nick Wren's horse was killed within thirty yards of the cannon, knocking him out cold as he slammed to the ground. Jack saw Nick fall and assumed he was dead. As they reached the first cannon, Bud leaned under the neck of Lightning and shot a soldier through the spokes of the cannon wheel. Ben and four rangers chased down seven others as they attempted to scale a dirt bank, killing them as they clawed their way to the top. The rangers captured the cannon, killing all the Mexican soldiers in the process. Jack looked back to see if the Texas army was advancing. To his dismay, they were still at the bottom of the hill. Some were already mounted and heading north. Jack and his thirty rangers had unknowingly advanced alone.

Anticipating the Texans would turn the cannons on them, General Woll placed women and children between his army and the rangers, using them as human shields. The General knew the weakness of the Texans.

Jack realized they wouldn't be able to hold the cannons without the army's help. The rangers found themselves in a perilous situation as the Mexicans had regrouped and around four hundred soldiers were moving toward the thirty rangers. The rangers had no choice but to rejoin the army at the base of the hill. Jack demanded an explanation for why the forces held back. When he was told it was a command issue, he let them know, in no uncertain terms, they had acted in a cowardly manner. When nothing could be settled Caldwell told the group, "I don't care who leads. All I care about is that we let Jack and his men down. I will follow Moore or Morehead. I say enough wrangling about who gets the glory. Let's go after the Mexicans while we can. We have lost the element of surprise. Now they are waiting for us, but I still say Mexicans be damned, let's go."

By the time the divided group came to an agreement, darkness had fallen. The next morning Jack, Bud, Ben, Big Foot and the other rangers were ready to ride at sunrise. Mayfield began to make excuses as to why it would not be wise to attack. Then Moore spoke, supporting Mayfield's sentiments. Since Caldwell had agreed that Moore would lead, he was in an awkward position. If he went with Hays, he would be disobeying orders; yet, if he failed to go with the rangers, he would be seen as a coward.

Jack Hays started to respond, but was too angry to say what was on his mind. He asked Ben McCullough to speak for the rangers. "It's clear to us the only reason you have for not fighting is the yellow streak down your backs. How in the name of God can you sit there and let that bunch haul our friends off to Mexico City? Woll has fifty-three of our finest, and because of your cowardice, they are being taken away in chains."

Mayfield avoided looking at Jack and Ben, literally hiding behind his horse to avoid further confrontation. His men were the first to head home. Soon John Moore saddled up and told his men to follow. As they left, others followed. They ignored Hays and McCullough's protests and chose to abandon the fight. Colonel Caldwell became distraught, his face flushed and tears streamed down his rugged cheeks. He felt they had let Jack and Ben down.

The blame for the Hondo River incident fell on Colonel Caldwell. He was humiliated and outraged that he should take the blame for the failed mission. Anyone who knew "Old Paint" knew he was a true Texas hero, one of the bravest men to walk Texas soil. When the Council House fight broke out, he had no gun, but wrestled a pistol from one of the Indians and shot one Chief, and then killed another with the butt of the weapon. Though stabbed in the leg, he managed to keep fighting, finally resorting to throwing rocks at the enemy. But the deplorable conditions he endured in a Mexican jail had extracted a heavy toll, and the fearless Indian fighter had no strength to stave off depression. Despair grabbed a foothold and like an angry bulldog, refused to let go. Caldwell died less than three months after the Hondo River debacle a bitter and broken man. Jack Hays' letter was on his bedside table with his reading glasses on top of the folded paper when he expired.

Mathew,

We have ridden side by side. I know your courage and think you should ignore those who try to slander your great name. Texas owes much to you. You have nothing to be ashamed of. If my words were curt that day, they were not directed at you, but at Moore, Mayfield, and Morehead. I knew your hands were tied. You have never failed to answer the call. I hope you can put this in the past and more forward in helping us protect and serve this great Republic of Texas.

Major John C. "Jack" Hays

Texas Rangers, San Antonio de Bexar

Bud was pleased to find his room waiting when he arrived back in town. He had two important letters to write. He sat down on the bed to remove his boots and before he could get his socks off, he leaned over and was asleep by the time his head touched the pillow. There would be no letter writing this night.

Chapter Thirty-Three
Change

Back in Galveston, a story of another kind was taking shape. A new Lutheran Church had been built and a minister appointed to pastor the flock. The minister, German by birth, was in his early fifties and had five children. Reverend Wilhelm Heinrich Gottlob immigrated to America and drifted south from one small congregation to another. When offered the opportunity to move to Texas, he told his wife it was God's will that he minister to the heathens in the new Republic. The Reverend's oldest son, Wilhelm Heinrich Gottlob Jr., "Junior", twenty-three, tall and blond, and with proper manners, would be his assistant pastor.

The Treptows were the first to invite the new minister and his family to their home for Sunday dinner. During the evening meal, the discussion turned to the men lost in the Woll invasion. Reverend Gottlob assured the Treptows that his minister son, Junior, would not kill a man. He expounded, "It is against the teachings of our Lord to take the life of another. We are conscientious objectors. We refuse to raise a firearm against one of God's people."

Mr. Treptow was a debater at heart and challenged his minister, citing the atrocities of the Alamo and Goliad. The Minister countered that in both circumstances, the men had ample time to leave and avoid conflict. Mr. Treptow shot back and reminded the minister of the savage Indian raids. In his thick German accent, Reverend Gottlob was quick to justify his opinion. "When man treads on the territory of another, he can expect retribution."

Helmut understood that the minister's thoughts were born of ignorance and nurtured by naiveté. To close the argument, Helmut simply responded, "I do believe you have a point. What you are saying is if we leave them alone, they won't trouble us."

"Precisely. Man cannot go around taking others' abiding places. They are bound to get an angry response from those who know not our Lord and Savior. We Christians are commanded to spread the gospel, and not slaughter the natives. I plan to make some changes in this Republic after my congregation grows to an influential size."

Helmut had similar beliefs when he moved his family to Galveston Island. He caught harsh criticism from the locals when he refused to go after a band of Indians that raided a ranch across the bayou, killing a family of five. He felt the scorn of the townspeople, and out of shame, rode along the next time the Comanche came near Galveston. He saw two traders scalped and gutted as a hunter does a deer, their bodies hung from a tree. The incident changed Helmut Treptow's attitude 180 degrees.

Six weeks later, the Treptows again invited the Gottlobs to their home for a fried chicken dinner. After a big meal, Virginia asked Junior if he would like to go horseback riding on the beach. He confessed he didn't own a horse and had ridden very little. Virginia responded, "My daddy has plenty of horses. Come with me and we'll pick one you like. We have a mare that's as gentle as a lamb."

Junior excused himself from the table and followed Virginia to the barn. She ordered one of the ranch hands to saddle a gentle gray brood mare for the tenderfoot minister. Virginia then mounted her spirited horse and the pair headed to the beach where she and Bud had ridden on many occasions.

Attitudes toward Bud Miller were changing in the Treptow home. Since he inherited a large sum of money, Helmut knew Bud would never be satisfied living on the Treptow ranch and being a part of their operation. Helmut saw how the ranger life changed Jack Hays into a fierce fighting machine, and he believed young Miller was cut from the same cloth. The Treptows encouraged Virginia to take Junior horseback riding; knowing Bud would no longer make the type of son-in-law they were seeking for their only child.

Junior finally opened up. "Virginia, I'll be delivering the sermon again next Sunday. I doubt if you know, but my father is not well. I know he appears to be strong as an ox, but the doctors have told him he only has a year or so to live. He wants me to be trained to preach so I can take the church when he goes home to be with God."

Virginia was shocked. She responded to the news with a question. "What's wrong with the Reverend?"

Junior looked into the ink blue water, the moon dancing across the sparkling smooth surface, and then back at Virginia. "He has advanced consumption. It's called tuberculoses. Mama says he should live in a drier climate, but I think you may have noticed how stubborn my father can be. He says he is ready to meet God, and if Galveston is the meeting place, then so be it. He is such an intrepid man. He believes God brought us here for a reason and nothing or no one can change his mind."

Virginia's heart sank. After Junior told her about the tuberculoses, she remembered how, from time to time, the Reverend would leave the house to cough. Even at the pulpit, he would turn his back on the congregation and cough into his handkerchief. She looked at Junior in the light of a full moon, his blond hair blowing in the soft ocean breeze. "Will you and your family stay here when your father goes to be with God?"

Junior didn't hesitate in giving his answer. "Without question. It's my goal to be ordained next month. I have been studying eschatology and theology for the past three years. I have already read the Martin Luther translation of the entire bible seventeen times. Today was my first sermon."

"First? This was your first sermon to the congregation?"

"Yes, this morning was my first sermon at the pulpit, but I do not want to mislead you. I have been preaching to the mirror and the cats and chickens for several years."

Virginia was impressed. "Well, you can count on me being in a front pew. I am sure you will deliver a wonderful sermon again next Sunday. I'm sorry to hear about your father, but I am glad you will not be leaving. You are such a brilliant and caring man."

A strange thing happened to Virginia. At that moment, she decided the cavalier attitude possessed by Bud was not for her. The last time they were together, he had spurned her advances, choosing to be with his ranger friends rather than remain a few more weeks at the ranch. She wanted a man with her father's disposition; a man who wouldn't leave for months at a time, is studious, and not always looking for greener grass on the other side of the fence. As they rode, Virginia wondered if she should write Bud or wait until she knew Junior was interested in her. She did not have to wait long. Junior gave her the answer she was hoping for when he asked, "May I come calling some evening when my family is not with me? I would like to see you as a girl and not because I'm the minister's son and you have to be nice to me."

Virginia did not hesitate. She immediately replied, "I would be most pleased to have you come calling and so will my mother and father. They like you, and I think you are a special gentleman."

Virginia thought there would never be a man who could replace Bud in her heart, but Junior was making deep impressions of his own. She and Junior rode until almost ten that night. When they returned to the ranch, Helmut and the Reverend were talking scripture on the front porch. They waved as the two galloped past on their way to the barn. The Reverend became serious in his demeanor as he said, "Helmut, I feel it is urgent I share something with you since you are an elder in the *Christ the Redeemer Church*. I implore you to keep this a secret. I am a dying man. I have tuberculosis and the doctor back in Missouri told me that I had less than one year to live. I have made a liar out of that doctor and already made it eighteen months, but I know I don't have much more time. I can feel the life slipping from my body and soon I will go be with the Lord. I want you to promise you will take care of my son. It is my wish that he will lead the congregation and build an edifice that will bring glory to our Lord and Savior Jesus Christ."

A stunned Helmut was blindsided by the minister's words. He took a deep breath and answered, "With God as my witness, I promise to give Junior all the support he needs. I feel it is God's will that a German pastor our church. Now, I don't want to hear any more talk about dying. You look as strong as a bull and twice as ornery."

The two men talked for a few more minutes, and then Virginia and Junior joined them. Virginia, ever the bold one, announced, "Daddy, the Reverend Wilhelm Heinrich Gottlob Jr. will be preaching again Sunday and he has asked permission to come calling one day next week. I was so sure you would approve, I told him it would be fine. I hope I'm correct in my assumption."

Mrs. Treptow and the minister's wife had come from the house onto the porch unnoticed. Mrs. Treptow answered for Helmut, saying, "Daughter, you have made a wise choice. Wilhelm is a splendid young man from a proper family and it will be our honor to have him come calling. You are both adults and know how to conduct yourselves in a Christian manner."

After saying goodnight, Reverend Gottlob and his family boarded their buggy and headed home. On the ride home, Junior was silent, knowing he would have a hard time sleeping. The full moon disappeared behind a cloud, leaving him to think in the darkness. He recalled hearing the old timers talk of being "lovesick", and now he knew the emotion. As much as he would miss his father, he now had someone to fill the void. He could hardly wait until he could see Virginia again.

Upon retiring for the evening, Virginia began thinking about Bud. His free spirit and enthusiastic way of describing his dreams, hopes and ambitions was unparalleled, his fearlessness, unrivaled. She knew she would be trading security and good standing in the community for a chance to be married to a man who might one day be President of Texas. There was never an ounce of doubt in her mind Bud Miller would become a leader of men, and should he select politics, he could go as far as he chose. As she was drifting off to sleep, she realized it didn't matter what she wanted, but what pleased her parents that mattered. She knew she had no choice except to write Bud a "Dear John" letter the following morning.

Coincidentally, the same day Bud was visiting with Jack Hays and Ben McCullough. Major Hays was thirty, and Captain McCullough thirty-two. Each man was handsome and successful and Bud had certainly noticed that women found them attractive; yet, both of the older rangers were unmarried. Bud wanted to know why. Jack's answer was that he was married to Texas and didn't have time for another woman. Ben's bright blue eyes glistened as he teased, "No woman in her right mind would have me." The two rangers gave Bud what he was seeking: permission to not rush into marriage.

After leaving the rangers, Bud ran into Maria with her three small children. He stopped and gave the two older children a piece of rock candy and talked with Maria for the first time since she brought him cake in Galveston. She was much heavier and looked thirty-five, even though she was Bud's age, twenty-one. She told him she had never married. Men didn't marry girls like her. Bud started to walk away then stopped abruptly. Reaching into his jacket pocket, he removed a twenty-dollar gold piece. In a soft, sympathetic voice, he said, "Maria, you will always be a lady to me. You were the first girl to make my heart pound. Thinking about you helped me endure being locked up. I want to give you this money so you can purchase some food, new clothes and other things for your babies. If you ever need a friend, you can count on me. I have some money and will do what I can for you. Lady, I owe you my life."

Maria's eyes watered up as she spoke. "Thank you. I wish I could have met you before I was forced to start working in the *Brass Monkey*. You are not like any man I have ever known. I do thank you for the money and I will spend it wisely."

Bud gave her a strong hug, patted the older children on their heads and walked away wondering how different things might have been if he had found her after his release from jail. Perhaps he could have rescued her. Bud fought back tears as he returned to his small room.

Pondering the comments of his two ranger friends, Bud decided that not rushing into marriage was the right choice for him. Besides, he was not sure he liked Virginia better than Charm. There was something about Charm. His heart fluttered when he held the simple handkerchief she had given him. That little white piece of cloth had become brown from being removed from his vest pocket so many times. That night in the candlelight, he wrote:

My Dearest Virginia,

With pen in hand, I write not to hurt you, because nothing on this earth could make me do that. I write because I care very much for you and respect your family greatly. I need to be beaten with a pepper stick for not having written sooner. You probably have heard the news about us driving General Woll and his Mexican Army from Texas. I was wounded a few times, but nothing serious. Thank God, Lightning didn't get hurt. Jack Hays' warhorse was shot and died on our way back to San Antonio. Jack loved that horse as much as I love Lightning. I will ever be grateful to your father for giving me such a magnificent mount. There is no better horse in all of Texas.

I think it would be dishonest for me to lead you on. I have decided to follow Major Jack Hays and Captain Ben McCullough's example. Neither of them has married because they didn't want to have to leave a family home alone with no male protection. With sadness in my heart, I have to tell you that at this time, I cannot take a wife. There is talk of us invading Mexico. I have a feeling if we do invade Mexico, I may not return. Fighting in Mexico will be different than on ground we are familiar with. We rangers think it is a foolish idea, but we cannot let the army down if President Houston chooses to seek revenge for the Dawson slaughter. Texas is building an army and it is my understanding war is imminent. I have a premonition if we do go, I will be killed, yet it is my duty to defend my country.

This letter is my way of setting you free. Don't wait for me. Even if I return, we still have the Comanche issue to contend with. I'll be twenty-two by the time you read this letter. I own a home I have yet to move into. I've been in Texas six years and still have not visited the spot where my father was killed.

Please pray there will be no war. Thank your sweet mother and generous father for me. I will always be your friend and at your aid in a heartbeat should you ever call.

With deep affection,

Bud

Virginia was up early, staying in her room until she could compose a letter to Bud, a long overdue letter, and one to which she had given much thought. She was careful with her words, hoping not to hurt him or cause him to do something reckless. She had no way of knowing their letters would soon cross paths somewhere around the Brazos River.

To my friend Benjamin Miller,

I am not sure how to say what I must without hurting you. I have to speak straight. I know that is what you would want. You never speak with a forked tongue. With some reservation, I want to call off our engagement. God has presented me with an opportunity to become acquainted with a young minister. We both share the same faith. Unlike you, he is not a womanizer and adventurer. He wants to settle down and raise a Christian family.

I do hope this letter will not cause you too much grief or cause you to do something rash. I do not expect a return letter. Be safe. Do not take too many chances. I can truthfully say my family will miss you, and so will I, but your neglect in writing has made it clear to me you have other birds on your stove.

Your friend,

Ginny

Virginia failed to take into consideration that Bud never proposed. Marriage had been her and her family's conversation, without Bud ever taking part in the discussion. Ten days after Bud sent his letter, the crumpled envelope was delivered to the Treptow home. Virginia was livid at the audacity of Bud writing such a presumptive letter. She stomped through the house, screaming. How dare he dump her? She completely ignored her own rapier epistle.

Jack Hays was deep into a pressing survey job that needed to be finished before he could get involved in the invasion of Mexico. Bud took a few days to check on his Bastrop home and perhaps drop by to see Charm. Traveling at night to avoid detection, he reached his Bastrop home while the sun was still resting. He watered Lightning and staked him in belt-high grass.

The next morning, Bud left for town to find someone to clear his yard. He didn't have to go far. His neighbor, Willie Hill, was struggling with a spirited dun mule as Bud approached. "Hi, I'm Bud Miller. I have the place next to yours, the Bastrop house." Bud forgot they were in Bastrop, and of course, all the homes would be Bastrop houses.

Willie spoke to his mule. "Whoa, Brownie." Removing his big floppy hat, he wiped the sweat from his brow, and asked, "What house is that?"

"The house the Baron de Bastrop built."

"Oh, I see. You are the youngen that folks been talkin' 'bout. You made quite a stir the last time you wuz here. Not everyone was happy with the Baron, but he did right by me and my woman. You will never stick a plow in better soil. What kan I do fur ya, son?"

Bud jumped effortlessly from Lighting, landing light as a feather on the freshly- plowed field. "Sir, I would like to hire you to plow the grass around my house and then drag a rake and level the soil. The Johnson grass is so tall I can hardly get in the door. I'm thinking I might want to show some folks my place and don't want them to see it in such poor condition. What would you charge me to clean up around the house about fifty yards?"

Willie scratched his head and put his hat back on. His speech was slow and deliberate. "Sonny, since you are my neighbor, I guess I kan do it fur ya tomorrow."

"How much?"

Willie looked puzzled. "There ain't no charge. We's neighbors."

"Sir, I do appreciate your generosity. If you will not let me pay, then I want to give your wife a present. Bud flipped Willie a five-dollar gold piece. As the coin tumbled over and over in the air, Bud said, "Mr. Willie, give this to your wife so she can buy some cloth."

Willie looked at the five dollars and then back to Bud. He had not held this much money in his hands in a long time. His face blushed. He wanted to hand the money back, but knew how much they needed the funds. His voice cracked. "Youngen, you don't have to do this. I'm your neighbor and glad to hep when I kan. I'm gonna keep the money 'cause the truth is we got five kids and they all kan use some clothes. Molly kan sew as good as any woman and better than most. This money will come in mighty handy. Thank ya."

Bud grabbed his saddle horn and swung his leg over the seat in one fluid motion. He reached in his saddlebag, then said, "Willie catch" as he tossed another five-dollar gold piece to his new friend. "I will need for you to keep an eye on my place and make sure the grass doesn't invade my yard. You will know when to clear the yard, so I'll leave that up to you. I'm a ranger and we have our hands full right now. Mexican bandits and Santa Anna's men both want to do damage to Texas, and it looks like we will be invading Mexico to retrieve a bunch of our captured men. They took Judge Hightower and Sam Maverick back to Mexico City in chains."

Willie looked skyward instead of at Bud, and with praise in his voice, said, "Thank you Lord for your bountiful blessings on me, your humble servant." Then he looked at Bud with gratitude, asking, "Youngen, how kan I thank you? I've been prayin' for the means to get some salt and sugar. I never expected to be able to buy clothes for my babies and my Molly. I won't never forget your kindness. In all my born days, I sure kaint recall havin' so much money. My Molly is gonna cry. Mr. Miller, you are a good man. Sure as the sun comes up in the east, that is how sure you can be I'll do ya proud. Me and a couple of my kids will go over tomorrow. I suspect the house can use a good scrubbin' so Molly will take some ashes and clean your floors sparkling clean."

Bud's ride to the Hempsteads was uneventful. He saw no one and the weather was perfect; just enough coolness for Lighting to be high spirited. When he reached the farm about four in the afternoon, the men were working in the field. Bud wanted to go to the house directly, but thought it proper to visit the men first. Charm's older brother was the first to spot him. He dropped his plow and dashed to greet him. "What brings you to this neck of the woods? Don't tell me. Let me guess. I bet you just happened to be passin' by and wanted to return my sister's handkerchief." Then Charlie gave Bud a bear hug and motioned to follow him to the house, talking as they jogged.

"I have to be there to look at Charm's face when she sees ya. You are all she talks about."

Bud smiled. "Now what makes you think I'm not here to just visit you?"

"'Cause I saw the letters you wrote Charm."

When they reached the house, the kitchen door was open, but Bud stood to one side to prevent Charm and her mother from seeing him as he knocked. When Charm saw Bud's boot extended into the doorway, she screamed, "Mama. It's Bud!"

As he stepped into the doorway, his body filled the space.

Charm, still standing at the stove, exclaimed, "Mercy mama, look how big he is!"

Mrs. Hempstead, in a coy voice, answered, "He has become a tall drink of water."

Bud removed his hat, kicked the dust from his boots, and washed his hands and face before entering the house. He spoke to Mrs. Hempstead first. "Ma'am, I have already visited with Charlie. I'm here to call on Charm, that is, if I have your permission."

Mrs. Hempstead appeared taken aback. She wiped her hands on her apron and motioned for Bud to have a seat. Then she looked at her daughter asking, "Did you know this boy was coming for a visit?"

"No mama. Isn't it wonderful?"

"Yes dear. You know we all think Bud is a fine young man."

Charm could wait no longer. She rushed over and threw her arms around Bud's neck, pressing her face against his chest. She surprised even herself showing such an outburst of emotion, especially in front of her mother. Words failed to come out of her mouth. She just squeezed him tight. So often she had longed to see him again, to hear his voice, but thought that may never happen. Travelers passing through gave them tidbits of information from time to time. They knew Bud was involved in the battle of Salado Creek and helped drive General Woll from Texas. One traveler had told them Ranger Miller was shot up pretty bad at the battle of Hondo River. Her hand touched his neck where a Mexican bullet had cut the flesh. The wound was crusted over, and she wondered how many more wounds he might have endured.

Bud was not sure if he should hug her back, but tossed caution to the wind and placed his arms around Charm's waist. Speaking loud enough for her mother to hear, he said, "You are even more beautiful than I remembered. Your mother named you well. You are the most charming girl in all of Texas. I want you to know I still have the handkerchief you gave me, right here in my vest pocket."

Mrs. Hempstead knew for sure the moment she saw Charm looking into Bud's eyes that her daughter was head-over-heels in love. Her maternal instincts took over and she worried Bud might not feel the same toward Charm. She did not want her daughter to suffer a broken heart. She herself was crushed by her first love spurning her affections; Charm's father was her second choice. Their relationship was not her only worry. After Bud told them of the battle with the Mexicans and the possibility of the Texans invading Mexico, she had a feeling her two oldest sons would want to join the war; a day she had long dreaded. A family she strove to hold together was getting ready to splinter, all because too many young adventurers had planted seeds of glory and excitement in the hearts of her eldest sons. Too many evenings at the dinner table, her boys had expressed their interest in fighting for the Republic. Mrs. Hempstead's intuition was correct. After the day's work was done, the boys hovered around Bud at the supper table, wanting to know what Texas was going to do about the Mexicans. Bud explained that General Alexander Somervell was putting an army together with the intention of rescuing the sixty or so Texans held prisoner in Mexico. Then he excused himself to unsaddle Lightning before dark.

While he was gone, the two oldest boys, Charles and Edward, asked their father if they could go with Bud and join the fight. He had no choice but to allow them to leave. He knew if Texas did not stop the Mexicans now, they would return with a much larger army and drive his family from their farm. He told the boys they could pick the best horses and take what supplies they needed. Then he lowered his head and prayed, "Our Holy Father, we thank you for the food we are about to partake. Amen."

That evening, Bud and Charm rocked on a swing dangling from an oak tree in the front yard, talking for hours. The conversation mostly was about what each had done since they last saw each other. Then, unexpectedly, Bud told Charm that he would like her to see his house in Bastrop. "It's not all that far from here. Maybe your brothers can take you over. The tall pines reach up to the heavens and the Colorado flows nearby. There is no place in Texas more tranquil or beautiful. I have good neighbors and there is some property adjacent to mine that I can purchase once we finish with the war."

Charm didn't hesitate. "I would be honored to see your home. I can only imagine how beautiful it is, but Charlie and Edward cannot take me. I heard them talking with papa and mama. They are planning on going back with you to the war."

Bud stopped the swing. Her words shocked him. "Charm, are you saying they plan on joining the army? I apologize. I made fighting sound too glorious. I have been scared on many occasions and wondered if I would live to see another day. I have seen many friends killed or wounded. I will do my best to discourage them from going. We should have enough experienced men to fight without your brothers."

"Bud, please don't be upset. It's not your fault. We have guests often at the supper table and they all tell of how adventurous it is to be in a big battle, cannons firing and rifles cracking. We all knew it was just a matter of time before the two older boys wanted to join the fray. I will get papa to take me over to see your home. I just want you to be very careful. If I were to lose you, I don't know what I would do. There has never been anyone like you in my life. My mama says you are handsome."

Bud, lightened the conversation as he replied, "Being perfect does have its price."

They both laughed. Bud gave Charm a tight hug and thanked her for listening. He also thanked her for making an effort to visit Bastrop. He didn't tell her that one day he might want to ask her to live in the house, and had decided that when he returned to San Antonio, he would draw up his will leaving the Bastrop property to her in the event he didn't make it back. He had strong feelings the trip into Mexico would end up leaving him buried on foreign soil. His many visits with men captured by the Mexicans had made him determined never to be taken prisoner. Mathew Caldwell was dead because of the horrendous treatment he received while in a Mexican prison. Jose Navarro was still living in squalor in a dungeon deep in the heart of Mexico City. Death would be welcomed rather than suffering Navarro's fate.

The following morning, Bud, Charlie and Edward left shortly after breakfast. Charm's tears flowed down her rosy cheeks as she waved goodbye to three men she cared for so deeply. Mr. Hempstead refused to watch his sons leave, but Mrs. Hempstead joined Charm and waved until the trio was completely out of view, and then consoled her daughter as they embraced.

Houston's old nemesis, soldier, Indian fighter, and Statesman, Edward Burleson was in San Antonio inflaming the sentiment for war with Mexico. As Brigadier General, Burleson had defeated Mexican insurrectionists under Vicente Cordova. He intercepted a Cordova agent with proof that Mexico had formed an alliance with the Cherokee and other tribes. Under orders from President Lamar, he defeated the Cherokee led by Chief Bowles, and had sent the slain Chief's hat to Houston. That incident created deep animosity between Burleson and Houston and Sam would never forgive Burleson for his inhumane actions toward his beloved Cherokee. Now, Burleson had organized an army of twelve hundred troops and was whipping up public support for the army's march all the way to Mexico City. Texans were crying out for revenge and demanding Woll's head on a stick in the same manner Santa Anna had dealt with the rebels in Mexico.

President Houston immediately dispatched Brigadier General Alexander Somervell to San Antonio, instructing him to defend Texas' liberties with the knife, but not invade Mexican soil. Houston knew should the Republic take the war south of the Rio Grande it would be Texas' demise. Thus, General Somervell's mission was to stop the invasion, while at the same time make a cautious display of resolve. Somervell was to shadowbox his way to the border and then come up with a plausible reason to retreat.

When Bud, Edward, and Charlie arrived in San Antonio, they were surprised to find twelve hundred armed men spread around the city in seven or eight different camps. The second day in San Antonio, General Burleson gave a rip-roaring oration from a window in the Alamo. The mob was ready to march on Mexico that day, but Burleson told them to go home and return in one month for the invasion. Before Burleson finished speaking, General Somervell rode into town and took command of the Army. Vice President Burleson reluctantly gave the power over to General Somervell.

Charlie and Edward Hempstead joined a group of men from their area and lived in their camp awaiting orders. The young Hempstead boys took a lot of ribbing from some of the older men, some trying to scare them with stories of seeing men's head blown up like watermelons from rifle shot. The brothers were new to war; however, they had heard many, many stories over their dinner table from visitors who were true Texas war heroes. Both Hempstead boys joined the fight so they could tell their own war stories across the supper table.

Jack Hays was not satisfied with the actions of General Somervell and complained bitterly to the President and Secretary Hamilton. Houston instructed Hamilton to send Jack a letter imploring him to do what he could to assist Somervell. In November, Major Hays wrote G.W. Hill, the Secretary of War:

> *I was compelled to incur a debt for ranger expenses of some $400 for which amount I became personally responsible, having full confidence that as soon as circumstances would permit, I would be furnished for the payment of same.*
>
> *I have also the pleasure to report that the western settlements have, for several months past, enjoyed almost entire immunity from the incursions of Indians. The only source from which danger is now apprehended is the robbing parties of Mexicans which may be expected to increase since disbanding of the larger companies that have, until recently, been employed by the Mexican government upon the frontier, composed chiefly of men destitute of principles and without the resources to obtain an honest livelihood. Many, it is thought, will be ready to engage in any enterprise, however disreputable or hazardous, that may promise to afford them the means of subsistence.*
>
> *There are now many Mexicans who depend wholly for their subsistence upon robberies. A small force could be kept up of well-mounted men sufficient to keep them in check, which might be done at small exposure to the government. At the same time, I would suggest the officer in command should receive from your Department particular instruction as to the manner in which those who were formerly citizens of the Republic and joined the enemy should be treated on their return, some of whom are known in San Antonio and no doubt will be ready to do the country what injury the advantage of living among us may give them. We have many spies in San Antonio.*
>
> *Major Jack C. Hays*

Jack made a hint to Juan Seguin at the bottom of his letter. No one was more disappointed in Juan going over the other side than Jack. He felt if Juan had confided in him, the problems could have been worked out. Sam Maverick and Deaf Smith were leaders in San Antonio. If they had been aware of the mistreatment he was receiving from the new arrivals, they would have surely helped relieve the pressure on Juan and his family.

President Houston was disgusted with Somervell's failure to organize his army and his tardiness to report any news of progress. Somervell received a severe censure from the War Department, reminding the general that President Houston faced similar odds in building an army for San Jacinto. Finally, the general gave the order for the men to follow him. Major Jack Hays, who by now had raised 140 rangers, would use his men to act as scouts. Falcco and 15 Lipan Apaches joined Hays' ranger group and went ahead of the army. The rangers stayed a day's ride ahead so, in the event they encountered a Mexican force, the army would have ample time to find a suitable battleground.

Fall rains began to impede their progress as sheets of water poured from the skies daily. At night, the fog was so dense that visibility was only a few feet. The clay ground under the scrub oak trees became mushy and extremely difficult for the horses to traverse. By the time the army reached the oak groves, their horses were knee deep in mud. Each night, Jack would find a grove of large oaks for their campsite and had his men sleep sitting up, with their backs against the trees. The ground around the roots was slightly elevated, offering relief from the mud, and the trees' sprawling canopies served as nature's umbrella, keeping the men relatively dry.

When Hays reached the Nueces River, the rains had turned the shallow water into raging whirlpools. Seeing it was impossible to ford the river and keep their powder dry, Jack dismounted and suggested his men do the same. He removed his clothes and using his belt, tied them around his neck. Holding his rifle high in the air, he mounted and swam across on the back of his horse. Not one of his men lost any precious gunpowder. Before all were across, Jack sent Henry McCullough and another ranger back to tell General Somervell he would need to build barges to haul his forces and supplies across the river.

Somervell's recruits were ill prepared for the cold nights and the blistering rains that now besieged them daily. Somervell ordered his men to kill some deer, tan the hides, and make more suitable buckskin clothing to protect them from the elements. Large white tail deer were highly populous in South Texas and easy to harvest, and the troops were able to kill over three hundred deer in two days. Only cutting the choice meat for rations, the soldiers left the carcasses behind. A large group of carnivorous wildlife trailed behind the army, feasting on the remains.

The nights were filled with the eerie cries of wolves, coyote and mountain lions. The knowledge that Indians often used animal sounds to communicate with each other added to the soldiers' uneasiness when darkness came. There was no glory or adventure in being constantly wet and cold, and sleeping with one's eyes and ears open.

When Major Hays and his rangers reached the edge of Laredo, Mexican spies spotted them. Knowing an army would follow, the scouts rode full out back into town, warning the Mexican soldiers and bandits to flee south across the Rio Grande. Shortly thereafter, Jack sent scouts ahead to Laredo, and when they reported there were no Mexican soldiers present, the Texans entered the town unabated. City officials met them at the city limits and offered to provide them with whatever supplies and food the citizens could afford. Somervell made a show of force, parading his troops right through the middle of town. As he did so, citizens turned out to welcome the Texans. As Jack rode beside the general, he knew better than to trust the waves of the "friendly" crowd. He had received similar welcomes in San Antonio and he knew how devious those waving citizens could be when the Texans' backs were turned. He suggested the general move his men away from the city because it was most likely filled with spies. Somervell heeded Jack's advice and gave the order to continue marching all the way through town. Reluctantly, the army left town empty-handed and camped six miles east along the banks of the Rio Grande.

Shortly after making camp, whiskey stolen as the army passed through town began to appear. A contingent of the men started to drink in excess. Edward and Charlie were not drinkers, only helpless bystanders as the army turned into an angry, uncontrollable mob. "Let's go back. Let's go back. Let's go back," the drunken men chanted. They began squabbling and anonymously calling their General slanderous names for not furnishing them with better supplies. They slandered his mother and questioned the circumstances of his birth. Within an hour or so, the men developed whiskey courage and two-dozen grabbed their rifles and started back toward Laredo. Two hundred more followed, against General Somervell's orders. This time, the men took what they wanted. No woman or young girl was safe from the predatory actions of the Texas militia that night. Somervell was powerless to control his men as the mob plundered the town, raping and pillaging to a disgraceful proportion. They ransacked private residences and looted stores. Anyone who tried to stop them was murdered in the street. Without question, the *Pillage of Laredo* was the most despicable of acts ever perpetrated by Texas men. Not even the barbarous Santa Anna was guilty of such wanton debauchery. Had Houston been the commander, he would have ordered the first men to leave the camp shot as deserters. One dead soldier would rapidly have brought the remaining mob under control.

The two hundred who plundered the town returned empty handed because the Mexicans of Laredo had nothing worth stealing, and the majority of women had fled into the countryside when word came the Texans were returning as an angry mob. The following morning, the men with throbbing hangovers were told they could leave the army and go home without being given a dishonorable discharge. Two hundred men accepted the discharge and immediately left camp. The remaining five hundred soldiers ignored Somervell's command to disband and began to march, stepping over and around the dense chaparral as they followed the river toward the Gulf of Mexico. Around three in the afternoon, the group reached an open area across the Rio Grande from the village of Guerrero, Mexico, six miles from the Rio Grande along the banks of the Rio Salado. In behind Guerrero, at the mouth of the Rio Salado, was a rather large Indian camp. Hays and McCullough confiscated a long boat from an Indian, rowed across the river, and then walked to Guerrero. The town was larger than either had expected. There was a bustling population and the streets crowded with people selling, begging, or taking a siesta. They received a surprisingly warm welcome from the Mayor. Jack's observant eyes spotted a couple dozen Mexicans on horseback in the mountains overlooking the village. "Ben, the hills are alive with men who might at any moment come swooping down and kill us." He nudged Ben and they began a brisk trot back to the long boat. They returned to camp and told Somervell what they had seen, and were surprised with his reply. "Go back and tell the Mayor I want one hundred horses or I'll level his town to the ground. If they don't have that many horses, then I'll settle for five thousand dollars."

"I am confident the poor Mexicans of Guerrero don't have a hundred horses, and I know there is not two-thousand dollars among them. You are wasting your time General." Jack spoke the truth.

Somervell insisted that no harm could come from making the demand. With reluctance, Jack and Ben rowed back across to Guerrero. The Mayor told them all the horses had been taken into the mountains. Then Jack demanded the five thousand dollars. The mayor, in a panic, rushed through town trying to raise the ransom money. After a frantic meeting with anyone he thought might be able to contribute, he was only able to gather four hundred dollars. Knowing Somervell would not be happy, Jack asked the mayor to return with them to explain to General Somervell that the town had no funds. When the general met with the mayor and learned that four hundred dollars was all that could be collected, he decided raiding the town was not worth the risk. He had accomplished what President Houston wanted.

The rangers then captured a spy who confirmed that General Woll had moved the Texas prisoners two or three hundred miles into the heart of Mexico. Somervell knew his army had no supplies and would perish if they crossed the Rio Grande seeking to rescue the captured men. The general announced he was closing the expedition down and the men should march to Gonzales where they would be discharged. Thomas Jefferson Green began chanting, "Go home, HELL NO. Go home, HELL NO. Go home, HELL NO! We come to kill us some Meskins!"

Thomas Jefferson Green was born in North Carolina, and like Fannin, attended West Point. He came to Texas just before the Alamo to establish a colony. When General Cos captured San Antonio, Green was promoted to General in the Texas Army and returned to the United States to raise funds, supplies, and men for the war. He considered himself a military man in spite of the fact that he had never fought a battle. Jefferson Green had an almost pathological passion to apply what he had learned at West Point.

"Go home, HELL NO. Go home, HELL NO. Go home, HELL NO!" the men continued shouting at the top of their lungs.

The very vocal William Fisher, who had served as Houston's secretary of war in his first administration, jumped on a wagon and vigorously spoke out against aborting the expedition. Fisher had long held a vendetta against Houston for not taking the war south of the Rio Grande. He told the men the expedition had been a fraud perpetrated by Houston; there was never any intent of going after the Texas prisoners. Somervell reminded the two officers they were disobeying a direct order and could face a firing squad. Fisher bellowed back, "We get our marching orders from a higher power. God is our leader and He has told us 'an eye for an eye.' We are not cowards and we will pursue those brown men to the ends of the earth. Who do they think they are coming into our country and dragging away the pillars of our communities?"

Three hundred men gathered in a tight group and elected Fisher to assume command and lead them into Mexico. They had not come this far to tuck tail and run. Bud pleaded with Edward and Charlie Hempstead not to follow Fisher, but to return home with General Somervell. Charlie replied, "We have yet to see any action. We came here to kill Mexicans. We cannot leave without our chance for glory."

"Charlie, there won't be any glory if a Mexican spy shoots you in the back. Listen to Jack Hays. This is a trap waiting to be sprung," Bud implored.

Before leaving, General Somervell made one last try to convince them to leave, re-reading the letter he received from President Houston before the expedition:

Alexander,

You will proceed to the most eligible point on the Southwestern frontier of Texas and concentrate with the force now under your command all troops who may submit to your orders and if you can advance with a prospect of success into the enemy's territory, you will do forthwith. Our greatest reliance will be upon light troops and the celerity of our movements; hence the necessity of discipline and subordination. You will therefore receive no troops into service, but such as will be subordinate to your orders and the rules of war.

You may rely upon the gallant Jack Hays and his rangers, and I desire that you should obtain his services and cooperation. Insubordination and disregard of command will bring ruin and disgrace upon our arms.

Respectfully,

Samuel Houston

President of the Republic of Texas

Only 189 men joined General Alexander Somervell in returning to Gonzales, where the army was disbanded. His mission was a colossal failure, one of the greatest military blunders in the history of the Republic of Texas.

Companies led by Captains Charles Reece, Claudius Buster, John Goodlow, Ewan Cameron, and William Eastland joined up with Commander William Fisher. The leaders assembled three hundred men and were prepared to march when a scout came rushing into camp. The scout reported discovering a number of flatbed boats tied up across the river near the Indian camp. Traveling downstream by boat would be faster and less tiring for his men, so Fisher immediately assembled a squad to acquire the boats. They then loaded their supplies, baggage, and men into the confiscated boats and set off down the river toward Mier.

Jack's friends and former rangers Samuel Walker and Big Foot Wallace had climbed into the long boats in spite of Jack's stern warnings. Fearing Mexican snipers might start shooting at his friends like sitting ducks, Jack and his rangers followed along the banks, ready to fire on any who might attempt to attack the convoy. The rangers moved downriver, staying close to the bank, watching for any movement in the hills above. On their right were Jack Hays and his men, and on the left, their horses driven by seven privates: Sidney Callender, Frank Hancock, Virgil Phelps, George Walton, Guildford West, Michael Cronigan and Thomas Warren. These men would live to tell what they saw from the Texas banks of the Rio Grande that day.

Thomas Jefferson Green's boat took the lead. He raised a cadium-red flag from the bow, conveying his intent was to take no prisoners. Charm's brothers, Charlie and Edward were in Green's boat, their hearts pumping at the prospect of action. Without question, the single purpose driving the entire group of Texans was revenge. Hatred ran deep and confidence was at an all time high as the long boats made their way across the river.

When Hays' rangers reached the riverbank adjacent to Mier and found no movement or army camp, he sent Bud to tell Fisher that as far as they could ascertain, there would be minimal resistance in taking the walled town. Once Fisher's men were on shore, Jack instructed his rangers to cross back over onto Texas soil. Ben McCullough, Nelson Lee, and a small group of rangers and Lipan Apaches protected the boats from the Texas side of the river.

William S. Fisher and his three hundred Texans disembarked and marched to the gates of Mier two days before Christmas. The mayor and several locals met Fisher and two of his officers, and offered a warm welcome. Fisher immediately demanded money and supplies. The mayor told him the town would provide what they could, but the men would have to carry the provisions on their backs to the boats. Fisher was not planning to return to the boats; he needed the supplies for the Texans' long march into the heart of Mexico. He instructed the mayor to gather the provisions and he would return the next day to pick them up. To ensure the Mexicans carried out his demand, Fisher held the mayor captive, transporting him back over to the Texas side.

Jack Hays and Ben McCullough crossed back over to inspect the town's defenses. What they found was not good; Mexican troops were now assembling along the river. The two rangers advised Fisher against crossing back in to Mexico, insisting he abandon the expedition. "To go back over will be suicidal," Jack told him bluntly. When their advice went unheeded, Jack paused to give Big Foot Wallace a strong handshake and wished him safe return.

When Jack and Ben told their rangers to prepare to leave, John Regan Baker, the sheriff of Refugio County, convinced several of the new rangers to stay, saying, "Our mission is to give our brothers safe passage and protect them from ambush." Several rangers, caught up in the excitement of the moment, and against Jack's orders, followed the sheriff.

All day Christmas Eve, the Texans waited in vain for delivery of the goods. A.S. Holderman foolishly crossed the river alone to look for horses and was immediately captured by a small detachment of Mexican cavalry. To his good fortune, the Mexicans wanted information; otherwise, he would have been killed on the spot. On Christmas day, the Texans captured a Mexican soldier who was freer with his information than Holderman. He told Fisher that General Pedro de Ampudia had descended from the hills and prevented delivery of the supplies. Fisher became infuriated and made the decision to go after their rations. Fisher and Green knew that without the necessary provisions, they would be unable to penetrate the interior of Mexico and fulfill their mission. They placed Oliver Buckman in charge of 42 men to guard their horses and pack animals. This move left them with less than 260 Texans for the expedition; nevertheless, they crossed the Rio Grande with Mier on their minds.

The wise Mexican General Ampudia knew the mindset of his enemy. When the rations were not delivered as promised, the Texans re-entered Mier on Christmas day, just as he knew they would. Heavy fighting ensued and continued into the following afternoon. The Mexicans outnumbered the Texans ten to one, but with superior marksmanship, the Texans repeatedly found their target with deadly accuracy. The Mexican casualties mounted, with over 200 wounded and 600 killed. No matter how many fell, the brave Mexican soldiers continued their resistance. One of Fisher's men who survived, later said, "I have never seen a more fearless group of fighters than those tiny Mexicans. They had to know we didn't miss, but nothing deterred their advance."

The Texans had lost only nine men, with twenty-three wounded as the battle was tilting in their favor. That is, until Fisher was wounded. With no single leader in command, the men started to lose their resolve, and chaos and confusion sifted through the Texans' ranks. They were hungry and thirsty, their powder supply was almost exhausted; however, it would be their lack of discipline that sealed their fate.

Ampudia sent up a white flag of surrender, which was only a ruse to stop his men from being killed. Ampudia was successful; falling for the deception the Texans abandoned the fight. Ampudia then captured to exhausted Texans. In the terms of surrender, the Texans were promised they would be held as prisoners of war along the south bank of the Rio Grande. In truth, Ampuda did not intend to keep them anywhere near Texas.

The first to die was a private named George Bush. Then Edward Hempstead fell next to his brother, a musket shot to his head. Charlie cradled his brother in his arms, remembering Bud's pleas, and wished they had listened to him. Those who were unable to walk were left in the Mier hospital, while Charlie, Commander Fisher, and all the men who could walk were marched to Matamoras. No water or food was provided the first day. Only when General Ampudia felt confident the men could not break free and make it back into Texas did he stop and allow them to eat and drink.

Two soldiers, Tom Smothers and Hank Wilson, had escaped from Mier as the battle was waning. Under the cover of the black gun smoke, they swam across the river and warned the camp guards. Because of their brave escape, five of the Texans guarding the horses escaped, with the exception of George Bonnell and Richard Hicks. Bonnell tarried, not realizing the urgency and was killed while saddling his horse. Hicks, in the brush using the toilet when the Mexican cavalry crossed the river, was unable to get back to his horse in time to flee, and was hunted down and shot as he ran across the flat land.

The captured Texans were sentenced to execution, but on December 27 General Ampudia had the decree reversed. Ampudia also had done an honorable deed when he left the wounded Texans in the small

Mier hospital. Once healthy enough to walk, the wounded men got together and planned their escape. They saved bread, dried goat meat, and gourds for water. When the next full moon waned, the men slipped away into the darkness and swam across the river into Texas. In the group were George Pilant, James Rice, John Bideler, Henry Weeks, William Rupley and Lewis Hays. Once across the Rio Grande, they made their way safely to Corpus Christi.

From the survivors of the Mier battle, Bud learned the fate of his friend Edward, and the capture of Charlie Hempstead. A sick feeling came over him, filling his heart with deep despair. He was unable to hold back the tears and blamed himself for not being more aggressive in preventing the brothers from following Fisher. Jack tried to offer solace, reiterating how hard they both had tried to convince Fisher and his men of the futility of the invasion. "I told Fisher he was walking into a trap. Ben and I made sure all the men understood there were no official orders to invade Mexico. I accept no responsibility whatsoever for Fisher and the men who followed him. You must not either. My young friend, you must take no responsibility as to the death of Edward Hempstead or the capture of his brother. Rest assured Charlie will eventually be set free. The Mexicans grow tired of feeding the Texas prisoners and send them home. It may be a couple of years, but he will return."

Jack led the rangers back to San Antonio. Henry McCullough suggested to Bud that he be the one to deliver the news to the Hempsteads rather than them hearing about their sons' fate from a stranger. Bud agreed and said he would go as soon as they returned to San Antonio.

Hearing of the incursion into Mexico, President Houston stated the men had acted without authority of the government. His pronouncement left the impression they were not entitled to treatment as prisoners of war unless the Mexican government wished to do so as a humane gesture. The truth of the matter was that Houston had no choice except to distance his administration from the Fisher invasion; otherwise Santa Anna would have a perfect excuse to wage war against Texas.

In a letter shortly after the battle, General Ampudia gave his version of what took place during the battle of Mier:

To the Most Excellent Secretary of War and Navy, Sir Jose Ma Tornel:

In Reynosa, I met Jesus Cardenas, who was awaiting my arrival in order to mobilize all the inhabitants and Auxiliaries who did not stand in the field already under Mr. Canales. Without a moment's loss, I organized the citizens of Reynosa and Camargo into Companies, entrusting to the above leader that he join me when ready, with the precaution of leaving small squads to observe the invaders at close range. Not taking heed that my Infantry was worn out to exhaustion, as soon as they had choked down their ration, I undertook the crossing of San Juan River, a maneuver that started at 4 o'clock in the afternoon and ended at 2 o'clock in the morning since I had no other means of transportation other than a small raft and two canoes. There, my Adjutant Aznar reported to me, after having come through the enemy lines, bringing instructions from Your Excellency from General Headquarters that the previously mentioned 20,000 pesos be delivered in Monterrey instead. In spite of the impression that such an announcement caused in my subordinates, and of their real weariness, I started my movement toward that town, and Mr. Canales fell in with me at four leagues (16 miles) toward the Southeast of it, leading the 100 Sappers and 137 horses.

As the enemy had occupied Mier, my troops were barely left time to eat some roasted meat in the ranks before we marched off again, sending out small parties in all directions to spy out the enemy so as to calculate whether I ought to establish myself here for the night, or not. My spies returned, assuring me that the town had already been evacuated by the enemy who had moved back to Chapeho on the left bank of the Bravo, 4 leagues to the northeast, taking along Mayor Francisco Perez as hostage until he would receive the ransom demanded. On the strength of this news, I decided to enter the town, which I did at 8 o'clock that night, warning my column not to sound any drum or trumpet, to keep our entry secret. Surrounding myself with small cavalry advance posts, I sent the rest of the army to turn their mounts out to pasture, half a league (2 miles) to the east, behind a hill.

On the 24th, irked that the enemy did not undertake a new incursion into this town, I resolved to go and look for him in his encampment located on both banks of the Rio Bravo with five large rafts and four canoes as communication, which craft he had brought with him down river all the way from Guerrero. Notified on the march that the enemy was moving with the flow of the river, I too, changed direction by my right flank to await him at the confluence of the river and the small creek that waters this vicinity, choosing that point as being militarily more advantageous because of its dominant situation. There, I remained in ambush nearly an hour. Since the day was drawing to a close, and at the same time, word reached me that the Texans had already come to a halt at Casas Blancas, I countermarched to Mier to let my men and their animals get some food just in case the enemy had planned to occupy the place tonight. Our scouts captured two Texan spies who, questioned when caught, admitted that their comrades were determined to wreak depredations on the other three towns before reaching the outskirts of Matamoros.

On the morning of the 25th, I set out again toward the confluence of the rivers, but before reaching it, another two prisoners declared that they were just concluding the crossing of the Bravo, to occupy the town. Again, I turned about and countermarched and achieved the objectives of my desires, namely to make the enemy attack me in the base of operations where I had planned it from the beginning. I ordered Mr. Luciano Garcia, in command of the scouts, to start firing on the enemy alternately, drawing them closer to my line, and by 7 o'clock at night, the flashes of firing revealed to me the direction of the enemy's advance. Intentionally, I left unoccupied and at his disposal a few of the houses close to the lower part of the Alamo River while I emplaced my Infantry on the higher elevations, setting up my two cannons at the entrances to the town square, toward the side where the affray began.

In a sudden and headlong rush, they tried to penetrate to the center, but the havoc that greeted them from the rooftops and the running rain of projectiles threw them back on the spot. They crenellated various houses and a deadly exchange of fire commenced, sustained so steadfastly by both armed sides that, were it not for the solidity and consistency of the buildings due to the thickness of their walls and the materials of which they were constructed, this action would have unquestionably concluded very quickly and would have cost less victims than the ones sacrificed on the altars of the Fatherland. During this interval, I disposed that the Cavalry move up to the rear of the Texans to prevent them from retreating to the gullies and brambles whence they had started, taking advantage of the darkness of night and the incessant rain. I also constantly maintained within the square a column of 100 Infantry with bayonets fixed, to lend a hand wherever it might have been necessary. A rainy dawn broke, and the firing increased progressively on both sides. Noticing the enemy fire was causing me many losses among my brave men posted on the rooftops, and that the gunners of one of the pieces were nearly all down, I ordered the other cannon rolled around to my right, the enemy's left. Supported by 70 infantrymen to molest them more actively by crowding them together, while at the same time 100 of the defenders were to tether their horses and, taking advantage of the stonewall fences, attack him from the rear. This measure rendered the results I expected and the frontal fire instantly started to grow weaker.

The other cannon, serviced by Sappers, and I myself taking care of aiming it through a large aperture I had caused to perforate in the Town Hall wall, likewise contributed to the enemy's loss of the strong corrals where he had entrenched himself. Unable to reach them with the piece I had thrown against their left flank, I had it transferred to the hills, where the cavalry was stationed, to strike them from the rear. Pressed from all sides and realizing that they would be put to the knife at the first signal, for the sake of humanity and as proof of magnanimity of the Mexican heart, I offered them a chance to surrender within 5 minutes. They asked that I go over to talk to them, but the field and company officers at my side prevented me from doing this. In my stead, Colonel Vega did it and at the end of a short conference, he conceded them, in my name, an hour during which to decide to lay down their arms at the feet of our intrepid soldiers. At the end of the hour, they acceded. With part of our Infantry in battle formation, without the rest of them leaving their positions, the haughty conquerors started to march past in platoons, depositing their rifles, pistols and daggers on the ground in front of the unconquered and faithful defenders of the integrity of the great Nation to which we by good fortune belong.

Fearing that I may tire the attention of His Excellency (referring to Santa Anna), The President, and of Your Excellency, I enclose instead, in a separate folder, the detailed listing of resplendent merits and important services contributed and rendered during this notable action. I describe by the gentlemen, field and company officers, soldiers of the Army, Auxiliaries, authorities and civilians of the frontier, requesting that they be remunerated according to justice. I likewise enclose for Your Excellency the nominal lists of prisoners, a statement of arms they had surrendered, of the dead and wounded we had, of the ammunition consumed, a description of the material encountered in their camp, and the original letter that the chief of the Texans, William Fisher, passed on to me soon after the surrender.

I congratulate the Supreme Government again on this signal victory, remitting through the bearers, Brevet Colonel, Battalion Commandant Jose Ma. Carrasco and Ensign Cayetano Ocampo, the only flag found among their humble equipment that was returned to them, since the garments they wore during this combat were tattered to little pieces, as I had already notified Your Excellency in my previous note. May Your Excellency kindly accept the considerations of my constant appreciation and profound respect.

God and Liberty

Mier, 29 December 1842

Pedro de Ampudia

General Ampudia was careful not to mention the heavy casualties he sustained against the much smaller group of Texas fighters. Had the Texans not run out of gunpowder, food and water, the victory would have gone against the arrogant Mexican general. To his credit, he did allow the wounded Texans to be cared for. There is little doubt, had Santa Anna been present, he would have killed those who surrendered, as well as the wounded, as he had done at the Alamo and Goliad.

The Texans were not expecting to be moved further inland; the terms of their surrender gave the impression they would remain near the Texas coast. When the order came for them to march to Matamoros, they were taken by surprise; however, since the town was still fairly near the coast, most did not protest. A few did protest, only to have a bayonet shoved into their ribs. Ampudia kept the prisoners in Matamoros for a week and then ordered them transferred to Monterey. Those too weak from their wounds were left in the Matamoros hospital. They also would later escape and make the difficult journey back to Texas.

The Texans were then moved to Saltillo, where a few of the prisoners from the Woll invasion were being held. In Saltillo, an officer named Barriagan was put in charge of the prisoners. He placed the captives in chains, marched them a hundred miles west, and locked them in a large courtyard at the Hacienda Salado. Realizing they were being transported to a hellhole in the rugged mountains of the interior, the Texans started plotting their escape. They chose thirty-six-year-old Captain Ewen Cameron, a massive Scottish Highlander by birth, as their leader. Cameron was the ideal leader for such a daring operation. When Cameron had arrived in Texas, he set up his base of operations in the Victoria-Goliad region. Once established, he traded cattle until 1842 when he formed a militia known as the "Victoria Cowboys". Until then, the word cowboy was a derogatory term, but after the courage and daring displayed by Cameron's cowboys, the word came to represent valor and honor even though the Victoria Cowboys were, in fact, outlaws, confiscating cattle from Mexican ranches in the region south of the Nueces River. Since they were Texas cowboys doing the stealing, the term "cowboy" eventually came to be associated with the rugged, righteous men of the West.

Captain Cameron had been in fights with the Mexicans before. He had fought alongside the Mexican Federalists in their unsuccessful attempts to regain control of Mexico and establish the *"Republic of the Rio Grande."* While serving under Samuel Jordan in 1840, Cameron lost his horse and finding it in the possession of a Mexican, demanded his animal returned to him. Colonel Antonio Canales, Commander in Chief of the Federalists, ordered Cameron to give up the horse. After drawing his pistol and refusing, Colonel Canales ordered Cameron court-martialed. He was later exonerated, and his horse returned, but the incident made the two men bitter enemies. Cameron's "in your face" attitude made him a Texas hero.

Cameron solicited the aid of Samuel Walker, trusting Samuel's ability to think under pressure. While planning their escape, one of the captive Texans tipped off Barriagan. Upon learning of this betrayal, Cameron and Samuel suspected Phillip Dimitt and a runaway slave by the name of Swaney had been the informants. They decided they had to put their plan into action immediately. Cameron would grab a guard and Walker would seize his rifle. Just before the sun filled the morning sky, the two men moved quickly. Cameron's arms were like a steel vice as he restrained the guard and Walker's aim was perfect. The men then stormed the supply house and armed themselves. The shooting woke the other guards and the cavalry. As the Mexicans rushed the gate, they were killed. Five Texans died and fourteen wounded in the early morning battle. The Texans then made an agreement with Barriagan: The Mexican officer in charge to care for their wounded comrades in exchange for the lives of Cameron's men. The Mexicans agreed and Cameron led the reminder of the Texans out the gate and onto the road to Saltillo. Philip Dimitt and Swaney, the suspected traitors, were allowed to leave camp with the other Texans and travel with them in silence. When they reached Molino del Rey, the two suspects were locked up. Dimitt committed suicide. His actions confirmed he was the traitor, so the other suspect, the runaway slave, Swaney, was released. He remained in Mexico and eventually married a Mexican woman.

In the first hundred miles, the escaping Texans saw no Mexicans nor any sign of being followed. The men skirted the town and picked up the road to the Rio Grande. About fifteen miles from town, Cameron decided it was safer to leave the main road; this would prove to be a colossal blunder. By selecting the desolate, desert route, Cameron sealed their doom. The men's tongues swelled so thick from thirst, they were unable to close their mouths. Some broke into the thorny cacti to extract drops of water. Samuel Walker stuck a piece of leather between his teeth, allowing him to suck a little moisture, a trick he learned from an old Indian trader. The only food available was snakes, lizards, grasshoppers, roots, and cacti. The Texans eventually discarded their rifles to lighten their load.

The Mexicans sent a small cavalry of sixty-five soldiers to track down the escaping Texans. When the Mexicans started finding the Texans' weapons on the ground, they knew they were closing in. After days of wandering in the wilderness without direction and provisions, most of the escapees surrendered without incident to Colonel Domingo Huerta. The cavalry rounded them up like cattle and marched the weary men back to Salado. This time, the captors took no chances, placing the skeletal men in chains. Five men died in the desert, four other men vanished without a trace and were presumed to be either dead or living with Indians. Five men miraculously made it back to Texas: John Blackburn, William Morehead, George Anderson, William Oldham, and Lieutenant Thomas Washington discovered help in an unlikely place as a band of Indians provided them with food and water. Once they were fit to travel, they were given corn and gourds of water and shown the direction to travel. Two months later, the sun-baked survivors arrived in Gonzales. Their tattered clothing, matted hair and beards like wild men were a testament to their ordeal.

The 176 recaptured Texans were returned to Salado in chains. When Santa Anna learned of the escape, he ordered those who had fled be executed. His decree splashed shock waves around the world. Britain, France, and the United States all sent vigorous protests of his brutal decision. Governor Francisco Mexía of the state of Coahuila refused to obey the order, and foreign ministers stationed in Mexico were able to get the decree modified. Rather than alienate his country from the powers of the world, Santa

Anna acquiesced to their demands and canceled the death sentences. He mulled over what to do next. One of his aides gave him an idea, which involved a game of chance. Santa Anna ordered every tenth man be executed in what became known as the *Black Bean Episode.*

The Mexican executioners filled a black pot with 151 white beans and 17 black beans. Big Foot Wallace watched closely as the Mexicans poured the beans in the clay pot and noticed they put the white ones in first, and then the black ones. Decatur Cocke, a pro-Lamar man and former newspaper editor, was the first to draw a bean, not knowing the black beans were nearest the top. He raised the tiny round black bean high in the air and shouted, "Boys, I told you so. I never failed in my life to draw a prize." Big Foot followed and struggled to get his big hand in the mouth of the pot. Using his long fingers, he reached to the bottom and pulled out a white bean. As he passed back down the line, he whispered the secret to his old rangers friends, like Samuel Walker. Each one he told walked up to the front of the long line and reached deep into the pot, pulling out a white bean. No one objected to another person going to the front of the line because each man stood in fear of being unlucky. Ewen Cameron followed Samuel Walker, and to the consternation of Colonel Canales, drew out a white bean. Canales was enraged. How could he let the leader of the escape attempt live? Canales wrote His Excellency, Santa Anna, pleading his case. Santa Anna, who wanted all the Texans dead, had no problem issuing a death warrant for Cameron. Colonel Canales personally removed Cameron from his cell and marched his nemesis to the edge of town so the local children would not witness the killing. As the colonel escorted him outside the walls of the town, Cameron whistled an old Irish tune. As Cameron walked next to the banty rooster Canales, the giant Scotsman spat a wad of chewing tobacco on the Colonel's boot. Cameron was offered a blindfold, which he refused, saying is Spanish, "I want to look you in the eye so you will live with my murder in the dark of the night and remember you killed a man for no reason. I defy your cowardice."

Canales pushed one of the nine men in the firing squad aside, and grabbing his rifle, shouted, "Fire at will. Kill him and shut his mouth!"

As the nine bullets ripped Ewen Cameron's flesh, the big Scotsman kept a smile on his face. On April 25th, 1843, even as he was being executed in cold blood, Ewen Cameron still beat Colonel Canales; Cameron's attitude in death haunted the diminutive Colonel for the remainder of his days. Each year following Cameron's death, as the 25th of April approached, Canales became despondent and a recluse for weeks. Even in death, Cameron continued to torment his enemy.

The remaining captives were marched to the edge of Mexico City and locked up in Molino del Rey for seven months. During the months of June, July and August of 1843, the Texans did roadwork in and around Mexico City. Big Foot Wallace was harnessed to a two-wheel oxcart like a workhorse. When he got angry, he would run through town, pulling the cart, knocking over tables and crashing into walls.

A few Texas prisoners managed to escape from Mexico City by bribing the corrupt guards. They purchased horses and made it to safety north of the Rio Grande, while those without means had to double their work efforts. In September, the Texans were transferred to Perote Prison, where the San Antonio prisoners the Mier expedition had sought to liberate were being held. Located in the Mexican state of Vera Cruz, some sixty miles into the jungle, the structure was originally the Castle of San Carlos, built to guard one of the main trade routes and serve as a depository for treasure awaiting shipment to Spain. The massive stone fortress stood on twenty-six acres of land surrounded by a moat. When Santa Anna came to power, he turned the castle into a torturous dungeon in which to house work prisoners.

The Texans were forced to work in unbearable conditions enclosed behind the castle's massive stonewalls. When they were taken outside to work on roads, the Mexicans kept them under heavy cavalry guard. Subjected to the extreme heat and humidity, and lack of nutrition, two-dozen Texans died in Perote

Prison, their bodies dumped in shallow graves outside the castle walls. Big Foot Wallace reported seeing a pack of half-starved wild dogs fighting over a human skull. Their only relief in the sweltering jungle was in the monsoon season when the skies opened, dumping heavy rain for hours on end. The Texans stood in the courtyard facing skyward with their arms open, letting the cool water clean the perspiration from their bodies and filthy clothes.

On April 25, 1843, the same day Ewen Cameron was executed, William Thompson, Ed Wright, and Cyrus Gleason discovered an open prison gate. Without any consultation, they looked at each other and simultaneously dashed through the exit. The escapees made their way to the Gulf coast in three days, eating tree bark and foliage. Once on the beach, they followed the thin ribbon of sand back toward Texas. After two days on the beach, they came upon a Catholic priest. Cryus, who spoke fluent Spanish, was able to convince the priest that their English ship sank at sea and they had floated to shore on debris. Believing they were nothing more than shipwrecked sailors, the priest was more than willing to provide them with food and gourds of water.

Once back in Texas, the trio exposed the deplorable conditions they and their associates had endured. The near-death stares on their gaunt faces and their skeletal appearance personified the credibility of their claims. The three traveled across the Republic, telling of the deplorable, inhumane conditions of the dungeons of Perote. Ed Wright then met with President Houston. Ed's description of the horrendous conditions caused Houston to sob with emotion; many of those held prisoner in Mexico were his dear friends. Houston acted with alacrity, writing a long letter to his friend Waddy Thompson, the U.S. Minister to Mexico. In the letter, the President informed Waddy that his cousin, Sam Maverick, and 49 other Texans captured in San Antonio were in Perote Prison along with the remaining Mier prisoners.

The plight of the Texans held in Perote aroused sympathy across the United States. President John Tyler instructed Waddy Thompson to negotiate the release of the Texans and demand the liberation of all United States citizens imprisoned in Mexico. The Texas Congress granted money for humanitarian relief for the men at Perote; however, the money never reached the prisoners. The traitorous courier, Eddie Bell absconded with the funds for his own gain. The isolated prisoners came to believe their country had forsaken them. They had no knowledge of the diplomatic efforts that were taking place nor were they aware that the president had sent money for their needs. The silence made things appear no one was making an effort to secure their release.

Not all prisoners were treated with brutality and disdain. George B. Crittenden, the son of Senator Crittenden from Kentucky was released almost as soon as letters could be exchanged. A number of others were released through the intercession of influential friends and family in the United States. Orlando Phelps was indeed fortunate to have Santa Anna as a benefactor. His cowardly conduct was severely criticized by his comrades on the Mier Expedition, but upon learning he was the son of Dr. James Phelps, Santa Anna bought him new suits and gave him a room at the National Palace. Young Orlando's father was the physician responsible for housing Santa Anna after his surrender at San Jacinto. When an angry mob descended on the doctor's home and tied Santa Anna to a massive oak tree, intent on killing the dictator, Mrs. Phelps threw her arms around the Mexican President's body, protecting him with her life. Santa Anna never forgot the Phelps' kindness, and to demonstrate his profound gratitude, he provided Orlando safe passage back to Texas.

Another prisoner to grab the awareness of Santa Anna was John Christopher Columbus Hill. At fourteen, Hill was the youngest member of the Mier Expedition. His courageousness during the battle won him the admiration of General Ampudia. After his capture, the general enrolled Hill in a Matamoros school before marching the main body of prisoners southwest. At President Santa Anna's request, a military escort transferred the young man to Mexico City. Santa Anna was intrigued with young John and so were Generals Valentine Farias and Jose Tornel. The three men persuaded him to attend Mexican schools, where he completed his education at the College of Mines. Hill's special relationship with the Mexican president enabled him to win the early release of his father and brother, although he did not return with them to Texas. Hill married a local girl and remained in Mexico as a citizen, becoming a successful mining engineer.

Small groups of the Perote prisoners were released from time to time through the heavy persuasion of Waddy Thompson and the British minister, Lord Packenham. Santa Anna did not want conflict with the United States so on March 23rd, 1843, Sam Maverick, W.E. Jones, and Judge Anderson Hutchinson were released after having spent eight-and-a-half months in the Mexican prison. On May 4th, Sam arrived in La Grange and back into the loving arms of his wife, Mary. He told Mary his only sadness was he had gained release while so many of his friends had been left behind. On September 16th, 1844, the remaining 105 Texas prisoners were released. One of the darkest periods of the Republic came to a close, but deep animosity on both sides of the Rio Grande remained.

Every man, woman and child in Texas heard of the appalling conditions and the humiliating treatment the Texans had been subjected to while prisoners of war. Vendetta without mercy became the battle cry among the survivors. Outrage spread across the Republic, and small groups of angry men grew into substantial fighting forces demanding retribution. President Houston knew the powder keg was full and the wick lit. He was convinced that not even *he* would be able to prevent war with Mexico, so he prayed, knowing their only hope for victory would be a prolonged fight that would draw the United States into the fray. His prayers were answered when, after ten years as a Republic, Texas became part of the Union. In April of 1846, the Texas Rangers led the way for the U.S. Army to challenge those who had perpetrated such horrific atrocities upon their countrymen.

Chapter Thirty-Four
Sorrow

Jack Hays and Ben McCullough watched from the Texas banks of the Rio Grande as over two thousand Mexican fighters overwhelmed their friends. Jack knew it would be suicide if his men joined the fight. His motto was never to run from a fight if there was any possibility to win, but never rush into a death trap just for revenge. From their vantage point, the rangers could see the entire battlefield. What was Fisher thinking? He had ignored both Jack's scouting report and the direct order of his Commander in Chief and forged ahead, leading his men to certain death.

When Jack saw the Texans raise a white flag, he ordered his rangers to move inland, knowing the Mexicans would come across the river in large numbers. Their horses were tired and so were the men. Jack stopped on the San Antonio side of the Nueces River to rest, kill some game, and let their horses graze on the tall bottomland grasses. None of the rangers ever knew how dejected Jack was. He was able to maintain his equilibrium in the face of extreme disappointment and the deaths or capture of his close friends. Much like Matt Caldwell and Bud Miller, he blamed himself for their misfortune and held himself responsible for not being able to prevent Fisher from pursuing the deadly mission. Jack didn't think it cowardly to not stand and fight when the enemy was larger than his small number could defeat. He thought back to the time when his survey crew of five men came upon a hundred Comanche. They did not stick around and face such a large group of hostile Indians. The odds were too great. Jack knew Fisher's vengeful mindset had clouded his thinking. No rational man would think 275 men could invade Mexico and retrieve captives from a well-supplied army of over 1,500. After two day's rest, Ben and his men headed to Gonzales and Jack's forces headed to San Antonio. As they rode, Bud took the opportunity to seek Jack's counsel. "Major, how do I go about telling Mr. and Mrs. Hempstead about their sons?"

Jack removed his floppy hat and scratched his head as if contemplating what to say. Finally, he plopped his hat back on and answered, "I have been in that uncomfortable position more than once. It never gets easier. If I were you, I would not wait. Go immediately and tell them. They will be able to read your face anyway. You can give them assurances the Mexicans will not keep their boy but a couple of years."

Bud rode silently beside his wise leader for a while before explaining, "What makes it rough is my caring for them so deeply. Edward and Charlie seemed like brothers to me even though I had not known them all that long. I am rather fond of their sister, Charm, and I know the news is going to break her heart. I doubt if the Hempsteads will ever speak to me again."

Bud had hoped Jack would offer some encouraging words. What he did say put a knife in Bud's heart as surely as if his words had been made of steel. "It wouldn't surprise me if the sister blames you. Most of the time in this sort of thing, the loved ones look to place fault on others. I had to tell my best friend's parents that their son William had been killed fighting Comanche. William's pa asked me point-blank if his son had been scalped. I crossed my fingers behind my back and told a half-truth. I told them we were able to give William a Christian burial and read scripture over his grave. I pray God will forgive me for not being completely truthful, but I could not bear the thought of his parents spending the rest of their days haunted by visions of William's body being defiled. Even so, William's father blamed me for his son's death. He has not spoken to me since. Bud, do what you have to do to ease their pain."

Without hesitation, Bud replied, "I was thinking of writing Santa Anna and telling him I'm willing to exchange places with Charlie. What do you think?"

"I think you have rocks in your head. Don't you know they are aware of who you are? They know you are a ranger who rides with 'Devil Jack'. You go down there, and you will be killed. Don't get me wrong, if I thought an exchange could be made, I would leave that decision up to you."

When Jack arrived in San Antonio, the town was buzzing with the news of a recent raid by the cowboy bandit known as Perez. Perez's spies knew that Jack Hays was gone, so Perez and about a hundred bandits raided the town, killing one citizen and looting homes. The locals demanded Jack and his men go after the bandits. Jack understood their anger, but his rangers had personal matters that needed their immediate attention, and besides, the bandits had been gone for three weeks; tracking them would be impossible.

Jack realized that as long as he lived in San Antonio, he was in a den of Mexican spies and his every word passed on to either Santa Anna or the bandit gangs roaming the area south and west of town. He called his men together in the Military Plaza and when they were gathered in close, he said, "I don't want to be the only one without a chair when the music stops. I have to get out of this town or the spies will lay an ambush for me. This town has more spies than flies, and we all know how thick they are. I am going to relocate in Leon Springs and suggest you do the same. Don't tell a living soul where we are going to make camp. I believe our lives may very well depend on how well we keep our location secret."

Jack headed north up the mountain into Leon Springs where he owned a small cabin, more of a lean-to, really. Leon Springs was a viridian valley tucked in between two mountains with one of the best fresh-water springs in all of Texas. The tall, round mountain to the west of his cabin provided a perfect lookout post. He could see for miles in every direction. Jack told his men they would use Leon Springs as their new meeting place, and invited them to build cabins and shelter for their animals on his land. He had no choice. If he remained in San Antonio, the enemy could never be surprised. The walls had ears.

Bud opted not to go with Jack, but remained in town. The next day he would leave early to visit the Hempsteads. He spent the night restlessly tossing and turning, his heart heavy with sorrow. One son dead and the other might as well be. He fought back tears as he saddled his powerful stallion early the next morning. As he sat on the strong back of Lightning, listening to the pounding hooves on the hard surface, he contemplated what he would say over and over in his mind, changing the wording from mile to mile. The second day, when it was nearly dark, he reached his house in Bastrop and stopped to fill his gourd with fresh well water. The house was spotless and the yard level and clean. His neighbor had more than earned his money.

Bud wanted to hide in his house and never tell the Hempsteads. He rationalized that after the grueling two-day ride from San Antonio to Bastrop, his horse needed a rest. Even for a horse as strong as Lightning, forty-five miles a day was pressing the limits. The truth was that he was overcome with dread at the thought of facing Edward and Charlie's parents, and more than that, their sister, Charm. It was not difficult for Bud to convince himself not to continue until the following day. As Lightning ate, Bud stoked up a fire, and then took a warm bath. He had no trouble falling asleep after rolling up in his blanket. He awoke early the next morning, cooked breakfast, shaved, and put on a new store-bought shirt and brown wool jacket. He rolled up his buckskin clothes and tied them to the back of his saddle, mounted up, and was off. As he rode, he wrapped a magenta sash around his waist similar to the one Buck Travis was wearing when he was killed in the Alamo. The next twenty-five miles seemed like three hundred. As he turned off the Camino Real onto the road leading to the Hempsteads, he met a rider who seemed to be in a hurry. Bud held up his hand and summoned the man to stop. It was Noah Smithwick, who had been in New Orleans on business and was on his way to Austin, not realizing the capital had moved.

"Great to see you, Noah. I have lots to tell," Bud said, reaching over and vigorously shaking his friend's hand. "Will you please ride back to the Hempsteads with me? I have some horrible news to tell them and could use your moral support."

"I'd love to, but have to get to Austin to meet with President Houston."

Bud smiled. He knew Noah would have to ride with him partway if he wanted to meet with the President. "Noah, you are going in the wrong direction. President Houston up and moved the capital back to Washington-on-the-Brazos. Seems they are giving the government free rent. You know President Houston. He will squeeze a dime out of nickel."

"When did this all happen?"

"Right around the time Woll invaded San Antonio. President Houston's moving of the capital caused quite a ruckus among some of the folks up in Austin. That bunch was ready to shed blood rather than give up the archives."

Noah turned his horse saying, "Guess I will ride with you since I have to go that way to reach Sam."

As the pair of old friends followed the road along the banks of the Colorado River, Noah wanted to know all about Mier and the men taken from court in San Antonio. A variety of rumors had floated back to New Orleans, with many of the stories too outlandish to be true. Noah depended on George Kendall's newspaper for most of his information, but the majority of news was third and forth generation hearsay. Noah listened intently as Bud told him of the Dawson massacre, the victory at Salado Creek, and Jack Hays' frustration at being denied the army's assistance in chasing down Woll. Bud spoke of his contempt for the actions of those who pillaged Laredo, and the insane attack led by Fisher on Mier. Suddenly they heard screaming and dogs barking up ahead. The two rangers gave their mounts rein, spurring them in the flanks. As they rounded the bend, they saw a fourteen-foot alligator dragging a young Negro girl by her arm toward the river. She had fainted as the angry beast progressed toward the water. Several Negro men and women were screaming at the alligator as it dragged the young girl, but the dogs' vigorous barking and the helpless bystander's screams did not dissuade the alligator.

Bud pulled Lightning to a sliding halt and dismounted in the mass of dust. The alligator was only ten yards from the riverbank, and Bud knew he had to act fast. He shoved his way past the frightened slaves and jumped on the back of the alligator with both boots. The angry animal tried to shake Bud off, thrusting his lethal tail back and forth. Bud started jumping up a down as if he were on a trampoline. His actions caused the big alligator to release the girl and concentrate on the man jumping on his back. Like a Brahma bull, the gator rolled his skin, making it impossible for Bud to remain on top of him. He lost his balance and tumbled to the ground, rolling over and over to escape the gator. The angry alligator turned toward the ranger, but Bud managed to get to his feet and make a dash toward the riverbank. Just as they both reached the water's edge, Bud jumped up, grabbed a tree limb and swung his feet out of reach. The alligator looked up at Bud dangling over him. Bud didn't know if alligators could stand on their back legs and tails like a prairie dog. He hoped not. He could hear the Negroes crying and the strong voice of Noah Smithwick shouting, "Hang tight. He is getting ready to go back into the water."

Just as Bud's grip was failing, the alligator swished his tail and slid over the red clay bank into the dark water and out of sight. After dropping to the ground, Bud turned to see Noah applying a tourniquet on the little girl's arm. To everyone's amazement, the alligator did not inflict severe damage; she received only minor cuts that would heal in a matter of weeks.

The twelve family members had recently escaped from the Groce Plantation and were on their way to Mexico to seek their freedom. They were frightened, thinking Bud and Noah would take them back to the plantation for the reward. Most slave owners would pay $100 for the return of a male slave, and $25 for the women and children. Bud and Noah had no such intent. They didn't judge those who owned slaves, but would never consider taking another person's freedom away. The rangers gave the family part of their corn and beef jerky and Noah drew a circuitous route around San Antonio that would take them onto the old road west of town. Noah had lived in Mexico as a young man and smuggled tobacco into the country, trading his contraband for silver. He spoke fluent Spanish and knew the customs of the Mexican population. He told the male slaves they would need to work their way toward Monterey if they hoped to find employment.

Bud then cut two thin poles and using his blanket, made a travois to pull the little girl until she was able to walk. He then gave the eldest man his shotgun and some ammunition, saying, "You will need to kill a mustang, wild pig, cow or deer for food. I would give you my long rifle, but it was purchased for me by some good friends." The gray-haired Negro slave didn't know what to say. He lowered his head before responding to the rangers' kindness, "Thank yous, Massa Miller 'n Massa Noah. Yous is good men, and we be much obliged you dun saved our baby gurl. May the Lord Jesus smiles on you and yours."

It was now late in the afternoon. Bud knew he was only a mile or so from the Hempstead home. It was then Noah said, "I cannot go with you. I've seen too many people cry since I got to Texas sixteen years ago. If you will promise not to tell a living soul, I'll tell you why I need to meet with President Houston."

Bud looked Noah in the eyes and answered, "On my mother's grave, I promise not to reveal a word you tell me in confidence."

"That's good enough for me," Noah responded. "Sam sent me to New Orleans to see if I could sell some of the Republic's Navy ships. I think I have the original shipbuilders talked into buying the vessels back at a reduced price. The Republic is broke and needs the funds desperately. Sam told me in confidence that we could not afford to sail the ships and don't have the money to pay the sailors."

"Thank you for having confidence in me. Your secret is safe. I sure wish you would go with me to face the Hempsteads. I dread telling them. I suspect they will not let their daughter Charm even talk with me after I tell them."

"I can tell you from experience, your stock is going to ascend with showing so much compassion. Seriously, you are showing true grit. Most men would just let someone else deliver the bad news."

As the men reached a bend in the road, they heard another terrifying scream. Bud grabbed his rifle, followed closely by Noah. As they rounded the corner, at the edge of a thicket stood a wild mustang stallion, intent on stealing Noah's mare. The roan wild stallion stood his ground. Both rangers realized he was most likely master of a large heard of mares until a younger, stronger stallion took his place. He had been roaming the countryside, seeking mares to build a new remuda.

"It's a real shame," Noah said with a tinge of sadness in his voice. Then he raised his rifle and before Bud could stop him, he pulled the trigger. The wild stallion fell to his knees, and then crumpled to the ground.

Bud shouted, "Why did you do that? We could have run him off. He was not bothering us. That was a pretty sick thing to do!"

Noah just smiled as he retrieved his horsehair rope from his saddle. "I just creased him. He'll be fine. If I can break him, he will make me a great war horse. He's exactly like one I coveted when I was in Mexico smuggling tobacco." Noah's voice was as calm as a lake in the morning.

Bud had heard of "creasing" horses with a bullet along the crest of the neck, stunning them for a moment; however, he had never seen anyone actually perform the act. He watched in amazement as Noah made a halter and tied the stunned stallion to a tree. Moments later, the stallion struggled to his feet, only to discover he was now the property of Noah Smithwick.

Before they parted ways, Noah said, "When I reach forty, I will marry, settle down and become a tamed man. Right now, a woman would only get in my way. There are still places I want to see. One day I want to go west and see the Pacific Ocean. One day, California will be like Texas and a man of my skills will be needed. I'm not for annexation, but remember this: In five years, Texas will become a state in the Union. You know this to be true. Sam is not going to give up until he outsmarts those bluebloods up north."

Bud didn't believe that Texas would give up her independence to become part of the United States, but he did not argue with the seasoned ranger who taught him to ride and shoot from the back of a horse.

Bud was still trying to delay delivering the unpleasant news to the Hempsteads. To change the subject, he asked, "What's the story on you smuggling tobacco into Mexico?"

Rolling a cigarette, Noah removed his flint and steel and lit a smoke. "Bud, when I was a couple years younger than you, I got the bright idea to smuggle tobacco into Mexico. It was too hard to get the stuff into New Orleans. At that time, the Mexicans kept a good eye on the border. John Webber, me, and a couple other men put together a thousand pounds of some of the best tobacco ever grown in Texas. We cut it down into 100-pound bales and John and I took half, tied it on five mules and then headed for Laredo, only to find other smugglers got there first. The other two wanted to try Monterey, and John and I headed upriver. Mind you, we didn't have a map or local guide. After awhile, our food ran out. John shot a wild mustang colt. I had never eaten horsemeat and was repulsed by the idea. I fasted for three days watching John cook thick, juicy horse steaks…"

Bud interrupted, "You had never tasted horse steaks? They are great. The first one I ate, I didn't know it was horse and gobbled it down. Then one of the old-timers told me it was mustang meat."

"Yeah I know that now, but back then I couldn't stomach the thought of eating a horse. By the third day, I was famished. Webber cooked some horse fat to grease our pack straps and leather lariats. When he got the grease he needed, he placed the cracklings on a rock close to me. He never said a word. The smell made the pit of my empty stomach growl. Finally, I reached over and picked one up, took a bite, and dad-gum-it, I liked it. Before I knew it, I had gobbled down all the cracklings. Then I cooked me a thick horse steak. Webber made a believer out of me."

The wild mustang's neck now covered with blood, the injury looked a lot worse than it was. He angrily fought the rope as Noah mounted his mare and wrapped the lariat around his saddle horn. His halter squeezed the nose of the mustang, making it uncomfortable for him to resist. Bud rode Lightning at the rear, slapping the mustang on his rump to speed him along. After a few hundred yards of fighting the lariat, he gave in and started following like a trained dog. The two friends came to a crossroads where one trail turned north to the Hempsteads, and the other main road led to Washington-on-the-Brazos. Bud thanked Noah again for helping him become a ranger, and watched as Noah and his prize mustang trotted around a bend in the road.

Bud nudged his mount and headed toward the Hempsteads. He could see smoke rising from the chimney and hear the ringing of the supper bell. This meant he would have to face George and Mabel Hempstead, the boys, and Charm all at once. He got a sick feeling in the pit of his stomach. He slowed from a trot to a walk. He was still beating up on himself for letting Edward and Charles go with him in the first place. The knot in his stomach tightened when Mr. Hempstead spotted him coming up the dirt road, rushed into the house and brought the entire family out front to await his arrival. As Bud neared the house, George shouted, "Welcome home. We have kept you in our prayers ever since we got word about our dear Charles and Edward. We were so afraid you were among the causalities."

When Bud heard George's words, he pushed Lightning into a gallop. As he dismounted, he said, "I really tried to get Edward and Charles not to go with Fisher. We knew it was a trap and Major Hays did his best to make Fisher and his men understand the overwhelming odds they faced."

Mrs. Hempstead saw the guilt on Bud's face and quickly interrupted, "Son, a wagon full of men couldn't have stopped those two boys. They had their minds set on fighting and no one, not even you, could have prevented them from going with Fisher. Little Ralph Gilpin, who was left with the horses on the Texas side came through yesterday and told us about Edward being killed and Charles being taken prisoner. He assured us you did all you could to persuade them not to cross the river. He told us that you and Major Hays had already been on the Mexico side and spied the enemy soldiers in the mountains. Please don't be upset. It was preordained by the Lord to take Edward Home from a desolate place like Mexico. Please come inside."

Charm stepped from the family, put her arms around Bud and whispered, "God answered my prayers. You are back safe." Then taking his hand, she led him into the rustic cabin.

Charm placed another wooden plate on the table and gave Bud a cane fork, and a knife made with a blade of steel stuck into a dear antler. When everyone was seated, George bowed his head and prayed, "Oh Heavenly Father, we, your obedient servants can never question your will. We know Charles is in your protective care and Edward is sitting in Heavenly places far above all principalities, power, might, and dominion, next to our Lord Christ Jesus. We bless you for returning young Miller to us unharmed. We humbly thank you for this food and your blessings upon our family beyond our fondest imaginings. Amen."

Bud never expected to find such a gracious reception and he was humbled. He was also greatly relieved they did not blame him for their sons going to war. His appetite was constrained, but after watching the family eating venison steaks covered with white gravy, Bud finally picked up his fork. For the first time since hearing the news of Edward's death, and Charlie's capture, Bud relaxed. Charm poured him a large gourd of fresh grape juice squeezed from wild mustang grapes, which grew in abundance in Texas. Bud reluctantly took a sip; slightly concerned it might blister his lips. He had eaten wild mustang grapes and they did blister, but this juice was sweeter and didn't cause such a drastic reaction.

Charm broke the silence, blurting out, "Papa took me to Bastrop to see your house. You didn't tell us it was a mansion. It is so big and beautiful. I loved the tall pines and seeing the Colorado River protected by the giant pecan trees. The pine floors were so beautiful. I just had to sweep up the dust. I couldn't stand for something so gorgeous to remain dirty. You even have water in the kitchen. We had never seen a home with a water well inside."

"Don't give me the credit. The Baron de Bastrop is the man who designed the home with the well pumping inside the kitchen," answered Bud. "Are you saying the inside of the house was dirty when you got there?"

"Yes, why?"

"Well, I paid my neighbor's wife to clean the house so it would be nice and clean when you arrived. I plan to have a word with them."

Suddenly the table went silent. George asked, "You don't know, do you?"

"Know what?" asked Bud.

"He was killed, and the Comanche captured her. His blood is still on your front porch where he struggled to reach his rifle. Poor fella. It must have been horrible seeing his wife carried off. They removed his scalp while he was still alive, and it is my guess he lived a day or so, too weak to go for help. We understand a local family took the children in. Did you know they had five little ones, ages three to nine?"

"I cannot believe this. Dang. I hate I asked him to clean my property. The least I can do is see the children have what they need. I'll see to it that the folks caring for them get some money."

Mrs. Hempstead responded, "I'm sure they will appreciate any help you can give them. Frank and Judy Foster are dirt framers from Alabama, and already have nine children of their own. They are a good Christian family." Mabel then posed a direct question to Bud, asking, "How long do you plan to stay with us?"

"I was hoping to remain a couple of days. I can stay longer if you need me."

Charm anxiously waited to see what her father was going to say. George spoke words that took Bud off guard. "We need you to cut us some firewood," he said. "With the older two boys gone, we have not been able to find time to do any choppin'. Can you cut fire wood?"

Bud did not hesitate. "Can an owl hoot? Sure I can cut wood."

Charm began with a soft giggle, and the other children followed suit. Soon the giggling turned into uncontrollable laughter. Even stone-faced George was laughing so hard he started coughing. Mrs. Hempstead, ever the lady, could not restrain herself and burst out laughing as well. The laughter was a welcome release of the family's pent-up sadness. Finally, when George could catch his breath, he asked, "Do you know what a cord and a rick of wood are?"

Bud answered, "Sir, I have heard the term when I was a boy back in Kentucky, but I cannot say I know what they are."

"Cords and ricks are the way we measure firewood. A cord is four feet wide, four feet high and eight feet long. Since stoves and fireplaces won't accommodate a four-foot log, we cut a rick, which is two feet wide, four feet high and eight feet long. It takes two ricks to make a cord. Don't jump up and rush out the door, but we could use five cords; that way, me and the smaller boys can tend the crops 'til Charlie is back with us. Can you handle that?"

Bud answered without hesitation. "If that is what you need, then that is what I'll do."

Charm quickly interjected, "I will stack the wood and measure the cords. I'll also make Bud some soft doeskin gloves tonight to protect his hands. His gloves are too rough and will give him blisters."

George looked up from eating, and with a mouthful of food, inquired, "Do you know the difference between a Shin oak and a Burr oak?"

"Yes sir. You have to know trees if you are going to be a ranger. Lots of times when we are riding, we talk about the different kinds of trees so we can find our way back home. Trees change from one area to another. Burr oaks are the great big tall ones that grow to about eighty feet high and more than three feet around. You have a batch of them growing on the north side of your farm. One of the rangers told me they got their name from the burr look of the top of the acorn. The Shin oaks are the ones that have the thin, gray flaky bark. Up in limestone country, they are short and scrubby, but down here, in this good soil, they grow to about twenty feet. I like the smell of 'em when they are fresh cut."

"You know your trees," George responded as he continued to eat. "I need you to cut the Shin oaks nearest the farm over on the west side." George needed the trees next to the field cleared so he could expand his farmland.

I'll get started early," Bud replied.

The Hempsteads could have done without Bud's help; George and the boys could manage to find time to chop a fresh supply when the weather was too cold to work the fields. What he and Mabel really wanted was for Charm to have time to get to know Bud. They were well aware of their daughter's serious interest in him and hoped the feeling was mutual. Mabel had little doubt; she had seen Bud's eyes glaze over when he was speaking with their vivacious daughter.

The following morning, Bud was up early. He had no choice. The roosters roused him at dawn. After shaving in cold water, nicking his face in a couple spots, he joined the family for breakfast. There was no chatting. Everyone ate quickly, and then Charm led Bud to the barn where the wood ax was stored. She accompanied him to a large Shin oak tree and showed him how to notch one side and then cut through from the other. The tree fell exactly where she had predicted. From time to time, George glanced in their direction, not saying anything, but observing the pair working in tandem.

Bud started off doing very well, but as the day wore on, his production significantly dropped. To the embarrassment of his daughter, George walked over and asked, "How many times have you sharpened your ax today?"

"He hasn't," answered Charm. "I didn't think it was my place to say anything."

The giggling started again. Mrs. Hempstead, who was bringing them water, joined in the laughter. "What in the heck is so all fired funny?" Bud asked laughingly.

"Son, when cutting wood, it is necessary to stop and sharpen your ax every hour or so. The duller the blade, the less wood you can cut."

"Boy, do I feel stupid. I was wondering why I was falling behind my morning pace. Now I see why you all were laughing." Reaching his blistered hand behind Charm's neck, pretending to be shaking her, he joked, "Just wait till I get you alone."

That evening at the dinner table, George asked, "Know anything about the Osage orange trees, Bud?"

He hesitated before answering, "Sir, I hope this isn't a trick question. Someone, I can't remember who, told me they are the trees we call Bo-dark?"

George nodded his head as he took a sip of steaming coffee. "Yep. When the French traders first arrived, they named the tree *Bois D'Arc*. They only grow around here and up through east Texas. The Osage Indians use the limbs to make their powerful bows; they make such strong bows, the Osage also use the branches for barter with other tribes. I plan to plant sprigs around my plowed ground. They will eventually grow to three feet in diameter and are extremely sturdy. I thought if I planted them three feet apart, as they branched out they would form a solid wall. In a year or so, the thorny trees will make it impossible for man or beast to pass through. Mama and me were thinking maybe you would stay and help Charm sprig the Osage orange trees on the south and west side of our field. Can't pay you much, but we can feed you some of the best food in Texas. What say you?"

Bud was in a tight spot. He felt he needed to be back in San Antonio, yet to spend another week with Charm was too appealing to turn down. "Any way I can help, I'm willing to give it a shot. You have a fine daughter, and it would be my pleasure if she gave me guidance in planting the sprigs. If you don't mind, Sir, I'll finish cutting the wood. I think one more day with a 'sharp ax', and I'll have your winter wood."

George nudged his knee against his wife's leg, signaling his approval. "Son, I think you may feel some responsibility for our boys and I want to put you at ease. They both left with Mama and my blessings. They are grown men and capable of making choices for themselves. They talked of going to fight long before you came into our home, and if they had not left with you, it would have been with someone else. I also want you to know we are proud of you. You are a credit to Texas. Please don't stay just because you feel bad about our sons. They both are in God's hands. Edward has gone Home, and one day Charlie will come riding up that sandy trail."

Bud was quick with his reply. "Mr. Hempstead, please rest assured I'm not trying to replace either of your sons. I'm not man enough to do that. I'm staying because, frankly, I want to spend the time with you and your family."

Normally George ate and left the table, but seeing Bud had not finished eating, he asked Charm for a second cup of coffee. "What are you going to do with that fine home and piece of land down at Bastrop?"

Bud was chewing a piece of tender meat and not able to answer immediately so he raised his hand, signaling he would answer in a moment. "I hope to live on the place once I marry. You have seen my house and the general area. There are 1,147 acres adjacent to my property that I can buy for a quarter an acre. I would like your opinion about me buying that tract of land. I have the money to pay cash."

Puzzled, George inquired, "What would you do with all that acreage?"

"I have thought about that a lot. I want to raise horses and cattle on part of the land and work out a deal with someone to farm the parcel on the north end. I'd build them a house and trade them a place to live and work in exchange for corn for my horses. You know, like the sharecroppers do back in the states. Only I want to make sure whoever does the farming gets more than enough to live on."

"Couldn't you buy a Negro family to run the farm?" Mabel inquired.

"Yes Ma'am, I could, but I'm not one for owning people. I know how much I love my freedom, and I can't see taking that away from any other person. Freedom is worth dying for. That is why Travis, Crockett, Bowie, Bonham and all the other brave Texans made their stand at the Alamo."

George looked at his wife and then scanned around the table before speaking. No one uttered a word because they knew Mr. Hempstead was collecting his thoughts. "Son, me and Mama are not in favor of buying slaves either. I need to preface that statement by saying we can't afford to buy one, but if we had the money, we would not. Back home in Tennessee, we were sharecroppers and were essentially slaves to the landowner. Here in Texas, we have our own place. It's not a big spread, but a place we can plant our roots. I can tell by talking with you that you're not the kind of man to take advantage of someone working your crops. I suspect when Charlie is set free, he would like nothing better than to work your place. He has a girl he is going to marry when Santa Anna pardons him. Mind you, I'm not trying to get a place for my son, but I don't believe you will find a harder worker."

"I knew Charlie planned to marry when he returned, but I had never thought of him working my place. That would work just fine. When I finish cutting the wood and sprigging the fence line, I'll go buy that land and contract to have a nice house built near the spring on the northern edge. With the tract the Baron left me, and the extra pasture, I will have plenty of land to start my cattle business. I visited with Mr. Taylor White and learned a great deal about cattle. Horses, I learned about from a German breeder on Galveston Island." Bud was careful not to mention Mr. Treptow's name or hint about Virginia.

George stood up and looked Bud in the eyes for a moment before speaking. "Why don't you go on down and buy that property, and then me and the boys will clear off a tract of farmland so all Charlie will have to do is move in and start planting. I have enough seed corn to get him a starter crop. Nothing would please me more than to have my son and his family near us."

Bud also stood, and answered, "Mr. Hempstead, I have a better idea. I'll have three hundred acres of top farmland surveyed off, build them a house, and give the place to Charlie and his bride for a wedding present. If Charlie is not released in time to plant, you and the boys can drop the corn in the ground. I know a perfect spot right along the banks of the Colorado."

Charm squeezed Bud's arm and then boldly, in front of her parents, stood on the tips of her toes and kissed him on the cheek. Bud turned beet-red. Then Charm surprised everyone, saying, "Bud Miller, you are the kindest man I have ever met. I feel like crying when I think of my brother owning a farm and having a house waiting when the Mexicans let him go. You are so generous. It's no wonder everyone who knows you loves you."

Bud glanced down at Charm's enchanting face and saw tears forming in her eyes. He had to fight to hold back his tears as he addressed the family. "When my work here is done, I will go get a contract and have a two-room dogtrot house constructed. When I get the land plotted, I'll have the surveyor bring the paperwork up here. Mr. Hempstead, once you get the plot plan, you can go and prepare the soil for planting. As rich as the riverbank is, I don't think much will need to be done."

George didn't need to think; he already had an answer. "A hundred dollars for us to build the house. The only reason I would charge anything at all is that we need some new farm implements and Mama is short on cloth for clothes. That amount will go a long way to getting us what we need and it'll be our pleasure to build the house for our son."

Bud's jacket was hanging on one of the coat pegs protruding from the entrance wall. He walked over and removed three 50 dollar gold pieces, and placed them on the table in front of George. "Sir, here is 150 dollars. Part is to build the house and the rest is for my room and board. No need for you to wait to get the cloth and things you need. I know you will do a fine job building the house. I cannot wait to see Charlie's face when he gets home and you take him to his new farm. Now, I need to get to bed. Tomorrow will be here before we know it."

Charm spoke before her father could respond. "Daddy, may I walk Bud to the barn?"

Mr. Hempstead looked at his wife, waiting to see what she would say. Mabel knew it was on her shoulders to make the decision. The wise country woman knew she could trust Bud. She also knew her strong-minded daughter would be terribly disappointed if not allowed to say goodnight. She pondered before speaking her mind. "We know we can trust both of you. What I'm going to say has nothing to do with trust, but appearances. Charm dear, it's not proper."

George heard his wife speak and knew the answer was final. "Let's go boys. It will be daylight soon enough if we just sit around here."

Before they could leave the table, Carl, their third oldest son, spoke up. "I could walk with them. It should be okay if I go along. What do you think Papa?"

Carl was now seventeen and even larger than Charlie. His father placed the palm of his hands in the center of his back, stretching like a dog waking from a deep sleep, "I don't know. What do you think mother?"

"Well, son, you came up with a good idea. With you along as a chaperone, I see no reason why Charm cannot accompany Mr. Miller to the barn."

The work progressed steadily and within nine days, the wood was stacked neatly beside the house, and two sides of the field were sprigged. This goodbye was less painful because everyone knew Bud would return.

Bud's neighbor, Clematis Boggs, was allotted 1,147 acres for his service in the Texas Army, but his wife and children died from yellow fever before he could build them a house. Boggs wanted to sell the land and return to Virginia, where he had family. Bud had no trouble finding him at the only saloon in Bastrop. He was leaning against the bar and talking to a stranger when Bud approached. Tapping Boggs on the shoulder, Bud asked, "Ready to sell your land?"

Stunned, Boggs turned and asked, "Hey, you are Stump Miller's boy, ain't cha? I talked to you not long ago. Does a Billy goat butt? You dang tooten I'm ready, as long as you don't try to steal it from me. I will not take a dime under twenty cents an acre."

"Mr. Boggs, you told me twenty-five cents. Have you lowered your price?"

"Did I tell you twenty five? I should have kept my big mouth shut. Now the cat is out of the bag. My price is twenty and not a cent less."

"I'm not here to cheat you, Mr. Boggs. You risked your life fighting Santa Anna. Didn't you tell me you had some plows and other farm equipment?"

"Yeah. I wuz ready to build a home for my family 'til the yeller devil took 'em. There's a small barn up near the fresh water springs full of plows, hoes, and a harness. Why do you ask?"

"I want to buy your farming equipment and the land. I'm ready to pay you in gold right now. Is it a deal?"

"Do I look like a fool? The place and what equipment I have is yours, including the wagon. It's like new. You git it all for twenty cents an acre."

Bud asked those standing in bar room: "Any of you know how to fill out a land transfer?"

The bartender dried his hands on his apron before answering, "We now have a lawyer in town. William Boone is his name. Says he's related to Daniel Boone of Kentucky. You can find him set up in front of the hardware store. They rented him a table in the corner to do his business."

"Well Mr. Boggs, let's go over and visit Mr. Boone. I have some shiny gold dollars just itchin' to get into your hands."

"Much obliged, fur shore," Boggs replied. "Soon as we sign them papers, I'm on my way back to my family. I've had all the dad-gum Injuns and Meskins I ever want to lay my eyes on."

William Boone was a short, balding man, with thick wire-rim glasses and a thin goatee. His voice was high pitched and his hands were milky white. He stood to introduce himself, and Bud's hand engulfed the lawyer's as they shook hands.

"I'm here because I need for you to draw up and record a deed for me, Mr. Boone. I'm buying Mr. Boggs' place."

"The fee will be five dollars for the deed and two more to record it. Do you have that much money?"

"I think I can scramble together that amount," Bud replied. "While we're at it, I want to hire you to find someone to survey the north three-hundred acres, and I want that parcel deeded to Charlie Hempstead. Can you handle all of this for me? I cannot stick around. I ride with Major Jack Hays and he's expecting me in San Antonio soon."

Bud was Boone's first paying client. Sweat beads covered his forehead as he strung out his reply, "I---m yooour maaan!"

"Catch your breath, Mr. Boone. Get your paper and pen and let me go over once more what I need. I'm paying $290 in gold to Mr. Boggs for his 1,147 acres. Out of that, I want to divide off three hundred acres and deed that parcel to Charlie Hempstead. On second thought, I think that should be Charles, Charles Hempstead. Then I'm giving you an additional twenty dollars in gold to have the land surveyed. Do we have a deal?"

Boone's speech morphed into a professional tone. "Mr. Miller, I can assure you that I am the man to act as a fiduciary of this transaction. I have my law degree from the University of Virginia and was among the top twenty in my class."

Bud smiled to himself, thinking there were probably only twenty in the class, with the pudgy lawyer at the bottom. Pulling up a three-legged stool, Bud sat down and drew a map of the land to be surveyed. Then he wrote instructions with his name and Charlie's on the paper. He stood up and gave the lawyer his fee in gold, with firm instructions, "Mr. Boone, if this job is not completed in haste, you can expect me to be extremely angry upon my return. If you run, rest assured I will track you down. I will enlist the help of my fellow rangers and see you dangle from the end of a rope on the backside of that hillock."

Once Boggs penned his signature on the deed, he saddled his gray mustang mare and headed up the Camino Real in the direction of Nacogdoches. From there, he would make his way back home to Kentucky, a rich man. He turned in his Mexican saddle, waving at Bud before kicking his wiry little horse in the flanks. Boggs' luck didn't hold. Five Comanche waylaid him along the road and soon his shaggy red hair was proudly displayed on the belt of one of the warriors. For an equal divide, three took the coins, one took Boggs' horse, and the fifth brave took the flaming-red scalp, a prize the Indians believed would ward off evil and give the warrior superpowers in battle. Boggs' mistake was wearing a hat. If the Indians could have seen his crimson mane, they never would have attacked him. An amber glow painted the morning sky as Bud made ready for the two-day ride to Leon Springs. The only person he encountered along the way was a bee hunter heading for the San Antonio Missions. The old man sat humped over in his saddle as he pulled four reluctant pack mules loaded down with bee's wax and honey. As Bud cantered past the buckskin-clad hunter, he tipped his hat, but said nothing. As he rode, Bud's thoughts drifted back to Charm and her family. He recalled how when time came for him to leave, George couldn't stand to watch him ride off, but rather busied himself in the barn. The younger boys, Mabel and Charm saw him off, watching until the thick fog engulfed him a few hundred yards from the house. Both women cried; Mabel for her daughter and Charm because she would desperately miss her brave hero. They knew there were pressing ranger duties and that Bud needed to visit his father's grave. He had avoided and found excuses not go to Goliad for many years. Now it was time he learned the truth. Was his pa a hero or a coward? Did he leave property or had he gambled the title away in a card game as many had said? Then there was a promise to fill. Before he left, Charm had extracted a vow that he would visit Goliad. She knew if he said he would, nothing short of death would stop him.

Lightning's rhythmic hooves pounding the clay surface was music to Bud's ears as each step confirmed he was making the right choice; Charm. Even though his mentors, Noah, Jack and Ben argued against marriage, this time he would not follow their advice.

Chapter Thirty-Five
Houston

The year of 1843 swept in on a dark storm cloud, bringing with it grave consternation for President Samuel Houston. He lost the Archive War to an angry woman with a cannon, and more than four hundred of his beloved Texans remained incarcerated in the worst hellhole imaginable deep in the jungles of Mexico. He was also facing being fifty-years-old in three months and about to become a legitimate father for the first time. His children with Indian women didn't fit into his equation. His sickly wife, Margaret was experiencing a difficult pregnancy. The fledgling Republic was destitute and the treasury was not even able to pay his meager salary. Just when he didn't think things could get any worse, his mother-in-law Nancy Lea arrived on a stagecoach.

Nancy Lea had moved to Texas in 1842 to be near her six children. She moved to New Cane, about twenty miles north of Liberty, and purchased fifteen hundred acres of land and built a home. Her youngest daughter married Bill Bledsoe, who owned a successful sugar cane plantation there, and all of her children, with the exception of Margaret, lived in New Cane. When Nancy learned of Margaret's difficult pregnancy, she did what Nancy did best: She took control. Nancy Lea strutted into Sam's small office demanding her daughter live with her until the baby was born. Houston thought of standing up to his mother-in-law, but when he saw the determination in her eyes, he backed down. Sam didn't want his wife to leave, but he was not about to deal with Nancy's wrath. His mother-in-law loved to brag how she told the President: "You may have conquered the wretched Santa Anna, but you will never conquer me."

As long as Margaret was with Sam, he may have been tempted to take a nip, but out of respect to his wife, suppressed his desire to imbibe. The stress of being alone, the Republic's destitute condition, his concern for the constant Indian conflicts, and concern for his fellow Texans locked away by a brutal warlord, created the perfect storm and lowered his resistance. A few weeks after Margaret left, Sam's old drinking buddy, Major B.M. Hatfield, who ran a local saloon and rented the upper floor to Congress for a modest fee, dropped in for a visit. He had just received a shipment of Sam's favorite drink, Madeira, a rarity in Texas. Produced on the island of Madeira off the coast of Portugal, the wine was made from black paint grapes planted in the rich volcanic soil along the island's hillsides. The fine wine owed its success to the primitive shipping conditions of the seventeenth century. By accident, some wine left in tubes in the bottom of a ship crossed the equator and the journey inexplicably mellowed the wine. The winemakers reasoned that if one crossing of the equator was good for the wine, two crossings had to be better. By the late 1700s, pipes of Madeira were placed in the bottom of ships and sent on round-trip voyages to all parts of the world. This unique maturation technique became known as *vinho da roda* (*wine of the round voyage*). Exposed to constant rocking and extreme heat, why the wine was not ruined was a mystery, but the results were astonishing. When Sam refused to accept the wine, Hatfield suggested the wine could be a gift to the Lockharts for allowing him to stay in their home rent free. Sam finally relented and accepted the wine for himself. After visiting with Major Hatfield, Sam retired to his room for the night. He placed the gallon of Madeira on the night table and began reading under the dim lamplight. He kept glancing at the bottle until finally he thought maybe just one sip before bedtime wouldn't hurt. One sip turned into two, and two into three, and slowly the jug began to empty. Around 3 AM, Sam finished off the gallon of wine. Drunk, sprawled across his bed, he started screaming for Frank, the Negro slave provided him by Congress. When Frank rushed into the room, he found Sam wrapped in a wool quilt in the center of his bed, bellowing, "I'm surrounded by the enemy! Get your chopping ax and cut them down."

Frank answered, "Yes, Massa Houston. I kaint sees 'em. Shore hopes you kan."

Frank returned with his ax and upon Sam's instruction, proceeded to cut the posts off the bed, which happened to be one of Mrs. Lockhart's prized possessions. The mahogany four-poster bed had belonged to her grandmother, and imported to Texas at great expense. Needless to say, the Lockharts were none too thrilled the following morning when they discovered their priceless antique bed had been destroyed. Sam had no excuse. He simply said nothing. He washed his face, drank a large cup of black coffee, and put on his Sunday best before saddling his favorite mule, Bruin. Bruin was rested and ready to take the president to see his wife.

Nancy Lea met her son-in-law at the front door with her hands braced on her hips. "What on God's green earth brings you here? You should be running the government."

Sam removed his hat, wiped the dust from his face with his sleeve and kissed his mother-in-law on the cheek. The short, pudgy, black-haired Nancy gave him her patented smirk as Sam ducked down to enter the doorway. Speaking in a humble tone, he asked, "May I see my lovely wife in private?"

"She is in the bedroom resting, if you must disturb her," Nancy snarled, like a mother lion protecting her cub.

It was clear she was not pleased to see her son-in-law with the smell of a hangover lingering on his breath. He knew he had a job to do, so Sam brushed past Nancy and headed straight to his wife's room. She was reading the bible when Sam entered. As he knelt beside her bed, his injured leg ached. Before either said a word, Sam kissed Margaret on the forehead and gently brushed her hair to one side.

Concerned, Margaret softly asked, "What is it, Sam?"

With his head lowered, he answered, "I have sinned, my dearest wife. Without your strength, I gave in to the devil drink. Last night, the Devil himself walked into my room carrying a bottle of his poison. You have taught me the Devil is a snake and liar, and I am sad to admit I believed his lie. He whispered tempting words. He told me one small drink would ease my unbearable loneliness for you and fill the void in my heart that arose in your absence. Please forgive me for trusting the cloak of evil. Please forgive my failure."

Margaret rose up on her elbows and looked deep into her husband's repentant eyes. "My dearest, sweet Sam. Of course, I forgive you. What else can I do since our Savior has washed away your sins in His blood?"

The next day Sam rented a wagon, and over Nancy's objections, returned Margaret to Washington-on-the Brazos. There was a price to be paid to have Margaret back; Nancy Lea's condition for allowing her sick daughter to leave was that she come along with them.

Sam failed to mention the bed incident to Margaret and didn't tell her they were no longer welcome in the Lockhart's home. He rented a small rustic log cabin at the edge of town. The rental cabin was hastily constructed and in poor condition. The parlor doubled as a bedroom. Nancy used the lean-to bedroom, and instructed the slaves build themselves a shelter under a large hackberry tree.

Calling Washington-on-the-Brazos a town stretched the meaning of the word. One street ran through the middle of town, with towering burr oak and magnolia trees lining both sides. The stumps from fallen trees remained in the street, forcing horses and wagons to maneuver around them. Margaret was happy to be back with Sam, but Nancy felt the place was beneath her status and never missed an opportunity to express her disdain to the president. Margaret grumbled to her mother, but never to Sam.

With Margaret back in his arms, Sam walked the line, returning to the pressing matters of state. He signed a "Treaty of Friendship" with King William of the Netherlands. The King personally signed the agreement, which Sam showed to everyone entering his office, and made sure the news of the treaty reached the highest levels of office in the United States. Houston then arranged a meeting with Captain Charles Elliot, the British *charge de affaires* in Texas, asking Elliot to intervene on behalf of the Texans held in Mexican jails. The President requested Elliot convey to Santa Anna that the Santa Fe Expedition had only sought to secure commerce and good faith trade with Santa Fe; the military presence was only to protect the caravan from hostile Indians. Houston did some tap dancing when he discussed the Mier incident. He explained the men illegally entered Mexico as independents; however, since they had surrendered in battle, they were entitled to humane treatment as prisoners of war. He inferred that Santa Anna must realize that if Texas enters the Union, the Americans will seize the western part of Mexico all the way to the Pacific Ocean. The Raven desired the Eagle to stop playing war games with Texas because, with an independent Texas, there would be no justification for an American invasion. His logic was sound and Elliot immediately understood what Sam was suggesting; an Independent Texas was clearly a better option for Mexico. Sam also wanted the Mexican dictator to think it would be easier to deal with Texas as a Republic than if it became the twenty-eighth state.

Believing Elliot would successfully negotiate the release of the Texans held in Mexico, Houston could focus his attention on negotiating peace with the Indians and convened a pow-wow at Washington-on-the-Brazos. Before the summit, one of Sam's envoys, who worked with the Indians, sent the following dispatch:

Mr. President,

Please excuse the brevity of this letter. Old Chief Falcco, the father of Chief Falcco riding with Major Jack Hays is concerned for the safety of his son. He is seeking information. It is his understanding his son is dead. Would you please shed some light on the matter?"

Respectfully,

Ben Bryant

The President had already received another letter concerning Falcco from Major Jack Hays:

To My Esteemed President Samuel Houston,

Your honor, it is with much sadness and a broken heart I take this pen in hand. I am sad to say my companion in many battles and one of the bravest men I've ever known has been murdered. On December 24, I asked Chief Falcco, an elderly mute Lipan, and two Mexicans to drive our horses back to San Antonio. I finally had to give up trying to talk some sense into Colonel Fisher. He refused to see the truth, no matter how clearly it was placed in front of him. On our way back to San Antonio, I was horrified to happen upon the body of Falcco and the old Lipan. The two cowardly Mexicans slit my dear friend's throat during the night, killing him and the mute Indian. They stole our horses and sold them in San Antonio. I know who they are and with God as my witness, I will hunt them down like the wild beasts they are. Anger flows through my blood and sadness fills my heart for Falcco. I give you my word no harm will come to the Lipan Nation as long as I am alive. They have been more than friends.

Yours truly in the service of the Republic,

Major John C. Hays

President Houston knew who killed Falcco when he answered Ben Bryant's letter. Knowing that the death of such a respected Lipan Apache Chief would provoke retribution, Sam was not completely truthful with the great warrior's father and intimated that the cowardly Mexicans south of the Rio Grande had killed his son. Sam included a long letter praising Falcco's bravery and asked that Ben Bryant carefully translate what he had written. In the letter, Sam told old Falcco he would not blame the Lipan Apache and their friends for joining the five thousand Creeks the president had already relocated to the Rio Grande. As a group, they could prevent Mexico from invading Texas. He urged the Chief not to kill women and children. Houston made it clear he would never shake the hand of a warrior who shed innocents' blood.

The pow-wow lasted six weeks. They ate heartily and to the consternation of the local citizens, Indians mingled in the streets as they pleased. When the gathering was over, Houston had his treaty. He could rest assured his citizens were safe, with the exception of the Comanche, which the rangers were keeping under control. Sam gave the Indians small gifts to seal the agreement, suggesting they return immediately to their respective tribes and share the news of peace and prosperity.

Then, on 25 May 1843, the fifty-three-year-old President became a father. The birth was difficult as Margaret labored twelve hours before giving up the 9-pound healthy baby boy. Sam offered various suggestions for the child's name, without much influence; Margaret would consider no other name than Samuel Houston Jr. for their first-born son.

September found the wily Raven working once more to lure his nemesis, the Mexican Eagle, into a trap as he had at San Jacinto; only this time, Houston's lure was political posturing, rather than battlefield tactics. His British scheme worked as he hoped. Santa Anna was now very worried. What if Houston did allow Texas to become part of Britain or the U.S.? He would have to defend his country all the way to California. He did not have the manpower or the capital to expand into California. Houston had no intention of "going British", even though he referred to England as the "Grandmother" and the Union as the "Mother". This time, he came at Santa Anna with an unexpected move on the chessboard, assigning Hockley and Williams to administer the immediate release of all Mexican prisoners held by Texas. They were to inform Santa Anna that President Houston wanted to exchange prisoners in good faith. The move to release the Mexican prisoners was a win-win proposition for Sam Houston; Texas could not afford to feed and care for the Mexican prisoners, and international pressure would be brought to bear on Santa Anna to reciprocate and free the Texans.

Like a professional poker player, the Raven was holding a deuce and seven in a Texas Hold 'em game. He had to do a lot of bluffing if he was going to win the pot. He sat at the table with the United States, England, France, Mexico, and about half of the Texas population. England believed he wanted to invite them in, those for annexation had no doubt about him wanting Texas to be a state, and Santa Anna was worried. Even Sam's dear friend Andrew Jackson was concerned that Houston was serious about joining the British Empire. From his sick bed, Jackson implored Sam not to link up with the "limeys". Jackson, in one letter, told Houston if Texas went to the British, they would have an iron-grip around the Union's neck. England was already in the West Indies, and with Texas, they could move westward and control the land to the Pacific. Sam remained coy.

As if Santa Anna's saber rattling and sneak invasions were not troublesome enough, the Regulators and Moderators feud flared up again in the piney woods of east Texas. A megalomaniac from Mississippi, Charles Moorman, took control of the Regulators, amassed a force of more than three hundred armed men and decided to restart the feud with the Moderators. Rumors drifted back to the President that the Regulators were plotting a coup to remove him from office. Houston was sick with fever; nonetheless, he knew the problem must be resolved quickly. He contacted Travis Brooks, merchant and postmaster of San Augustine, telling his old friend to assemble a militia of six hundred men and join forces with General Jim Smith. He then sent word to Rusk to join him in New Cane. On August 15, the president and General Rusk entered Shelby County, leaving the militia under the commands of Brooks and Smith camped a few miles away. Houston and Rusk then entered the town. Sam, weak from fever, sat down on a cord of wood and removed his pocketknife. He started whittling and as the people arrived, he gave them a father-son talk. Sam, determined to quell the trouble without any bloodshed, sat on a stump seat, whittled, and reasoned with both sides. The Moderator and Regulators feud followed the structure of most feuds: Eighty percent of the men didn't want a fight, ten percent rode the fence, and the radical ten percent wanted blood. When Sam had things sorted out, he sent his men to bring in the leaders from each group. The Moderators' came freely and almost immediately, while Moorman and his Regulators were not so eager. Finally, Moorman realized it was futile; if his Regulators went to war with both the Texas militia and the Moderators, they would not stand a chance. Before the day was over, Sam had a signed peace treaty.

Completely exhausted after the intervention, one of the men saddled Sam's mule and assisted the ailing president into the saddle. When he arrived back in New Cane, he was too weak to unsaddle his mule, and one of slaves had to assist the president in to the house. To his surprise, Nancy showed deep concern and made a bed ready for her son-in-law, treating him as if he were a sick child. Margaret sat beside his bedside, washing his face with a cool cloth and reading passages from the scriptures for his comfort. Margaret and her mother feared Sam was going to die. What they couldn't see was his strong will to live. He was determined to be able to play with his son, to be with his beautiful wife, and to fulfill his role as President of the fledgling Republic. In two days, he was sitting up in bed asking for pen and paper. He had letters to write and a country to lead. His most urgent business was making peace with the Comanche. The lower Chiefs were willing to come to council, but Chief Buffalo Hump refused to speak with anyone other than "Chief Houston". By October of 1844, Sam was feeling stronger and arrived at the council site north of Washington-on-the-Brazos in good spirits. Houston began the parley, saying, "Texas has had the misfortune of having the evil Chief Lamar as our leader. He did much harm to your people, your Comanche Nation, and to my Cherokee family. As you know, Chief Lamar killed The Bowl, who was like a father to me. I cannot change the evils done by Chief Lamar. All of you know I am an adopted Cherokee and have lived with the red man for many moons. I know your desire to be free. I understand your anger at the white man. We will cease hunting you as if you were deer if you will stop stealing our horses and killing our people. The white man wants to live in harmony with our Indian brothers, and this includes the Comanche."

Houston's ploy to blame Lamar was an effective one and shifted the heat off the general population of Texans. Buffalo Hump pondered for several minutes and then held a caucus with his lower Chiefs. They talked amongst themselves in their native tongue for some time, arguing back and forth. Finally, Buffalo Hump answered in broken English, "We will not harm your brothers, steal your horses, or take your property. We want freedom to go where we want in Texas. You give the Comanche our freedom and we will live in peace with the white man. We respect you, Chief Raven."

Sam knew the last element of the agreement was going to be a concern to his people. Comanche riding freely through the interior of Texas was not going to be an easy sell, but Texas had no other option; he had to agree to Buffalo Hump's terms or the bloodletting would continue, and probably escalate. A peace treaty was drawn up, and each Chief made their mark. Then, that evening, Sam supplied tobacco and Buffalo Hump supplied a pipe, and the leaders sat around the campfire for several hours, passing the peace pipe.

After the council, Houston returned to New Cane, picked up his wife and son, and retreated to their home at Cedar Point on Galveston Bay. Finally out from under the iron fist of his mother-in-law and alone with Margaret, Sam was at peace. Their evening strolls along the bay, with Sam carrying the baby, were some of the happiest moments of his life. Bliss at last. He wanted those days to last forever.

A few days after Thanksgiving, Sam returned Margaret and the baby to New Cane. Leaving them with Nancy, Sam headed for Washington-on-the-Brazos and the eighth session of Congress. He arrived in Washington on December 4th only to find few had joined him. He waited in town for four days, but no one else arrived. With no quorum, he returned to New Cane and celebrated Christmas at the Bledsoe plantation.

Annexation was never far from Sam's mind. He knew something needed to be done; therefore, he penned anonymous letters to *The Houston Telegraph* and the *Texas Register*. Both papers were sympathetic to his desire for annexation. Gail Borden, an old friend, was more than willing to publish Sam's anonymous and somewhat transparent messages in his newspaper, *The Houston Telegraph*. Gail Borden, Jr. was born in Norwich, New York in 1801. In 1816, the family moved to New London, Indiana, where Gail received two years of formal schooling. Shortly thereafter, he moved to Mississippi where he learned how to survey in his spare time and taught school to support himself. After arriving at Galveston Island on Christmas Eve, 1829, Borden farmed and raised cattle, and did some surveying in Fort Bend County. By February 1830, he took over his brother, Thomas' job as surveyor for the Stephen F. Austin colony. Then, in 1835, he and his brother started Texas' first newspaper. Borden published the *Telegraph* in San Felipe until March of 1836 when news reached San Felipe that Santa Anna had taken the Alamo. With the enemy on their doorstep, they moved the printing press to Harrisburg. As Santa Anna closed in, two of Gail's men remained as long as possible setting type and were able to print two hundred copies detailing the massacres at the Alamo and Goliad. Those two hundred newspapers passed from person to person until all of Texas knew the atrocities perpetrated by the invading Mexican dictator. Gail joined Houston's forces, and after San Jacinto, moved to Houston and was the primary surveyor of the city. There, he set up a prosperous newspaper, *The Houston Telegraph*.

Houston now needed Borden and the other newspapers to spread the word about annexation without it appearing that he was the slightest bit interested. Houston's sly maneuvers did not go unnoticed in Washington; the issue of Texas annexation became the central focus of the 1844 presidential debates between Henry Clay and James Polk. Clay was no friend of Houston or Texas. Anytime the annexation issue waned, Clay dumped wood on the fire, making the words *slaves* and *slavery* synonymous with Texas and Texans. This was Clay's fifth and final run for the office of President of the United States and Houston knew, without any doubt, if Henry Clay won the presidency, Texas would have to wait four more years for the matter of annexation to be resolved. On the other hand, James K. Polk was a close, personal friend of the Republic's President Houston and protégé of "Old Hickory". Polk was born in Mecklenburg County, North Carolina in 1795. Studious and industrious, he graduated with honors in 1818 from the University of North Carolina. As a young lawyer, he entered politics and served in the Tennessee legislature where he became friends with Andrew Jackson and Sam Houston. James Polk served as Speaker between 1835 and 1839, leaving the House to become Governor of Tennessee. Until circumstances raised Polk's ambitions, he was a leading contender for the Democratic nomination for vice president in 1844. Both Martin Van Buren, who had been expected to win the Democratic nomination for President, and Henry Clay, the Whig nominee, tried to take the Expansionist issue out of the campaign by declaring their opposition to the annexation of Texas. Polk, however, publicly asserted that Texas should be "re-annexed" and all of Oregon "re-occupied." Jackson, correctly sensing the people favored expansion, urged the choice of a candidate committed to Manifest Destiny. His point of view prevailed at the Democratic Convention and Polk won nomination on the ninth ballot. "Who is James K. Polk?" Whigs jeered. Democrats replied Polk was the candidate who stood for expansion. He linked the Texas annexation issue, popular in the South, with the Oregon issue, popular in the North. Polk also favored acquiring California, by force if necessary, from Mexico. Even before he took office, Congress passed a joint resolution offering annexation to Texas. In so doing, they bequeathed Polk the possibility of war with Mexico while Polk's stand on Oregon risked war with Great Britain.

The 1844 Democratic platform claimed the entire Oregon area, from the California boundary northward to latitude 54/40, the southern boundary of Russian Alaska. Extremists proclaimed "Fifty-four forty or fight," but Polk knew neither the Americans nor the British would benefit from such a war and offered to settle by extending the Canadian boundary along the 49th parallel from the Rocky Mountains to the Pacific. When the British minister declined, Polk re-asserted the American claim to the entire area. Finally, the British agreed, with the exception of the southern tip of Vancouver Island and signed the treaty in 1846.

Polk then set his sites on grabbing Texas for the Union before England could gain a stronger foothold in the new Republic. Even Polk believed Houston's bluff.

Prior to Polk's narrow victory, Benjamin Harrison, who stood firmly against Texas becoming part of the Union, was elected President. The Whigs, seizing on a political opportunity, in 1840 presented their candidate William Henry Harrison as a simple frontier Indian fighter, living in a log cabin and drinking cider. "Country boy" Harrison was in sharp contrast to the aristocratic, champagne-sipping Van Buren. The Whigs nominated Tyler for vice president, hoping for support from southern "states righters" who didn't care for "Jacksonian" democracy. William Harrison was a hero of the battle of Tippecanoe in 1811, and thus, the slogan "Tippecanoe and Tyler Too" was born. Harrison easily won the race, becoming the Union's ninth President. While giving his face the Nation address, the weather turned cold and sheets of rain pelted his body. The inclement conditions gave him a cold, which turned into pneumonia. On April 4, 1841, Harrison became the first President to die in office. The Whig party had counted on the fact that, as vice president, Tyler would wield minimal power. Now, suddenly President "Tippecanoe" Harrison was dead and "Tyler Too" was in the White House as the tenth President. Dubbed "His Accidency" by his detractors, John Tyler was the first vice president to be elevated to the presidency by the death of his predecessor.

At first, the Whigs were not too disturbed by the sudden turn of events, and remained optimistic that Tyler would accept their agenda. They soon became disillusioned. Tyler was ready to compromise on the banking question, but Henry Clay would not budge. He would not accept Tyler's "exchequer system", and Tyler vetoed Clay's bill to establish a National Bank with branches in several states. Congress passed a similar bank bill, but again, on "states rights" grounds, Tyler vetoed their bill as well. In retaliation, the Whigs expelled Tyler from their party. His entire Cabinet resigned, with the exception of Secretary of State Daniel Webster. A year later, when Tyler vetoed a tariff bill, the first impeachment resolution against a president was introduced in the House of Representatives. Representative John Quincy Adams knew President Tyler leaned toward Texas statehood and thought if he could impeach the president, he could cut the snake's head off before he could garner much support for annexation. A committee headed by Representative Adams charged that Tyler had misused his veto power, but the resolution failed. In 1842, Tyler signed the tariff bill, the "Webster-Ashburton Treaty", which protected northern manufacturers and ended the Canadian boundary dispute.

The year of 1843 ended on a high note for President Houston as Texas brought in a bountiful grain harvest, the largest in the brief history of the new Republic. Texas was selling grain to the Americans for record amounts of hard currency, backed by gold. Texas had money in the bank and finally some back salaries could be paid. Houston started to walk with a swagger as he had after the battle of San Jacinto, and his enemies were at a loss on how to attack the popular president. Talk of making Houston Dictator of Texas floated around like dandelions in the wind. When Sam heard the rumors, he dismissed the offer, still preferring Texas statehood; nevertheless, he didn't tip his hand.

The question of Texas annexation had been around since the days of the Louisiana Purchase in 1803. At that time, Thomas Jefferson asserted the true southern limit of Louisiana was the Rio Grande, and many Americans agreed. Naturally, the Spanish objected to this interpretation. In 1819, the United States and Spain signed the "Adams-Onis Treaty" in which Spain relinquished Florida to the U.S. in exchange for the U.S. abandoning their claim to Texas.

In late 1843, President Houston received a visitor sent by the Queen of England. Captain Charles Elliot of the Royal Navy, hero of the Opium Wars of China, and honorable servant to his Queen landed in Galveston with no place to sleep. He and his wife shared a board covered with a blanket alongside the docks, certainly not the accommodations to which the Captain was accustomed. Elliot was a self assured, courteous gentleman whose deep blue eyes reflected the solitude of serving in remote lands for two decades. He wore a big floppy hat and constantly smoked a long-stemmed pipe. His speech was curt, his voice crystal clear, and he carried himself with an aristocratic, and some said arrogant air found among British officers. He visited with the locals, getting their thoughts of the president, and then boarded a barge for the town of Houston. The barge ran into a sandbank and the passengers were forced to evacuate. As they were departing in the darkness, Elliot stepped through a hatch and badly bruised his ribs. Ever the stiff upper lip Englishman, he ignored the pain and pressed on. They spent the night at Pamela Mann's Hotel and enjoyed the pleasures of a duck down featherbed. Two days later the Englishman arrived in Washington-on-the-Brazos. Even though he had been forewarned, Captain Elliot was stunned to find the president operating in such raw conditions.

That evening, Margaret served cornbread, cabbage, beefsteak, and fried okra. The Captain didn't want to hurt Margaret's feelings, so he whispered, asking Sam what they called the "sawdust" bread. In all of his travels, Elliot had never tasted anything like the food the Texans ate. Sam laughed, explaining to the Englishman he had been living the easy life and didn't know what real food was.

Margaret eased the tension by playing her piano. The young beauty charmed the Captain and his wife with delightful songs and even played *God Save the Queen*, captivating the British couple with her civilized, cultured demeanor. Sam sat back and basked in her performance as he watched her entertain their guests.

After two weeks in the Republic, Elliot felt he had enough information and penned a letter to the Queen:

"President Samuel Houston has had a large career in a raw, rugged land. Houston is a habitual drunkard who lived for several years among the Cherokee Indians as a Chief. He came to Texas on the orders of President Andrew Jackson, took leadership, defeated the Mexicans led by General Santa Anna and had the good fortune to marry a young, beautiful, pious woman half his age. She tamed the lion and he has become an effective leader. His wife brought the fear of Almighty God into their home and conquered the General's desire for strong drink. Whatever General Houston has been in the past, it is plain to see now he is the fittest man in Texas for his present station. His education had been imperfect; nevertheless, he possesses great sagacity and penetration, surprising tact in the management of men, trained as they are in these parts. Houston is perfectly pure handed and moved in the main by inspiring motive of desiring to connect his name with a Nation's rise in power.

General Houston has two sides to understand, one very clear indeed and the other impenetrably dark. Let him speak of men or public affairs or the tone and temper of other Governments, and no one can see farther or more clearly. The moment he turns to financial arrangements, you find that he has been groping on the dark side of his mind.

Captain Charles B. Elliot of Her Majesty's Navy

The good Captain misread Houston. Sam was a brilliant administrator of his Republic's finances. Elliot, like so many others, fell for the "dumb ol' country boy" act Houston liked to perform. One of Houston's strongest traits was to make people underestimate him.

The first thing England wanted to know was when Texas won independence "Will the Republic be permanent?" The Texans answered that question with iron-fist resolve: In spite of their day-to-day struggles, the Republic was able to survive and prosper independently. A month after the victory at San Jacinto, the British Minister of Mexico wrote: "Mexico can never re-conquer Texas. Texas has crushed the Mexican yoke and will remain free."

England stood to attention as Houston started turning Texas around after Lamar's malfeasance in office had driven the economy into the ground. Word in England was Texas would be conquering Mexico, not the other way around. With the perception of Texas being the victor, the decision to recognize them as a new republic hastened, the slavery issue placed on the back burner. After the recognition, the Queen summoned Captain Charles Elliot back to England to give her his assessment of Texas. Houston's plan was working like a well-oiled machine. Elliot's arrival was exactly what Houston needed to place a burr under the Americans' saddle and to hint to England that Texas was growing stronger and might expand into California. France picked up her fiddle and joined the band, trying to get Texas to dance to a French tune. In each case, Houston told them courteously his dance card was currently full, explaining that the people of Texas were not ready to give up their freedom. Yet, he hinted he was open to offers. Houston's Texas flirted, but never committed.

Houston was a master at using distractions to conceal his tricks. He did such a skillful job that he had England, Mexico, France, the United States, most of Texas, and President John Tyler wondering about the future of Texas. Twice during the summer of 1843, President Tyler made overtures indicating the United States would be interested in reopening the question of annexation.

Houston responded to President Tyler's overtures in a letter:

Mr. President,
Were Texas to agree to annexation, the good offices of the European powers would, it is believed, be immediately withdrawn and were the treaty to fail of ratification by the Senate of the United States, Texas would be placed in a worse position than she

is at the present. We would be without a friend and faced with an unsettled Mexico. Better to trust in the proven good offices of England and France than the doubtful promises of the United States, which might again return the apathy and indifference towards us as had always until now characterized that government. We have been led to the altar and jilted before by those from the North. I am reluctant to be spurned again.

With Respect,

Sam Houston

Houston's letter lit President Tyler's fire to bring Texas under the wing of the Union. He knew his mentor, Old Hickory had dreamed of Texas opening the door for Manifest Destiny. He and many Americans believed it was God's will that the United States should reach from sea to shining sea.

Houston's message reached his old mentor, Andrew Jackson. Though he was on his deathbed, the old leader struggled to make his wishes known. He wrote to Houston in his wobbly hand:

My Dear General,

"I have put down everywhere I have heard the slanders of British intrigue circulated against you. The rumors of you selling out to the Mexicans. I know the English cannot dupe you and all the gold of Santa Anna could not buy you. None could seduce you from a just sense of duty and patriotism. My strength is exhausted and my meeting with my Maker is near. I must close. Please write to your friend.

Sincerely,

Andrew Jackson

The heinous slander against Houston didn't stop. The feeble hand of Jackson wrote again:

My Dear General,

I tell you in sincerity and friendship if you will achieve annexation, your name and fame will be enrolled amongst the greatest Chieftains of the age. Now is the time to act and that with promptness and secrecy, have the treaty of annexation laid before the United States Senate, where I am assured it will be ratified. Let the threats of Great Britain and Mexico then be handled by us. If war they wish, our fleet and army will freely fight them. I am scarcely able to write. The theme only inspires me with strength.

Your friend,

Andrew Jackson

P.S. Please write, even if it is only three lines.

Houston sat down immediately to answer Jackson's letter with tears flowing down his cheeks. The water from his eyes dropped on his paper, causing the ink to run. He had to compose his thoughts, and drying his eyes, he started again. Instead of the three lines Jackson requested, Sam wrote three hundred lines. In part, his letter read, "Texas could do well without the United States, but the Union couldn't do without Texas." In the core of the long letter, Sam offered an analogy to his dying friend, "You will perceive that Texas is presented to the United States as a bride adorned for her espousal. If the Union should reject her, she would be mortified. The shame of being left at the wedding altar would be devastating. The act would be indescribable. She has been sought by the United States three times. Were she spurned a fourth, it would forever terminate the possibilities of annexation."

Sam sent one of his most trusted aides to hand deliver the letter, giving him a message to whisper in the ear of his mentor to assure his friend that he was working behind the scenes to achieve Texas becoming the twenty-eighth state. Houston could not allow Jackson to die with a heavy heart. Jackson read the long letter with a sad countenance. Then the courier leaned over and whispered, "Fear not. General Houston said to tell you he would rather die than let you down. Texas will become the twenty-eighth state. His exact words were 'Chief, I won't disappoint you.'"

Houston had carefully examined the situation in Washington and was not sure the treaty could muster the three-quarters vote required to pass. To cover, he had a man in Washington working secretly to push the annexation through, without it appearing Sam was involved. He knew a smart woman made a man chase her until she let him catch her. He wanted the Union to chase Texas rather than Texans beg for statehood; Sam realized he would have more power if he could make the Union pursue Texas. On April 12, 1844, President Tyler signed the treaty and sent the document to the Senate. The treaty was like throwing fifty tomcats into one cage as fur flew on the floor of the Senate. Loud voices and uncivilized words bounced off the chamber's ceiling, but when the dust settled, the Texas Treaty was ratified. Before the citizens of Texas learned of the treaty, General Murphy rushed home and met with President Houston in Washington-on-the-Brazos. Sam cleared off his plank desk as Murphy carefully unwrapped the document. As Sam read over the treaty, Murphy whispered in his ear the solemn promise of President Tyler: "Tell General Houston I guarantee Texas will be protected during the pending of the treaty." Sam gave Murphy a nod of approval to show his appreciation for the generous offer of Tyler, and for the haste with which Murphy delivered the news.

Houston told the Englishman Elliot in private: "Ninety percent of the Texans I have talked with favor annexation to the United States. It is my understanding the leaders in Washington and across the states are in favor of annexing Texas. I do concede the Whigs, abolitionists, and those who hate liberty will scream like a stuck pig, but will be helpless to stop the inevitable. Texas can choose her suitor." Sam purposefully left the impression that he held the power to decide whether Texas would join with the British or the Union.

Knowing it would soon be time for him to relinquish the presidency, Sam chose to support Dr. Anson Jones as his successor. Born in Massachusetts in 1798, Jones became a physician at the age of 22, but was a restless young man and spent time at Harper's Ferry, Philadelphia, and in Venezuela, never making much of a success anywhere. In 1832, he gave up medicine, and tried his hand as a commission merchant in New Orleans and went broke within a year. In October 1833, at the suggestion of Jeremiah Brown, Jones drifted to Texas. He soon had a medical practice at Brazoria worth $5,000 a year. This was the first success Jones ever experienced. At first, he resisted becoming involved in the tensions between Texas and Mexico, but eventually came to support independence. When the revolution came, Jones served as surgeon in the San Jacinto campaign at the insistence of General Houston. He served Sam well during both of his administrations, but started to pull away from Sam in the last few months of his presidency. Jones wanted Texas to remain an independent Republic and expand its boundaries west, fulfilling the dream of Houston's nemesis, ex-president Lamar. Jones sincerely thought Texas could become a dominant power in the Western World and planned to make his mark on history as the architect of a Great Republic. Even though Jones distanced himself from Houston, Sam felt he could control Anson when it came to important issues. He believed that a weak President Jones was better than a "Lamar man". With Houston's support, Anson Jones became President of the Republic of Texas.

President Houston's second term ended on December 2, 1844, and he and Margaret moved back to the city of Houston. She could be near her friends and Sam was in a position to keep an eye on Mexico.

He felt sure Texas would have to fight the Mexicans again and he wanted to be in position to lead, should that happen. Texas was ready this time. The Anglo population in Texas had grown from thirty thousand to slightly more than one hundred thousand. Of that hundred thousand, the majority were men and boys of fighting age. Texas now was getting on her feet financially and could afford to buy powder and supplies for a substantial army. Santa Anna was cognizant of the rapid growth in the population of Texas and the challenges another invasion would pose. He was beginning to fear Texas would invade northern Mexico and seize another large chunk of his empire. Mexico did not have the money or manpower to withstand a major invasion, and the once-aggressive dictator became conciliatory in tone when dealing with Texas.

Margaret soon grew tired of her husband entertaining the masses passing through Houston and wanting to meet the man who carved Texas from the stone mountain of Mexico. Sam welcomed rich and poor, famous and infamous, with equal vigor. Margaret punished him by holding back her affection for his lack of attention toward her. Sam attempted to devote more time to Margaret, but like a drunk, he fell off the wagon every time someone of "interest" ventured into town and wanted to meet him. Margaret wanted out of Houston, and deep down, so did Sam. He had fallen in love with the Huntsville area and they took a trip to find a place to locate a plantation. The area reminded him of Virginia, and he purchased a large tract fourteen miles south of town. Margaret loved the area and agreed this was a perfect spot to raise their family. While in town, Sam sketched out a design for their new home, Margaret made small changes to the design, and then Sam contracted a local man to build their home; a home the "Old Chief" would call *Raven Hill*.

Houston felt there was one final letter he must write, one that had been pressing on his mind for months:

His Excellency,

The satisfaction with which on yesterday I laid down the cares and responsibilities of Government, was greatly heightened by the recollection that your Excellency had recently released from confinement all the men save one, who has been retained in prison. Your gracious act did not disappoint me and the only regret is the knowledge that your Excellency has thought proper to withhold the same kindness and set free Jose Antonio Navarro. I ask this favor as a private citizen and ask a personal favor for the liberation of Jose Navarro.

I cannot close this note without tendering to your Excellency my unaffected condolence in the bereavement which you have had the misfortune to sustain the loss of your late, most excellent spouse.

Respectfully,

Samuel Houston

Sam's message reached Santa Anna too late. Santa Anna was in exile, and Navarro had already escaped. A sympathetic general had allowed Navarro the freedom to walk the ramparts of the prison, where friends secured a boat and rowed the patriot to safety. He then boarded a British mail ship for a fast trip to Havana and from there to New Orleans where George Kendall greeted him. The two spent a few days recounting the atrocities of the failed Santa Fe Expedition, and then Kendall gave Jose new clothes, a horse, and guns for his trip to San Antonio. Navarro spent four years in the most deplorable living conditions imaginable because of Santa Anna's hatred. Because Navarro was Mexican, he was not treated as just another captured soldier, but as a traitor to his race. If Santa Anna had remained in power, would he have granted Houston's request? Probably not.

Houston was not the only one sending messages to Santa Anna. Jones was extremely disappointed with the United States offer to annex Texas. He wanted Texas to remain an independent Republic, with him as its ruler. For years, he stood in the shadow of the two giants Houston and Lamar, and now believed this was his time to shine. He immediately sent messages to the French and British ambassadors in Mexico, urging them to persuade Santa Anna to recognize Texas' independence. Jones was either stupid or naive. He asked for a ninety-day reprieve to give Santa Anna time to respond. Houston already knew the answer; Santa Anna would rather lose his other leg than give in and allow Texas her independence.

Word spread like snow in a windstorm about the annexation. The Texans began having small meetings, which quickly grew in magnitude. The British did bring some favorable news to Jones, saying Santa Anna would consider the offer; however, by the time the message was received, it was too late. The Texas Congress called a special session on July 4th, and with only one negative vote cast by Richard Bache, approved annexation. When asked why he voted against annexation, Bache answered, "Because I left my wife in the United States. I didn't want to vote myself back into the same country with her."

Jones watched helplessly as his power eroded.

Chapter Thirty-Six
Maverick

The Mexican prison system allowed inmates to buy blankets, food and other necessities. The warden encouraged the prisoners to shop at the local stores because the merchants gave him a kickback on their purchases. Sam Maverick and some of the other wealthy prisoners helped the less fortunate, giving funds to the indigent so they did not have to exist on the worm-infested pig slop served at Perot.

As the prisoners became familiar with their location, they realized they were forty miles straight up from the Gulf of Mexico. They also realized escape was rendered almost impossible by the dense jungle canopy that blocked the night sky and prevented using the stars for navigation. The prisoners learned from the mistakes of previous escape attempts, and eventually became expert at finding their way through the mass of vines and trees to reach the Gulf and follow the beach back to Texas.

Sam Maverick knew he didn't need to risk escaping; he had friends in high places. He had a significant amount of pull since his cousin by marriage was the American General Waddy Thompson assigned to Mexico. Once Waddy learned of Sam's capture, he started working for his release. There was a strong case for the release of Sam Maverick; he was not engaged in acts of hostility against Mexico, but only in court minding local affairs when taken captive. Waddy was able to have Sam and two of his friends transferred to Mexico City. Not long after the transfer, he secured their release and arranged for each man to have a good horse and a rifle and powder in the event they encountered bandits along their journey home. Released with Sam were W. E. Jones and Judge Anderson Hutchinson, whose court was in session when General Woll captured them in San Antonio. The trio left Mexico City April 12th, 1843 and one month later, Sam arrived at his home in La Grange.

Mary was not expecting to see her husband. At first, she thought she was dreaming when she heard, "Anybody home?" Mary was so shocked that she waited for Sam to yell a second time before she responded. By the time she got to the front door, her husband was unlocking the front gate. Mary ran to him, throwing her arms around his neck and swinging both legs around his waist. Tears of joy flowed as she started kissing his face. Finally, her lips met his and the lovers froze in place until Jinny broke their trance, saying, "Massa Sam, we dun mighty glad yous home."

Still clinging to Sam, Mary added, "You are loved in Texas and the people would have no one but you represent them. I assured everyone that you were going to be set free because Waddy was helping with your release. My darling husband, you have been re-elected to Congress."

"I missed you too! Did you miss me?" Sam asked as he swung her around and around, her legs still clinging to his waist.

"You are as silly as ever. You know I missed you. My darling Sam, I am ever grateful that our Lord brought you home safely, and by all appearances, in good health."

"Mary, I'm as strong as an ox. I cannot begin to tell you how many nights I have thought of sleeping in your arms or, I guess I should say, you sleeping in my arms. I am glad to have this behind us and I look forward to getting back to business."

This was not what Mary wanted to hear. The months of captivity in the worst jail in the world could not slow down the energetic land speculator; Sam didn't tarry long before resuming his business. The first afternoon back, he was already making a deal to purchase an additional twenty-six acres adjacent to their house. The next morning after breakfast, he sought out a local contractor and arranged to build an addition onto their house. After being home for two weeks, he was ready to get back to San Antonio. People owed him money and there were legal matters needing his attention.

Once more Mary showed no tears or sadness as her husband mounted his best horse. Once Sam rode out of sight, she broke down, crying uncontrollably. Jinny offered her apron skirt to dry her eyes. Mary's deep-seated fears were that the Mexicans would return and once more capture her husband. Sam assured her that scouts now encircled the city; there would be no more surprise attacks, but his promises did nothing to allay her fears.

Time seemed to have stood still in San Antonio. Everything looked as it did the day he left. His office was dusty, but all the papers were still in place. Sam hired a local Mexican lady to clean his office, and then opened his doors for business. His old clients welcomed him home and provided him with plenty of work. Aside from his legal matters, Sam also had debts to collect. He was successful in being paid by most; however, Silas Bumstead, a struggling cattleman, simply did not have any hard cash. Silas owed him $1,200, a considerable sum to write off. Sam pressed hard for payment, but only got delays and excuses. It was almost time for Congress to convene over in Washington-on-the-Brazos, so Maverick had to forgo collecting until another time.

Mary was happy to have her husband come home for a couple of weeks before leaving for Congress. While in La Grange, he got word of a large tract of land for sale by Thomas DeCrow, down on Matagorda Bay. Sam Maverick was always interested in land. He would amass over 300-thousand acres of Texas land, making him the second largest landowner in North America. Only Thomas O'Connor, who owned over a half million acres, owned more. Sam tendered an offer in a letter to DeCrow; seven strong male slaves in exchange for the ranch land. He then left for Congress. When he got to Washington-on-the-Brazos, no quorum showed up. He remained a week, spending time with President Houston and apprising him of the horrid conditions of the Mexican jail system. When it became apparent that not enough representatives were going to show up, Houston suggested they all go spend Christmas with their families and try again in January.

When Maverick arrived back home, he had received a letter accepting his low offer to trade slaves for the Matagorda Bay land on the southwestern end of the peninsula. DeCrow's Point had many names: DeCros Point, Decros or DeCrow's Landing, Port Cavallo, Port Cabello, and Paso Cavallo. DeCrow's

Point received its original name from Daniel D. DeCrow, one of Stephen F. Austin's original three hundred immigrants. Daniel was part of the seafaring DeCrow family from Maine. His son, Thomas, built a home and raised cattle on the property. He also constructed a wharf and piloted vessels through Pass Cavallo into Matagorda Bay for a modest sum. When his wife died, Thomas decided he wanted to be a cotton farmer, thus the need for slaves. After Sam's father died, he had an abundance of slaves to barter. Each of the traders got what they wanted.

Sam had seen the land once, but could not visualize the terrain as well as he felt necessary to consummate the purchase. After Christmas dinner, he saddled a big black Tennessee Walking Horse and took along three well-armed slaves in case he ran into bandits. The strip of land was two miles wide and five miles long, Matagorda Bay on one side, and the Gulf of Mexico on the other, with a narrow bridge of land connecting the barrier island to the mainland. Sam was pleased to find that DeCrows Point was an idyllic place to raise cattle. They could drink fresh water from the bay and eat until they were too fat to walk in the thick, tall grasses. The large house on the property was currently being used as a custom's office, where General Somervell, the Revenue Officer, lived and collected import taxes. Maverick struck a deal with the general to rent him a room once he purchased the house and land. Somervell had no objections; in fact, he relished the thought of having company. Maverick returned to San Antonio and registered the deed for the ten thousand acres of land. Then he looked up Silas Bumstead, the man who owed him a substantial sum of money. He told Silas, "I have a way for you to pay me what you owe."

"How is that? You know I don't have any money."

"You have cattle?"

"Yes, I have some nice cows and a few good bulls. Why?"

"Well Silas, my friend, I have decided to let you pay me in cattle. You being an honest man, I'll let you pick four hundred of your prime cows and a dozen bulls, and deliver them to my ranch on Matagorda Bay."

Silas was relieved. He could raise more cows, but getting his hands on $1,200 was an insurmountable task. Bumstead immediately accepted Sam's offer. Sam drew up the papers, and had the local blacksmith make a branding iron with his initials as the brand. He gave the branding irons to Silas and asked him to put the S. A. M. brand on each animal.

Sam worked another month in San Antonio before returning to La Grange to pick up Mary and the children. Mary was sick, so the slaves made a board and covered it with quilts and blankets, lifting her into the large carriage. Mary rode in the carriage on her back the entire way. Sam was on his Tennessee Walker and all but three of the slaves rode in the wagons. Three slaves with rifles flanked Sam. The children switched from riding with Sam, to the wagon, and back to the carriage with their mother. The group made their way to Matagorda Bay, staying with friends, in unoccupied houses, and a few nights sleeping in the open. A cold north wind at their backs kept them pushing forward to warmer weather. Due to the inclement weather and lack of roads to follow, some days they only traveled two or three miles. On good days, they were able to travel almost twenty miles. The last day, they rode fourteen miles along the wide beach with white sand dunes on one side, and the warm azure Gulf of Mexico on the other. The sound of the pounding surf lifted Mary's spirits. She made Sam promise to take her swimming in the salt water as soon as she was stronger. Finally, on December 7th, the Mavericks arrived on the island and were greeted by the boisterous laughter of General Somervell. Mary was feeling much better and riding in the front seat when they arrived. The warmer weather and gentle sea breeze improved her health. In addition, the laughter of General Somervell had a healing affect.

Less than two weeks after their arrival, the Mavericks had company. Prince Carl Solms, the son of the Grand Duke of Braunfels was on his way to the colony of New Braunfels, which he founded two years earlier. Mary was relieved that their isolated location did not mean they would have no visitors. Quite the contrary; they constantly had new and interesting guests. The busy port brought many notable people to visit the Mavericks. Sam, as usual, always had pressing business and regularly made trips that ranged from several weeks to several months. He would pop in for a few days, and then be off to Houston, Galveston, New Orleans, or perhaps San Antonio, Austin, Nacogdoches, Washington in the States or Washington-on-the-Brazos. When he was home, he made up for lost time. He seemed to find time to make more Mavericks; Mary eventually birthed ten children.

The winters on the Matagorda Bay Peninsula were mild compared to San Antonio or La Grange. The summers were hot, but not humid because of the breeze off the water. When Sam was home, he and Mary swam in the salt water. The Gulf water was never very cold, even in the dead of winter. A few months out of the year, during hurricane season, seaweed or small sticks of bamboo covered the beaches. Once Mary discovered a palm tree with coconuts still attached that floated all the way from Florida or Cuba. A Frenchman spending a week at Tiltona asked, "Do you know where the word hurricane comes from?"

No one knew, not even Sam, who was one of the better-educated men in Texas.

They answered, "No, please tell us."

The Frenchman was anxious to show off his intellect to the backwoods Texans. He leaned back in the homemade chair and with an aloof attitude, hissed out, "Hurricane derived from 'Hurican', the Carib god of evil. Hurricane has different names according to the island. I have visited many of the islands of the Caribbean and have made a study of this word. Some of the names used by the natives are foracan, foracane, furacana, haracana, haraucane, hurricano, urycan, jimmycane. The Carib god Hurican comes from the Mayan god Hurakan. Hurakan is one of their creator gods who blew his breath across the chaotic waters and brought forth dry land and later destroyed the men of wood with a great storm and flood."

Sam, always the diplomat, responded, "Thank you for such a wonderful explanation. As you have been able to observe, we don't have the intellect of an astute gentleman like yourself. I assume you will want an early breakfast. I know you have pressing business inland and are ready to venture into Comanche territory where they collect scalps as you do words."

The Frenchman said nothing for the remainder of the evening and left early the next morning, without eating breakfast. Sam had given the pompous Frenchman something to worry about. He knew enough to realize Sam was not joking about the Comanche, and instead of going inland, he decided to board a ship leaving for New Orleans. His excuse was he wanted to go where people spoke his language, but the truth be known, Sam scared the living daylights out of him.

The second spring, Sam sailed to New Orleans and two months later returned with a big surprise. He purchased a sailboat and had it slipped into the bay without Mary or General Somervell knowing. The following Sunday, he took them down to the water with an invitation to ride the *Mary Ann*, named in honor of his wife. Sam was not a veteran sailor, but he knew the basics of maneuvering a sailing vessel, and over the next several months, they had a grand time exploring the coast and enjoying the glass smooth ride on the Gulf waters.

During the summer, Mary insisted Sam take their visitors out on the sailboat. Two couples from San Antonio came to spend a few weeks with the Mavericks and Sam was eager to show off his sailing skills. Mary had the slaves pack a picnic basket and the six of them boarded the *Mary Ann*. The wind was ideal for some fast sailing, so Sam put the boat through her routine. Around four in the afternoon, Mary noticed a dense fog off shore and suggested they head in. Sam had planned for them to see the sunset over the bay; however, he realized his wife was correct. He turned the sailboat and started home. No sooner had he turned around than they were surrounded in fog. With no compass, they soon were lost. Tacking the sailboat right and left, Sam could only guess their position, while each passenger expressed a different idea of the direction home. Suddenly the boat slammed into shore, knocking all but Sam to the deck. One man injured his arm and others received minor scrapes and bruises. Sam suggested they spend the night on the boat, because with such a dense fog, should they push free, they would be at the mercy of the darkness. The women went down into the cabin, and as soon as they closed the hatch, a summer rainstorm began pouring down on the men. Sam pulled down one of the sails and made a makeshift tent for the men to sleep under. No one got much sleep that night.

A cold, wet morning greeted the weary sailing party as they arose at dawn, hungry and freezing. The men pushed the sailboat offshore. When they got their bearings, Sam realized they were two miles across the bay from their home. They hoisted the sails and headed home. As they neared the shore, they saw five large bonfires blazing on the beach. During the night, the slaves and neighbors constructed the fires as a beacon for Sam to find his way home. Once their sails were visible, riotous shouting broke out on shore. More than two dozen adults were waiting as Sam pulled the boat alongside the dock. Sam soon traded the *Mary Ann* to a neighbor on the opposite side of the bay in exchange for a thousand acres of land. Mary had no objections. Their joy of sailing vanished into the fog that frightening night.

Eventually, Sam, Mary and the children moved back to their large home in San Antonio. Mary missed giving the large social gatherings and Sam needed to spend more time in his law practice. He left three slave families to care for the cattle and their home. Food and water were in abundance, and the slaves only had to wait until the calves were born, and brand them. The only problem with that idea was that Sam failed to teach them how to use a branding iron; the slaves did not know to get the iron white-hot and only singed the hair off the animals. At first glance, the brand was clear and ownership established, but within a year, the brand faded and eventually was not visible at all. Sam was gone so often, he never realized what was happening. His herd multiplied; however, the only ones with a permanent Maverick brand were the original cattle branded by Silas Bumstead.

When part of the Maverick cattle operation moved to the new property across the bay, a large number of his cattle no longer had visible brands. Other ranchers started cutting the poorly branded cattle out of the herd and sizzling their own brands on them. Soon, anytime the locals found a grown cow or bull without a brand, they called it a "maverick". Over time, the meaning of the word evolved to describe all untamed, trail-blazing men, who refused any one group's brand.

Chapter Thirty-Seven
"Devil Yack"

Jack and his rangers scouted southward toward Corpus Christi. They encountered no bandits or Indians and were feeling great when they reached Laguna Madre Bay, directly west of a barrier island on the Gulf of Mexico. They camped for a week, catching fish and swimming in the warm bay waters. Then the rangers started home, moving up the Nueces River. On their second day inland, they captured two Frenchmen who had made illegal entry into Texas. Jack remembered Sam Maverick's episode with a Frenchman and braced for another encounter of brilliance, only to find them very cooperative. When Jack questioned them, they readily gave up what information they knew about the Mexicans' intent, telling Jack that the fort across the Rio Grande had less than four hundred Mexican soldiers. This lack of military build up meant Santa Anna was not planning another immediate invasion of Texas. Jack immediately dispatched Henry McCullough to deliver the good news to the president and his cabinet.

The following morning, the rangers pressed homeward, pushing hard that day and the next. The third night, they made camp early, hobbling their horses by tying a soft cotton rope around the ankle of their horse's right foot. Digging a hole about eighteen inches deep, the rangers made a ball knot at the end of the rope and dropped it in the hole. Then they covered the knot with dirt and packed the soil with their boot heels. This simple trick made it impossible for the horses to pull free, yet allowed them to graze a larger area.

The unit turned in early as both the rangers and their horses were exhausted. Normally Jack would have posted a guard, but he knew how tired everyone was and felt they were in a safe area, having seen no sign of any Indians or bandits since leaving the Mavericks. That night, Leandro Garza and about eighty of his men discovered the rangers' camp. Garza had been a Lieutenant of Agaton, the top Mexican bandit in the Nueces strip. Garza was just as evil and had assembled his own meanest-of-the-mean gang of killers and thieves. Garza's men surrounded the rangers. As the night worn on, the bandits murmured among themselves, debating on how best to kill the rangers. The myth of Devil Jack was the topic of conversation among the Mexicans as they pondered what to do next. Did they dare try? Was Devil Jack luring them into a trap? The mystique of Jack Hays was powerful. With the breaking of the morning light, the Mexicans decided any attempt to kill Devil Jack was not worth the risk. They left without firing a shot.

At daylight, Jack discovered the bandits' tracks and estimated the number to be more than seventy-five. The signs were clear; the bandits came within fifty feet of where the rangers were sleeping. Major Hays could not know it was his fierce reputation that drove the bandits to retreat.

No sooner had the rangers unsaddled in Leon Springs than they received word that a Comanche band was in the hills just to the north, not far from the Blanco River. Jack did not wait. The rangers picked up the Comanche trail near the community of Comfort and continued deeper into the hill country, following the trail to Big Spring in west Texas. It became obvious the Indians were going to stay out of his reach, even if the rangers followed them all the way to Oregon. Jack kept hoping the two hundred Comanche would want to turn and face the smaller ranger unit, but the Comanche knew the leader was "Devil Yack", and wanted nothing to do with him.

The rangers' return ride home was long and tiring. Tommy Mason, a new ranger, accidentally discharged his pistol and shot himself in the right leg, another banged his head on a tree limb and six others came down with dysentery. By the time the unit arrived in Leon Springs, almost half of Jack's men were injured or sick. Miguel Lopez was waiting with news Jack did not want to hear. "Cap'n Jack, Cap'n Jack, me got muy bad news. Dat bandito Perez, he not far frum Medina River with a hundred men. They goin' to San Antonio and kill all gringos. Cap'n Jack, you must stop Perez."

Jack refilled his saddlebags with food and supplies and assembled a group of fourteen men to accompany him. The sun was blazing hot, with the temperature sitting squarely on 100 degrees as the rangers reached San Antonio about three thirty in the afternoon. Jack rang the warning bell at the Military Plaza. He didn't dismount, but gave his men permission to visit one of the local watering holes for a beer or a shot of whiskey. He allowed them a moment to relax, knowing that they would soon be in a battle for their lives. Jack waited for the townsfolk to assemble in the Plaza. "I called you here to tell you Perez and a hundred of his killers are at the edge of town. He wants to kill all Anglos and any Mexicans who help us. If for any reason, we are unable to stop them, I want you to be prepared. Go to your homes and make sure you have a sufficient supply of powder and lead. Clear areas around your homes so there will be no hiding places for the bandits. You will be safe within the thick rock walls of your homes. I am certain that after we kill forty or so, they will tuck tail and run. Just make sure you have water and enough food in the event there is a longer siege."

He dismissed the crowd with a wave of his hand, sending them away to prepare their defenses. By the time Jack finished speaking to the local citizens, his men began to re-assemble in the Military Plaza. He was pleased to see a familiar blaze-faced sorrel stallion trotting in his direction. As Bud got closer, he could see the strain on Jack's face and knew something serious was about to come down. "Captain, what's happening?" he asked.

Jack didn't correct Bud that he should have addressed him as Major, and quickly answered, "I'm glad to see you, Bud. We need your guns and fresh horse. We are going after Perez. It will not be an easy task. I understand he has a hundred men."

The rest of the rangers came out one by one, shielding their eyes from the bright sunlight. "Let's go kick Perez six ways to Sunday," shouted Henry McCullough. Henry then led the way as fifteen rangers followed in single file, with Bud and Jack pulling up the rear. People peered from their houses, praying the rangers could stop the invading killers. The only visible signs of life were dogs wandering the streets and an occasional squirrel scurrying up a tree. The mayor sent spies to the edge of town so he could warn the people when they spotted Perez and his men.

"Devil Yack"

As the ranger unit passed the city limits, Hays and Miller rode point. Five miles west of Helotes, one of Perez's scouts spotted the small group of rangers. He fired a wild shot and then made a run for Perez and his band of killers. Jack knew it would not be long before the Mexicans would be coming over a small cedar-covered hill about two hundred yards ahead.

"Dismount!" Jack shouted. "Take your positions."

The men spread out and awaited Jack's order to fire. The rangers heard the shouting and the pounding of hooves long before the Mexicans crested the hill. As the first wave topped the ridge, Jack gave the signal to fire at will. The Texans' long rifles cracked in unison and twelve Mexicans tumbled to the ground, one horse fell, and two others mortally wounded as their mounts tumbled over the fallen horse. The rangers reloaded their long rifles. Bud's heart pumped wildly as he mentally set for the second wave. Suddenly, a line of black smoke rose from the top of the ridge. "Perez is using an old Indian trick," Jack shouted to his men. "He is setting the grass on fire. He wants the protection of the smoke so we won't have much time to draw a bead on 'em. Don't rush your shot."

Jack was wrong. Perez had dashed down into a dry creek bed after setting the fire, using the smoke to cover his escape. He wanted no more of the perfect shooting he just faced. Knowing the rangers' horses were too tired to give chase, Jack ordered, "Mount up men. Let's head back to Leon Springs. Bud, I need you to swing by San Antonio and let the good folks know we have turned Perez back. They have nothing to fear presently. Make sure and tell them he will try again when his spies tell him we are not around."

As Bud cut off from the group, Kit Adkins shouted, "If you've got a couple of dollars, pick up some coffee beans and a wad of chewing tobacco." Henry McCullough got into the act and ordered some sugar and salt, not really expecting Bud to get the supplies. Bud waved his hand toward them, shouting back, "Get outta here." Nevertheless, he did purchase coffee beans, sugar, salt and a couple rolls of chewing tobacco. He also picked up two bottles of bourbon. As he was loading the supplies on Lightning, Maria and her children walked past. He tipped his hat and used his finger to signal the older child to come to him. Bud removed a dime from his pocket and spoke in Spanish, telling the lad to give the money to his mother so she could buy them each a chunk of rock candy. When the child handed the money to Maria and told her what Bud said, she bowed toward him saying, "Thank you Mr. Bud, you are always so thoughtful."

Bud swung his leg over the saddle cantle and waved at Maria and the children as he left for Leon Springs. His heart went out to Maria and he felt sorry that she faced such a hard life.

Jack introduced Bud to the new men. He was the talk of the camp because of the supplies he brought with him, especially the bourbon. Bud also purchased some extra powder and lead, knowing the rangers were running short. The government had been unable to pay salaries or give the men money for supplies. Jack Hays was footing some of the bill out of his own funds, and Henry McCullough and Big Foot Wallace freely gave as well. The unit made do by each sharing what they could.

The next day, Bud found Jack heating up some horse fat to oil his tack. Jack asked, "How did Charlie and Edward's folks receive the news of what happened to their sons?"

"Better than I had expected. Mr. Hempstead was especially gracious. They had already heard the news from a young man who had become close friends with Charlie and Edward. He stopped by the Hempsteads on his way to San Antonio, absolving me of all guilt. Charm seemed glad to see me and we spent some time together. She is a special girl. Speaking of girls, I hear you have been hanging around a judge's house over in Seguin. Is there any truth to the rumor?"

Bud caught Jack completely off guard; he never saw that question coming. Jack's face turned red and his thin eyes gave Bud a cold stare. Bud knew his question had struck a nerve as the Major shot back, "Who told you?"

Bud didn't let up. "Everyone knows, so you may as well tell me the rest of the story."

Jack stopped rubbing the horse grease on his bridle and remained silent for a minute or longer before answering, "Last Thanksgiving, I stopped in Seguin on my way to meet General Houston and some friends asked me to stay through Christmas. While in Seguin, I had the opportunity to visit with an old acquaintance, Judge Jeremiah Calvert."

Bud prodded, "And?"

Jack answered with a question, "And what?"

"You know what?"

"Who told you?"

"I'll tell you who told me, but you have to finish answering my question."

"Fair enough. So tell me who is meddling in my business."

Bud could hardly keep a straight face. He had never seen Jack squirm. Bud was grinning like a Cheshire cat as he answered, "I was talking with the Riddles while buying supplies yesterday and they told me some very interesting things. Seems they introduced you to Judge Calvert and his family, and in the family are three very attractive young ladies. Right?"

Jack walked over to the fire and poured two cups of freshly brewed coffee, and returned to the log where Bud was now sitting. "Then you know about Susan Calvert?"

"Yep, I know about Susan." Bud tried to sip his coffee, but it was too hot. He sat and blew the steam off the top and waited for Jack to continue.

Realizing Bud was going to be relentless, Jack burst out talking. "Judge Calvert moved his family from Alabama a couple years back and settled in Seguin. While the Judge, his wife, and three daughters were visiting San Antonio, the Riddles hosted a social gathering. Susan and I met and became friends and I just happened to find her attractive. She is seventeen, medium height, with long black hair that turns deep blue in the sunlight. Her eyes sparkle, and are so black, it's hard to see her pupils. Now I told you about her, are you satisfied?"

"Almost. Sounds to me you're getting a little sweet on her."

"Mind your business or I'll put you on permanent midnight guard duty."

Bud had to get the last word. "Maybe, if I were to marry Charm, we could ask the preacher to perform a double wedding."

Jack didn't answer, but his uneasy shuffling told Bud he thought it was possibly a good idea. As Bud stood to walk away, Jack hollered, "Susan is one fine Southern lady. Reminds me of the one General Houston brought in from Alabama."

Bud's inquiry triggered Jack's fond memories of Susan and the time he spent with her in Seguin. That night, he wondered if he should give up being a ranger, and get married and settle down. He could earn an excellent living surveying. Jack felt very strongly that it was only a matter of time until an arrow pierced his heart or a Mexican sniper's bullet found its mark. He buried many brave men in Texas soil and knew that, but for the grace of God, he would be planted with his feet pointing east, awaiting the Rapture.

"Devil Yack"

Bud worked steadily for two weeks, helping repair guns and gear. One Sunday morning, Jack approached him, saying, "Bud, I need a favor."

"Sure, what is it?"

"I need you to leave here and go to Washington-on-the-Brazos and speak to General Houston. I would go, but the Comanche are on the warpath, hitting small farms west of San Antonio. We have to go and slow them down."

"I'd rather you send someone else and let me take part in the fighting."

Jack replied, "I have given it a lot of thought. You are the best man to gain the general's ear. He knows you, and when what I have to say comes from you, I think he will act. As you are aware, my men have not been paid a thin dime in six months. Some are starting to grumble and it won't be long before I will be seeing good men pack up and head home, not because they want to, but because they have no choice. We need some money fast. You know. You had to buy us some grub out of your own pocket."

Bud knew Jack was right; he needed to go. "I'll pack and be on my way. If there is nickel in Washington, I'll bring it back."

"I knew I could count on you. Why don't you spend the night so we can talk, and you can leave with us at daybreak?"

Early the following morning, Bud said goodbye and spurred Lightning into a steady gallop. Jack chose fifteen men to ride with him. Thirteen were rangers who had been with him for several years, and two were new men. H.R. "Lefty" Block was a six foot two, raw-boned young man from Virginia who came to Texas to be a ranger and pestered Jack until he couldn't say no. The other new man was Paddy O'Toole, a red-faced Irishman and experienced soldier with the warmest personality of any in the unit. His paunch added to his humorous looks, yet he was a man of true bravery and daring. He was an accomplished marksman and his horsemanship skills were better than most. What he lacked in athletic ability, he more than made up for with extraordinary courage.

Hays didn't like using new men on dangerous excursions; however, he had no choice. Many of his regulars were either sick or recovering from serious wounds suffered in battle. Two sustained broken legs, one a broken right arm, and four were dealing with infection from Indian arrows, making the camp look like a battlefield triage unit. There was no time to give the new men a minor battle; they would have to learn to be a ranger in the heat of a serious fight.

The second day out, the rangers entered Nueces Canyon and headed west. After less than a mile, one of the men stopped and rose up in his stirrups and shouted, "Bee tree, I found a bee tree."

The thought of fresh honey was too tempting to pass up. Even Jack couldn't refuse, telling his men, "Dismount and let your horses graze, but be ready to move fast. We need to stay alert."

With their horses tied, the rangers plopped down on the grass under the welcome shade of the sprawling tree. Noah Cherry had the unenviable task of chopping a hole large enough to extract the honeycomb. He shinnied up the tree, carrying a small ax. The oak around the opening of the beehive was rock-hard. He whacked and whacked while the anxious rangers below shouted instructions and frivolous suggestions. Jack sat and watched, but said nothing. His gut feeling was telling him not to get too comfortable. Noah stopped cutting for a moment to wipe the sweat from his brow and caught a glimpse of a frightening sight. "God Almighty, I see a thousand Comanche coming straight at us," he yelled.

At first, the men thought he was joking, but when they saw the speed at which he descended from the tree, they knew otherwise. Jack flipped to his feet in one swift motion, shouting orders, "Bridle up and get ready, boys. We got a fight on our hands. Get ready. Make sure your powder is dry and all of your guns are loaded."

Hays was the first one ready, his long rifle placed across the seat of his saddle and his horse turned broadside to shield him. Suddenly dust filled the base of the canyon as over two hundred Comanche charged toward the rangers with blazing speed. When the war chiefs saw the rangers standing behind their horses, they urged their men on with shrill screams and wild war cries, which bounced off the canyon walls and echoed down onto the rangers' position. Jack could see a few of his men were getting a little edgy and showing signs of fear. They had good reason to be afraid. The Indians were closing the gap between them every second. With raised lances and pounding hooves, the moment of engagement was approaching rapidly. Jack did not want his rangers to fire prematurely. He lowered his left hand as a signal for them to wait, and exclaimed, "HOLD YOUR WATER! Let 'em get closer. Stay calm boys and make sure of your shot. Trust me; we can whip this bunch of savages."

As the band of screaming Comanche were about to overrun the rangers' position, Jack fired his weapon. Simultaneously, fifteen ranger rifle shots cracked. Horses fell and braves dropped right and left as every round found its mark. Those immediately behind the fallen fell to the ground as the rangers' deadly fire caused bodies and horses to stack up. The main body could not turn around because of the press of braves behind them and could not move forward through the dam of the dead. The rangers' pistols found easy targets as the Indians panicked. Thirteen more fell. The next volley took down ten more. It was like shooting ducks in a pond. Finally, one Chief found his way through the carnage and others followed his retreat, forcing their horses over the dead bodies. Jack grabbed his saddle horn and swung his lithe body onto his horse, shouting a command: "Mount up. We can't let the red bastards escape. Keep on 'em. They can't have room to turn around."

The rangers were able to close in quickly because the vast number of fallen braves and horses blocked the Indians' escape from the narrow canyon. Jack and the rangers yelled in Spanish, "Run you yellow bellies, run."

The rangers continued shouting as they closed in on those trapped in the rear. At Jack's urging, the rangers opened fire. The fighting was so close that gunpowder burned the Indians as the lead penetrated their bodies. One ranger's pistol blast was close enough to set the braves shirt on fire.

Jack encouraged his men, shouting, "Powder burn 'em. Kill all you can. We can't let 'em turn." This was a wise move on Jack's part because had the Chiefs been able to reverse the band's path, they would have easily overwhelmed the small ranger force.

With each crack of a ranger's firearm, the terror in the Comanche horses increased. Braves leaned over, pleading in their horse's ears to run faster. The Chiefs in front were like being in front of a herd of longhorns running wildly in a thunderstorm. Nothing could prevent the petrified braves from running their fear out. The Chiefs had to keep moving, or be trampled.

One brave on a blue mule darted from the crowd and headed up a small embankment. Kit Adkins decided he wanted that beautiful blue mule. He split off from the group and followed the brave up the embankment. Kit was on his fastest horse and felt that in no time he would be upon the Indian and kill him, secure the mule, and then get back into the fight. The blue mule was so scared it left Kit behind as if his horse was standing still. He gave chase for a few hundred yards, but realizing he would not be able to catch his prey, he whirled around and rejoined the one-sided battle. About the time Kit caught back up, the fight was over.

"Devil Yack"

The rangers dismounted and walked their exhausted horses the mile or so back to the bee tree. When they reached the tree, Jack told them to unsaddle their horses and let them cool off after the hard chase. Noah Cherry once more scaled the tree and finished whacking away until he reached the nectar. Soon, he was able to start handing down big chunks of honeycomb. The men were relishing the sweets and talking about how many Indians they killed. They estimated there was close to fifty Indians dead and no rangers killed in the fight. Only two rangers sustained significant wounds. Lefty Block had experience in dressing wounds, so the nursing chore went to him. Jack was very pleased none of his men died and wanted them to know how proud he was of them. He commented, "Enjoy your honey. Rest your bones. After a bit, we will head back to Leon Springs. The Indians won't come back for their dead till after dark, and maybe not even then. I want to thank Mr. Cherry for extracting the honey. You are the bravest of the brave." The men laughed, and continued to eat the honey, made exceptionally sweet by wild rose nectar.

Paddy O'Toole didn't sit down. He kept pacing and looking down the canyon. Finally, he blurted out, "I saw one of them redskins go into that clump of bushes on the left, not a hundred yards from here. I think I'll go kill him."

Jack stopped eating and looked up at Paddy. Cocking his head to one side, he asked, "Are you crazy? That wounded Indian will kill you if you enter his hiding place. Let him be. He will die later or starve to death. Sit down and enjoy this delicious honey."

Paddy argued, "With all due respect, I'm not afraid of a crippled savage."

Jack glanced back, shaking his head in a negative motion before responding, "Paddy, if you go in there, he will kill you. Leave him be. We all know you are not afraid. You have nothing to prove to us. Sit down and tell us one of your stories. He is not going anywhere. When we finish eating, we will all go down and get him."

Paddy looked down at Jack and then back toward the thick brush. "I'm going in there and kill that savage and take his scalp as a trophy to mail to my wife and children back in Baltimore." With those words, he threw out his chest and off he went, rifle in hand. Jack said nothing more.

Moments later, a shrill scream that sounded like a dying panther came from the brush. The men knew instantly it was Paddy. Before Jack could stand, Kit, Lefty, Henry and Cherry were up with their rifles in their hands. Jack didn't need to give them an order. They ran to the brushy area and fanned out, crouching to their knees. Kit noticed a small branch move slightly. He fired, and a mummer came from behind the branch. Suddenly three more shots filled the tight compound of trees. The four rangers reloaded and converged on the spot. The Indian was not dead, even though he had a broken leg and four bullet wounds. His eyes told the rangers his thoughts. He wanted them to end his suffering. Kit fixed his gaze on the wounded Indian as he contemplated whether to oblige or ignore the dying man's request. He shrugged his shoulders and said, "Let's find Paddy."

As they walked away, the wounded brave shouted out in Spanish, "Help me stop hurting." His pleas were ignored.

The rangers didn't have to go far to find Paddy. Not twenty feet away they discovered the big Irishman flat on his back with an arrow in his heart. Kit broke off the shaft of the arrow and tossed it aside. The four men managed to drag Paddy from the brush, and carried his body to the base of the honey tree.

Jack grabbed a shovel and snapped, "No buzzard is gonna taste this brave ranger's flesh."

As soon as his arms grew tired of digging, he ordered Kit to take his place. The ground was stone hard, so the grave would have to be shallow. The men cut small saplings about six feet long and Jack made a cage around Paddy's body with the green poles. Using Paddy's leather lariat, they tied the poles around his body so if an animal smelled the grave and dug up the body, they wouldn't be able to chew through the green poles. By the time the poles rotted, the body would have returned to dust. While the men finished making the burial cage, Jack retrieved his New Testament from his saddlebag and read First Corinthians Chapter 13:

> *"Though I speak with the tongues of men and angels and have not love I am become as sounding brass or a tinkling cymbal.*
>
> *And though I have the gift of prophesy and understand all mysteries and all knowledge and though I have all faith so that I could remove mountains and have not love, I am nothing.*
>
> *And though I bestow all my goods to feed the poor and though I give my body to be burned and have not love it profiteth me nothing.*
>
> *Love suffereth long and is kind; love envieth not itself, love vaunteth not itself, is not puffed up.*
>
> *Doth not behave itself unseemly, seeketh not her own, is not easily provoked, thinketh no evil.*
>
> *Rejoiceth not in iniquity, but rejoiceth in the truth.*
>
> *Beareth all things, believeth all things, hopeth all things, endureth all things.*
>
> *Love never falleth; but whether there be prophecies, they shall fail, whether there be knowledge, it shall vanish away.*
>
> *For we know in part and we prophesy in part.*
>
> *But when that which is perfect is come, then that which is in part shall be done away.*
>
> *When I was a child, I spake as a child. I understood as a child. I thought as a child; but when I became a man, I put away childish things.*
>
> *For now we see through a glass darkly; but then face to face; now I know in part; but then shall I know even as also I am known.*
>
> *And now abideth faith, hope and love, these three, but the greatest of these is love."*

When Jack finished reading the scripture, he closed by saying, "Please Father, take him Home. Paddy will make the angels laugh as he did us in the brief time we had the privilege of riding with him. Amen."

Kit placed a chunk of honeycomb on the poles over Paddy's mouth. The gesture was Kit's way of saying here is food for your journey home. Jack tossed the first shovel of dirt over the body. Soon the other men joined in. They packed the dirt tight with their boots. Cherry and Lefty made a heavy wooden cross to mark the grave. Not that anyone would ever return to Paddy's grave, but at least for a while, strangers riding through the canyon bed would see the marker.

There was no more time for mourning. Jack told the men to saddle up; they were going back to Leon Springs. He allowed his men to pick up Comanche souvenirs: Bows, arrows, lances, tomahawks, and shields with painted symbols. There would be no scalping; Jack Hays would not permit desecration of the dead.

The rangers were in camp for five days when Bud Miller returned, grinning like a Cheshire cat. He brought back pay for all the rangers on Jack's list. Paddy's money was put in the general supply fund. In addition, Bud gave Jack three hundred dollars for powder, lead, and much needed supplies. In his saddlebags was a gift of two gallons of Kentucky bourbon from Sam Houston. The president had given up drinking, but he felt nothing wrong in sending such a treat to his rangers. Neither Jack nor Bud drank, but knew most of the men could bend an elbow with the best. Jack thought a celebration was in order. Kit sang some old Tennessee songs, strumming along on his rusty guitar. To the men, he was a virtuoso of the highest standard, and the more whiskey they drank, the better Kit's playing and "sangin'" sounded. The rangers stayed up until after midnight telling Paddy O'Toole stories and laughing at the funny things the big Irishman said and did while he was with them.

The compound at Leon Springs had grown from a few lean-tos into a small fort. The scrub oaks of the area didn't provide the material to duplicate Fort Parker; nevertheless, there was a raised blockhouse on one corner and rifle portholes on all sides. The walls were only eight feet tall, but Jack cut the tops of the logs to a sharp point, making it difficult for anyone to climb over without being punctured. The location Jack selected placed the compound next to a running stream. He had the rangers build a dam across part of the stream, giving them a steady water supply in the event of a long siege. He also made sure the fort had plenty of beef jerky, corn, salt, and honey on hand. He fully expected an attack by cowboy bandits or Comanche once they learned of the rangers' location. The blockhouse was manned most of the time; they could never be sure when an Indian band would stumble upon them or worse yet, seek them out. The longer they lived in Leon Springs, the more risk they faced because the rangers, especially Devil Jack, had plenty of enemies.

Major Hays and his men rested up and let the wounded heal. There were so many sick or wounded, Jack didn't have enough men to make another Indian chase. There was no money to hire new rangers or call his regulars back into service. He had plenty of adventure seekers wanting to join the rangers, but Jack needed special men. He didn't want men who came to Texas just to kill "redskins and greasers", but rather those of good character and exceptional courage, like Paddy O'Toole.

Since there were not enough healthy men to withstand a large battle, Jack accepted a land surveying job southwest of San Antonio, about half way between Uvalde and Laredo. He employed eleven rangers, including Bud, Samuel Walker, and Robert Addison Gillespie, who hailed from Tennessee, the son of Robert and Patsy (Houston) Gillespie. He moved to Texas in 1837 with his two brothers, Houston and Matthew. In January 1838, the trio formed a mercantile and land partnership at Matagorda Bay, not far from the land Sam Maverick would later purchase. James furnished the money for the enterprise, known as *Gillespie and Brothers*. At the end of 1839, the Gillespie brothers moved to La Grange, and established a mercantile store and continued to buy Texas bounty land certificates. They learned from Sam Maverick how easy it was to purchase the certificates from soldiers not wanting to settle down. Addison then fought with Henry Moore in the upper Colorado River Expedition. In 1842, he took part in the battle of Salado Creek and was a member of the Somervell Expedition, where he became friends with Jack Hays. After General Somervell disbanded his army, Addison joined Jack Hays' rangers. He was the perfect ranger for Jack Hays' unit. Addison's good judgment in choosing not to participate in the Mier invasion showed Hays his new ranger had brains and was not afraid to use them.

Surveying was a new experience for the rangers and they were amazed how something so simple proved to be so difficult; Bud had not walked so much since he was sixteen. Poor Lefty was wearing moccasins and the goat head grass burs were lethal on his feet. Most of the trees and bushes had a thorn of some kind, and the area was rife with rattlesnakes. Rangers knew no fear, with the exception of the sizzling sound of a diamondback rattler. The first night, Bud's feet and calves hurt so much he could hardly sleep. He was not alone, as all the men were suffering. Jack was hurting as well, but he concealed his pain so he could tease the men, calling them sissies.

At the end of six weeks the horses were fat, rested, and ready to go. The day the survey group arrived back in Leon Springs, a message was waiting for Major Hays. An unknown band of Indians was harassing settlers around the perimeter of San Antonio. Jack handpicked fifteen rested men, which included Kit Adkins, Sam Walker, Addison Gillespie, Bud Miller, Lefty Block, and nine other experienced Indian fighters. The rangers left as soon as supplies were loaded on their horses. Jack wanted to get his men to the heart of where the Indians were launching their raids. He selected Walker's Creek, north of Lulling and not far from the San Marcos River for his headquarters. The area sat in a triangle between San Antonio, Austin, and Gonzales and provided a permanent location to store their food and extra clothing. The running creek provided water and some protection in the event they were attacked.

Two hours ride from camp, the rangers sensed they were being followed. When Sam Walker looked back, he saw ten Indians sneaking into the trees. The rangers stopped and turned to face the enemy. Four braves ambled out from behind the trees, trying to lure the rangers into chasing them. The rangers proceeded with caution. Soon, a group of 120 Mexicans and Comanche under the leadership of Chief Yellow Wolf emerged from the tree line. At first, the hostiles formed a battle line and waited for the rangers. When Jack and his men got within rifle range, Chief Yellow Wolf signaled a retreat down into the deep ravine and up a steep hill, the apex of which stood three-hundred feet above the rangers' position. Yellow Wolf started screaming in Spanish, "Charge us, cowards! Charge us, you sons of a mother dog!"

Getting no response, he rode down the hill, raised his middle finger as an insult and then charged back up, gesturing for the rangers to follow. He kept challenging them to fight. If they were so brave, then why not show it? He then singled out Jack Hays, shouting, "Devil Yack, your mother is a pig. You are a cowardly suckling." The wise Chief was trying to provoke the rangers to attack his superior position. After the Chief's verbal assault, his braves and Mexican associates began a relentless barrage of slander, questioning the rangers' mothers' martial status at the time of their birth and using every insulting name they could think of. Jack realized that the Indians and their companions were getting his men agitated and feared someone might do something rash. Even Bud and Samuel Walker, the normally cool and collected pair, were riled up. Before things got out of control, Jack nudged his horse forward a few feet and using his hands as a megaphone, screamed, "Yellow Dog, son of a mother dog. The Comanche liver is yellow, the color of a coward."

Jack's words got under Yellow Wolf's skin. The Chief became so upset he almost fell off his massive bay stallion. His gestures exaggerated and his braves became more animated in their insults. Jack had seen their tricks and heard their profanities before and he was not going to let emotions play a part in the battle. Let the Comanche and their Mexican friends say what they wished; he would fight when he knew the time was right.

The longer the rangers sat on the bank looking up, the louder the Indians voices screamed like a wildcat caught in a trap. When Jack started down into the ravine, the Indians got very excited. Could it be the stupid white men would come up the hill and face their guns and strong bows? That was not going to happen. Once all of his men were in the ravine bed, Jack motioned for them to stay quiet and follow him. Because of the curve of the hill, the Indians couldn't see into the base of the ravine. Jack led the rangers in a 180-degree circle, placing them at the rear of the enemy. Waiting on the high ground, eyes glued to the ravine below, the braves' bows were loaded and the Mexicans' rifles primed and ready, just waiting to fire when the stupid white men stuck their heads above the precipice.

When Jack felt they were directly behind Yellow Wolf's band, he signaled his rangers to check their guns and move silently up the backside of the hill. There was open ground all the way to the ridge, allowing the rangers to climb undetected. When the sixteen rangers reached a spot where they could look over the edge of the ridge, they saw the enemy looking down in the opposite direction.

"Steady your horses and pick you a man," Jack whispered. "Sam, Bud and the men on my left, pick a Mexican to kill. They can do more damage with their guns. You, on my right, take out the Indians in the middle. We want to divide 'em."

Jack squeezed his knees and his horse edged ahead a few more yards. The movement caused one Indian to turn and look. Jack's bullet tore a hole in the middle of his skull, splattering blood over the brave next to him. An instant later, Bud's lead hit a Mexican in the back of the head. Each ranger's bullet found its target; fifteen enemy killed and one mortally wounded. Before the rangers could reload, the Mexicans and Indians dashed for their horses in fear of being the next to fall. Before the Indians could mount, ranger bullets killed eleven more and struck down five horses. The rangers rushed the enemy position, creating even more confusion. Instead of standing their ground, the Indians and Mexicans chose retreat. Had they remained calm, they could have easily cut down the sixteen rangers.

The chaos didn't last long before the brilliant Yellow Wolf got his men under control. He lost twenty-two men and knew he couldn't lose many more if he wanted victory. The Chief galloped through his men, calming them down and at the same time, urging them to fight. No matter how the battle started, he would have victory. No matter how few men he had left, it was time for "Devil Yack" to die. Yellow Wolf's men encircled the outer perimeter of rangers' position. Jack countered by moving his rangers into a tight circle, back-to-back on their horses.

"We only have one chance with our rifles. Wait until you are sure of your shot. Then place your rifles in your saddle scabbard and use your pistols. Eight of you move forward and empty your pistols, and then drop back into the circle so the other eight can take your place. We cannot have all our guns empty at the same time. Stay calm, we can whip this bunch," Jack ordered.

Yellow Wolf, sitting like a Greek god on his marvelous bay stallion, rallied his frightened men. To instill confidence in his men, the Chief started moving around the rangers. With each circle, the Chief tightened the circle around the small band of defiant Texans. Jack countered once again, making a tight circle within the Indians' larger one. He wanted a man facing all directions should one group decide to charge. Jack encouraged his men, "Boys, this won't be easy, but we can whip 'em. Just stay calm and steady. Every shot has to kill if we are going to drive 'em back."

Bud was in the first eight to move forward, along with Walker and Gillespie. The Indians and Mexicans charged. In their excitement, the Mexicans shot high. The rangers obeyed Jack's orders and remained calm. Bud was the first to pick off a Mexican riding a pinto at a distance of 250 yards. Walker took the next one down, a Comanche at the same distance. The rest of the rangers fired, killing three more men and taking down a few horses. Jack knew Yellow Wolf was not going to let the rangers continue using their long rifles to kill off his men one by one. Jack issued another order: "Put away your rifles and get out your pistols. Yellow Wolf is getting ready to charge. If you can't get a clear shot, then take a horse down. We cannot allow them to run over us." The rangers braced for the charge.

Yellow Wolf followed Jack's script. He stopped circling and began a slow march toward the clustered group of rangers. The sight of such a large force gave the rangers reason to pause and make sure they were right with God. Bud wondered if he would ever see Charm again. He was aware they were facing almost impossible odds, but believed Jack Hays had the cunning to beat impossible odds, having done so on many occasions. Then he heard the comforting commands of his Major: "Every other man step forward and the others drop back. When the first group has emptied your pistols, drop back and the others will take your place. Each of you has ten shots. Stay steady. You are the best shots in the world and those poor souls don't know what they are riding into. I pity them. Boys, I didn't bring you up here to lose. We will win. Keep a cool head and hot hand and we will be eating supper in no time."

Fire shot from the pistols of eight rangers until eighty bullets had been fired. Not all hit their target and those that did were not always a kill. Bud's group killed nine and wounded at least twenty. The Indians were truer with their lances than the Mexicans were with their guns. One lance tore through Gillespie's thigh and another slashed through Walker's left bicep. Both men were bleeding profusely, but there was no time to stop and apply a tourniquet. Not one ranger escaped injury during the fierce battle. Bud was hit twice. One Indian got close enough to split his skull with a lance. If Bud had not ducked, the point would have penetrated his Adam's apple. In the adrenaline of battle, Bud felt nothing. He remained calm and maintained deadly aim with each round.

The second unit then stepped forward, taking all eighty of their rounds to repel the charge. As the second unit emptied their pistols, Bud and his group had reloaded and stepped forward. They didn't have to shoot. Yellow Wolf decided he would do better in a running fight and led his men down the hill and into the ravine bed.

Jack shouted, "Follow them. Get close enough to use your pistols."

The chase was on. Down into the ravine raced Yellow Wolf and his men, with the rangers in hot pursuit. The Texans were having a difficult time getting close enough to use their pistols when Yellow Wolf suddenly turned the fleeing group. That was a mistake on his part because the rangers killed five more of his men. The chase was on again as the Indians ran another two miles before Yellow Wolf decided to make another stand. Jack remained confident, once more bellowing instructions, "Bud, you, Lefty, Kit and me will shoot first. You other six, be ready. When we are empty, you step forward." Jack looked at Bud's blood-covered face and asked, "Can you see to shoot?"

"Bet your boots, your best boots. I'm just nicked."

Bud patted Lightning on the neck, relieved that a gunshot or lance had not hit his horse. A broken arrow still sticking from the pummel of his saddle was proof of how close Lightning came to being hit. On the other hand, Jack's horse had two arrows in his shoulders and one in his flank. Jack observed the condition of his men and for the first time in the battle, he felt vulnerable. Gillespie could hardly sit in his saddle. Bud didn't look all that healthy. Lefty was in immense pain. Kit had a broken arrow shaft protruding from his leg, leaving the flint in his body.

Yellow Wolf was down to thirty-five men, but they were all healthy, with some of his better warriors and a few of the bravest Mexicans remaining. Yellow Wolf was an exceptional battlefield technician and strong leader. He lined up his men for one last charge. The Chief knew he had the numbers to reach the rangers before they could respond strongly enough to impede his advance. The Chief rode in and out among his men, telling them their destiny was to rid the country of Devil Yack and now was the time. The warrior who killed the Devil would be rewarded with one hundred of the Chief's horses, and ten horses for each of the other rangers slain. Yellow Wolf felt his prey was wounded and cowering. All he had to do was take down Devil Yack and the others would unravel. He underestimated the resolve of the Texas Rangers; Yellow Wolf would have to kill all ten if he was to claim victory.

Once the Chief felt his men were in the perfect mindset, they formed a long line and began a forward movement on the rangers' position. Without their long rifles, the rangers would have to wait until the enemy was close enough to use their deadly bows or muskets before they could defend themselves. Jack realized the rangers' only hope was to take down Chief Yellow Wolf himself.

"Anybody got a loaded rifle?" Jack asked, not expecting a positive answer.

Bud answered, "I can load fast."

The injured Addison Gillespie, about to fall from his saddle, answered in a southern drawl, "I got my rifle primed. I wanna take the shot."

"Then dismount and kill that wicked Yellow Wolf. If you don't kill him, we cannot stop them this time. Our lives are in your hands."

Lefty helped the weak, but confident Gillespie down from his horse. Removing his rifle from his saddle scabbard, Addison placed the long barrel in the well-worn saddle seat. Chief Yellow Wolf continued to move forward, keeping his buffalo shield between him and Gillespie's rifle. The rangers grew anxious as the enemy closed in. Addison Gillespie remained calm and patient. He was feeling faint, but told his mind he could not let his comrades down. Yellow Wolf confidently moved forward, his big bay prancing sideways with his knees high and nostrils flared. The powerful Comanche Chief was within thirty yards when he raised his right hand to signal his warriors to prepare to charge. Yellow Wolf's shield remained in place, protecting his body. Addison had only one option; he would have to aim for the Chief's head. A small moving target was risky. If he missed, they all would be killed. Gillespie slowly squeezed the trigger and his lead shattered the Chief's forehead, knocking a large hole in his skull. Blood and brains covered his horse, causing the bronze stallion to lunge forward. Like a raw colt, the bay started bucking and tossed the Chief over his back and onto the ground.

"Great shot!" yelled Jack.

The rangers shouted with joy as the frightened Indians turned to retreat. Jack quickly turned his attention to the weak condition of Gillespie and his other men. Lefty Block was losing blood fast. He had been stuffing a rag in his leg, but the Mexican bullet had severed an artery. Jack told Kit to build a fire while he and Bud went to retrieve the injured. Jack carried an iron rod in his saddlebag for just such occasions. He knew he had to cauterize the wounds to prevent infection. Kit Adkins produced a bottle of whiskey to help the men withstand the pain. While the iron was heating up, Jack asked Bud, "Do you want a shot of whiskey while I sew up your head wound?"

Bud shivered at the thought of a needle in his scalp; however, he didn't hesitate with his answer. "My mama would turn over in her grave if she saw me drinking. Do what you gotta do. I know the bleeding has to be slowed down or it will do me in."

Bud placed a leather strap between his teeth and bit down so he wouldn't flinch. Jack removed a needle from the flames and doused it with water from his canteen. He then strung some thread through the eye and proceeded to sew together the five-inch gash in Bud's skull. In a brief time, Jack said, "You'll be fine. The stitches will rot out in a month or so. Pour a dab of whiskey on the other cut and keep it clean."

Samuel Walker's wound was still bleeding profusely. He didn't refuse a few shots of whiskey. He knew what was coming. Two rangers then held Walker down so Jack could sear the wound closed. Bud couldn't stand to watch and turned away, but was unable to escape the smell of burning flesh. He wanted to vomit. He didn't wait around for Jack to sear the other men's wounds and headed for the nearby stream to wash the blood from his face and hair.

Addison Gillespie was passed out when Jack stuck the white-hot iron to his wound. The pain startled him awake and the familiar smell told him what was happening. One by one, Jack tended to each of his men. Kit and Bud rounded up some Indian ponies for the two rangers who had lost their horses. The unit camped for four days so the wounded could recover enough to make the trip home. Even then, traveling was slow. Ten to twelve miles was all Jack felt he could push the men. He never shared with the others how close he came to death. A Mexican bullet had creased his side and if it had gone two inches further in, it would have punctured his intestines. A ruptured intestine on the battlefield would have meant a slow and painful death.

Jack and the wounded rangers limped into San Antonio five days later. Jack took those in the weakest condition to stay with Mrs. Jacques until they recuperated. She was a nurse of sorts and experienced as anyone in San Antonio in caring for the ill.

Bud approached Jack and asked, "Is it alright if I get my wounds dressed and go to Goliad? I have avoided going to my father's grave for nine years and I think it is time. Dillard Cooper, one of the men who escaped the massacre, is living down in that area. I need to go talk with him, and the padre at the Mission."

"Go with my blessings," Jack answered without hesitation. "I have to report to President Jones, which I'm not all that pleased about. He has turned out to be more like Lamar and less like General Houston."

Bud slapped Jack on the shoulder and with deep concern in his voice said, "My friend, God be with you. For Texas and our future, I pray you will find success with President Jones. I know that if he can be turned, you are the man for the job. I'll let you know how things work out down in Goliad." The two shook hands and Bud went to prepare for his trip.

Jack assigned Henry McCullough to run the ranger camp at Leon Springs while he remained in San Antonio with the wounded. Jack would regret remaining in town where he was swarmed with newspaper reporters seeking a hero story. Jack refused to give an interview, stating, "Yellow Wolf is the bravest and finest opponent we have ever faced on the battlefield. I thank God there was only one Yellow Wolf. If the Comanche had a dozen leaders like him, there would be no Republic and we would not be standing here today. I salute Yellow Wolf as the greatest warrior, other than my friend Falco, I have ever encountered. Now, if you don't mind gentlemen, I have some brave men of my own to attend to."

The reporters had found their hero story in the few words of John Coffee "Jack" Hays. Every Texas newspaper wrote of his heroics, and the news soon crossed into the United States. Young boys across the country played Rangers and Indians, and they all wanted to be Jack Hays. He became a larger than life figure without ever seeking fame and glory.

The following morning, Jack checked on the health of his men, and with growing apprehension, headed east to meet with President Jones. He hoped to also visit Raven Hill and speak to General Houston. Even though Jones was the new President, Hays still considered Houston the man in charge of the Republic. Jack planned to do his best to show President Jones the reasons why Texas needed to annex into the Union. Texas didn't have enough trained men nor enough money to defeat the superior Mexican army. Jack wanted an independent Republic as much as the next man, but understood that without annexation, Mexico City would join with hostile Indian tribes and drive the white man back into the United States. He would do everything in his power to see Texas become the twenty-eighth state.

Chapter Thirty-Eight
Goliad

Bud led Lightning to the livery stable and paid for new shoes and board. He stocked up on supplies and made sure all of his guns were in excellent condition.

He then paid his landlady back rent, and finally retuned to the comfort of his room, where he noticed a letter propped up against the kerosene lamp. The handwriting looked vaguely familiar. Bud removed his pocketknife and slit open the flap on the envelope. The moment he started to read, he knew the author.

My Dearest Boy,

I am sorry to be the bearer of bad news. That sweet young little rich girl you were courting has abandoned you for another. Sunday after church, she was married to the minister's eldest son. I attended the wedding so I could report the news to you. I hope this doesn't break your heart. You are being so brave to protect us from the Red Savages and she does this horrible thing to you. I say she stuck a knife in the middle of your back while you were away fighting for freedom and our Republic.

Now that you are free from that untrustworthy woman, I pray you will consider moving back to Galveston Island and living with me. I have a new large home on the beach with a barn you can keep your horse in. I was thinking perhaps you could run for sheriff and replace that piece of trash Leland Maples. He is more crooked than a side-winding rattlesnake. My new home is yours and there is sufficient room. The best news is you can stay with me rent-free.

Affectionately,

Your admiring Teacher, Horace

The news of the wedding was a great relief to Bud. He had been concerned how he was going to leave Virginia for another without causing her pain. The letter from Horace made him realize he had neglected writing to Charm. He sat down in the rickety handmade chair and began to write. His mind started to drift, his thoughts turning to Charlie. While on the Indian mission, word had reached him that Charlie was home and soon to be married. Bud was anxious to find what Charlie's reaction was to his new farm and home. His mind kept wandering and he decided to wait to pen the letter to Charm when he was less exhausted. He lay down on the top of the quilt and didn't wake up until twenty hours later when his landlady came into his room and shook him vigorously, fearing he was dead.

While Bud shaved, even though it was three in the afternoon, she prepared him a large breakfast of four eggs, several strips of lean bacon, hot coffee, and fresh biscuits and cream gravy. After eating until his stomach hurt, he went onto the front porch. He sat in the swing hanging from the roof joist, and wrote an eight-page letter to Charm. He detailed the fight with Yellow Wolf and, for the first time, admitted how close he came to death; only the remarkable shot by Gillespie saved their lives. He neglected to mention his scalp wound. He didn't want her to worry. On page seven, he wrote:

Facing death makes a man to stop and ask what is really important. I remember feeling in my pocket for the handkerchief you gave me as the Indians moved in on our small band of rangers. I realized I want to spend the remainder of my life looking into your eyes and listening to your laughter, but if I was going to die, I wanted you to be in my final thoughts. I said a prayer and placed your image in my mind.

The moment it began to look like we had lost all hope, I was thinking we must make a victorious stand. We must turn back this final assault. Then Major Hays asked if anyone had a loaded rifle. Addison Gillespie was weak from the loss of blood from a severe lance wound. He said his rifle was primed. I started to ask Addison if he would let me use his rifle, but I could see he wanted revenge. He made the best shot I've ever seen under such circumstances. He split Yellow Wolf's skull with one shot. I am able to write because of the bravery of Addison Gillespie.

By the time you read this letter, I will be at the place where my father was murdered. This is why I came to Texas and I can wait no longer.

With deeper love than you can possibly realize,

Bud

P.S. I managed to obtain two books. I cannot wait to share them with you. Washington Irvin's, 'A Tour of the Prairies' and 'The Adventure of Captain Bonneville'. I was able to purchase these first editions from a book peddler passing through San Antonio. I was told Mr. Irvin is considered the first American Man of Letters. On that, I cannot extrapolate.

The road to Goliad took Bud through places where Texas history was made. As he rode past the Alamo, he paused to reflect on the brave men who lost their lives in the old mission. He followed the mission trail down past a chain of five missions established along the San Antonio River in the 18th century. Built primarily to expand Spanish New World influence northward from Mexico, the missions also served to convert the natives to the Spanish God. It was at Mission Concepcion that Jim Bowie and his men served the Mexicans their first major defeat. Bud stopped in San Jose and San Juan, but it was at Mission Conception that he lingered. Espanda was the last mission along the river. One of the padres told him the missions had originally been in east Texas and later re-established along the river. Bud was beginning to understand the importance of Goliad. In the mission chain, Goliad was the key to the Gulf of Mexico for the supply route.

When he came to the edge of Goliad, he discovered the Mission Espiritu Santo sitting away from the Fort La Bahia. He had erroneously assumed they were both in one structure. He stopped at Espiritu Santo first because he spotted a padre's brown robes as he walked up from the river carrying water. As he approached the priest, he offered a friendly greeting: "Howdy, I'm Bud Miller. I came to see if you could help me learn what happened to my father. He was killed in the Goliad massacre."

"Welcome my son. Please tie your horse and enter God's house with me. I am confident you could use a cold drink of water and perhaps a morsel of food. I will be pleased to share my limited knowledge with you."

Bud obeyed. Once inside, the padre squatted so the buckets on each end of the yoke reached the floor. Standing back up, he placed his hands on his back and stretched, and then addressed his new friend, "My name is Father Colon. I'm afraid I'm getting too old to manage carrying the water. We used to have Indians doing this kind of work. Now it's only Father Manuel and me. Now, how may I help you?"

"I understand the prisoners were housed in your mission before Santa Anna ordered them marched out and slaughtered," Bud answered.

"No, someone has misled you. You are thinking about The Lady of Loreto Mission (named after the sweet smelling laurels growing in the area. Loreto means laurel) inside Fort La Bahia. I can understand the confusion. This entire area was known as La Bahia until 1829 when it was renamed Goliad. Now La Bahia is called Fort Defiance. Father Manuel is up at The Lady of Loreto Mission helping an indigent Indian family. He has been here the longest and I suggest you ride up and see him. He will know more about the massacre."

"Thank you Father."

"God bless you, my child. I will say a rosary for you tonight."

As Bud entered the mission, he found the silver-haired Father Manuel, his back hunched over from years of hard work. When he got closer, he could see that the unforgiving Texas sun had cut deep creases into the padre's face. Bud could also see Father Manuel's demeanor projected love and compassion as he tended to the frightened Indians. When the padre was finished, he turned his attention to his new guest. "What brings you into the House of God?"

"My name is Bud Miller. My father was Joshua "Stump" Miller who was among those imprisoned in your mission along with Colonel Fannin."

The mission room was small with a beautiful fresco on the rear wall. Bud felt beset with sadness knowing the last day of his father's life was spent in the very room in which he now stood. He was amazed at how small the chapel was and queried in his mind how over three hundred men could be confined in such a small space.

"My son, I'm not sure I remember your father. We have a list of the men who died in that horrible insult on humanity. There are graves on the hill on the southeast side of the compound. I am sure you want to place some flowers on his grave. I will say a prayer for you."

"Perhaps you can help me find someone who would know what took place here."

"We did have a nice young man set free before the unthinkable happened. His brother and sister-in-law live just south of here, near San Patricio. The distance is not more than a half day's ride."

"Can you tell me if my father left me any property?"

"Follow me." The two went into long, thin room off the sanctuary, the padre carrying a beeswax candle to light their way. He dusted off the spines of the books until he found a volume dated in the timeframe that Stump would have recorded a deed. "My son, carry this for me into the courtyard so we can have sufficient light to read."

They walked outside and found the page where his father recorded a land grant for 1,140 acres. Next to his father's signature was the name of the man the land was deeded to, a man Bud knew very well. In brown ink written on the yellowed paper was the bold signature of Samuel A. Maverick. Now Bud knew why Sam had never warmed up to him when they rode together as rangers. Perhaps Sam thought Bud would challenge him in court for his birthright. He thanked the kind padre and walked to the hill where the prominent burial mound stood. Under this pile of dirt were the remains of his father. Good or bad, he was his blood. Seeing the grave made Bud want to know more. He would not wait until the next day to leave. It was dark before he found the O'Boyle's home, so he decided to make camp a couple of miles away and wait until the next morning to pay them a visit.

Edward and Mary O'Boyle didn't have to wait for Bud to knock on their door; their coonhounds put up a ruckus when the young ranger was a thousand yards away. They were waiting outside when he rode up. Dismounting, he extended his hand to Mr. O'Boyle, introducing himself. "I'm Bud Miller. I understand you might have known my father or the truth of what happened at the Goliad massacre."

Edward's hands gripped Bud's with the power of a blacksmith's vice as he answered, "Welcome, we are getting ready to eat breakfast. Mama, put another plate on for this lad. Son, we are glad to have you in our humble abode. Come in and we can talk over breakfast. I'll get one of the boys to care for your stallion."

Mary O'Boyle was red-faced Irish through and through. She was a short and stocky woman whose smile would melt butter. She was the talker and Edward seemed pleased to sit back and listen. Bud spoke fondly of the Lipan who rode with the Texas Rangers when something in the conversation triggered him to mention the Indian tribes down in their area being very different from the Comanche. Mary jumped in, saying, "The Karankawa, Copane, Cujanes and Cosos inhabited the coastal bend country. All are gone now, with the exception of the Karankawa. Some people call them Caranchua. Either way, they are mean and dirty. They smell horrible. They grease their bodies with alligator or skunk oil to keep the mosquitoes away. The men ran around naked both summer and winter. There are still a few living on North Padre Island."

The minute she mentioned the Karankawa, Bud sat up in his chair and exclaimed, "The Baron de Bastrop told me about them. He told me they are cannibals. I didn't know they were still around. I might not have come down here alone with them running around."

Mary looked at Edward and back to Bud. "Son, you need not worry. They all retreated across the Laguna Madre from Corpus Christi to North Padre, a barrier island less than 2 miles wide and 120 miles long."

When Mary paused for a moment, Bud turned to Edward, saying, "Sir, if you wish, you can use Lightning. He has a strong bloodline. His foals look just like him."

"Thank you, boy. I have two mares ready to mate. If you will excuse me, I'll be heading to the barn and take you up on your offer." With those words, Edward grabbed his hat and left before Bud could change his mind.

As if there had been no interruption, Mary continued, "I was telling you about the Karankawa. Right after we moved here in 1833, they captured two white men and strapped them to a tree. Those savages proceeded to cut chunks of skin off the men's bodies and cook it over the campfire, making the men watch while they feasted on the flesh. One of the men lost so much blood he died, but his companion escaped and lived to tell the tale. We had a trader through here last year who told us that after the Karankawa fled to North Padre Island the tribe's men killed all the women and children. When the few remaining men die off, their race will vanish. Their tribe was slowly dying out anyway because a third of the men born are hermaphrodites. I suspect from inbreeding."

Bud didn't have a clue what a hermaphrodite was and certainly was not going to ask. He knew it was not desirable and left it at that. "You are telling me the men killed their own women and little ones?"

"That is what we were told, and I have no reason to believe otherwise. The old trader told us they made a shelter out of a Spanish shipwreck and are surviving on oysters, snakes, rats, rabbits, shore birds, and fish."

Bud leaned back in the cowhide chair, and with distress on his face, commented, "That is pretty sad. I cannot imagine waiting for my race to die off."

"You wouldn't wet your eyes for them if you knew the Karankawa like we do. You have no idea how horrible those Indians are, but the history of the vilest Indians to ever live is not what you came seeking. How may we help you?"

"The padre told me you could tell me the story of how Mr. O'Boyle was set free and some information on what happened in Goliad."

"Edward was in New Orleans on business, so I was here alone. Colonel Francisco Garay came through here with General Urrea and asked to stay the night in our home as it was late in the day to continue, and I consented. The next morning when Colonel Garay was about to leave, he thanked me for my hospitality and said that if there was anything he could do to repay me, he would do so cheerfully. I told him that that my husband's brother was under Fannin's command at Goliad and if, in the fortunes of war, he could do him a favor, I would be much appreciative. He asked me for his name and then wrote it down in his notes. On the morning the prisoners were led forth for execution, Colonel Garay rode up the line asking if there was a man named Michael O'Boyle present. Michael raised his hand. Colonel Garay instructed Michael to follow him to the hospital, and then to his personal quarters, thus sparing Michael's life."

"Ma'am, that is pretty amazing. Tell me more, please."

Mary obliged. She loved telling the Goliad story as if she were reciting a part in a school play. "On the 17th of March, the enemy appeared on the opposite side of the river from Fort Defiance or, as it was called back then, Goliad. Fannin sent a skirmishing party under Captain Jack Shackelford's command to engage the Mexicans as he watched from the ramparts. We have been told Fannin was scared to death. After the Mexicans retreated to the Old Mission Church, Colonel Fannin recalled Shackelford. On the following day, the Mexicans appeared in force at the same place. That was when Fannin gave orders for the men to gather bread, dried beef and rations sufficient for several days. The cannons were taken down from the bastions and orders were given to be ready to march before daylight the following morning." Mary suddenly stopped speaking and poured Bud and herself a fresh cup of coffee. Then without missing a beat, she continued, "For reasons unknown, Fannin didn't evacuate the fort until 9 o'clock the next morning even though his men were up before six, packed and ready to march. The three hours he lost cost them their lives. Fannin marched his men down to the river crossing without any difficulty. He opted to cross at the lower crossing instead of the upper ford in front of the Old Mission, thinking they could avoid a confrontation with the Mexicans. Fannin later said his plan was to get into the interior of Texas and join Houston's army. They continued to march until they crossed Manahuilla Creek, about three miles from the lower river ford. Traveling was slow because of the cannons and oxen-drawn baggage wagons. As you know, no one rushes oxen. Fannin then made another mistake. He halted the men so they could eat. There would have been time to eat once they were safe. Eating took over an hour of precious time. I can promise you this: Without his West Point education, he would not have been given command of a dogsled."

"I gather you don't like Colonel Fannin," Bud responded, feeling he needed to say something.

"I personally think Fannin was a good man. He just got in over his head." Not wanting to get sidetracked from her story, she continued, "After breakfast, the march continued without incident until around noon when the Mexican army appeared unexpectedly, descending from the left and the rear. The cavalry approached very fast with the intention of cutting the Texans off from the timber along the edge of Coleto Creek. They fired a few shots warning Fannin to halt. That is when the Colonel exclaimed, 'That's the signal for battle. I won't retreat another foot.' The men unlimbered the six cannons and formed into a hollow square, placing the baggage wagons, hospital wagon, and magazine in the center. Colonel Fannin, realizing too late that the Mexicans' objective was to cut off his army from the timber, ordered the men to load the cannons and continue their march. The Texans left the main road, marching in an oblique direction toward the nearest trees. They were within three-quarters of a mile of the timberline when the enemy's infantry overtook the slow-moving oxen. Fannin said they had no option but to stop. In hindsight, they should have shot their way through the smaller Mexican cavalry and taken up battle positions in the oaks.

The fighting continued until near dark, leaving twenty-five Texans dead or wounded. Michael was wounded in the leg in the first volley of gunfire about two thirty in the afternoon. Colonel Fannin received a wound in the thigh. Then abruptly, the Mexicans stopped firing and pulled back. The real trouble commenced after the Mexicans retreated. The Texans were out of water. The wounded were suffering with nothing to drink. A few men dug for water while the rest built up entrenchments. The Alabama Red Rovers and New Orleans Grays urged the Colonel to make a fight for the trees, but he declined, saying it would be too risky. Michael was one of those who urged the colonel to make the move, telling Fannin the cover of the thick trees would provide a superior position for the fight. They could have made it through, even if they had to leave the cannons behind. Our Texans with long rifles could have plucked off the cavalry any time they got within 250 yards."

"I gather from what you are saying that Fannin just didn't understand his men's strengths?" Bud commented, being careful not to slander the colonel.

The round-faced Irish woman snarled at the mention of Fannin's name and continued, "The following morning, with fresh reinforcements, the Mexicans moved in closer. They fired a few cannon shots, all of which passed over the Texans' heads. After the first cannon volley, the Mexicans hoisted a white flag. Fannin answered, raising a white shirt. He then gathered his officers for a consultation. After a brief discussion, they agreed to capitulate, realizing it was hopeless to continue the struggle trapped in an open field. The wounded men suffering from their wounds and lack of water. I will admit he showed some character when he expressed his determination not to abandon any of his men. I will give him credit for his loyalty. Fannin then sent two officers to parley with the Mexicans. An agreement was reached guaranteeing the Texans' safety upon surrender. Michael said Fannin's officers agreed to give up all government property in their possession, and to remain as prisoners of war until they were either honorably exchanged, or sent to the United States. Upon parole, the men had to promise never to return to Texas. Both parties signed these articles and the surrender was complete.

Those able to march were taken to Goliad. The wounded waited two or three days for Mexican carts to carry them. Their suffering was intense. The men were in dire need of water and medical attention. Upon arrival at Goliad, the wounded were placed in the hospital, while the rest of the command was put under guard in Fort Defiance. As you know, just one week after the surrender, the men were marched out in three divisions and slaughtered in cold blood. Your father was in the third group."

"I know," answered Bud. "I visited my father's grave. The priest told me the bodies were torn apart by wolves, dogs, buzzards, panthers and even bobcats. General Rusk went to bury the dead, but had to gather up what bones he could find and put them all in one large grave. My friend Jack Hays helped with the burial."

Mary acknowledged what Bud said, and then continued, "Michael told us that a Mexican officer came into the hospital ordering him to tell all those able to walk to go outside. Shortly thereafter, four Mexican soldiers came in and began to carry out the severely wounded. Two of Michael's friends, who were only slightly wounded, assisted him. As they passed through the doorway, Michael overhead an officer saying the prisoners were all to be shot and relayed the information to the men.

The wounded were placed in the corner of the yard, next to the church doors. A company of soldiers formed in front of them and loaded their pieces with ball cartridge. Then a file of men under a corporal took two of our men, marched them out toward the company and tied bandages over their eyes. The Mexicans made them get on their bellies, with their faces to the ground. No sooner than the men got down, the Mexicans placed their musket muzzles to their heads, killing them. About this time, an officer of distinction came into the yard asking whether anyone named O'Boyle was there. Michael was near him as he entered and answered at once. He ordered Michael taken to the officers' hospital to have his wound tended to. Mr. Brooks, aide to Colonel Fannin was there, his thigh badly shattered near the hip. Michael told us that upon informing him what was going on, Brooks replied, 'I suppose it will be our turn next.' In less than five minutes, four Mexicans carried Brooks out, cot and all, placed him not fifteen feet from the door, and shot him dead. Then the bloodthirsty devils took his gold watch, and anything else of value was stripped from his body."

Bud sat spellbound listening to Mary. She was so confident and informed, as well as a great storyteller. He didn't know what to say, so he asked another question, "What happened after Michael came to stay with you?"

"Keep in mind; we knew nothing of the battle of San Jacinto until the end of April, though we had noticed Mexican troops traveling toward the Rio Grande in large numbers. A dragoon rode up one day and asked us to sell him two bits worth of dried meat. I told him he could have all the meat he wanted if he would answer a few questions. He consented and I learned for the first time that a battle had been fought on April 21st near San Jacinto Creek. We learned that General Santa Anna had been taken prisoner and the remainder of the Mexican forces was in full retreat. We were filled with joy. Hearing the good news lifted Michael from his depression. Colonel Garay arrived a few days later, stopping in to see us as he rushed toward Mexico. He told Michael he would need to accompany him to Matamoras. We later got a letter explaining Garay had no choice; an order came down that no Texan who had been a prisoner in Mexican hands at any time could remain in Texas. Garay informed him that all prisoners would be placed under heavy guard, but he would allow Michael the freedom of the city if he didn't try to escape. About three weeks later, Garay invited Michael to accompany him to Mexico City as his guest. He thanked the colonel, but said he was anxious to see his father in the United States. Colonel Garay released Michael from parole and set him free to make his way to Louisiana. He experienced some problems in obtaining a permit to leave the city, but finally succeeded in passing himself off as the son of an old Irishman who had a passport for New Orleans. Six days later, Michael arrived safely in New Orleans."

Bud stood up and stretched his arms over his head, and asked, "Where is Michael now?"

"It is with some sadness I have to tell you he has changed his name and now goes by Andrew Boyle. I understand he is getting rich in the States. We never hear from him. It's like he wants to forget Goliad and anything and anyone that makes him remember."

"Then I guess you really don't know what happened at the massacre," replied Bud.

"I know what I've heard, but I think the man you need to visit is Dillard Cooper of the Alabama Red Rovers. Do you know where the community of Smiley is?

"I can't say as I do. Seems I've heard the name. One of the rangers I know was from around there, but never mentioned exactly where it was."

Mary loved being able to give advice. "Of course you know where Cuero is."

Bud was pleased to answer, "Yes, I came through there on my way to Goliad. I purchased some supplies at the general trading post."

"Well, you were not far from Smiley. When you get to Cuero, take the old road to San Antonio and it will run you smack dab through the middle of Smiley. Ask anyone; they can tell you how to find Dillard. If I were you, I would go find Mr. Cooper while he is still alive. The last we heard, he was not in good health."

Bud thanked Mary and offered to help with the dishes, only to be rebuffed for offering to do woman's work. He thanked her again and joined Edward as he was leading Lightning back into his barn for a reward of shelled corn. Edward insisted Bud spend the night and leave early the following morning. Bud didn't want to get involved in another conversation with Mary, so he declined the offer. Edward would not let him leave without stocking up on bread and dried beef.

Lightning was full of energy. His nostrils flared as he pranced past the mares. Bud pushed the big sorrel into a gallop. Just as the darkness began to fall, Bud stopped to make camp and lit a fire to cook the rabbit he shot along the way. The rabbit roasted over the open flames while Bud made his bed. Suddenly, he heard a crack in the brush. His first thought was the Karankawa Indians. Mary painted such vivid pictures of the cannibals, Bud felt sure they would swarm him from all directions, cut his flesh and cook it up, and then force him to watch as they ate. He backed away from the campfire, and listened. There was more crackling of the underbrush. His heart pounded. He knew he had ten shots. He stood with his back against a large oak tree and waited. Almost simultaneously, three small brown-faced men in big floppy hats emerged from the shadows. "Mexicans," he whispered under his breath.

In broken English, one of the men pleaded, "We friends. We no banditos. No guns. We hungry."

Bud stepped into the light, still holding his belt pistols. "I'm cooking up some rabbit. You are welcome to eat."

The three Mexicans explained they had been part of a supply train attacked by cowboy bandits and had managed to escape. Their twelve companions were not as lucky. As they told their story, Bud felt sorry for them. He forgot about them being Mexican. His hatred dissipated into the darkness and he knew he had to help these men reach Mexico. They had families who loved them. They were hard-working men whose only misfortune was delivering supplies to an area filled with bandits.

The following morning, Bud made a big pot of coffee. He then saddled Lightning as the three young men, fresh from a near-death encounter, prepared for their long journey home. Bud gave the English speaking man his old shotgun, explaining they could use it to hunt for food. Mexico was a long, long walk.

In Cuero, Bud purchased a new shotgun. He needed to replace the old one anyway because the stock had cracked in a hand-to-hand fight with a Comanche. He replenished his supply of corn and jerky and purchased a quart of whiskey. Bud suspected Dillard might be a man who drank, like so many who fought in the war, perhaps to forget seeing friends die or to drown their fears, he thought.

Smiley was not a town, rather just a small trading post and some farms clustered closely together. Bud tied Lightning to a hitching post in front of the rugged log building and went in. A man standing six foot three and barely weighing 145 pounds was busy stocking a shelf when Bud startled him, saying, "Hi there."

"Dad-gum-it, boy. You done scared the liver outta me. I didn't hear you come in. Kan I hep you?"

"Sure can. I'm looking for Dillard Cooper's place," Bud answered as he placed a bag of shelled corn on the rough-hewn counter.

"Poor ol' Dillard. Been to hell and back. He came home from the war and started makin' youngens. I think his brood is up to four, with one in the hopper. The Republic ain't able to pay him a pension so he makes his livin' huntin' coon, fox, and wolves. He tans the hides and trades 'em for food and such. He's got all them kids and the sweetest little wife. I kaint recall her name. It's one of them odd names. Anyway, he is holed up in his cabin about three miles due south. You kaint miss his place. Jus' follow the wagon tracks through those two big live oak trees on the other side of the road. The Cooper place will be the third cabin on the right."

As Bud was paying for his supplies, he noticed a jar of rock candy. He filled a brown paper bag, adding it to his bill. He had mixed emotions about finally meeting a man who knew his father, and perhaps had witnessed his death.

Suddenly, the tall thin merchant blurted out, "Lucenda. Yep, her name is Lucenda Fondren Cooper. I know 'cause my mama's maiden name was Fondren."

"Much obliged, Sir. I appreciate the information. I'll give the Coopers your regards."

"You come back, ya hear?"

As Bud was packing his saddlebags and loading his shotgun, he heard horses approaching. He looked up and saw a group of forty Texas soldiers swirling dust skyward as they approached in columns of four. The unit stopped in the middle of the narrow road and dismounted and dozen of the men entered the trading post. Some cared for the horses while others waited outside because the store was not large enough to accommodate but a few at a time.

Captain Cletus Johnson was the commanding officer. Bud didn't know him; nevertheless, he introduced himself. "Good afternoon Sir, I'm Benjamin Miller, but folks call me Bud."

"Nice to meet you, Miller. Are you the Texas Ranger Miller by any chance?"

"Yes Sir. That would be me. I've been riding with the rangers for five years."

The captain's face lit up. "I got someone who will faint when I tell him who I'm talkin' with. You are famous! Wow, Bud Miller! Please, wait here."

Bud didn't know what to say. Within moments, a strapping young lad came running up, threw his arms around Bud and started hugging him. "Boy, this is my lucky day! I can't believe you are here," the boy said as he released his bear hug and stepped back.

Bud looked for a moment and then asked, "Is that you A.D.?"

"In the flesh. Mama and Jim let me join the army when I turned eighteen. This is my first real mission. We are going to Matagorda to guard the port. With all this annexation talk goin' around, there is no telling what is gonna happen."

Bud, standing with a hand placed on each hip, cocked his head to one side in disbelief as he took in the sight of the grown-up A.D. "Satterwhite, this is a pleasant surprise. How are your ma, the children and Jim?"

"Jim is the greatest man you'll ever meet. He has treated us as if we were his own. He loves mama and provides us with a good life. We built a real house with glass windowpanes and five rooms. Jim put a water pump in the kitchen so all mama has to do is prime it and out comes the water. Jim said you told him 'bout yours. The ferry is making money now that we enlarged it to pull wagons over. Jim sent me down to the Groce Plantation so I could go to school. I learned to read and write. Now Ruthann is at the plantation gettin' her schooling."

Bud listened with delight, then inquired, "How's your ma?"

"For a long time she had nightmares. The past few years, God seems to have delivered her from fear. Jim and Ma have been busy making babies. I now have two brothers and a sister. The best part is Jim earns enough money to care for us all. He is smart and works hard. I'm proud to call him my Pa."

The two talked until it was A.D.'s turn to go into the store. Captain Johnson took young Satterwhite's place, asking Bud if he could hold his belt pistols. Bud obliged the new captain, watching the awestruck young man cradle the firearms in his hands.

"I bet you have killed a lot of Indians with these."

Bud didn't want to brag and modestly replied, "They have killed their share of cowboy bandits and Comanche. Frankly Captain, I don't know how many. I mostly depend on my long rifle. I like to keep them as far away as possible. If you find yourself in a battle with Comanche, shoot their Chiefs as quickly as you can. Aim for their heads. They wear a breastplate that will repel your shots. Have your men make the first volley hit their mark. When you start killing the Comanche, they tuck tail and run. They cannot afford to lose men in big numbers."

Robert Sollers, a first lieutenant, thought he heard the name Bud during his captain's conversation. Leading his horse over and waiting for his superior to finish speaking, he asked, "You happen to be Bud Miller, the ranger?"

Bud didn't have time to respond. The captain shot back, "This is the Indian hunter in the flesh."

Robert turned white and his hands became sweaty. "Sir," he said as he extended his hand. "Sir, I have some news from Colonel Jack Hays for you."

Bud wondered what the message could be. He assumed Robert misspoke, referring to Jack as Colonel, and inquired with some reservation, "What news would that be?"

"President Jones has promoted Major Hays to the rank of Colonel and you to Captain, Sir. Colonel Hays knew we were coming in your direction. I guess he selected me to deliver the message 'cause my older brother was a ranger with him in his first unit."

Bud felt lightheaded. Did he say Captain? Jack a Colonel? This was startling information. He didn't know how to reply. Finally, he answered, "Thanks. I'll see Jack in a few days and congratulate him on his promotion."

Feeling uncomfortable with his celebrity, Bud mounted Lightning and left before A.D. exited the store. He assumed young Satterwhite was telling his companions a famous ranger was outside, and he was about to be swarmed by wide-eyed young men wanting to hear Indian war stories. Bud and Lightning headed down the dusty path to Dillard Cooper's place.

Chapter Thirty-Nine
Dillard

Time passed quickly as Captain Miller traveled through the thick timber and open prairies. It was not long before he saw a small two-room dog-run log house off in the distance. Smoke rising from the chimney and twisting upward into the cloudless sky gave the impression of a tranquil storybook home. As Bud dropped off the road, a pack of coon dogs poured off the porch and from under the house. He quickly counted sixteen. Bud's first thought was how does Dillard feed so many dogs? Then he remembered the lanky storeowner had told him Dillard hunted animals for their pelts. He assumed the dogs ate the carcasses after the animals were skinned. The barking alerted Dillard, who stepped out onto the porch with his long rifle ready. Bud continued toward the house with the dogs surrounding his horse. Dillard shouted out a command: "Silence!" All but one small pup stopped immediately. Then, as if on cue, an older dog walked over to the pup, bared her teeth, and the yelping stopped.

Bud hollered to Dillard, "Thanks, they are a loud bunch. I guess you are Mr. Cooper. I'm Bud Miller, a Texas Ranger. I think you knew my pa."

Dillard leaned his gun against the side of the house and came off the porch to greet his guest. "I see you already know who I am and you think I knew your pa. I served with three or four Millers. Which one was your father?"

Bud dismounted and tied Lightning to the hitching post. "My father was Joshua Miller, but folks called him Stump."

Dillard reached out his bony, callused hand to greet Bud. His grip was strong in spite of his skinny frame. He spit a wad of tobacco at one of the dogs trying to sniff his visitor. "So you are Stump Miller's boy? I can't believe a runt like Stump dropped a lump like you. I'd say you are six feet one or more."

Bud was not able to free his hand from Dillard's firm grip. He pushed his broad-brimmed hat back with his left hand and grinned as he replied, "'Bout six two. Everyone tells me my pa was not very tall, but I don't remember him much. He left for Texas when I was very young."

Dillard finally released Bud's hand, and looking his guest up and down, he said, "Stump Miller's boy. Son, come up on the porch. We don't have but two chairs. I'll bring 'em out and have the lady of the house make us some grape root tea. I knew your father well. He was a good friend of mine."

Dillard's willingness to talk about his father was not something Bud expected. Even more surprising was his speech. Considering the meager living conditions, Bud naturally thought Dillard would speak like an ignorant backwoodsman, but he was obviously well educated.

Dillard brought the chairs out onto the porch and they both sat down. Bud's chair was hand hewn with a deerskin back and seat, and Dillard's was sheepskin. Bud glanced into the room with the kitchen and noticed two beds. In the darkness, he also noticed a frail woman standing behind the door, four small children clinging to her apron. The size of her stomach told him she had to be at least six months pregnant. He excused himself and walked over to Lightning, removing the small brown bag. As he stepped back on the dog run, he handed the bag to Dillard. "Give this to your children. It's some rock candy."

Dillard didn't know how to respond. His children had never tasted candy. He handed the bag to Lucenda, saying, "Honey, this is from Stump Miller's boy. I told you about him. I suspect you will need to show the children how to eat their candy."

Water filled her eyes. Her voice quivered with excitement as she asked, "Dill, do we save the candy for Christmas so we will have something to put under the tree?"

Bud was not sure if he should interrupt; however, he leaned back in his chair and said, "Mrs. Cooper, don't worry about candy for Christmas. I'll buy another bag for you to put under the tree on my way out of town and Mr. Cooper can pick it up the next time he goes by the trading post."

Dillard brought out two tin cups of steaming root tea, handed one to Bud, and then retook his seat. He looked out on his field of corn and tobacco, remaining silent for quite a while. Time seemed to slow down in the silence. Finally, Dillard just started talking. "Stump was some kind of special man. He had a weakness for cards, but he was also one of the bravest men I've ever known. You should be proud of your father. I suspect you are here to get me to tell you what happened to us at Fort Defiance."

"Sir, I have to be honest. I have sought you out to see if you would be willing to tell me about the massacre. I know you don't talk about the murder of our Texans at Goliad, and I will not press. I understand the pain you must be suffering. I know from my limited battle experience what it is to see friends die."

Dillard sat straight up in his chair. His face grim, he looked straight into his guest's face and responded, "That's right. You did say you are a ranger."

"Yes Sir."

"Well, I'm glad to hear you say so. I admire you rangers. Nobody tougher. That little John Hays is a legend and so is Ben McCullough. I have an idea you know these men."

Bud was proud to answer, "Jack and Ben are friends of mine. I ride under Major Jack Hays. I guess I should have said Colonel. I understand President Jones just gave him a promotion. He is, without question, the most courageous man I've ever known. Not only is he brave, he is smarter than a pair of mockingbirds."

Dillard sipped the hot tea, causing his brow to furrow as he said, "It's sorta bitter till you get used to it."

Bud seized the moment to offer some of his coffee to Dillard. "Let me get some coffee beans from my bag. It's time you had a real cup of coffee. I also have some salt and sugar that I suspect you can use." Bud returned with the three items and handed them to Dillard so he could give them to his wife. While Lucenda ground the coffee and boiled a pot of water, the men made small talk. Dillard suddenly changed the conversation, saying, "That Stump was something else. Yep, he was a pistol. Your pa wanted to make a fight for the trees. We Red Rovers agreed with him and so did those brave New Orleans Grays. That night we were trapped on the open prairie, the Mexican cavalry rode around us playing *Sentinel Alerto*. They played that dang song all night. I remember your father picking up our bugle and playing the song right back at them. He climbed up on one of the wagons and blasted as loud as he could. He called them names in Spanish. I spoke enough Spanish to understand your pa was giving it to those fleas in the darkness. It was down right stupid for us to stay in that open field. The tree line was not very far. Sure, some would have died trying, but looking back, maybe we could have saved two hundred or more. As it turned out, only a few of us survived."

"Thank you Sir. Your words mean a lot to me."

Dillard abruptly switched the direction of the conversation again. "I have trouble sleeping. I jump at the slightest sound. If the dogs bark at night, I see Mexicans in the shadows when nothing is there. I just can't seem to shake the memory of the enemy chasing me. I know why you are here and why you have been so kind. It is obvious you gave us the salt, coffee, sugar and candy for the babies because you want me to tell you what I know about the death march."

Bud blushed. "Sir, I'd have given you the food without you saying a word. I'm not here to buy information. As a ranger, I understand what you are trying to block from your memory. I have memories I struggle to forget, yet I never experienced anything like the horror you endured. I came to Texas when I was sixteen and it has taken me nine years to get the courage to visit Goliad. I came to kill Mexicans and ended up spending most of my time fighting Comanche to protect Mexican families. I finally got the nerve to visit my father's grave and to go to San Patricio, where the O'Boyles were kind enough to tell me how Michael was spared. Just getting to meet you and hear the story of the bugle is a treasure I will never forget. You have been most kind to tell me that story. I'll finish my coffee and be on my way."

Lucenda brought the coffee pot out onto the porch, careful not to look at Bud as she motioned to Dillard. He quickly tossed his root tea onto the ground, offering his cup for fresh coffee. Bud did the same. "Mama, get you a cup and pour yourself a treat. Been a long time since we drank the real McCoy." Dillard's words were more of an order than a request; his frail wife obeyed.

Bud sat silently, watching three pups play in the dirt yard. The larger pup was being chased around and around by the two smaller ones. He knew not to press Dillard. The two sat drinking their hot coffee, trying to prevent the tin cups from blistering their lips. Dillard then turned and looked Bud directly in the eyes. "I don't want you to leave. You have the right to know the truth. I am confident no living man knows what happened to your father better than me, and I feel I have a duty to share with you what I remember. Perhaps one day you can write all of this down. I thought of doing it myself, but each time I take quill in hand, I cry for my dear friends who were not so fortunate. I have had some who escaped try to tell me that Jack White and Hank Rosenbury were cowards for hiding under blankets in the hospital. I thought they came up with a good plan, and I tip my hat to those two boys for being smart enough to see what was about to take place. The truth of the matter is most of us did not see it coming. We got so caught up in the belief we were going home, we didn't even notice they gave us no provisions for a long march. Funny how many little things we failed to notice. Had we been thinking clearly, we would have known what they were up to, like them dressing in their finest uniforms and assembling no supply wagons for our journey. Those signs were enough for any thinking man to smell a rat."

Dillard was rambling about names and events Bud was not aware of, so Bud requested, "Sir, if you plan to tell me the story, would you please start at the beginning? I promise to chronicle your account so all the world will know the brutality of Santa Anna and the bravery of the men who served in Goliad."

The tattered survivor took another sip of coffee, his eyes fixing on Bud's before continuing, "We had the most beautiful flag in the world. Johanna Troutman designed it. She has never been in Texas, but she knew our dream. When the Georgia Battalion of Volunteers under Captain William Ward marched from Macon on their way to Texas, Miss Troutman presented the troop with a flag to carry with them. The flag was white silk with an azure five-pointed star on both sides. Under the star, she wrote in Latin: *'Where Liberty Dwells, There is my Home.'* Fannin raised that flag over Fort Defiance."

Bud could visualize the flag with the lone star in brilliant blue fluttering in the wind over the citadel. Maybe his father had helped raise the flag. It was difficult waiting for Mr. Cooper to speak; yet, Bud understood he was asking Dillard to rip open old wounds. He waited patiently.

Finally, Dillard started to speak again. "The March of Death is a horror the world needs to hear about, but I can't go out and tell people what happened. It's not that I couldn't speak, it's just I would break down and never finish. You seem very articulate and well spoken and perhaps God has sent you to me so you can be the messenger of the truth. I have decided to break my silence. I will go back to the beginning so you will have the entire incident delineated in detail, allowing you to pass the story to future generations. What I'm getting ready to say is the Gospel truth, so help me God."

"Mr. Cooper, don't tell me if it's going to cause you to have bad dreams. You have shared more than I expected. I will always remember my father blowing the bugle in rebellion."

"Miller, you do need to hear the entire story," Dillard answered firmly. "I remember one lad, not more than fifteen, telling everyone to stand and look the Mexicans in the eyes and shout, 'Hurray, hurray for Texas. May she ever remain free!' He was a brave boy. I don't recall his name. Your father, standing between Robert Fenner and me tore open his shirt and told one of the soldiers in Spanish, 'Shoot here,' pointing to his heart." Dillard abruptly stopped and yelled into the kitchen. "Mama, get us some more coffee. We are going to be here a spell."

"Thank you, Sir. I am pleased to learn he was not a coward. You have done more than enough. Are you sure you want to further open the wounds?"

Dillard didn't hesitate. "It is time. I have tried to hide in this house in the woods long enough. I am pleased you found me. I need to tell the story."

Dillard started again, this time from the beginning. "I was with the Alabama Red Rovers who came to Texas on the steamboat *Yellow Stone* under the command of Dr. Jack S. Shackelford. That was my first, and last, ship ride. Can't say I want to go over the ocean again. God Bless Jack's soul, the good doctor lost a brother and young son in the massacre.

James Walker Fannin took command at Goliad in the latter part of January of '36. Houston had yet to get involved in the military; Sam was in east Texas engaged in treaty negotiations with the Indians until early in March. In January, we received information that Santa Anna was leading a large force into Texas. They were coming to subdue her and retaliate for the severe beating they sustained at the hands of our boys at San Antonio and Concepcion. Santa Anna was riled that the Texans sent his brother-in-law running home like a scared rabbit.

Houston was in favor of withdrawing to east Texas and consolidating the army into one unit. Fannin, Grant, and Johnson wanted to meet the Mexicans on the border and keep the war out of Texas. At first, I believed it would be a good idea to take the fight to them. Then, after General Houston assumed supreme command, he ordered Fannin to shut down Goliad and go help the men in the Alamo. Fannin disobeyed the order. On 23 February, Santa Anna appeared in San Antonio where only a feeble garrison under Travis was waiting for the depraved dictator. As you know, Travis withdrew into the Alamo, where Santa

Anna's superior force besieged them. Colonel Travis had less than two hundred men, but I am confident that with our four hundred fighters, we could have held them at bay until General Houston organized a larger force. I place blame for the deaths in both the Alamo and Fort Defiance squarely on the back of that pompous Fannin. He was a poor student in West Point, graduating near the bottom of his class, a major slave trader, and I hear tell, a swindler. Had he survived, he surely would have been court-martialed for his failure to obey a direct order. Guess you can tell what I think of him."

Bud finished his coffee, and as he placed the tin cup on the plank floor, he asked, "Sir, are you telling me General Houston gave Colonel Fannin a direct order to evacuate Fort Defiance?"

The seasoned veteran fixed his gaze on Bud. "As sure as God makes little green apples. Dr. Jack Shackelford was there and heard the messenger tell Fannin. In fact, Dr. Jack read Houston's order. I got to know Bonham, and I was there when he begged that ignorant Fannin to come help his fellow countrymen. Fannin was certainly not going to the Alamo and let a young whippersnapper like Travis or ruffian like Bowie serve as his commanding officers."

Bud never expected such an outpouring of information or the strong opinions he was getting from the frail, hollowed-eyed veteran of the Goliad massacre. Bud was honored to be speaking with a heroic survivor of the battle that took his father's life. "Mr. Cooper, Sir, I cannot begin to tell you how important your account is; not just to me, but to all Texans. Everyone knows the story of the Alamo, but so few lived to tell the truth about Goliad. It's time the truth was known and you are the man who can pull back the covers."

Dillard nodded his head to indicate he understood how important his information was. He removed a plug of homegrown tobacco from his pocket and offered Bud a chew. The new captain declined. With his wad of homegrown tobacco stuffed in his jaw, Dillard continued, "Like I was saying, that high-minded Fannin thought it ill-advised to aid Travis and Bowie and gave orders for us to strengthen Fort Defiance. We went to work. Under the direction of Chadwick and a few Polish engineers, we strengthened the walls and rebuilt the stronghold along the southern side. We built a covered way northwest of the fort down to the river to supply water. He was making ready to withstand a long siege. I didn't like the idea of remaining cooped up in the fort. I still felt we should get into the cover of the trees and let our sharpshooters shine, but I was not an officer and my thoughts couldn't buy a cup of coffee. It was not long before some of our men clashed with the local citizens of La Bahia. Some of Fannin's men got sloppy drunk and went on night prowls outside the fort, breaking into local homes, molesting the women, and robbing and plundering. I'm proud to say that not one single Alabama Red Rover participated in the crimes committed against the citizens of La Bahia, which, by the way, is what Fort Defiance was called before they changed the name to Goliad. Gets sorta confusing with so many names for one place." Dillard smiled for the first time. "After Fannin's men terrorized the locals, Father José Valdez and rancher Don Carlos de la Garza organized the citizens of La Bahia and some members of the Power-Hewetson Colony and moved them down to the Don Carlos Ranch, a thriving settlement, with a blacksmith shop, church, and general store ten miles south of the San Antonio River.

The morning of the death march, Don Carlos sent one of his men into our camp and told John and Nicolas Fagan to bring a side of beef down to the river. They didn't want to leave, so Don Carlos sent his men again. This time, the Fagans went to the river and waited. Not long afterward, they heard the slaughter taking place. Even though Don Carlos fought with the Mexicans and his men scouted for General Urrea, he was an honorable man and saved his Anglo neighbors.

By the end of February, we learned Urrea's Army was heading our way. Johnson and four or five others fleeing San Patricio barely escaped with their lives, and warned us that three thousand troops were only a day's ride away. Even after hearing that news, Fannin pussyfooted around. General Houston wanted us to retreat to Victoria and take up a position on the Guadalupe River more suitable to defend. In spite of the order from General Houston, now recognized by all, Fannin still refused to leave."

Dillard paused as if trying to piece together the suppressed details. "I believe it was on March 11th, David Kent alerted Ben Highsmith about the arrival of General Houston and his staff the previous evening in Gonzales. In the afternoon Highsmith delivered a letter from Fannin to General Houston stating he was not going to the Alamo. That same evening, Anselmo Borgara and Andres Barcena, who lived outside San Antonio, arrived in Gonzales and informed General Houston of the fall of the Alamo. General Houston implied the two Mexicans were spies and took them directly into custody in order to suppress the information. I don't fault the General for that. He had to keep the small force together if we were going to have a chance.

If my memory is correct, Houston's order to evacuate and blow up the fort came to Fannin on March 12th or maybe 13th. All of that gets a little fuzzy. I saw Ben Highsmith and David Boyd deliver the order in person and hand it to Fannin. I saw Fannin read the order. There is no doubt Fannin knew his orders were to destroy the fort and go help Houston. For five days, Fannin made no move. The evening of the 17th, one of our scouts, John White Bower, came into the fort telling us a large force of Mexicans was on the other side of the river. Only then did that dim-witted Fannin prepare to leave. I am still mystified as to why he disobeyed so many orders. Some claim it was because Lt. Governor Robinson told him not to retreat, but to wait for reinforcements. Others claim he was waiting for King to return from Refugio. I personally believe his bitter jealousy of Houston and not wanting to serve under the general was the more likely explanation. I know he did not go to the Alamo because Travis would have been his commander. I do want to inject this: Fannin was no coward. He was a brave man, even though his leadership qualities may be questionable. In my anger, I might have implied differently. Not so. He would stand toe-to-toe with anyone. There was not a smidgen of yellow in his blood." Dillard grinned and added, "No room 'cause his ego crowded it out."

"I know I asked you this question before, but let me get this clear. You are saying he disobeyed direct orders because he didn't want to give up his position and serve under another's command?"

Dillard didn't hesitate. "Sure am. That is the Gospel truth. He fell into the devil's snare and succumbed to the green-eyed monster as sure as my hounds bark. Now where was I?"

"You were telling me about Fannin's inability to make a decision."

"That's right. Well, Urrea's dragoons found Johnson, Grant, and Morris with about ninety-seven men in and around San Patricio. The Texans, for some reason, naively split up their forces. General Urrea overtook them, and following the Mexican protocol, butchered all but five or six. Johnson escaped along with Captain Placido Benavides, a wealthy Mexican from Victoria, who later fought bravely at San Jacinto. One man wounded and captured, but spared execution was Reuben Brown of The Georgia Volunteers. Brown later credited his escape from death to the intercession of Señora Alavéz, 'The Angel of Goliad'. She saved several young men from the Miller unit, another Miller, unfortunately. Not your brave father."

Afraid to interrupt Dillard's train of thought, Bud reluctantly asked, "Would you please tell me a little more about the Angel of Goliad? I have heard of her, but no one seems to know the details of her story."

Dillard spit a slug of tobacco at one of the dogs that was venturing too close and the wad hit the canine square between the eyes. He yelped and scurried out of sight. In a melancholy tone, he answered, "Ah, the Angel of Goliad. She was a quite a lady. History tells no finer story than that of the Angel. Her merciful heart, unyielding courage, and fearless exertions saved so many of our young boys. She persuaded General Urrea's officers to help her, and in so doing, disobey Santa Anna's strict orders to shoot all prisoners. That included the sick and young. She single-handedly saved twenty-seven lives, mostly young boys. She was the beautiful young wife of Captain Telesforo Alavéz, commander of the Mexican Central forces under General Urrea. I understand Captain Alavéz later took her to Mexico City, where he dumped her; I suspect because of pressure from the Mexican Government. No doubt, they knew she had helped a number of young boys escape the slaughter. Santa Anna didn't like disobedience. I have been told she now lives in Matamoros, broke, and on her own. Someone told me she was going to move to south Texas."

Dillard raised his hand up to his floppy hat as if giving her a salute. "To Señora Alvaréz: May the gates of heaven be open when you arrive."

"I never knew the "Angel" was the wife of a Mexican officer. I am impressed with her daring and defiance, and her courage to do the right thing. I wonder how many Texas women would have done the same if the circumstance was reversed."

Bud could see the struggle as Dillard tossed his head back, challenging his mind to focus. By sheer force of will, he began again, "It must be remembered that when Señora Alvaréz came to Texas, she could have considered us as rebels and heretics. Yet, after everything that occurred to represent the worst of Texas men, she became engaged in saving our boys' lives. Her name deserves to be recorded in letters of gold among the angels, a woman whose memory should be sacred in every Texan's heart. I am glad you made me reflect on this brave soul. Someone needs to go to Mexico and find her. All Texans need to know her name and honor her while she is alive. I wish I was stronger, I'd go and bring her here myself."

Bud reached his hand over, touching Dillard on the leg. "I need to excuse myself, Mr. Cooper. The coffee is getting to me."

"There is a two-hole shed out back on the other side of the big magnolia tree. I'll show you the way." Dillard was feeling comfortable with Bud. He liked the young ranger.

As the two returned from the privy, Dillard continued his story, "As you already know, Fannin wasn't inclined to follow orders; on the contrary, he was determined to face the enemy in the fort. I recall him giving us orders to march to the Alamo earlier. We camped on the other side of the river and expected to break camp for San Antonio the next morning when he ordered, 'Go back to the fort.' Fannin changed his mind during the night. Simple as that. We Red Rovers and the New Orleans Grays raised a stink. Trust me. We all tried to persuade the pompous colonel to march to San Antonio, but our efforts were in vain. While we tarried, Santa Anna closed the noose around the Alamo. Fannin could not be moved to evacuate our fort because he still believed that the men at the Alamo, if they so desired, could pull out. This is the only reason I can think of to justify his action, or should I say, his inaction.

We got a large consignment from Lavaca Bay and slaughtered eight hundred head of cattle, which we cut into jerky strips. The blood from the cattle ran down a ditch, making the river run red. Darndest sight you have ever seen. Little did we know that in a few days, that ditch would flow red again with our blood. We continued to stock up on supplies in preparation for a long siege. Then, unexpectedly, on March 19th, Fannin ordered our retreat, and instructed some of the men to burn the town of La Bahia. The Colonel burned our food as well, several months worth of food. With no supplies, we could not stand and fight. All the cannons, with the exception of two four-pounders, were spiked and left behind. Discarded objects trailed behind us as we dropped our baggage and excess items along the way. Chests filled with musket provisions and other belongings disappeared into the waves of the San Antonio River. What horses and oxen we had left, we used to pull the remaining supplies.

Our route led us through little prairies, alternating with thin forests of oak without any undergrowth. Frequently we saw herds of black Mexican cattle grazing on the viridian grasses beside immense herds of deer that watched with amazement as our little army wound its way through the tall grass. I will never forget the noble Andalusian horses and the sight of those magnificent animals' proudly arched necks, tails dragging the ground as they pranced in close formation across the undulating prairies.

Eight miles from Goliad, there is a treeless strip of land known as the nine-mile prairie. It was over this prairie that our army slowly advanced five of the nine miles by three o'clock that afternoon. We Red Rovers were bringing up the rear guard about two miles behind the main group. We were under the directive to keep a watchful eye on the thick grove of trees several miles away to the left of us. There was no evidence of any Mexican presence as we moved cautiously forward. As if by providence, one of our Red Rovers turned around and spotted a figure in the trees about four miles back. It looked like a man on horseback. The figure did not move, so we concluded that it was only a tree. Without looking back again, we moved on.

We were gaining on the army, so we decided to slow our pace. Sid, I forget his last name, spotted a long, black streak in the distance. It was impossible for us to tell what it was. A few thought it was a massive herd of cattle. As the object neared us, we observed a moving and twisting in the dark mass that grew larger and larger as the form moved closer. It was an enormous number of Mexican cavalrymen approaching at a full gallop. We took off at full speed toward them. I can say with assurance the Grays, the Rovers, and the rest of the men welcomed the fight. Dr. Jack suggested we make a rush to the trees. Fannin exerted his authority and ordered us to form a square instead of pushing the short distance to the dense trees. He sealed our fate by attempting to stand and fight a much superior force on the unfavorable open terrain."

Bud moved to the edge of his chair; Dillard had his full attention. It was like reading James Fenimore Cooper's, *The Last of the Mohicans*. He didn't need to worry about Dillard getting off point. He had a story to tell and no one was going to stop the flood of words pouring from his lips. "We hunkered down in the field of Coleto or as the Mexicans say, *Encinal de Perdidos*. They came within about five hundred yards and fired off a round, which had no effect because their guns could not reach that distance. Standing next to me was a young lad named Thomas Camp. Thomas was our youngest soldier. I don't know why the Angel of Goliad didn't rescue young Camp. Perhaps she didn't know about him. We remained calm, letting the Mexicans move forward until they were in range of our cannons. Our men waited patiently for the opportune moment to reply to the Mexicans' unholy greeting. The moment arrived, our ranks opened and our artillery hurled death and bereavement upon the enemy. The Mexicans' horses became confused and reared up wildly, totally out of control. I saw riders tumbling to the ground. Horses were running without riders, while others were wallowing in blood and kicking furiously. Our cannons had stopped the Mexicans' advance. With the cavalry in a state of confusion, we began to move forward again. We were soon threatened with a new attack. Fannin ordered a halt in spite of the fact that their cavalry was pushing through the darkness of the trees to our left. There was no doubt their intention was to cut us off from the woods, allowing their other group to confine us from the rear. Either Fannin did not grasp the danger of the situation, or his ego held him back because someone else had figured out the Mexicans' maneuver before he did. Finally, after repeated protests, we felt obligated to tell Fannin we were going to march off alone, but by then, it was already too late. The Mexicans had moved to a small hill overlooking our position. We had two choices; we could fight our way through to the trees or make a stand from the unfavorable position Fannin had placed us in. The cavalry converged from all sides at lightning speed, yelling profanities and firing on us."

Dillard's face grew grim and determined. He froze his expression, allowing Bud to speak. "Mr. Cooper, I'm beginning to get a clear picture of why you got trapped. I could never understand why Fannin would select the open area to make his stand. I have been in enough scrapes to know the advantage in battle goes to those with the superior location. Jack and Matt Caldwell whipped General Woll because they were well protected."

Dillard shook his head as if to clear his trance. He didn't respond to Bud's statement, but went back into his story. "The Mexicans' screaming and shouting, which they thought would intimidate us, stood in clear contrast to our composure. We ignored their antics and waited for a good opportunity to shoot. Just like as hunting deer. You can't get 'buck fever' when a big one steps into the open. The thunder of our artillery soon rolled peal upon peal and the balls flew devastatingly into the Mexicans. So far, their cavalry attack had been ineffective. The Mexican infantry arrived and put all of their forces into motion, attacking us from all sides simultaneously. Besides the army, there were three hundred Indians lying in the tall grass on the left of us, toward the San Antonio River. We were not aware of them until their bullets brought down a number of our men. One clipped the tip of my cap, ripping a hole in the bill. When we discovered the savages' location, we sent a few loads of grape shot into the tall grass and they took off like scared jackrabbits. Meanwhile, the Mexican infantry merged with the cavalry and started closing in on our position." Dillard stopped.

"What's wrong?" Bud asked.

"Nothing, I was just caught up in reliving the battle. I had pushed most of this into the recesses of my mind. Sorry I got distracted. As I was saying, we were very careful to make every shot count. You know, you have fought the Indians and Mexicans. The difference between our fighters and theirs is we don't randomly fire; we choose our targets wisely and shoot to kill. The smoke got so thick, we couldn't see; the entire prairie became shrouded in black smoke. You could only see the flashes of artillery through the darkness, accompanied by the relentless thunder of our cannons and the crack of our rifles. The Mexicans were encouraging their men with bugle blasts. The clarion call of bugles and the roar of the cannons would inspire even a dead man to fight. I have to be honest. I loved being in battle. One never thinks of dying. There is too much excitement in the air. There was not a coward on either side of the battlefield that day. We advanced toward the enemy through the dense smoke. Foolhardily, I now freely admit."

When Dillard paused to take a sip of his cold coffee, Bud took the opportunity to interject, "I know what you mean. Even when it looked as if we had no hope against Chief Yellow Wolf, we focused on not missing our shot, not on the fear of death. I'm being honest when I tell you I didn't think about death until the next day. Then, in the stillness of the night, I felt the full gravity of the situation. When the guns are popping and the arrows flying, your mind is fixed on protecting your friends and killing the enemy."

"Precisely, you see my point," Dillard said, feeling a sense of relief that Bud understood. "I somehow got out in front of the other men and found myself standing in the middle of the Mexicans. In the confusion, I got lucky. They didn't realize I was the enemy and I made a mad dash back to the Rovers. On my way back, I saw scores of wounded or dead Mexicans. Our camp was in no better condition. I counted my blessings and thanked the Lord for delivering me unharmed from such a perilous place. All the Poles manning our cannons were dead, except one. Their bodies formed a wall around the cannons. Bud, it was an appalling sight. The entire battlefield was covered with death. I found Colonel Fannin in a pool of blood. He had three wounds. The third ball cut through his trousers and a pocket of his rubber overcoat, and then came to a rest in a silk handkerchief stuck into his flesh. It was the oddest thing; the ball didn't tear the silk handkerchief. When Dr. Jack pulled the handkerchief from his wound, the ball fell to the ground. The colonel let out a scream so shrill I can still hear it. Some of my worst dreams are the ones in which the colonel's screams tear through my head."

Bud raised his hand to gain Dillard's attention, softly asking, "Sir, what time of the day was this happening?"

Dillard pulled another plug of tobacco he answered, "It was getting late in the day, the sun was setting over the treetops. I'm guessing it was around six. The Mexican cavalry tried to penetrate our lines, but our boys' marksmanship repelled each attempt. Likewise, their infantry was forced to withdraw. It was difficult to count, but there had to be seven hundred dead or wounded Mexicans covering the battlefield like a crimson blanket. I know of no other battle where more men fell.

Darkness came and gave us time to tend to our wounded, and I'm sad to say, use our dead as a breastwork. That night, a fine mist began to fall and so did the temperature. Our guns became damp and useless. The moonless night made making a dash for the trees extremely perilous. We could have ended up traveling in circles. The bigger dilemma was that we would have been forced to abandon our wounded. Dr. Jack wouldn't hear of us leaving them to the brutality of the Mexicans. Since we couldn't transport our injured, we had no choice but to remain and fight.

We did have some hope. Captain Horton and his horsemen were still out in the woods and we hoped they would hear the cannons and go to Victoria and bring a large militia to assist us. Our battlefield was only ten to twelve miles from Victoria. Finally, about midnight, Dr. Jack and some of the other officers made an appeal to Colonel Fannin to use the pitch darkness as a shield and make an effort to reach the trees. They explained if we didn't, all of us would be killed. We did not have enough water or food for a long siege. Colonel Fannin had other plans. He decided we needed to dig trenches and strengthen our position during the night. I recall the drizzling rain beating on my body. The night air was filled with the sounds of dying men on both sides, the Mexicans less than 200 yards from our position. I felt helpless that night. I think I would have been willing to go to the aid of the dying Mexicans just to stop their screams."

"Sir, if I may," Bud interrupted, "I have heard the death moans of too many men; a sound that stays in your mind. Sometimes, when I close my eyes, I can hear the screams and see the dying writhing in pain."

Dillard nodded an affirmative. "That's why I'm telling you this story. I know you have walked in my shoes. One of the reasons I have remained silent is because not everyone understands the horror of war, the sights and sounds that never fade away…Colonel Fannin called the officers to him. I happened to have been standing nearby and I remember his words as if it were yesterday. He said, '*Comrades, grant my words of consideration. Listen to the cries of pain of our brothers whom the skilled hand of a surgeon can free from the grip of death. Are we willing, are the Red Rovers and Grays of New Orleans, willing to leave their wounded brothers to horrible death that the barbarous enemy has sworn to inflict upon them? Friends, again I beseech you by the patriotic and humanitarian feelings that live in our hearts, do not forsake the helpless ones here. At least offer them protection until daybreak. If no help arrives by that time, fellow citizens, do your duty; I will follow you!*'

As you can imagine, we felt the gravity of the moment and the extreme responsibility. During the night, the Mexican cavalry passed back and forth, sounding the death song. I wandered from camp and noticed dark figures moving in the shadows. The Indians were removing their dead so we would not be able to count their losses.

At daybreak, we lost all expectation of help arriving from Victoria. We had hoped all night in vain. There were no forces in the trees ready to break out and save us. I saw that the digging we had done during the night was useless. We could see the Mexicans positioning their cannons. They had a superior position, making our trenches open graves. I looked around and realized we were, as they say, up the creek without a paddle. Mind you, this was my first battle, but I was smart enough to surmise the most likely outcome. I remember being jarred out of my thoughts by the deafening silence that surrounded me; the cries from the wounded had ceased, and I am ashamed to say, I thought to myself, 'why didn't they die earlier so we could have escaped into the trees?' I admit this was a terribly selfish thought on my part."

"Dillard, don't be ashamed. I was thinking the same thing as you were telling me the story. That is nothing to lower your head about; you had a natural human reaction," consoled Bud.

"Thank you. I needed your words of support. Seems I can't get past the 'what ifs'. As I was saying, I glanced around and saw dead and dying Mexicans strewn across the pasture. I guess in the darkness, the enemy had not been able to locate them or perhaps thought it was not worth their effort to retrieve them. Some of the Grays went over to view the dead bodies. One of them found the banner of the Mexican army under a pile of dead riders and horses, and brought it into camp. No one rejoiced. We all knew the deciding moment of victory or defeat lay ahead.

By the time the sun was shining that morning, it was painfully clear we were not going to get help. We later found out that Horton and about forty of his men were in the trees, watching, but it would have been instant death for them to try to reach our position."

"But Sir, I was told some of Horton's men fell asleep and that is why you were surprised in the first place," Bud blurted out, without thinking.

Dillard looked over and realized the young ranger had some familiarity with what took place. His eyes caught Lucenda standing in the doorway. He spoke in a compassionate tone. "Honey, it's alright for you to come out here."

Lucenda shook her head 'no', holding up the coffee pot, offering the two men a refill. Bud handed his cup to Dillard who kept talking as she poured him another cup of coffee. "Four of Horton's men were left behind to keep an eye open for the Mexicans. They did fall asleep. Before you condemn them, I want you to know just how worn out we all were. I admit I was plenty riled when they rode full bore past us heading for the woods, but in reflection, I'm sure they felt they would fare better remaining outside the death trap. Fannin had selected the worst possible place to fight; we had no chance. I'm not saying Fannin was stupid. I just think the pressure of war was more than he could handle. General Houston is the exception, not the rule.

Our wake-up call came in the form of a wad of grapeshot from one of the Mexicans' cannons as it announced the beginning of a new day. The Grays and Rovers decided it was time to fight our way to the trees. We were getting ready to leave when we spotted three men on horseback holding a white flag. Two Mexicans and one German. The German was the architect who built the castle Mango de Clavo for Santa Anna. I think his name was Holzinger. He became a colonel in the army and served as an interpreter. We sent men out for the parley, and after a lengthy discussion, they came to an agreement of surrender. I want you to know the Alabama Red Rovers, and the New Orleans and Mobile Grays protested the signing of any agreement with General Urrea. Everyone knew about the capture and brutal murders of Captain King and Colonel Ward. By then, we also knew about the brutality of Santa Anna at the Alamo. Even though there was a written agreement stating we were to give up our arms until we were put on a ship in Copano or Matamoros for New Orleans, we didn't trust them. Perhaps Fannin was weak from the loss of blood, in pain, or just confused. He could not have been thinking clearly to trust the Mexicans."

"I know what you mean," Bud responded. "We have dealt with enough spies to shy away from trusting them. Of course, I suspect they don't trust us either, and for good reason." Bud didn't want to paint all

Mexicans with the Santa Anna brush. He knew General Urrea had made an effort to spare the Goliad prisoners.

Dillard was not as forgiving. His voice rose with a tinge of anger. "Dr. Jack told Fannin if we were going to die, then let us die fighting. He told the colonel 'we may not all make it the trees, but we could take a hundred Mexicans to meet their Maker with us. Bowie's two hundred defeated two thousand.' Fannin closed his eyes to Tampico, San Patricio, and the Alamo. He turned his back on our murdered brothers and placed his trust in the untrustworthy.

The Mexicans collected our guns and marched us back to Goliad. I was saddened to see our wounded left behind. Some remained in the field untreated with no food or water for two days. As we were being marched off, the Mexican cavalry discovered Horton and his small group. They gave chase, but Horton, knowing the area, escaped unscathed into the dense ten-foot canebrakes and over the Guadalupe River. I only got a glimpse of Horton, but it was a good feeling knowing they had returned, even if they couldn't help rescue us. We later learned they were prepared to cover our break; they would have engaged the Mexicans and given us a fighting chance. I am confident if we had fought for the trees, Horton and his men would have come to our aid.

We got back to Goliad just before dark, tired and hungry. Some were rejoicing while others, like our group and the Grays, did not feel very secure. Unlike our night in the field, there was not a cloud in the sky and the moon cast a blue glow as we crammed into the small church sanctuary. The cramped conditions in the chapel were deplorable. There was no room for all of us to sit down. Fortunately, the ceiling was thirty some feet high or we would have suffocated. Espiritu Santo Bay was thirty miles south, and the Gulf of Mexico about fifty. That's how close we were to freedom, but it may as well have been a thousand miles."

Bud interjected, "I have been in that chapel. I don't see how all of you could have fit into such a small space. I cannot imagine how horrible it was being jammed so tightly together, unable to find a place to sleep."

Dillard mused for a moment before replying. "We ended up sleeping standing up, like horses, leaning against each other. Our most pressing problem was the lack of water. When they finally brought some to us, it disappeared like a drop on a hot rock. We got no food the following day and, again, very little water."

Bud felt claustrophobic just listening to Dillard describe the conditions, and asked, "Mr. Cooper, what was their reason for starving you and keeping you in such cramped quarters when they had the open courtyard to house you?"

"Bud, I have thought about that question a lot. I do know they had the cannons pointed at the entrance of the church. I honestly think Santa Anna was trying to provoke us into charging out so he could shoot us down like dogs and finish us off. This way Santa Anna and his thugs could announce they were compelled to kill us to save their own lives. This is the only explanation I can think of. I will say this: The commander in charge of guarding the church was more compassionate than Santa Anna was, and finally gave us small chunks of raw meat. We scrounged up some planks and started a fire. Only a few at a time could gather around to cook their meat. It took all night for some of the men to get to the fire and even then, some didn't get to cook their meat. I ended up eating mine raw and was mighty thankful to have it.

The stench of human waste permeated the sanctuary. After three days of confinement, we were allowed go in to the courtyard. I think they realized we were not going to give them an excuse to kill us. There was a soft mist in the air as we left the church; I never smelled air so sweet. We should have suspected something, because of the heavy guard placed around us. The Mexicans didn't feed us, but allowed us to buy corn tortillas from the señoras who frequented the fort. We all shared freely with those without funds. To our delight, that afternoon we each received almost a pound of beef. This time, I roasted mine to perfection.

The Mexicans then ordered us to surrender all our possessions. I had to give up my waterproof blanket. I treasured that blanket and considered fighting to save it. They offered us no compensation for the things they took. We should have seen what was next. I do fault us for not spotting the trend and overpowering the guards. We could have captured the fort and their cannons. We were lulled into thinking that soon we would be on our way home. On the morning of the seventh day, the Mexicans brought an additional one hundred prisoners into the compound. They were volunteers from New York under Colonel Miller, captured immediately after landing at Copano Bay. When they were brought to the fort, Miller's men had freedom to move about, as did the doctors and their aides. I think they were originally to be killed along with us, but Urrea changed his mind, or perhaps it was Santa Anna's call all along.

We felt the time was near for us to depart for home. I recall your father joking and laughing with some of his men. He seemed to maintain hope no matter how bleak the situation. I guess the one thing I remember most about Stump was his positive attitude; he was never down or blue.

Unbeknownst to us, a courier arrived during the night with orders from Santa Anna. When we were escorted from the fort, we were divided into three groups. Soldiers in dress uniforms surrounded each group. All of us who could walk left the compound, with the exception of Captain Miller's group. I have not asked, was Captain Miller related to you?"

"No Sir, I believe Captain William Miller was from Tennessee. It's possible we are related, but I cannot claim a connection to that brave and honorable man."

Dillard's face grew tight as he continued his narrative. "That day was March 27th, Palm Sunday. We were ordered to line up quickly and prepare to march. We were just about to leave when I saw quite a number of ladies standing with Colonel Holsinger. Two ladies of distinction were in the crowd who I now know to be Lady Urrea, the General's wife, and Señora Alvaréz, the Angel of Goliad. Suddenly Señora Alvaréz grabbed a thirteen or fourteen-year-old boy and pulled him out of our line, saving him from certain death. Holsinger had us counted and divided into three separate detachments under the guise that we were going to Capono, and from there, on to New Orleans. Our group was marched out in double file. When we got about half a mile southwest of the fort, we came to a brush fence and lined up, single file, halfway between the guards and the fence. I'd say about eight feet apart. The commanding officer came up to the head of the line and asked if any of us could speak Spanish. Several of our men could, but no one acknowledged it. The officer ordered us to turn our backs to the guards. When the order was given, not one man moved an inch. A skinny, mean-eyed and extremely irritated officer stepped up to the man at the head of our column, took him by the shoulders and physically turned him around, demonstrating what they wanted us to do. By now, despair overcame us. I remember one young man who had been a strong Christian, but had backslid somewhat because of bad company, falling to his knees, crying aloud for God's mercy and forgiveness. Other men attempted to plead for mercy from the merciless Mexicans.

Wilson Simpson stood on my right and Robert Fenner on my left, your father next to him. In the midst of the horror that now engulfed most of the men, I heard your father calling out to us, 'don't take on so, boys. If we have to die, let's do it like men.' He stood like a stone sculpture, looking the Mexicans in the eyes and baring his chest. At that moment, I saw the flash of a musket. I instantly threw myself forward onto the ground. Robert Fenner's limp body fell on me with such force, he almost knocked me out."

Dillard stopped for a moment. He saw Bud's eyes water over. Bud was trying to choke it back, but the tears gushed forth. He was ashamed to be crying in front of Dillard, but facing his father's death was more painful than he ever imagined. When he regained his composure, Bud implored, "Please excuse my outburst of emotion. For a moment, I could envision my father being shot. The pain was excruciating. Please, continue."

"Are you sure you want to hear more?"

Bud wiped his eyes on his sleeve. "Yes, please."

"Well, I attempted to get up, but Robert's body had me pinned to the ground. I saw my friend Simpson leap to his feet and run toward an opening in the brush fence. I managed to push up and dislodge Robert, following Simpson through the opening. There was a two-mile-wide open prairie between Simpson and I and the nearest trees. When we first escaped, Simpson and I were together, but then he took a direct course across the prairie. I was putting distance between those pursuing me when I saw three Mexicans after Simpson. In order to avoid his pursuers, he took a circuitous route, causing them to go around in circles. There were two points of timber projecting into the prairie, one of which was closer to me. I was making for the furthest point, but as Simpson entered the trees, the Mexicans turned toward me and cut me off. Our Rover uniforms were red, round cloaks fastened with a clasp at the throat. As I ran, a Mexican cavalryman charged upon me, jabbing his sword through my cloak. I grabbed the clasp with both hands, managing to tear it off and escape the Mexican's lance. I then started for the point where Simpson had entered the trees, but they turned and cut me off from that. I stopped running and began walking slowly toward them. No doubt, thinking I was about to surrender, they stopped and waited. When I was within sixty yards of them, I wheeled and ran into the timber. Just as I was about to enter the trees, they fired, but did not follow me. As soon as I entered the timber, I saw Simpson. He and I ran together for about two miles in the underbrush. We stopped when we reached the river, getting our heads together on the best way to conceal ourselves. I proposed climbing a tree, but Simpson objected, saying that if the Mexicans discovered us, we would have no way to escape. I accepted his argument. Before we could take action, we heard someone coming. This really frightened us. I jumped into the river, while Simpson ran a short distance up the bank, but then seeing me, he also jumped into the water. The noise continued from the bank immediately above the spot where Simpson had been hiding. I could see the place very plainly and soon realized it was two of our comrades, Zechariah Brooks and Isaac Hamilton. Both of Hamilton's thighs had wounds; one a gunshot wound and the other from a bayonet. In spite of his wounds, he managed to run to safety.

We all four swam the river and traveled a short distance upstream until we got to a bluff near a thick screen of brush. This is where we first selected to hide ourselves. We did not dare proceed any further that day because the Mexicans were swarming the woods and Hamilton's wounds had become so painful, it was impossible for him to walk. We remained there until about 10 o'clock that night. We then started moving again under the cover of darkness. Simpson and I carried Hamilton. Brooks, though severely wounded, was able to walk. We had to proceed very cautiously and of course, extremely slowly. We kept proceeding in a circle, in a northeasterly direction. We found ourselves back pretty close to the fort and we couldn't understand why there so many fires burning. Our question was answered when we smelled the sickening stench of burning flesh. We later learned some of our boys were still alive when they were thrown into the flames. We passed the fort and stopped when we reached a fresh water spring. This is where we stopped for the rest of the day and planned how we would reach freedom.

We agreed we would resume walking when it was dark, but the night turned foggy and we became disoriented. It was not long before we found ourselves back at the same spring where we had spent the day hiding. This was very frustrating and frightening. We realized we had too much at stake to sink into despondency. Once more, we carried our wounded companion, thinking we could not miss going in the right direction this time. Wrong. When daybreak came, we discovered we had been going in circles, and for the third time, arrived back to that same spring. It was too late to try again because we dared not travel during the day, so we concealed ourselves by crawling into the thick undergrowth once again. We managed to sleep, even under such dire conditions. When we awoke, we were starved. I discovered an elm bush nearby. We broke off the branches and ate them as if they were beefsteaks. Then, about mid-morning, we heard heavy marching. The Mexicans passed within a few yards of our hiding place. We remained safely concealed the rest of that day and resumed our escape after dark.

When we reached the vicinity of Lavaca, we were finally ahead of the Mexicans. We traveled all night and on the ninth morning discovered an abandoned house within a few hundred yards of the river. We approached with caution and when we reached the house, we were relieved to find that the owner had fled. Once inside, we discovered a quantity of corn, some chickens, and a nest full of fresh eggs. Our stomachs were weak and revolted at the idea of eating raw eggs. We looked in vain for something to light a fire. As a last resort, we tried starting a cooking fire with a grindstone and an old chisel. We were finally so desperate, we cracked open the eggs and ate raw eggs and corn until we were full."

Bud glanced over his shoulder and saw a small cotton-headed boy with freckles sprinkled across his nose and cheeks standing behind him. "This your oldest?" Bud inquired.

"That boy is William. We call him Will. Yes, he is my first-born. I named him after an ancestor in England, William Cooper from Warwickshire. I understand he was a nobleman who lived in a massive stone castle. Quite a contrast to our meager surroundings. There are three more youngens hiding in the house: Albert, Melissa and Elizabeth. Good kids, just a little shy. They don't see many strangers."

"Mr. Cooper, you have a fine place and a fine family. With Texas coming into the Union, you will see an improvement in your ability to earn money. As young as you are, there is a promising future just waiting for you to grab it by the horns."

Bud got a response he had not expected. "With annexation will come war. I understand Santa Anna is out, but the new ruler will go to war to keep Texas, rather than let her be gobbled up by the United States. I know I'm in the minority, but I'd like to see us remain an independent nation. Too many will be killed if the United States goes to war with Mexico."

Bud didn't argue, even though his "Houstonian" viewpoint favored annexation. His voice was apologetic as he said, "I interrupted your story. Please continue."

Dillard had lost his train of thought and asked, "Where was I?"

"You were in a small abandoned cabin eating raw eggs and corn."

"That's right. Thank you, my mind seems to slip from time to time. I guess it's old age."

"Old age!" You are not much older than I am. When were you born?"

"September 10, 1814," Dillard answered. "I'm thirty, but I just don't seem to have the gumption I once did. I guess Goliad has taken its toll on me. I should not complain; I did get this land. Anyway, as I was saying, we rested in the abandoned cabin. As Simpson was putting on his shoes that morning, his feet were raw and bleeding from the rocks and rough terrain, as were mine. He got one shoe on when he remarked, 'Boys, we would be in a tight place if the Mexicans were to come upon us now.' For some reason, perhaps our 'Angel's' intervention, he walked to the window and to his horror, saw the Mexican army was not more than a mile and a half off, and fifteen to twenty horsemen approaching at full speed within two hundred yards of the cabin. We grabbed our wounded friend and dashed outside into the undergrowth. We got into the timber and concealed ourselves between two fallen trees. The tops fell together, forming an almost impenetrable screen above and around us. Again, our Angel had a hiding place ready for us. We had scarcely hidden from view when the Mexicans were all around us. We heard them from time to time all throughout that day and night. Early the next morning, just before daybreak, the noise ceased. Simpson asked me to go with him to get his shoe from the cabin. It would have been almost impossible for him to travel without it, so I consented to go and get it for him. I got to the edge of the timber, and seeing no Mexicans, I proceeded to the little cabin. Once inside, I found his shoe, grabbed some corn and a jug of water and returned to the other men. We were confident the Mexicans were gone, so we sat down, drank the water and ate an ear of corn. Brooks then asked Simpson to go with him back into the house, saying they could get a couple of chickens we could eat raw. They hardly got to the edge of the timber when we heard the sound of hooves pounding at blazing speed. A short distance away, the Mexicans appeared from every direction. Soon I heard something in the brush near us. I didn't know if it was my friends or the Mexicans. It turned out to be our boys, who had crept safely back into our hiding place. Within a few minutes, four Mexicans rode by, within a few feet of us. They were so close we could hear their horses breathing. It seemed to me they could have heard my heart pounding. I felt more frightened than I ever had in my life and feared that at any moment I would feel a lance between my shoulder blades. The Mexicans passed and re-passed our hiding place throughout that entire day. We dared not move. Finally, the majority of the cavalry moved on, leaving a small detachment to search for us.

About 10 o'clock the second night, we held a consultation. We felt it was not wise to remain in our hiding place any longer. I felt the Mexicans were aware we were still hiding in the area and would discover us the next day. We all agreed to leave. I was somewhat familiar with the local area, having hunted in the nearby woods while stationed at the fort, so they asked me to lead the way. I told them we would have to crawl through the underbrush until we crossed the road near the Mexican pickets. Hamilton's wounds were so painful, we could only move at a snail's pace. It must have taken us two hours of crawling to move two hundred yards. When we passed the edge of the timber and reached the road, we stopped to make a careful survey of the situation. I could see the Mexicans placed along the road about a hundred yards on each side of us. The full moon was shining, but once more, our Angel was looking out for us. A cloud drifted over the moon, casting a shadow across the road. We continued to crawl until we had traveled far enough away from the guards, and then stood up and walked. Although Hamilton was in a great deal of pain, he had managed to crawl, but it was impossible for him to walk. His wounds, by then, were so inflamed he could barely stand to be carried. We traveled a few miles that night, and then hid ourselves in a thicket near a pond. Brooks had been trying to persuade us to leave Hamilton. Although our progress was impeded by having to carry him, I would not consider the idea for one moment. I indignantly refused. That didn't stop Brooks; he seized every opportunity to persuade us to abandon our wounded companion. He said our escape was in jeopardy, burdened as we were with Hamilton. I could only acknowledge he was telling the truth. It was desperate times for us.

The next morning, Brooks and Simpson took a bottle we picked up at the cabin and went to fetch some water. As they were returning, Hamilton and I overheard Brooks urging Simpson to leave our wounded friend. Brooks was saying that if we remained with Hamilton, we would certainly lose our lives. Hamilton's wounds were very grave, and I honestly felt he was dying. I realized we were doing him no good and placing ourselves in peril by carrying him. But mind you, Brooks had never carried him a step; yet he was the first to propose abandoning him. Although there was a great deal of truth in what Brooks was saying, I got angry listening to him. Hamilton did not say a word. He just buried his face in his hands for quite awhile, then finally looked up and said, 'Boys, Brooks has told you the truth. I cannot travel any further and if you stay with me, all of us will die. Go and leave me. If I rest, I may recover.' Having known Brooks back in Alabama, Hamilton handed him his gold watch and $40, telling him to give them to his mother. He spoke so reasonably, we were convinced he was being sincere. Maybe he was just saying what we wanted to hear. After a brief discussion, we decided to go on without him. All three of us shed tears as we turned to leave. I couldn't find it in my heart to walk away and said, 'Boys, let's not leave him.' No matter what I said, Simpson and Brooks were determined to move on. That was when I told them I would stay with Hamilton and do my best to save him. They walked off without me. However, Hamilton pleaded so strongly for me to leave, I finally gave in and soon caught up with the other two.

We thought we were safe traveling during the day because of the torrential rain. The Mexicans would be hunkered down, trying to avoid drowning. You know Texas weather. We had not gone more than half way through the next prairie when the rain abruptly stopped. That's when we saw the entire Mexican army camped at Texana, no more than two miles away. Thank God, we saw them before they saw us. Brooks broke and ran for the timber along the bank of the Navidad River, with Simpson and I hot on his heels.

About eight o'clock that night, we started out once again to seek our freedom. We followed the road forged by the thousands of Runaway Scrape refugees. On the twelfth day, we reached the Colorado at Mercer's Crossing. The river current was exceptionally swift due to the recent rains. We were exhausted, and I suggested we rest on the riverbank before attempting to cross. While we rested, a dog on the opposite side of the river began to bark. I cannot express what exhilaration we felt when we heard that mangy dog barking. That was the first time since the day of death that any of us smiled. In fact, we looked at each other and burst into laugher. We found a dead log to use to ferry us across. I was at the back, Simpson in the middle, and Brooks the front. We clung to that big hollow log and dog paddled our way to the other side. We climbed the bank to freedom and ran to the little log house. I don't know where we got the energy to run, but we sure did. The Texans welcomed us warmly; we couldn't eat all the food they placed before us. The ladies sewed us some new buckskin breeches and shirts and we used some of their tanned hides to make some new shoes. We must have slept twelve hours straight through and the following morning, we ate till our stomachs hurt. We borrowed some horses and headed off to join up with General Houston's forces, but before the three of us could reach San Jacinto, our boys had already defeated Santa Anna."

Bud sat spellbound. He finally asked, "What ever happened to Mr. Hamilton? I assume he died."

"I admit I thought the same thing. In fact, I was angry with myself for leaving him. A year or more passed before I heard anything about Hamilton. He remained nine more days at the pond, soaking his body in the spring water, easing the pain and healing his wounds. We had left him a dozen ears of corn and that and leaves sustained him. At the end of nine days, he improved enough to walk toward freedom. Hamilton later said the best food he ever had in his life was when he reached an abandoned campsite and ate the meat off the rawhides left behind by the Mexicans. He almost made it to Dimmitt's Landing when he was recaptured. Not long after, other soldiers came and tied him onto a mule; he was so weak that he kept fainting along the way. When he fainted, the Mexicans would untie him, lay him on the ground and throw water in his face until he revived. Then they would plop him back on the mule and be on their way. He remained in the Mexican's hands for some time. The guard assigned to care for him became quite fond of him. One morning, he woke Hamilton and told him if he wanted to live another day, he must make his escape that night. The guard had learned that Hamilton and two other prisoners were to be shot the next morning. Hamilton quickly arranged a plan of escape for him and his two cellmates. The three escaped, and after almost starving to death, the tattered trio reached Texas soil."

Dillard leaned back in his chair and looked over at Bud, checking his facial reaction. Bud stood and stepped over to Dillard. The Goliad survivor responded by standing as well. The two men stood face to face. Dillard started to reach out his hand when Bud gave him a strong bear hug and said, "Words fail to express how much your stories mean to me. You did have a Guardian Angel watching over you. It was very important for me to learn about the way my father died. Dillard Cooper, you are a special man. If I were a writer, I'd pen a book about your exploits."

Dillard hugged Bud back, and amid the overwhelming emotional release of sharing his story, managed to say, "Bud, your coming here is what I needed to get out of my malaise. I was sitting here feeling sorry for myself. Seeing you has made me want to fight for Texas again. When Texas joins the Union and we go to war with Mexico, as I am certain we will, I plan to join the army and extract my revenge on those murdering barbarians."

Bud had heard the talk of war with Mexico and the United States from several sources. Even Jack Hays suggested war would follow annexation. He knew Dillard was speaking the truth. Mexico was a proud nation and would not allow the Union to take what they felt was theirs without a fight. Bud also knew Dillard would be one of the first to sign up and the rangers would be at the front of the line.

Bud stayed for a supper, which consisted of hot cornbread, cabbage, fried venison, and corn on the cob. Before he left the table, he slipped a twenty-dollar gold piece under his tin plate. He thanked Lucenda, rubbed little Will on the top of his head, and walked out and mounted Lightning. He couldn't stay any longer or he would break down. Dillard had touched him deep inside and had made him proud to be a Miller. Dillard, surprised by Bud's abrupt departure, reached up his bony hand and offered Bud a handshake. The two held their firm grip for quite a while before Dillard said, "May God grant you safe passage and a promising future." With those parting words, the new ranger captain galloped away, never looking back.

Lightning drank from the cool stream while Bud washed his face and then cupping his hands, joined his sorrel stallion and quenched his thirst. There was one thing he had to take care of as soon as possible for his life to be complete, but first, he would need to return to San Antonio and locate Colonel Hays. That night, the moon shadows danced in and out as the southern breeze gently pushed the clouds across the Texas sky. Bud rolled up in his blanket with his head on his saddle and didn't awake until an angry crow raised a ruckus after discovering him to be too near her little ones.

When he arrived at the Smiley trading post, he refilled his saddlebags with supplies, purchasing shelled corn for Lightning and candy for Dillard's children as he had promised. He then followed the narrow path west by northwest toward San Antonio. As the sun set, he decided it was safer to get a few hundred yards off the trail and move into the woods to camp for the night. After unsaddling and staking Lightning, he ate without making a fire. He then made his bed by cutting several small branches and covering them with his saddle blanket, using his saddle as a pillow. Sleep didn't come easy. He tossed and turned, trying to clear his mind. He kept seeing visions of his father standing in defiance. Just as he was dozing off, he heard an owl to the south. Then one from the north answered, followed by hoots on the west and east of him. Bud had heard those kinds of owl calls before; Comanche used birdcalls to signal each other. The voices from the dark surrounded his position. The owls from the four winds spoke again and unless his imagination was playing tricks on him, they were getting closer. Why would a dozen hooting owls encircle him? He knew the answer. The signals had to be man made. His mind raced. Could he saddle and flee in time or would he be forced to make a midnight stand?

Chapter Forty
Statehood

Once the prospect of statehood became a reality, the floodgates opened. Lured by the promise of unbridled opportunity and inexpensive land, people flooded across the border into Texas in rickety wagons, fine carriages, on horseback, on foot, and by boat. They came from every state in the Union and Europe. In their motley ranks were land speculators with over-the-top ambition, and slave owners seeking cheap land on which to expand their empires. Blacksmiths, gunsmiths, lawyers, doctors, ministers, teachers, carpenters, and merchants joined the entrepreneurs. Along with the good, came the bad and the ugly. Murderers, swindlers, gamblers, and women of ill repute also flooded into Texas seeking their piece of the dream. Some were running from their sordid pasts, hoping to start over, while others came hoping to continue in their evil ways. The enemy would not be as easy to find; no war paint, no Mexican sombrero to sort the bad people from the solid citizens. The bad would have to be ferreted out one by one. There was a certainty awaiting those who sought to inflict their evil intent on Texas: a thirteen-loop hangman's knot and plenty of strong oaks. Along with the riff-raff and undesirables, the rich and pompous, the majority of citizens coming into Texas were poor, hardworking people armed only with their hope for a better life.

The roads were little more than dirt paths cutting through the landscape, either choking with dust or bogged down with mud from torrential rains. A few turned back, which was the right thing for them; the rugged frontier of Texas was no place for the weak, cowardly, or undecided.

Galveston Island was the arrival point for a select group of wealthy Americans and Europeans. The largest number of wealthy immigrants, other than Americans, came from Germany, followed by the French, Belgians, Irish, and Swedes. The majority of foreign immigrants clustered together: New Braunfels was set aside for the Germans. The Irish went south to San Patricio. Mexicans sought out San Antonio.

The birth of Texas statehood would prove to be just as complicated as the formation of the Republic. England and France offered support if Texas would remain free of the stars and stripes. The new ruler in Mexico gave hope of finally recognizing Texas as an independent Republic. Both Mexico and the United States were unrealistic. The United States was foolish in expecting Mexico to part willingly with nearly half of its territory. Mexico was not seeing the larger picture clearly in expecting to hold back the inevitable march southward. Anyone with logic realized Mexico could not repel the more powerful

United States military. Both sides remained obstinate and resolved to win the tug-of-war, which would only lead to cutting an erratic and bloody path through the territory.

President Anson Jones, sworn in December 9, 1844, said it would be over his dead body that Texas would annex into the Union. Jones felt he had been born to be the President of Texas and to fulfill the destiny of westward expansion, an independent Republic encompassing the lands between Louisiana and the Pacific Ocean. Nothing else would be acceptable.

General Houston had worked for sixteen years for Texas to become part of the United States. Back as far as the early 1830s and his first exploratory trips, he wanted to be the man who brought the prize to the United States. Houston focused all of his energy to make statehood a reality, and now Jones was trying to undo what he put in motion. The two-term President had worked tirelessly to ensure Jones' victory and Sam was deeply hurt by his friend's betrayal.

He turned to his old roommate, Dr. Ashbel Smith for help. When Smith arrived in the newly formed Republic in the spring of 1837, he became Houston's roommate and close friend. Houston later appointed Smith as Surgeon General of the Army where he created an efficient medical system and established the first hospital in Houston. Smith would earn the titles of *The Father of Texas Medicine* and later, the *Father of the University of Texas*. Houston recognized Smith's diplomatic ability and sent him to negotiate a treaty with the Comanche. In 1842, he traveled to Europe as the *chargé d'affaires* and secured ratification of an amity and commerce treaty with England, and improved relations with France.

Then, in 1845, as Secretary of State under President Anson Jones, he worked to give the people of Texas a choice between remaining independent or becoming the twenty-eighth state. At this time, he also negotiated a treaty with Mexico and received their acknowledgment of the independence of Texas. This treaty, known as the Smith-Cuevas Treaty, angered many Texans who strongly favored annexation. The citizens of Galveston and San Felipe burned Smith in effigy. He could not walk the streets of these towns in safety. But, if push came to shove, Sam believed he could count on Ashbel Smith to help him tip the scales in favor of annexation.

Smith had recently returned from Europe and was home resting when he heard the clomping of boots and the jangling of spurs on his front porch. The door flung open and a tall figure filled the doorway. The blazing sun at his back, his cape blowing ominously in the breeze, the figure blocked out most of the sunlight as he stood squarely between the door jams, quirt in hand, like a bronze statue. Smith knew only one man would enter his home is such a dramatic fashion. It had to be General Houston. Before he could ask Sam to come in and have a seat, the General gruffly said, "I have come to leave Houston's last words with you. If the Congress of the United States shall not, by the fourth of March, pass some measure of annexation which Texas can accede to, Houston will take the stump against statehood." Sam gave the startled Smith a bear hug, as was his custom, and then clicked his heels and exited the doorway. Smith knew he would need to act with alacrity for his dear friend. Houston had no bigger admirer in the Republic than Ashbel Smith.

President Polk promised Anson Jones and Houston protection from the Mexicans while the issue of annexation was under consideration, and sent General Zachary Taylor and a group of skilled soldiers to Corpus Christi. President Polk then sent a message to the Congress on December 2, 1844, recommending annexation by a joint resolution requiring only a simple majority in both houses. In late January 1845, the U.S. House of Representative responded, passing an annexation resolution by a vote of 120 to 98. The Senate modified the amendment the night of February 27, 1845, the bill passed with a vote of 27 to 25. The Senate version called for Texas to be a state, and not a territory and the adjusted amendment also included a provision for Texas to divide into four states, should the need or desire to do so arise. In addition, they allowed Texas to fly her Lone Star at the same height as the United States' Stars and Stripes. Texas would be the only state allowed to do so. The resolution went to Texas on March 3, 1845, nine years and one day after the brave men met in Washington-on-the-Brazos to hammer out a constitution for the new Republic. President Polk came through for Texas and his old friend Sam Houston.

In May, the Houstons took their two-year-old son to New Orleans for a shopping trip with intentions of also visiting Tennessee to show off the baby to Sam's relatives and of course, his mentor, Old Hickory. When they arrived at the dock, an open carriage was waiting to escort the trio to the home of a friend. The streets were lined with people trying to catch a glimpse of the hero of Texas. Sam stood up in the open carriage waving at the throngs of admirers. As they turned in to the French Quarter, they heard chanting on both sides of the street: "*Lone Star State. Lone Star State. Lone Star State.*" A team of wild horses could not have pulled the smile from Sam Houston's face. He was in his glory. That evening, he spoke to a standing room only crowd at the Arcade. People began applauding when he stepped to the podium and kept on clapping, preventing the moderator from making his introduction. When he was finally able to speak, he simply said, "I give you General Samuel Houston, who, it is obvious, needs no introduction."

The audience began once more to applaud for several minutes. Sam raised his right arm, motioning for them to be seated. Slowly, they obeyed. "My friends," he began, in a boisterous voice. "I have been accused of leading myself to England and France, but I assure you I have only been coquetting with them." Once more, the crowd applauded enthusiastically. "I hope not to weary your patience in listening to matters personal to myself, but I feel compelled to answer back to some of the worst of the newspaper editors who have been abusing me for their own amusement. They are alleging a sale of Texas to interests in Europe, which would leave me a wealthy man. Will my fellow citizens forgive me for lowering myself sufficiently to even acknowledge these menacing creatures?"

A shout came from the front row. "Amen brother Houston."

Sam looked down and replied, "Bless you brother. I give an Amen to your Amen."

Sam then pounded the lectern with his massive fist, almost splitting the pine board top. His face turned red and anger resonated in his voice. "That Willard Richardson of *The Galveston News* is too mean to steal. That is fortunate for the inmates of the penitentiary, because they are not likely to be disgraced by his being their associate." Sam knew he made a strong point, so he paused to let the crowd respond. They did. His statement prompted roaring laughter. He waited. Then, like a Pentecostal Preacher, Sam strutted back and forth on the podium, basking in the glory of the supportive audience. "Francis Moore of *The Houston Telegraph* is another example," he continued. "Moore is a one-armed man. You would never forgive me for abusing a cripple, but I must admit his one arm can write more malicious falsehoods than any man with two. I must admit in retelling their slanders, these two men are compelled to tell some truths. I did direct our Minister at Washington to withdraw the application of Texas for annexation and commence entertaining England and France. Because of public policy, I have not been able to give an explanation. Now, however, I will explain my reasons for doing so. Annexation did not meet respectful consideration. To my great surprise, annexation met with a decidedly insulting rebuff. I admit that I have recommended treaties of reciprocity be made with England and France, squinting even to the future extent of slavery in Texas, while at the same time turning public opinion in the United States in favor of annexation. I can justify myself with the following illustration. Suppose a charming lady has two lovers. One of them is inclined to believe he would make a better husband, but he is a little slow to make appealing propositions. Do you think if she were a skillful practitioner in Cupid's Court, she would pretend that she loved the other more and be sure her favorite would know? I have been told that a smart woman will let a man chase and chase until, at the last moment, she allows him to grab her; she will run, but not too fast to be caught." Once more, Sam's words brought the house down with screaming laughter. He patiently waited for them to finish applauding and laughing. "If ladies are justified in making use of coquetry in securing their annexation to good and agreeable husbands, you must excuse me for making use of the same means to annex Texas into the Union."

As he and Margaret left the Arcade, the mayor of New Orleans joined them at their open carriage. Grabbing Sam's arm before he stepped into the carriage, the mayor said, "General, you are a Mississippi gambler of the truest nature. You bluffed them out of their poker chips. I darn sure would never want to get in a card game with you."

Sam smiled and thanked the mayor, and then said, "Mr. Mayor, sometimes I find things difficult when I discover my opponent has been dealing from the bottom of the deck. The northern states have a vitriolic hatred against Texas statehood, and many would only be happy if the Lone Star Republic was effaced. With great men like you in our corner, we will prevail, even if they are cheaters."

A.J. Donelson was in New Orleans on his way to Texas when he was surprised to discover the Houstons were in town. A.J. had delivered the elderly President Jackson the letter from Sam assuring his mentor that he was doing all in his power to make Texas the twenty-eighth state. Sam wanted Jackson to know his courting of England and France had been a bluff to force the Union President and Congress to act on annexation. President Jackson rose from his bed and with palsy hands, read the long letter. His voice quivering, he dictated his reply to Donelson:

General Houston,

I now behold the great American Eagle with her Stars and Stripes hovering over the Lone Star of Texas with cheering voice welcoming it into our glorious Union and proclaiming to Mexico and all foreign governments in a stentorian voice, you must not attempt to tread upon Texas, that the United Stars and Stripes now defend her. Glorious result, in which General, you have acted a noble part, the new state constitution must forbid banks and corporations. Texas must close its borders to further foreign colonization. If Providence spares me to next summer, of which I have great doubts, I hope to see you, your amiable lady and charming boy at the Hermitage, where you will receive a hearty welcome, not on your way only to see your relatives, but on your way to the Senate of the United States to take your seat with the sages of our Union.

Your friend,

Andrew

A.J. gave Old Hickory's letter to Sam, and delivered the grave news of Jackson having but a brief time to live. Sam felt an urgency to bid farewell to his mentor, and told Margaret they must act with haste to reach the Hermitage before it was too late. Sam and Margaret were on the way when a courier met them with the news of Jackson's death. Houston's mentor, friend, and second father breathed his last breath June 8th, 1845, but did not meet his Maker without knowing his dream of annexation was becoming a reality. President Jackson was in a chamber of mourning when the trio arrived. Sam held his son up so he could look at the deceased President and said, "Son, I pray you will remember this giant among men." Sam then handed his son to Margaret, placed his head on Old Hickory's chest, and wept uncontrollably. Sam's only consolation was that Jackson knew Sam was doing all in his power and using the cunning of a fox to assure Texas statehood.

After the funeral, the Houstons visited with relatives, and then returned to Texas before the annexation vote. Sam took to the stump and zigzagged back and forth across the Republic like a circuit preacher, spewing out brimstone and hell fire. Only Sam was spreading the gospel of good news about annexation.

Once the Texans who feared an invasion from the south saw that Union President Polk was keeping his word by sending Union troops into Corpus Christi, they had no problem voting for annexation. On October 13, 1845, Texas approved annexation by a wide margin of 4,254 to 267, and President Polk signed the Texas Admission Act on December 29, 1845.

Anson Jones' hopes of his election to the United States Senate vanished as the citizens swept two Texas heroes, Sam Houston and Thomas Rusk into office. Anson Jones would never get over his defeat for the Senate or his unsuccessful efforts to prevent annexation.

Bud Miller rustled around for a short time under his blanket and then heard another hoot only a few yards away. This was the last straw. He saddled Lighting and was on his way in record time. Bud would never know if he was running from Comanche or owls.

Once back in his own bed in San Antonio, he slept the remainder of that afternoon and into the next day until the large fist of Noah Smithwick banged on his bedroom door, jolting him from his stupor. He sat on the side of his bed and with a yawn, muttered, "Who is it?"

"Captain Miller. It's Noah. Got some exciting news. Get your britches on."

Bud had difficulty getting oriented. He fumbled with his pants and couldn't find one boot. Glancing in the mirror on his wall, he could see he needed a shave. "Uh-okay, give me a minute," he answered.

"Hurry up. You don't have to get pretty. I'll be outside so I can spit my tobacco."

Bud's eyes were puffy, and his need for a shave and bath obvious as he stepped outside, shielding his eyes from the bright morning sun. Noah took one glance at Bud and exclaimed, "Son, you look like you have been trampled by a herd of buffalo.

Bud grumbled his reply. "Two herds. What's up?"

Noah's face conveyed more excitement than Bud had ever seen in his normally laid-back friend.

"You know about the celebration in seven days?" Noah asked.

Bud's eyes opened wide as he inquired, "Celebration? Seven days? What's going on?"

Noah was quick with his answer. "Statehood! That's what. There is going to be a big celebration in Austin when we turn Texas over to the Union. Everybody who is anybody will be in there. Colonel Hays and Ben McCullough think it wise for several rangers to be in Austin, just in case some cowboy bandits or Comanche try to spoil the party. I have dreamed of this day for a decade. Wild horses couldn't keep me away."

The news of statehood shot a rush of adrenalin through Bud, but before even reacting to Noah's news, he asked, "Think I have time to go to Bastrop?"

"Sure. You should have plenty of time. Today is only the 11th."

"Thanks, my friend. Tell Colonel Hays I'll see him in Austin. Tell him I have a Charm to see about. He will know what I mean."

Bud slapped Noah on the shoulder, thanking him profusely for delivering the news, and then rushed back to his room. His landlady was preparing breakfast as he entered the small adobe house. "Do I have time to shave and wash up before breakfast?" he asked.

"If you hurry. Don't want your eggs and biscuits to get cold."

Bud ate quickly, and then told his landlady he probably would not be renting the room in the future. He gave her ten dollars and a hug. He thanked her for caring for his needs and left quickly, before she started crying.

The livery stable owner had fitted Lightning with new shoes, brushed him to a shine and fed him all he could eat. The stallion was rested and ready to go. The hide on his back quivered as the cold blanket slid over his withers. Bud then tossed the saddle over the blanket and tightened the girth. The big sorrel stallion felt the urgency in Bud's movements. Lightning was eager to obey his master and carry him swiftly to his destination.

The Maverick's house was one street over from the livery stable. Bud had one small matter to attend to before he could be on his way. Mary saw the high stepping stallion pounding his way down the street and immediately knew it was Lightning. She began to wave a hundred meters before Bud reached her. Bud waved back and when he got within hearing distance, shouted, "Mary, Mary, how does your garden grow?"

Mary was equally as quick with her response. "Not full of weeds, I pray. I bet you have come to see Sam about your furniture."

"Yes Ma'am," Bud replied with a broad smile.

"Well, Sam is not here, but he said to tell you he picked you out some beautiful new furniture in New Orleans, including a four poster bed, and returned with forty dollars left over. Our slaves delivered the furniture to your house about a week ago. I sent one of the girls to make up the beds, put the dishes on their shelves, and mop and clean the place. Now all you need is a bride."

Mary snapped her fingers and a young black girl came to her. "Tiny, go and look on my bed table. Count out forty dollars for this gentleman and bring the money to me. If you can't count, then get Jinny to help you."

"That Sam doesn't dally around. I didn't expect the furniture for two more months."

Mary's pride in her husband overflowed. "Sam is an industrious man and always does what he says, and quicker than you except. That's what makes him such a great lawyer."

"Where is Mr. Maverick, if I may ask?" Bud's inquisitive mind wondered what could be so urgent for Sam to leave so soon after their long trip to New Orleans.

Mary handed him two twenty-dollar gold coins saying, "Sam is in Austin."

"Oh, the annexation. Is he there for the changing of the flags?"

Mary became confused. "I don't know anything about the annexation. Sam has a case in Judge Baylor's court. He's in Austin taking care of business. What's this about annexation? Frankly, I'd just about given up on Jones ever getting around to handing the reins over to the Union."

"Let me be the first to tell you. Mr. Maverick is going to be in Austin when Texas becomes the twenty-eighth state. The event is to take place in seven days."

"Are you serious?" Mary exclaimed with obvious joy in her voice. "You mean Jones is finally going to turn the keys over? I thought he would refuse to give up power and try becoming a little dictator."

"I'm as serious as a heart attack," Bud responded. "The annexation date is for real. I'm going to be in Austin on the 19th so one day I'll be able to tell my children and grandchildren I stood on the Republic soil until the very end."

He didn't need to nudge Lightning, just loosen his grip on the reins, and they were off. As he turned in his saddle, he saw a stunned Mary waving vigorously with both hands in the air, jumping up and down. He knew she would spend no more time in the garden; there were too many people to share the good news with. Bud turned forward in his saddle and set about making good time on his way to the Hempsteads. He knew no matter how hard he pushed, the ride would take the better part of two days. He wouldn't have time to stop by his house, even though he really wanted to see the new furniture. As he listened to the rhythmic pounding of Lightning's hooves, his thoughts drifted to The Baron de Bastrop; annexation was something his old mentor had hoped to see. The Baron, like so many others, started the dream and now Bud was going to see statehood for Bastrop's Texas.

He planned to follow the Camino Real until he reached the Hempstead's cutoff. There were so many more people on the road than when he first traveled this old passageway. The Republic was expanding, with new citizens arriving daily. The young ranger didn't need to press Lightning; his gallant steed seemed to grasp the urgency of this trip and took control of the situation. The powerful animal increased his strides, moving at a steady gallop. Bud was concerned they were moving too fast, but each time he tried to slow his horse down, Lightning chewed his bit and pushed onward, eager to carry his master to his date with destiny.

Bud left Lightning saddled as he stopped to cook and catch a few hours of sleep. He curled up in his blanket for only four hours. As he prepared Lightning for the day's ride, the stallion accepted the bit as if to say, "let's go." They were on the road before the birds began to sing and the first rays of sun peeked above the horizon.

Bud debated whether he should cut off to Austin. He only had a short time before he would be past the road leading northwest to capital. Maybe he should go on to Austin for the lowering of the flag, and then to the Hempsteads. He became confused. Lightning seemed to be able to read his mind and gave Bud the answer. When they reached a fork in the road, his stallion lunged past the Austin trail and continued up the Camino Real as if he sensed which destination was the most important.

Bud hoped they would reach the Hempsteads before dark, and his wishes were answered. As they made the turn onto the Hempstead's road, the sun was still shining above the treetops. Lightning knew where they were and started tossing his head as the two moved up the narrow lane. When they broke into the clearing near the farm, Bud couldn't believe how much the small fencerow of trees he and Charm planted had grown, casting long shadows across the plowed ground. In the distance, he saw a white flash, which then reflected the setting sun and turned to shades of pink. He realized who was behind the fluttering pink form; Charm was folding a bed sheet.

Charm spotted Lightning and screamed, "Mama, Mama, look. It's Bud."

Mrs. Hempstead dropped her sheet in the basket as her daughter grabbed her long skirt in each hand and ran to greet him. A ball of orange from the sun cut through the trees to the west, making their trunks appear to be on fire. An ethereal glow washed over the landscape as the lovers drew closer. Bud gave the rein, and Lightning responded. As they reached Charm, Bud leaned over, and with his powerful right arm, swept her up onto his horse. With her firmly on the saddle behind him, they proceeded toward the house. She clung to him with her arms locked around his waist. When they reached Mrs. Hempstead, Bud leapt to the ground, and reaching up, gently lifted Charm off Lightning. As her feet touched the ground, she grabbed Bud, announcing, "The answer is YES, YES, YES, I want to be Mrs. Benjamin Miller. Mama and papa have given their blessing!"

Bud felt a shot of happiness course through him and hugged her tighter. As the ranger's eyes surveyed the surroundings, his gaze fell on a welcome sight as Charlie stepped forward. Placing his hand on Bud's shoulder, he said, "You are a sight for sore eyes. I want you to know we love our house and thank you for the land. I just happened to be over here today to borrow a milk cow from papa. We are expecting any day, and the lady who is going to deliver the baby isn't sure my wife will have enough milk. Again, I want to thank you. I don't know how I'll ever repay you."

Bud blushed. The warm glow of the sunset made his cheeks appear even redder. "Charlie, the house is a gift. You don't pay for gifts."

Charm didn't want to share Bud, but she had no choice. Soon all the boys, her mother, and even her father gathered around him. Finally, Mrs. Hempstead said, "Come on in the house. Charm and I will fix supper and you men can talk."

As they started toward the house, Bud asked Mr. Hempstead to stop for a moment, and motioned for Charm to go on inside. He had a question to ask her father. He wasn't as nervous as he had expected. His manner was confident as he asked, "Sir, I would like permission to make your daughter my wife. I'll treat her with grace and never once lay a wrong hand on her. I will do my best to provide her with a good life. May I have your permission?"

"Bud, my son, I knew the purpose of your visit. Charm shared your letter with us. Yes, you and Charm have all the Hempsteads' blessing. Do you have a date in mind?"

Bud was relieved to have Mr. Hempstead's approval. "Sir, if we can find the preacher and Charm is willing, I would like for us to be married tomorrow. I want to take my wife to Austin so we can tell our children we were there when Texas became the twenty-eighth state."

Mr. Hempstead froze. "What did you say?"

"I said I wanted us to get married so we can be in Austin for the Annexation celebration."

"That is what I thought you said. The preacher part is easy. We have a Baptist Minister, Reverend John Trice renting a bed in the barn this week. The reverend is recovering from a rattlesnake bite and has been here waiting for the swelling to recede before he continues his evangelizing circuit. When did this annexation thing take place? I know about the vote, but I didn't realize Jones had set a date."

"Sir, Noah Smithwick informed me very early two mornings ago. He received word that President Jones is finally ready to give up his power and we are going to become a state. Noah said the official signing and transition celebration is the 19th. That gives us time, if we marry early in the morning. I'd like to buy a horse for Charm from you."

"Bud, she has her own horse. I gave her a mare so she could learn to ride after she read us your letter; especially the part where you told her you wanted her to learn to ride if she accepted your proposal. She has been on that horse every day in anticipation of your arrival. I was even able to trade an ox for a sidesaddle."

Charlie joined the two men as each took turns washing the dust and grime off their hands and faces before entering the house. Charm could not seem to take her eyes off Bud, so finally Mrs. Hempstead said, "I'll finish up. You go sit with your beau."

Charm thanked her mother and took her place beside Bud. Charlie broke the silence, saying with a big grin, "So you two are gonna tie the knot in the morning if Reverend John is up to standing on his leg?"

Bud could have wrung his neck. His eyes cut a hole in Charlie's forehead as he mumbled, "Wait till I get you outside."

Then he turned to Charm. "I apologize for the big mouth of your brother. I have your father's approval, but I need yours. Will you marry me tomorrow morning?"

"Are you serious? In the morning? I don't have my wedding dress finished."

"I know, I know. It's just that the annexation is almost here. There is going to be a big celebration. I want us to be in Austin so we can tell our children and grandchildren we were there when the Texas flag was lowered and the Stars and Stripes of the Union took her place. Besides, Reverend Trice is right here. I'll make him stand if I have to tie him to a tree."

Charm squeezed his arm and softly whispered, "You know it's fine with me, as long as we are together. I'd go with you around the world." She hesitated for a moment and then confessed, "I will admit I'm a little frightened to meet all those important people up in Austin."

"Charm, my beautiful young lady, you have already met the really important people of Texas. General Houston and men like him have spent the night in your barn and eaten at this very table. I promise you there is no reason to be concerned. We will be with friends."

Reverend John smelled the fried chicken and joined them at the table. He heard the mention of marriage and asked, "You two wanna get married? Well, I have some blank marriage licenses in the barn. We can do it tonight after supper if you wish."

Bud didn't want to begin his honeymoon with his in-laws. He didn't wait for Charm to respond, but quickly replied, "I want us to have a sunrise wedding and begin our new life with the blessing of the first rays of the sun announcing God is still on His throne. If it's all right with you, we will ask you to read the words before breakfast. Charm and I can pack tonight and I'll buy a pack mule from my 'almost' father-in-law." Then he turned to Charm, "Is this agreeable with you?"

"Benjamin Miller, you know it is."

John, the Baptist minister, said grace and then everyone dug in. No one spoke until Bud decided he would share some good news with the family. "I went to Goliad and saw where my pa is buried. Then I tracked down some folks who knew first hand about the massacre. Mr. Dillard Cooper witnessed my father's death. I am glad I went. I am also thinking Charm and I will set up a cattle operation while there are still longhorns roaming free. With crossbreeding, we can have a marketable product."

Charlie stopped eating, but kept on talking with food in his mouth. "Bud Miller, you are a genius. Of course crossbreeding will work. You will have cows that can live on cactus, go weeks without water, are tame as a cur dog and have a lot of meat on their bones, and best of all, can produce milk. I don't know why someone hasn't crossbred before."

Bud was in a talkative mood, so before anyone could speak, he answered, "Charlie, keep in mind, I have spent close to ten years riding back and forth across Texas. I have had the opportunity to see a couple of million longhorns and black Mexican cattle undulating across the great plains of the Republic. Looking at them and wondering what could be done got me to contemplating going in the cattle business. Spending time with Taylor White and seeing what Sam Maverick is doing down on the coast got my juices flowing. The Piney Woods are a hearty breed and they come from the original Spanish stock dating back to the Florida Crackers. Criollos I think they were called. They are heat tolerant and give a fair amount of milk. They don't get very big. An Englishman told me about his new breed. They are milk cows that, he said, produce an abundance of rich milk ideal for butter and cheese. The cow is from the Isle of Jersey. He just called them Jerseys. I'm not sure how well they would adjust to our neck of the woods. It would be my luck I'd go to the effort to get a bull shipped over here and the dang ticks would kill him the first month. The problem with domestic cows is that the purebreds, like the Durham and Devon, are susceptible to tick fever. Nothing causes those longhorns any problems. I'm thinking Durham and longhorns might make a good mix."

Mr. Hempstead listened intently. What Bud was saying made perfect sense. He coughed to gain the attention of the table. When everyone was looking in his direction, he spoke, "Longhorns are weak milkers. Their meat is tough as shoe leather and they have an ugly streak that shows up the minute a calf hits the ground. I know nothing of the other cattle you speak of, except the Durham. We had Durhams back home and I'm here to tell you that their bulls get big and mean as well. The cows are docile. Seems like you been doing' some studying."

"Yes sir, as much as I can; however, first things first. Charm and I must be married. I want her at my side so we can pursue this venture together."

Everyone at the table joined in, kicking Bud's idea around. Even the minister had some words of wisdom to add to the conversation. Reverend Trice mentioned President Jones owned several Piney Wood bulls and cows. His mention of President Jones sent coldness over the conversation.

Bud responded, "No thanks. I'm not interested in what Jones has to offer. I saw how he turned his back on General Houston. I have seen the Piney Wood cattle. They are not strong enough for my liking anyway."

Reverend Trice abruptly excused himself, "Bud, Charm, I will be ready when the rooster crows."

Both Charm and Bud tossed and turned all night. Bud was up long before daylight, and so was Charm. As the sun rose, the minister was the first to arrive, followed by Bud and Mr. Hempstead. Charm and her mother came out about the time the boys ambled out into the front yard. The reverend read a verse from the New Testament and then asked, "Is there anyone present who objects to Charm Hempstead and Benjamin Miller being joined in holy matrimony?" He quickly surveyed the family members, then continued, "Benjamin do you take Charm to be your lawfully wedded wife as long as you both shall live, to protect her with your life and honor and care for her, so help you God?"

"Yes Sir, I do."

Reverend Trice then turned to Charm. "Do you, Charm, take Benjamin to be your lawfully wedded husband, to cherish, honor and obey as long as you both shall live, so help you God?"

Charm didn't hesitate. "I do."

"With the powers vested in me by Almighty God and the Republic of Texas, I pronounce you man and wife. You may kiss the bride."

Bud blushed. He knew everyone would be watching as he gave his new bride a kiss. He made their first kiss tender but quick, then whispered to Charm there would be many, many more for the rest of their lives.

Knowing there was little time to waste if they were going to be in Austin for the celebration, the newlyweds said their goodbyes and left shortly after the wedding breakfast.

Days before the cerebration, jubilant crowds filled the streets of Austin. Citizens came from as far away as Nacogdoches and Galveston Island to witness the Stars and Stripes replace the Lone Star. A festive atmosphere was prevalent throughout the Republic as relief settled across Texas; finally they could stop worrying Mexico would declare war and draw them into a bloodbath. If there was war, the Union had a professional army and ample funds for a long campaign.

Houston and Rusk had their eyes on the U.S. Senate, and both arrived in Austin four days before the ceremony. From the moment they arrived, each began campaigning for the two available Senate seats. Sam was quick to remind any and all that he knew his way around, and was experienced in dealing with carpetbaggers. President Anson Jones left Barrington Farms at Washington-on-the-Brazos a week in advance so he could orchestrate the event and position himself in the best political light. When the vote proved to be overwhelmingly in favor of annexation, he immediately switched to pro-statehood and set his sights on becoming a Texas Senator. His political maneuvering was transparent, and rejected out-of-hand by all.

James and Millie Willingham arrived on the 18th with their children, except for A.D. Now a corporal in the Texas Army, he was on patrol along the Rio Grande. Little Ruthann had grown into a beautiful young woman, turning the heads of the young boys filling the streets of Austin. Jack Hays, Henry and Ben McCullough, Big Foot Wallace, Craig Winborn, and several other rangers arrived a day before the event and pitched camp on the capital grounds. Their mandate was to ensure there were no surprises and quell any unpleasant happenings should they occur.

All the rooms were booked at the Lubbock Hotel when Bud and Charm arrived, but after learning they were on their honeymoon, the manager, Mrs. Angelina Eberly, offered the young couple her room. The gruff and tough Angelina, who had single-handedly prevented the archives from leaving Austin, slept on a sofa in the lobby. Many visitors had to sleep on the cold ground, as every bed in town had been spoken for. Some of the wealthier citizens, like Jared Groce and Bobby Lay, brought tents and slaves to care for their needs, but they were the exception.

The hotel's dining room remained full from morning until night; when one group finished eating, another was waiting to take their place. As Bud and Charm pressed their way through the crowded room, he spotted General Houston. Over the roar of banging plates and lively conversation, Bud made his way toward the general's table, shouting, "General, General Houston."

Sam thought he recognized the voice. "Bud Miller. My lad, you have grown. You are almost as tall as me."

"Sir, no man in Texas is as tall as you. General, this is my new bride, Charm Miller."

Sam motioned for those seated at his table to move around and squeeze in tighter. He wanted Bud at his side. Sam recounted the Garza duel in graphic detail. The group gasped when they learned of Bud's bravery at such a young age, while Charm realized for the first time how close Bud came to dying in a duel. Bud tried to shift the conversation, asking, "Sir, how did we come up with our current Lone Star flag? I know we have had many flags." He knew General Houston would seize the opportunity to expound on the history of the Texas flag and forget talking about him.

"Interesting question Bud, and one that merits attention on the eve of such a momentous occasion. The Third Congress of the Republic adopted the current Lone Star design on January 25th, 1839. When Lamar was President, it was I who brought the matter to the floor. Before that, we used the Burnet flag, which consisted of a large golden star centrally located on an azure background. Although Lorenzo de Zavala proposed a flag of blue, with a white five-point star and the letters 'T E X A S' placed between the points, nothing further was done with the recommendation. I'm not sure why. Perhaps owing to our hasty adjournment of the Convention at Washington. In our hurriedness to leave, we also lost part of the Convention notes. I still think de Zavala's flag would have been a good choice; however, I did lean toward red, white and blue because of the association with the Stars and Stripes. This brings to mind why a single star in the first place. I guess you could say divine guidance was working behind the scenes. Henry Smith was the first Governor of pre-revolutionary Texas in 1835. A few days after his inauguration, a messenger arrived with important papers. In Henry's day, overcoats had large brass buttons, much like the ones on my topcoat. It happened that the buttons on Governor Smith's coat had the impress of a five-pointed star. After signing the papers, the Governor said, '*Texas should have a seal*' and forthwith, he cut one of the buttons from his overcoat and used it to seal the wax, stamping the impress of the Lone Star on the documents."

One man at the table, George Teulon, was not completely satisfied with General Houston's answer. "Sir, if I might add there was considerable Masonic influence in the adoption of a five-pointed star. Texas is a Masonic country; all of our presidents, including you General, our vice-presidents, and the majority of our officials are Masons. Freemasonry illustrates moral virtue with the symbol of the five-pointed star. May it ever bind us in the holy Bond of Fraternal Union and govern our social, Masonic, and political discourse."

Although he did not agree with Teulon's explanation, Sam responded, "Point well made, George. No pun intended. Texas is a Masonic Republic. Well, I guess I had better get accustomed to saying Masonic state." As rapidly as Sam had begun his dissertation regarding the Texas flag, he turned his attention back to the newlyweds. In a commanding voice so all could hear over the din, he continued, "Now Bud, tell us about your lovely bride."

When those seated at the general's table heard they were newlyweds, they stood and clapped. General Houston asked to be forgiven for not standing, citing his gimp leg. Bud talked and Charm blushed, dreaming of the day when great men like General Houston would be having dinner at Bud's and her table.

The District Court in Austin was in session when news reached the capital that President Polk had signed the Texas Admission Act and the U.S. Congress had approved it. It was official. Texas was now part of the Union. Judge Robert Baylor, who would later found Baylor University in Waco gave a proclamation, "No man should be considered intoxicated as long as he could pronounce the word Epson. Judge Baylor, also a Baptist minister, adjourned the court and joined in the celebration. They could find no working cannon so the joyous citizens spilled into the streets beating on anvils, buckets, and banging horseshoes or anything they could find to make noise. Guns were discharged almost constantly. Had any Indians been near, they would have thought the Anglos were insane and fled for their lives.

The heavens smiled on the Lone Star State, blessing her with a glorious day on which to enter the Union. The morning sky was crystal clear and the sun bathed the crowds gathered for the ceremony. February 19th, 1846, nine days short of a decade since Texas stood up to the tyrannical dictator Santa Anna, she became the twenty-eighth state.

Men like The Baron de Bastrop and Steven Fuller Austin were praised for their efforts in establishing the original Anglo settlements. Everyone expected to hear General Houston speak, but President Anson Jones wanted no one to share the spotlight and did not invite the general to address the audience. Jones stepped to the podium and in his high-pitched voice said, "May a gracious heaven smile upon the consummation of the wishes of the two Republics, now joined as one. May the Union be perpetual and may it be the means of conferring benefits and blessings upon the people of all the States…The final act in this great drama is now performed. The Republic of Texas is no more." Those words were his final official act as President of the Republic.

As the Lone Star of Texas lowered, General Houston pushed his chest out and stepping from the crowd, gently let the tri-colored flag drape into his open arms. He carefully folded the Lone Star flag so the star stood alone in the center of the triangle. Standing at attention, Sam then placed the folded flag over his heart as the Union Stars and Stripes rose up the same flagpole, unfurling in the wind. He thought of President Andrew Jackson and knew his old chief was smiling down on the glorious celebration. He could almost hear Old Hickory say, "Well done, my son."

Bud could taste the salt as tears rolled down his cheeks and ran into the corner of his mouth. Locking his arms around Charm's waist, he softly whispered, "Mrs. Miller, today is but one of the many joyful days we will share in our life together. I pledge my faithfulness, love, loyalty and trust to you. From this day forward, we are a world of two. I will never leave you nor will I ever break our vow."

Charm snuggled even closer to her husband's strong body. His words gave her comfort and security.

On this cloudless winter day, the golden sun illuminated the hopes and dreams of the new State of Texas. A thousand miles to the south, hovering over the tops of snow-tipped mountains, a menacing cloud began to gather strength. Those white-capped peaks would soon turn sangria with Anglo and Mexican blood. The belief in a Manifest Destiny and Mexico's anger over the Union's intrusion into their territory left little choice on either side. The Union was going to take the land west of the Louisiana border, by purchase or by force. Since Mexico refused the last offer of twenty-five million dollars, President Polk would opt for the second choice. Two years of war between Mexico and the Union would soon follow the dark clouds in the south.

The End